PETROGRAD

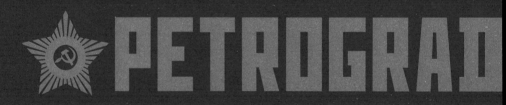

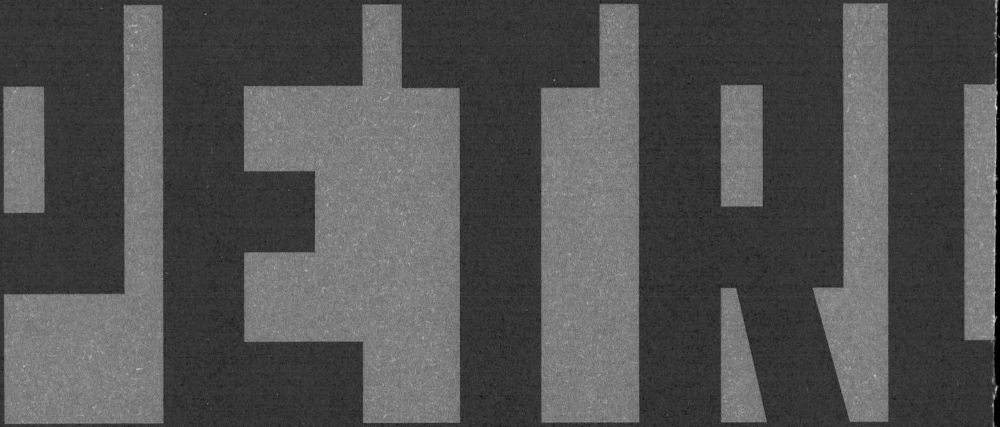

Written by
PHILIP GELATT

Illustrated by
TYLER CROOK

lettered by
DOUGLAS E. SHERWOOD

design by
KEITH WOOD
with
TYLER CROOK

Edited by
JILL BEATON

Oni Press, Inc.
JOE NOZEMACK, publisher
JAMES LUCAS JONES, editor in chief
GEORGE ROHAC, operations director
KEITH WOOD, art director
CORY CASONI, marketing director
JILL BEATON, editor
CHARLIE CHU, editor
DOUGLAS E. SHERWOOD, production assistant

onipress.com

First Edition, August 2011

ISBN 978-1-934964-44-6

Oni Press, Inc.
1305 SE Martin Luther King Jr. Blvd.
Suite A, Portland, OR 97214.

facebook.com/onipress • twitter.com/onipress • onipress.tumblr.com

10 9 8 7 6 5 4 3 2

Library of Congress Control Number: 2011922804

PRINTED IN CHINA

The city on the shores of the Neva River has known many names in its history.

For a long time it was known as St. Petersburg. But as the First World War dawned, that name was deemed too Germanic for a city at war.

For a long time after the First World War it was known as Leningrad. But for reasons beyond the scope of this book, that name was deemed too Communist for a country attempting re-birth.

Our story takes place between the two, during a time when the city was known as Petrograd.

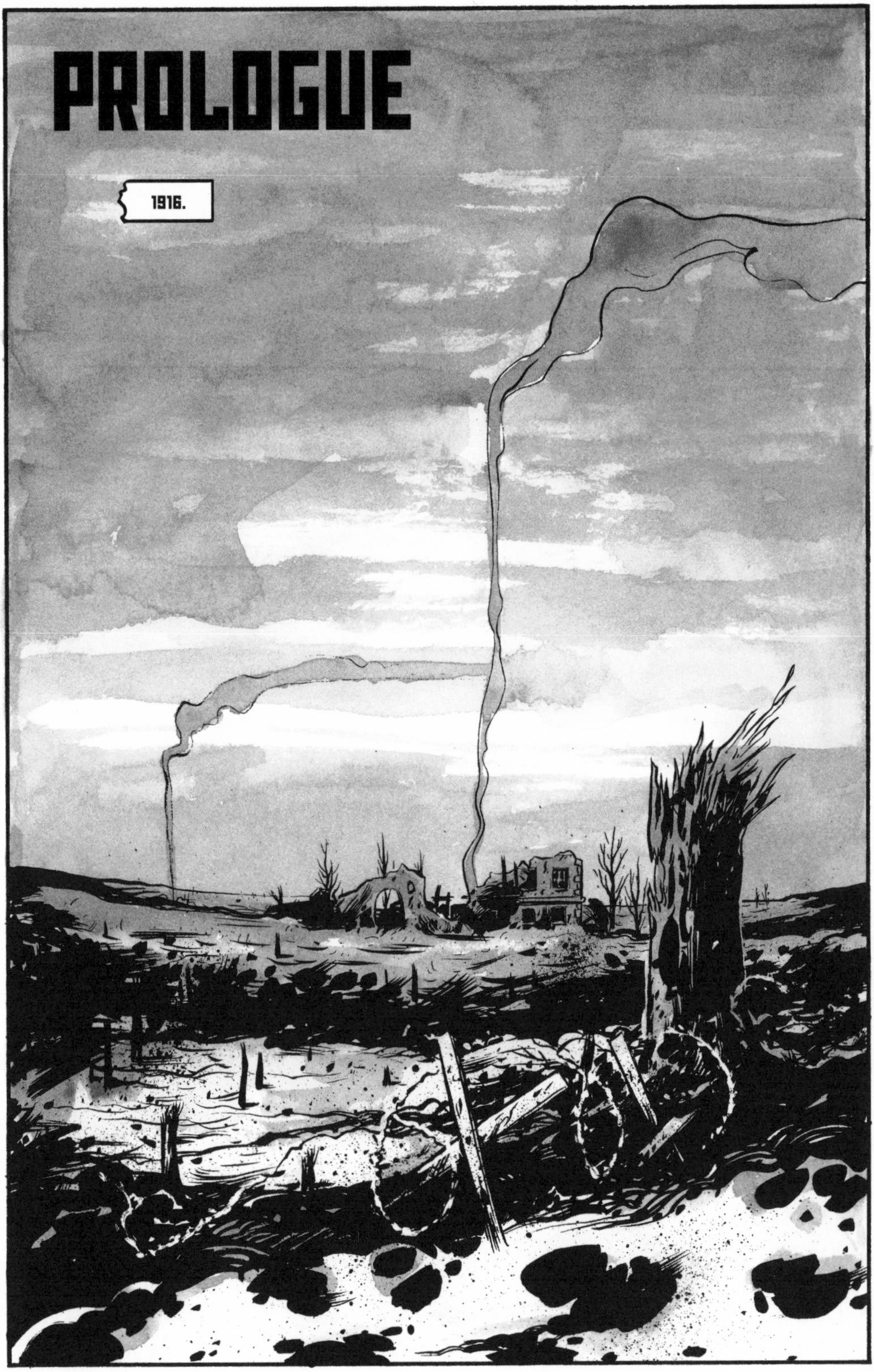
PROLOGUE
1916.

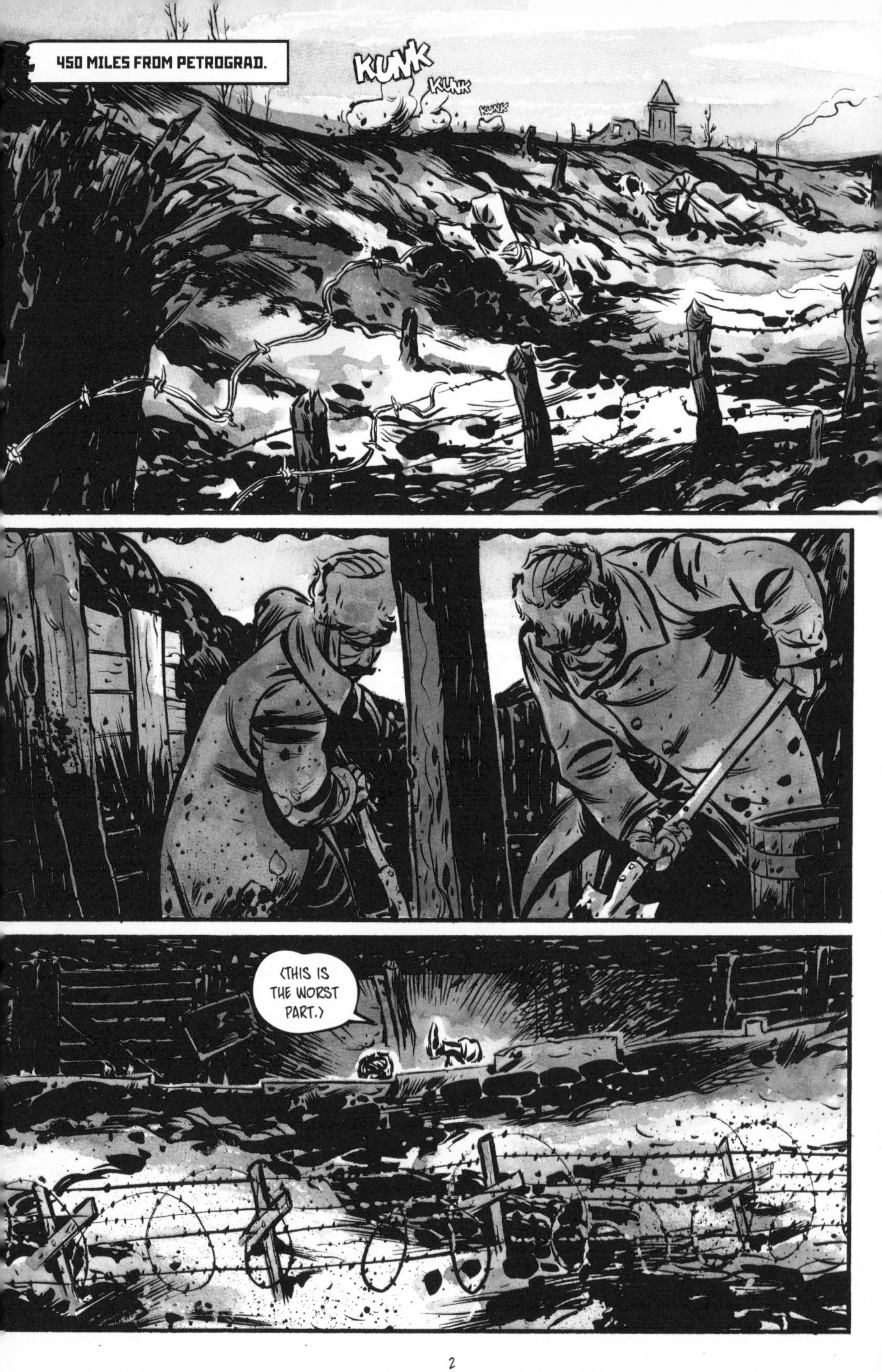
450 MILES FROM PETROGRAD.
KUNK
KUNK
KUNK
(THIS IS THE WORST PART.)

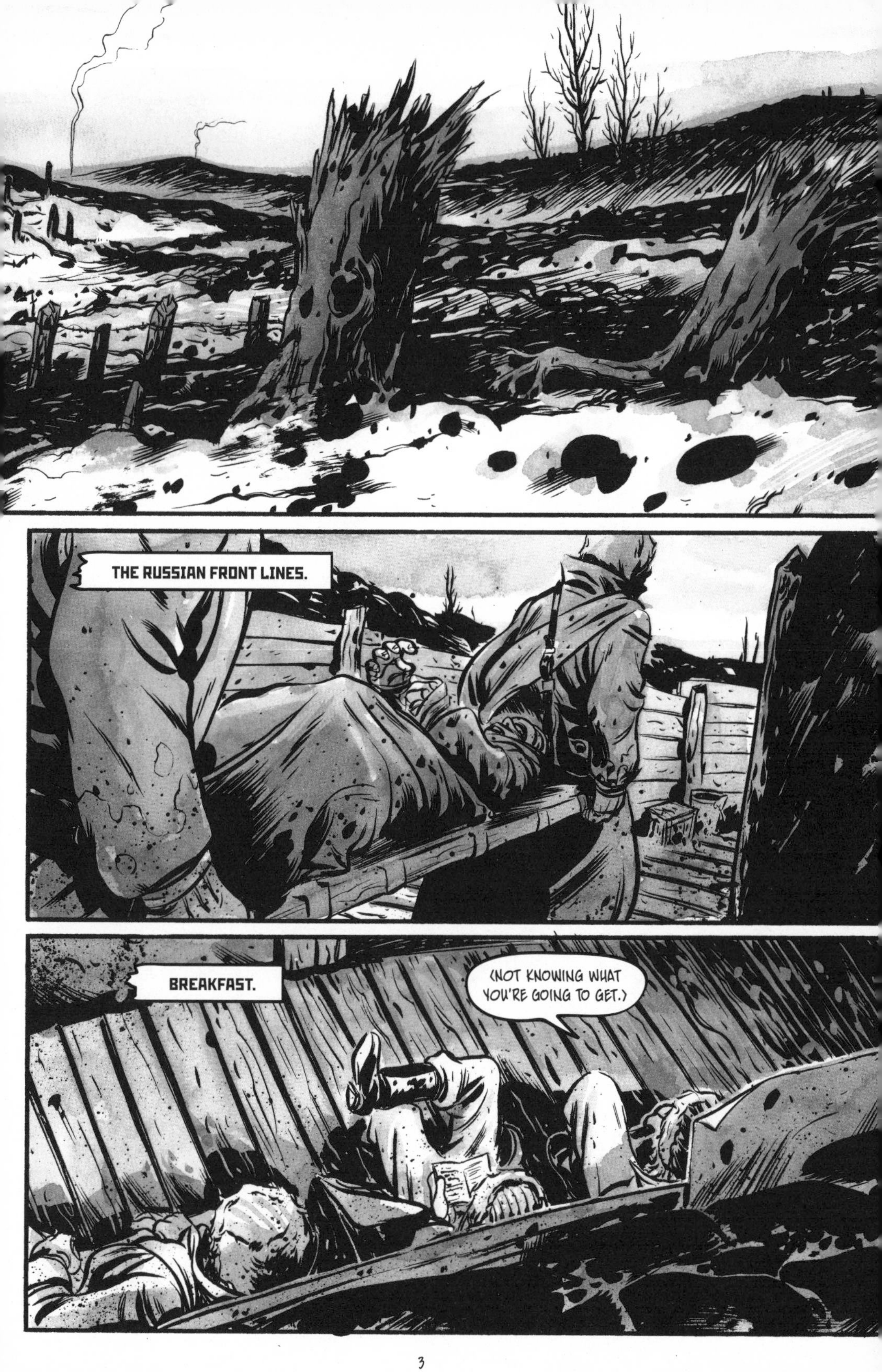
THE RUSSIAN FRONT LINES.
BREAKFAST.
(NOT KNOWING WHAT YOU'RE GOING TO GET.)

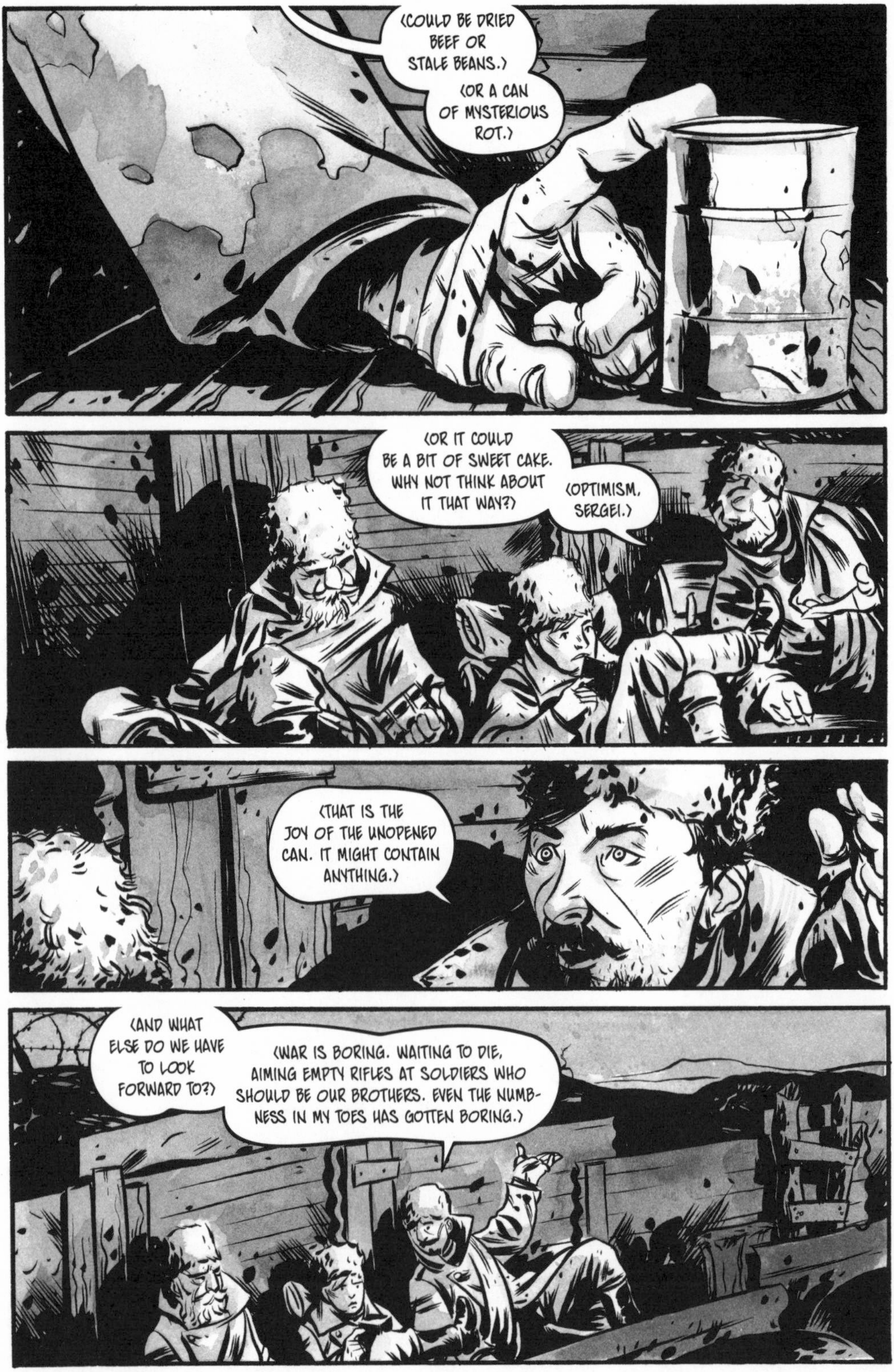
‹COULD BE DRIED BEEF OR STALE BEANS.›
‹OR A CAN OF MYSTERIOUS ROT.›
‹OR IT COULD BE A BIT OF SWEET CAKE. WHY NOT THINK ABOUT IT THAT WAY?›
‹OPTIMISM, SERGEI.›
‹THAT IS THE JOY OF THE UNOPENED CAN. IT MIGHT CONTAIN ANYTHING.›
‹AND WHAT ELSE DO WE HAVE TO LOOK FORWARD TO?›
‹WAR IS BORING. WAITING TO DIE, AIMING EMPTY RIFLES AT SOLDIERS WHO SHOULD BE OUR BROTHERS. EVEN THE NUMBNESS IN MY TOES HAS GOTTEN BORING.›

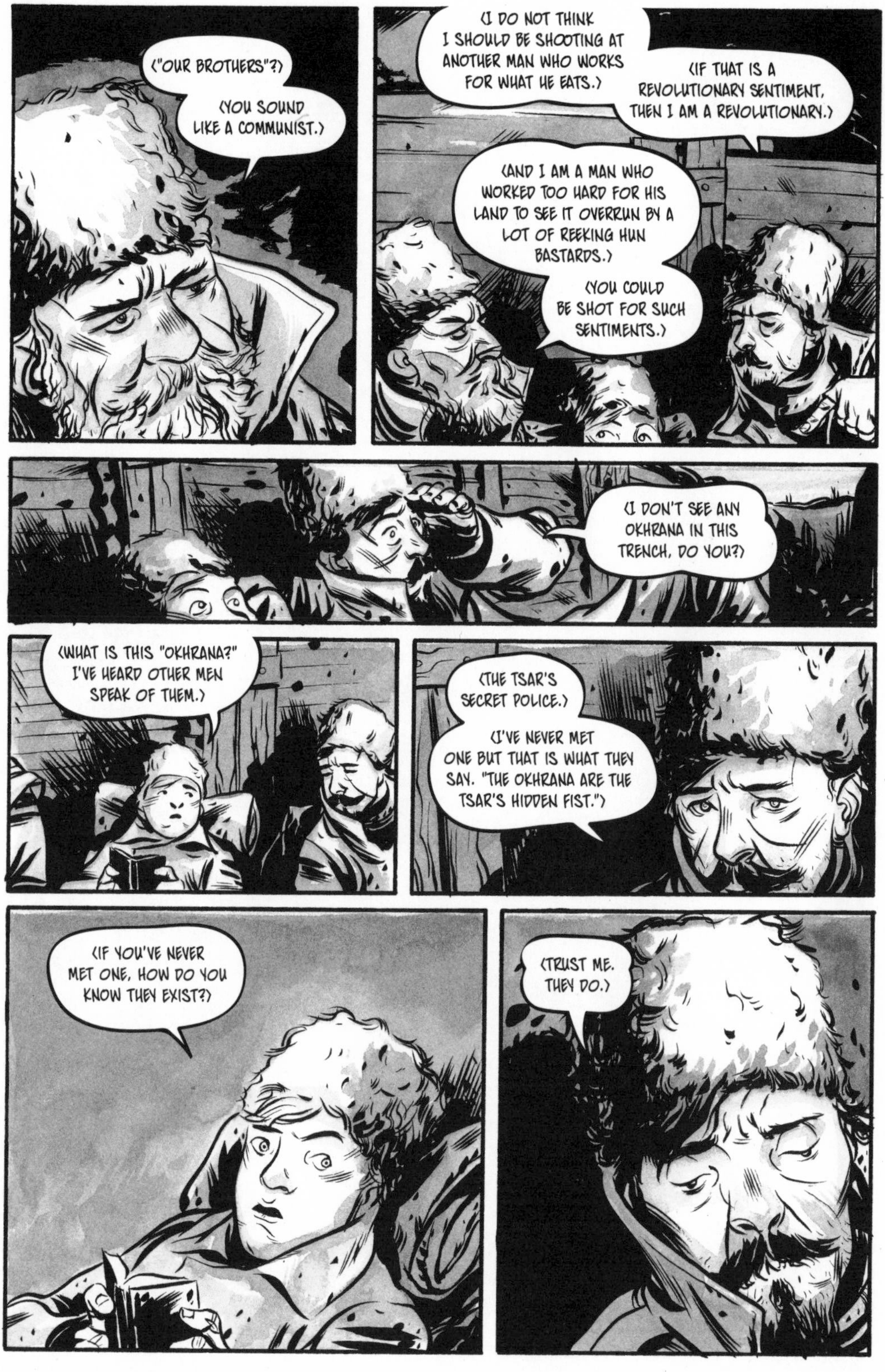
("OUR BROTHERS"?)
(YOU SOUND LIKE A COMMUNIST.)
(I DO NOT THINK I SHOULD BE SHOOTING AT ANOTHER MAN WHO WORKS FOR WHAT HE EATS.)
(IF THAT IS A REVOLUTIONARY SENTIMENT, THEN I AM A REVOLUTIONARY.)
(AND I AM A MAN WHO WORKED TOO HARD FOR HIS LAND TO SEE IT OVERRUN BY A LOT OF REEKING HUN BASTARDS.)
(YOU COULD BE SHOT FOR SUCH SENTIMENTS.)
(I DON'T SEE ANY OKHRANA IN THIS TRENCH, DO YOU?)
(WHAT IS THIS "OKHRANA?" I'VE HEARD OTHER MEN SPEAK OF THEM.)
(THE TSAR'S SECRET POLICE.)
(I'VE NEVER MET ONE BUT THAT IS WHAT THEY SAY. "THE OKHRANA ARE THE TSAR'S HIDDEN FIST.")
(IF YOU'VE NEVER MET ONE, HOW DO YOU KNOW THEY EXIST?)
(TRUST ME. THEY DO.)

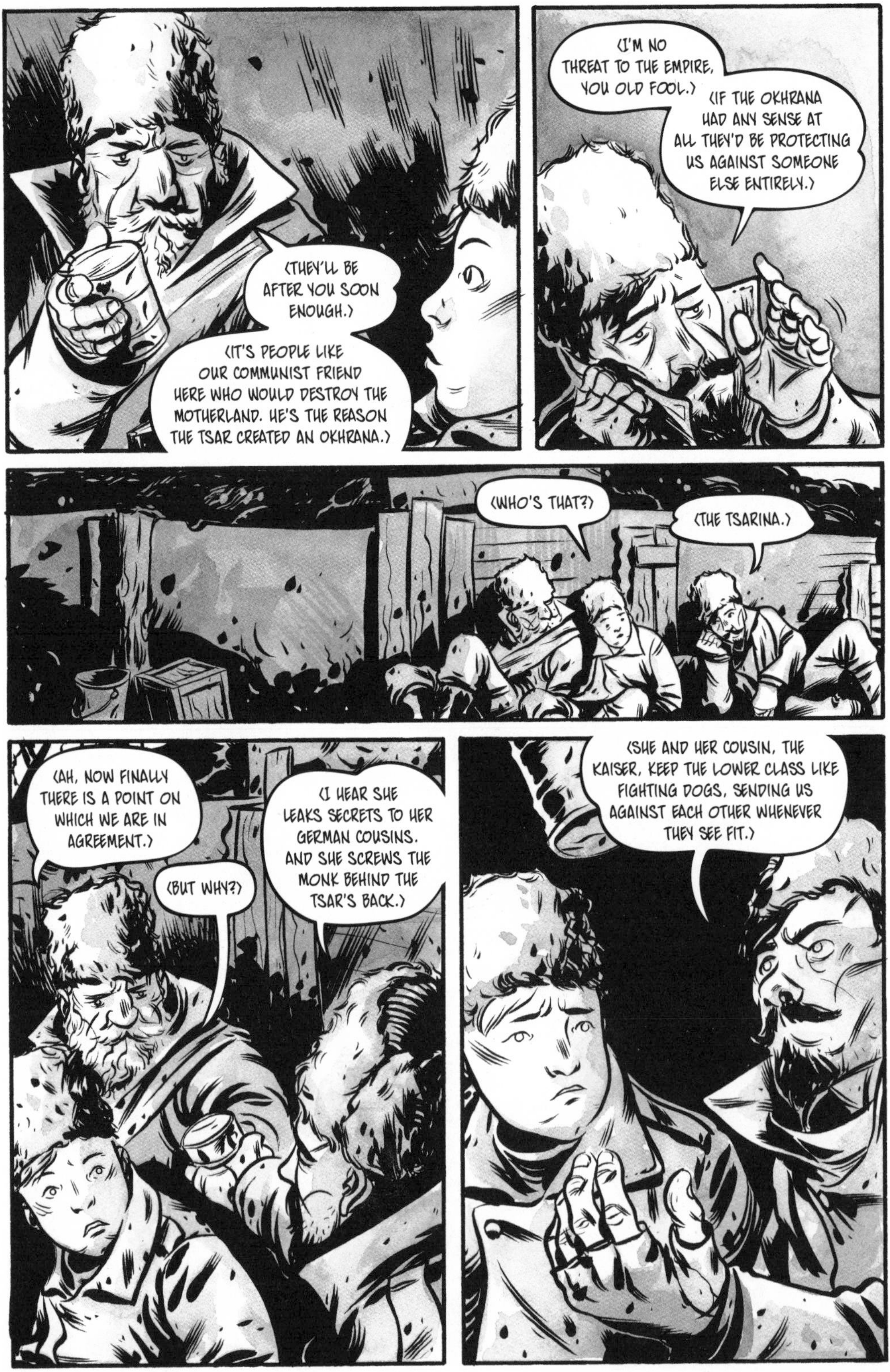
(THEY'LL BE AFTER YOU SOON ENOUGH.)
(IT'S PEOPLE LIKE OUR COMMUNIST FRIEND HERE WHO WOULD DESTROY THE MOTHERLAND. HE'S THE REASON THE TSAR CREATED AN OKHRANA.)
(I'M NO THREAT TO THE EMPIRE, YOU OLD FOOL.)
(IF THE OKHRANA HAD ANY SENSE AT ALL THEY'D BE PROTECTING US AGAINST SOMEONE ELSE ENTIRELY.)
(WHO'S THAT?)
(THE TSARINA.)
(AH, NOW FINALLY THERE IS A POINT ON WHICH WE ARE IN AGREEMENT.)
(BUT WHY?)
(I HEAR SHE LEAKS SECRETS TO HER GERMAN COUSINS. AND SHE SCREWS THE MONK BEHIND THE TSAR'S BACK.)
(SHE AND HER COUSIN, THE KAISER, KEEP THE LOWER CLASS LIKE FIGHTING DOGS, SENDING US AGAINST EACH OTHER WHENEVER THEY SEE FIT.)

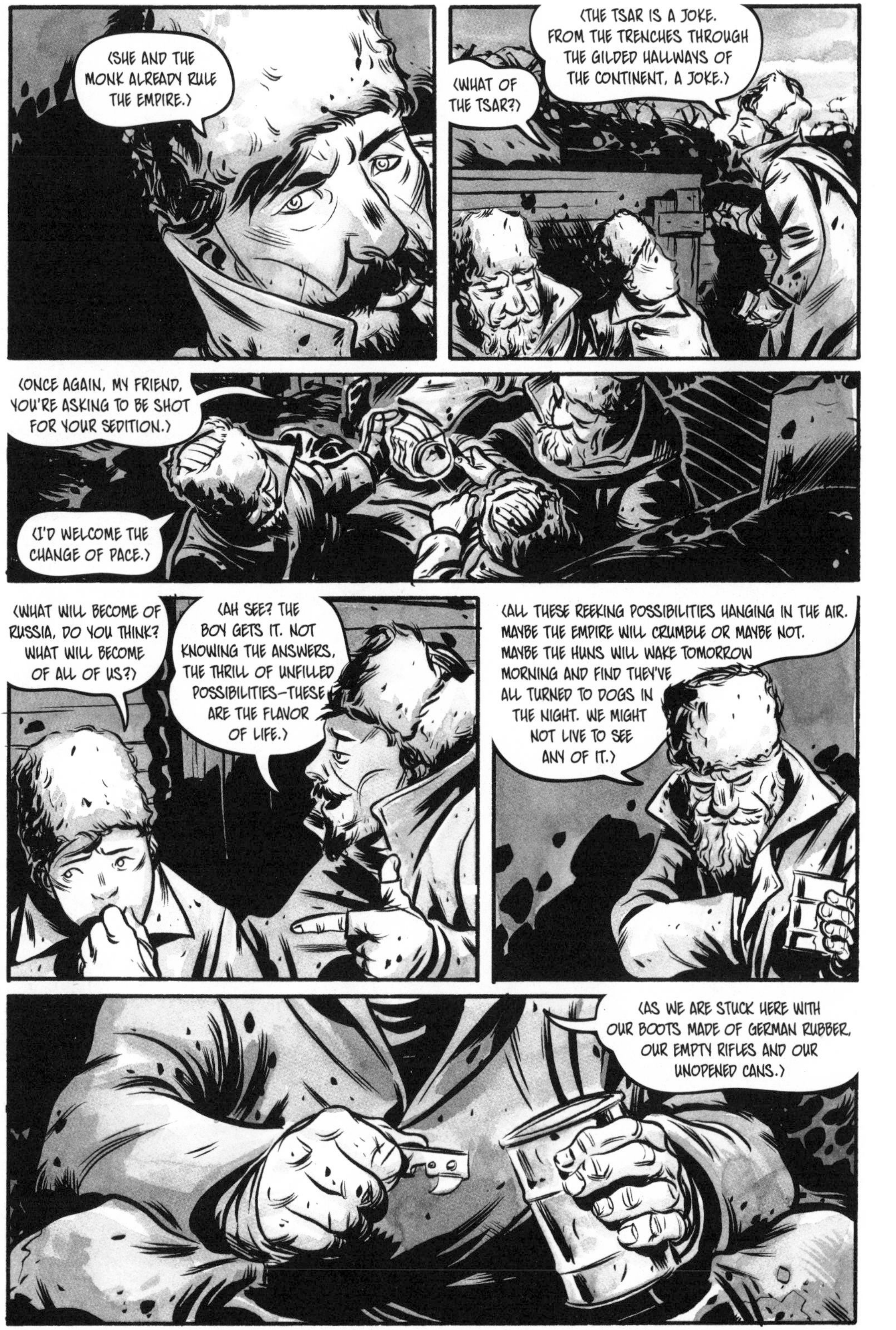

<SHE AND THE MONK ALREADY RULE THE EMPIRE.>
<WHAT OF THE TSAR?>
<THE TSAR IS A JOKE. FROM THE TRENCHES THROUGH THE GILDED HALLWAYS OF THE CONTINENT, A JOKE.>
<ONCE AGAIN, MY FRIEND, YOU'RE ASKING TO BE SHOT FOR YOUR SEDITION.>
<I'D WELCOME THE CHANGE OF PACE.>
<WHAT WILL BECOME OF RUSSIA, DO YOU THINK? WHAT WILL BECOME OF ALL OF US?>
<AH SEE? THE BOY GETS IT. NOT KNOWING THE ANSWERS, THE THRILL OF UNFILLED POSSIBILITIES—THESE ARE THE FLAVOR OF LIFE.>
<ALL THESE REEKING POSSIBILITIES HANGING IN THE AIR. MAYBE THE EMPIRE WILL CRUMBLE OR MAYBE NOT. MAYBE THE HUNS WILL WAKE TOMORROW MORNING AND FIND THEY'VE ALL TURNED TO DOGS IN THE NIGHT. WE MIGHT NOT LIVE TO SEE ANY OF IT.>
<AS WE ARE STUCK HERE WITH OUR BOOTS MADE OF GERMAN RUBBER, OUR EMPTY RIFLES AND OUR UNOPENED CANS.>

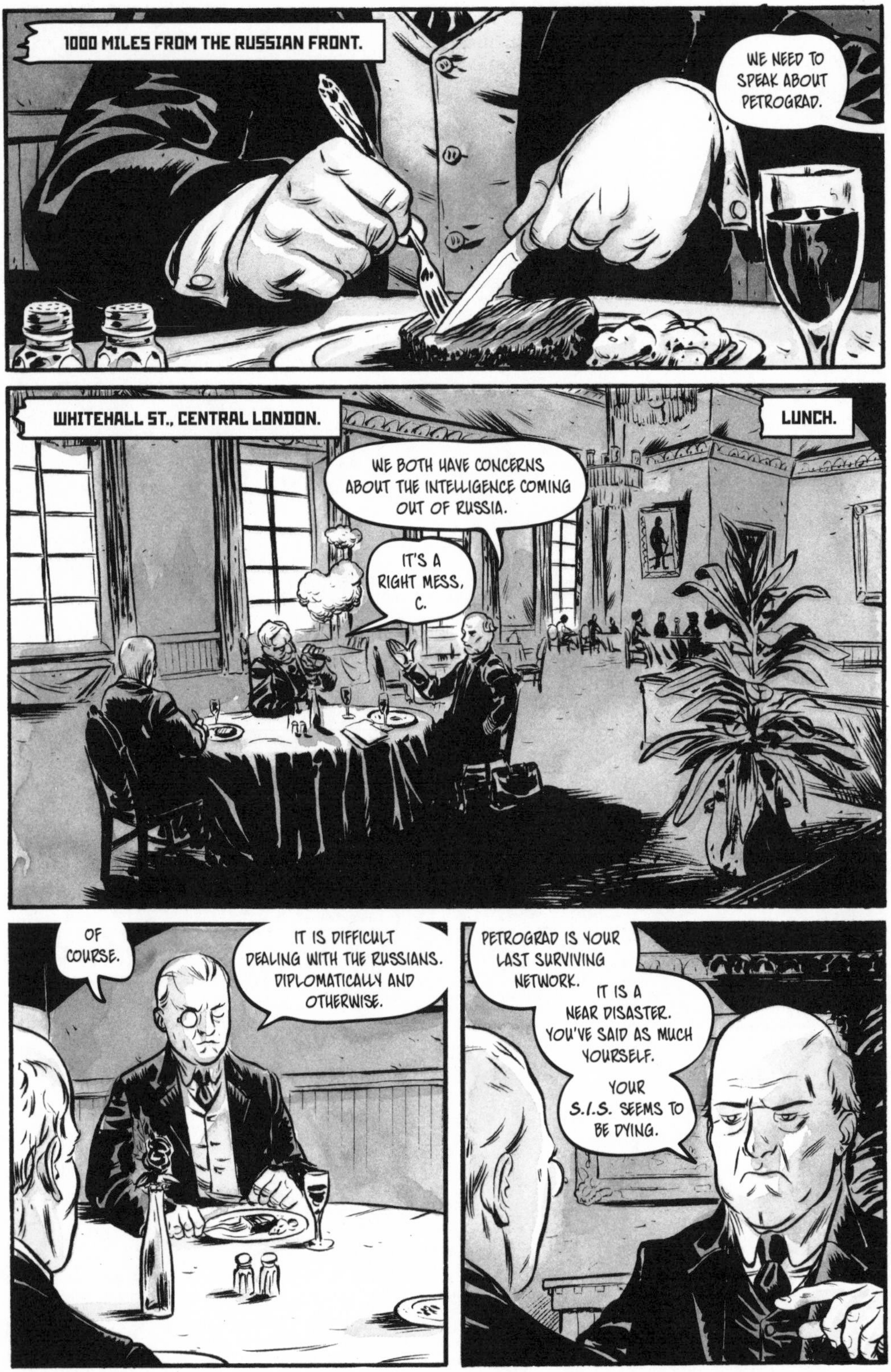
1000 MILES FROM THE RUSSIAN FRONT.
WE NEED TO SPEAK ABOUT PETROGRAD.
WHITEHALL ST., CENTRAL LONDON.
LUNCH.
WE BOTH HAVE CONCERNS ABOUT THE INTELLIGENCE COMING OUT OF RUSSIA.
IT'S A RIGHT MESS, C.
OF COURSE.
IT IS DIFFICULT DEALING WITH THE RUSSIANS. DIPLOMATICALLY AND OTHERWISE.
PETROGRAD IS YOUR LAST SURVIVING NETWORK.
IT IS A NEAR DISASTER. YOU'VE SAID AS MUCH YOURSELF.
YOUR S.I.S. SEEMS TO BE DYING.

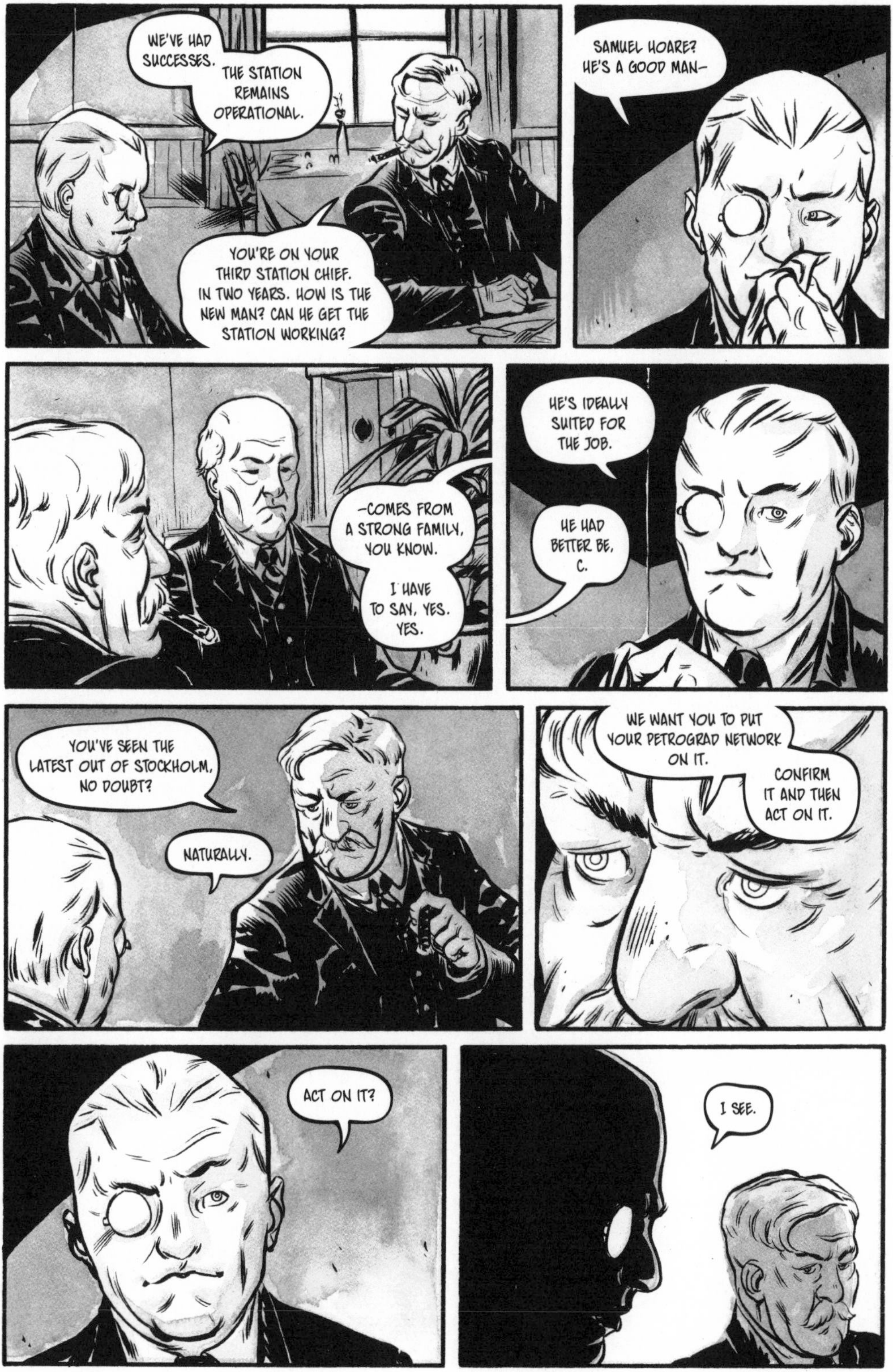
WE'VE HAD SUCCESSES.
THE STATION REMAINS OPERATIONAL.
YOU'RE ON YOUR THIRD STATION CHIEF. IN TWO YEARS. HOW IS THE NEW MAN? CAN HE GET THE STATION WORKING?
SAMUEL HOARE? HE'S A GOOD MAN–
–COMES FROM A STRONG FAMILY, YOU KNOW.
I HAVE TO SAY, YES. YES.
HE'S IDEALLY SUITED FOR THE JOB.
HE HAD BETTER BE, C.
YOU'VE SEEN THE LATEST OUT OF STOCKHOLM, NO DOUBT?
NATURALLY.
WE WANT YOU TO PUT YOUR PETROGRAD NETWORK ON IT.
CONFIRM IT AND THEN ACT ON IT.
ACT ON IT?
I SEE.

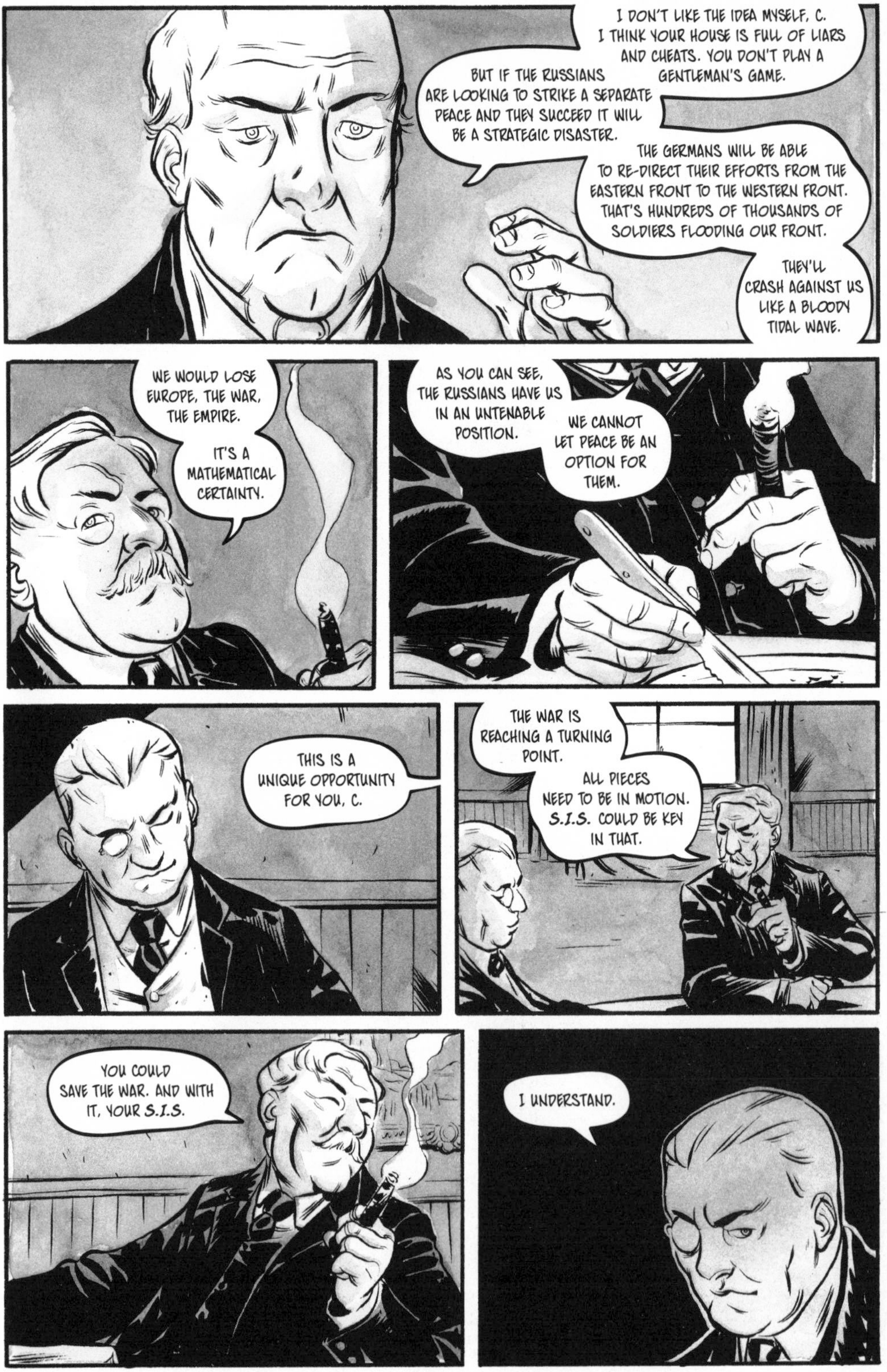
I DON'T LIKE THE IDEA MYSELF, C. I THINK YOUR HOUSE IS FULL OF LIARS AND CHEATS. YOU DON'T PLAY A GENTLEMAN'S GAME.
BUT IF THE RUSSIANS ARE LOOKING TO STRIKE A SEPARATE PEACE AND THEY SUCCEED IT WILL BE A STRATEGIC DISASTER.
THE GERMANS WILL BE ABLE TO RE-DIRECT THEIR EFFORTS FROM THE EASTERN FRONT TO THE WESTERN FRONT. THAT'S HUNDREDS OF THOUSANDS OF SOLDIERS FLOODING OUR FRONT.
THEY'LL CRASH AGAINST US LIKE A BLOODY TIDAL WAVE.
WE WOULD LOSE EUROPE, THE WAR, THE EMPIRE.
IT'S A MATHEMATICAL CERTAINTY.
AS YOU CAN SEE, THE RUSSIANS HAVE US IN AN UNTENABLE POSITION.
WE CANNOT LET PEACE BE AN OPTION FOR THEM.
THIS IS A UNIQUE OPPORTUNITY FOR YOU, C.
THE WAR IS REACHING A TURNING POINT.
ALL PIECES NEED TO BE IN MOTION. S.I.S. COULD BE KEY IN THAT.
YOU COULD SAVE THE WAR. AND WITH IT, YOUR S.I.S.
I UNDERSTAND.

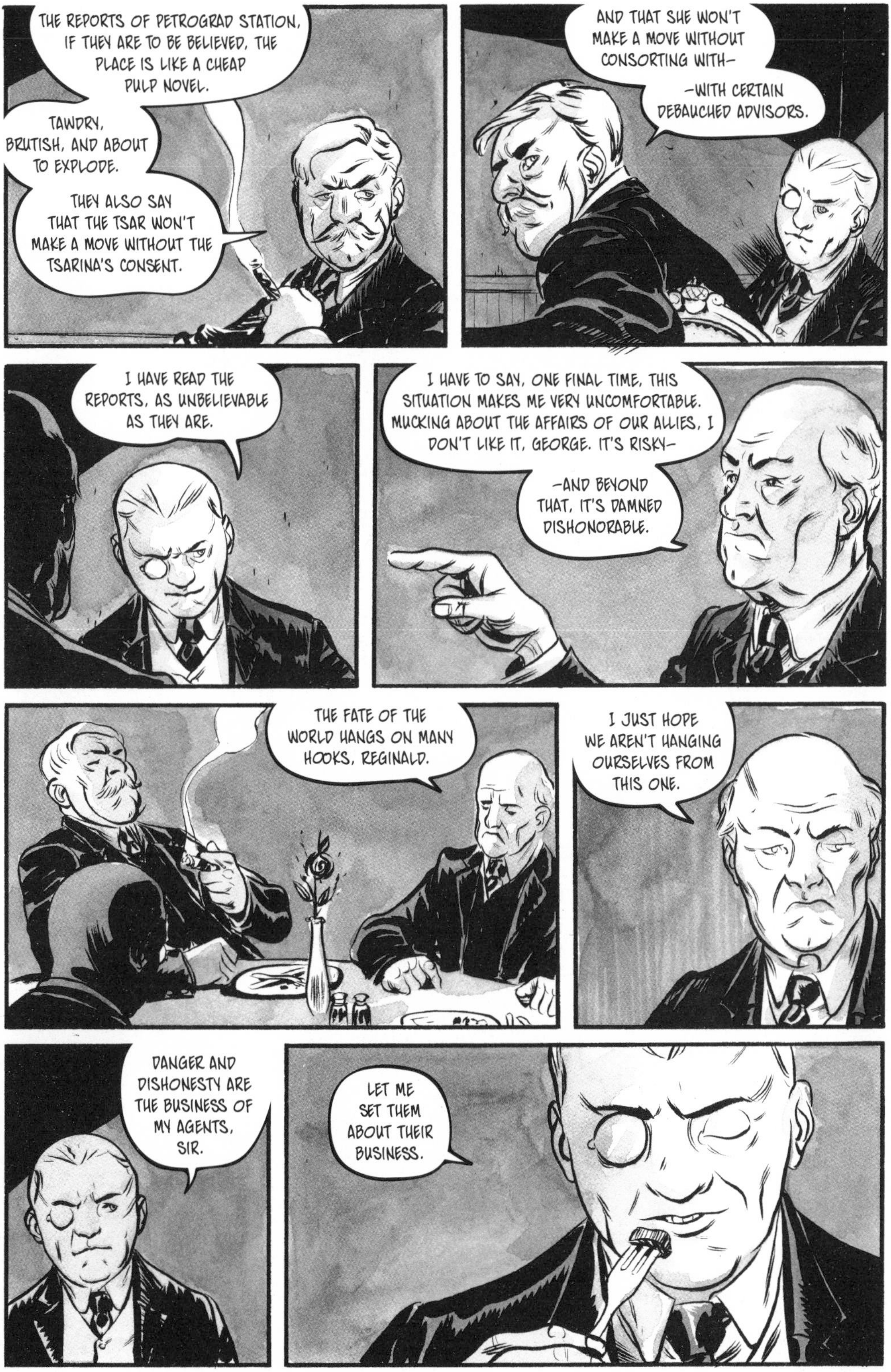
THE REPORTS OF PETROGRAD STATION, IF THEY ARE TO BE BELIEVED, THE PLACE IS LIKE A CHEAP PULP NOVEL.
TAWDRY, BRUTISH, AND ABOUT TO EXPLODE.
THEY ALSO SAY THAT THE TSAR WON'T MAKE A MOVE WITHOUT THE TSARINA'S CONSENT.
AND THAT SHE WON'T MAKE A MOVE WITHOUT CONSORTING WITH–
–WITH CERTAIN DEBAUCHED ADVISORS.
I HAVE READ THE REPORTS, AS UNBELIEVABLE AS THEY ARE.
I HAVE TO SAY, ONE FINAL TIME, THIS SITUATION MAKES ME VERY UNCOMFORTABLE. MUCKING ABOUT THE AFFAIRS OF OUR ALLIES, I DON'T LIKE IT, GEORGE. IT'S RISKY–
–AND BEYOND THAT, IT'S DAMNED DISHONORABLE.
THE FATE OF THE WORLD HANGS ON MANY HOOKS, REGINALD.
I JUST HOPE WE AREN'T HANGING OURSELVES FROM THIS ONE.
DANGER AND DISHONESTY ARE THE BUSINESS OF MY AGENTS, SIR.
LET ME SET THEM ABOUT THEIR BUSINESS.

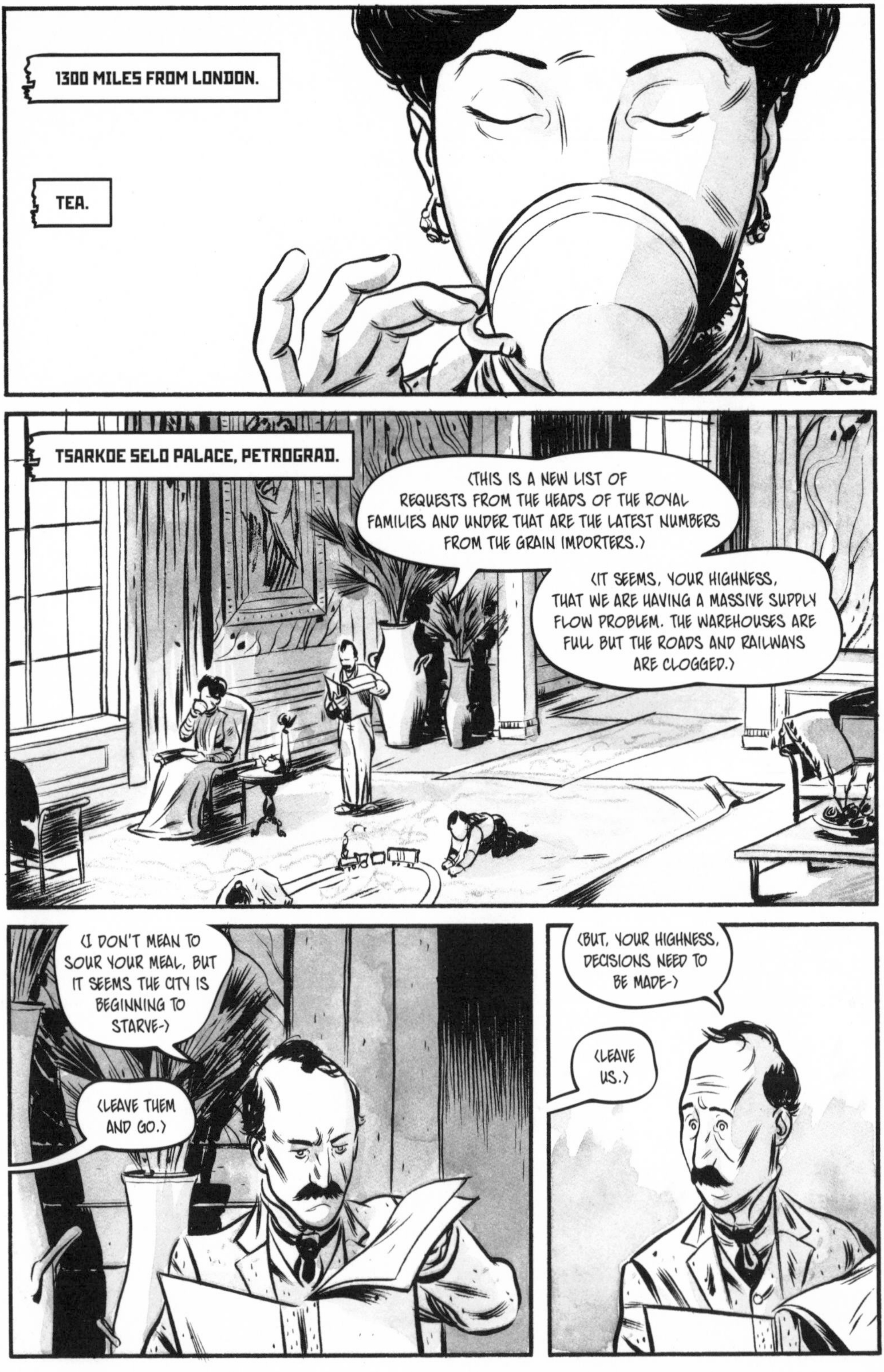
1300 MILES FROM LONDON.
TEA.
TSARKOE SELO PALACE, PETROGRAD.
(THIS IS A NEW LIST OF REQUESTS FROM THE HEADS OF THE ROYAL FAMILIES AND UNDER THAT ARE THE LATEST NUMBERS FROM THE GRAIN IMPORTERS.)
(IT SEEMS, YOUR HIGHNESS, THAT WE ARE HAVING A MASSIVE SUPPLY FLOW PROBLEM. THE WAREHOUSES ARE FULL BUT THE ROADS AND RAILWAYS ARE CLOGGED.)
(I DON'T MEAN TO SOUR YOUR MEAL, BUT IT SEEMS THE CITY IS BEGINNING TO STARVE-)
(LEAVE THEM AND GO.)
(BUT, YOUR HIGHNESS, DECISIONS NEED TO BE MADE-)
(LEAVE US.)

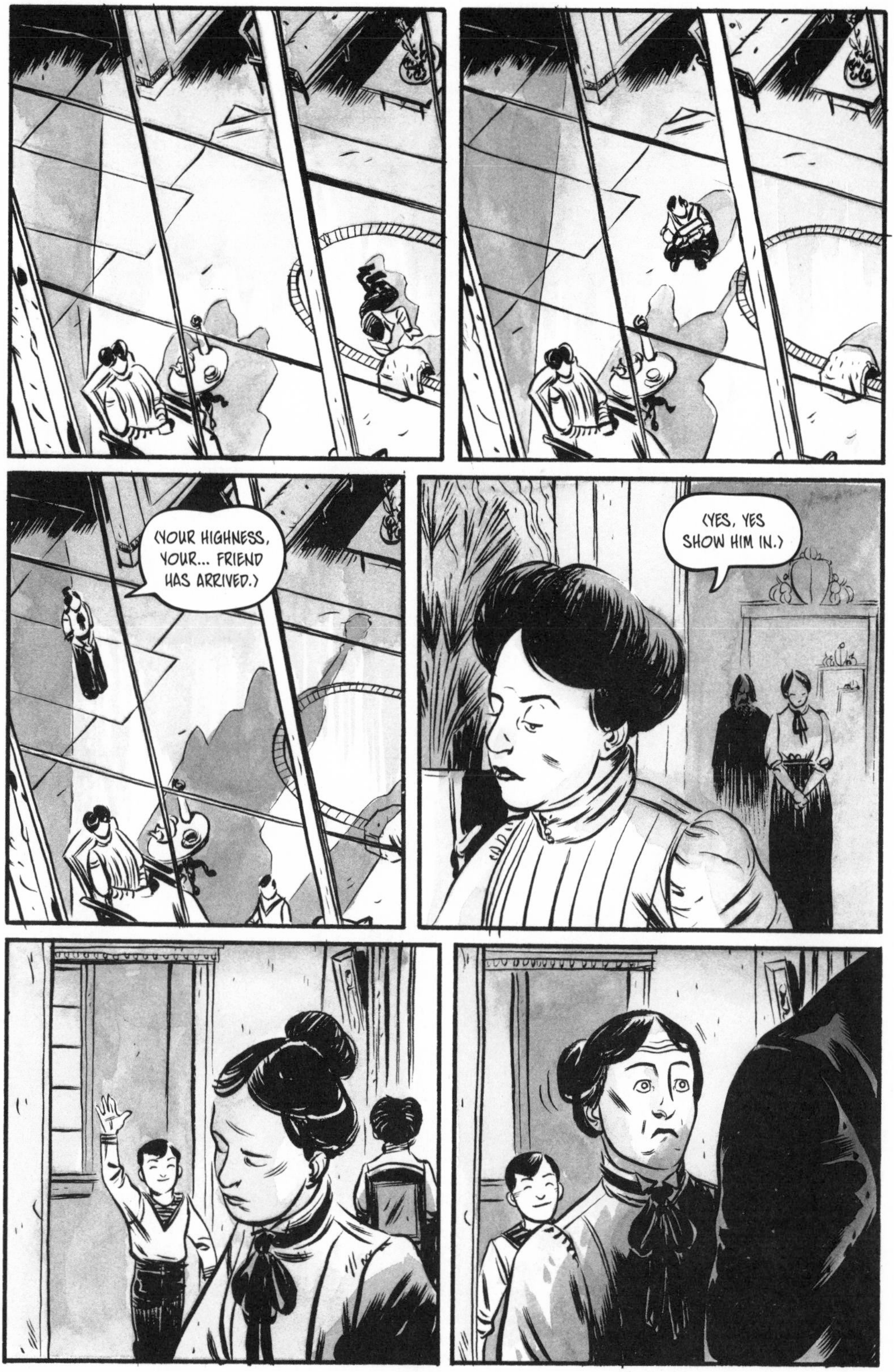
(YOUR HIGHNESS, YOUR... FRIEND HAS ARRIVED.)
(YES, YES SHOW HIM IN.)

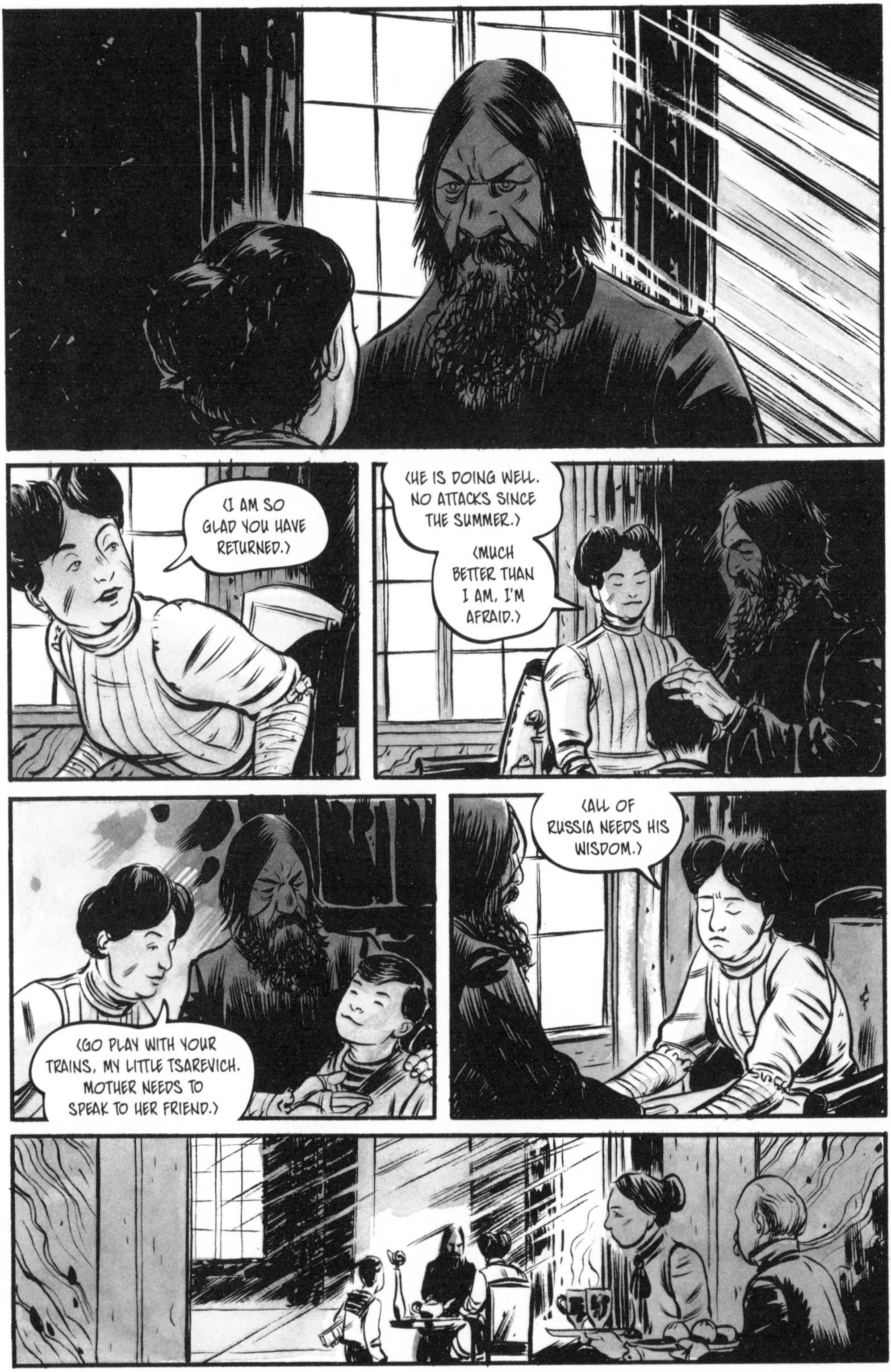
⟨I AM SO GLAD YOU HAVE RETURNED.⟩
⟨HE IS DOING WELL. NO ATTACKS SINCE THE SUMMER.⟩
⟨MUCH BETTER THAN I AM, I'M AFRAID.⟩
⟨GO PLAY WITH YOUR TRAINS, MY LITTLE TSAREVICH. MOTHER NEEDS TO SPEAK TO HER FRIEND.⟩
⟨ALL OF RUSSIA NEEDS HIS WISDOM.⟩

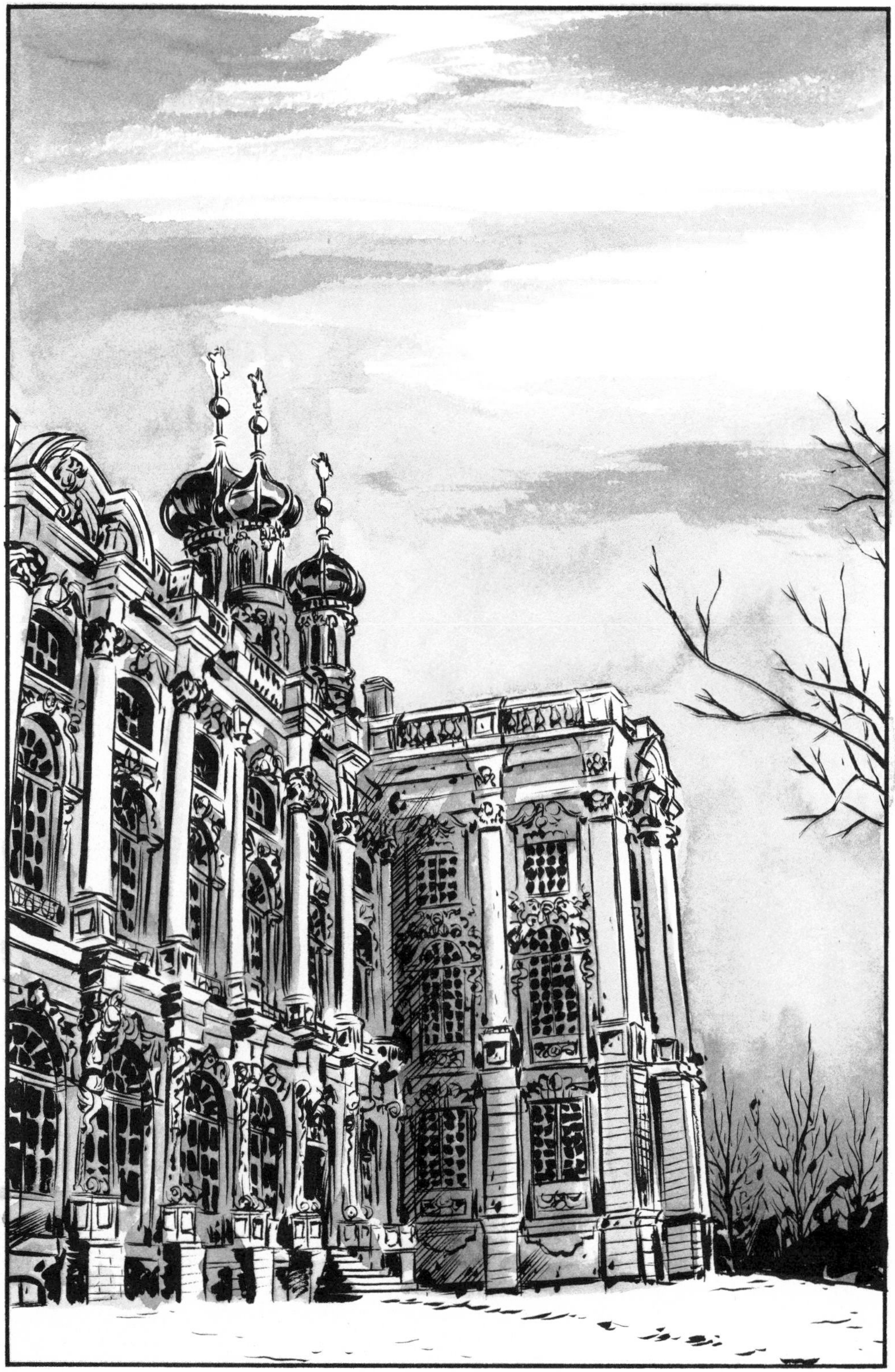

CHAPTER 1

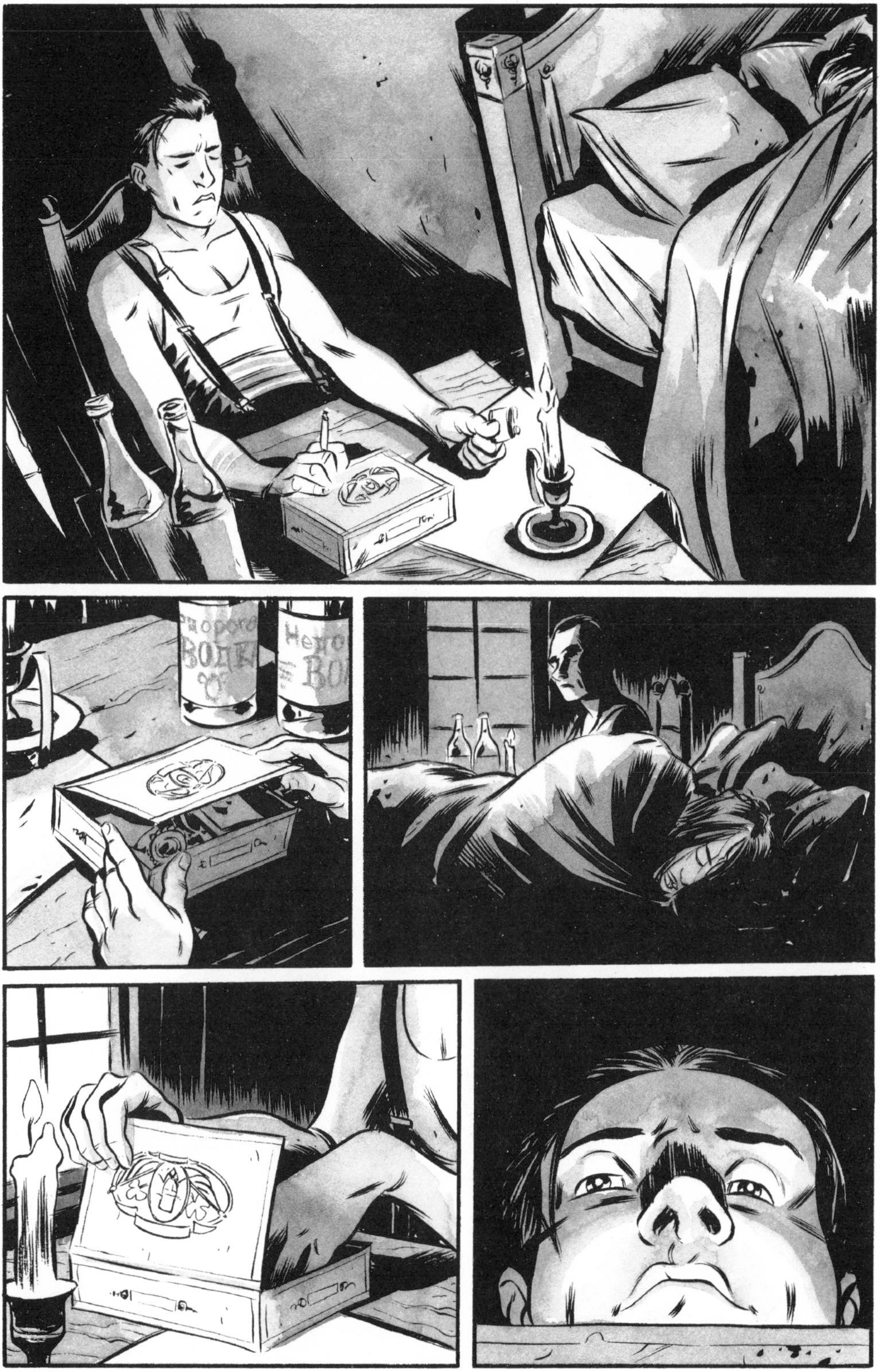

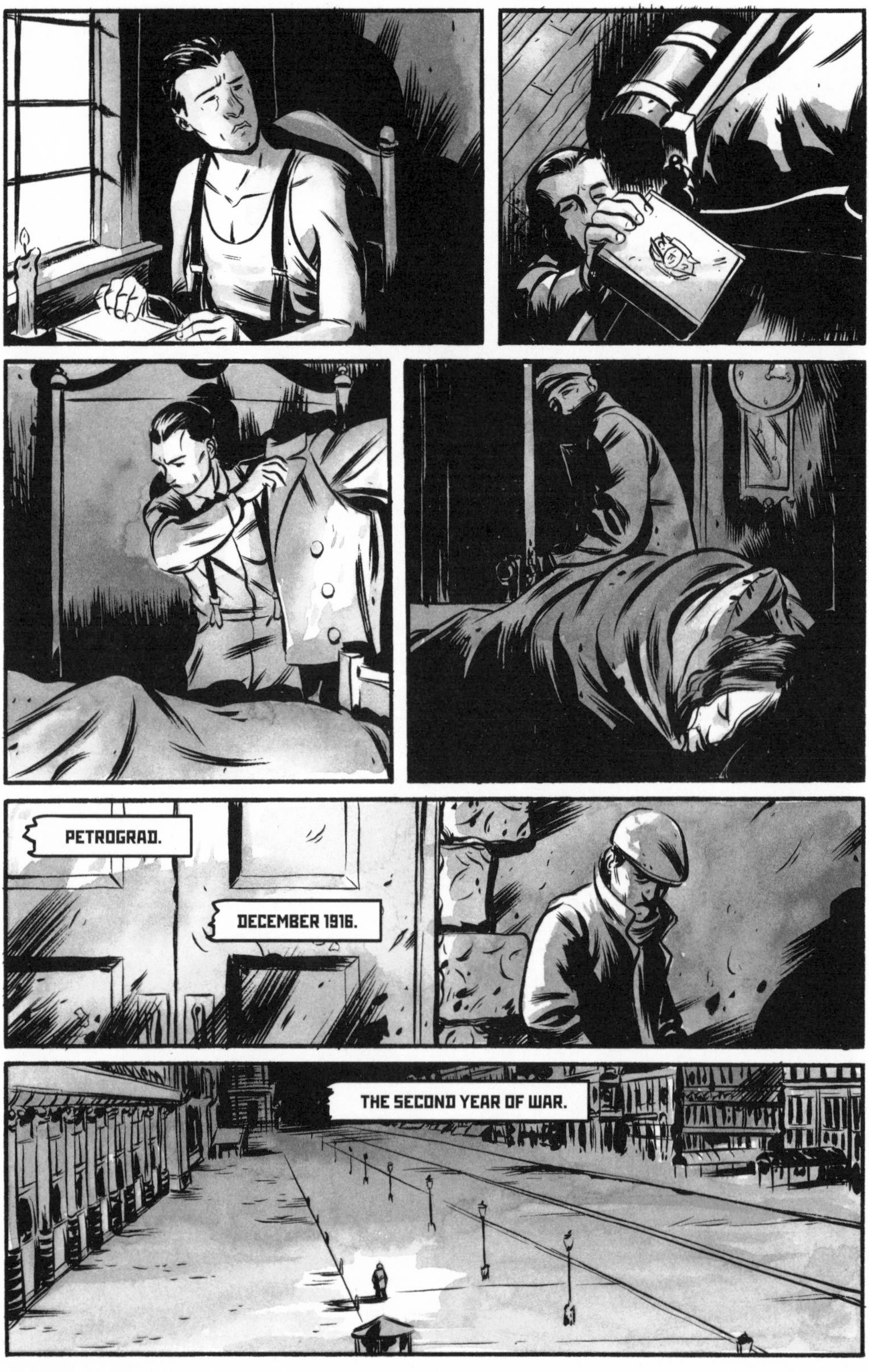
PETROGRAD.
DECEMBER 1916.
THE SECOND YEAR OF WAR.

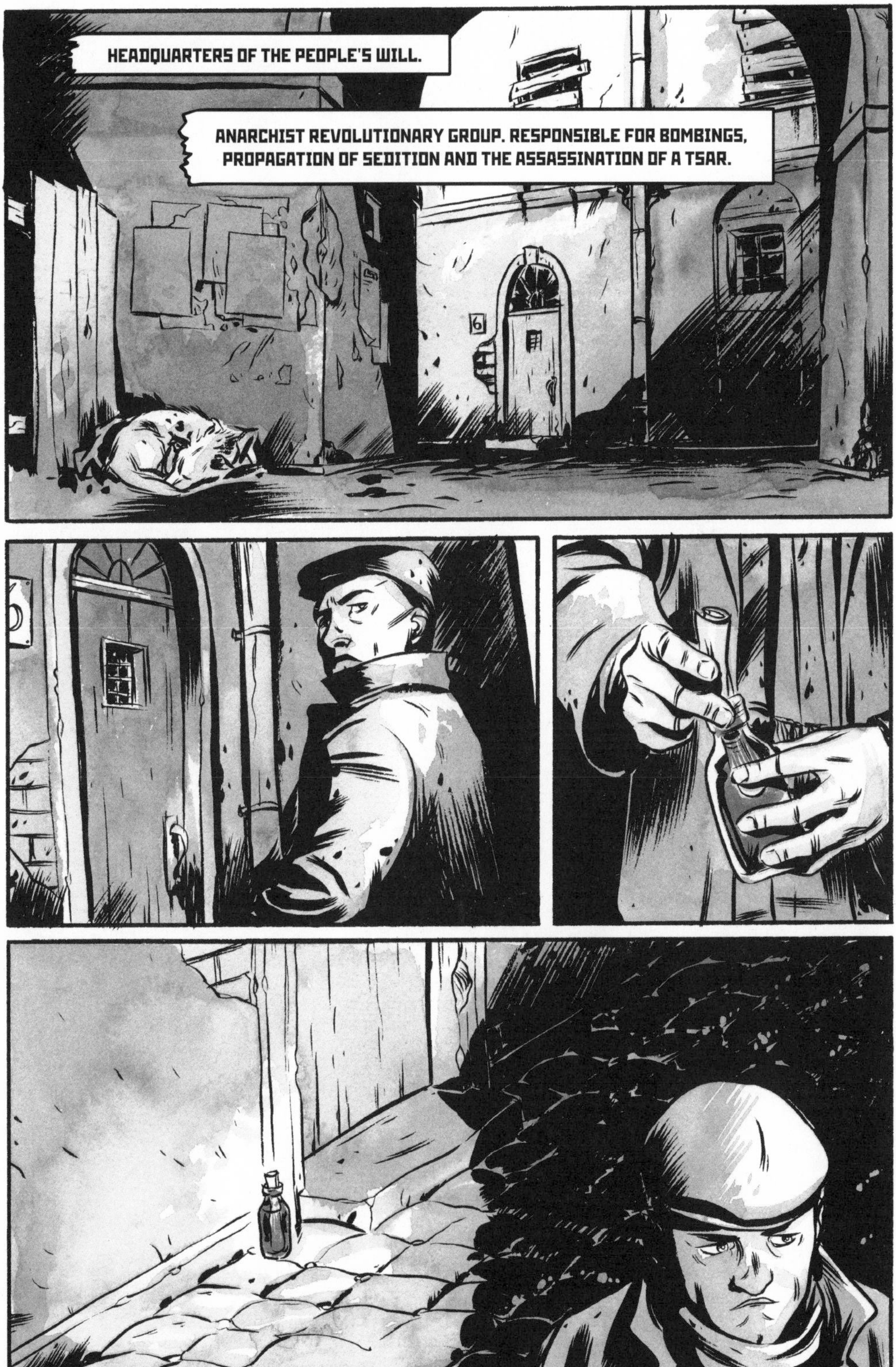
HEADQUARTERS OF THE PEOPLE'S WILL.
ANARCHIST REVOLUTIONARY GROUP. RESPONSIBLE FOR BOMBINGS, PROPAGATION OF SEDITION AND THE ASSASSINATION OF A TSAR.
6

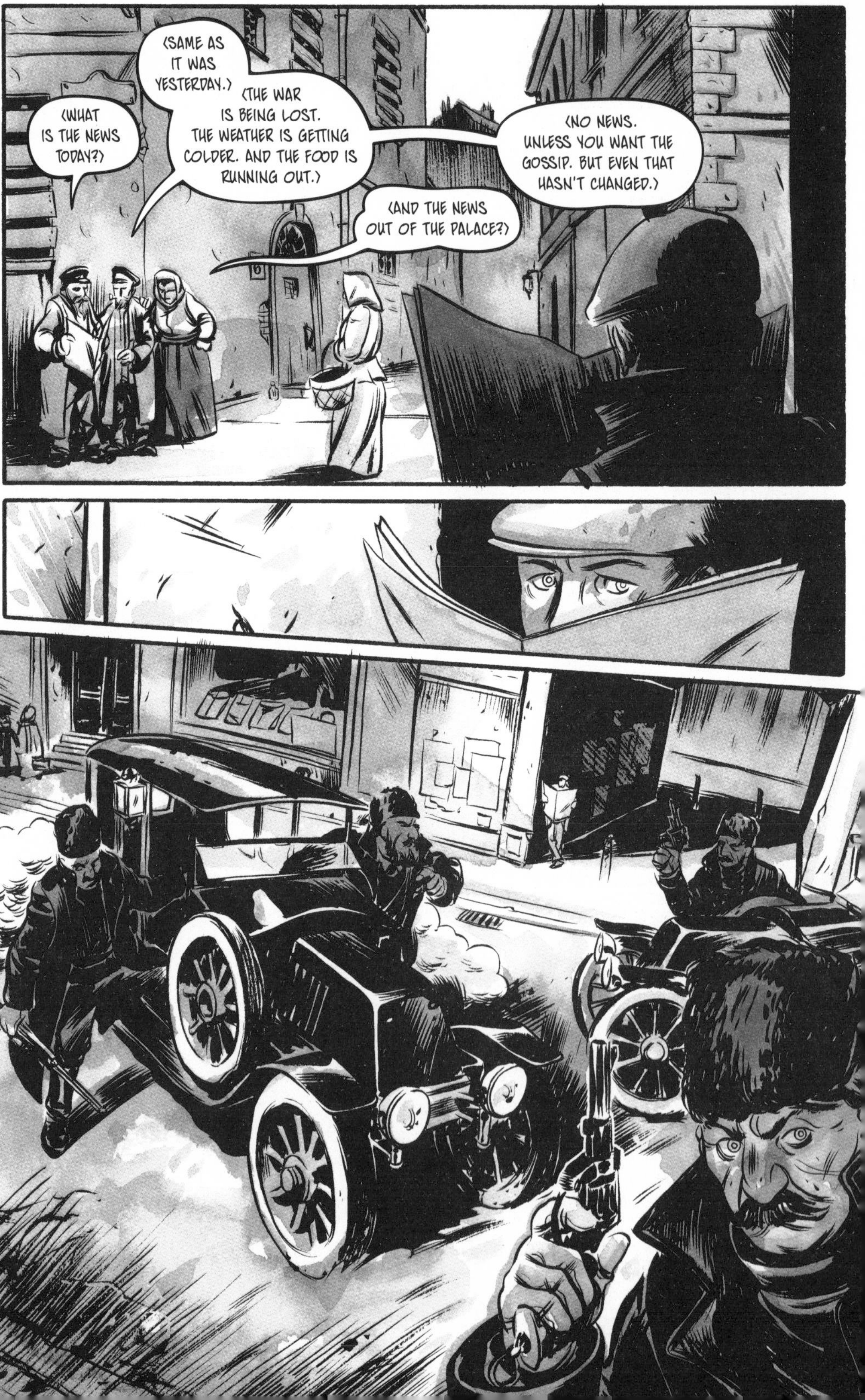
<WHAT IS THE NEWS TODAY?>
<SAME AS IT WAS YESTERDAY.>
<THE WAR IS BEING LOST. THE WEATHER IS GETTING COLDER. AND THE FOOD IS RUNNING OUT.>
<NO NEWS. UNLESS YOU WANT THE GOSSIP. BUT EVEN THAT HASN'T CHANGED.>
<AND THE NEWS OUT OF THE PALACE?>

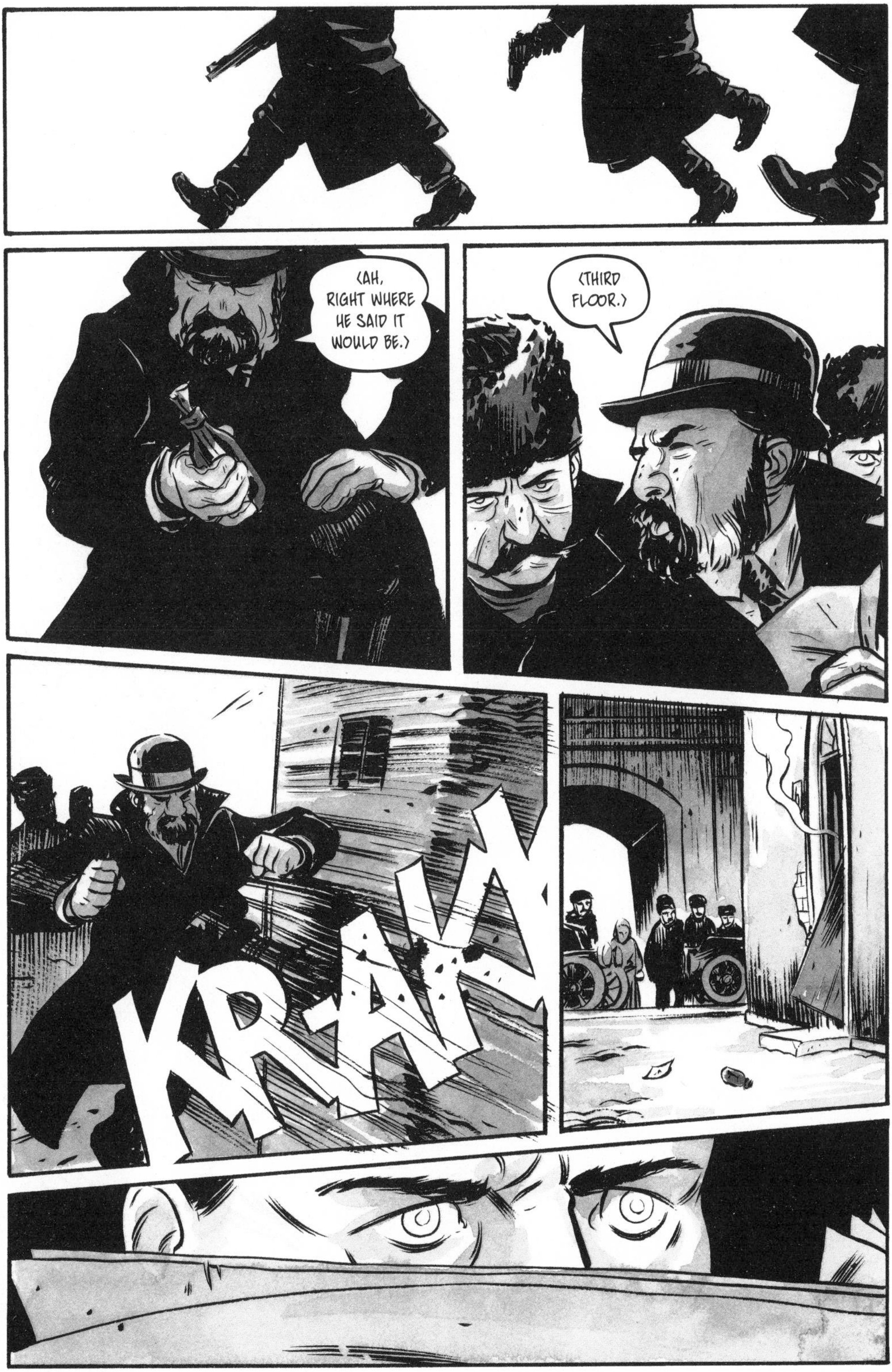
‹AH, RIGHT WHERE HE SAID IT WOULD BE.›
‹THIRD FLOOR.›
KR-AK

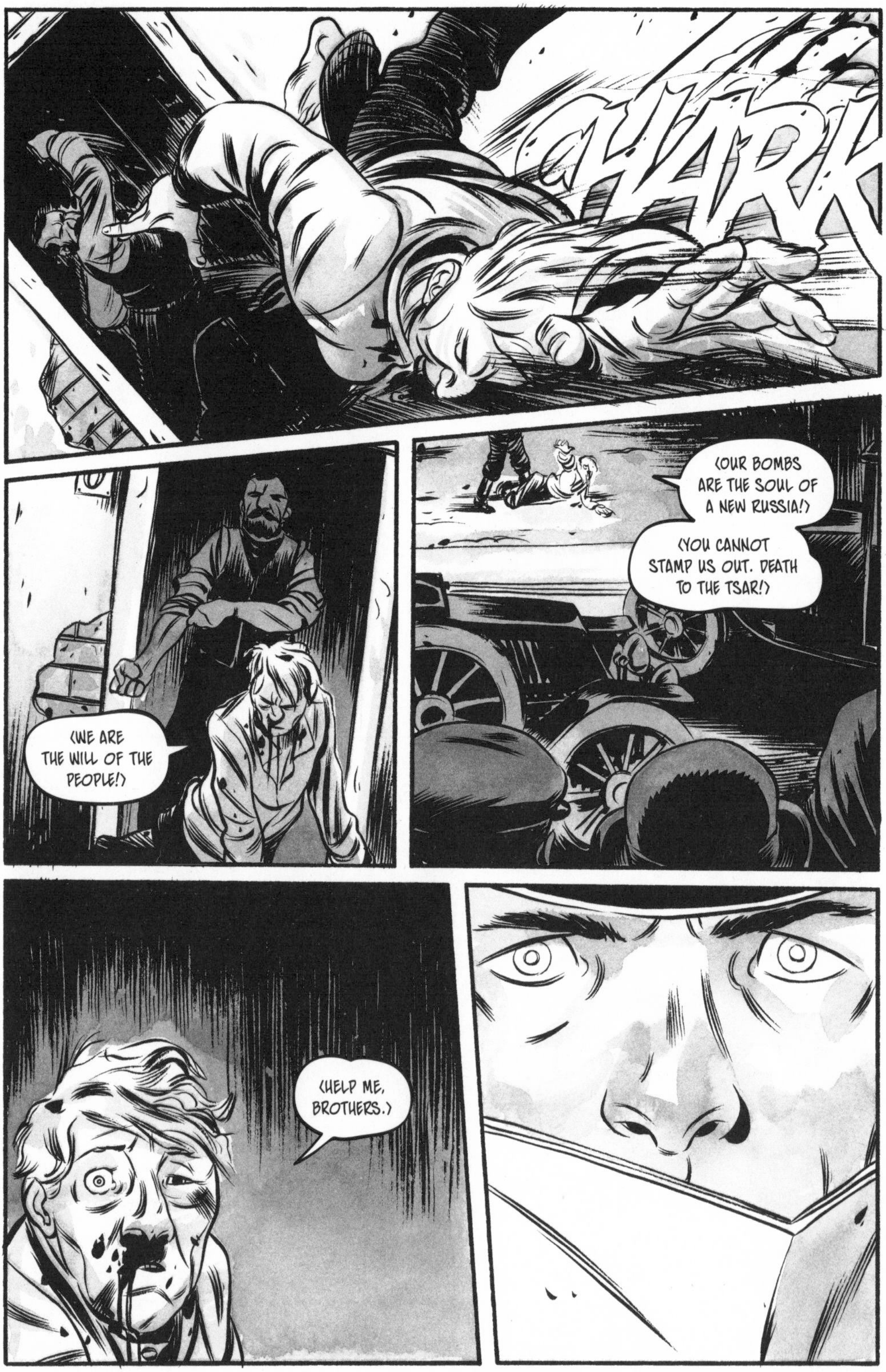

GHARK
‹WE ARE THE WILL OF THE PEOPLE!›
‹OUR BOMBS ARE THE SOUL OF A NEW RUSSIA!›
‹YOU CANNOT STAMP US OUT. DEATH TO THE TSAR!›
‹HELP ME, BROTHERS.›

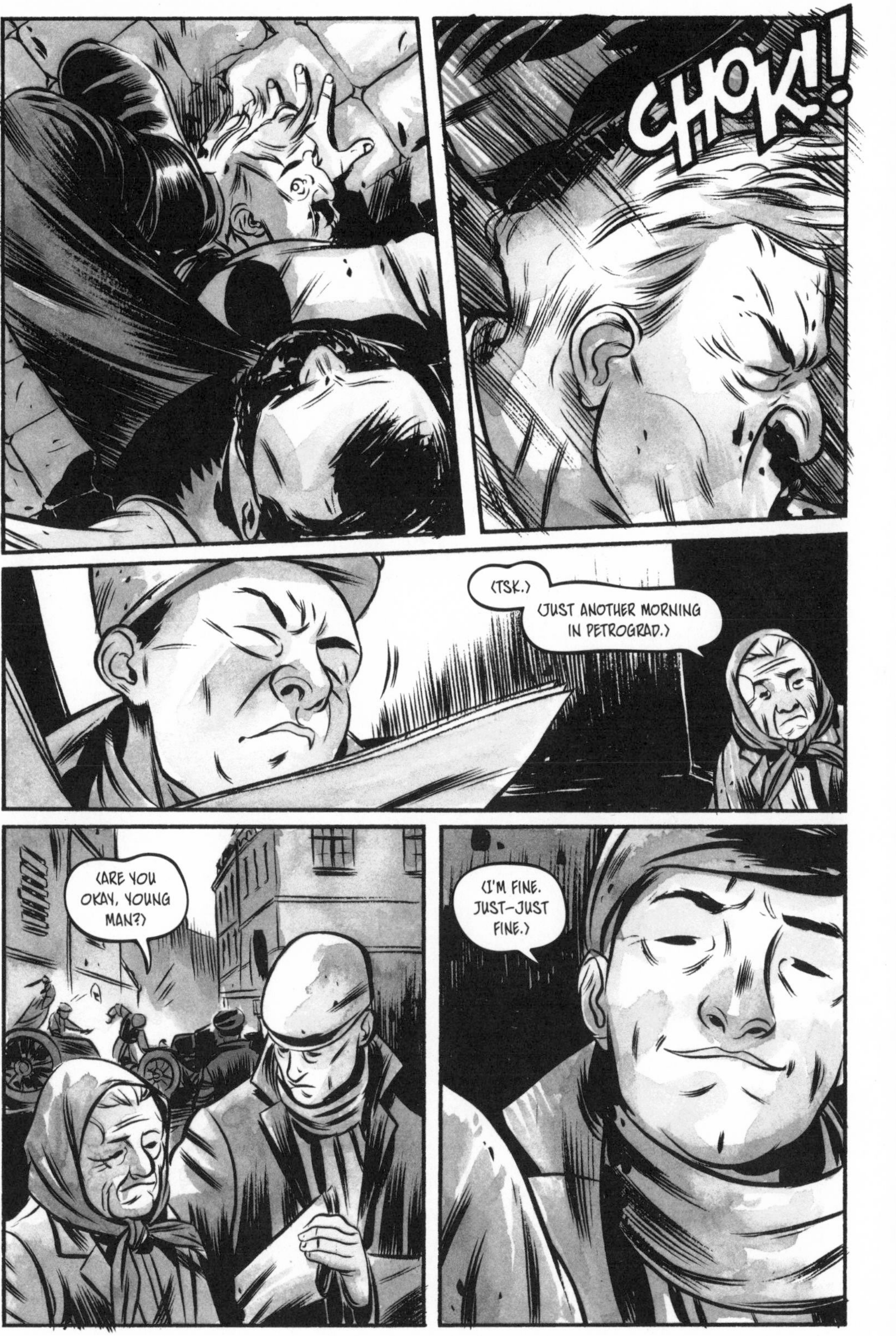
CHOK!
(TSK.)
(JUST ANOTHER MORNING IN PETROGRAD.)
(ARE YOU OKAY, YOUNG MAN?)
(I'M FINE. JUST—JUST FINE.)

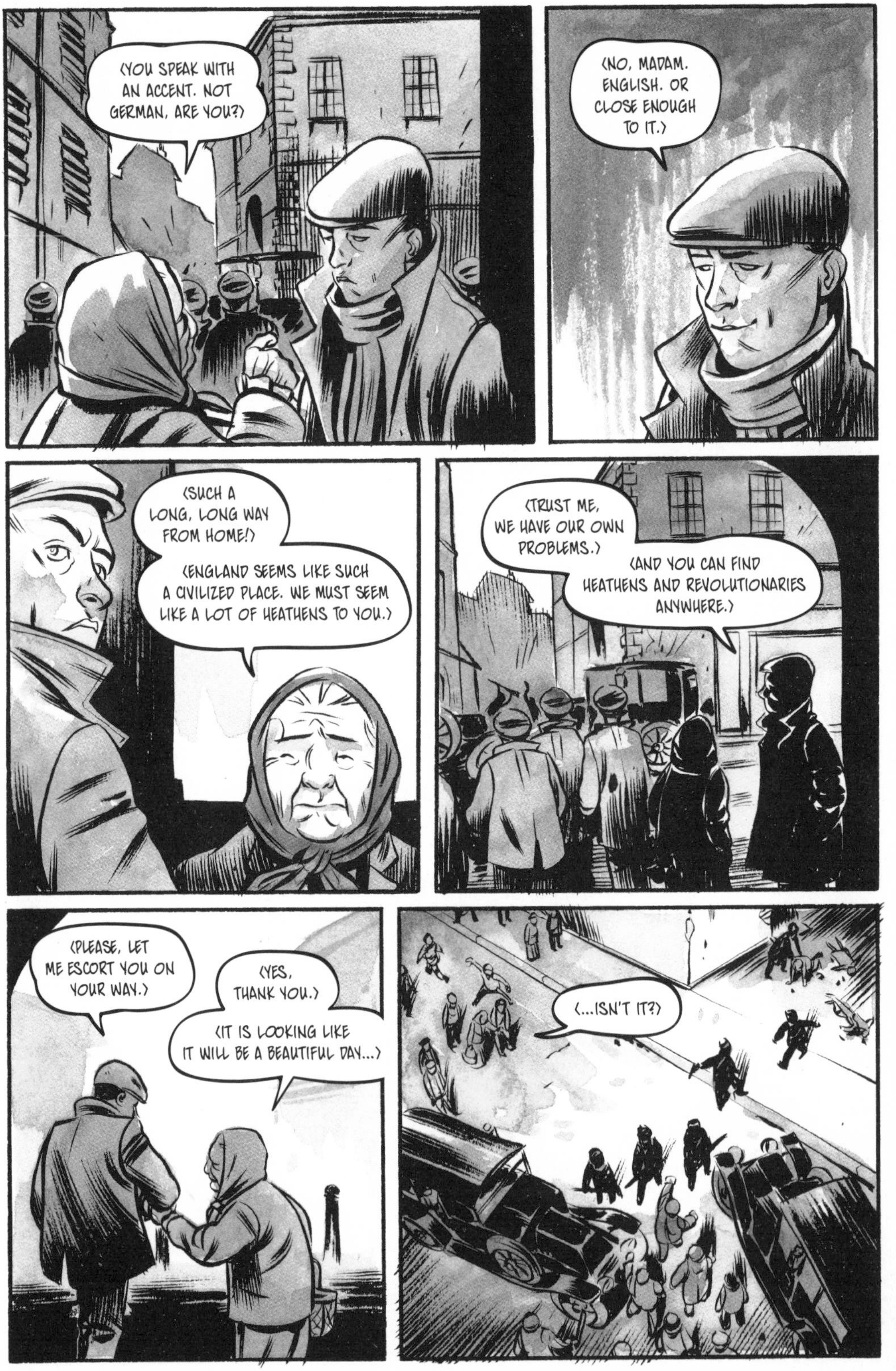
‹YOU SPEAK WITH AN ACCENT. NOT GERMAN, ARE YOU?›
‹NO, MADAM. ENGLISH. OR CLOSE ENOUGH TO IT.›
‹SUCH A LONG, LONG WAY FROM HOME!›
‹ENGLAND SEEMS LIKE SUCH A CIVILIZED PLACE. WE MUST SEEM LIKE A LOT OF HEATHENS TO YOU.›
‹TRUST ME, WE HAVE OUR OWN PROBLEMS.›
‹AND YOU CAN FIND HEATHENS AND REVOLUTIONARIES ANYWHERE.›
‹PLEASE, LET ME ESCORT YOU ON YOUR WAY.›
‹YES, THANK YOU.›
‹IT IS LOOKING LIKE IT WILL BE A BEAUTIFUL DAY...›
‹...ISN'T IT?›

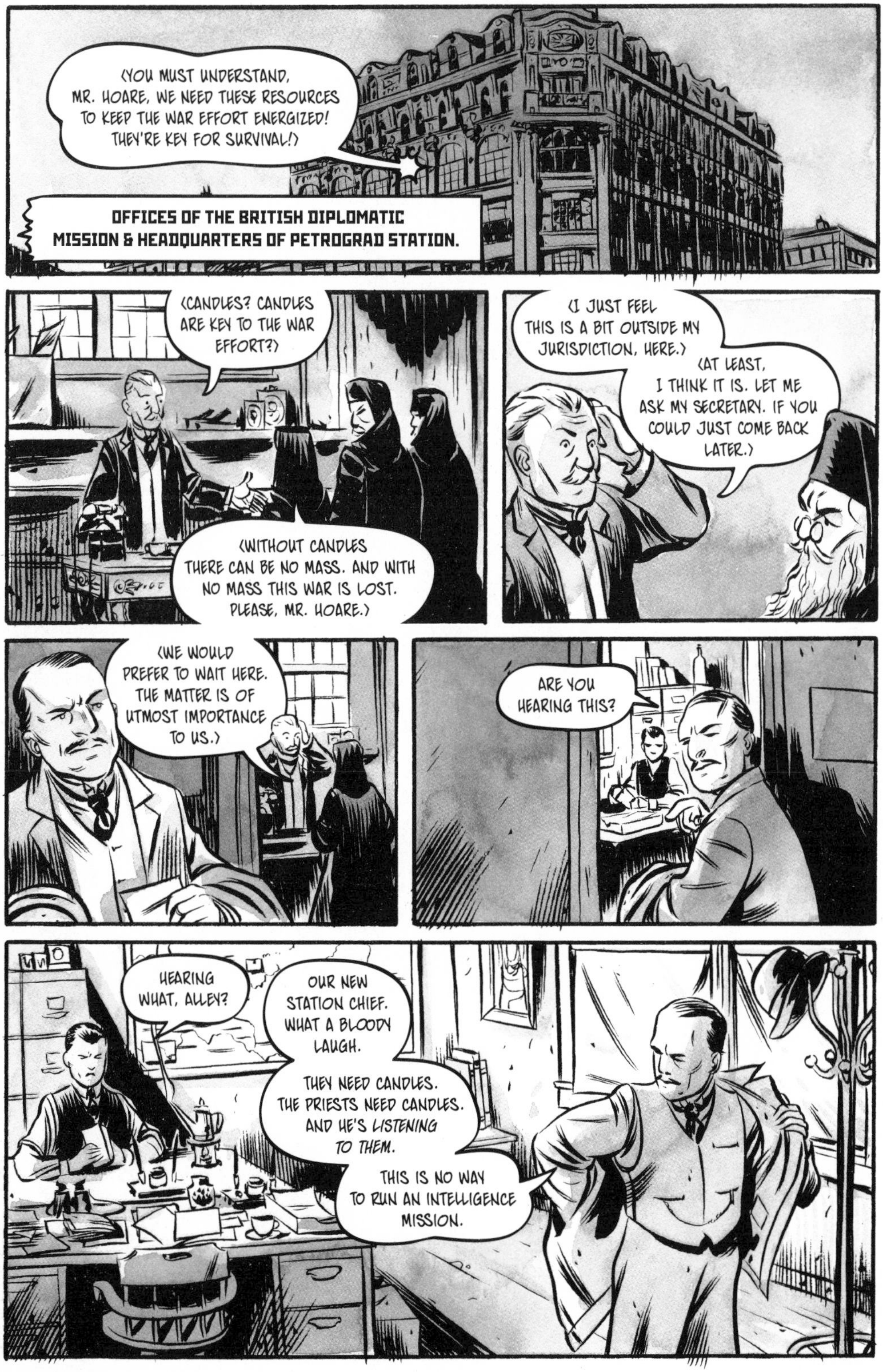
(YOU MUST UNDERSTAND, MR. HOARE, WE NEED THESE RESOURCES TO KEEP THE WAR EFFORT ENERGIZED! THEY'RE KEY FOR SURVIVAL!)
OFFICES OF THE BRITISH DIPLOMATIC MISSION & HEADQUARTERS OF PETROGRAD STATION.
(CANDLES? CANDLES ARE KEY TO THE WAR EFFORT?)
(WITHOUT CANDLES THERE CAN BE NO MASS. AND WITH NO MASS THIS WAR IS LOST. PLEASE, MR. HOARE.)
(I JUST FEEL THIS IS A BIT OUTSIDE MY JURISDICTION, HERE.)
(AT LEAST, I THINK IT IS. LET ME ASK MY SECRETARY. IF YOU COULD JUST COME BACK LATER.)
(WE WOULD PREFER TO WAIT HERE. THE MATTER IS OF UTMOST IMPORTANCE TO US.)
ARE YOU HEARING THIS?
HEARING WHAT, ALLEY?
OUR NEW STATION CHIEF. WHAT A BLOODY LAUGH.
THEY NEED CANDLES. THE PRIESTS NEED CANDLES. AND HE'S *LISTENING* TO THEM.
THIS IS NO WAY TO RUN AN INTELLIGENCE MISSION.

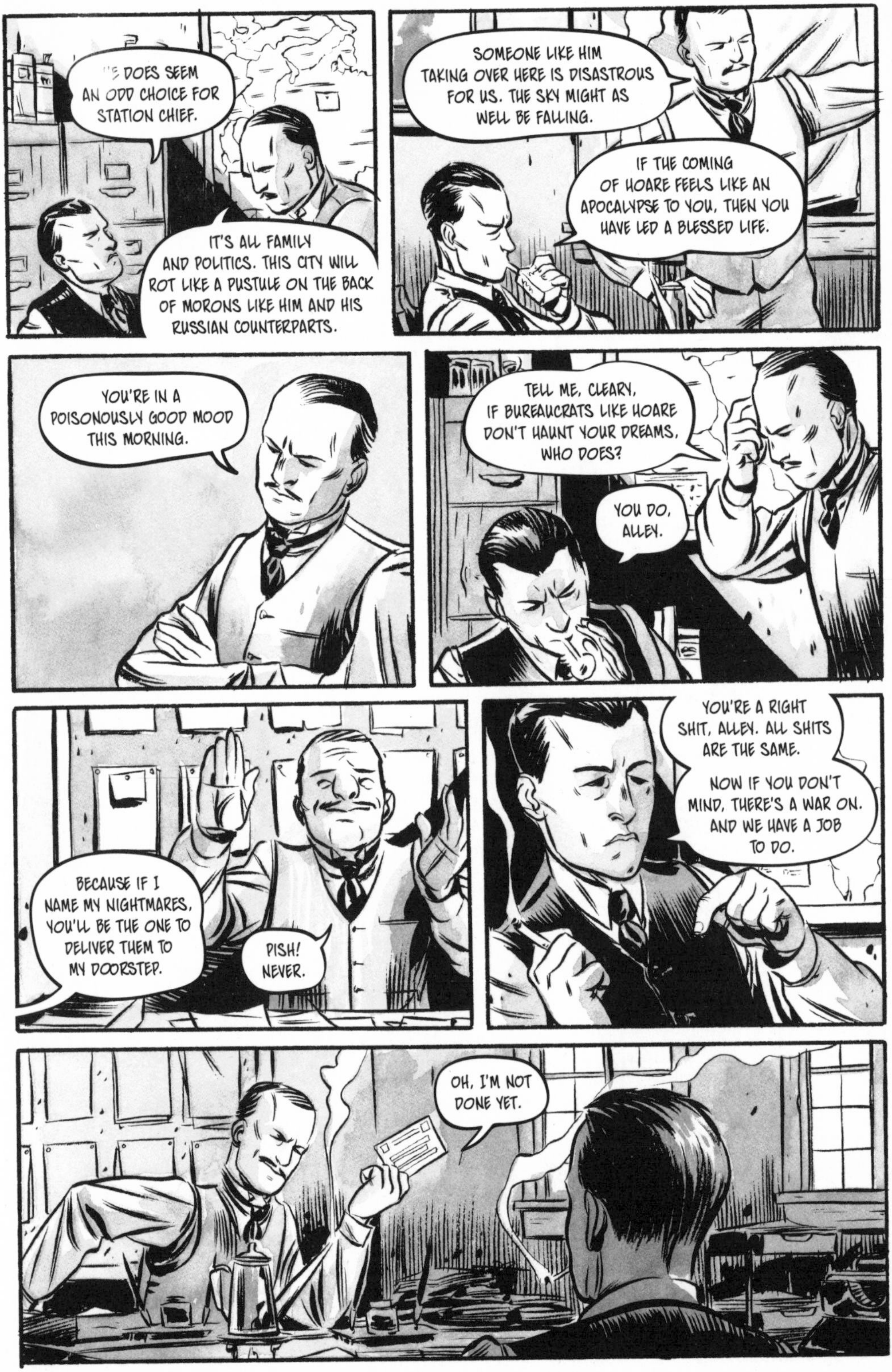

HE DOES SEEM AN ODD CHOICE FOR STATION CHIEF.
IT'S ALL FAMILY AND POLITICS. THIS CITY WILL ROT LIKE A PUSTULE ON THE BACK OF MORONS LIKE HIM AND HIS RUSSIAN COUNTERPARTS.
SOMEONE LIKE HIM TAKING OVER HERE IS DISASTROUS FOR US. THE SKY MIGHT AS WELL BE FALLING.
IF THE COMING OF HOARE FEELS LIKE AN APOCALYPSE TO YOU, THEN YOU HAVE LED A BLESSED LIFE.
YOU'RE IN A POISONOUSLY GOOD MOOD THIS MORNING.
TELL ME, CLEARY, IF BUREAUCRATS LIKE HOARE DON'T HAUNT YOUR DREAMS, WHO DOES?
YOU DO, ALLEY.
BECAUSE IF I NAME MY NIGHTMARES, YOU'LL BE THE ONE TO DELIVER THEM TO MY DOORSTEP.
PISH! NEVER.
YOU'RE A RIGHT SHIT, ALLEY. ALL SHITS ARE THE SAME.
NOW IF YOU DON'T MIND, THERE'S A WAR ON. AND WE HAVE A JOB TO DO.
OH, I'M NOT DONE YET.

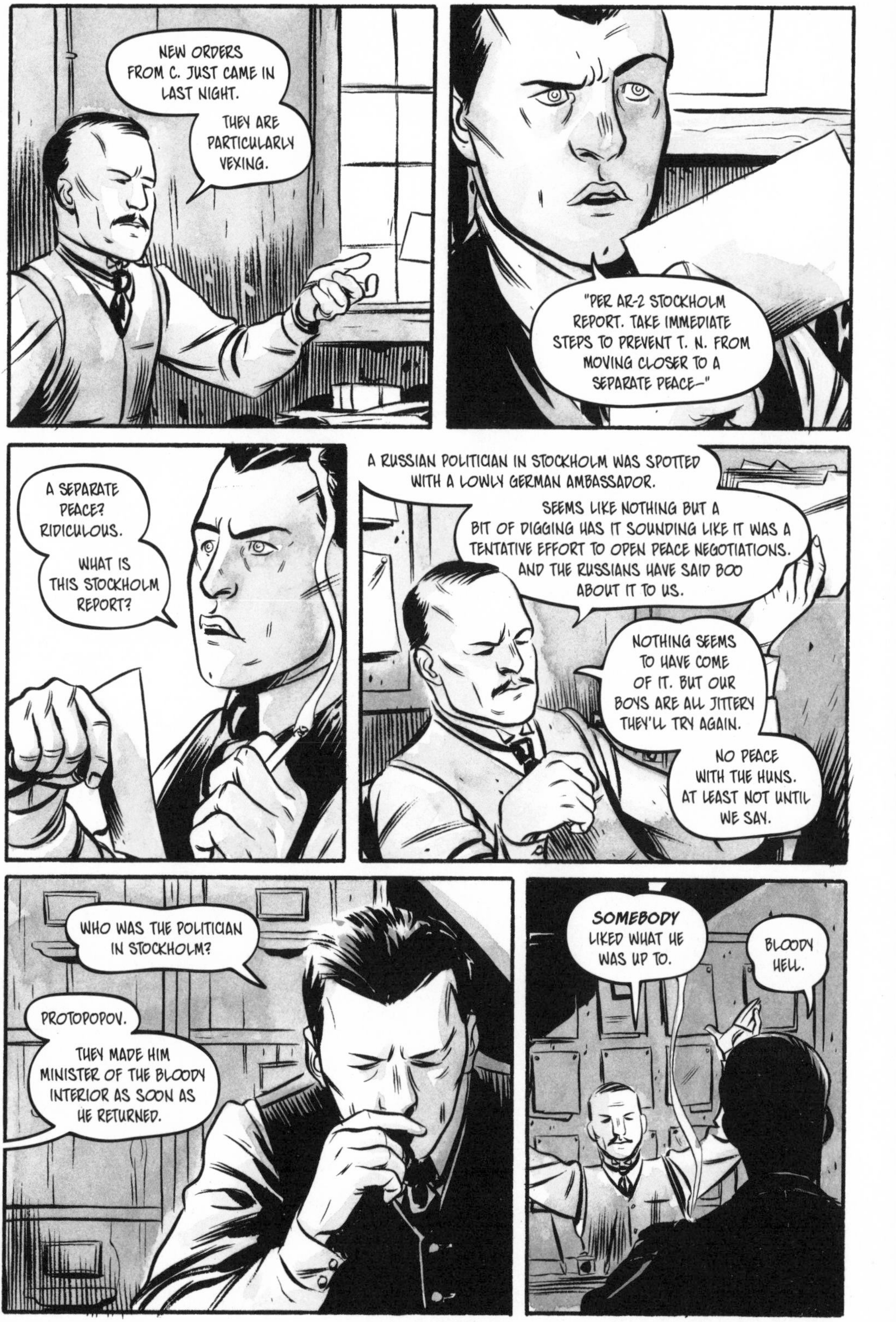
NEW ORDERS FROM C. JUST CAME IN LAST NIGHT.
THEY ARE PARTICULARLY VEXING.
"PER AR-2 STOCKHOLM REPORT. TAKE IMMEDIATE STEPS TO PREVENT T. N. FROM MOVING CLOSER TO A SEPARATE PEACE—"
A SEPARATE PEACE? RIDICULOUS.
WHAT IS THIS STOCKHOLM REPORT?
A RUSSIAN POLITICIAN IN STOCKHOLM WAS SPOTTED WITH A LOWLY GERMAN AMBASSADOR.
SEEMS LIKE NOTHING BUT A BIT OF DIGGING HAS IT SOUNDING LIKE IT WAS A TENTATIVE EFFORT TO OPEN PEACE NEGOTIATIONS. AND THE RUSSIANS HAVE SAID BOO ABOUT IT TO US.
NOTHING SEEMS TO HAVE COME OF IT. BUT OUR BOYS ARE ALL JITTERY THEY'LL TRY AGAIN.
NO PEACE WITH THE HUNS. AT LEAST NOT UNTIL WE SAY.
WHO WAS THE POLITICIAN IN STOCKHOLM?
PROTOPOPOV.
THEY MADE HIM MINISTER OF THE BLOODY INTERIOR AS SOON AS HE RETURNED.
SOMEBODY LIKED WHAT HE WAS UP TO.
BLOODY HELL.

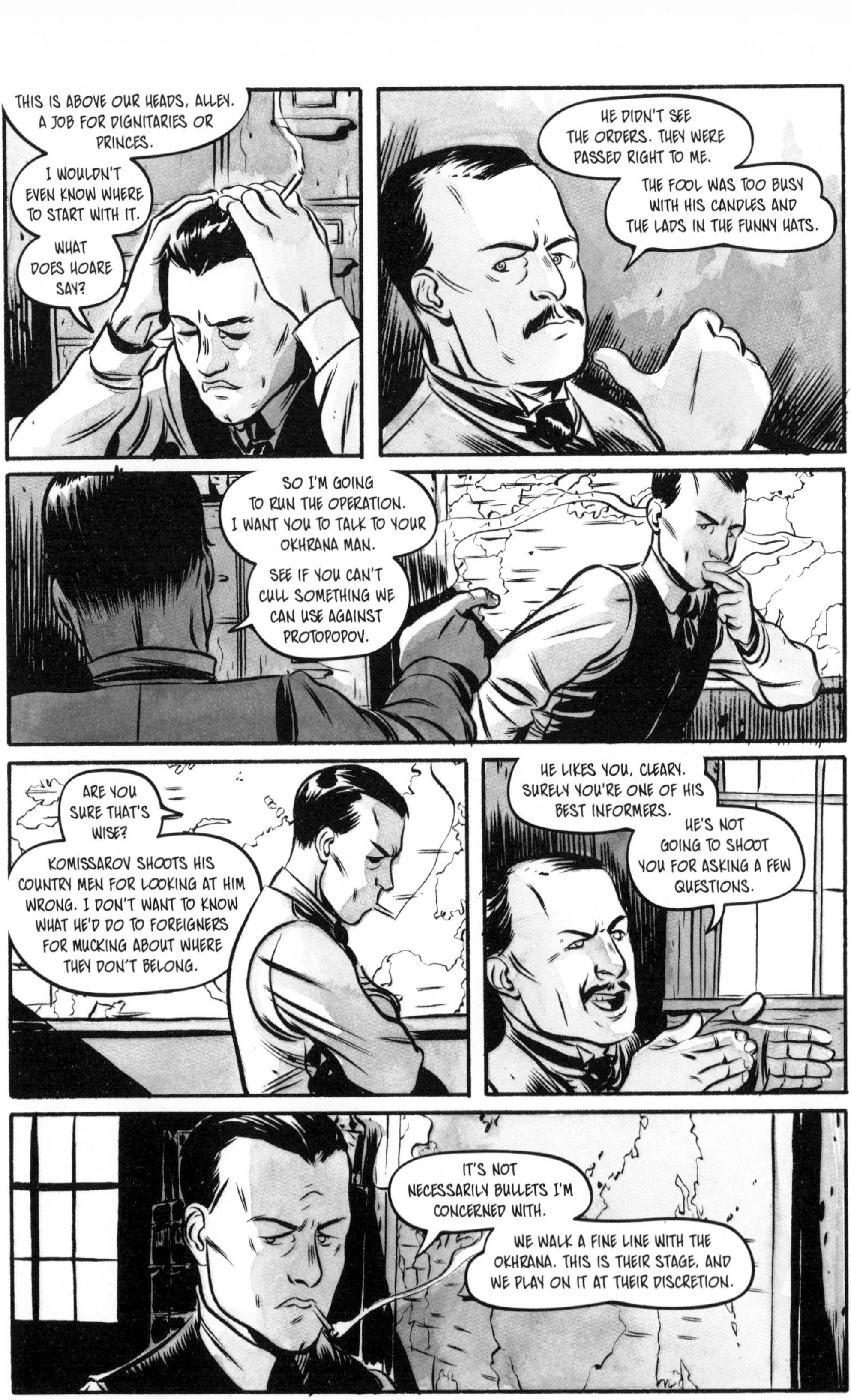
THIS IS ABOVE OUR HEADS, ALLEY. A JOB FOR DIGNITARIES OR PRINCES.
I WOULDN'T EVEN KNOW WHERE TO START WITH IT.
WHAT DOES HOARE SAY?
HE DIDN'T SEE THE ORDERS. THEY WERE PASSED RIGHT TO ME.
THE FOOL WAS TOO BUSY WITH HIS CANDLES AND THE LADS IN THE FUNNY HATS.
SO I'M GOING TO RUN THE OPERATION. I WANT YOU TO TALK TO YOUR OKHRANA MAN.
SEE IF YOU CAN'T CULL SOMETHING WE CAN USE AGAINST PROTOPOPOV.
ARE YOU SURE THAT'S WISE?
KOMISSAROV SHOOTS HIS COUNTRY MEN FOR LOOKING AT HIM WRONG. I DON'T WANT TO KNOW WHAT HE'D DO TO FOREIGNERS FOR MUCKING ABOUT WHERE THEY DON'T BELONG.
HE LIKES YOU, CLEARY. SURELY YOU'RE ONE OF HIS BEST INFORMERS.
HE'S NOT GOING TO SHOOT YOU FOR ASKING A FEW QUESTIONS.
IT'S NOT NECESSARILY BULLETS I'M CONCERNED WITH.
WE WALK A FINE LINE WITH THE OKHRANA. THIS IS THEIR STAGE, AND WE PLAY ON IT AT THEIR DISCRETION.

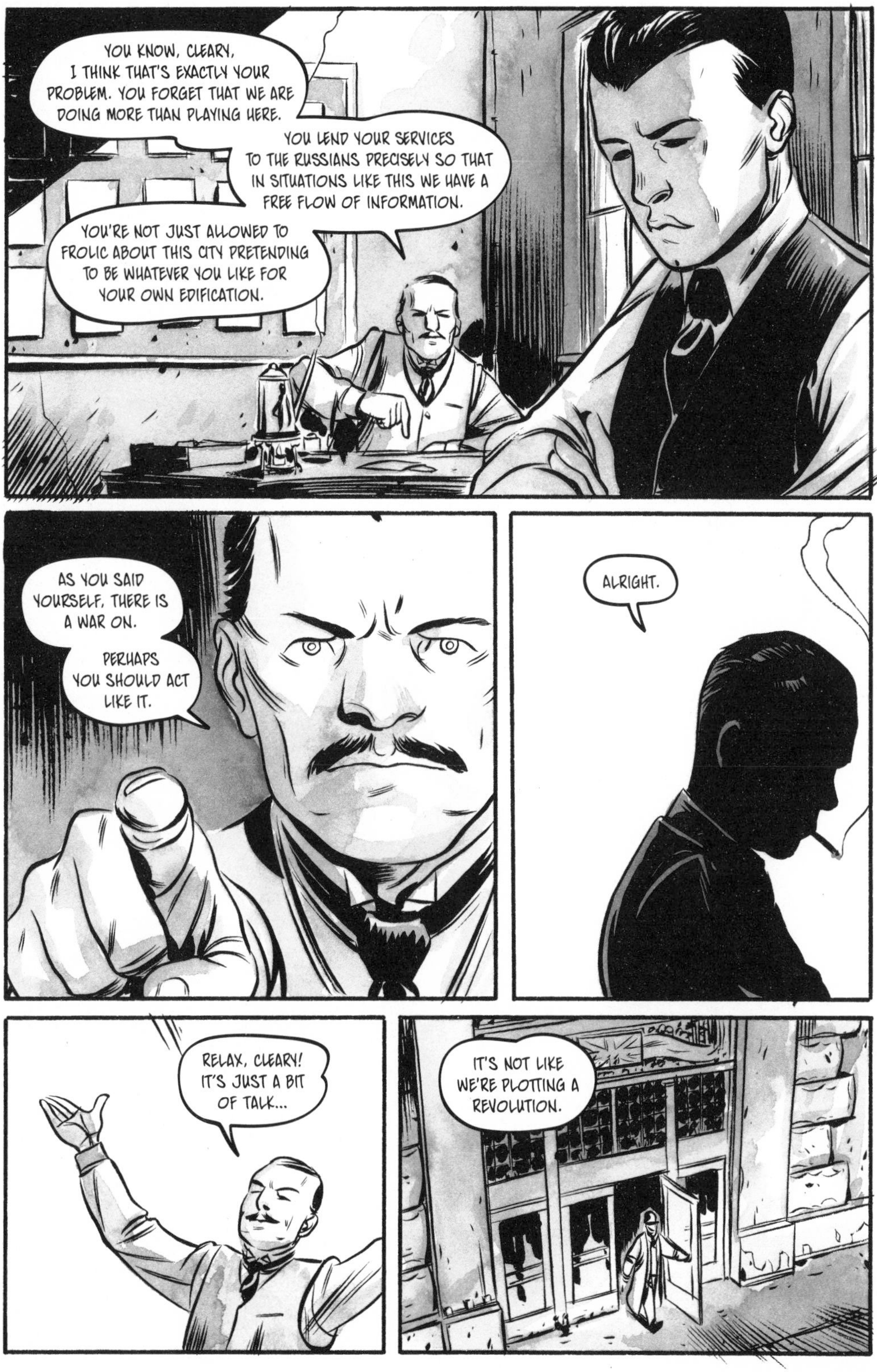
YOU KNOW, CLEARY, I THINK THAT'S EXACTLY YOUR PROBLEM. YOU FORGET THAT WE ARE DOING MORE THAN PLAYING HERE.
YOU LEND YOUR SERVICES TO THE RUSSIANS PRECISELY SO THAT IN SITUATIONS LIKE THIS WE HAVE A FREE FLOW OF INFORMATION.
YOU'RE NOT JUST ALLOWED TO FROLIC ABOUT THIS CITY PRETENDING TO BE WHATEVER YOU LIKE FOR YOUR OWN EDIFICATION.
AS YOU SAID YOURSELF, THERE IS A WAR ON.
PERHAPS YOU SHOULD ACT LIKE IT.
ALRIGHT.
RELAX, CLEARY! IT'S JUST A BIT OF TALK...
IT'S NOT LIKE WE'RE PLOTTING A REVOLUTION.

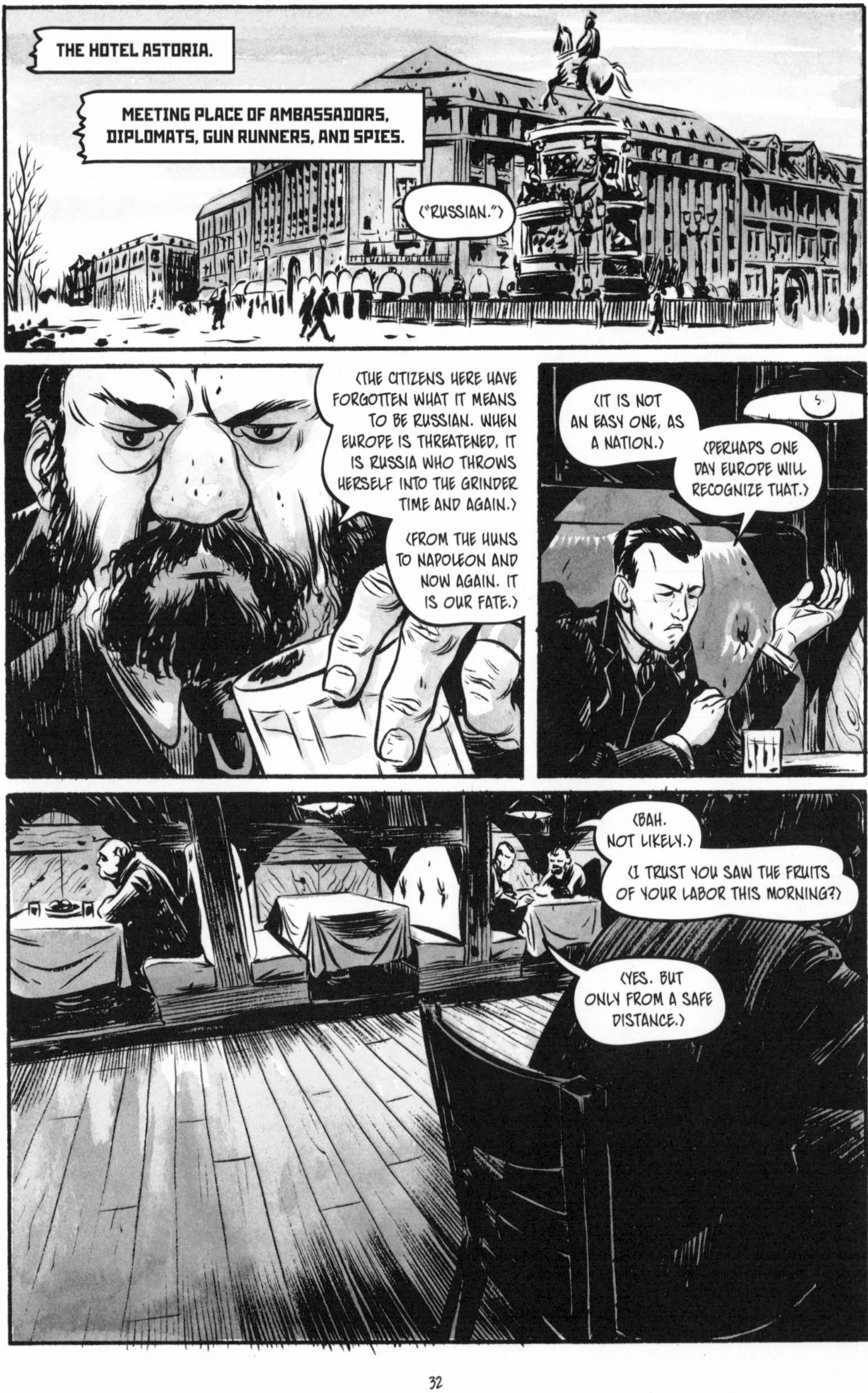
THE HOTEL ASTORIA.
MEETING PLACE OF AMBASSADORS, DIPLOMATS, GUN RUNNERS, AND SPIES.
("RUSSIAN.")
(THE CITIZENS HERE HAVE FORGOTTEN WHAT IT MEANS TO BE RUSSIAN. WHEN EUROPE IS THREATENED, IT IS RUSSIA WHO THROWS HERSELF INTO THE GRINDER TIME AND AGAIN.)
(FROM THE HUNS TO NAPOLEON AND NOW AGAIN. IT IS OUR FATE.)
(IT IS NOT AN EASY ONE, AS A NATION.)
(PERHAPS ONE DAY EUROPE WILL RECOGNIZE THAT.)
(BAH. NOT LIKELY.)
(I TRUST YOU SAW THE FRUITS OF YOUR LABOR THIS MORNING?)
(YES. BUT ONLY FROM A SAFE DISTANCE.)

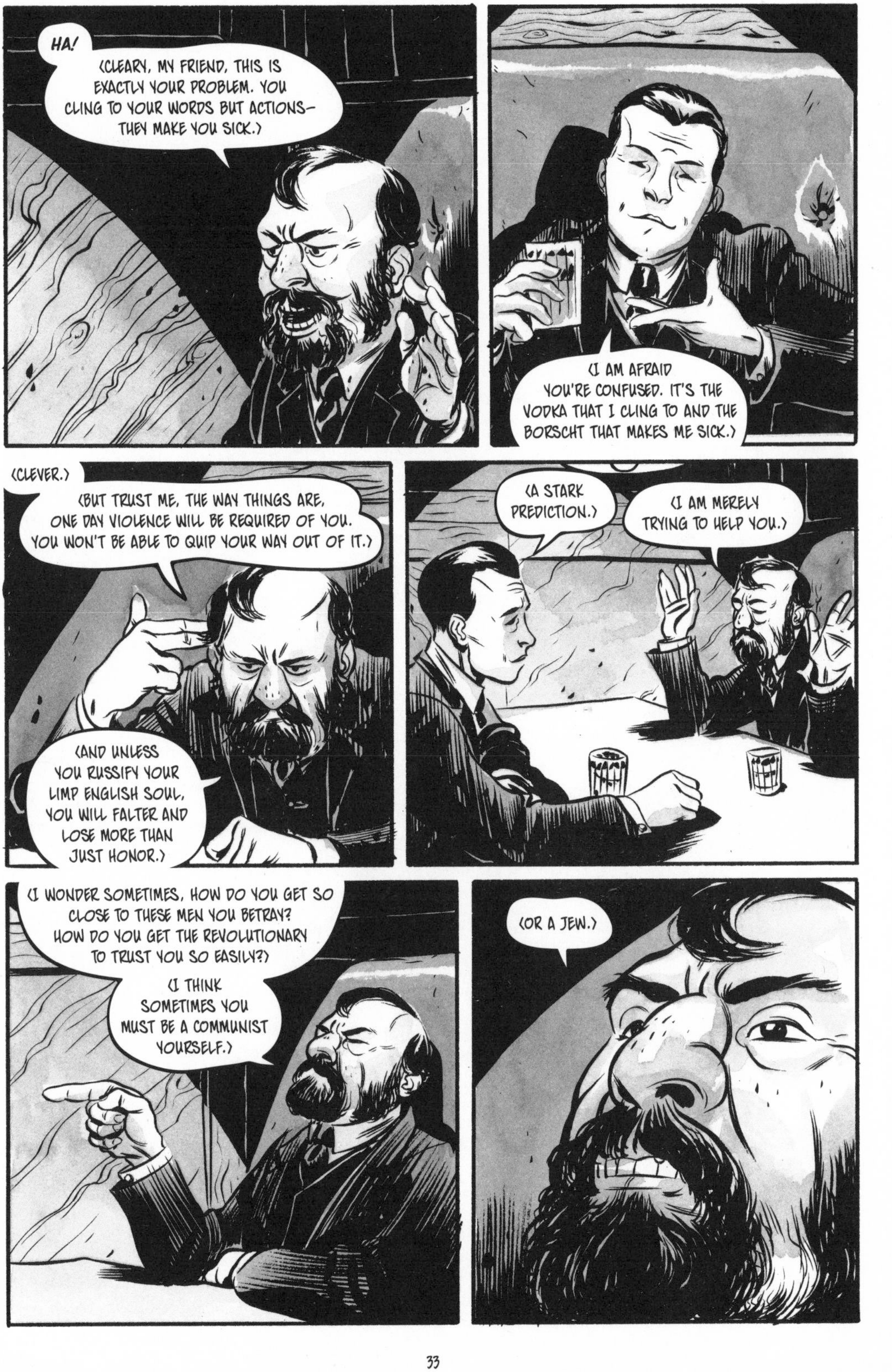
HA!
‹CLEARY, MY FRIEND, THIS IS EXACTLY YOUR PROBLEM. YOU CLING TO YOUR WORDS BUT ACTIONS— THEY MAKE YOU SICK.›
‹I AM AFRAID YOU'RE CONFUSED. IT'S THE VODKA THAT I CLING TO AND THE BORSCHT THAT MAKES ME SICK.›
‹CLEVER.›
‹BUT TRUST ME, THE WAY THINGS ARE, ONE DAY VIOLENCE WILL BE REQUIRED OF YOU. YOU WON'T BE ABLE TO QUIP YOUR WAY OUT OF IT.›
‹AND UNLESS YOU RUSSIFY YOUR LIMP ENGLISH SOUL, YOU WILL FALTER AND LOSE MORE THAN JUST HONOR.›
‹A STARK PREDICTION.›
‹I AM MERELY TRYING TO HELP YOU.›
‹I WONDER SOMETIMES, HOW DO YOU GET SO CLOSE TO THESE MEN YOU BETRAY? HOW DO YOU GET THE REVOLUTIONARY TO TRUST YOU SO EASILY?›
‹I THINK SOMETIMES YOU MUST BE A COMMUNIST YOURSELF.›
‹OR A JEW.›

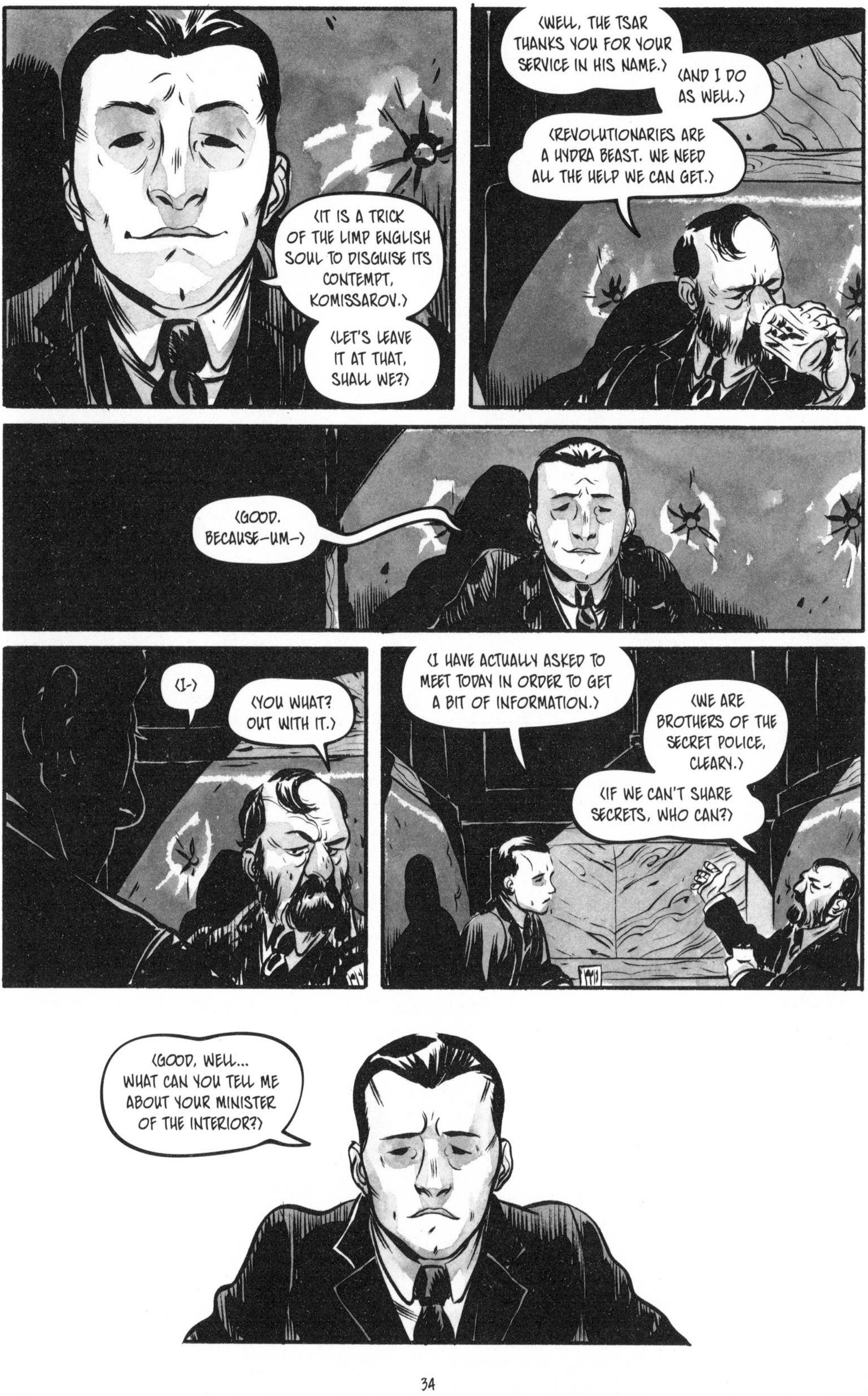
<IT IS A TRICK OF THE LIMP ENGLISH SOUL TO DISGUISE ITS CONTEMPT, KOMISSAROV.>
<LET'S LEAVE IT AT THAT, SHALL WE?>
<WELL, THE TSAR THANKS YOU FOR YOUR SERVICE IN HIS NAME.>
<AND I DO AS WELL.>
<REVOLUTIONARIES ARE A HYDRA BEAST. WE NEED ALL THE HELP WE CAN GET.>
<GOOD. BECAUSE—UM—>
<I->
<YOU WHAT? OUT WITH IT.>
<I HAVE ACTUALLY ASKED TO MEET TODAY IN ORDER TO GET A BIT OF INFORMATION.>
<WE ARE BROTHERS OF THE SECRET POLICE, CLEARY.>
<IF WE CAN'T SHARE SECRETS, WHO CAN?>
<GOOD, WELL... WHAT CAN YOU TELL ME ABOUT YOUR MINISTER OF THE INTERIOR?>

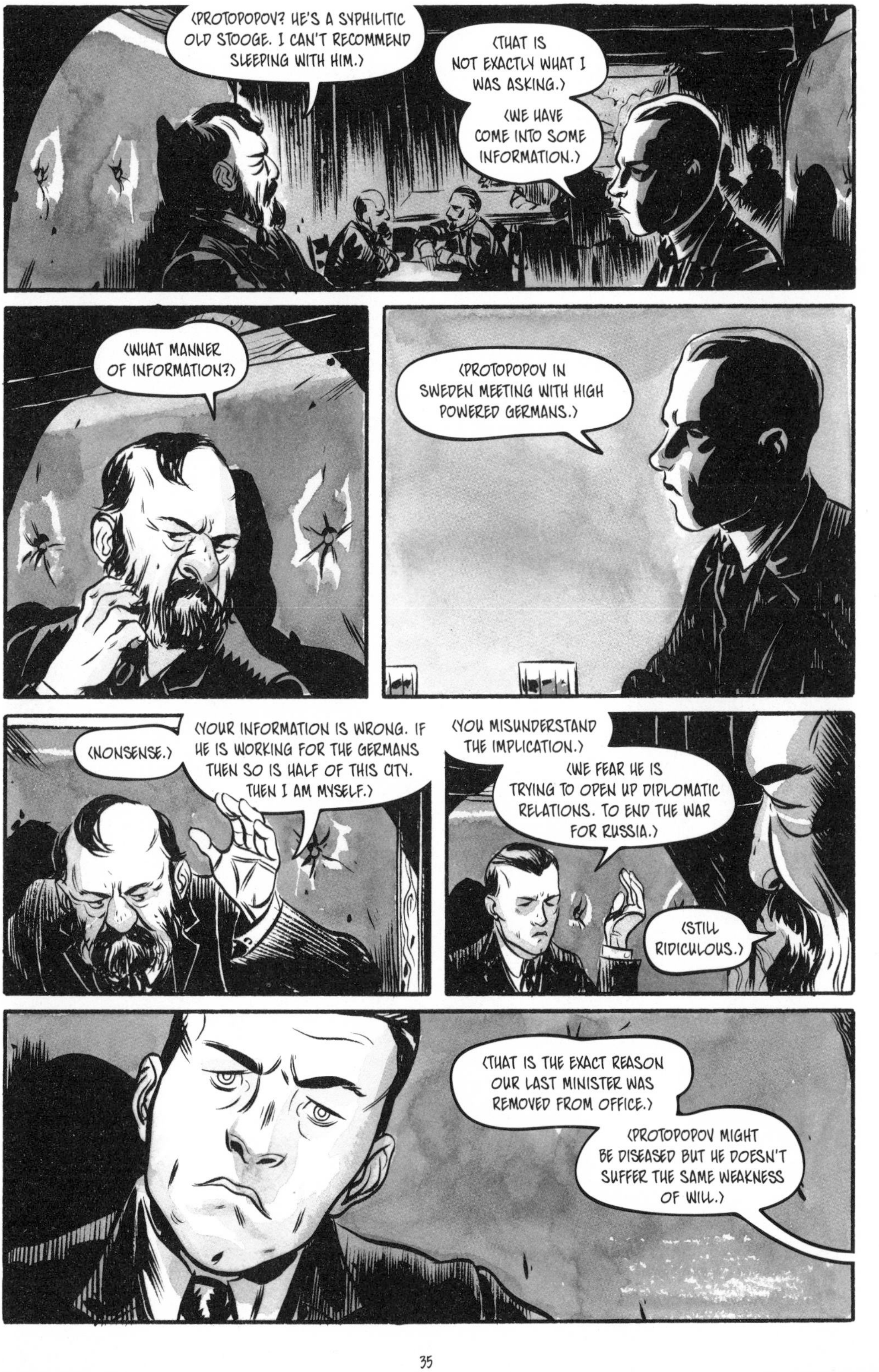
(PROTOPOPOV? HE'S A SYPHILITIC OLD STOOGE. I CAN'T RECOMMEND SLEEPING WITH HIM.)
(THAT IS NOT EXACTLY WHAT I WAS ASKING.)
(WE HAVE COME INTO SOME INFORMATION.)
(WHAT MANNER OF INFORMATION?)
(PROTOPOPOV IN SWEDEN MEETING WITH HIGH POWERED GERMANS.)
(NONSENSE.)
(YOUR INFORMATION IS WRONG. IF HE IS WORKING FOR THE GERMANS THEN SO IS HALF OF THIS CITY. THEN I AM MYSELF.)
(YOU MISUNDERSTAND THE IMPLICATION.)
(WE FEAR HE IS TRYING TO OPEN UP DIPLOMATIC RELATIONS. TO END THE WAR FOR RUSSIA.)
(STILL RIDICULOUS.)
(THAT IS THE EXACT REASON OUR LAST MINISTER WAS REMOVED FROM OFFICE.)
(PROTOPOPOV MIGHT BE DISEASED BUT HE DOESN'T SUFFER THE SAME WEAKNESS OF WILL.)

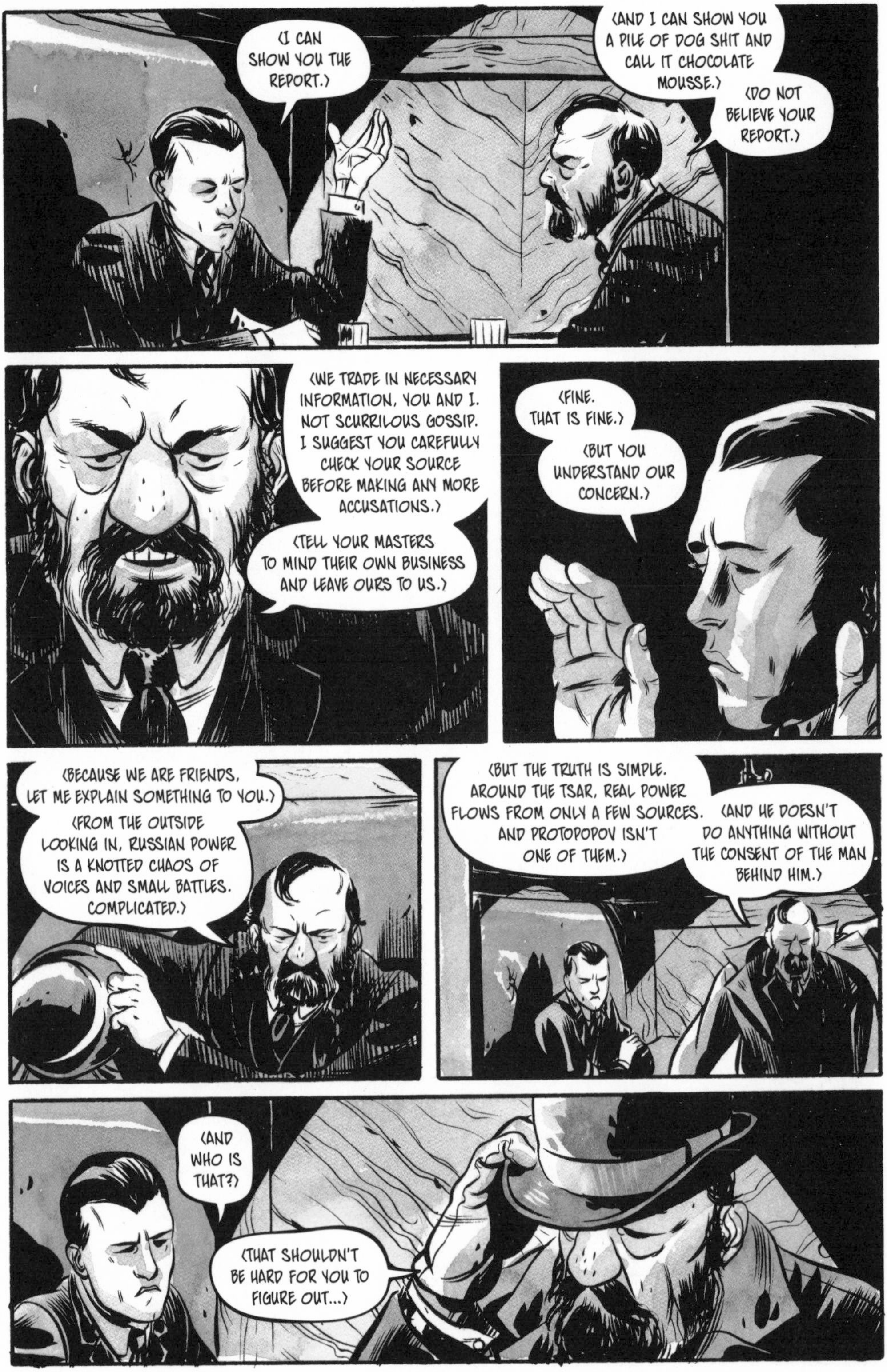
‹I CAN SHOW YOU THE REPORT.›
‹AND I CAN SHOW YOU A PILE OF DOG SHIT AND CALL IT CHOCOLATE MOUSSE.›
‹DO NOT BELIEVE YOUR REPORT.›
‹WE TRADE IN NECESSARY INFORMATION, YOU AND I. NOT SCURRILOUS GOSSIP. I SUGGEST YOU CAREFULLY CHECK YOUR SOURCE BEFORE MAKING ANY MORE ACCUSATIONS.›
‹TELL YOUR MASTERS TO MIND THEIR OWN BUSINESS AND LEAVE OURS TO US.›
‹FINE. THAT IS FINE.›
‹BUT YOU UNDERSTAND OUR CONCERN.›
‹BECAUSE WE ARE FRIENDS, LET ME EXPLAIN SOMETHING TO YOU.›
‹FROM THE OUTSIDE LOOKING IN, RUSSIAN POWER IS A KNOTTED CHAOS OF VOICES AND SMALL BATTLES. COMPLICATED.›
‹BUT THE TRUTH IS SIMPLE. AROUND THE TSAR, REAL POWER FLOWS FROM ONLY A FEW SOURCES. AND PROTOPOPOV ISN'T ONE OF THEM.›
‹AND HE DOESN'T DO ANYTHING WITHOUT THE CONSENT OF THE MAN BEHIND HIM.›
‹AND WHO IS THAT?›
‹THAT SHOULDN'T BE HARD FOR YOU TO FIGURE OUT...›

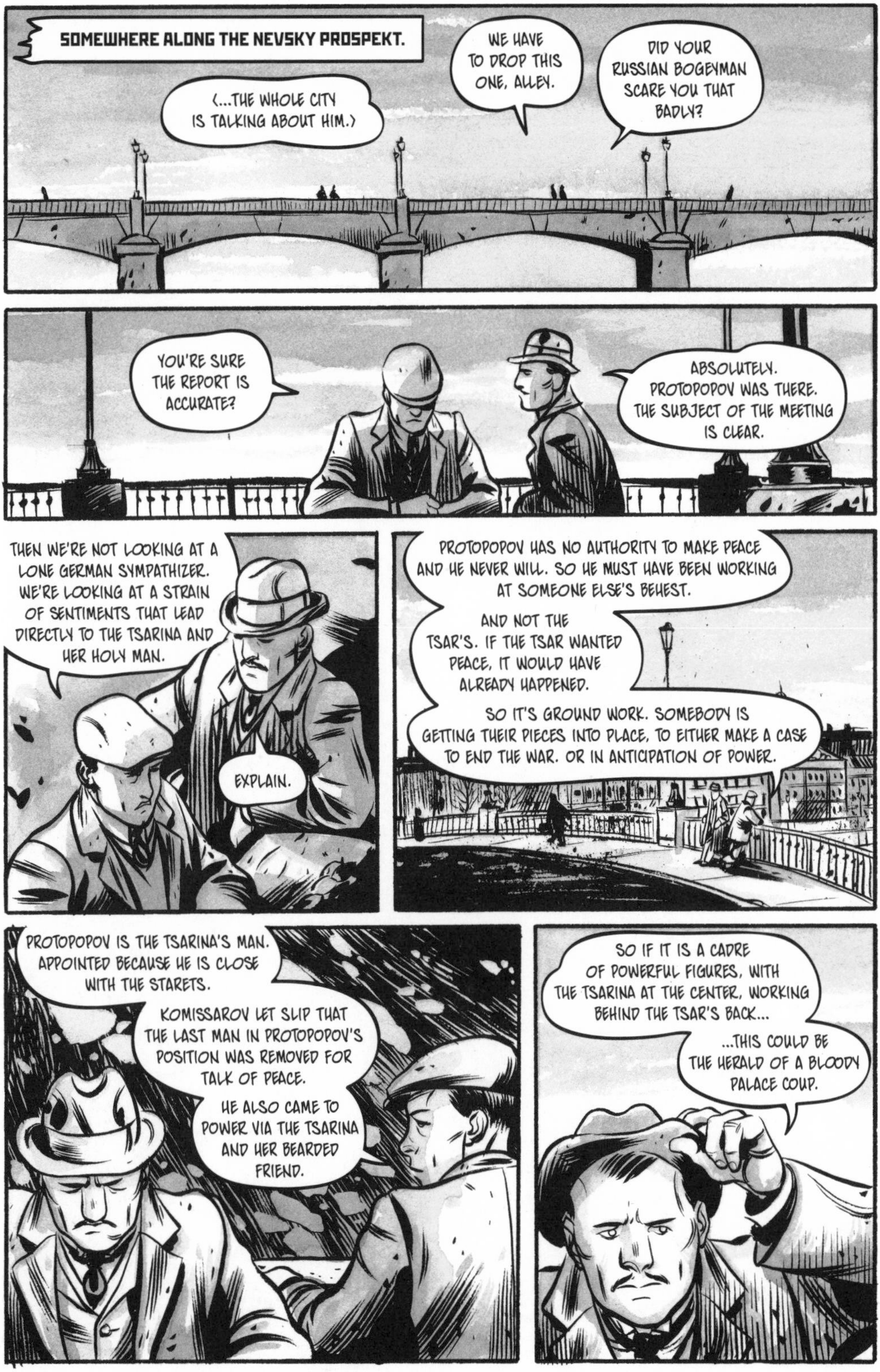
SOMEWHERE ALONG THE NEVSKY PROSPEKT.
(...THE WHOLE CITY IS TALKING ABOUT HIM.)
WE HAVE TO DROP THIS ONE, ALLEY.
DID YOUR RUSSIAN BOGEYMAN SCARE YOU THAT BADLY?
YOU'RE SURE THE REPORT IS ACCURATE?
ABSOLUTELY. PROTOPOPOV WAS THERE. THE SUBJECT OF THE MEETING IS CLEAR.
THEN WE'RE NOT LOOKING AT A LONE GERMAN SYMPATHIZER. WE'RE LOOKING AT A STRAIN OF SENTIMENTS THAT LEAD DIRECTLY TO THE TSARINA AND HER HOLY MAN.
EXPLAIN.
PROTOPOPOV HAS NO AUTHORITY TO MAKE PEACE AND HE NEVER WILL. SO HE MUST HAVE BEEN WORKING AT SOMEONE ELSE'S BEHEST.
AND NOT THE TSAR'S. IF THE TSAR WANTED PEACE, IT WOULD HAVE ALREADY HAPPENED.
SO IT'S GROUND WORK. SOMEBODY IS GETTING THEIR PIECES INTO PLACE, TO EITHER MAKE A CASE TO END THE WAR. OR IN ANTICIPATION OF POWER.
PROTOPOPOV IS THE TSARINA'S MAN. APPOINTED BECAUSE HE IS CLOSE WITH THE STARETS.
KOMISSAROV LET SLIP THAT THE LAST MAN IN PROTOPOPOV'S POSITION WAS REMOVED FOR TALK OF PEACE.
HE ALSO CAME TO POWER VIA THE TSARINA AND HER BEARDED FRIEND.
SO IF IT IS A CADRE OF POWERFUL FIGURES, WITH THE TSARINA AT THE CENTER, WORKING BEHIND THE TSAR'S BACK...
...THIS COULD BE THE HERALD OF A BLOODY PALACE COUP.

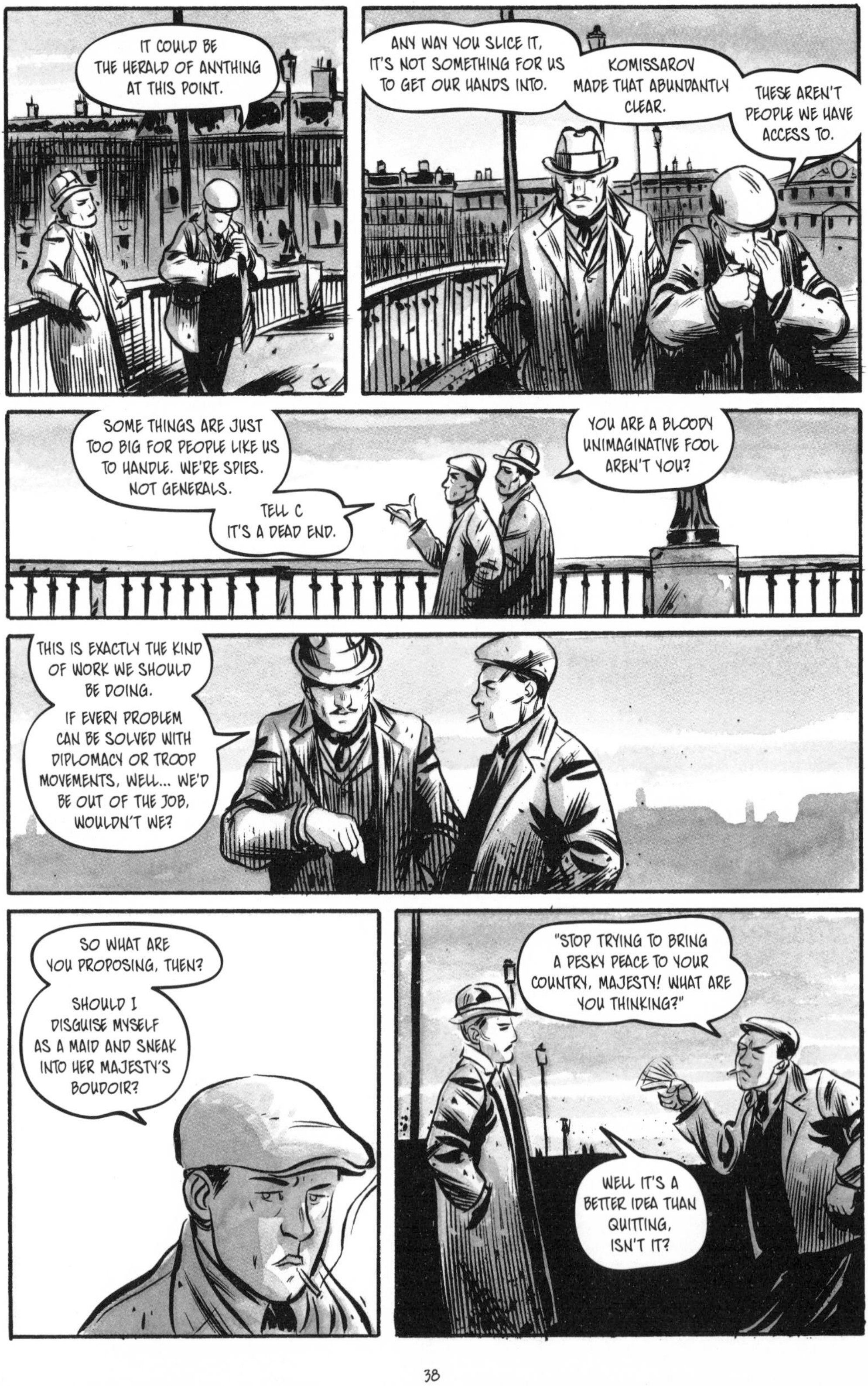
IT COULD BE THE HERALD OF ANYTHING AT THIS POINT.
ANY WAY YOU SLICE IT, IT'S NOT SOMETHING FOR US TO GET OUR HANDS INTO.
KOMISSAROV MADE THAT ABUNDANTLY CLEAR.
THESE AREN'T PEOPLE WE HAVE ACCESS TO.
SOME THINGS ARE JUST TOO BIG FOR PEOPLE LIKE US TO HANDLE. WE'RE SPIES. NOT GENERALS.
TELL C IT'S A DEAD END.
YOU ARE A BLOODY UNIMAGINATIVE FOOL AREN'T YOU?
THIS IS EXACTLY THE KIND OF WORK WE SHOULD BE DOING.
IF EVERY PROBLEM CAN BE SOLVED WITH DIPLOMACY OR TROOP MOVEMENTS, WELL... WE'D BE OUT OF THE JOB, WOULDN'T WE?
SO WHAT ARE YOU PROPOSING, THEN?
SHOULD I DISGUISE MYSELF AS A MAID AND SNEAK INTO HER MAJESTY'S BOUDOIR?
"STOP TRYING TO BRING A PESKY PEACE TO YOUR COUNTRY, MAJESTY! WHAT ARE YOU THINKING?"
WELL IT'S A BETTER IDEA THAN QUITTING, ISN'T IT?

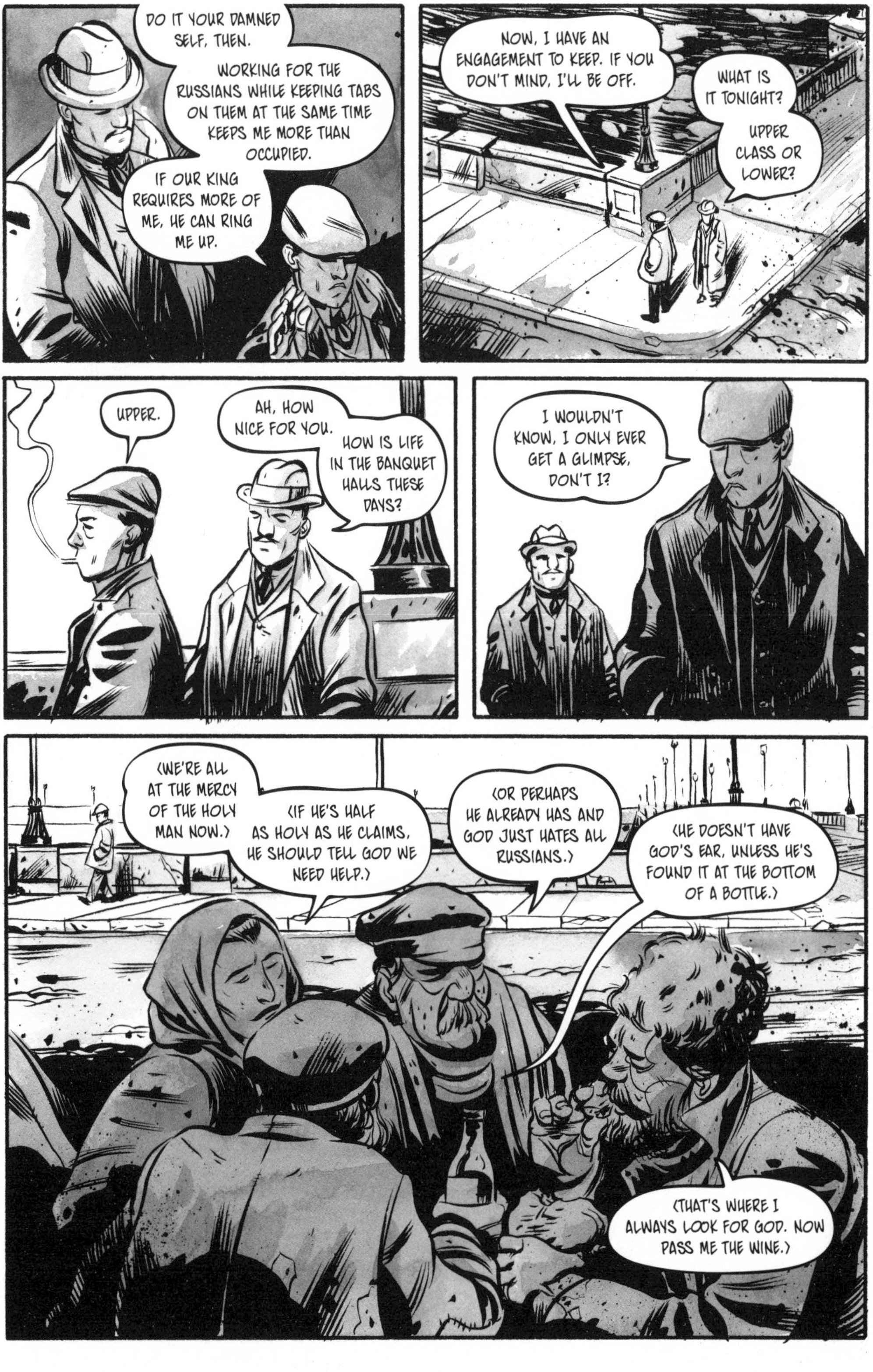
DO IT YOUR DAMNED SELF, THEN.
WORKING FOR THE RUSSIANS WHILE KEEPING TABS ON THEM AT THE SAME TIME KEEPS ME MORE THAN OCCUPIED.
IF OUR KING REQUIRES MORE OF ME, HE CAN RING ME UP.
NOW, I HAVE AN ENGAGEMENT TO KEEP. IF YOU DON'T MIND, I'LL BE OFF.
WHAT IS IT TONIGHT?
UPPER CLASS OR LOWER?
UPPER.
AH, HOW NICE FOR YOU.
HOW IS LIFE IN THE BANQUET HALLS THESE DAYS?
I WOULDN'T KNOW, I ONLY EVER GET A GLIMPSE, DON'T I?
‹WE'RE ALL AT THE MERCY OF THE HOLY MAN NOW.›
‹IF HE'S HALF AS HOLY AS HE CLAIMS, HE SHOULD TELL GOD WE NEED HELP.›
‹OR PERHAPS HE ALREADY HAS AND GOD JUST HATES ALL RUSSIANS.›
‹HE DOESN'T HAVE GOD'S EAR, UNLESS HE'S FOUND IT AT THE BOTTOM OF A BOTTLE.›
‹THAT'S WHERE I ALWAYS LOOK FOR GOD. NOW PASS ME THE WINE.›

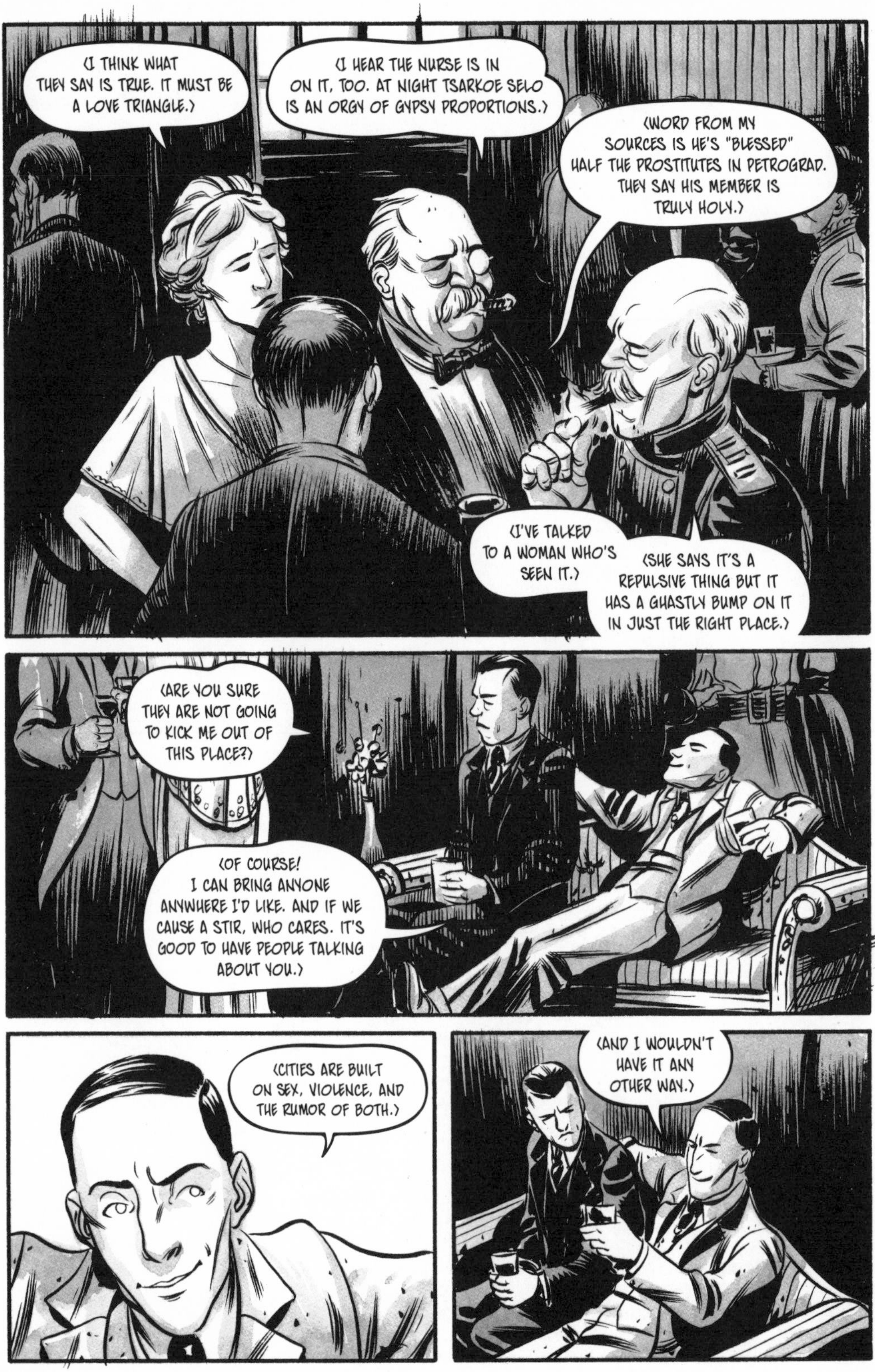

(I THINK WHAT THEY SAY IS TRUE. IT MUST BE A LOVE TRIANGLE.)
(I HEAR THE NURSE IS IN ON IT, TOO. AT NIGHT TSARKOE SELO IS AN ORGY OF GYPSY PROPORTIONS.)
(WORD FROM MY SOURCES IS HE'S "BLESSED" HALF THE PROSTITUTES IN PETROGRAD. THEY SAY HIS MEMBER IS TRULY HOLY.)
(I'VE TALKED TO A WOMAN WHO'S SEEN IT.)
(SHE SAYS IT'S A REPULSIVE THING BUT IT HAS A GHASTLY BUMP ON IT IN JUST THE RIGHT PLACE.)
(ARE YOU SURE THEY ARE NOT GOING TO KICK ME OUT OF THIS PLACE?)
(OF COURSE! I CAN BRING ANYONE ANYWHERE I'D LIKE. AND IF WE CAUSE A STIR, WHO CARES. IT'S GOOD TO HAVE PEOPLE TALKING ABOUT YOU.)
(CITIES ARE BUILT ON SEX, VIOLENCE, AND THE RUMOR OF BOTH.)
(AND I WOULDN'T HAVE IT ANY OTHER WAY.)

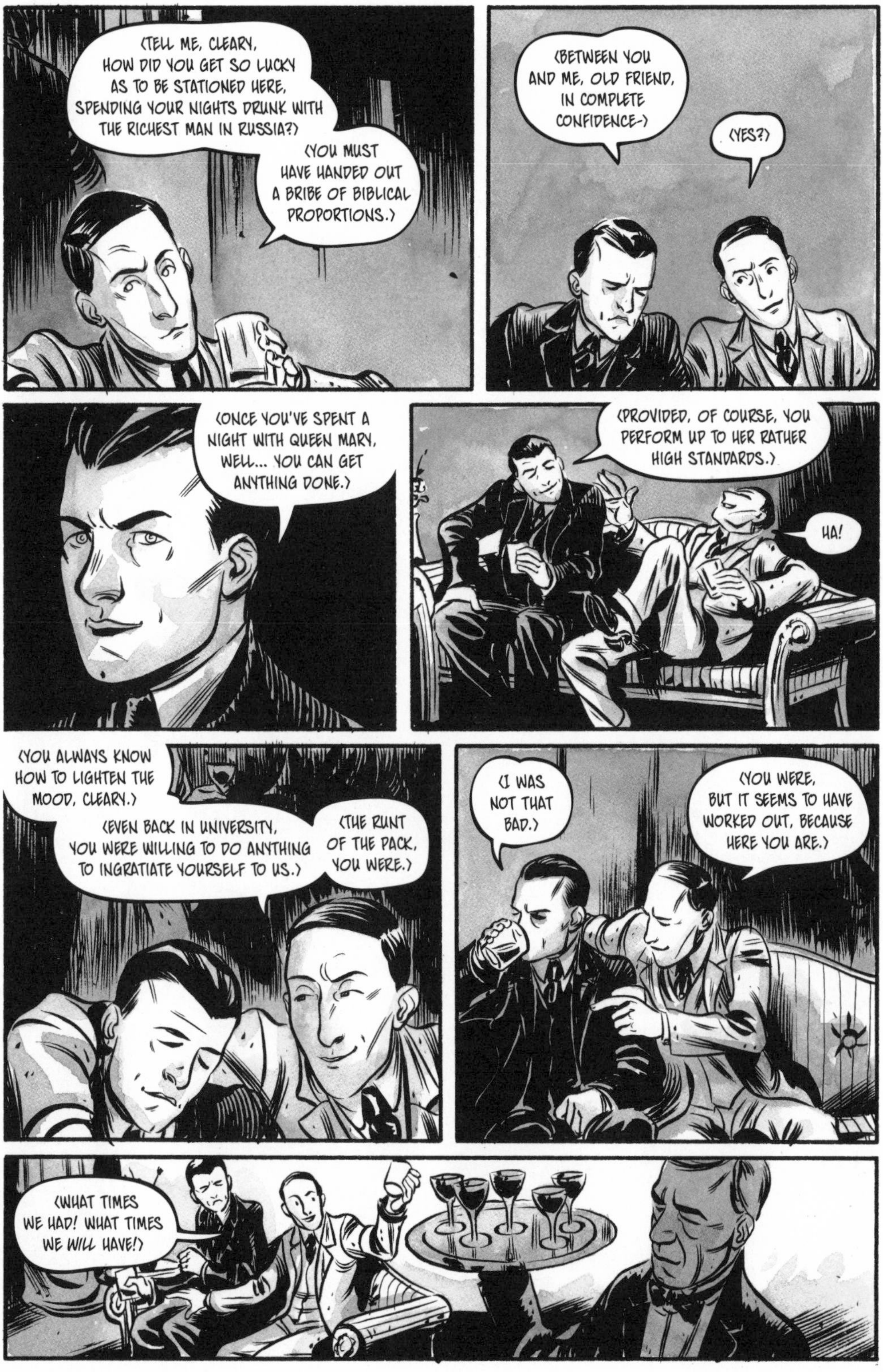
‹TELL ME, CLEARY, HOW DID YOU GET SO LUCKY AS TO BE STATIONED HERE, SPENDING YOUR NIGHTS DRUNK WITH THE RICHEST MAN IN RUSSIA?›
‹YOU MUST HAVE HANDED OUT A BRIBE OF BIBLICAL PROPORTIONS.›
‹BETWEEN YOU AND ME, OLD FRIEND, IN COMPLETE CONFIDENCE-›
‹YES?›
‹ONCE YOU'VE SPENT A NIGHT WITH QUEEN MARY, WELL... YOU CAN GET ANYTHING DONE.›
‹PROVIDED, OF COURSE, YOU PERFORM UP TO HER RATHER HIGH STANDARDS.›
HA!
‹YOU ALWAYS KNOW HOW TO LIGHTEN THE MOOD, CLEARY.›
‹EVEN BACK IN UNIVERSITY, YOU WERE WILLING TO DO ANYTHING TO INGRATIATE YOURSELF TO US.›
‹THE RUNT OF THE PACK, YOU WERE.›
‹I WAS NOT THAT BAD.›
‹YOU WERE, BUT IT SEEMS TO HAVE WORKED OUT, BECAUSE HERE YOU ARE.›
‹WHAT TIMES WE HAD! WHAT TIMES WE WILL HAVE!›

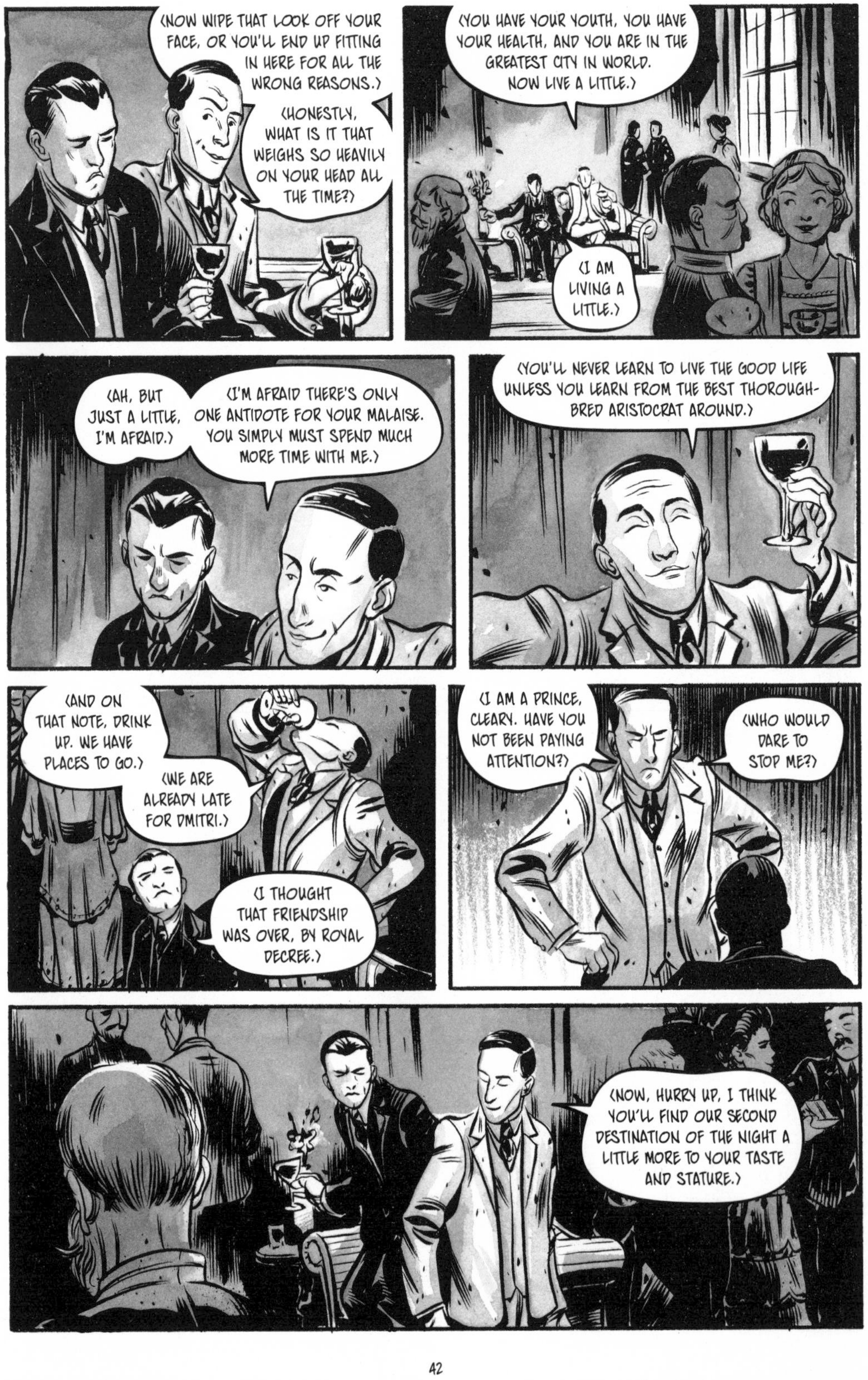
<NOW WIPE THAT LOOK OFF YOUR FACE, OR YOU'LL END UP FITTING IN HERE FOR ALL THE WRONG REASONS.>
<HONESTLY, WHAT IS IT THAT WEIGHS SO HEAVILY ON YOUR HEAD ALL THE TIME?>
<YOU HAVE YOUR YOUTH, YOU HAVE YOUR HEALTH, AND YOU ARE IN THE GREATEST CITY IN WORLD. NOW LIVE A LITTLE.>
<I AM LIVING A LITTLE.>
<AH, BUT JUST A LITTLE, I'M AFRAID.>
<I'M AFRAID THERE'S ONLY ONE ANTIDOTE FOR YOUR MALAISE. YOU SIMPLY MUST SPEND MUCH MORE TIME WITH ME.>
<YOU'LL NEVER LEARN TO LIVE THE GOOD LIFE UNLESS YOU LEARN FROM THE BEST THOROUGH-BRED ARISTOCRAT AROUND.>
<AND ON THAT NOTE, DRINK UP. WE HAVE PLACES TO GO.>
<WE ARE ALREADY LATE FOR DMITRI.>
<I THOUGHT THAT FRIENDSHIP WAS OVER, BY ROYAL DECREE.>
<I AM A PRINCE, CLEARY. HAVE YOU NOT BEEN PAYING ATTENTION?>
<WHO WOULD DARE TO STOP ME?>
<NOW, HURRY UP. I THINK YOU'LL FIND OUR SECOND DESTINATION OF THE NIGHT A LITTLE MORE TO YOUR TASTE AND STATURE.>

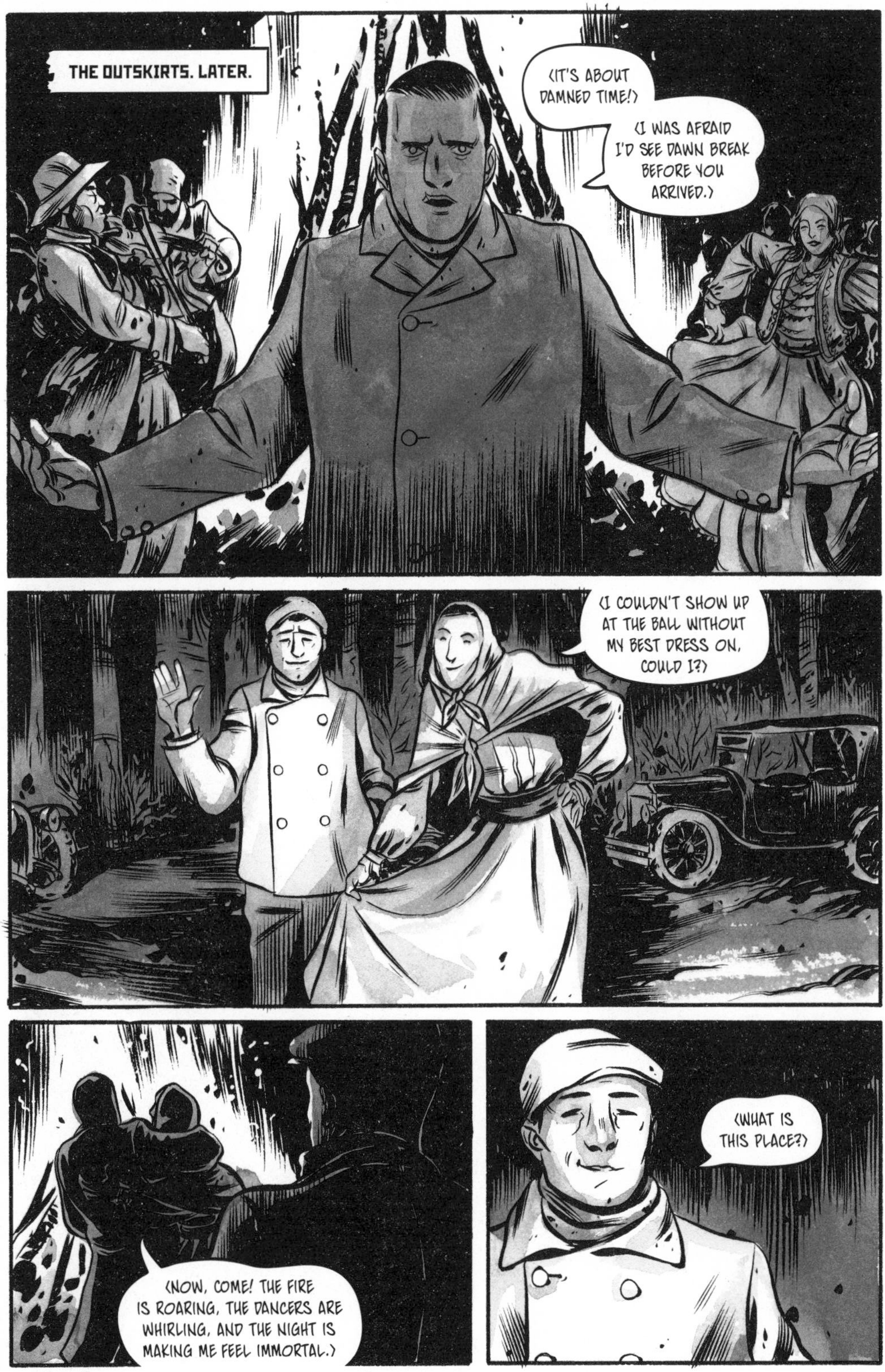
THE OUTSKIRTS. LATER.
‹IT'S ABOUT DAMNED TIME!›
‹I WAS AFRAID I'D SEE DAWN BREAK BEFORE YOU ARRIVED.›
‹I COULDN'T SHOW UP AT THE BALL WITHOUT MY BEST DRESS ON, COULD I?›
‹NOW, COME! THE FIRE IS ROARING, THE DANCERS ARE WHIRLING, AND THE NIGHT IS MAKING ME FEEL IMMORTAL.›
‹WHAT IS THIS PLACE?›

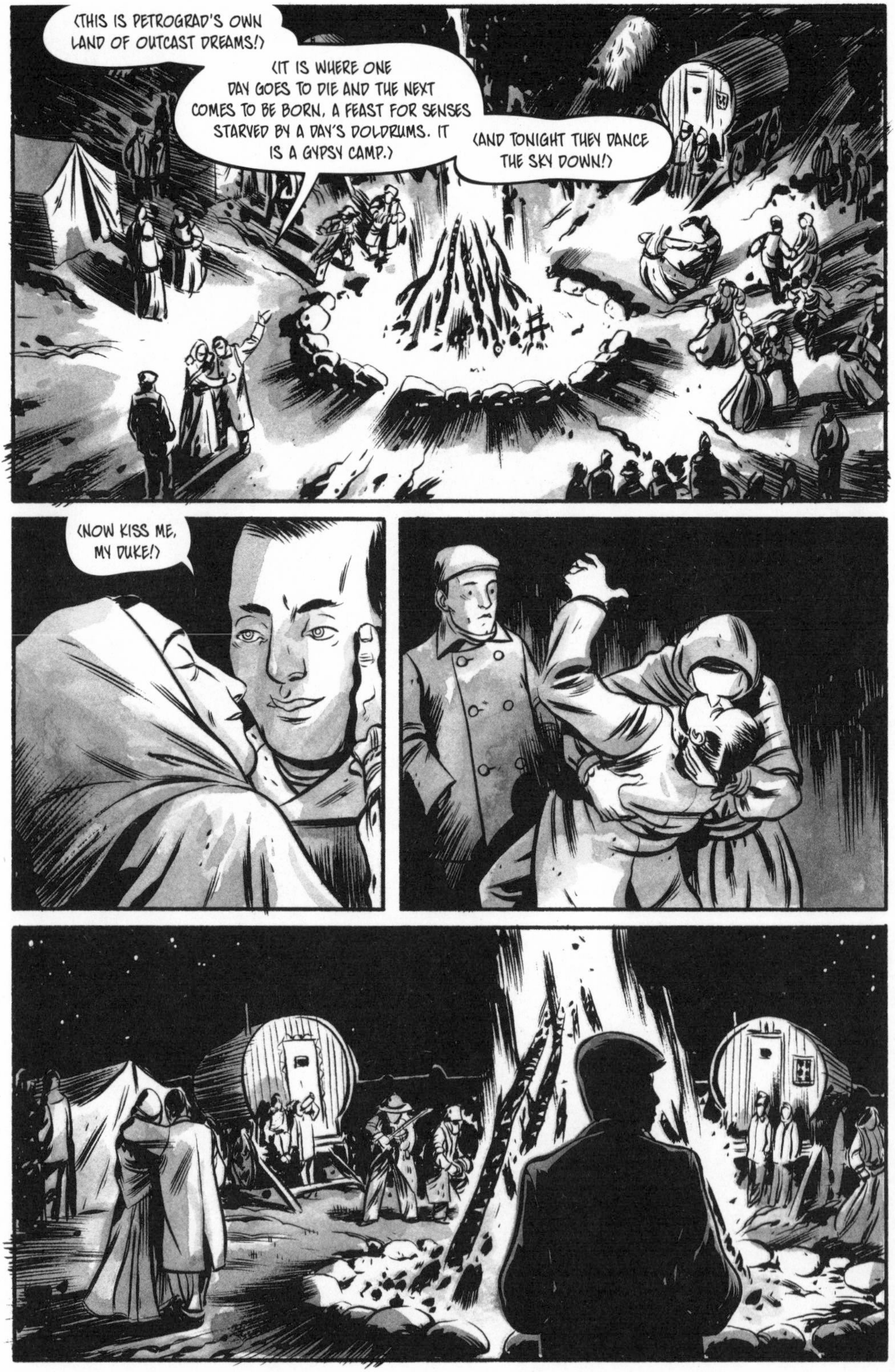
<THIS IS PETROGRAD'S OWN LAND OF OUTCAST DREAMS!>
<IT IS WHERE ONE DAY GOES TO DIE AND THE NEXT COMES TO BE BORN, A FEAST FOR SENSES STARVED BY A DAY'S DOLDRUMS. IT IS A GYPSY CAMP.>
<AND TONIGHT THEY DANCE THE SKY DOWN!>
<NOW KISS ME, MY DUKE!>

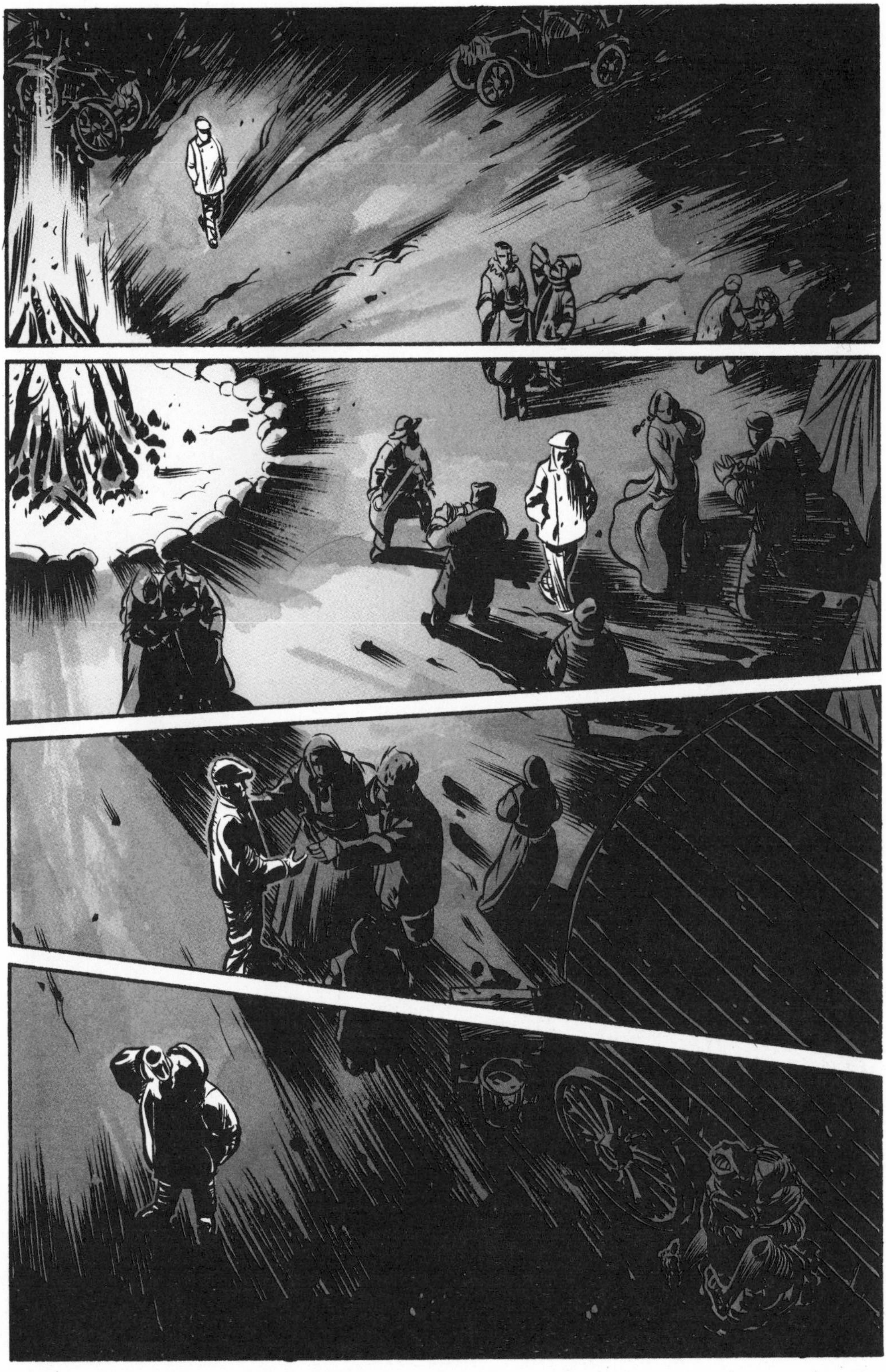

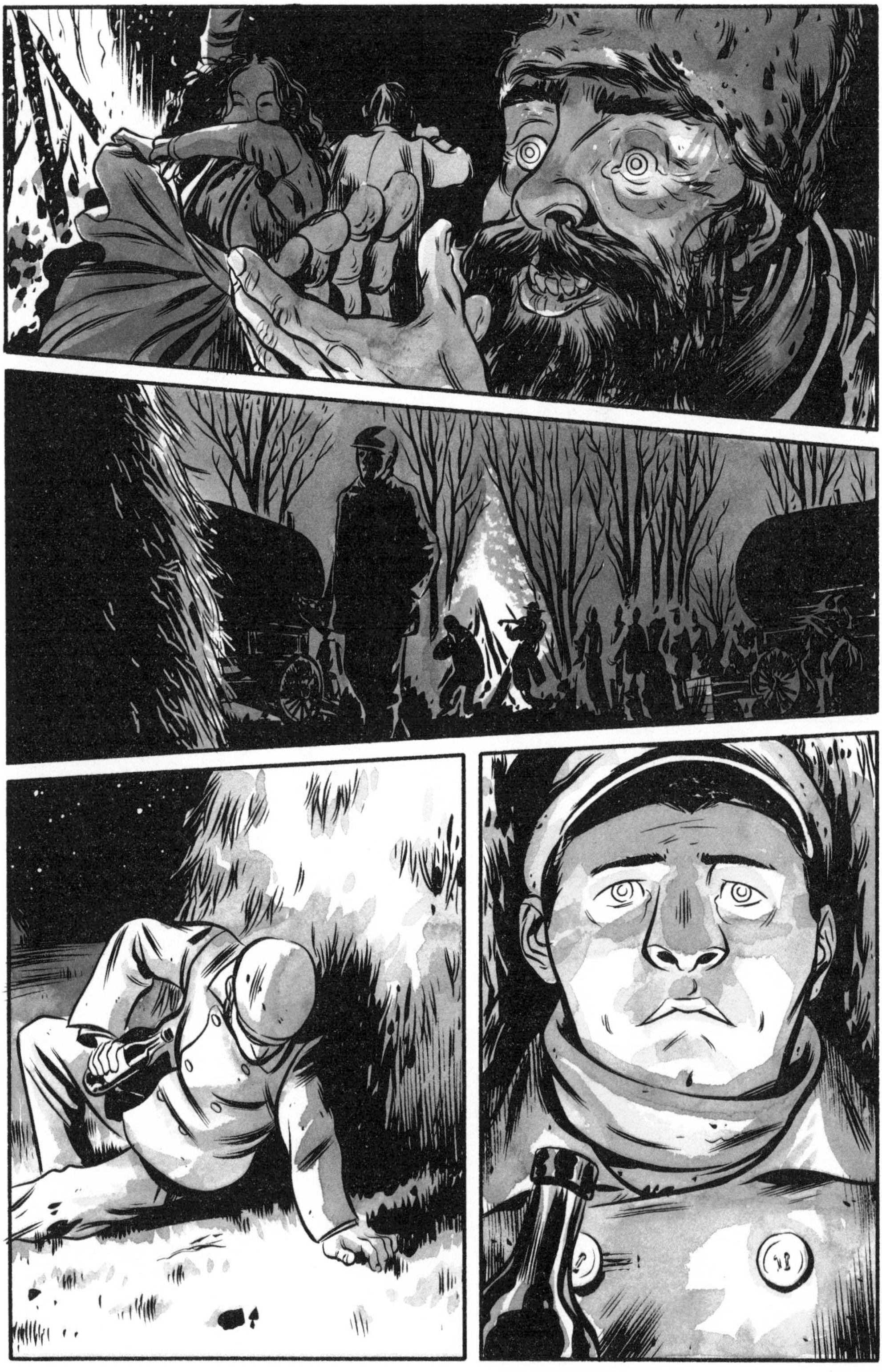

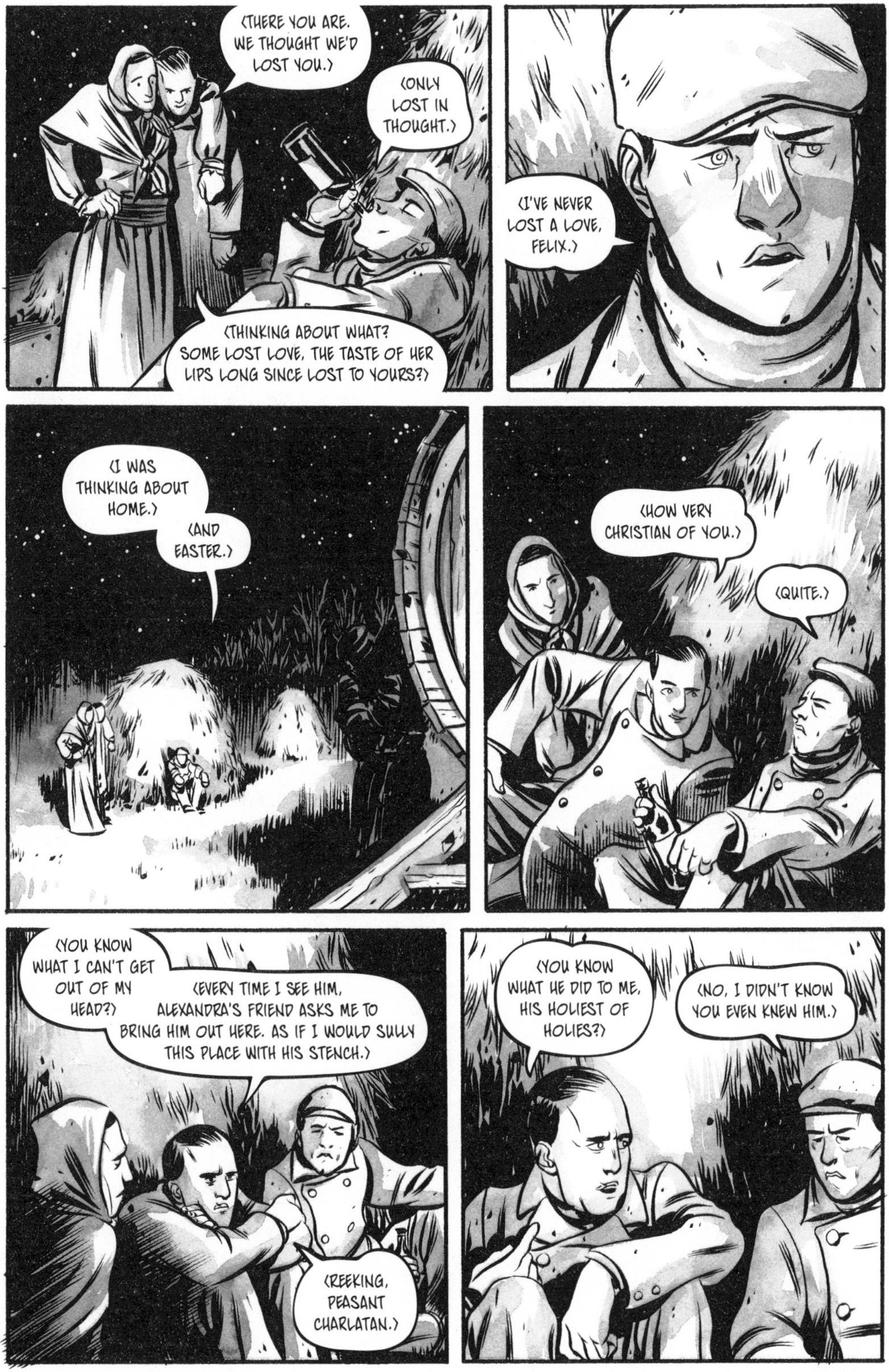

‹THERE YOU ARE. WE THOUGHT WE'D LOST YOU.›
‹ONLY LOST IN THOUGHT.›
‹THINKING ABOUT WHAT? SOME LOST LOVE, THE TASTE OF HER LIPS LONG SINCE LOST TO YOURS?›
‹I'VE NEVER LOST A LOVE, FELIX.›
‹I WAS THINKING ABOUT HOME.›
‹AND EASTER.›
‹HOW VERY CHRISTIAN OF YOU.›
‹QUITE.›
‹YOU KNOW WHAT I CAN'T GET OUT OF MY HEAD?›
‹EVERY TIME I SEE HIM, ALEXANDRA'S FRIEND ASKS ME TO BRING HIM OUT HERE. AS IF I WOULD SULLY THIS PLACE WITH HIS STENCH.›
‹REEKING, PEASANT CHARLATAN.›
‹YOU KNOW WHAT HE DID TO ME, HIS HOLIEST OF HOLIES?›
‹NO, I DIDN'T KNOW YOU EVEN KNEW HIM.›

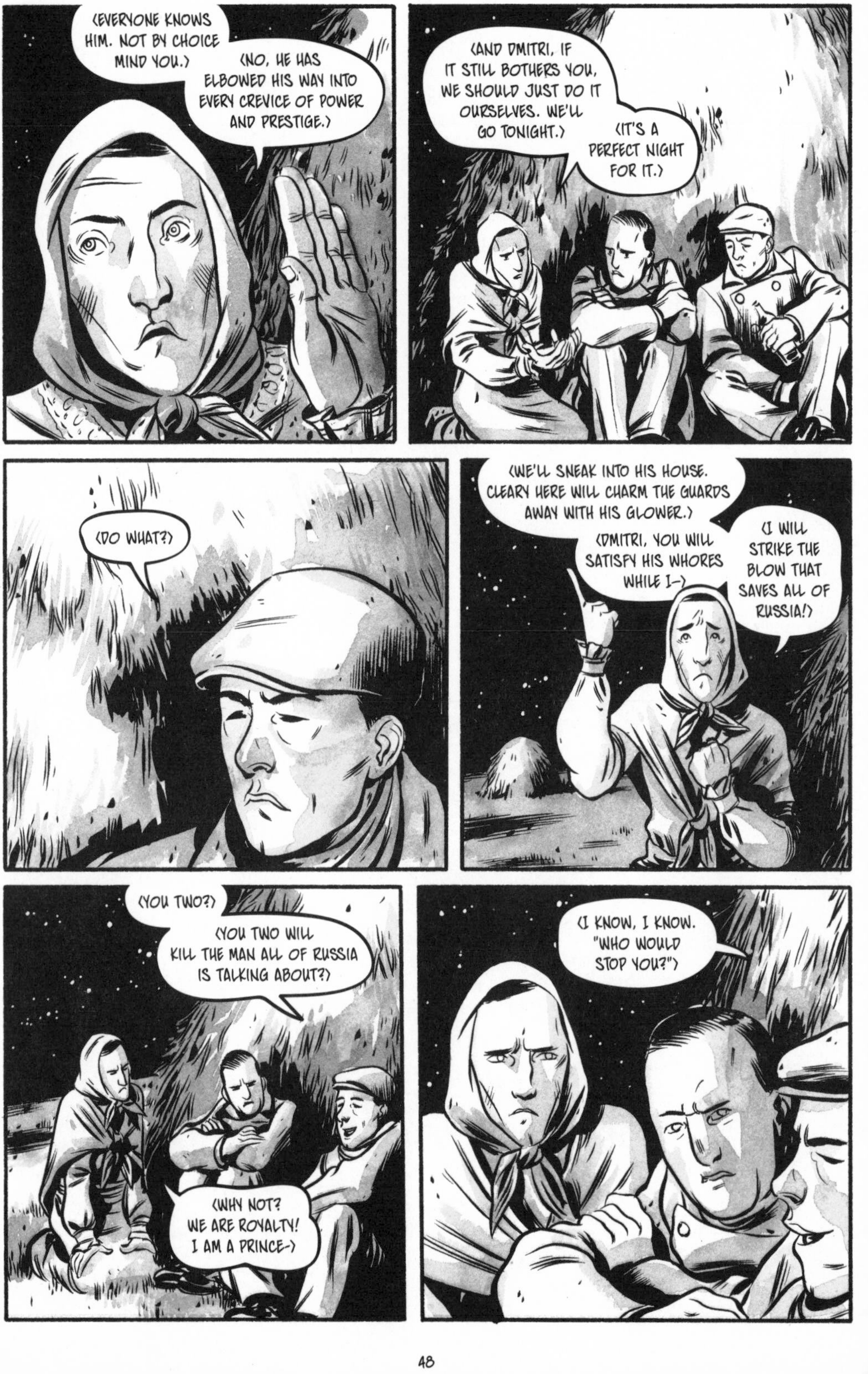
<EVERYONE KNOWS HIM. NOT BY CHOICE MIND YOU.>
<NO, HE HAS ELBOWED HIS WAY INTO EVERY CREVICE OF POWER AND PRESTIGE.>
<AND DMITRI, IF IT STILL BOTHERS YOU, WE SHOULD JUST DO IT OURSELVES. WE'LL GO TONIGHT.>
<IT'S A PERFECT NIGHT FOR IT.>
<DO WHAT?>
<WE'LL SNEAK INTO HIS HOUSE. CLEARY HERE WILL CHARM THE GUARDS AWAY WITH HIS GLOWER.>
<DMITRI, YOU WILL SATISFY HIS WHORES WHILE I–>
<I WILL STRIKE THE BLOW THAT SAVES ALL OF RUSSIA!>
<YOU TWO?>
<YOU TWO WILL KILL THE MAN ALL OF RUSSIA IS TALKING ABOUT?>
<WHY NOT? WE ARE ROYALTY! I AM A PRINCE–>
<I KNOW, I KNOW. "WHO WOULD STOP YOU?">

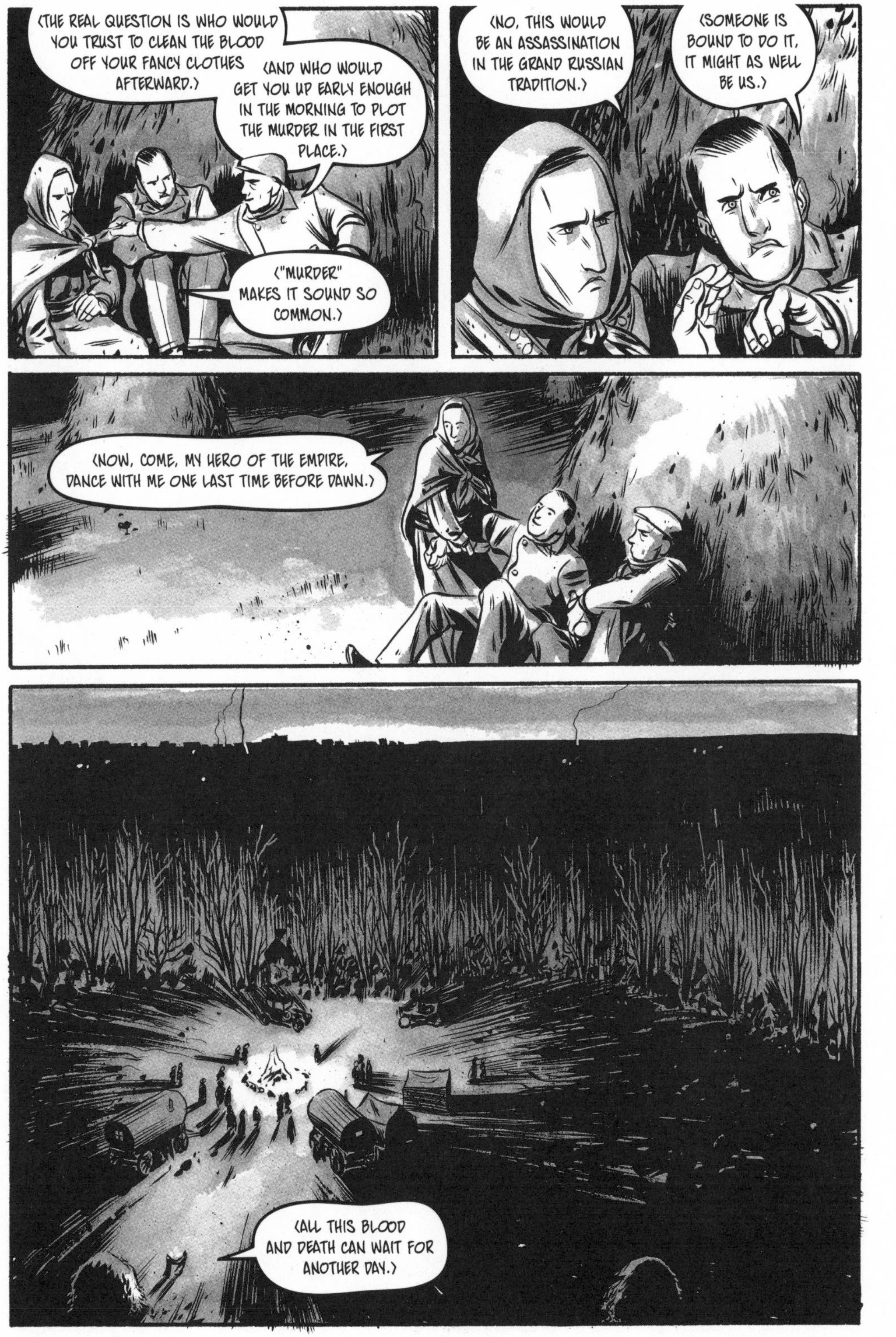
⟨THE REAL QUESTION IS WHO WOULD YOU TRUST TO CLEAN THE BLOOD OFF YOUR FANCY CLOTHES AFTERWARD.⟩
⟨AND WHO WOULD GET YOU UP EARLY ENOUGH IN THE MORNING TO PLOT THE MURDER IN THE FIRST PLACE.⟩
⟨"MURDER" MAKES IT SOUND SO COMMON.⟩
⟨NO, THIS WOULD BE AN ASSASSINATION IN THE GRAND RUSSIAN TRADITION.⟩
⟨SOMEONE IS BOUND TO DO IT, IT MIGHT AS WELL BE US.⟩
⟨NOW, COME, MY HERO OF THE EMPIRE, DANCE WITH ME ONE LAST TIME BEFORE DAWN.⟩
⟨ALL THIS BLOOD AND DEATH CAN WAIT FOR ANOTHER DAY.⟩

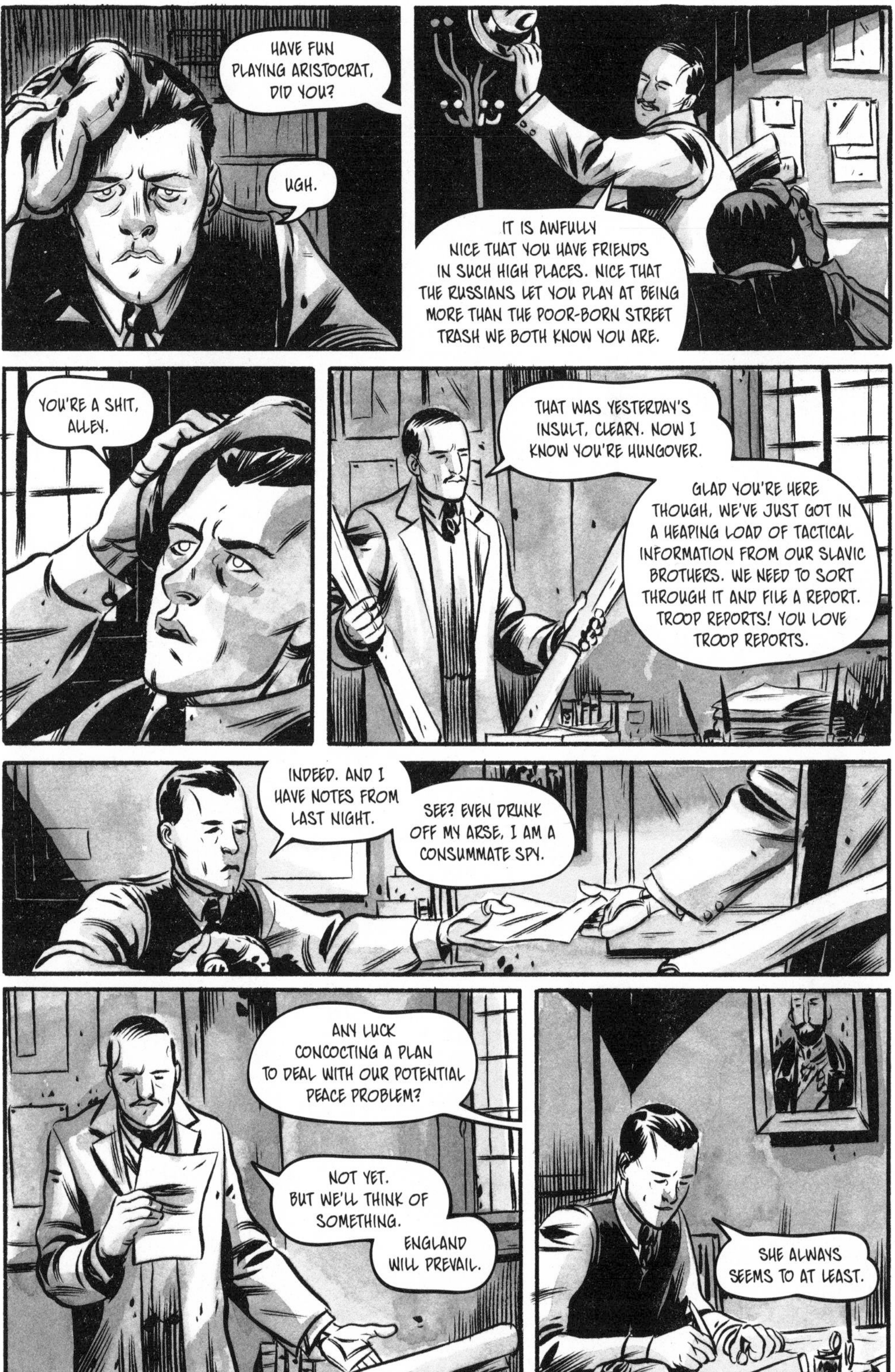

HAVE FUN PLAYING ARISTOCRAT, DID YOU?
UGH.
IT IS AWFULLY NICE THAT YOU HAVE FRIENDS IN SUCH HIGH PLACES. NICE THAT THE RUSSIANS LET YOU PLAY AT BEING MORE THAN THE POOR-BORN STREET TRASH WE BOTH KNOW YOU ARE.
YOU'RE A SHIT, ALLEY.
THAT WAS YESTERDAY'S INSULT, CLEARY. NOW I KNOW YOU'RE HUNGOVER.
GLAD YOU'RE HERE THOUGH, WE'VE JUST GOT IN A HEAPING LOAD OF TACTICAL INFORMATION FROM OUR SLAVIC BROTHERS. WE NEED TO SORT THROUGH IT AND FILE A REPORT. TROOP REPORTS! YOU LOVE TROOP REPORTS.
INDEED. AND I HAVE NOTES FROM LAST NIGHT.
SEE? EVEN DRUNK OFF MY ARSE, I AM A CONSUMMATE SPY.
ANY LUCK CONCOCTING A PLAN TO DEAL WITH OUR POTENTIAL PEACE PROBLEM?
NOT YET. BUT WE'LL THINK OF SOMETHING.
ENGLAND WILL PREVAIL.
SHE ALWAYS SEEMS TO AT LEAST.

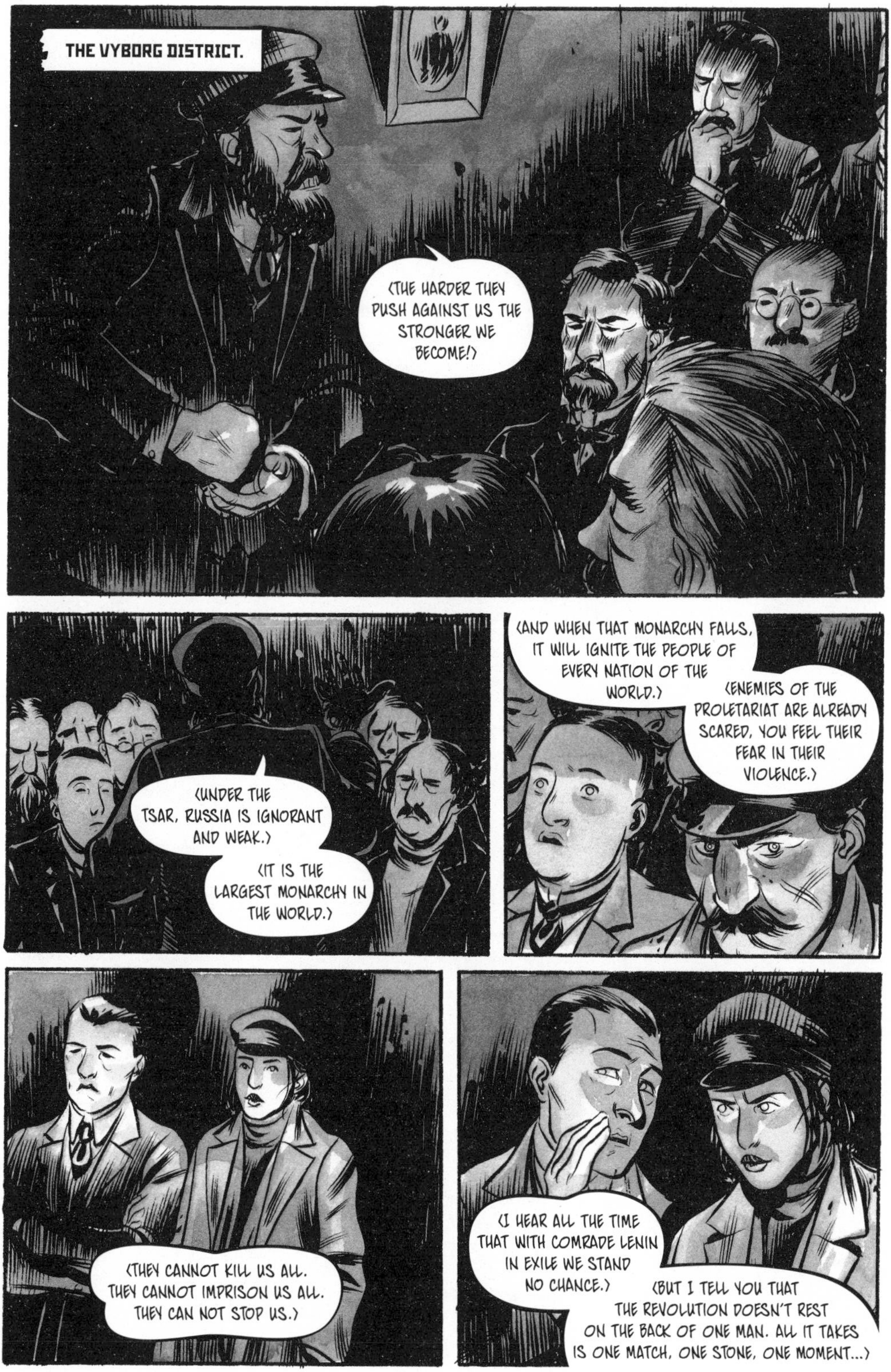
THE VYBORG DISTRICT.
‹THE HARDER THEY PUSH AGAINST US THE STRONGER WE BECOME!›
‹UNDER THE TSAR, RUSSIA IS IGNORANT AND WEAK.›
‹IT IS THE LARGEST MONARCHY IN THE WORLD.›
‹AND WHEN THAT MONARCHY FALLS, IT WILL IGNITE THE PEOPLE OF EVERY NATION OF THE WORLD.›
‹ENEMIES OF THE PROLETARIAT ARE ALREADY SCARED, YOU FEEL THEIR FEAR IN THEIR VIOLENCE.›
‹THEY CANNOT KILL US ALL. THEY CANNOT IMPRISON US ALL. THEY CAN NOT STOP US.›
‹I HEAR ALL THE TIME THAT WITH COMRADE LENIN IN EXILE WE STAND NO CHANCE.›
‹BUT I TELL YOU THAT THE REVOLUTION DOESN'T REST ON THE BACK OF ONE MAN. ALL IT TAKES IS ONE MATCH, ONE STONE, ONE MOMENT...›

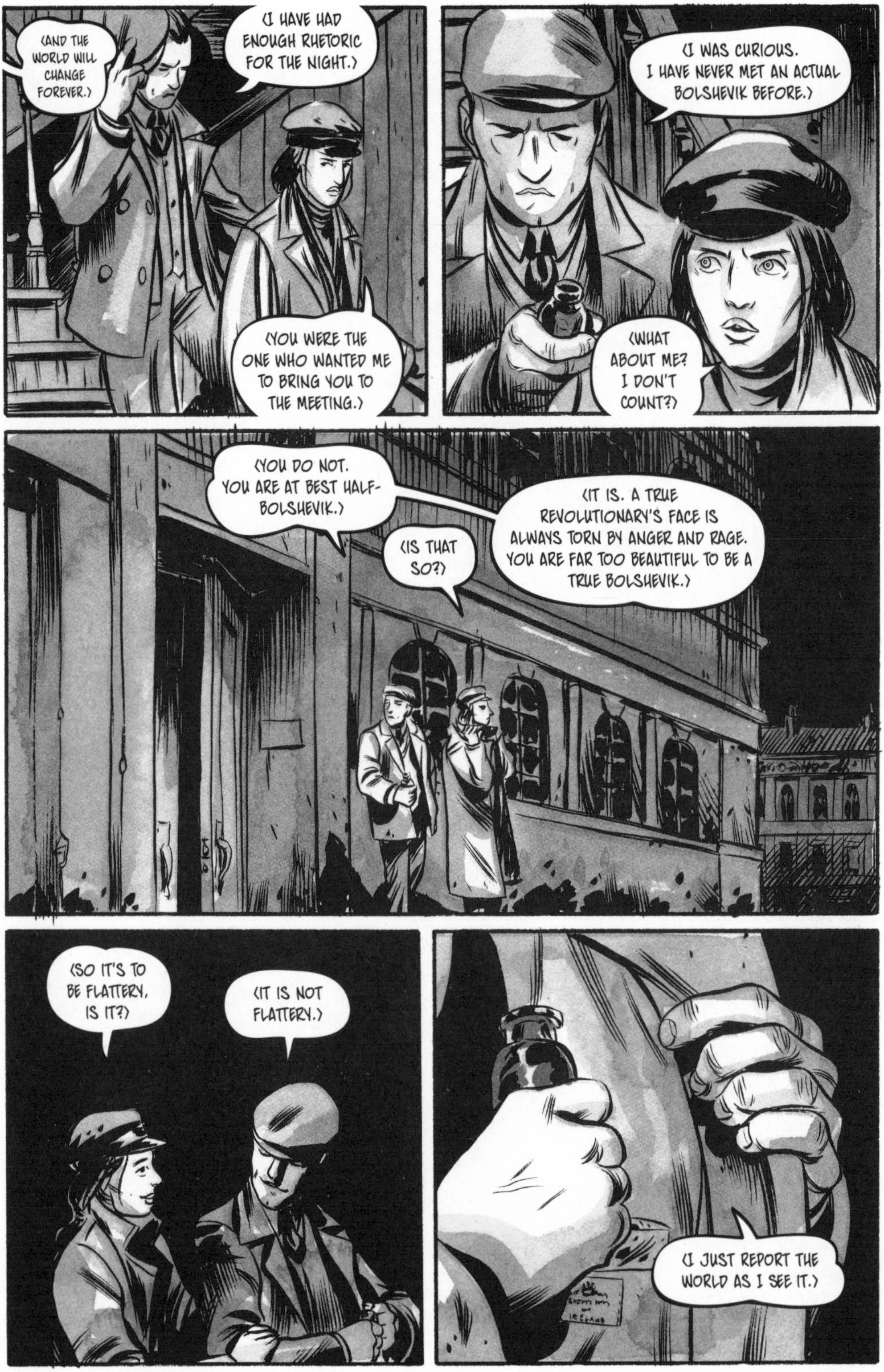

<AND THE WORLD WILL CHANGE FOREVER.>
<I HAVE HAD ENOUGH RHETORIC FOR THE NIGHT.>
<YOU WERE THE ONE WHO WANTED ME TO BRING YOU TO THE MEETING.>
<I WAS CURIOUS. I HAVE NEVER MET AN ACTUAL BOLSHEVIK BEFORE.>
<WHAT ABOUT ME? I DON'T COUNT?>
<YOU DO NOT. YOU ARE AT BEST HALF-BOLSHEVIK.>
<IS THAT SO?>
<IT IS. A TRUE REVOLUTIONARY'S FACE IS ALWAYS TORN BY ANGER AND RAGE. YOU ARE FAR TOO BEAUTIFUL TO BE A TRUE BOLSHEVIK.>
<SO IT'S TO BE FLATTERY, IS IT?>
<IT IS NOT FLATTERY.>
<I JUST REPORT THE WORLD AS I SEE IT.>

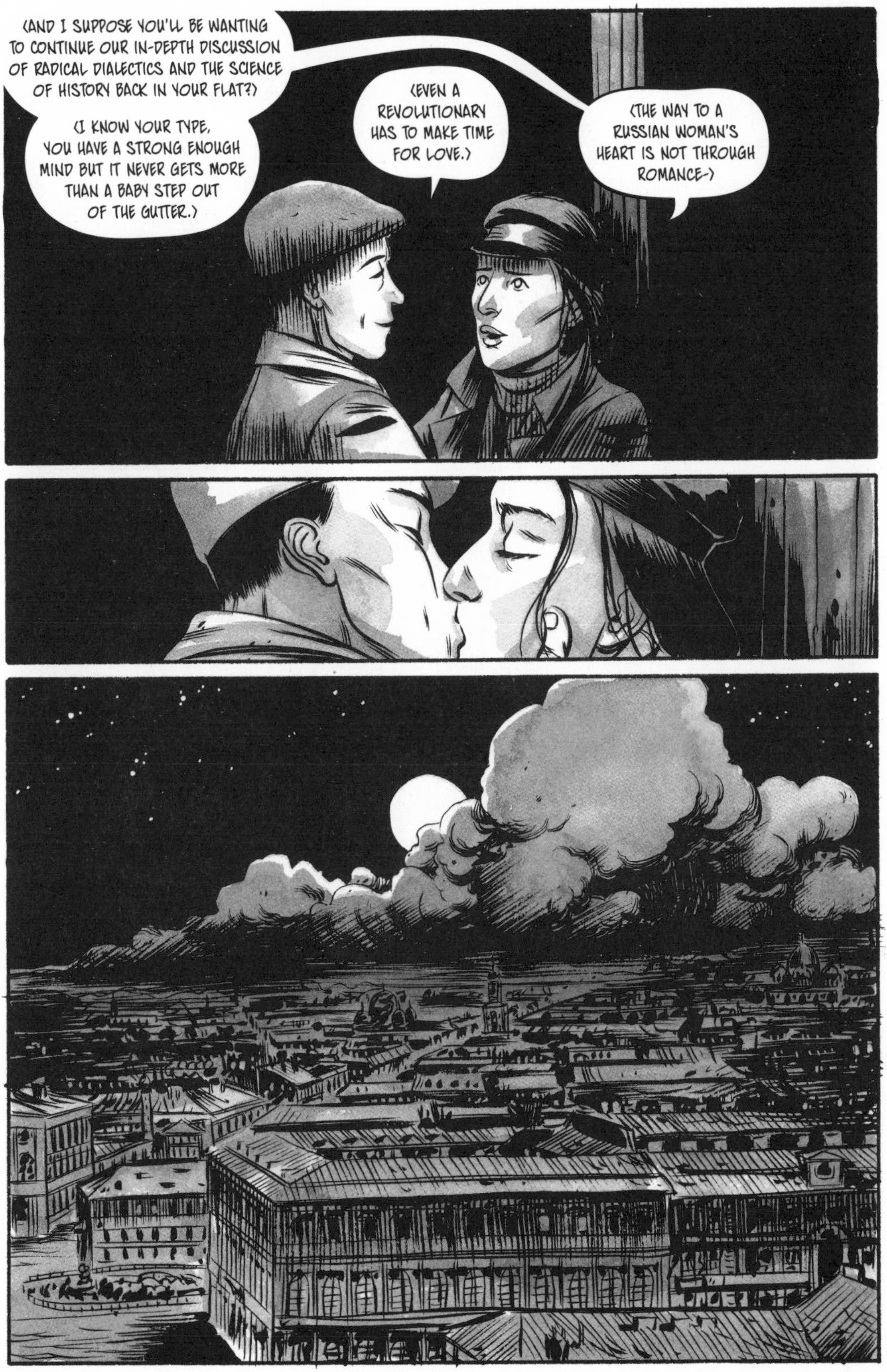
‹AND I SUPPOSE YOU'LL BE WANTING TO CONTINUE OUR IN-DEPTH DISCUSSION OF RADICAL DIALECTICS AND THE SCIENCE OF HISTORY BACK IN YOUR FLAT?›
‹I KNOW YOUR TYPE. YOU HAVE A STRONG ENOUGH MIND BUT IT NEVER GETS MORE THAN A BABY STEP OUT OF THE GUTTER.›
‹EVEN A REVOLUTIONARY HAS TO MAKE TIME FOR LOVE.›
‹THE WAY TO A RUSSIAN WOMAN'S HEART IS NOT THROUGH ROMANCE-›

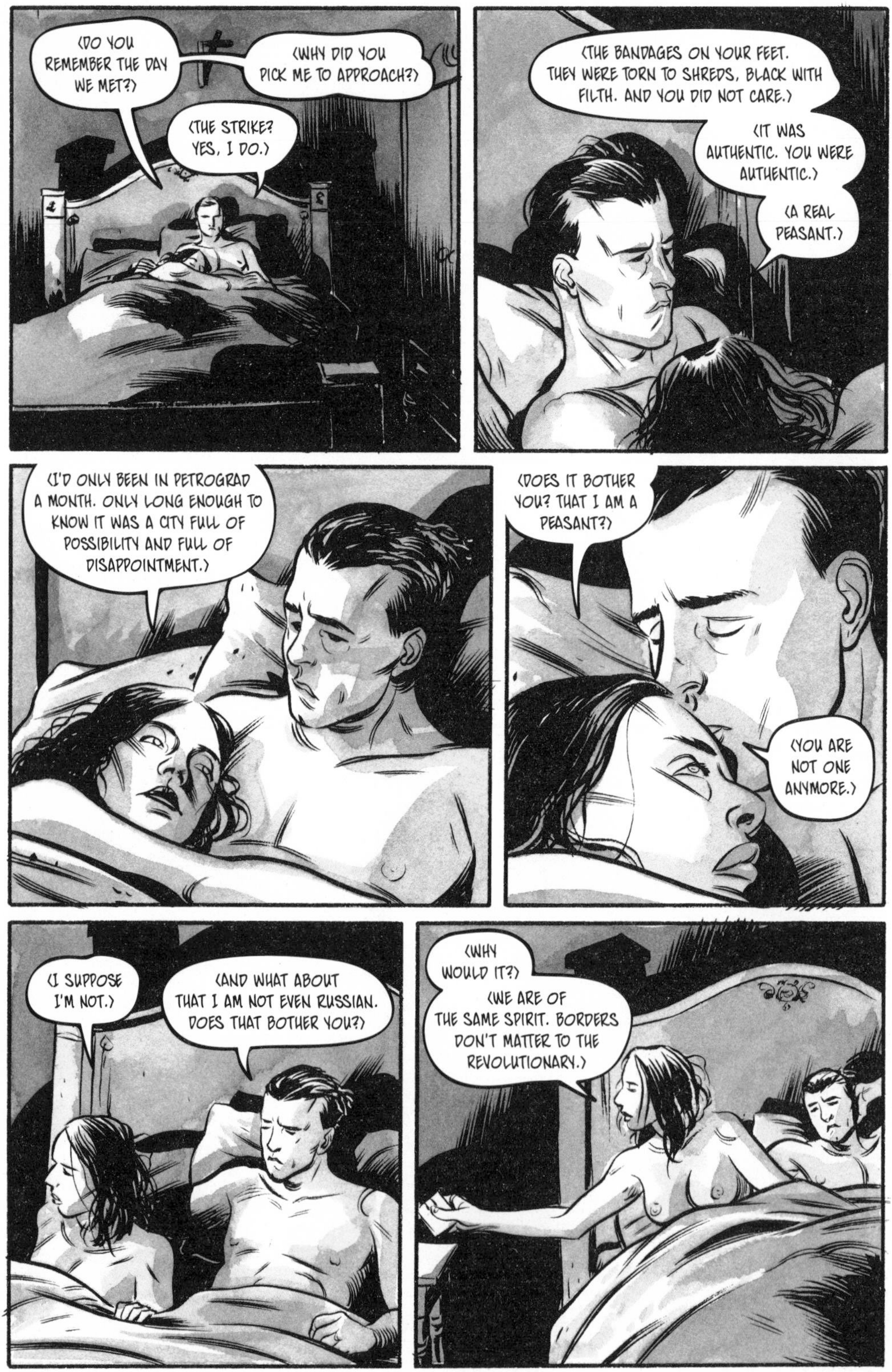
⟨DO YOU REMEMBER THE DAY WE MET?⟩
⟨WHY DID YOU PICK ME TO APPROACH?⟩
⟨THE STRIKE? YES, I DO.⟩
⟨THE BANDAGES ON YOUR FEET. THEY WERE TORN TO SHREDS, BLACK WITH FILTH. AND YOU DID NOT CARE.⟩
⟨IT WAS AUTHENTIC. YOU WERE AUTHENTIC.⟩
⟨A REAL PEASANT.⟩
⟨I'D ONLY BEEN IN PETROGRAD A MONTH. ONLY LONG ENOUGH TO KNOW IT WAS A CITY FULL OF POSSIBILITY AND FULL OF DISAPPOINTMENT.⟩
⟨DOES IT BOTHER YOU? THAT I AM A PEASANT?⟩
⟨YOU ARE NOT ONE ANYMORE.⟩
⟨I SUPPOSE I'M NOT.⟩
⟨AND WHAT ABOUT THAT I AM NOT EVEN RUSSIAN. DOES THAT BOTHER YOU?⟩
⟨WHY WOULD IT?⟩
⟨WE ARE OF THE SAME SPIRIT. BORDERS DON'T MATTER TO THE REVOLUTIONARY.⟩

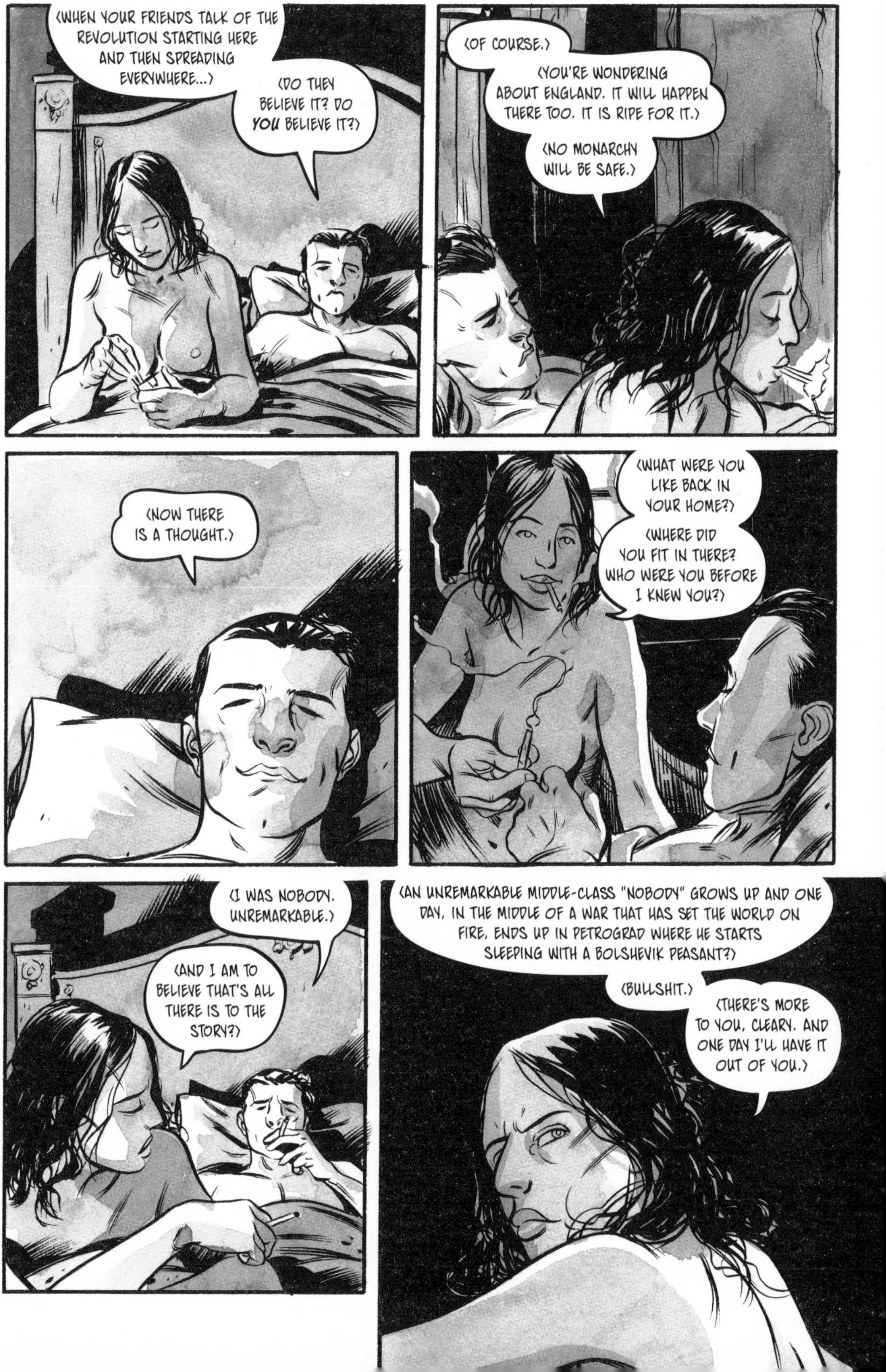
‹WHEN YOUR FRIENDS TALK OF THE REVOLUTION STARTING HERE AND THEN SPREADING EVERYWHERE...›
‹DO THEY BELIEVE IT? DO *YOU* BELIEVE IT?›
‹OF COURSE.›
‹YOU'RE WONDERING ABOUT ENGLAND. IT WILL HAPPEN THERE TOO. IT IS RIPE FOR IT.›
‹NO MONARCHY WILL BE SAFE.›
‹NOW THERE IS A THOUGHT.›
‹WHAT WERE YOU LIKE BACK IN YOUR HOME?›
‹WHERE DID YOU FIT IN THERE? WHO WERE YOU BEFORE I KNEW YOU?›
‹I WAS NOBODY. UNREMARKABLE.›
‹AND I AM TO BELIEVE THAT'S ALL THERE IS TO THE STORY?›
‹AN UNREMARKABLE MIDDLE-CLASS "NOBODY" GROWS UP AND ONE DAY, IN THE MIDDLE OF A WAR THAT HAS SET THE WORLD ON FIRE, ENDS UP IN PETROGRAD WHERE HE STARTS SLEEPING WITH A BOLSHEVIK PEASANT?›
‹BULLSHIT.›
‹THERE'S MORE TO YOU, CLEARY. AND ONE DAY I'LL HAVE IT OUT OF YOU.›

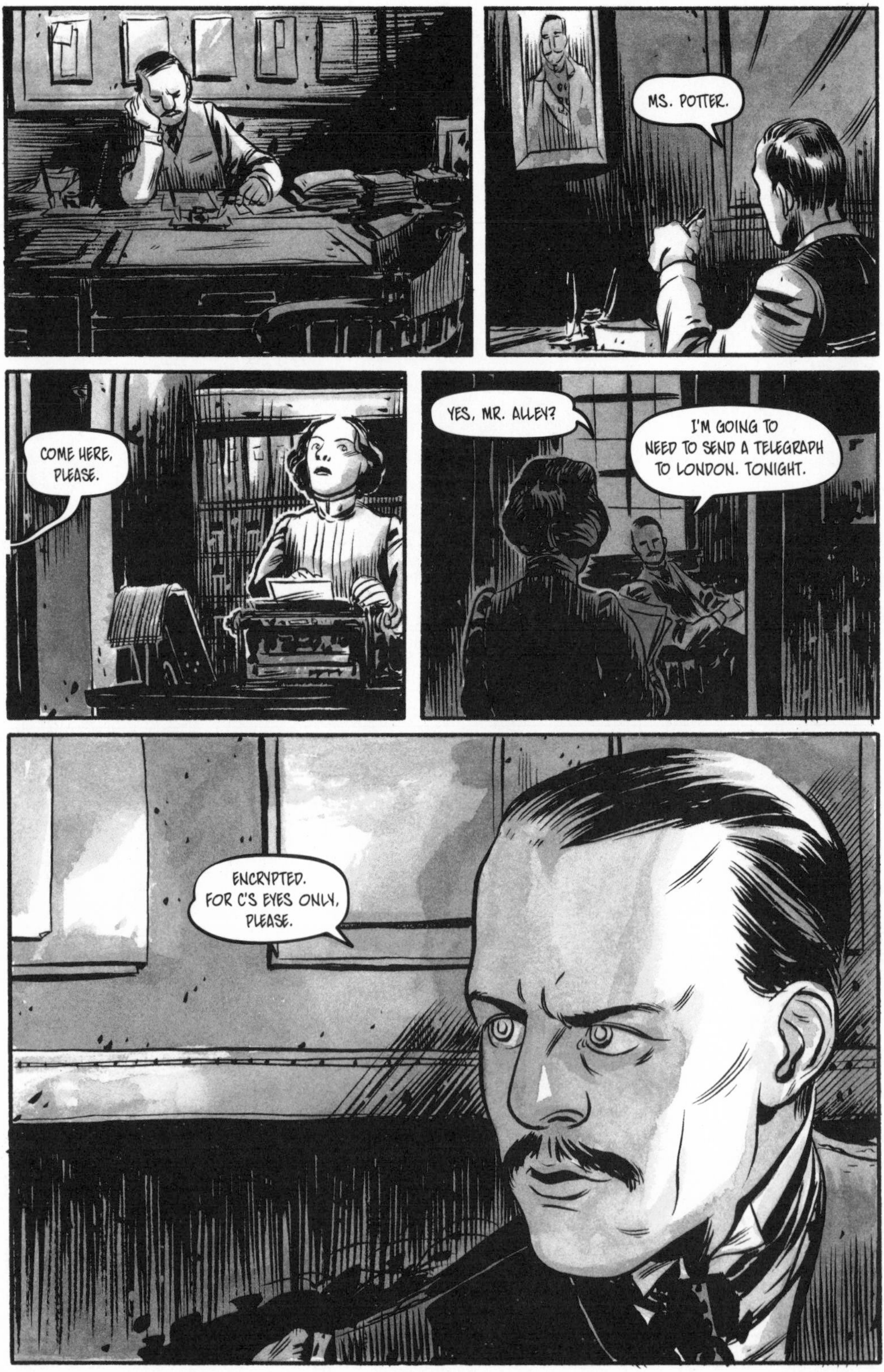
MS. POTTER.
COME HERE, PLEASE.
YES, MR. ALLEY?
I'M GOING TO NEED TO SEND A TELEGRAPH TO LONDON. TONIGHT.
ENCRYPTED. FOR C'S EYES ONLY, PLEASE.

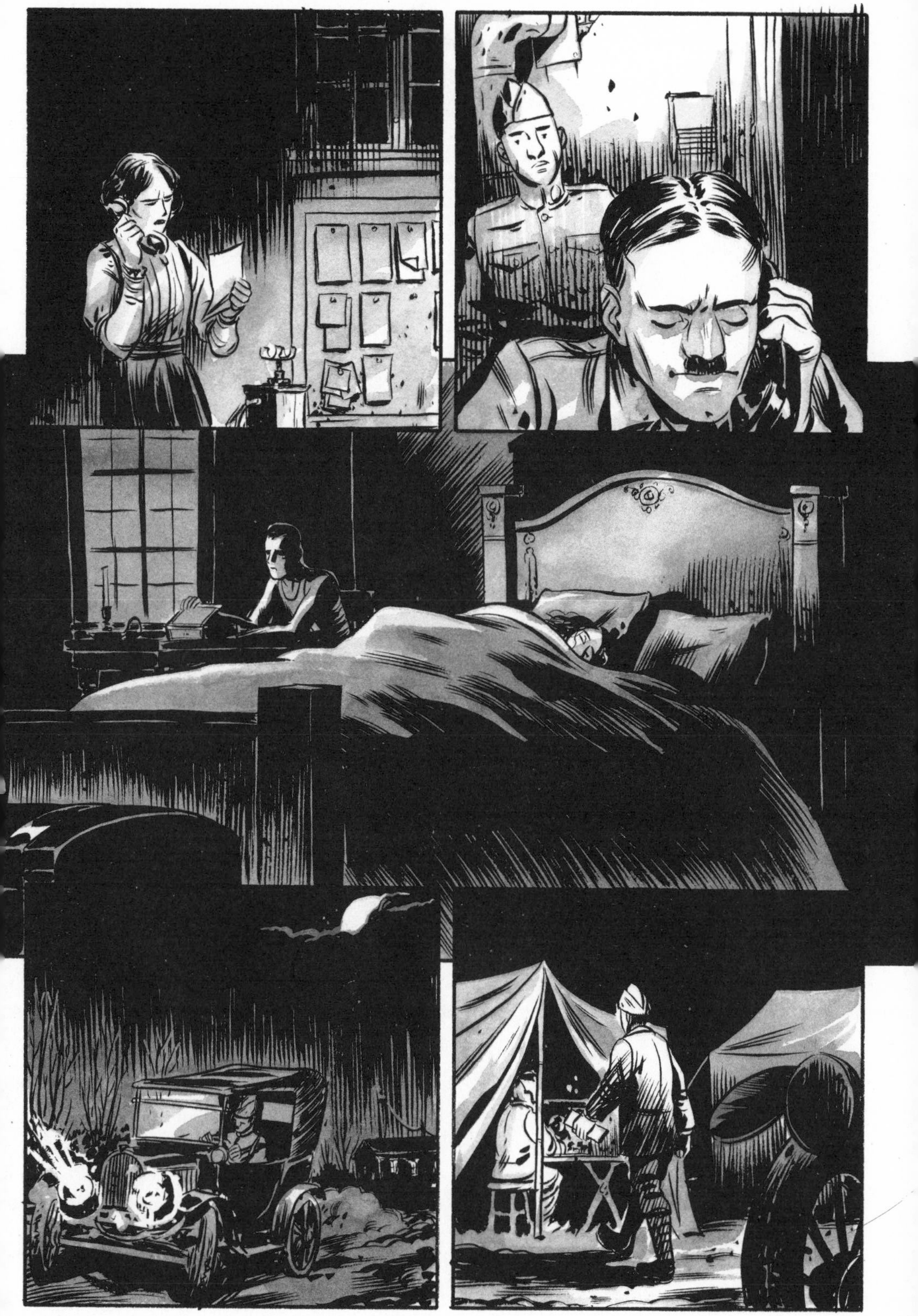

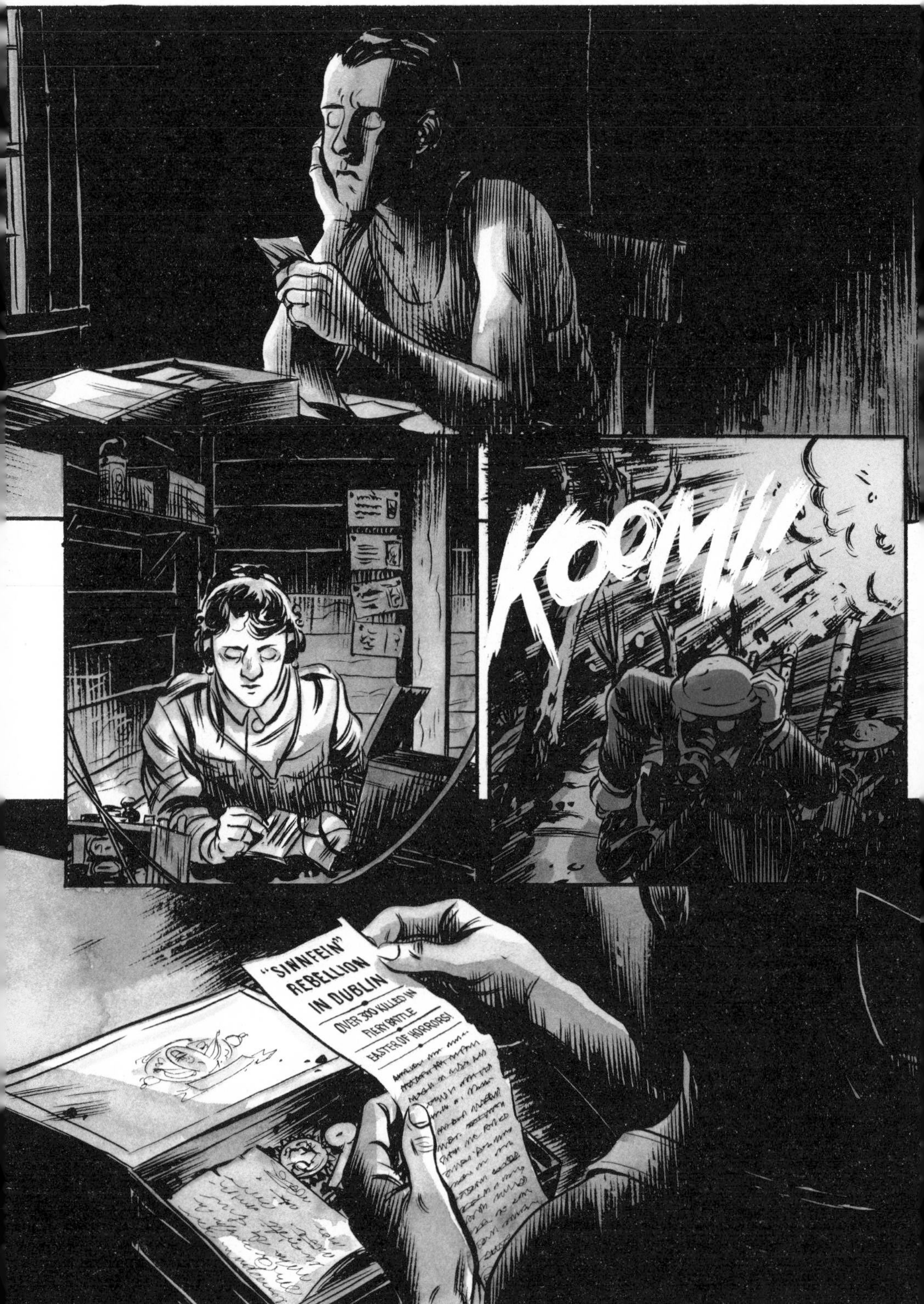
KOOM!!
"SINNFEIN" REBELLION IN DUBLIN
OVER 300 KILLED IN FIERY BATTLE
EASTER OF HORRORS!

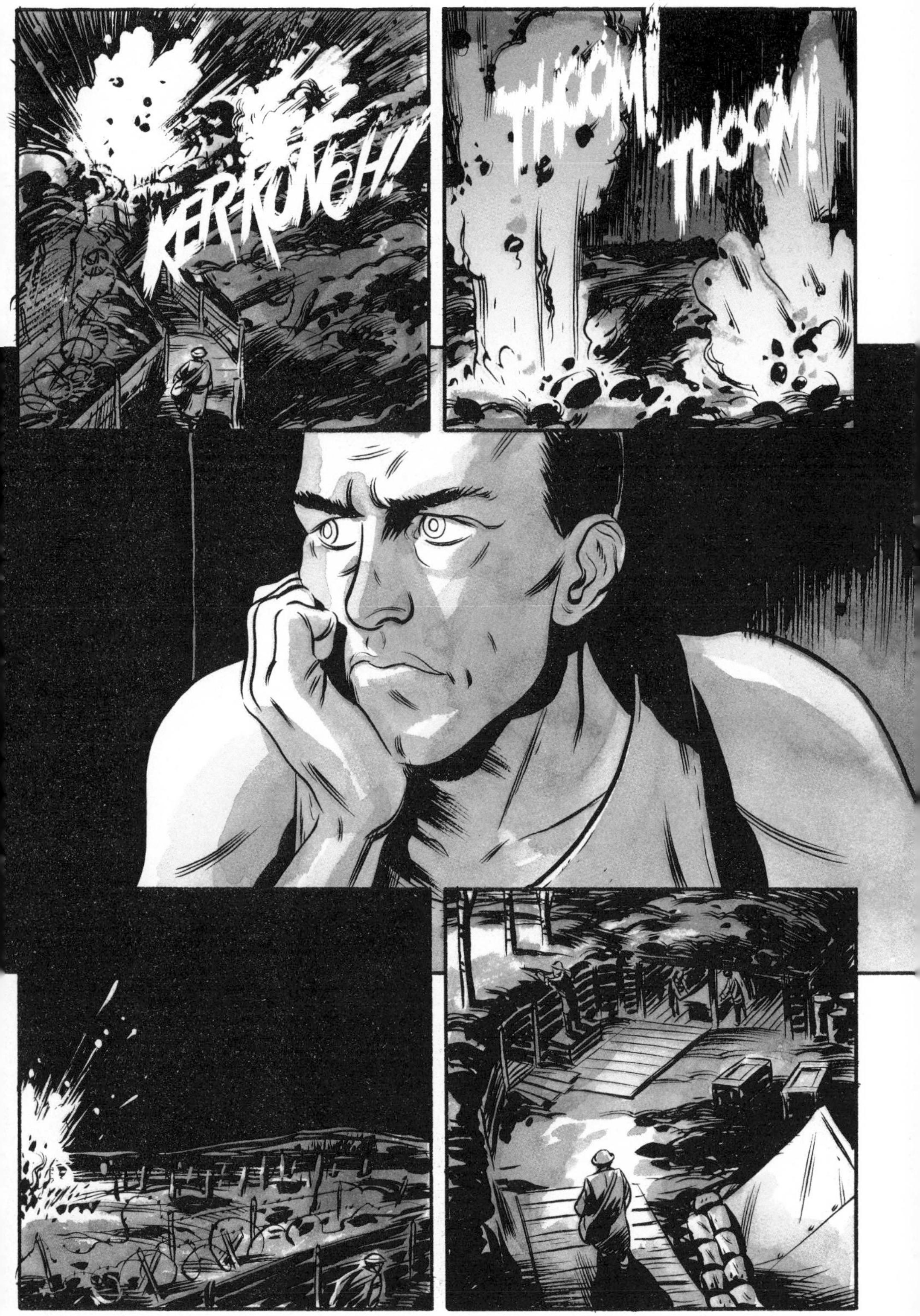
KERRUNCH!!
THOOM!
THOOM!

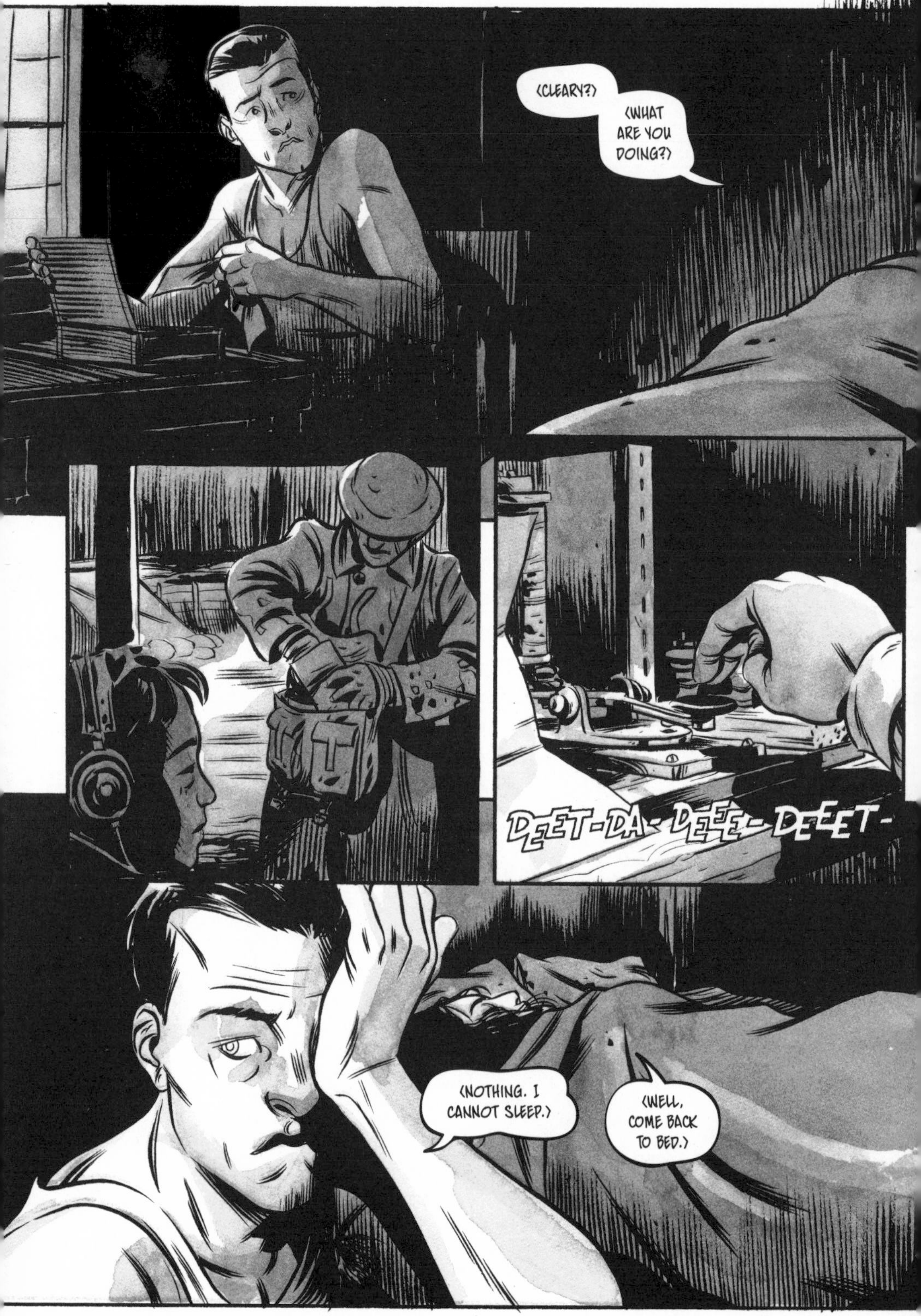

‹CLEARY?›
‹WHAT ARE YOU DOING?›
DEEET-DA-DEEE-DEEET-
‹NOTHING. I CANNOT SLEEP.›
‹WELL, COME BACK TO BED.›

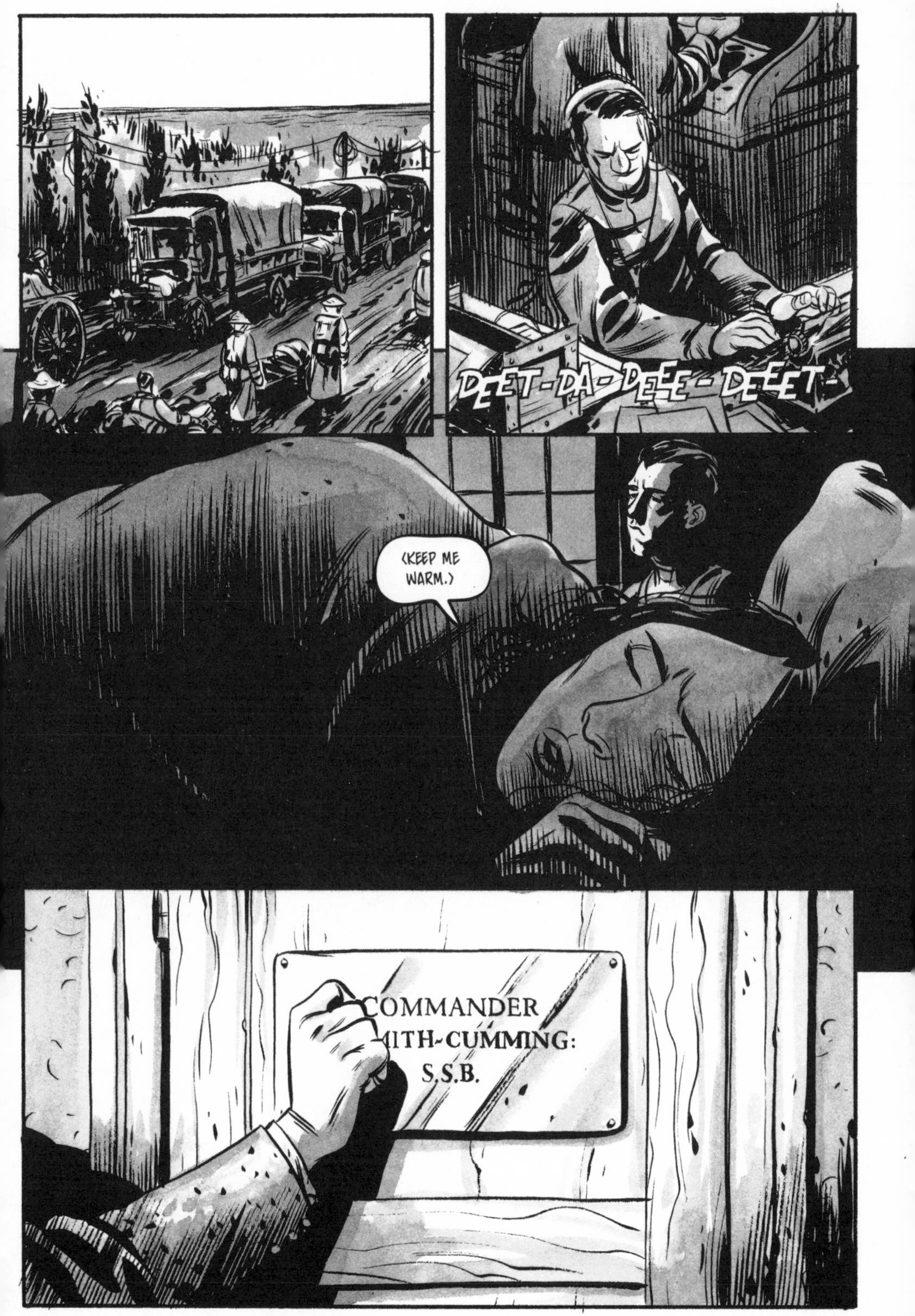
DEET-DA-DEEE-DEEET-
‹KEEP ME WARM.›
COMMANDER
MITH-CUMMING:
S.S.B.

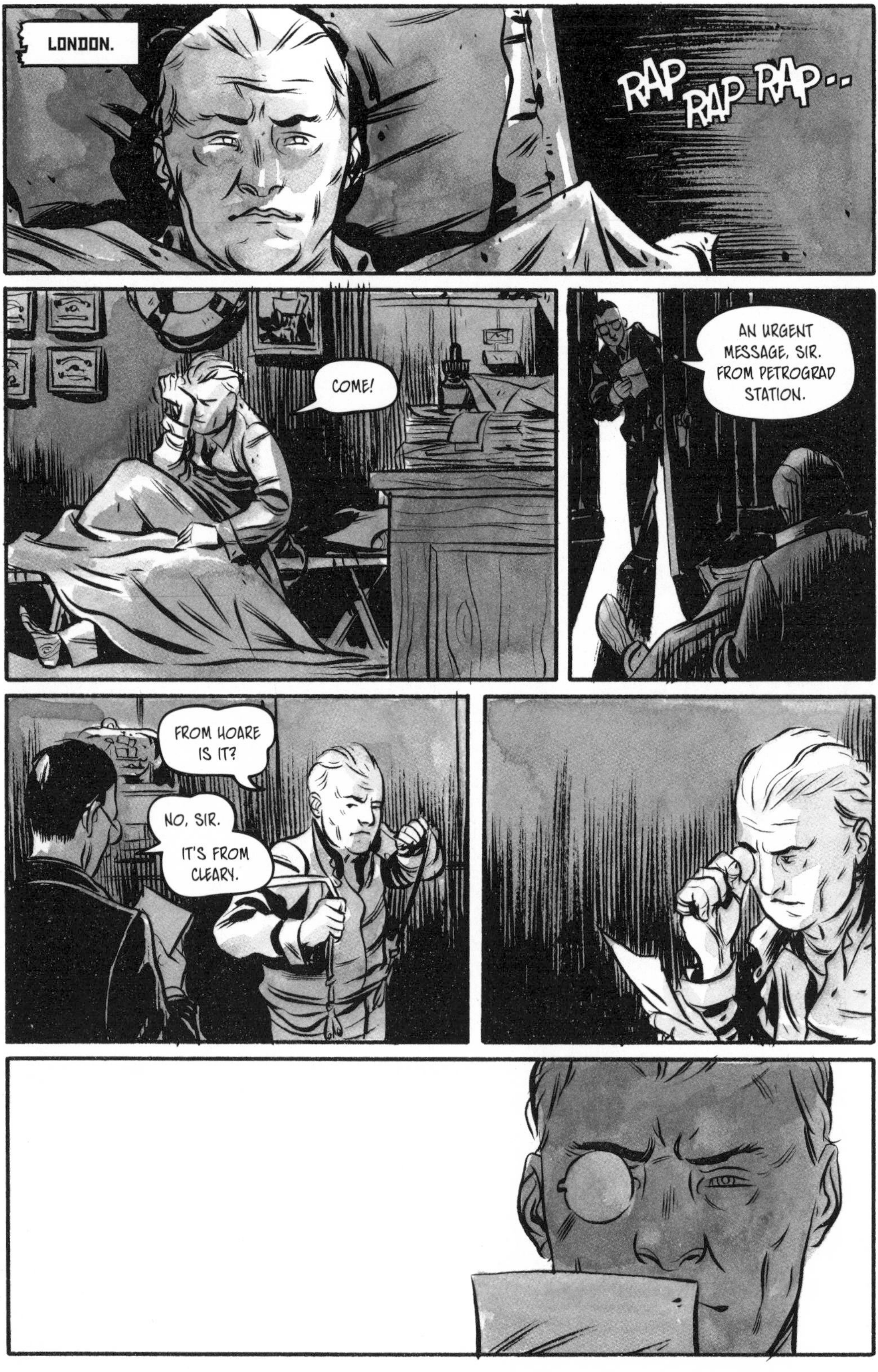
LONDON.
RAP RAP RAP..
COME!
AN URGENT MESSAGE, SIR. FROM PETROGRAD STATION.
FROM HOARE IS IT?
NO, SIR.
IT'S FROM CLEARY.

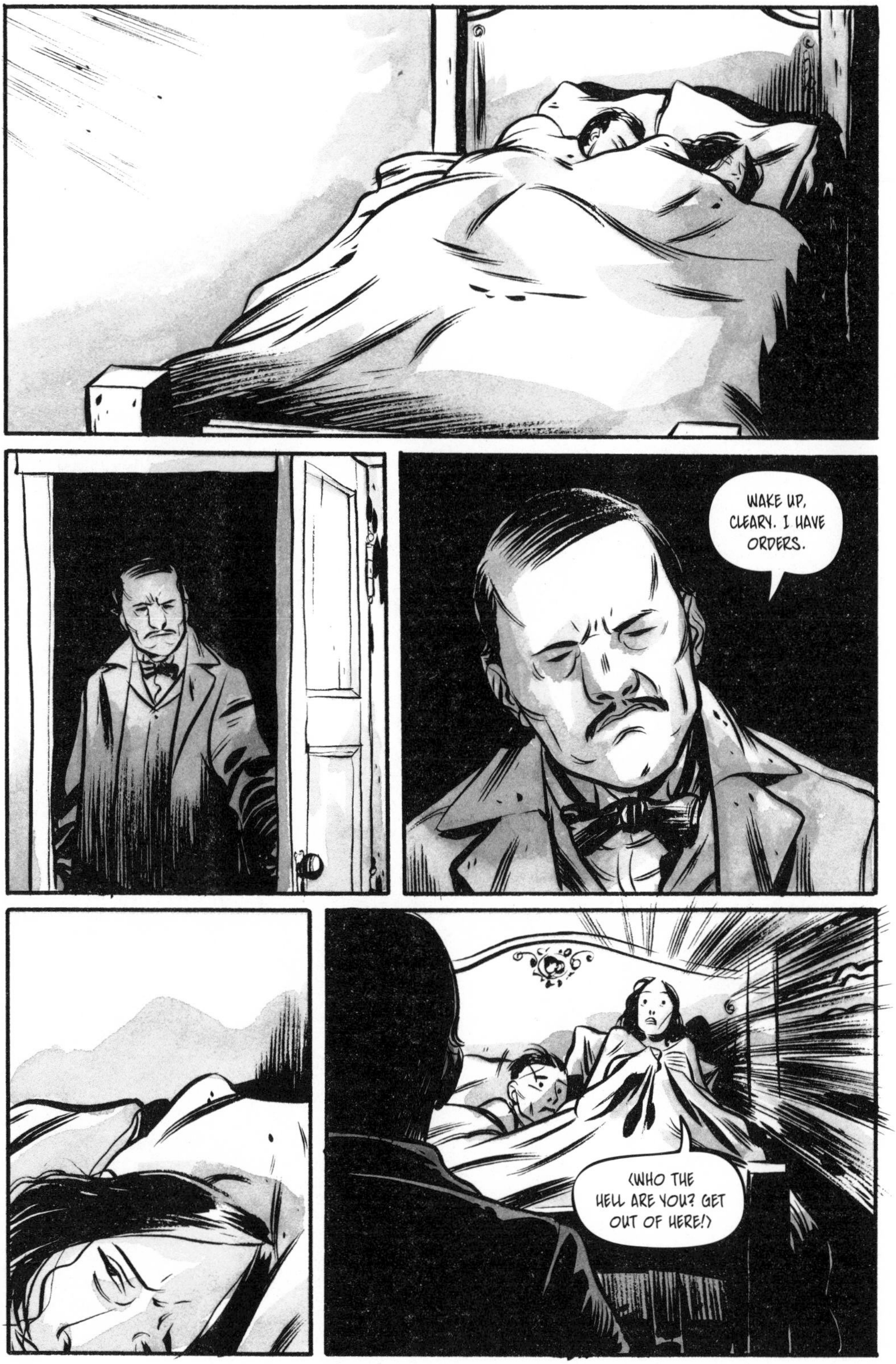
WAKE UP, CLEARY. I HAVE ORDERS.
<WHO THE HELL ARE YOU? GET OUT OF HERE!>

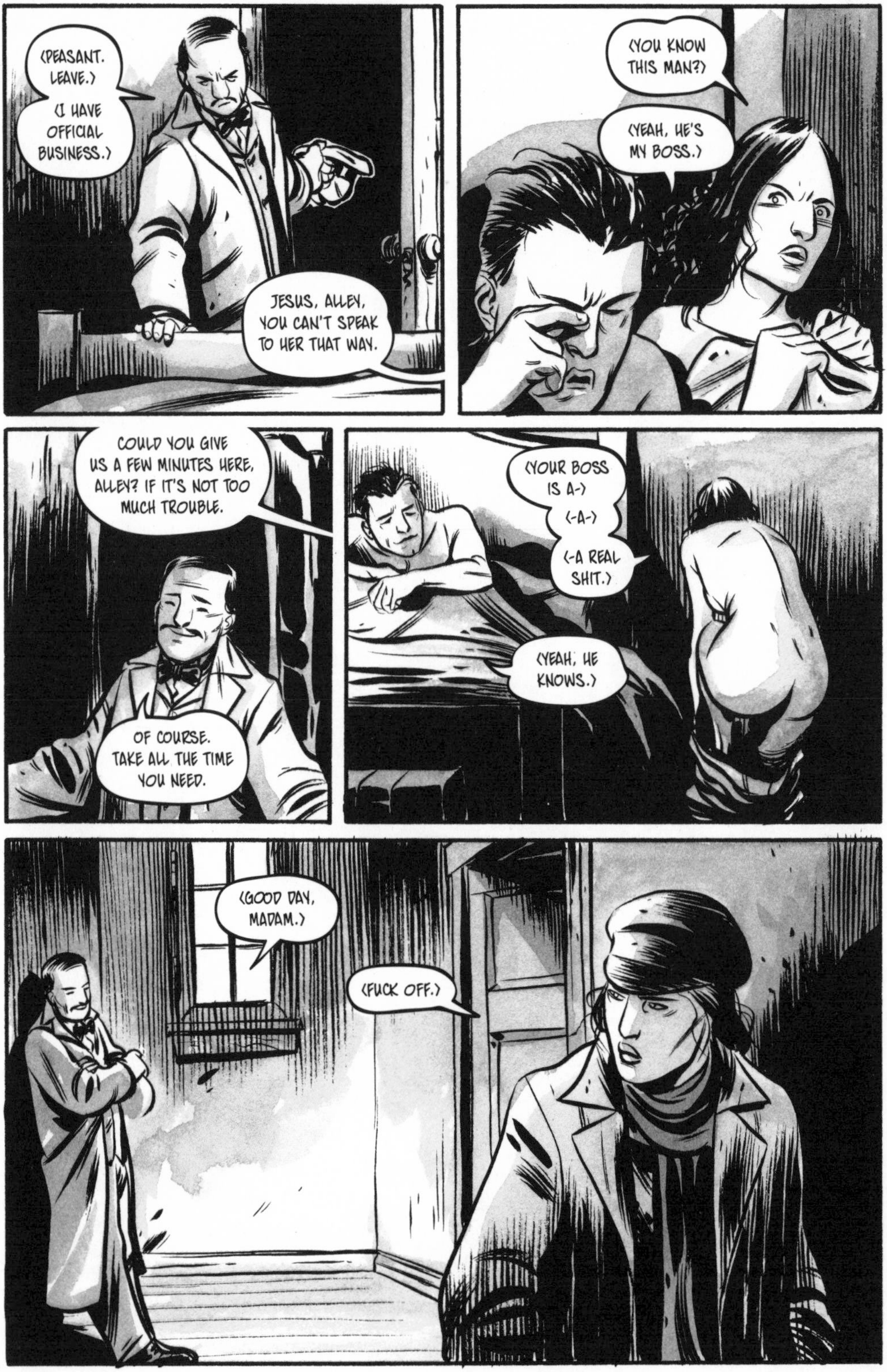
‹PEASANT. LEAVE.›
‹I HAVE OFFICIAL BUSINESS.›
JESUS, ALLEY, YOU CAN'T SPEAK TO HER THAT WAY.
‹YOU KNOW THIS MAN?›
‹YEAH, HE'S MY BOSS.›
COULD YOU GIVE US A FEW MINUTES HERE, ALLEY? IF IT'S NOT TOO MUCH TROUBLE.
OF COURSE. TAKE ALL THE TIME YOU NEED.
‹YOUR BOSS IS A-›
‹-A-›
‹-A REAL SHIT.›
‹YEAH, HE KNOWS.›
‹GOOD DAY, MADAM.›
‹FUCK OFF.›

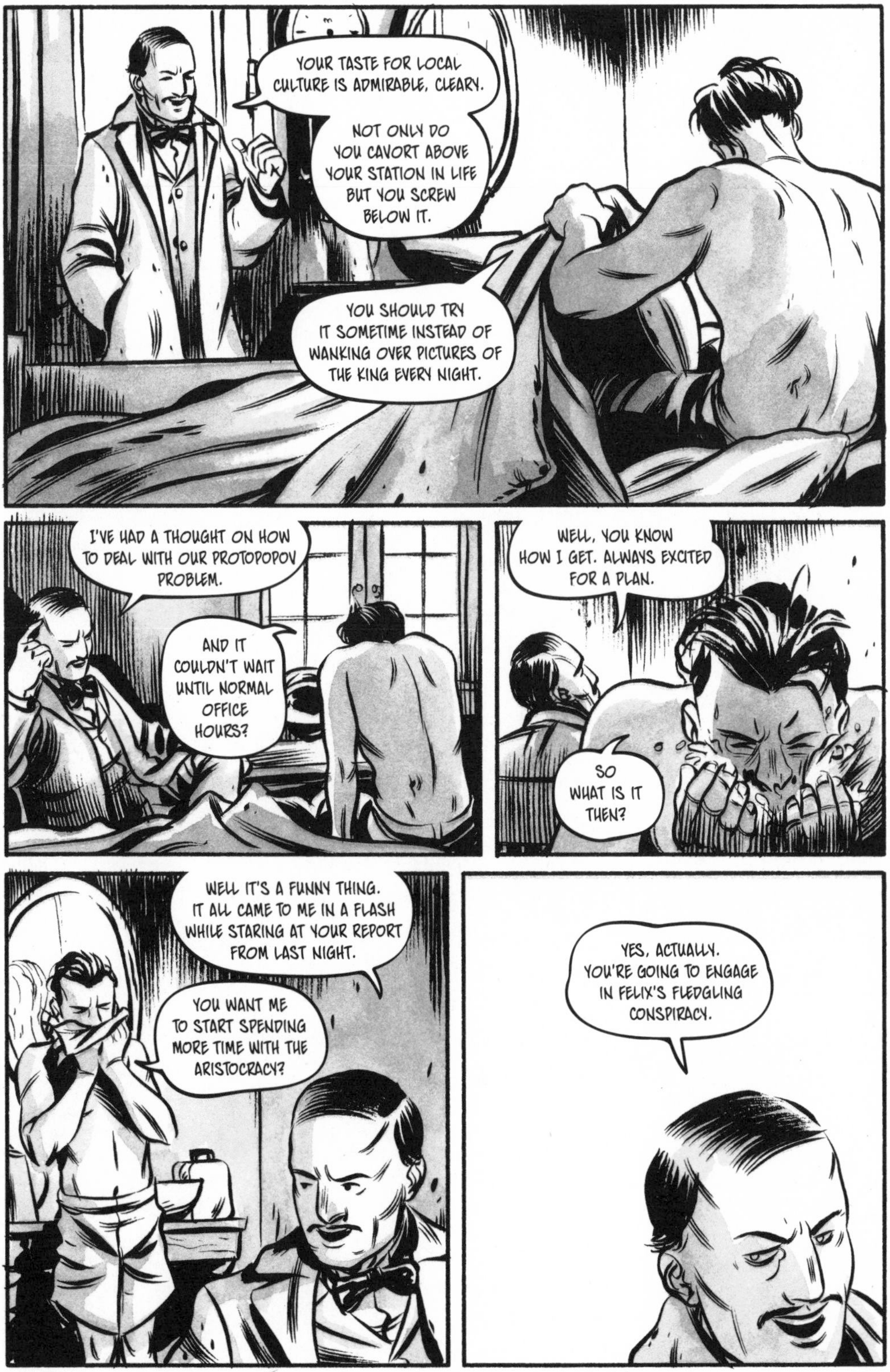
YOUR TASTE FOR LOCAL CULTURE IS ADMIRABLE, CLEARY.
NOT ONLY DO YOU CAVORT ABOVE YOUR STATION IN LIFE BUT YOU SCREW BELOW IT.
YOU SHOULD TRY IT SOMETIME INSTEAD OF WANKING OVER PICTURES OF THE KING EVERY NIGHT.
I'VE HAD A THOUGHT ON HOW TO DEAL WITH OUR PROTOPOPOV PROBLEM.
AND IT COULDN'T WAIT UNTIL NORMAL OFFICE HOURS?
WELL, YOU KNOW HOW I GET. ALWAYS EXCITED FOR A PLAN.
SO WHAT IS IT THEN?
WELL IT'S A FUNNY THING. IT ALL CAME TO ME IN A FLASH WHILE STARING AT YOUR REPORT FROM LAST NIGHT.
YOU WANT ME TO START SPENDING MORE TIME WITH THE ARISTOCRACY?
YES, ACTUALLY. YOU'RE GOING TO ENGAGE IN FELIX'S FLEDGLING CONSPIRACY.

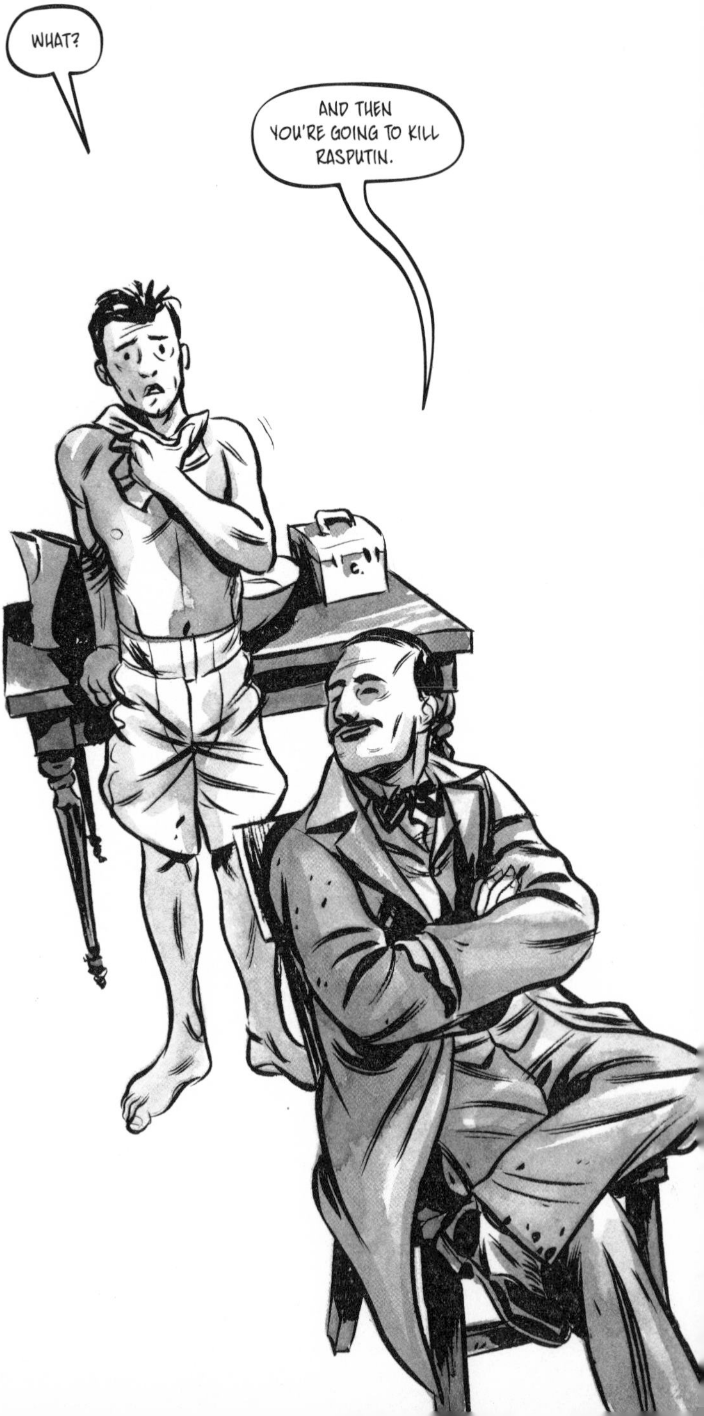
WHAT?
AND THEN YOU'RE GOING TO KILL RASPUTIN.

CHAPTER 2

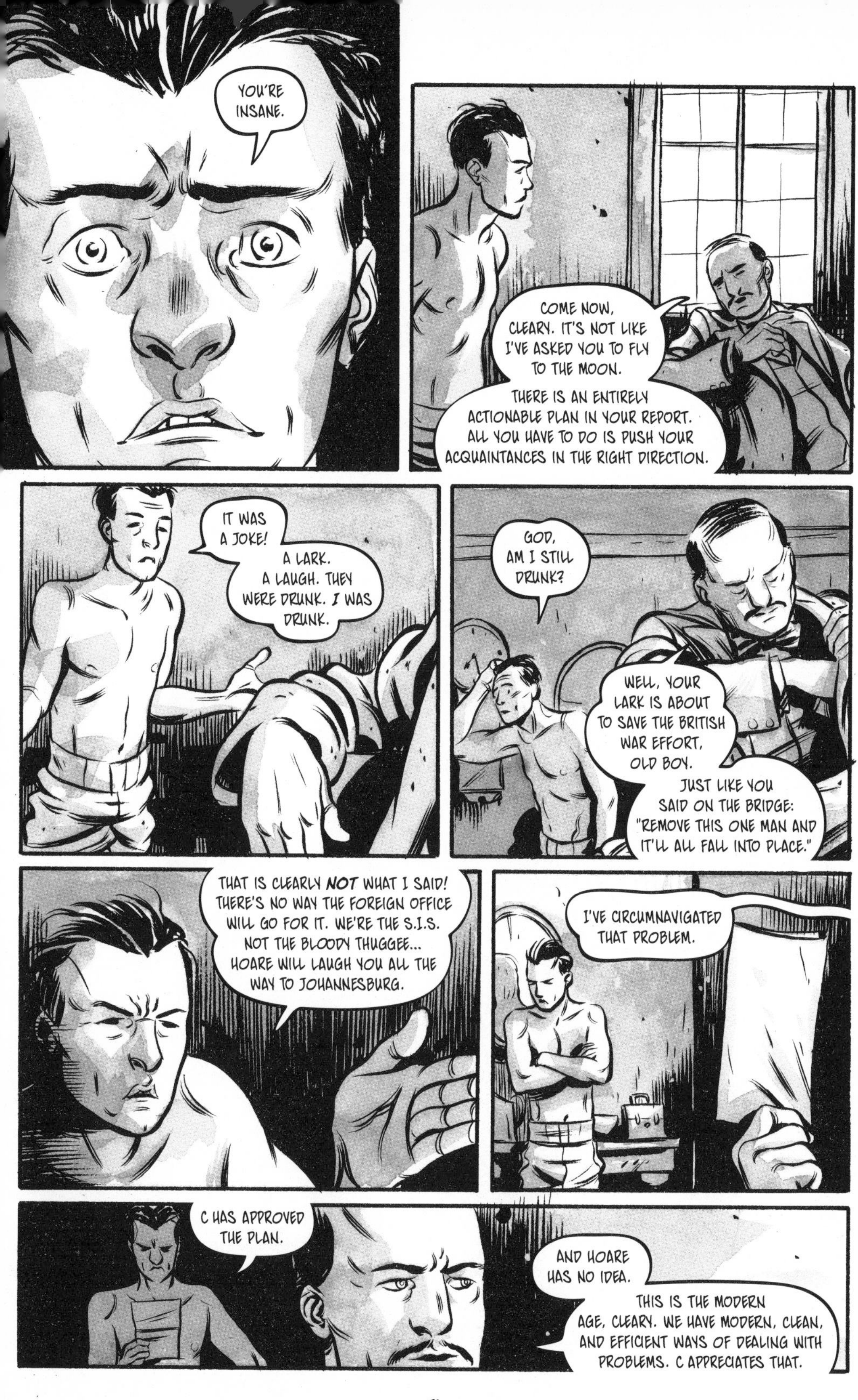
YOU'RE INSANE.
COME NOW, CLEARY. IT'S NOT LIKE I'VE ASKED YOU TO FLY TO THE MOON.
THERE IS AN ENTIRELY ACTIONABLE PLAN IN YOUR REPORT. ALL YOU HAVE TO DO IS PUSH YOUR ACQUAINTANCES IN THE RIGHT DIRECTION.
IT WAS A JOKE!
A LARK. A LAUGH. THEY WERE DRUNK. *I* WAS DRUNK.
GOD, AM I STILL DRUNK?
WELL, YOUR LARK IS ABOUT TO SAVE THE BRITISH WAR EFFORT, OLD BOY.
JUST LIKE YOU SAID ON THE BRIDGE: "REMOVE THIS ONE MAN AND IT'LL ALL FALL INTO PLACE."
THAT IS CLEARLY ***NOT*** WHAT I SAID! THERE'S NO WAY THE FOREIGN OFFICE WILL GO FOR IT. WE'RE THE S.I.S. NOT THE BLOODY THUGGEE... HOARE WILL LAUGH YOU ALL THE WAY TO JOHANNESBURG.
I'VE CIRCUMNAVIGATED THAT PROBLEM.
C HAS APPROVED THE PLAN.
AND HOARE HAS NO IDEA.
THIS IS THE MODERN AGE, CLEARY. WE HAVE MODERN, CLEAN, AND EFFICIENT WAYS OF DEALING WITH PROBLEMS. C APPRECIATES THAT.

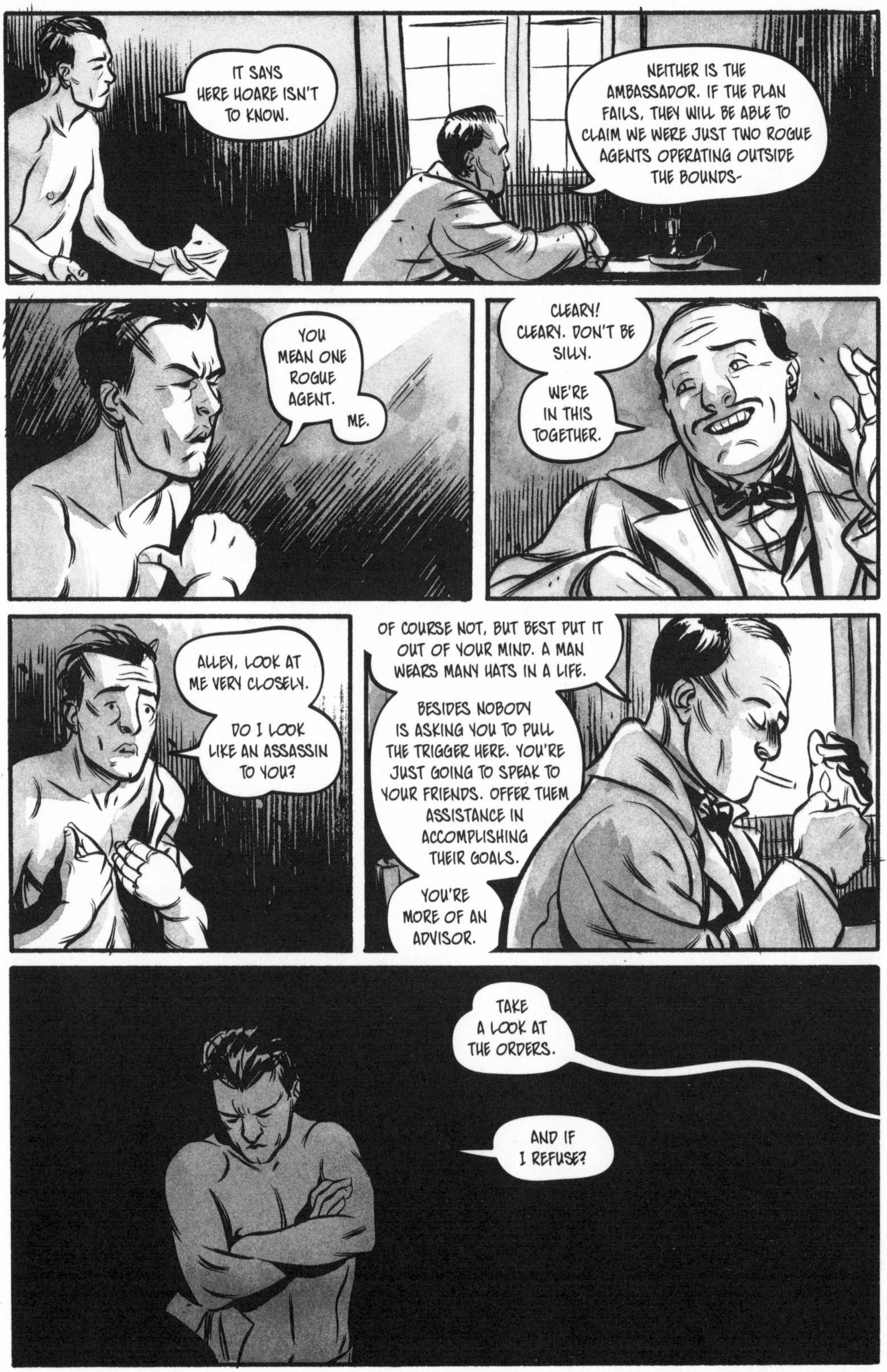
IT SAYS HERE HOARE ISN'T TO KNOW.
NEITHER IS THE AMBASSADOR. IF THE PLAN FAILS, THEY WILL BE ABLE TO CLAIM WE WERE JUST TWO ROGUE AGENTS OPERATING OUTSIDE THE BOUNDS-
YOU MEAN ONE ROGUE AGENT.
ME.
CLEARY! CLEARY. DON'T BE SILLY.
WE'RE IN THIS TOGETHER.
ALLEY, LOOK AT ME VERY CLOSELY.
DO I LOOK LIKE AN ASSASSIN TO YOU?
OF COURSE NOT, BUT BEST PUT IT OUT OF YOUR MIND. A MAN WEARS MANY HATS IN A LIFE.
BESIDES NOBODY IS ASKING YOU TO PULL THE TRIGGER HERE. YOU'RE JUST GOING TO SPEAK TO YOUR FRIENDS. OFFER THEM ASSISTANCE IN ACCOMPLISHING THEIR GOALS.
YOU'RE MORE OF AN ADVISOR.
TAKE A LOOK AT THE ORDERS.
AND IF I REFUSE?

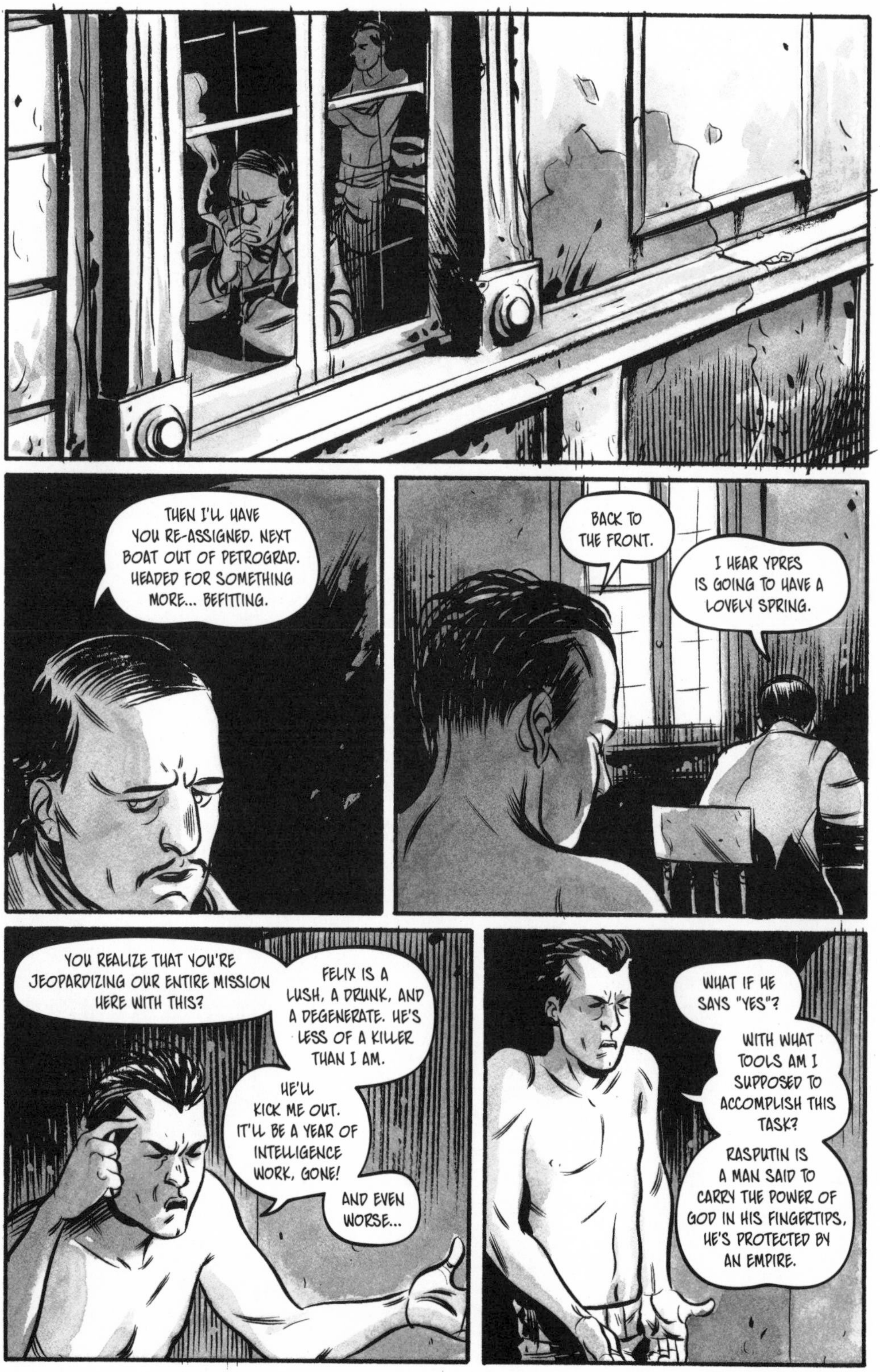
THEN I'LL HAVE YOU RE-ASSIGNED. NEXT BOAT OUT OF PETROGRAD. HEADED FOR SOMETHING MORE... BEFITTING.
BACK TO THE FRONT.
I HEAR YPRES IS GOING TO HAVE A LOVELY SPRING.
YOU REALIZE THAT YOU'RE JEOPARDIZING OUR ENTIRE MISSION HERE WITH THIS?
FELIX IS A LUSH, A DRUNK, AND A DEGENERATE. HE'S LESS OF A KILLER THAN I AM.
HE'LL KICK ME OUT. IT'LL BE A YEAR OF INTELLIGENCE WORK, GONE!
AND EVEN WORSE...
WHAT IF HE SAYS "YES"?
WITH WHAT TOOLS AM I SUPPOSED TO ACCOMPLISH THIS TASK?
RASPUTIN IS A MAN SAID TO CARRY THE POWER OF GOD IN HIS FINGERTIPS, HE'S PROTECTED BY AN EMPIRE.

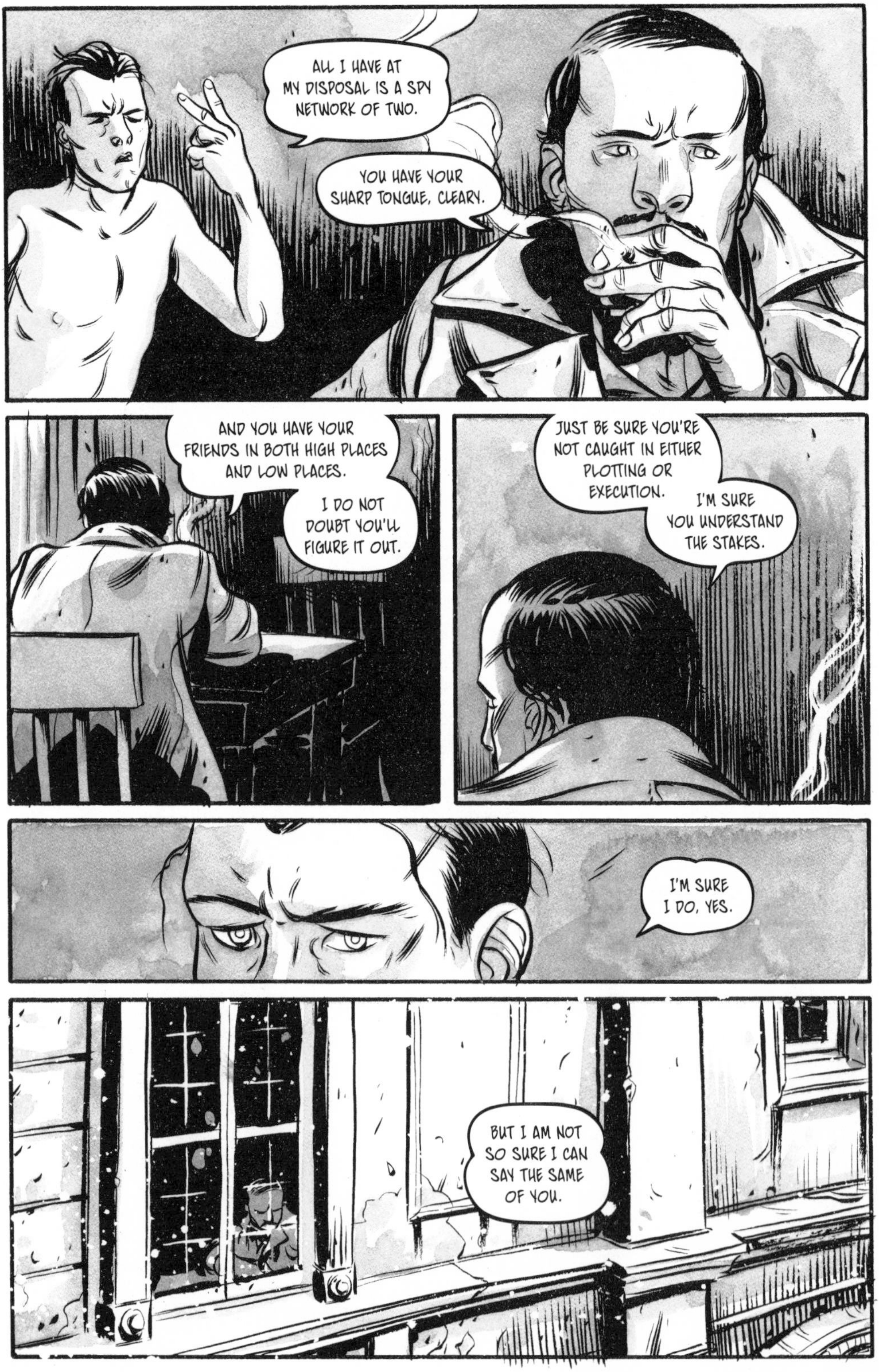
ALL I HAVE AT MY DISPOSAL IS A SPY NETWORK OF TWO.
YOU HAVE YOUR SHARP TONGUE, CLEARY.
AND YOU HAVE YOUR FRIENDS IN BOTH HIGH PLACES AND LOW PLACES.
I DO NOT DOUBT YOU'LL FIGURE IT OUT.
JUST BE SURE YOU'RE NOT CAUGHT IN EITHER PLOTTING OR EXECUTION.
I'M SURE YOU UNDERSTAND THE STAKES.
I'M SURE I DO, YES.
BUT I AM NOT SO SURE I CAN SAY THE SAME OF YOU.

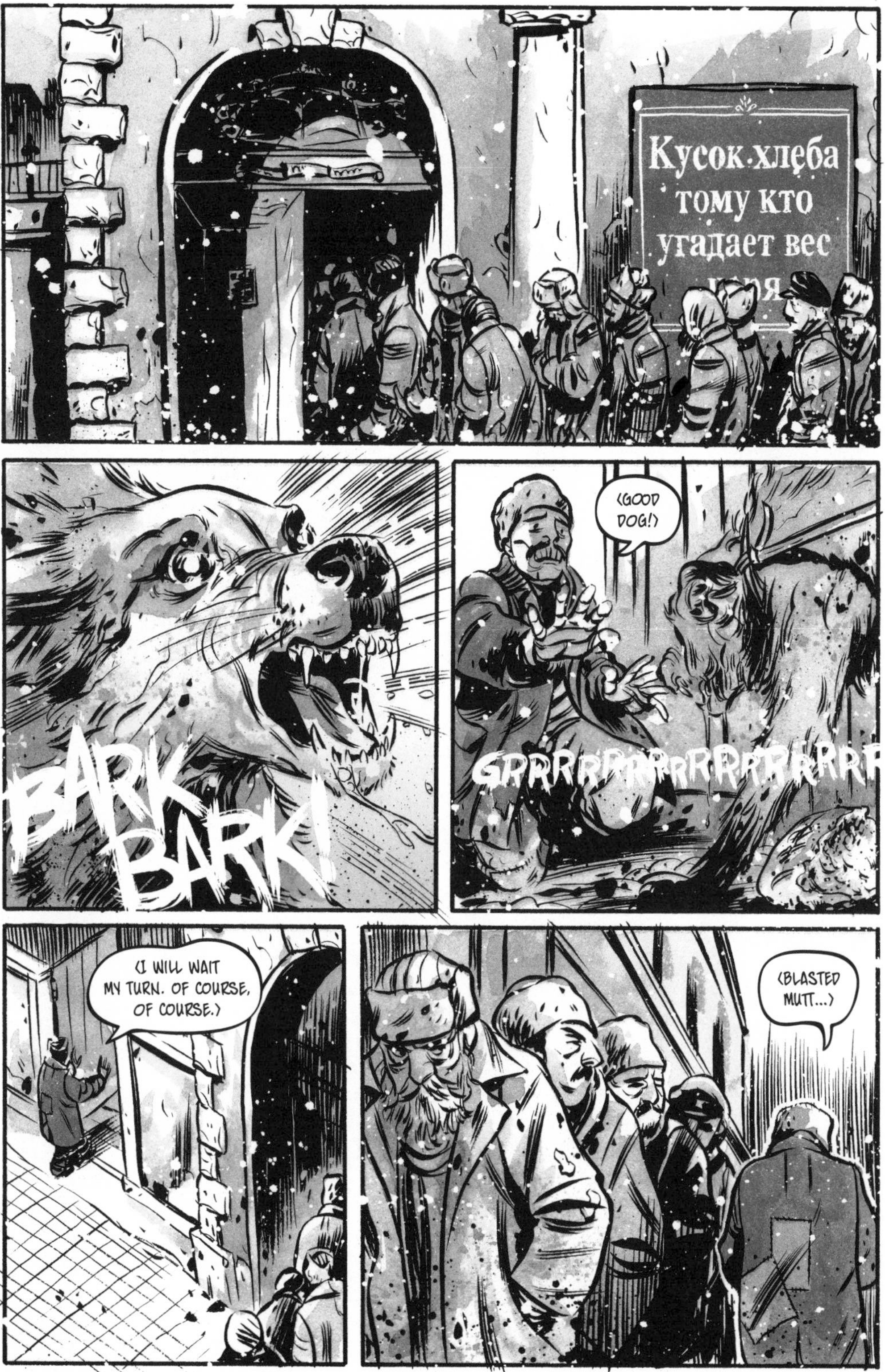
Кусок хлеба
тому кто
угадает вес
BARK BARK!
‹GOOD DOG!›
GRRRRRRRRRRRRRRRRR
‹I WILL WAIT MY TURN. OF COURSE, OF COURSE.›
‹BLASTED MUTT...›

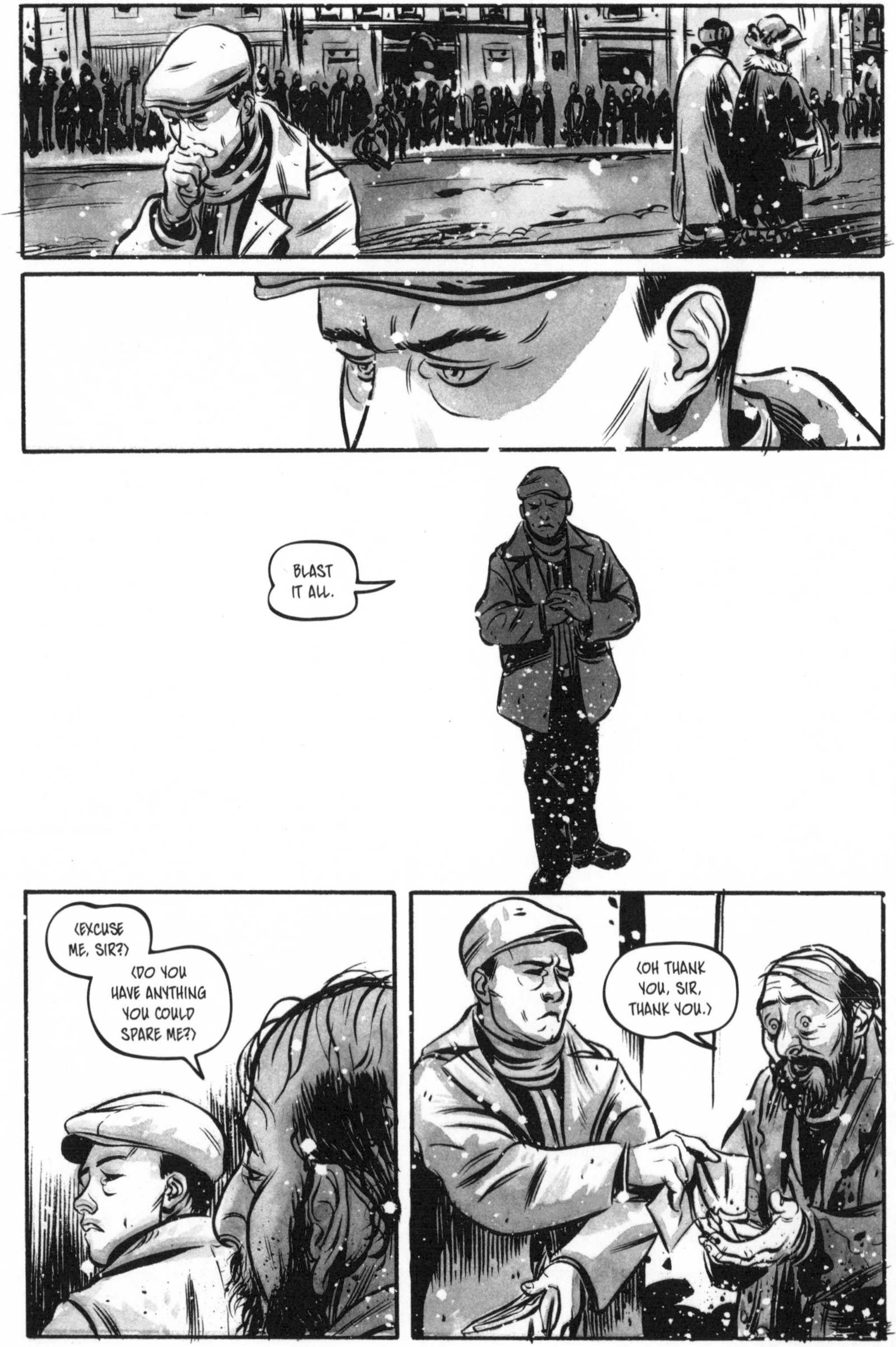

BLAST IT ALL.
‹EXCUSE ME, SIR?›
‹DO YOU HAVE ANYTHING YOU COULD SPARE ME?›
‹OH THANK YOU, SIR, THANK YOU.›

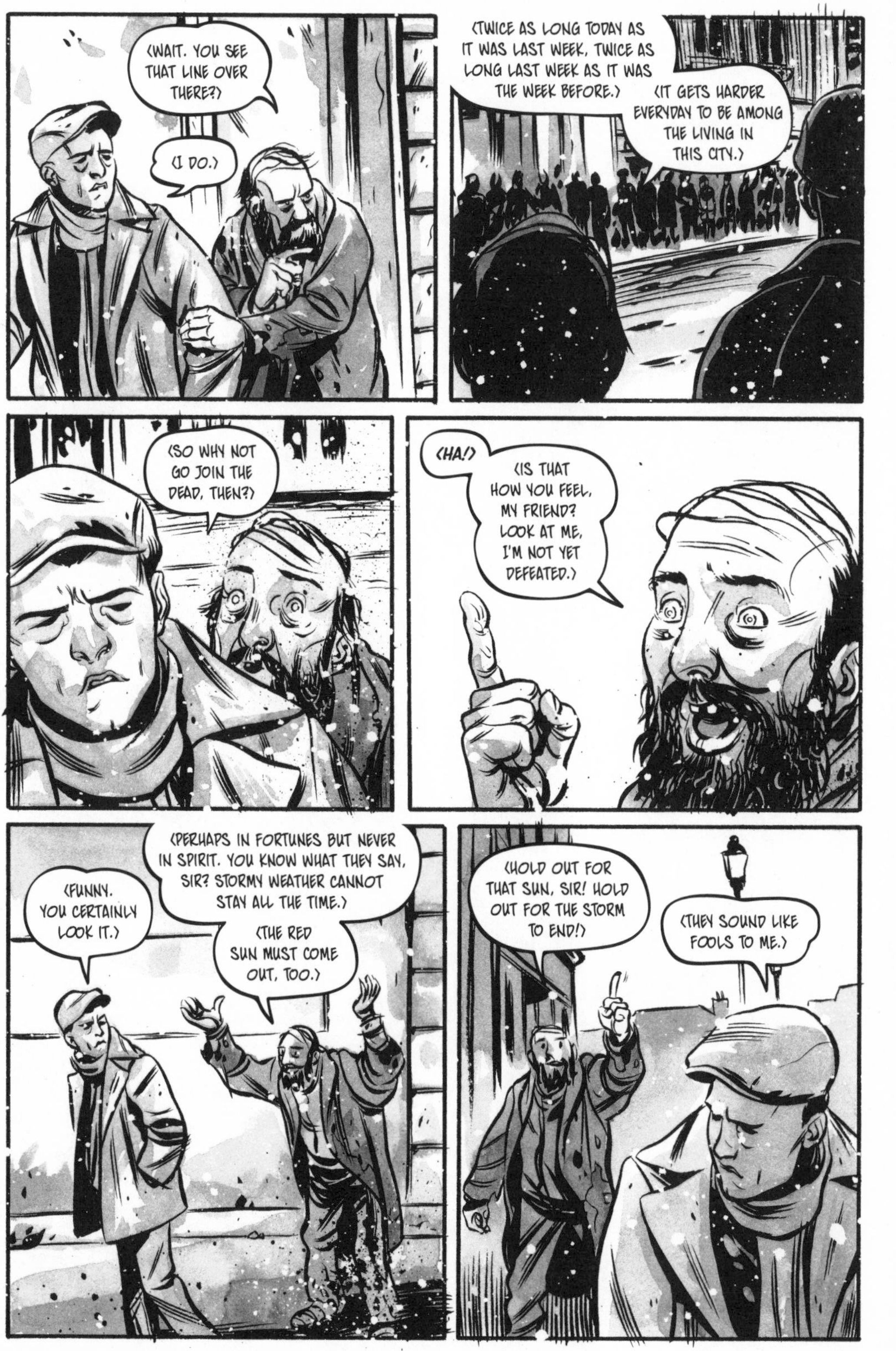

‹WAIT. YOU SEE THAT LINE OVER THERE?›
‹I DO.›
‹TWICE AS LONG TODAY AS IT WAS LAST WEEK, TWICE AS LONG LAST WEEK AS IT WAS THE WEEK BEFORE.›
‹IT GETS HARDER EVERYDAY TO BE AMONG THE LIVING IN THIS CITY.›
‹SO WHY NOT GO JOIN THE DEAD, THEN?›
‹HA!›
‹IS THAT HOW YOU FEEL, MY FRIEND? LOOK AT ME, I'M NOT YET DEFEATED.›
‹FUNNY. YOU CERTAINLY LOOK IT.›
‹PERHAPS IN FORTUNES BUT NEVER IN SPIRIT. YOU KNOW WHAT THEY SAY, SIR? STORMY WEATHER CANNOT STAY ALL THE TIME.›
‹THE RED SUN MUST COME OUT, TOO.›
‹HOLD OUT FOR THAT SUN, SIR! HOLD OUT FOR THE STORM TO END!›
‹THEY SOUND LIKE FOOLS TO ME.›

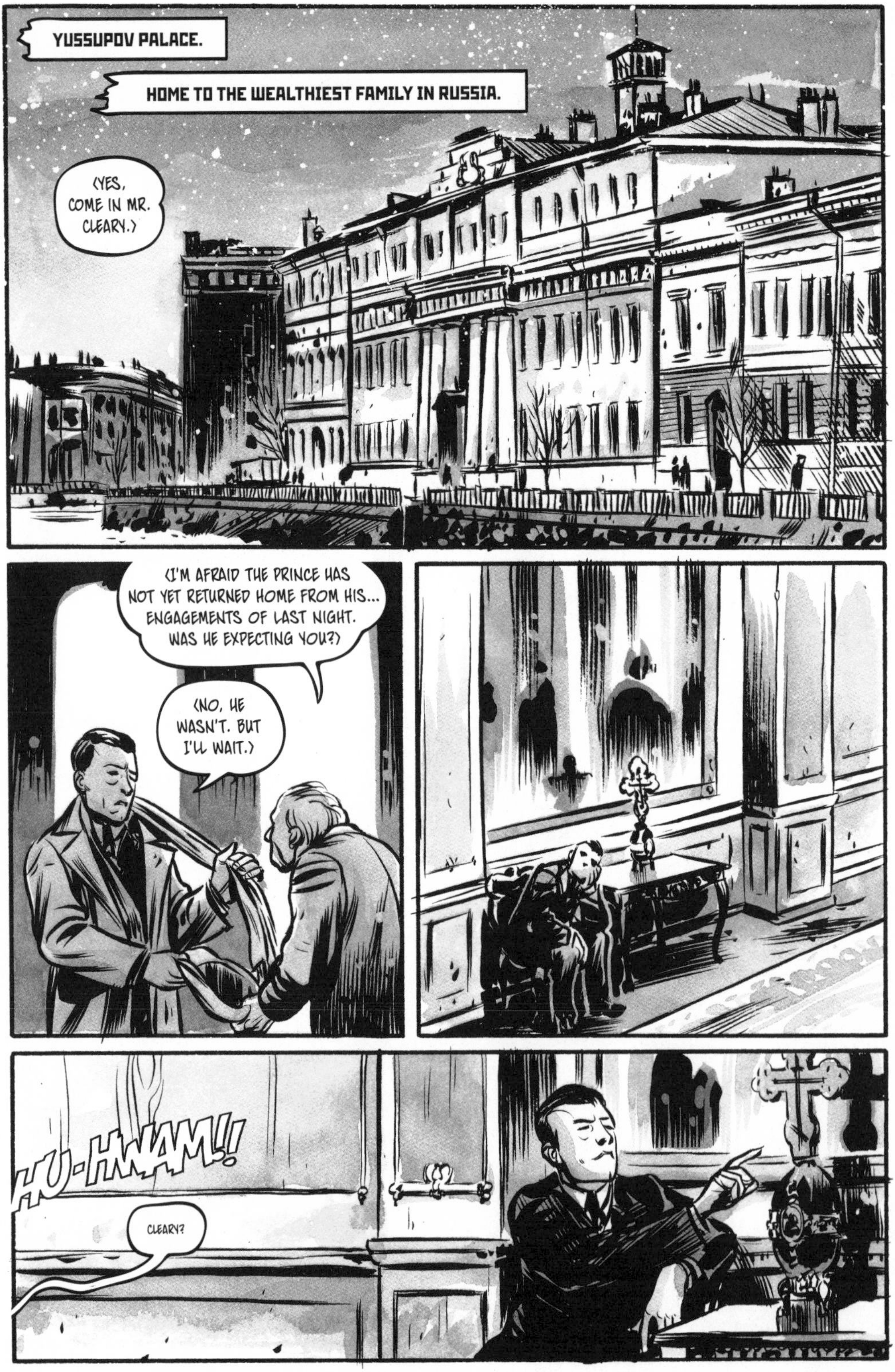
YUSSUPOV PALACE.
HOME TO THE WEALTHIEST FAMILY IN RUSSIA.
<YES, COME IN MR. CLEARY.>
<I'M AFRAID THE PRINCE HAS NOT YET RETURNED HOME FROM HIS... ENGAGEMENTS OF LAST NIGHT. WAS HE EXPECTING YOU?>
<NO, HE WASN'T. BUT I'LL WAIT.>
HU-HWAM!!
CLEARY?

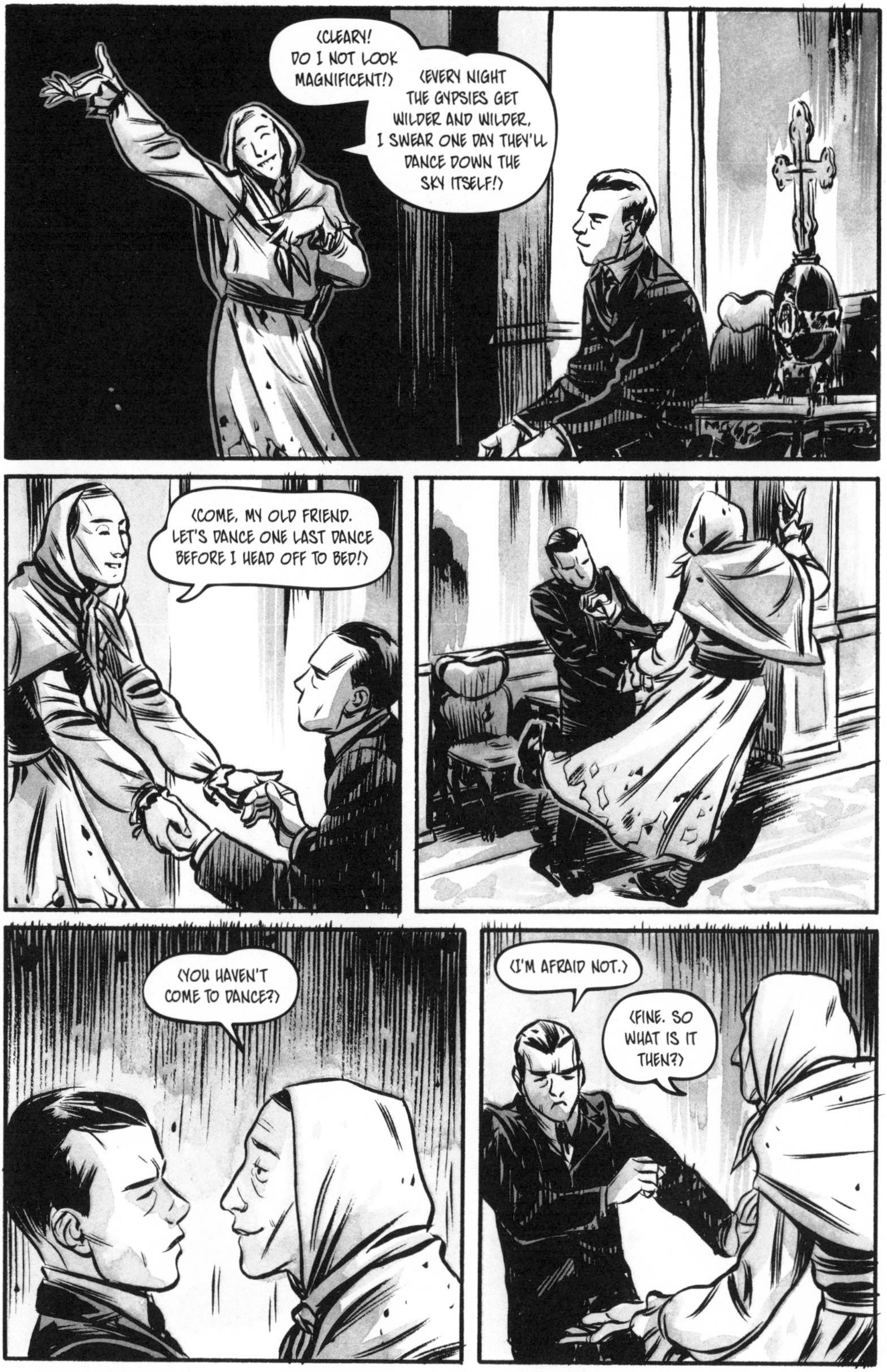
‹CLEARY! DO I NOT LOOK MAGNIFICENT!›
‹EVERY NIGHT THE GYPSIES GET WILDER AND WILDER. I SWEAR ONE DAY THEY'LL DANCE DOWN THE SKY ITSELF!›
‹COME, MY OLD FRIEND. LET'S DANCE ONE LAST DANCE BEFORE I HEAD OFF TO BED!›
‹YOU HAVEN'T COME TO DANCE?›
‹I'M AFRAID NOT.›
‹FINE. SO WHAT IS IT THEN?›

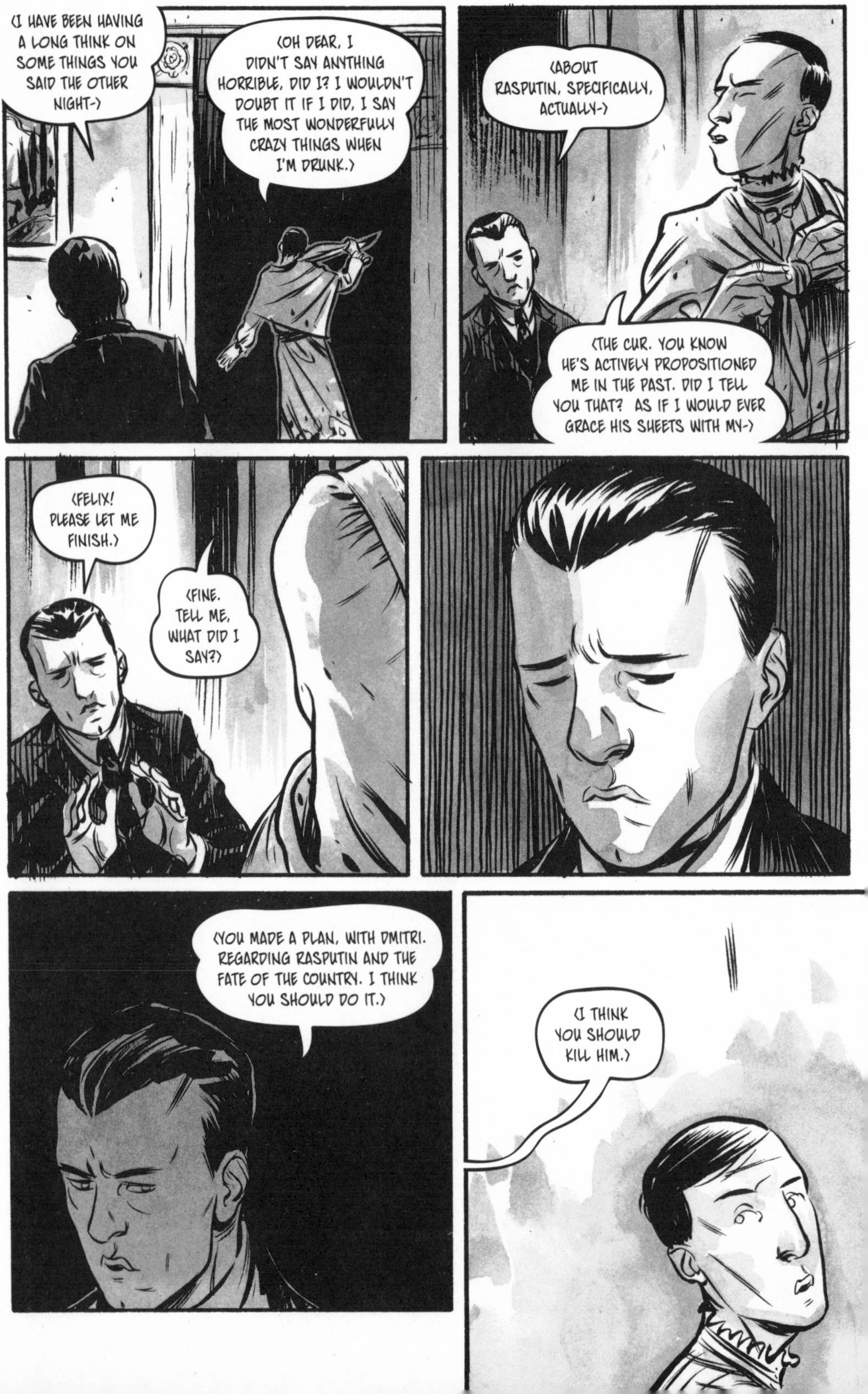

‹I HAVE BEEN HAVING A LONG THINK ON SOME THINGS YOU SAID THE OTHER NIGHT-›
‹OH DEAR, I DIDN'T SAY ANYTHING HORRIBLE, DID I? I WOULDN'T DOUBT IT IF I DID, I SAY THE MOST WONDERFULLY CRAZY THINGS WHEN I'M DRUNK.›
‹ABOUT RASPUTIN, SPECIFICALLY, ACTUALLY-›
‹THE CUR. YOU KNOW HE'S ACTIVELY PROPOSITIONED ME IN THE PAST. DID I TELL YOU THAT? AS IF I WOULD EVER GRACE HIS SHEETS WITH MY-›
‹FELIX! PLEASE LET ME FINISH.›
‹FINE. TELL ME, WHAT DID I SAY?›
‹YOU MADE A PLAN, WITH DMITRI. REGARDING RASPUTIN AND THE FATE OF THE COUNTRY. I THINK YOU SHOULD DO IT.›
‹I THINK YOU SHOULD KILL HIM.›

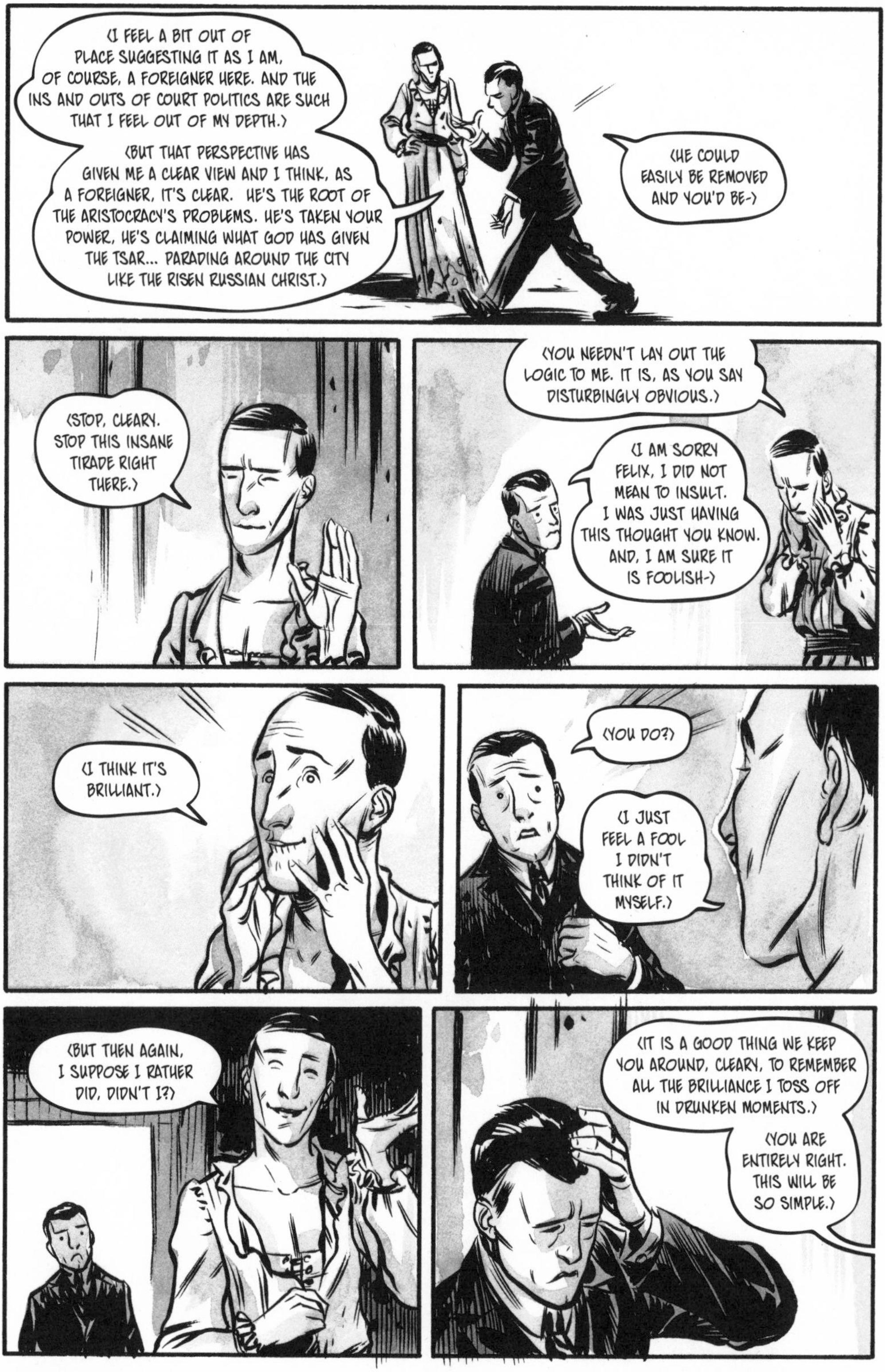
‹I FEEL A BIT OUT OF PLACE SUGGESTING IT AS I AM, OF COURSE, A FOREIGNER HERE. AND THE INS AND OUTS OF COURT POLITICS ARE SUCH THAT I FEEL OUT OF MY DEPTH.›
‹BUT THAT PERSPECTIVE HAS GIVEN ME A CLEAR VIEW AND I THINK, AS A FOREIGNER, IT'S CLEAR. HE'S THE ROOT OF THE ARISTOCRACY'S PROBLEMS. HE'S TAKEN YOUR POWER, HE'S CLAIMING WHAT GOD HAS GIVEN THE TSAR... PARADING AROUND THE CITY LIKE THE RISEN RUSSIAN CHRIST.›
‹HE COULD EASILY BE REMOVED AND YOU'D BE-›
‹STOP, CLEARY. STOP THIS INSANE TIRADE RIGHT THERE.›
‹YOU NEEDN'T LAY OUT THE LOGIC TO ME. IT IS, AS YOU SAY DISTURBINGLY OBVIOUS.›
‹I AM SORRY FELIX, I DID NOT MEAN TO INSULT. I WAS JUST HAVING THIS THOUGHT YOU KNOW. AND, I AM SURE IT IS FOOLISH-›
‹I THINK IT'S BRILLIANT.›
‹YOU DO?›
‹I JUST FEEL A FOOL I DIDN'T THINK OF IT MYSELF.›
‹BUT THEN AGAIN, I SUPPOSE I RATHER DID, DIDN'T I?›
‹IT IS A GOOD THING WE KEEP YOU AROUND, CLEARY, TO REMEMBER ALL THE BRILLIANCE I TOSS OFF IN DRUNKEN MOMENTS.›
‹YOU ARE ENTIRELY RIGHT. THIS WILL BE SO SIMPLE.›

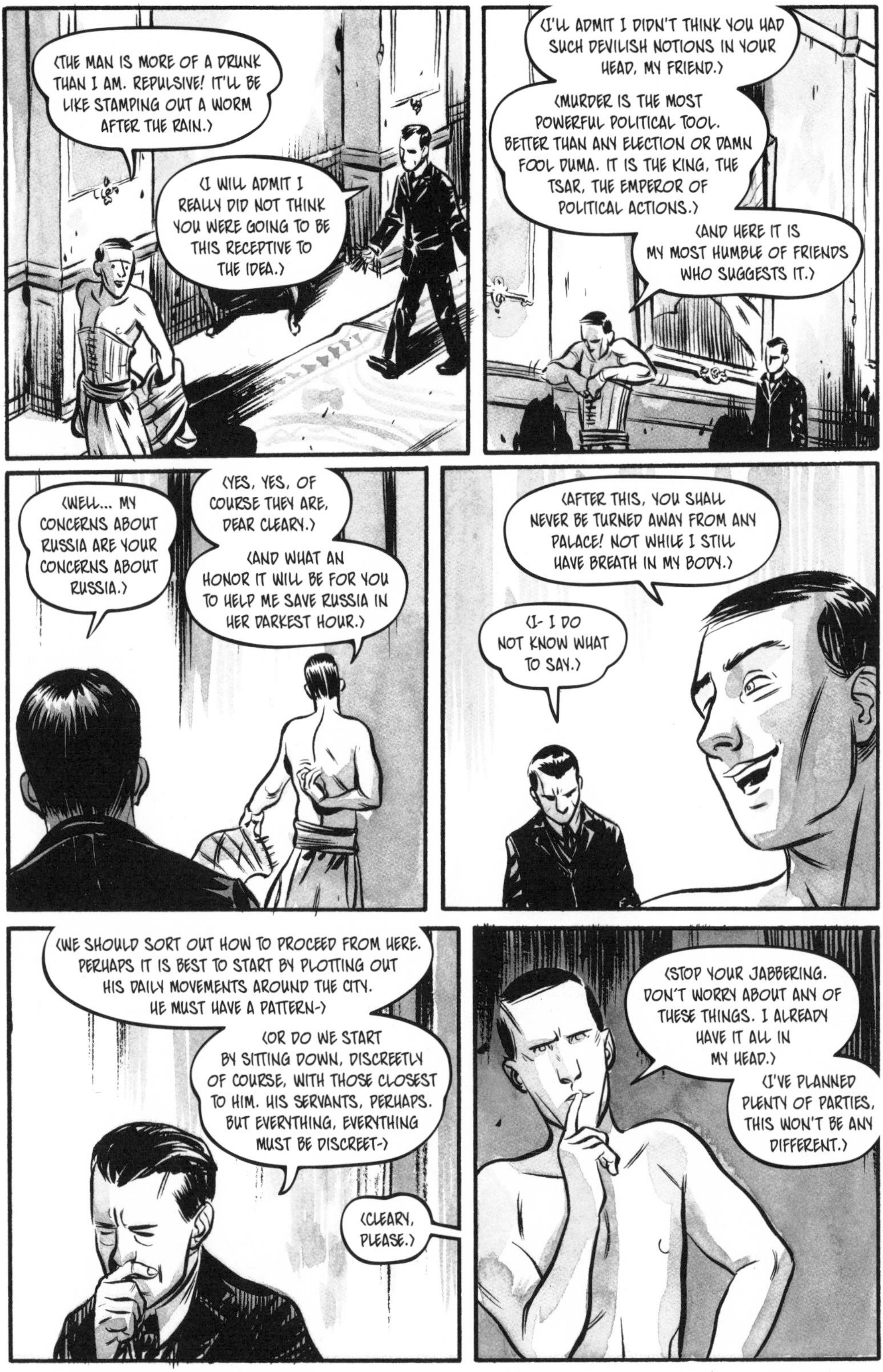

‹THE MAN IS MORE OF A DRUNK THAN I AM. REPULSIVE! IT'LL BE LIKE STAMPING OUT A WORM AFTER THE RAIN.›
‹I WILL ADMIT I REALLY DID NOT THINK YOU WERE GOING TO BE THIS RECEPTIVE TO THE IDEA.›
‹I'LL ADMIT I DIDN'T THINK YOU HAD SUCH DEVILISH NOTIONS IN YOUR HEAD, MY FRIEND.›
‹MURDER IS THE MOST POWERFUL POLITICAL TOOL. BETTER THAN ANY ELECTION OR DAMN FOOL DUMA. IT IS THE KING, THE TSAR, THE EMPEROR OF POLITICAL ACTIONS.›
‹AND HERE IT IS MY MOST HUMBLE OF FRIENDS WHO SUGGESTS IT.›
‹WELL... MY CONCERNS ABOUT RUSSIA ARE YOUR CONCERNS ABOUT RUSSIA.›
‹YES, YES, OF COURSE THEY ARE, DEAR CLEARY.›
‹AND WHAT AN HONOR IT WILL BE FOR YOU TO HELP ME SAVE RUSSIA IN HER DARKEST HOUR.›
‹AFTER THIS, YOU SHALL NEVER BE TURNED AWAY FROM ANY PALACE! NOT WHILE I STILL HAVE BREATH IN MY BODY.›
‹I- I DO NOT KNOW WHAT TO SAY.›
‹WE SHOULD SORT OUT HOW TO PROCEED FROM HERE. PERHAPS IT IS BEST TO START BY PLOTTING OUT HIS DAILY MOVEMENTS AROUND THE CITY. HE MUST HAVE A PATTERN-›
‹OR DO WE START BY SITTING DOWN, DISCREETLY OF COURSE, WITH THOSE CLOSEST TO HIM. HIS SERVANTS, PERHAPS. BUT EVERYTHING, EVERYTHING MUST BE DISCREET-›
‹CLEARY, PLEASE.›
‹STOP YOUR JABBERING. DON'T WORRY ABOUT ANY OF THESE THINGS. I ALREADY HAVE IT ALL IN MY HEAD.›
‹I'VE PLANNED PLENTY OF PARTIES, THIS WON'T BE ANY DIFFERENT.›

〈SPEAKING OF PARTIES, YOU REALLY MUST LEAVE ME BE NOW.〉

〈BUT-〉

〈THE DUKE AND DUCHESS OF THE UKRAINE ARE THROWING A BALL AND I MUST BE WELL-RESTED. HAVE TO BE ON MY BEST BEHAVIOR, YOU KNOW. MY WIFE MIGHT EVEN BE THERE, THE POOR DEAR!〉

〈I'D INVITE YOU BUT YOU KNOW HOW THESE THINGS ARE, I'M AFRAID YOU SIMPLY WOULDN'T FIT IN.〉

〈FELIX, WE NEED TO SIT DOWN AND DISCUSS THIS FURTHER. IT'S GOING TO BE A VERY DELICATE THING TO PULL OFF.〉

〈WHAT DID I SAY, CLEARY? DON'T WORRY ABOUT ALL THAT!〉

〈GO DO WHATEVER IT IS THAT YOU DO WHEN YOU'RE NOT WITH ME AND COME BACK IN A FEW DAYS!〉

TA-TA!

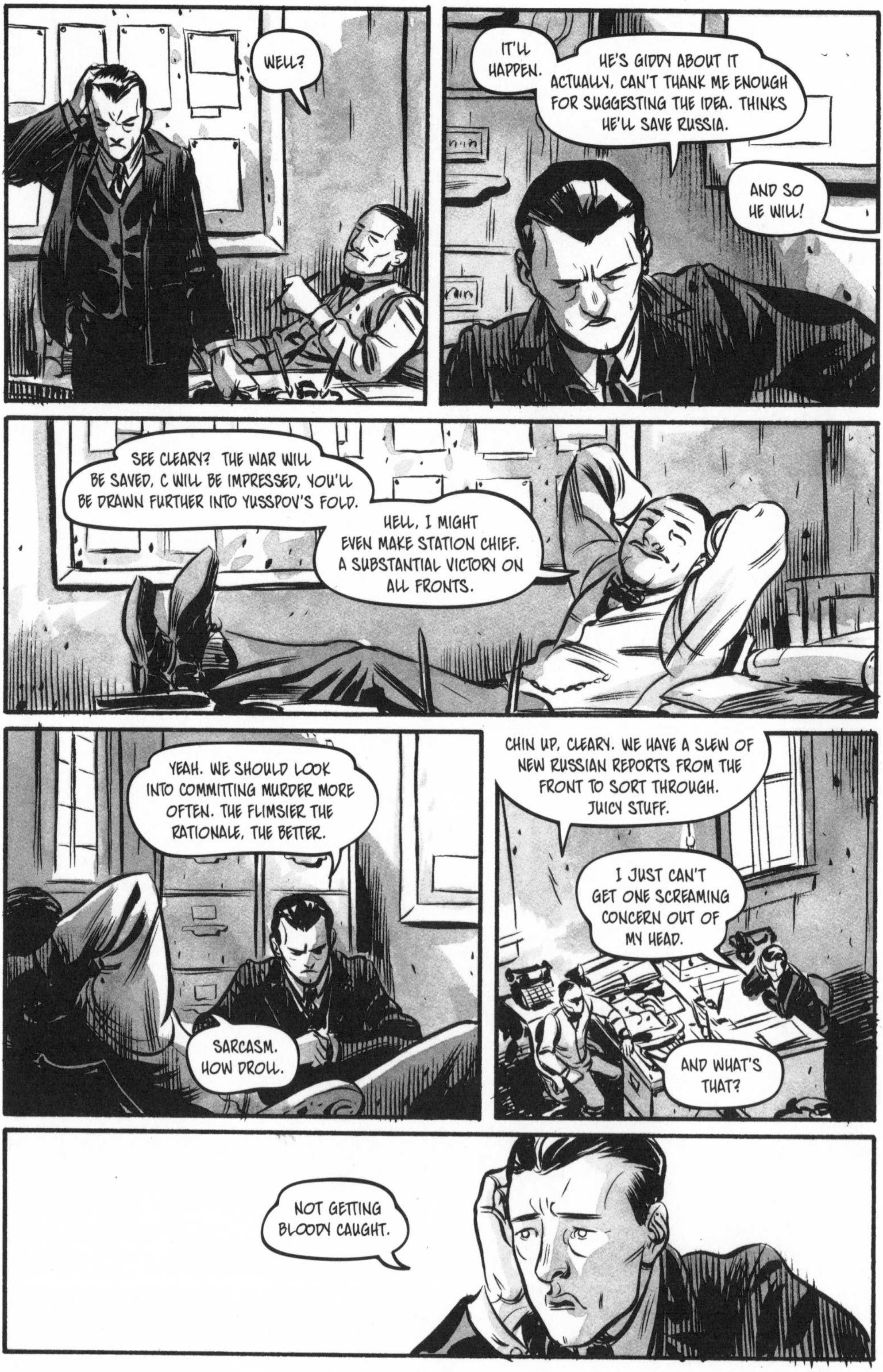
WELL?
IT'LL HAPPEN.
HE'S GIDDY ABOUT IT ACTUALLY, CAN'T THANK ME ENOUGH FOR SUGGESTING THE IDEA. THINKS HE'LL SAVE RUSSIA.
AND SO HE WILL!
SEE CLEARY? THE WAR WILL BE SAVED, C WILL BE IMPRESSED, YOU'LL BE DRAWN FURTHER INTO YUSSPOV'S FOLD.
HELL, I MIGHT EVEN MAKE STATION CHIEF. A SUBSTANTIAL VICTORY ON ALL FRONTS.
YEAH. WE SHOULD LOOK INTO COMMITTING MURDER MORE OFTEN. THE FLIMSIER THE RATIONALE, THE BETTER.
SARCASM. HOW DROLL.
CHIN UP, CLEARY. WE HAVE A SLEW OF NEW RUSSIAN REPORTS FROM THE FRONT TO SORT THROUGH. JUICY STUFF.
I JUST CAN'T GET ONE SCREAMING CONCERN OUT OF MY HEAD.
AND WHAT'S THAT?
NOT GETTING BLOODY CAUGHT.

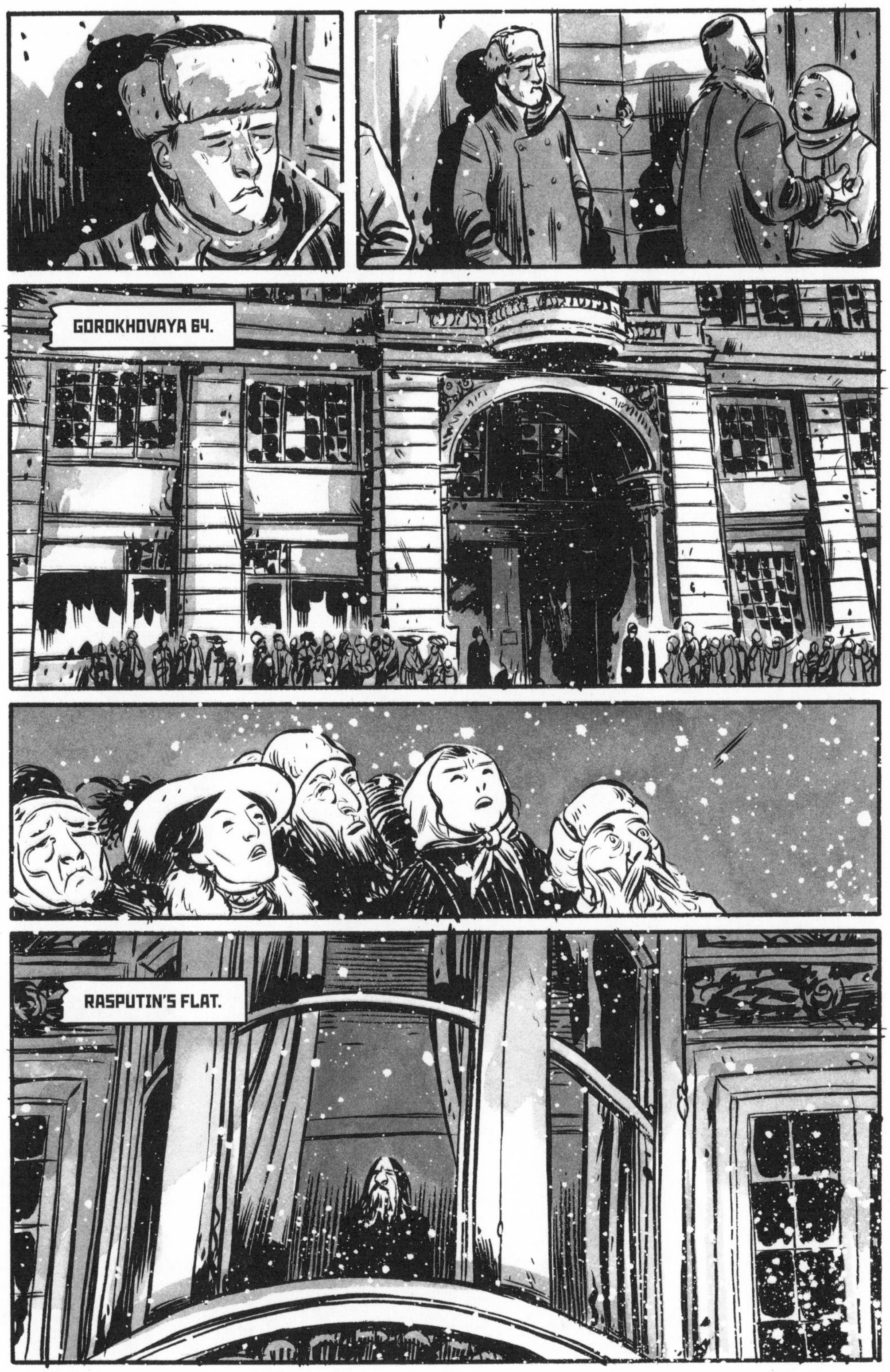
GOROKHOVAYA 64.
RASPUTIN'S FLAT.

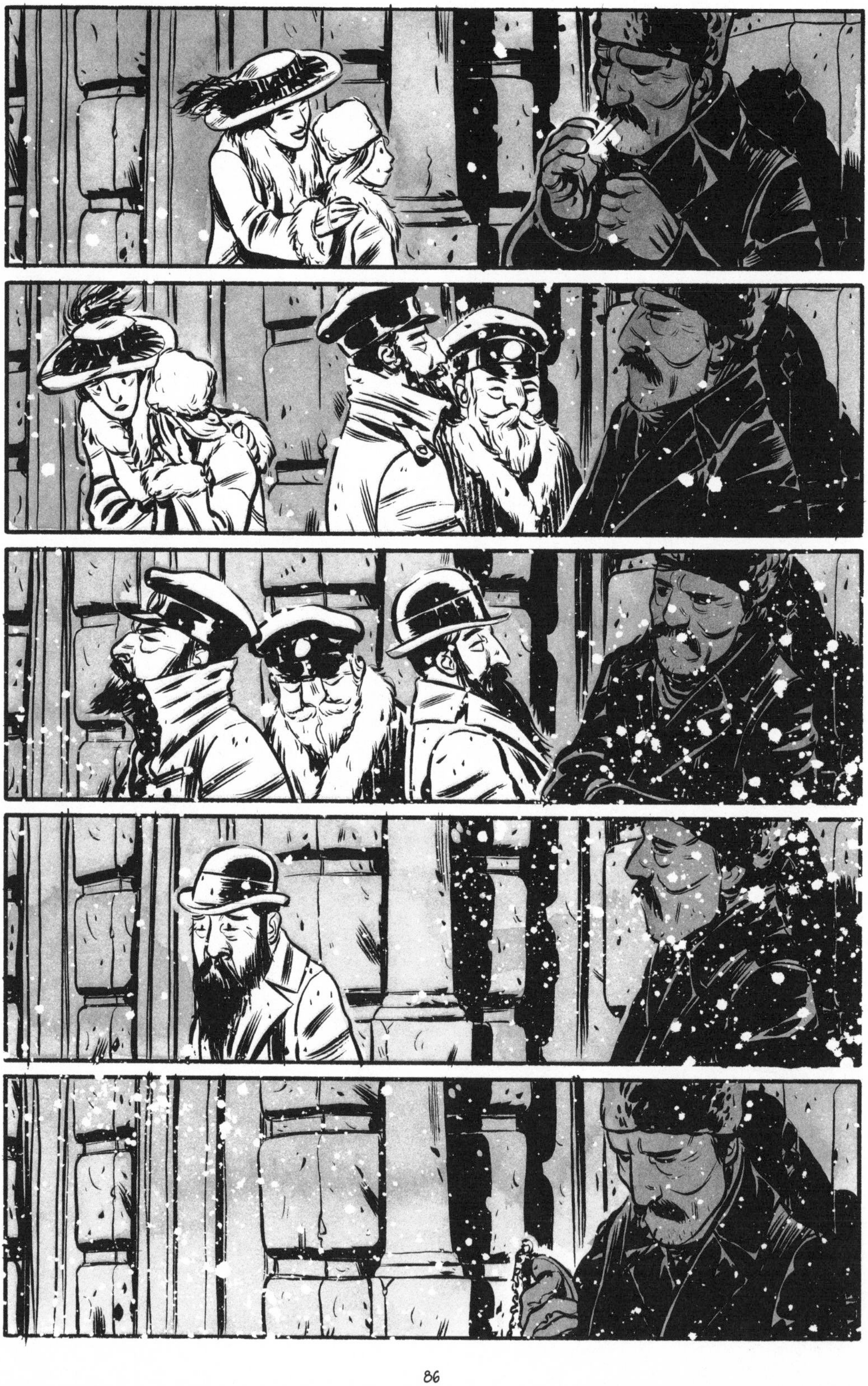

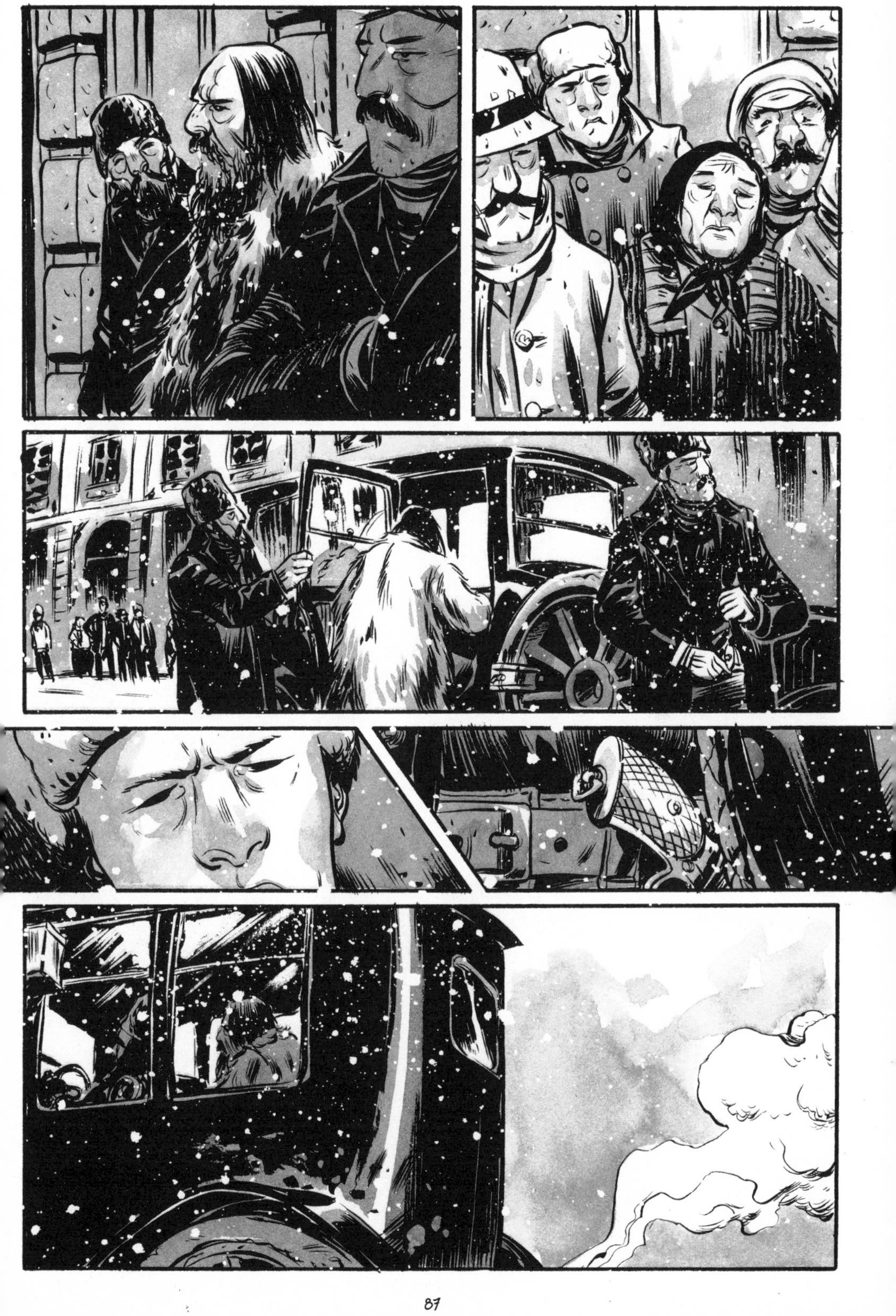

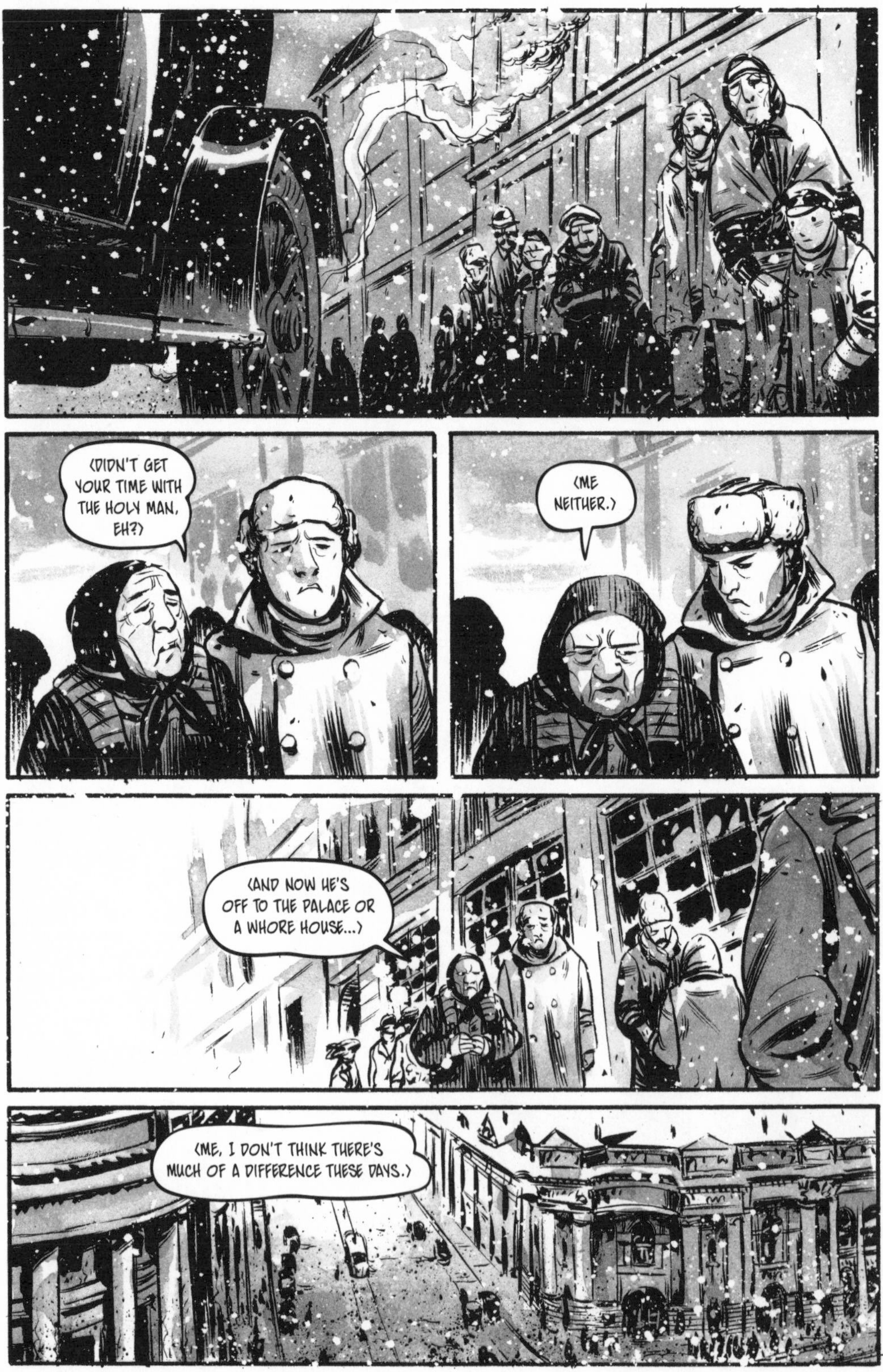

‹DIDN'T GET YOUR TIME WITH THE HOLY MAN, EH?›
‹ME NEITHER.›
‹AND NOW HE'S OFF TO THE PALACE OR A WHORE HOUSE...›
‹ME, I DON'T THINK THERE'S MUCH OF A DIFFERENCE THESE DAYS.›

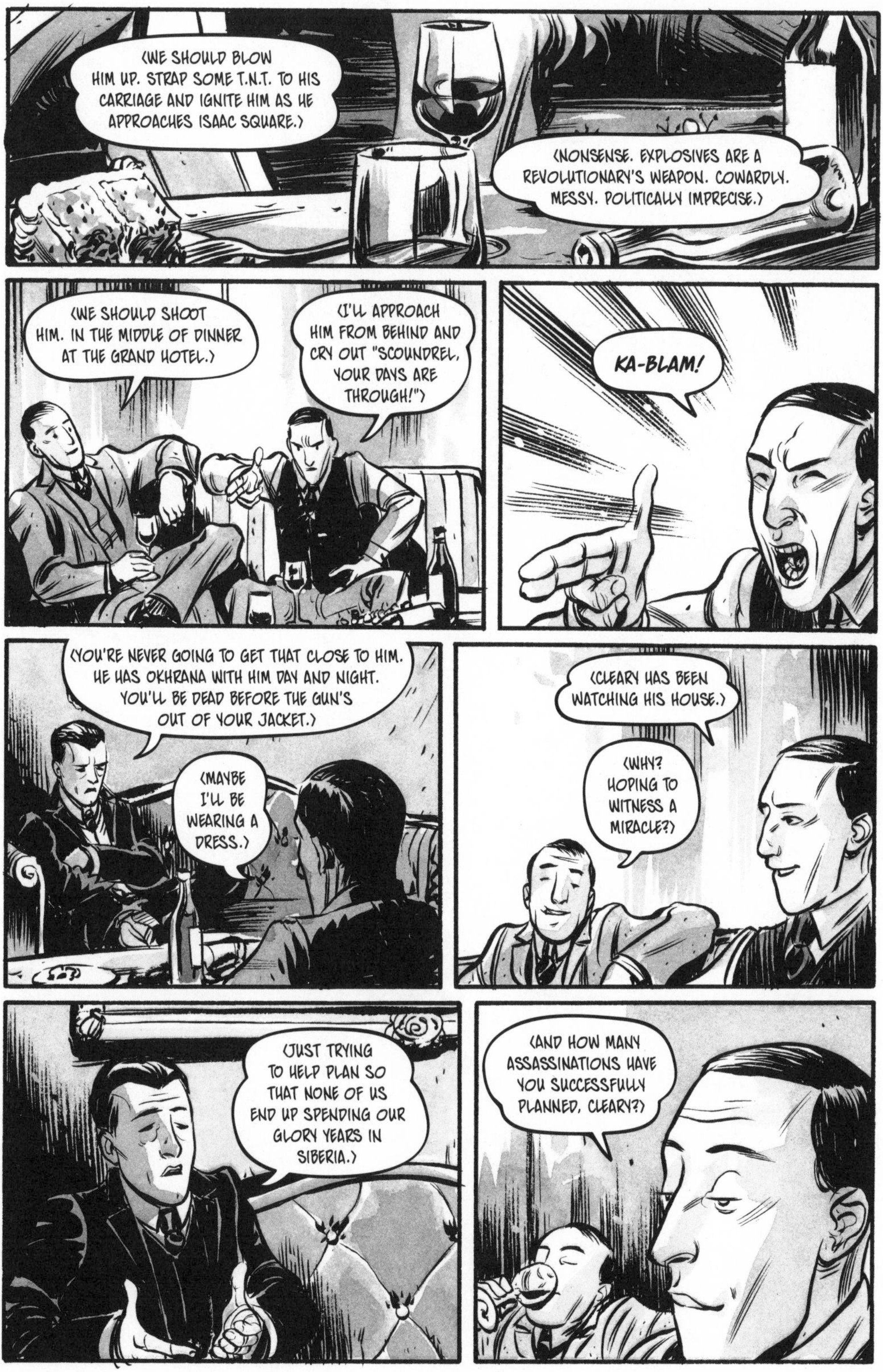
‹WE SHOULD BLOW HIM UP. STRAP SOME T.N.T. TO HIS CARRIAGE AND IGNITE HIM AS HE APPROACHES ISAAC SQUARE.›
‹NONSENSE. EXPLOSIVES ARE A REVOLUTIONARY'S WEAPON. COWARDLY. MESSY. POLITICALLY IMPRECISE.›
‹WE SHOULD SHOOT HIM. IN THE MIDDLE OF DINNER AT THE GRAND HOTEL.›
‹I'LL APPROACH HIM FROM BEHIND AND CRY OUT "SCOUNDREL, YOUR DAYS ARE THROUGH!"›
KA-BLAM!
‹YOU'RE NEVER GOING TO GET THAT CLOSE TO HIM. HE HAS OKHRANA WITH HIM DAY AND NIGHT. YOU'LL BE DEAD BEFORE THE GUN'S OUT OF YOUR JACKET.›
‹MAYBE I'LL BE WEARING A DRESS.›
‹CLEARY HAS BEEN WATCHING HIS HOUSE.›
‹WHY? HOPING TO WITNESS A MIRACLE?›
‹JUST TRYING TO HELP PLAN SO THAT NONE OF US END UP SPENDING OUR GLORY YEARS IN SIBERIA.›
‹AND HOW MANY ASSASSINATIONS HAVE YOU SUCCESSFULLY PLANNED, CLEARY?›

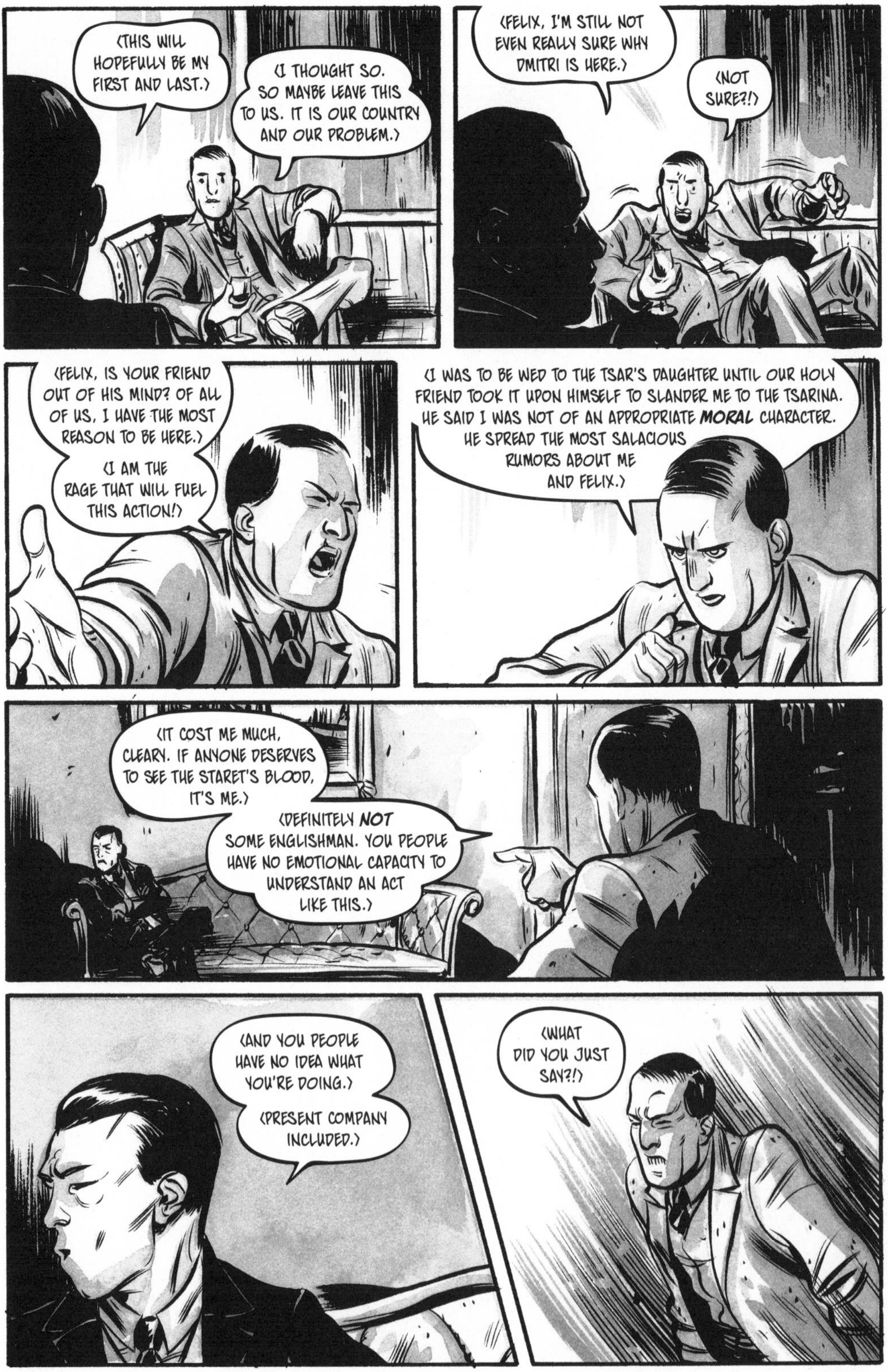

‹THIS WILL HOPEFULLY BE MY FIRST AND LAST.›
‹I THOUGHT SO. SO MAYBE LEAVE THIS TO US. IT IS OUR COUNTRY AND OUR PROBLEM.›
‹FELIX, I'M STILL NOT EVEN REALLY SURE WHY DMITRI IS HERE.›
‹NOT SURE?!›
‹FELIX, IS YOUR FRIEND OUT OF HIS MIND? OF ALL OF US, I HAVE THE MOST REASON TO BE HERE.›
‹I AM THE RAGE THAT WILL FUEL THIS ACTION!›
‹I WAS TO BE WED TO THE TSAR'S DAUGHTER UNTIL OUR HOLY FRIEND TOOK IT UPON HIMSELF TO SLANDER ME TO THE TSARINA. HE SAID I WAS NOT OF AN APPROPRIATE MORAL CHARACTER. HE SPREAD THE MOST SALACIOUS RUMORS ABOUT ME AND FELIX.›
‹IT COST ME MUCH, CLEARY. IF ANYONE DESERVES TO SEE THE STARET'S BLOOD, IT'S ME.›
‹DEFINITELY NOT SOME ENGLISHMAN. YOU PEOPLE HAVE NO EMOTIONAL CAPACITY TO UNDERSTAND AN ACT LIKE THIS.›
‹AND YOU PEOPLE HAVE NO IDEA WHAT YOU'RE DOING.›
‹PRESENT COMPANY INCLUDED.›
‹WHAT DID YOU JUST SAY?!›

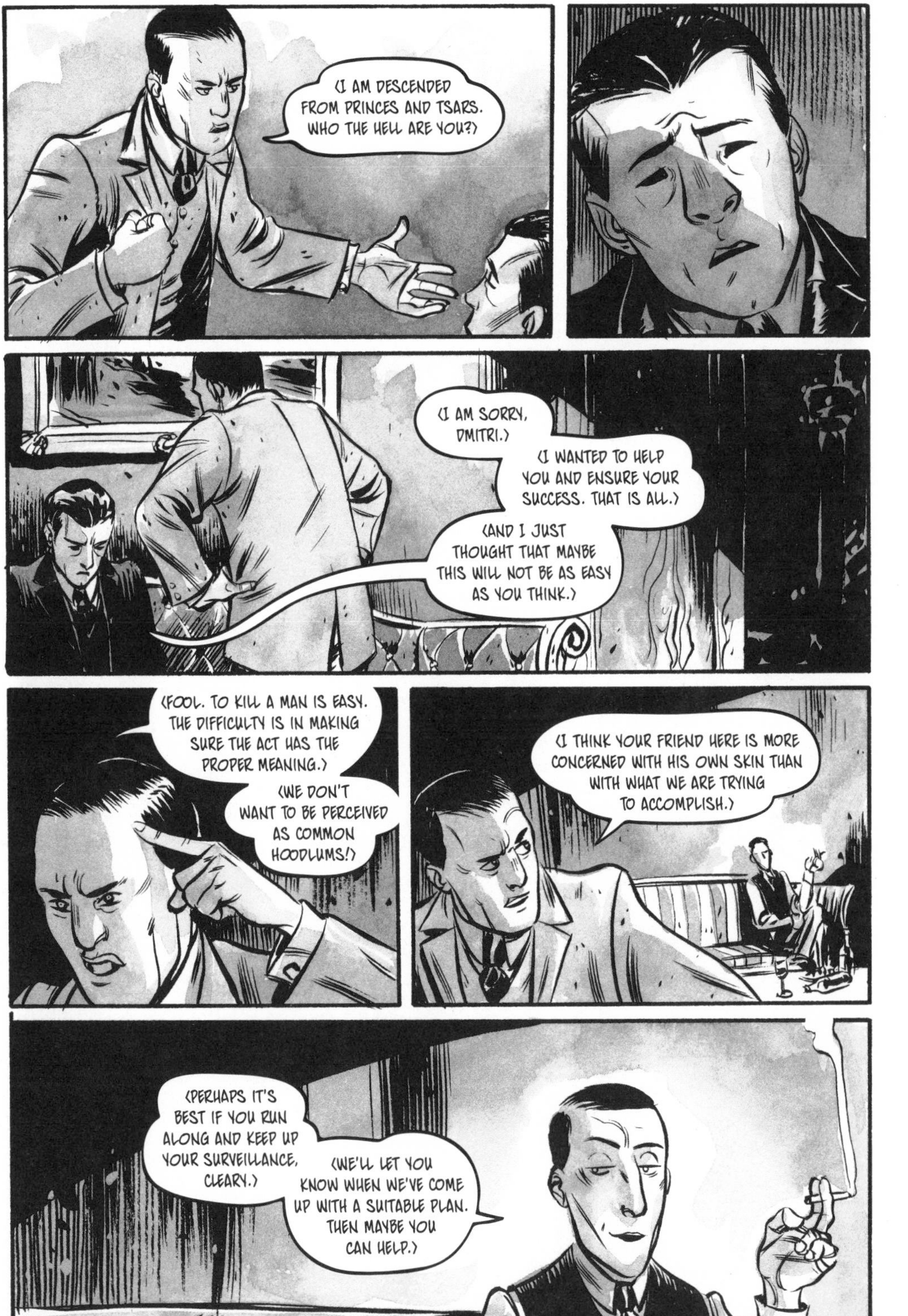
‹I AM DESCENDED FROM PRINCES AND TSARS. WHO THE HELL ARE YOU?›
‹I AM SORRY, DMITRI.›
‹I WANTED TO HELP YOU AND ENSURE YOUR SUCCESS. THAT IS ALL.›
‹AND I JUST THOUGHT THAT MAYBE THIS WILL NOT BE AS EASY AS YOU THINK.›
‹FOOL. TO KILL A MAN IS EASY. THE DIFFICULTY IS IN MAKING SURE THE ACT HAS THE PROPER MEANING.›
‹WE DON'T WANT TO BE PERCEIVED AS COMMON HOODLUMS!›
‹I THINK YOUR FRIEND HERE IS MORE CONCERNED WITH HIS OWN SKIN THAN WITH WHAT WE ARE TRYING TO ACCOMPLISH.›
‹PERHAPS IT'S BEST IF YOU RUN ALONG AND KEEP UP YOUR SURVEILLANCE, CLEARY.›
‹WE'LL LET YOU KNOW WHEN WE'VE COME UP WITH A SUITABLE PLAN. THEN MAYBE YOU CAN HELP.›

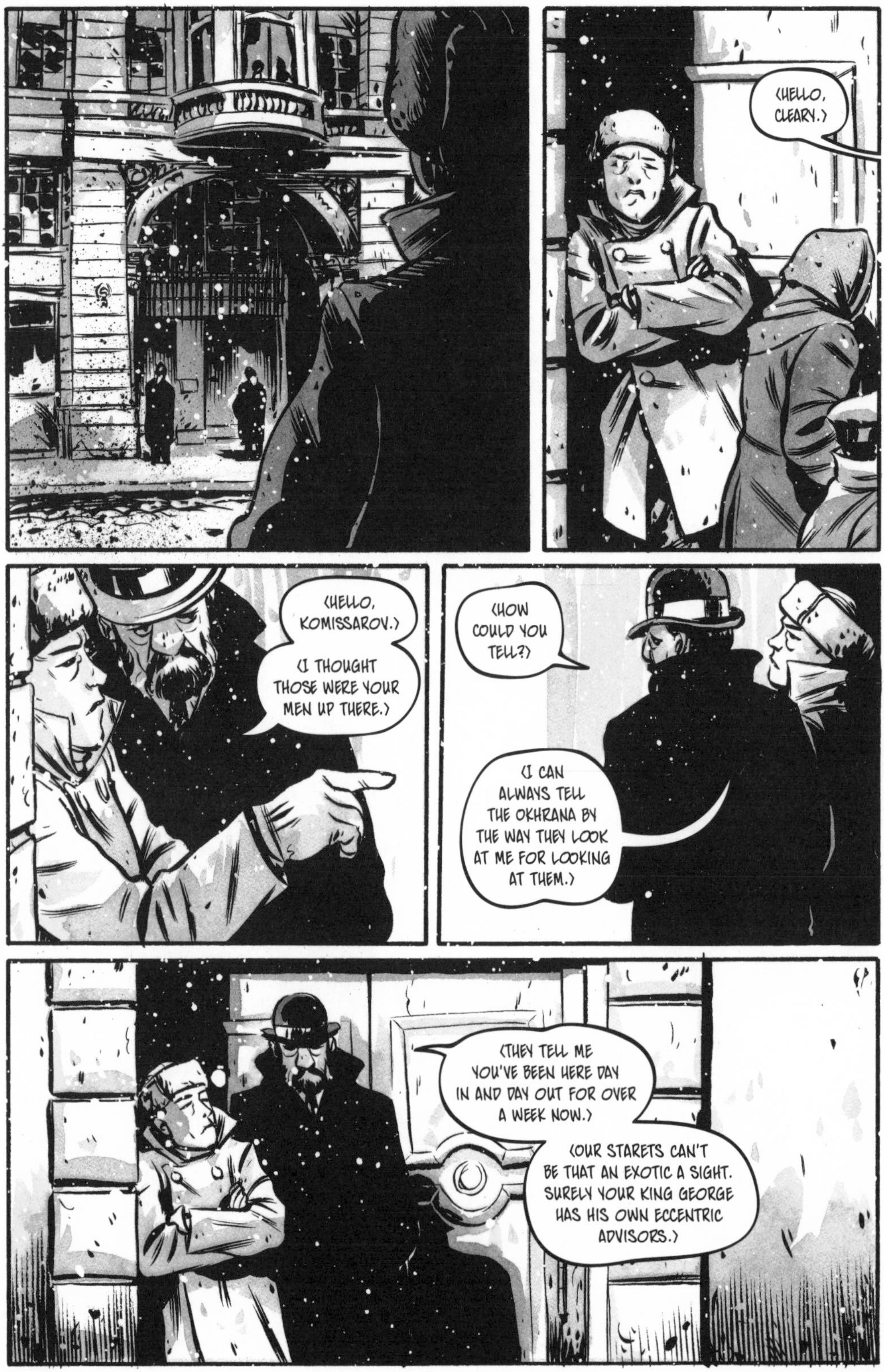
‹HELLO, CLEARY.›
‹HELLO, KOMISSAROV.›
‹I THOUGHT THOSE WERE YOUR MEN UP THERE.›
‹HOW COULD YOU TELL?›
‹I CAN ALWAYS TELL THE OKHRANA BY THE WAY THEY LOOK AT ME FOR LOOKING AT THEM.›
‹THEY TELL ME YOU'VE BEEN HERE DAY IN AND DAY OUT FOR OVER A WEEK NOW.›
‹OUR STARETS CAN'T BE THAT AN EXOTIC A SIGHT. SURELY YOUR KING GEORGE HAS HIS OWN ECCENTRIC ADVISORS.›

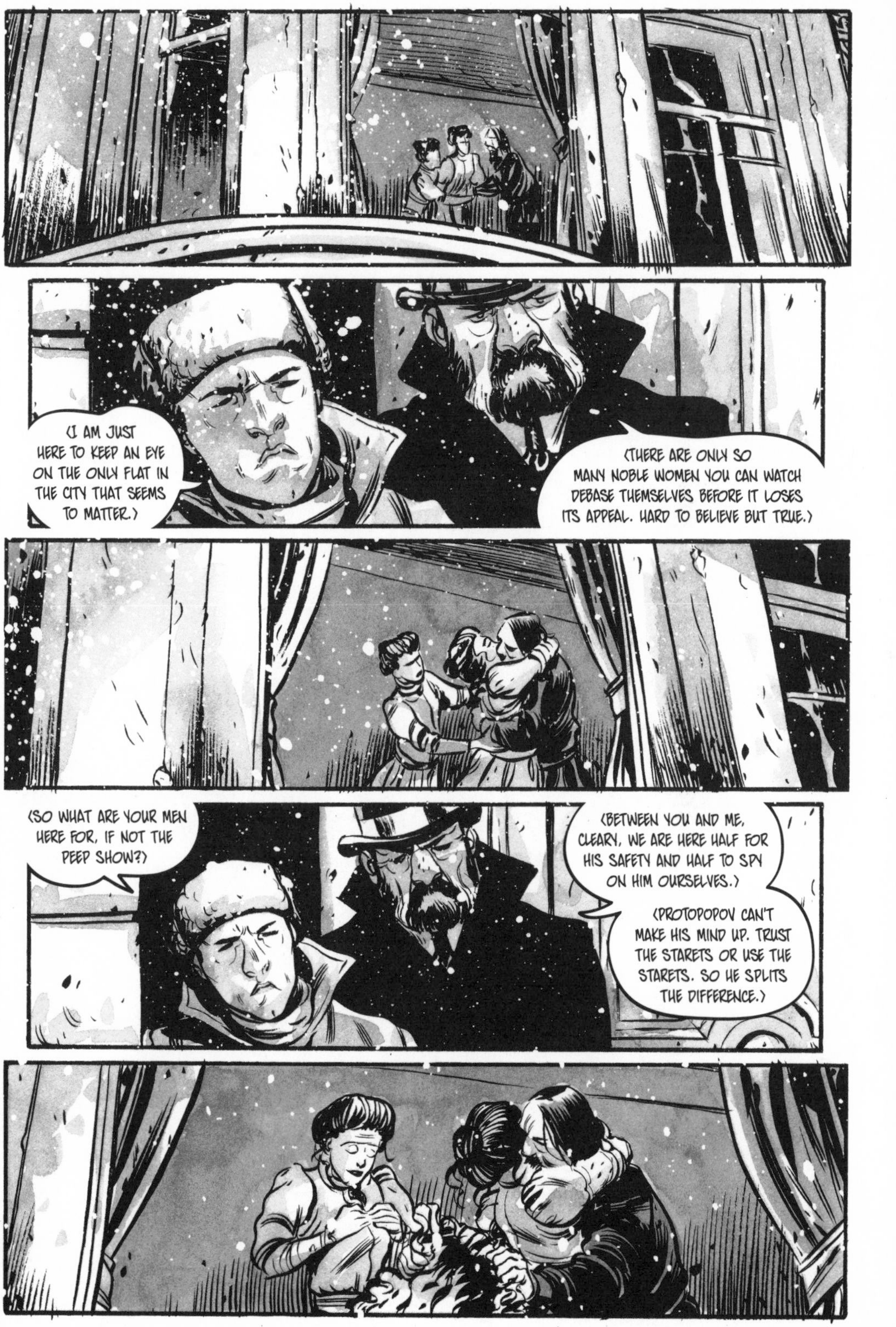

(I AM JUST HERE TO KEEP AN EYE ON THE ONLY FLAT IN THE CITY THAT SEEMS TO MATTER.)
(THERE ARE ONLY SO MANY NOBLE WOMEN YOU CAN WATCH DEBASE THEMSELVES BEFORE IT LOSES ITS APPEAL. HARD TO BELIEVE BUT TRUE.)
(SO WHAT ARE YOUR MEN HERE FOR, IF NOT THE PEEP SHOW?)
(BETWEEN YOU AND ME, CLEARY, WE ARE HERE HALF FOR HIS SAFETY AND HALF TO SPY ON HIM OURSELVES.)
(PROTOPOPOV CAN'T MAKE HIS MIND UP. TRUST THE STARETS OR USE THE STARETS. SO HE SPLITS THE DIFFERENCE.)

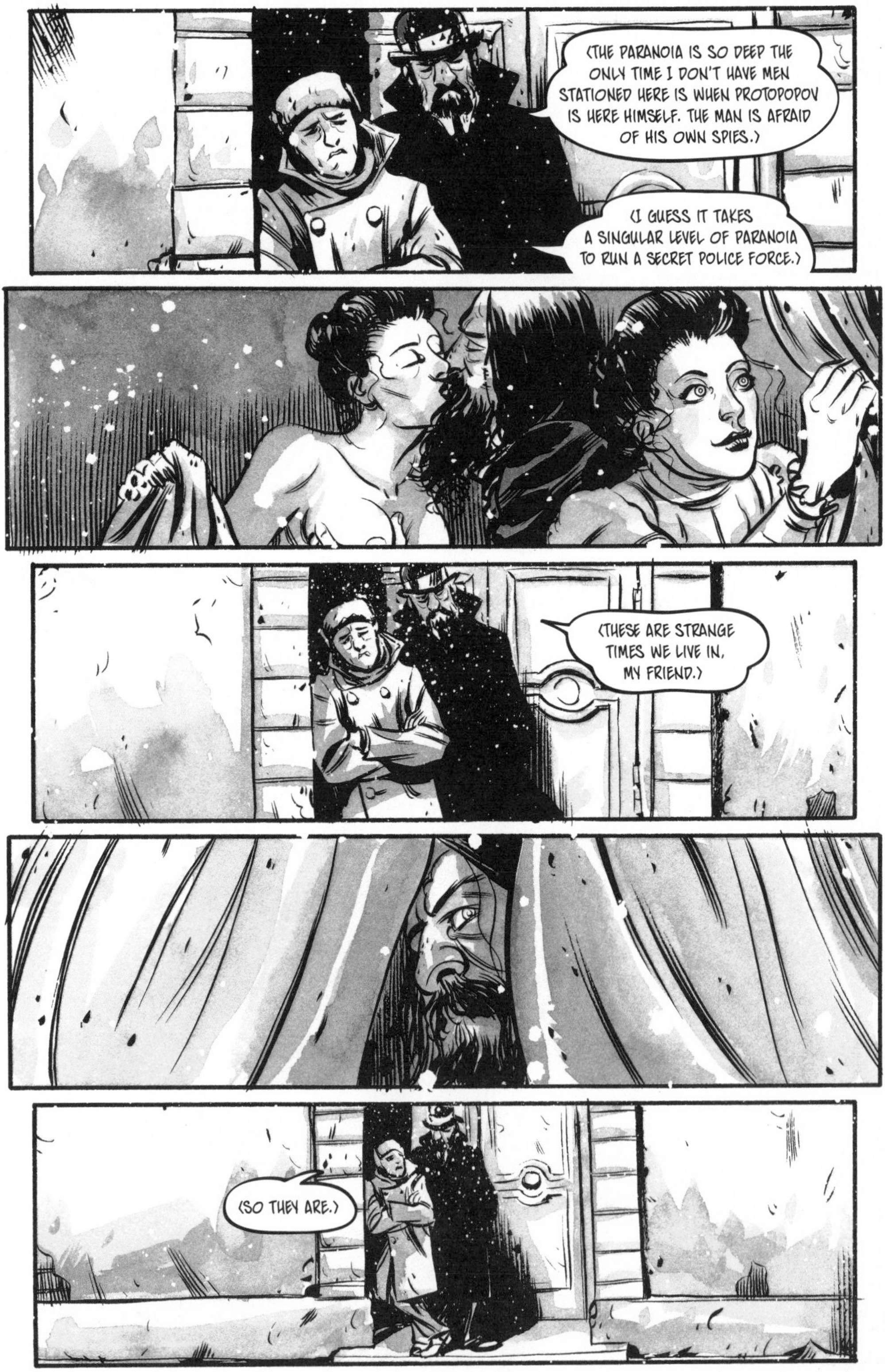
(THE PARANOIA IS SO DEEP THE ONLY TIME I DON'T HAVE MEN STATIONED HERE IS WHEN PROTOPOPOV IS HERE HIMSELF. THE MAN IS AFRAID OF HIS OWN SPIES.)
(I GUESS IT TAKES A SINGULAR LEVEL OF PARANOIA TO RUN A SECRET POLICE FORCE.)
(THESE ARE STRANGE TIMES WE LIVE IN, MY FRIEND.)
(SO THEY ARE.)

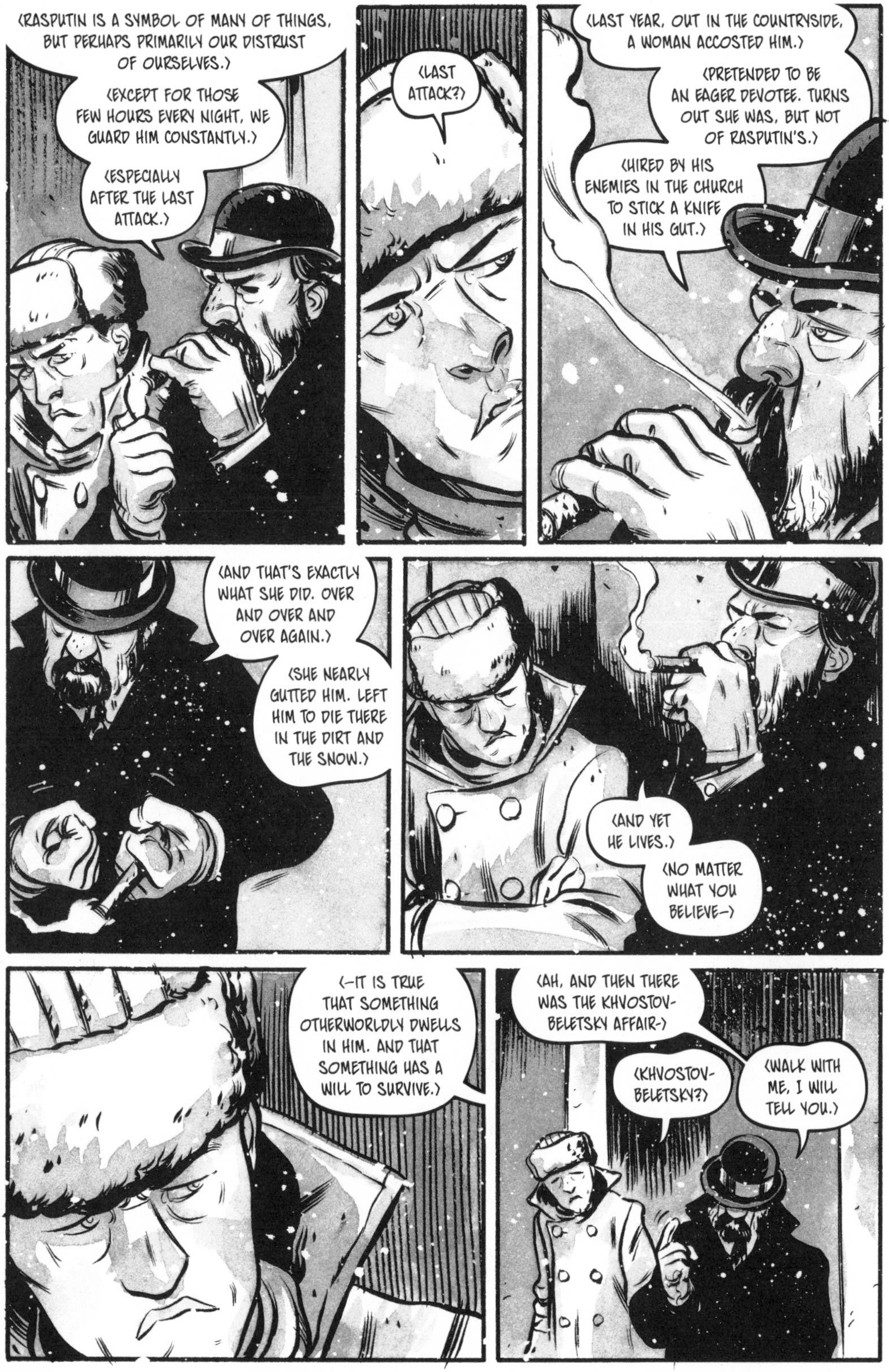

‹RASPUTIN IS A SYMBOL OF MANY OF THINGS, BUT PERHAPS PRIMARILY OUR DISTRUST OF OURSELVES.›
‹EXCEPT FOR THOSE FEW HOURS EVERY NIGHT, WE GUARD HIM CONSTANTLY.›
‹ESPECIALLY AFTER THE LAST ATTACK.›
‹LAST ATTACK?›
‹LAST YEAR, OUT IN THE COUNTRYSIDE, A WOMAN ACCOSTED HIM.›
‹PRETENDED TO BE AN EAGER DEVOTEE. TURNS OUT SHE WAS, BUT NOT OF RASPUTIN'S.›
‹HIRED BY HIS ENEMIES IN THE CHURCH TO STICK A KNIFE IN HIS GUT.›
‹AND THAT'S EXACTLY WHAT SHE DID. OVER AND OVER AND OVER AGAIN.›
‹SHE NEARLY GUTTED HIM. LEFT HIM TO DIE THERE IN THE DIRT AND THE SNOW.›
‹AND YET HE LIVES.›
‹NO MATTER WHAT YOU BELIEVE–›
‹–IT IS TRUE THAT SOMETHING OTHERWORLDLY DWELLS IN HIM. AND THAT SOMETHING HAS A WILL TO SURVIVE.›
‹AH, AND THEN THERE WAS THE KHVOSTOV-BELETSKY AFFAIR–›
‹KHVOSTOV-BELETSKY?›
‹WALK WITH ME, I WILL TELL YOU.›

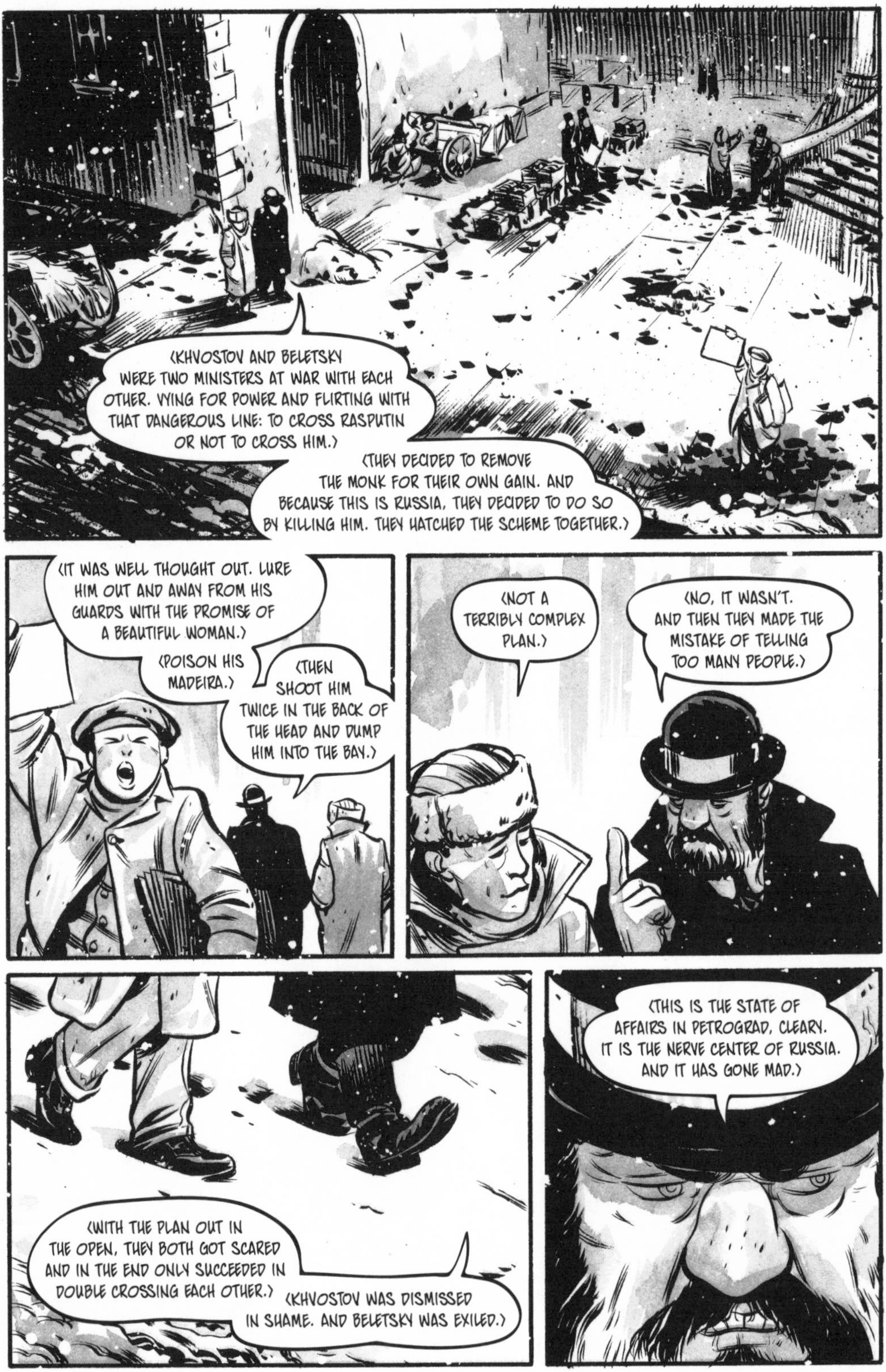

(KHVOSTOV AND BELETSKY WERE TWO MINISTERS AT WAR WITH EACH OTHER. VYING FOR POWER AND FLIRTING WITH THAT DANGEROUS LINE: TO CROSS RASPUTIN OR NOT TO CROSS HIM.)
(THEY DECIDED TO REMOVE THE MONK FOR THEIR OWN GAIN. AND BECAUSE THIS IS RUSSIA, THEY DECIDED TO DO SO BY KILLING HIM. THEY HATCHED THE SCHEME TOGETHER.)
(IT WAS WELL THOUGHT OUT. LURE HIM OUT AND AWAY FROM HIS GUARDS WITH THE PROMISE OF A BEAUTIFUL WOMAN.)
(POISON HIS MADEIRA.)
(THEN SHOOT HIM TWICE IN THE BACK OF THE HEAD AND DUMP HIM INTO THE BAY.)
(NOT A TERRIBLY COMPLEX PLAN.)
(NO, IT WASN'T. AND THEN THEY MADE THE MISTAKE OF TELLING TOO MANY PEOPLE.)
(WITH THE PLAN OUT IN THE OPEN, THEY BOTH GOT SCARED AND IN THE END ONLY SUCCEEDED IN DOUBLE CROSSING EACH OTHER.)
(KHVOSTOV WAS DISMISSED IN SHAME. AND BELETSKY WAS EXILED.)
(THIS IS THE STATE OF AFFAIRS IN PETROGRAD, CLEARY. IT IS THE NERVE CENTER OF RUSSIA. AND IT HAS GONE MAD.)

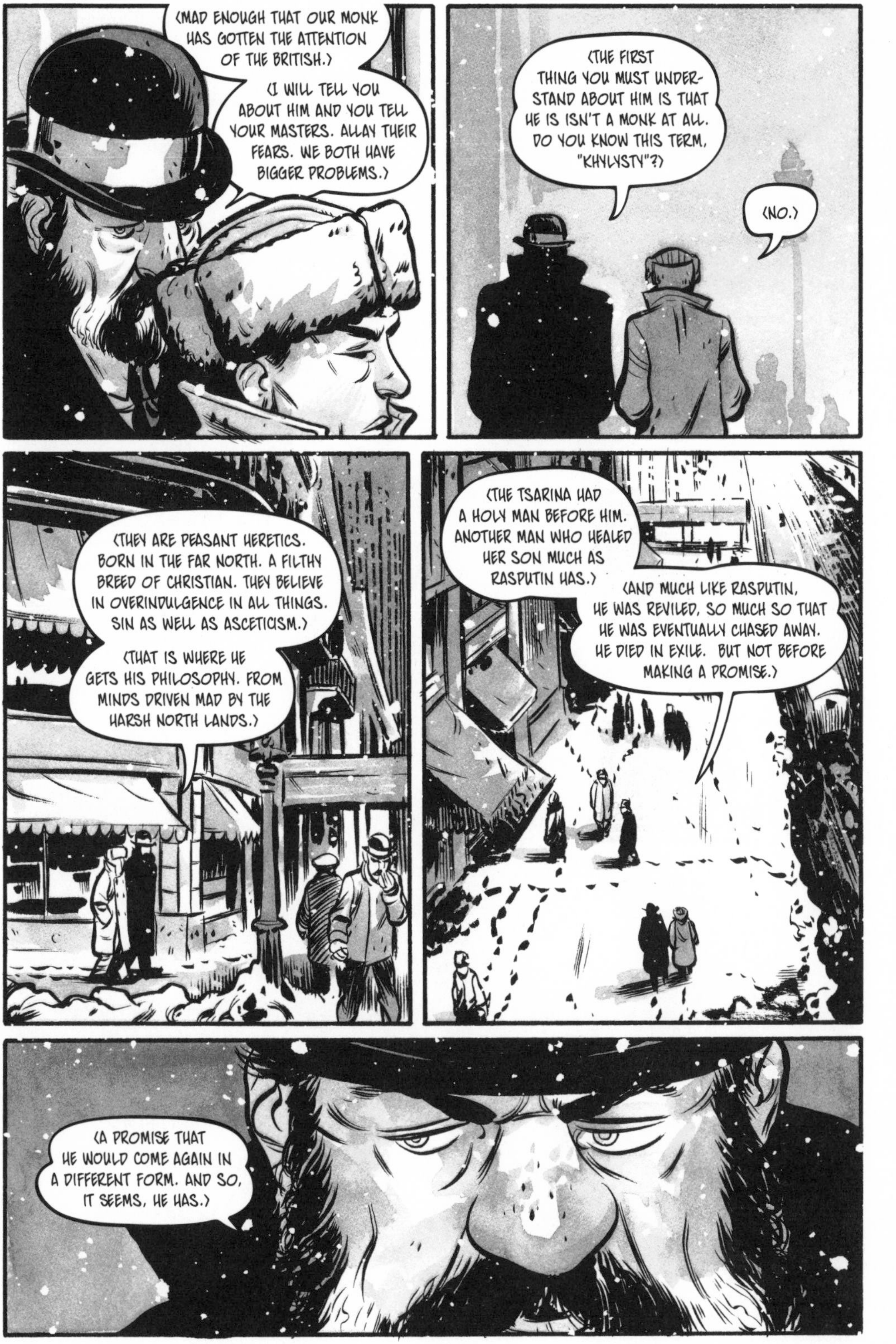
(MAD ENOUGH THAT OUR MONK HAS GOTTEN THE ATTENTION OF THE BRITISH.)
(I WILL TELL YOU ABOUT HIM AND YOU TELL YOUR MASTERS. ALLAY THEIR FEARS. WE BOTH HAVE BIGGER PROBLEMS.)
(THE FIRST THING YOU MUST UNDER-STAND ABOUT HIM IS THAT HE IS ISN'T A MONK AT ALL. DO YOU KNOW THIS TERM, "KHYLYSTY"?)
(NO.)
(THEY ARE PEASANT HERETICS. BORN IN THE FAR NORTH. A FILTHY BREED OF CHRISTIAN. THEY BELIEVE IN OVERINDULGENCE IN ALL THINGS. SIN AS WELL AS ASCETICISM.)
(THAT IS WHERE HE GETS HIS PHILOSOPHY. FROM MINDS DRIVEN MAD BY THE HARSH NORTH LANDS.)
(THE TSARINA HAD A HOLY MAN BEFORE HIM. ANOTHER MAN WHO HEALED HER SON MUCH AS RASPUTIN HAS.)
(AND MUCH LIKE RASPUTIN, HE WAS REVILED, SO MUCH SO THAT HE WAS EVENTUALLY CHASED AWAY. HE DIED IN EXILE. BUT NOT BEFORE MAKING A PROMISE.)
(A PROMISE THAT HE WOULD COME AGAIN IN A DIFFERENT FORM. AND SO, IT SEEMS, HE HAS.)

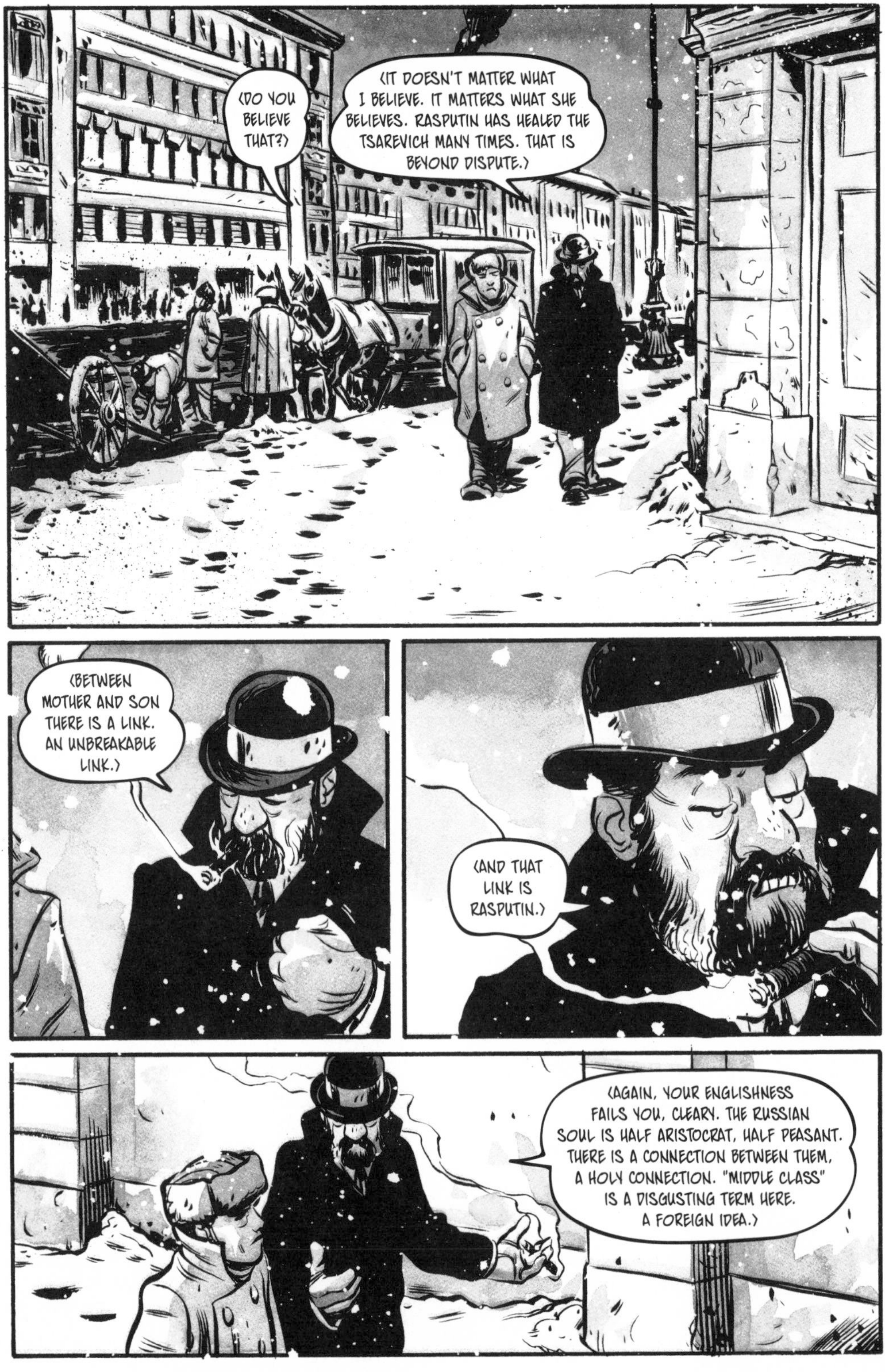
‹DO YOU BELIEVE THAT?›
‹IT DOESN'T MATTER WHAT I BELIEVE. IT MATTERS WHAT SHE BELIEVES. RASPUTIN HAS HEALED THE TSAREVICH MANY TIMES. THAT IS BEYOND DISPUTE.›
‹BETWEEN MOTHER AND SON THERE IS A LINK. AN UNBREAKABLE LINK.›
‹AND THAT LINK IS RASPUTIN.›
‹AGAIN, YOUR ENGLISHNESS FAILS YOU, CLEARY. THE RUSSIAN SOUL IS HALF ARISTOCRAT, HALF PEASANT. THERE IS A CONNECTION BETWEEN THEM, A HOLY CONNECTION. "MIDDLE CLASS" IS A DISGUSTING TERM HERE. A FOREIGN IDEA.›

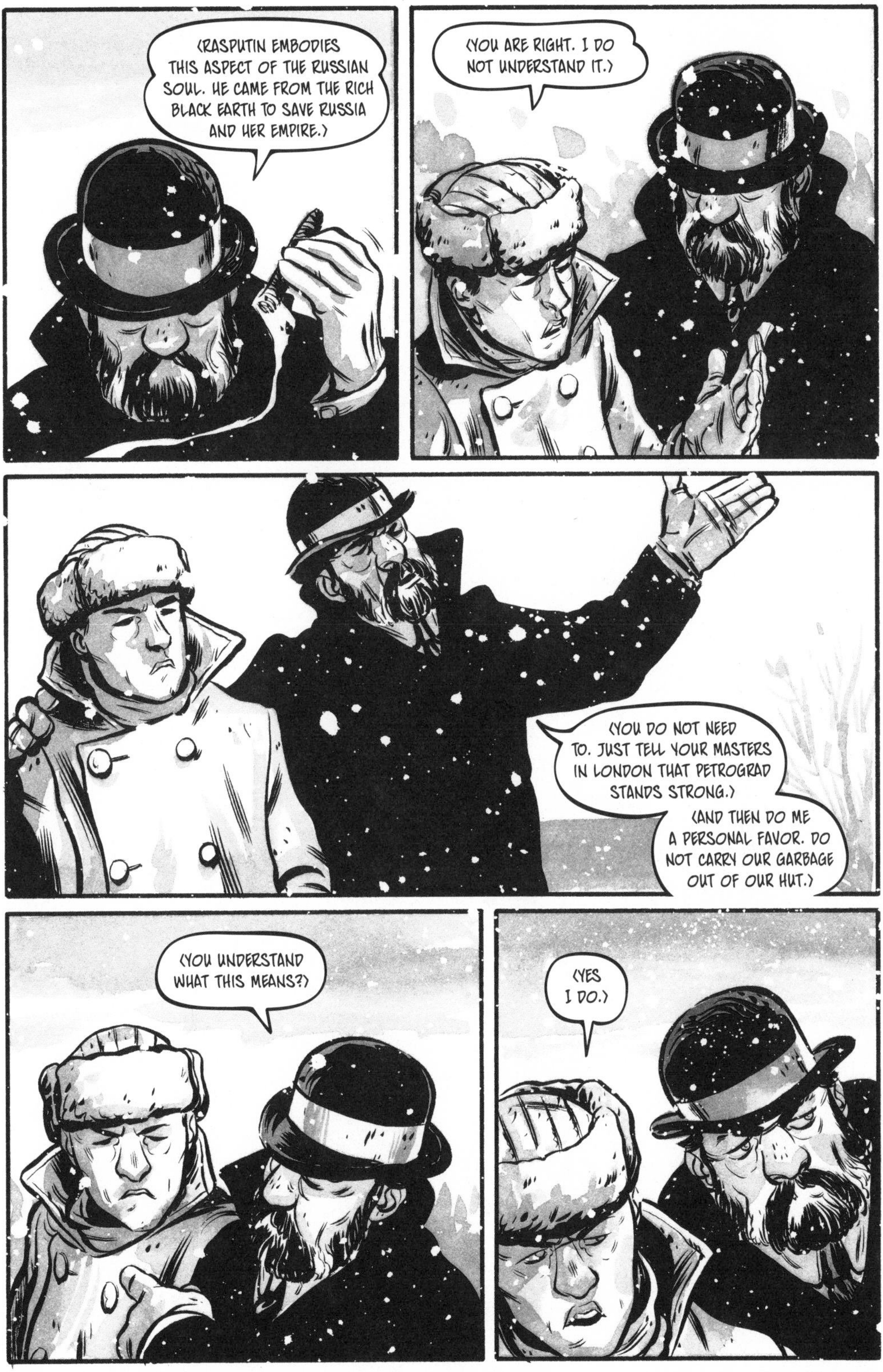
‹RASPUTIN EMBODIES THIS ASPECT OF THE RUSSIAN SOUL. HE CAME FROM THE RICH BLACK EARTH TO SAVE RUSSIA AND HER EMPIRE.›
‹YOU ARE RIGHT. I DO NOT UNDERSTAND IT.›
‹YOU DO NOT NEED TO. JUST TELL YOUR MASTERS IN LONDON THAT PETROGRAD STANDS STRONG.›
‹AND THEN DO ME A PERSONAL FAVOR. DO NOT CARRY OUR GARBAGE OUT OF OUR HUT.›
‹YOU UNDERSTAND WHAT THIS MEANS?›
‹YES I DO.›

〈FORGIVE ME FOR ASKING, BUT WHAT IF ONE OF THESE CONSPIRACIES HAD SUCCEEDED? WHAT WOULD HAVE BECOME OF THE TSARINA THEN? AND OF RUSSIA?〉

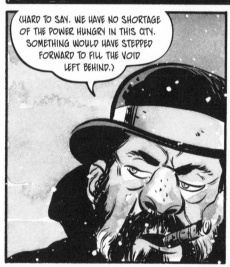

〈HARD TO SAY. WE HAVE NO SHORTAGE OF THE POWER HUNGRY IN THIS CITY. SOMETHING WOULD HAVE STEPPED FORWARD TO FILL THE VOID LEFT BEHIND.〉

〈I AM NOT DUMB, CLEARY. I KNOW RASPUTIN IS HATED. THAT HE IS A DANGER TO THE EMPIRE ITSELF.〉

〈BUT THEN AGAIN SO IS THE TSARDOM. SO IS THE PEASANTRY. SO IS THE WAR.〉

〈THESE ARE THE IRONIES OF OUR WORK. WE PROTECT THINGS WE KNOW TO BE HARMFUL, WE HUNT THINGS WE SUSPECT TO BE BENEFICIAL. WE GO WHERE WE ARE POINTED, YES?〉

〈YES.〉

〈THIS IS WHERE I LIKE TO COME TO THINK. IN THE SHADOW OF THE OLD TSAR.〉

〈HE KNEW HOW TO RULE THIS COUNTRY. UNAFRAID OF ACTION. DETERMINED. RUTHLESS AND STRONG.〉

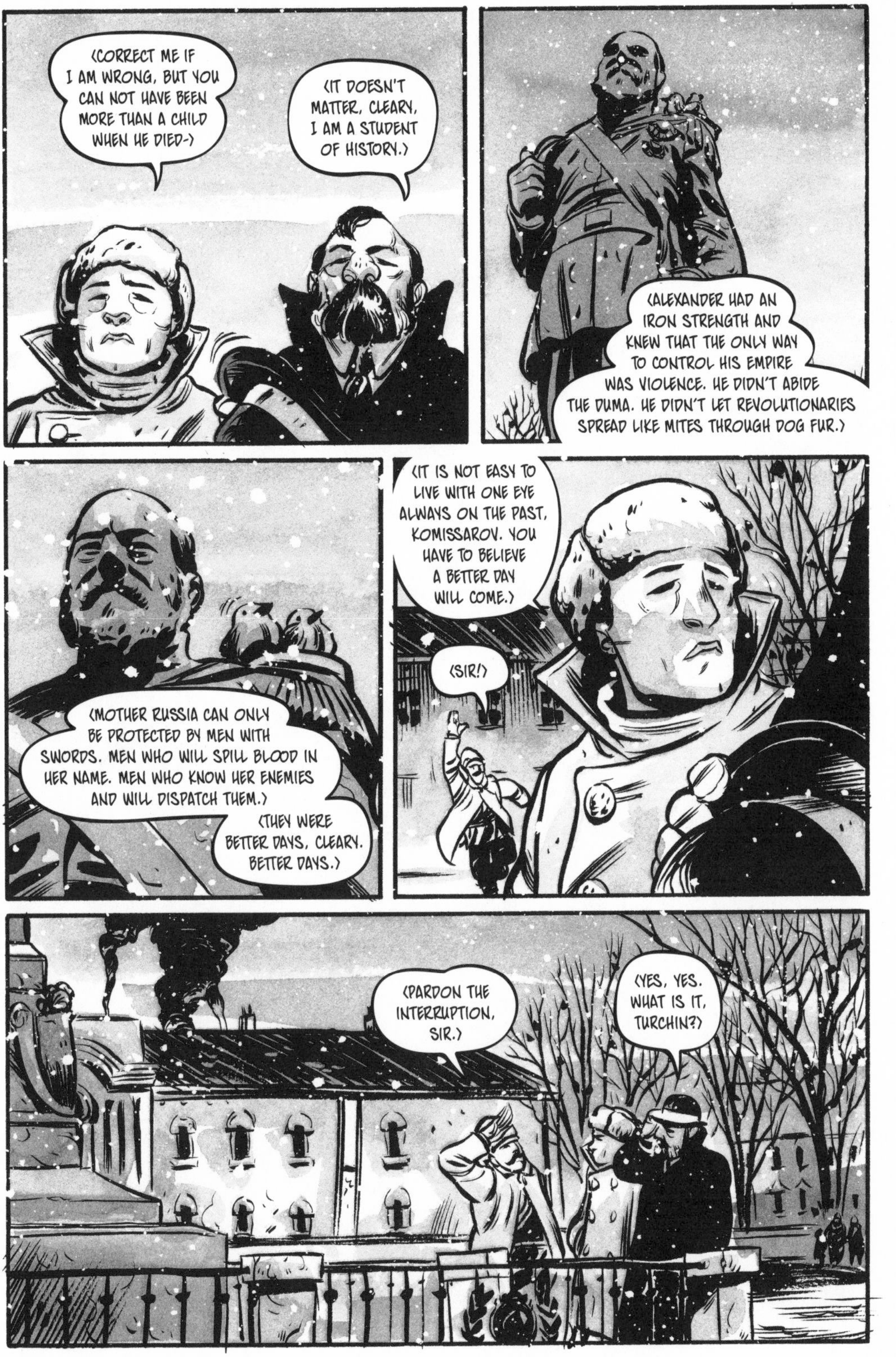

‹CORRECT ME IF I AM WRONG, BUT YOU CAN NOT HAVE BEEN MORE THAN A CHILD WHEN HE DIED-›
‹IT DOESN'T MATTER, CLEARY, I AM A STUDENT OF HISTORY.›
‹ALEXANDER HAD AN IRON STRENGTH AND KNEW THAT THE ONLY WAY TO CONTROL HIS EMPIRE WAS VIOLENCE. HE DIDN'T ABIDE THE DUMA. HE DIDN'T LET REVOLUTIONARIES SPREAD LIKE MITES THROUGH DOG FUR.›
‹MOTHER RUSSIA CAN ONLY BE PROTECTED BY MEN WITH SWORDS. MEN WHO WILL SPILL BLOOD IN HER NAME. MEN WHO KNOW HER ENEMIES AND WILL DISPATCH THEM.›
‹THEY WERE BETTER DAYS, CLEARY. BETTER DAYS.›
‹IT IS NOT EASY TO LIVE WITH ONE EYE ALWAYS ON THE PAST, KOMISSAROV. YOU HAVE TO BELIEVE A BETTER DAY WILL COME.›
‹SIR!›
‹PARDON THE INTERRUPTION, SIR.›
‹YES, YES. WHAT IS IT, TURCHIN?›

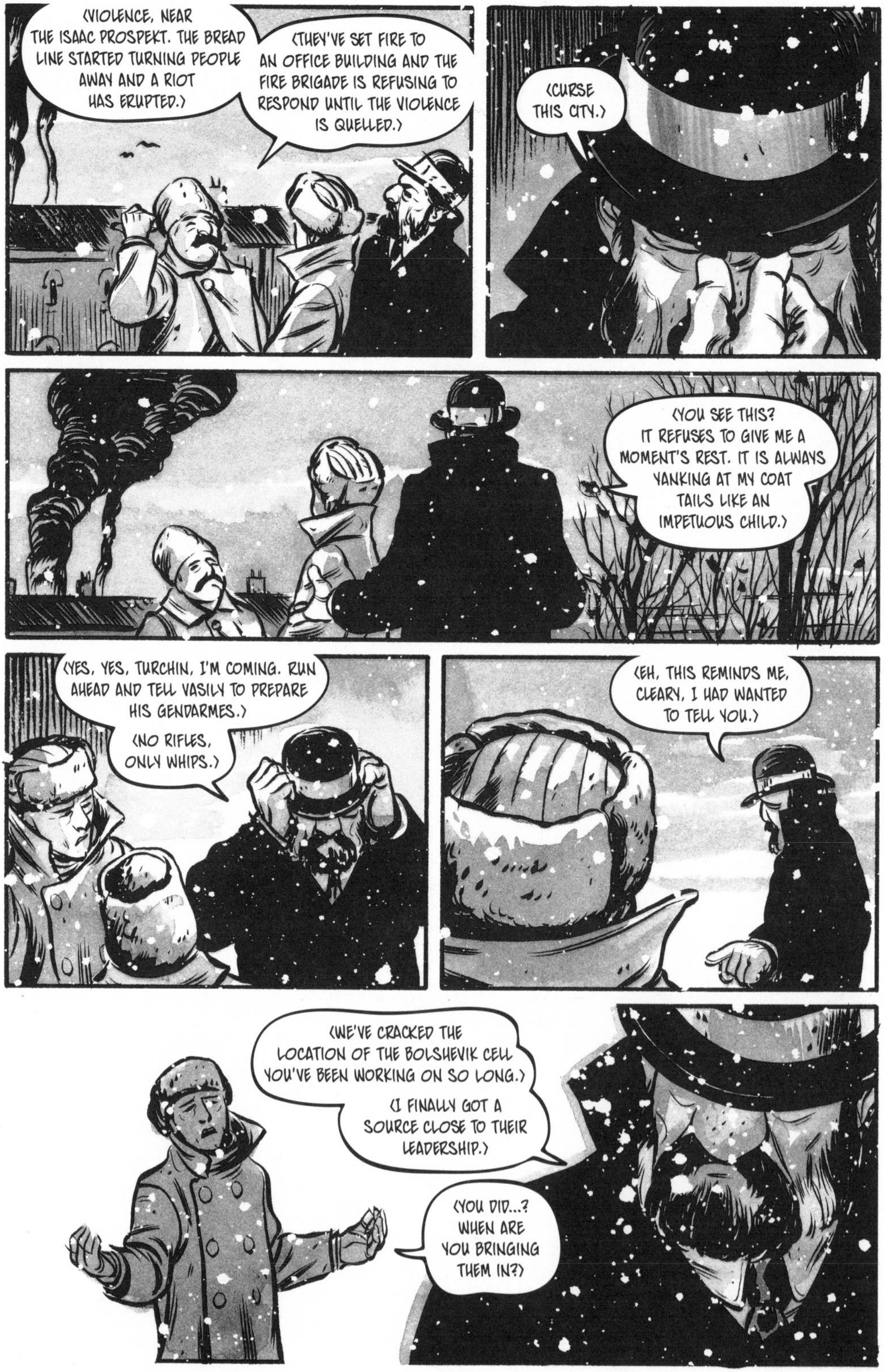
‹VIOLENCE, NEAR THE ISAAC PROSPEKT. THE BREAD LINE STARTED TURNING PEOPLE AWAY AND A RIOT HAS ERUPTED.›
‹THEY'VE SET FIRE TO AN OFFICE BUILDING AND THE FIRE BRIGADE IS REFUSING TO RESPOND UNTIL THE VIOLENCE IS QUELLED.›
‹CURSE THIS CITY.›
‹YOU SEE THIS? IT REFUSES TO GIVE ME A MOMENT'S REST. IT IS ALWAYS YANKING AT MY COAT TAILS LIKE AN IMPETUOUS CHILD.›
‹YES, YES, TURCHIN, I'M COMING. RUN AHEAD AND TELL VASILY TO PREPARE HIS GENDARMES.›
‹NO RIFLES, ONLY WHIPS.›
‹EH, THIS REMINDS ME, CLEARY, I HAD WANTED TO TELL YOU.›
‹WE'VE CRACKED THE LOCATION OF THE BOLSHEVIK CELL YOU'VE BEEN WORKING ON SO LONG.›
‹I FINALLY GOT A SOURCE CLOSE TO THEIR LEADERSHIP.›
‹YOU DID...? WHEN ARE YOU BRINGING THEM IN?›

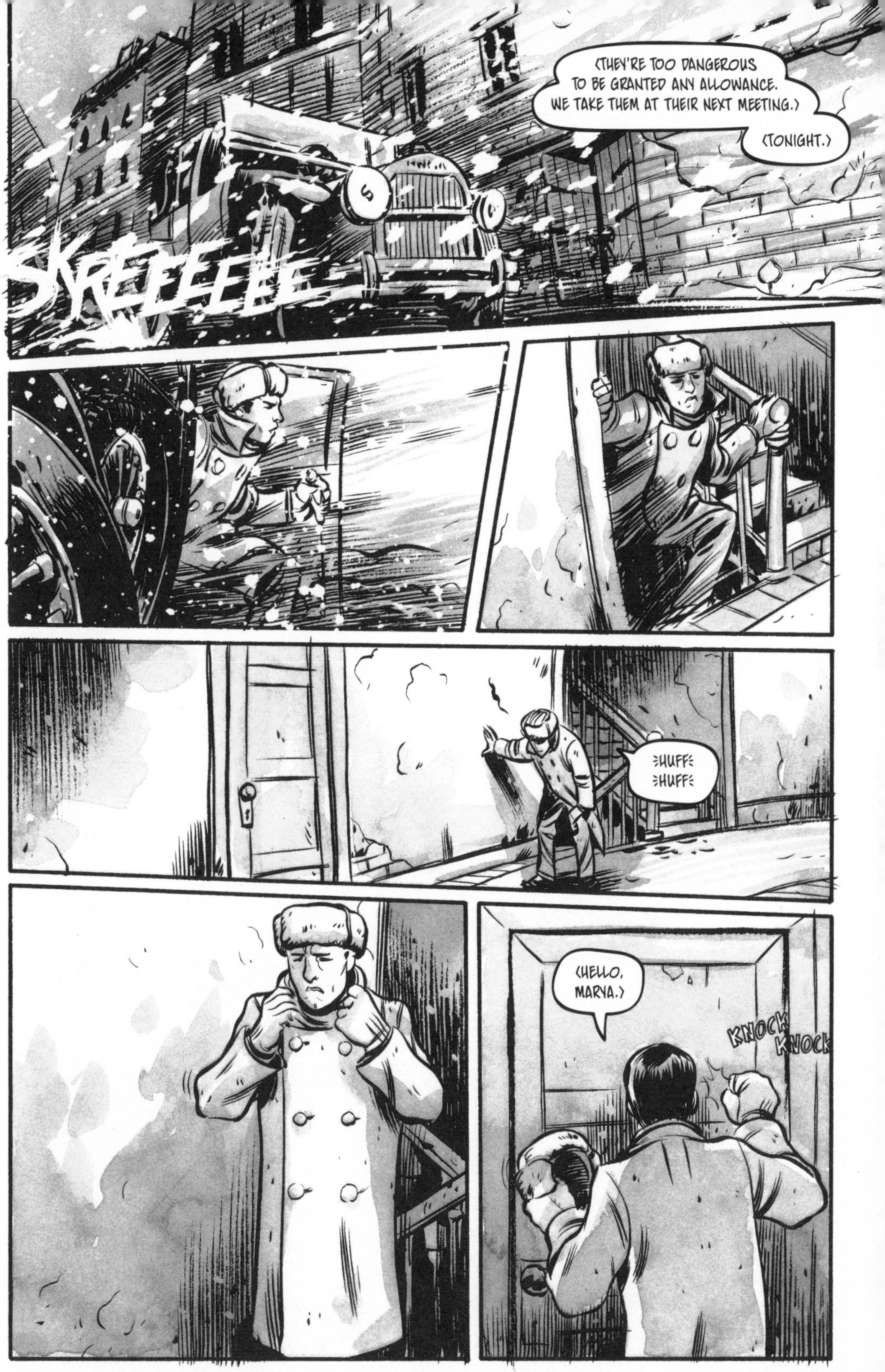
‹THEY'RE TOO DANGEROUS TO BE GRANTED ANY ALLOWANCE. WE TAKE THEM AT THEIR NEXT MEETING.›
‹TONIGHT.›
SKREEEEEE
HUFF HUFF
‹HELLO, MARYA.›
KNOCK KNOCK

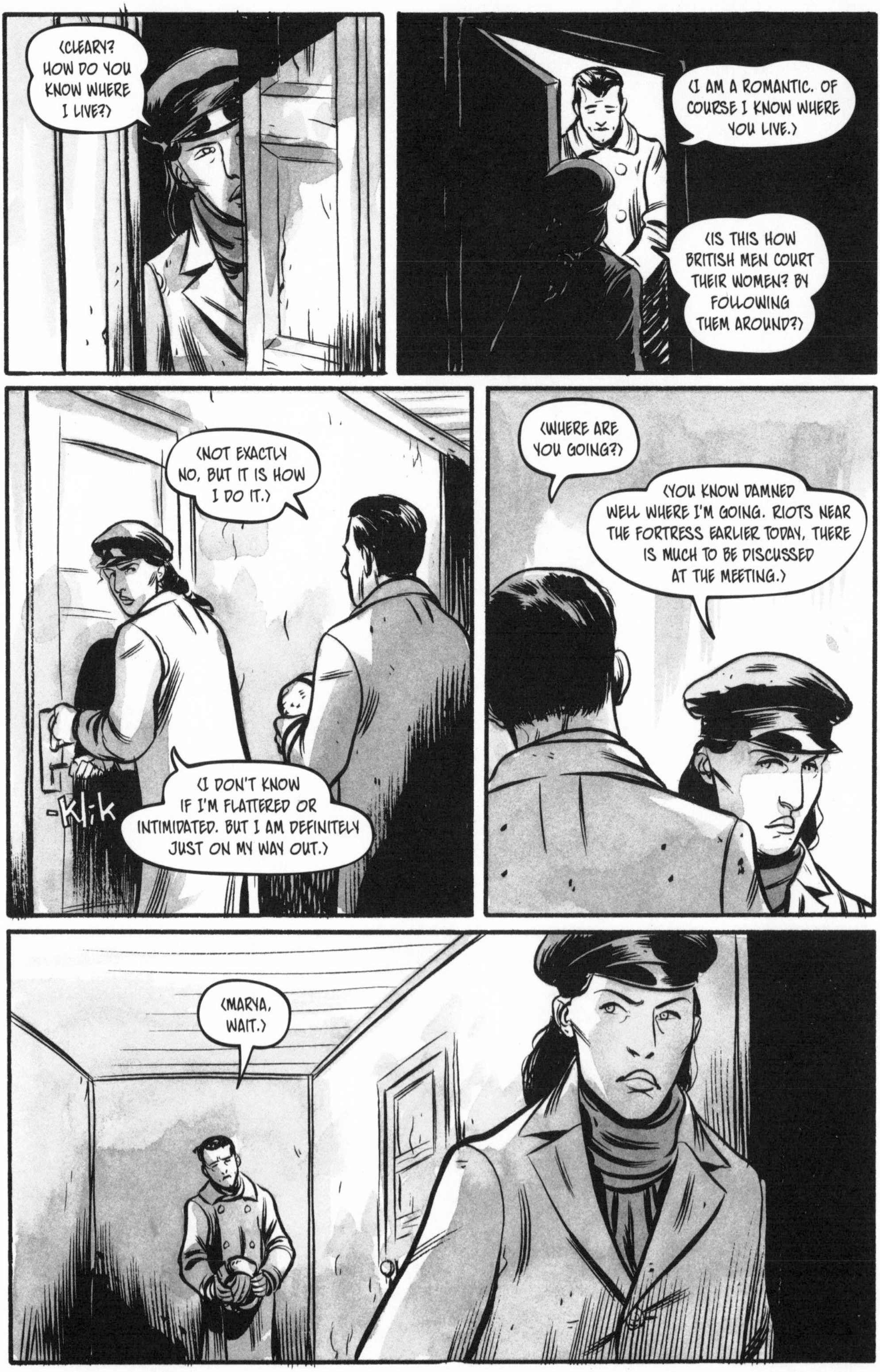
‹CLEARY? HOW DO YOU KNOW WHERE I LIVE?›
‹I AM A ROMANTIC. OF COURSE I KNOW WHERE YOU LIVE.›
‹IS THIS HOW BRITISH MEN COURT THEIR WOMEN? BY FOLLOWING THEM AROUND?›
‹NOT EXACTLY NO, BUT IT IS HOW I DO IT.›
-Kl-ik
‹I DON'T KNOW IF I'M FLATTERED OR INTIMIDATED. BUT I AM DEFINITELY JUST ON MY WAY OUT.›
‹WHERE ARE YOU GOING?›
‹YOU KNOW DAMNED WELL WHERE I'M GOING. RIOTS NEAR THE FORTRESS EARLIER TODAY, THERE IS MUCH TO BE DISCUSSED AT THE MEETING.›
‹MARYA, WAIT.›

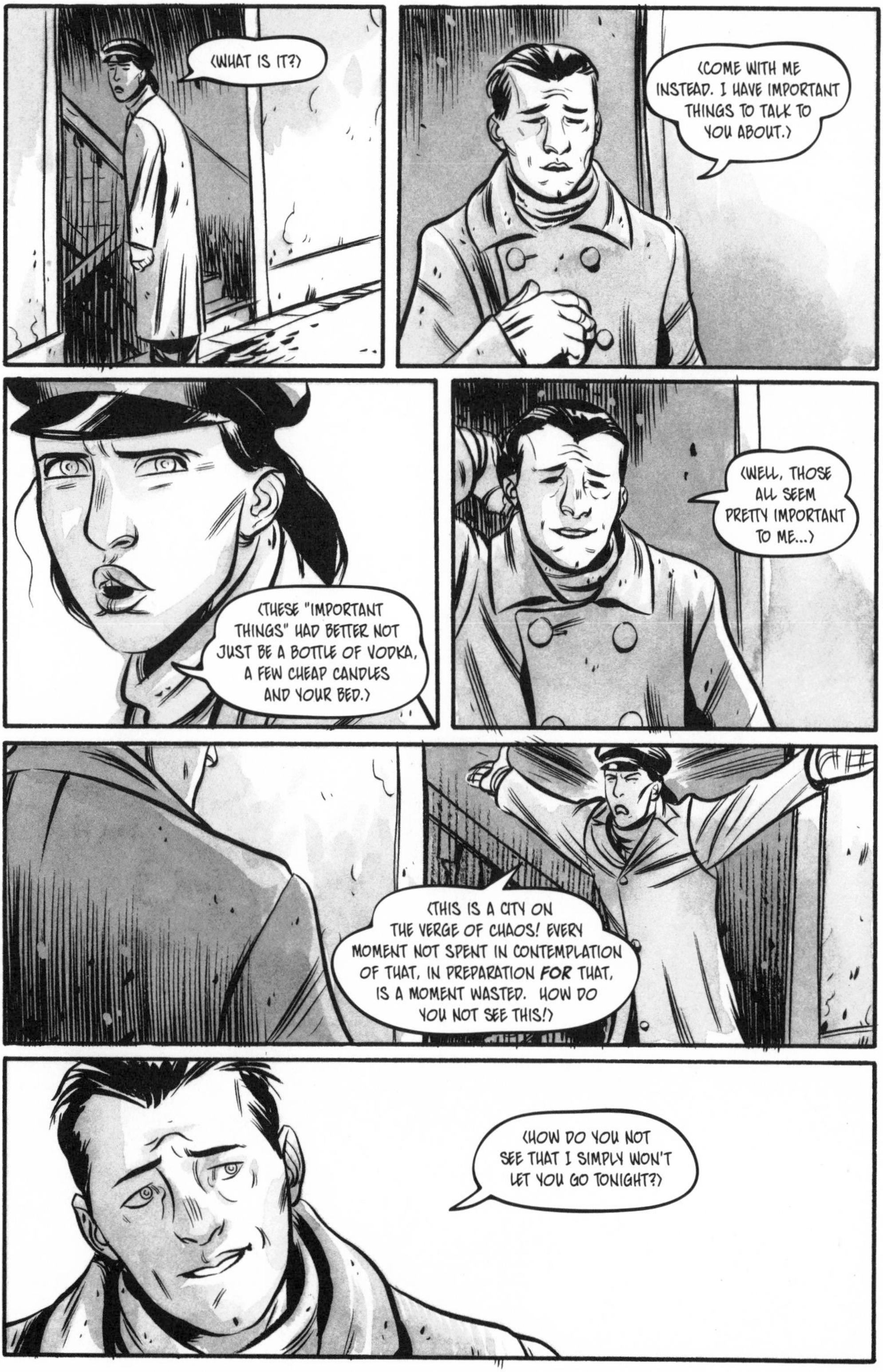
‹WHAT IS IT?›
‹COME WITH ME INSTEAD. I HAVE IMPORTANT THINGS TO TALK TO YOU ABOUT.›
‹THESE "IMPORTANT THINGS" HAD BETTER NOT JUST BE A BOTTLE OF VODKA, A FEW CHEAP CANDLES AND YOUR BED.›
‹WELL, THOSE ALL SEEM PRETTY IMPORTANT TO ME...›
‹THIS IS A CITY ON THE VERGE OF CHAOS! EVERY MOMENT NOT SPENT IN CONTEMPLATION OF THAT, IN PREPARATION FOR THAT, IS A MOMENT WASTED. HOW DO YOU NOT SEE THIS!›
‹HOW DO YOU NOT SEE THAT I SIMPLY WON'T LET YOU GO TONIGHT?›

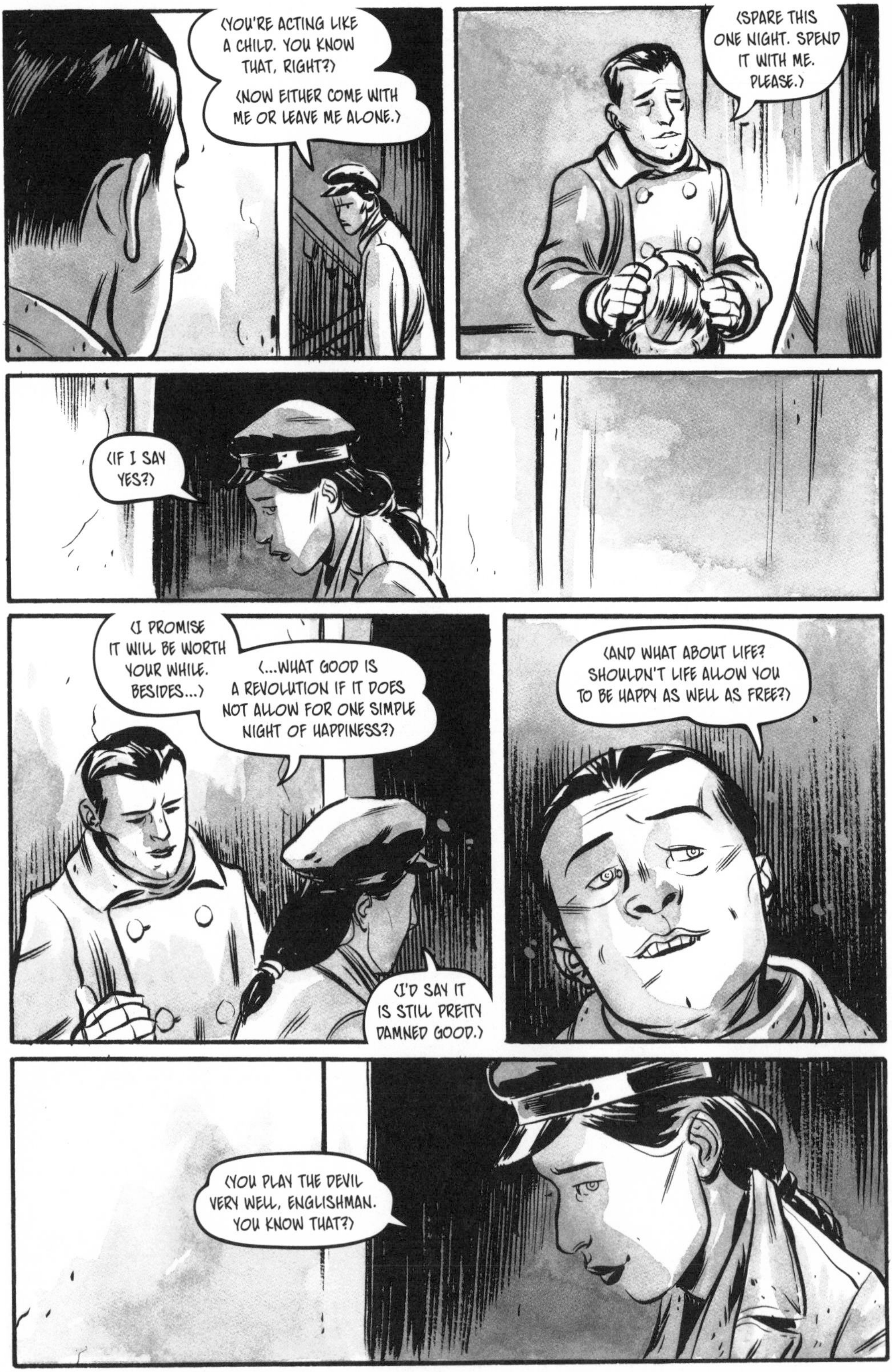
(YOU'RE ACTING LIKE A CHILD. YOU KNOW THAT, RIGHT?)
(NOW EITHER COME WITH ME OR LEAVE ME ALONE.)
(SPARE THIS ONE NIGHT. SPEND IT WITH ME. PLEASE.)
(IF I SAY YES?)
(I PROMISE IT WILL BE WORTH YOUR WHILE. BESIDES...)
(...WHAT GOOD IS A REVOLUTION IF IT DOES NOT ALLOW FOR ONE SIMPLE NIGHT OF HAPPINESS?)
(I'D SAY IT IS STILL PRETTY DAMNED GOOD.)
(AND WHAT ABOUT LIFE? SHOULDN'T LIFE ALLOW YOU TO BE HAPPY AS WELL AS FREE?)
(YOU PLAY THE DEVIL VERY WELL, ENGLISHMAN. YOU KNOW THAT?)

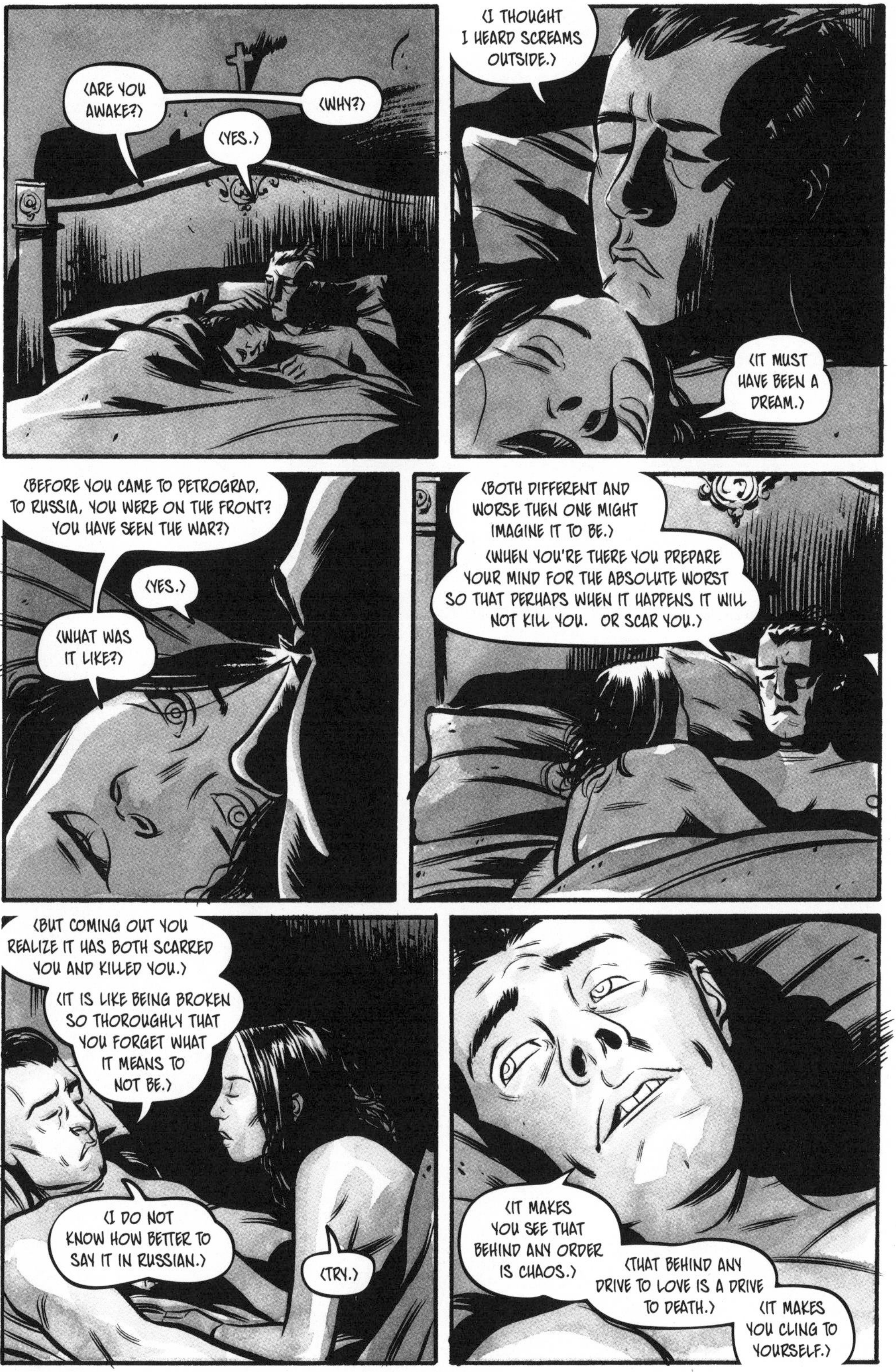
‹ARE YOU AWAKE?›
‹YES.›
‹WHY?›
‹I THOUGHT I HEARD SCREAMS OUTSIDE.›
‹IT MUST HAVE BEEN A DREAM.›
‹BEFORE YOU CAME TO PETROGRAD, TO RUSSIA, YOU WERE ON THE FRONT? YOU HAVE SEEN THE WAR?›
‹YES.›
‹WHAT WAS IT LIKE?›
‹BOTH DIFFERENT AND WORSE THEN ONE MIGHT IMAGINE IT TO BE.›
‹WHEN YOU'RE THERE YOU PREPARE YOUR MIND FOR THE ABSOLUTE WORST SO THAT PERHAPS WHEN IT HAPPENS IT WILL NOT KILL YOU. OR SCAR YOU.›
‹BUT COMING OUT YOU REALIZE IT HAS BOTH SCARRED YOU AND KILLED YOU.›
‹IT IS LIKE BEING BROKEN SO THOROUGHLY THAT YOU FORGET WHAT IT MEANS TO NOT BE.›
‹I DO NOT KNOW HOW BETTER TO SAY IT IN RUSSIAN.›
‹TRY.›
‹IT MAKES YOU SEE THAT BEHIND ANY ORDER IS CHAOS.›
‹THAT BEHIND ANY DRIVE TO LOVE IS A DRIVE TO DEATH.›
‹IT MAKES YOU CLING TO YOURSELF.›

‹DO YOU DREAM ABOUT IT OFTEN?›

‹YES. IT AND OTHER THINGS. THINGS I HAVE NOT SEEN WITH MY OWN EYES. THINGS THAT DO NOT EXIST YET I FEAR DO.›

‹TELL ME, WHAT IS THE BOLSHEVIK TAKE ON THE WAR?›

‹YOU CLAIM TO WANT PEACE, BUT YOU MUST REALIZE THAT THE LONGER IT GOES ON THE WEAKER THE TSAR BECOMES.›

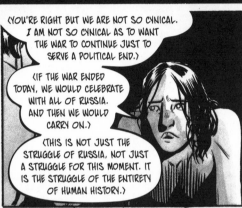

‹YOU'RE RIGHT BUT WE ARE NOT SO CYNICAL. I AM NOT SO CYNICAL AS TO WANT THE WAR TO CONTINUE JUST TO SERVE A POLITICAL END.›

‹IF THE WAR ENDED TODAY, WE WOULD CELEBRATE WITH ALL OF RUSSIA. AND THEN WE WOULD CARRY ON.›

‹THIS IS NOT JUST THE STRUGGLE OF RUSSIA, NOT JUST A STRUGGLE FOR THIS MOMENT. IT IS THE STRUGGLE OF THE ENTIRETY OF HUMAN HISTORY.›

‹I THINK ABOUT IT THIS WAY. THE PROBLEM IS NOT THAT WE HAVE A LEADER WHO IS UNJUST, CRUEL AND INCOMPETENT.›

‹THE PROBLEM IS THAT WE HAVE A LEADER AT ALL.›

‹IS THAT THE RUSSIAN VERSION OF ROMANCE? THE FIRE OF REVOLUTION BURNS EVEN IN BED?›

‹THAT IS THE BOLSHEVIK VERSION OF ROMANCE.›

‹AND TELL ME, MY LITTLE RED, WHEN THE REVOLUTION COMES AND IT IS NOT AS YOU THOUGHT IT WOULD BE, WHAT THEN?›

‹NOT POSSIBLE. YOU WILL SEE...›

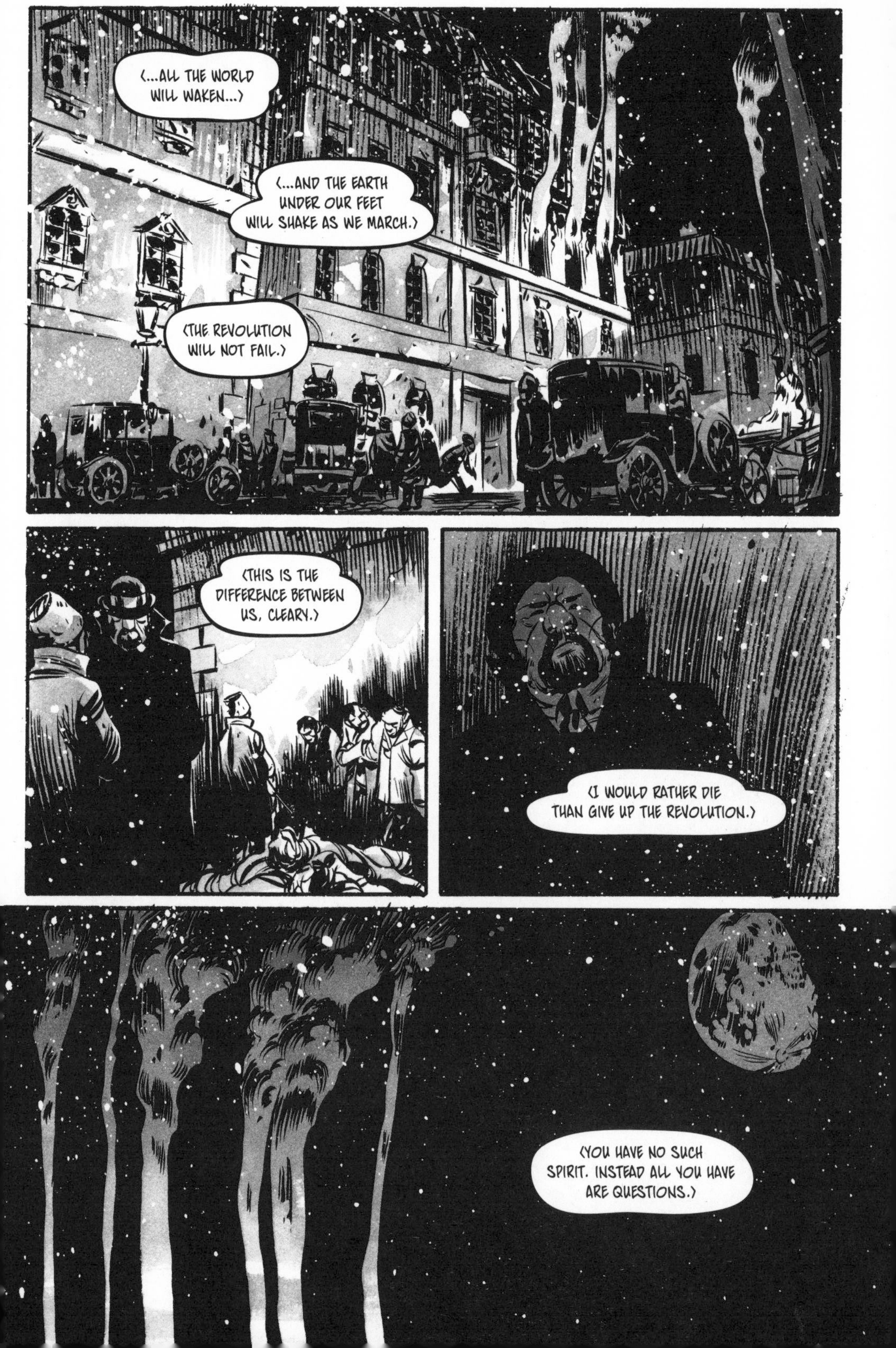
‹...ALL THE WORLD WILL WAKEN...›
‹...AND THE EARTH UNDER OUR FEET WILL SHAKE AS WE MARCH.›
‹THE REVOLUTION WILL NOT FAIL.›
‹THIS IS THE DIFFERENCE BETWEEN US, CLEARY.›
‹I WOULD RATHER DIE THAN GIVE UP THE REVOLUTION.›
‹YOU HAVE NO SUCH SPIRIT. INSTEAD ALL YOU HAVE ARE QUESTIONS.›

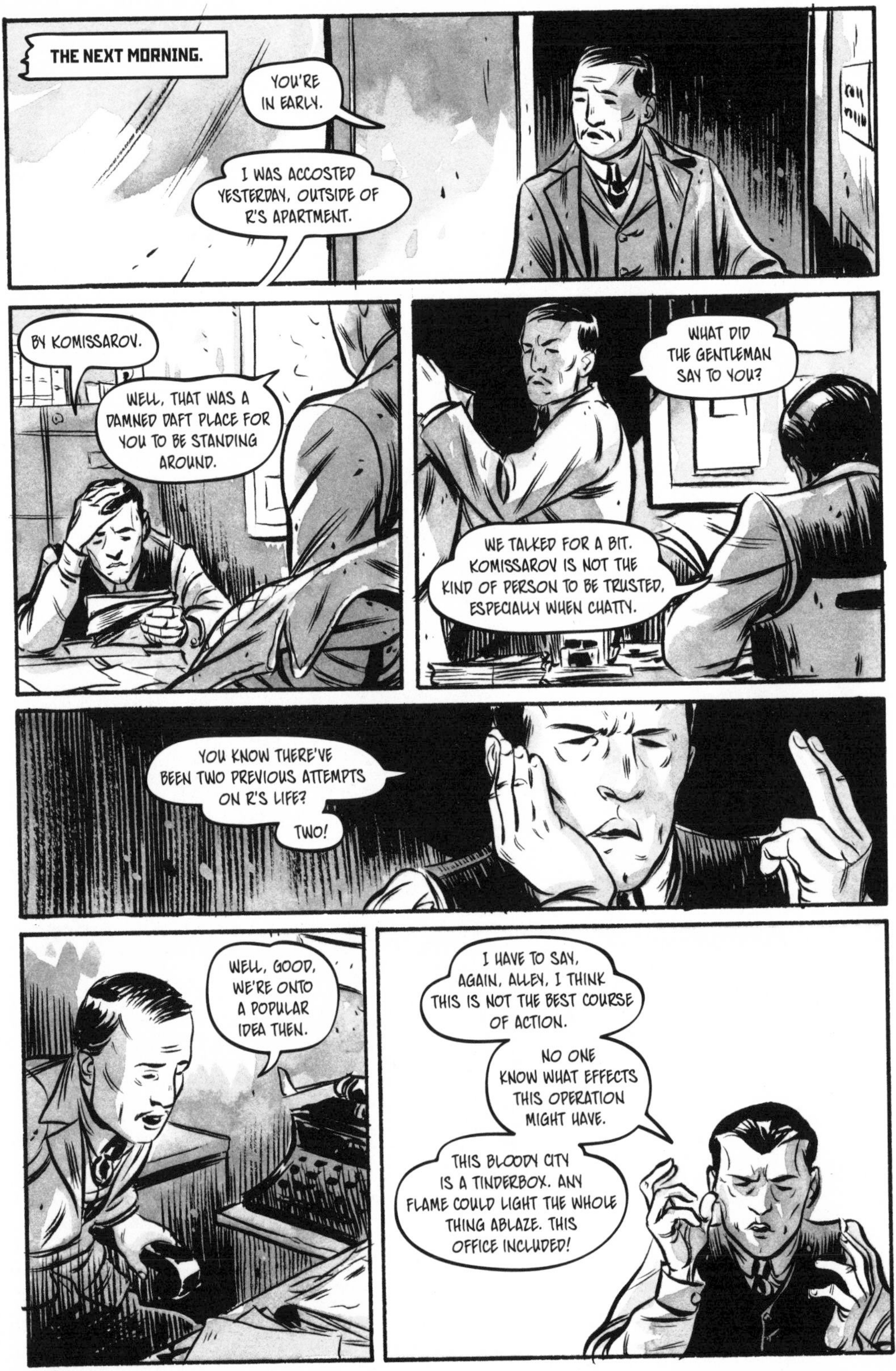
THE NEXT MORNING.
YOU'RE IN EARLY.
I WAS ACCOSTED YESTERDAY, OUTSIDE OF R'S APARTMENT.
BY KOMISSAROV.
WELL, THAT WAS A DAMNED DAFT PLACE FOR YOU TO BE STANDING AROUND.
WHAT DID THE GENTLEMAN SAY TO YOU?
WE TALKED FOR A BIT. KOMISSAROV IS NOT THE KIND OF PERSON TO BE TRUSTED, ESPECIALLY WHEN CHATTY.
YOU KNOW THERE'VE BEEN TWO PREVIOUS ATTEMPTS ON R'S LIFE?
TWO!
WELL, GOOD, WE'RE ONTO A POPULAR IDEA THEN.
I HAVE TO SAY, AGAIN, ALLEY, I THINK THIS IS NOT THE BEST COURSE OF ACTION.
NO ONE KNOW WHAT EFFECTS THIS OPERATION MIGHT HAVE.
THIS BLOODY CITY IS A TINDERBOX. ANY FLAME COULD LIGHT THE WHOLE THING ABLAZE. THIS OFFICE INCLUDED!

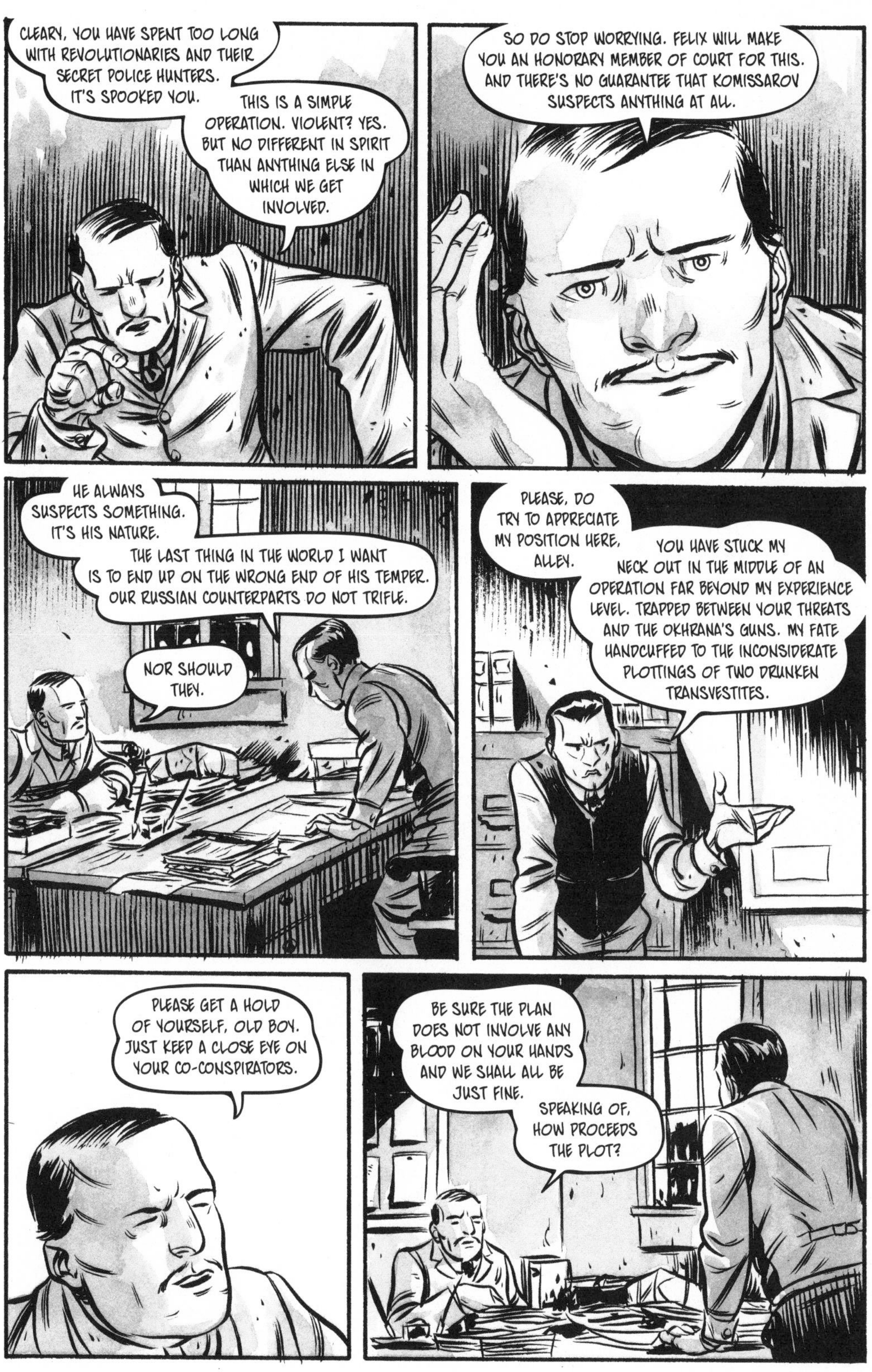
CLEARY, YOU HAVE SPENT TOO LONG WITH REVOLUTIONARIES AND THEIR SECRET POLICE HUNTERS. IT'S SPOOKED YOU.
THIS IS A SIMPLE OPERATION. VIOLENT? YES. BUT NO DIFFERENT IN SPIRIT THAN ANYTHING ELSE IN WHICH WE GET INVOLVED.
SO DO STOP WORRYING. FELIX WILL MAKE YOU AN HONORARY MEMBER OF COURT FOR THIS. AND THERE'S NO GUARANTEE THAT KOMISSAROV SUSPECTS ANYTHING AT ALL.
HE ALWAYS SUSPECTS SOMETHING. IT'S HIS NATURE.
THE LAST THING IN THE WORLD I WANT IS TO END UP ON THE WRONG END OF HIS TEMPER. OUR RUSSIAN COUNTERPARTS DO NOT TRIFLE.
NOR SHOULD THEY.
PLEASE, DO TRY TO APPRECIATE MY POSITION HERE, ALLEY.
YOU HAVE STUCK MY NECK OUT IN THE MIDDLE OF AN OPERATION FAR BEYOND MY EXPERIENCE LEVEL. TRAPPED BETWEEN YOUR THREATS AND THE OKHRANA'S GUNS. MY FATE HANDCUFFED TO THE INCONSIDERATE PLOTTINGS OF TWO DRUNKEN TRANSVESTITES.
PLEASE GET A HOLD OF YOURSELF, OLD BOY. JUST KEEP A CLOSE EYE ON YOUR CO-CONSPIRATORS.
BE SURE THE PLAN DOES NOT INVOLVE ANY BLOOD ON YOUR HANDS AND WE SHALL ALL BE JUST FINE.
SPEAKING OF, HOW PROCEEDS THE PLOT?

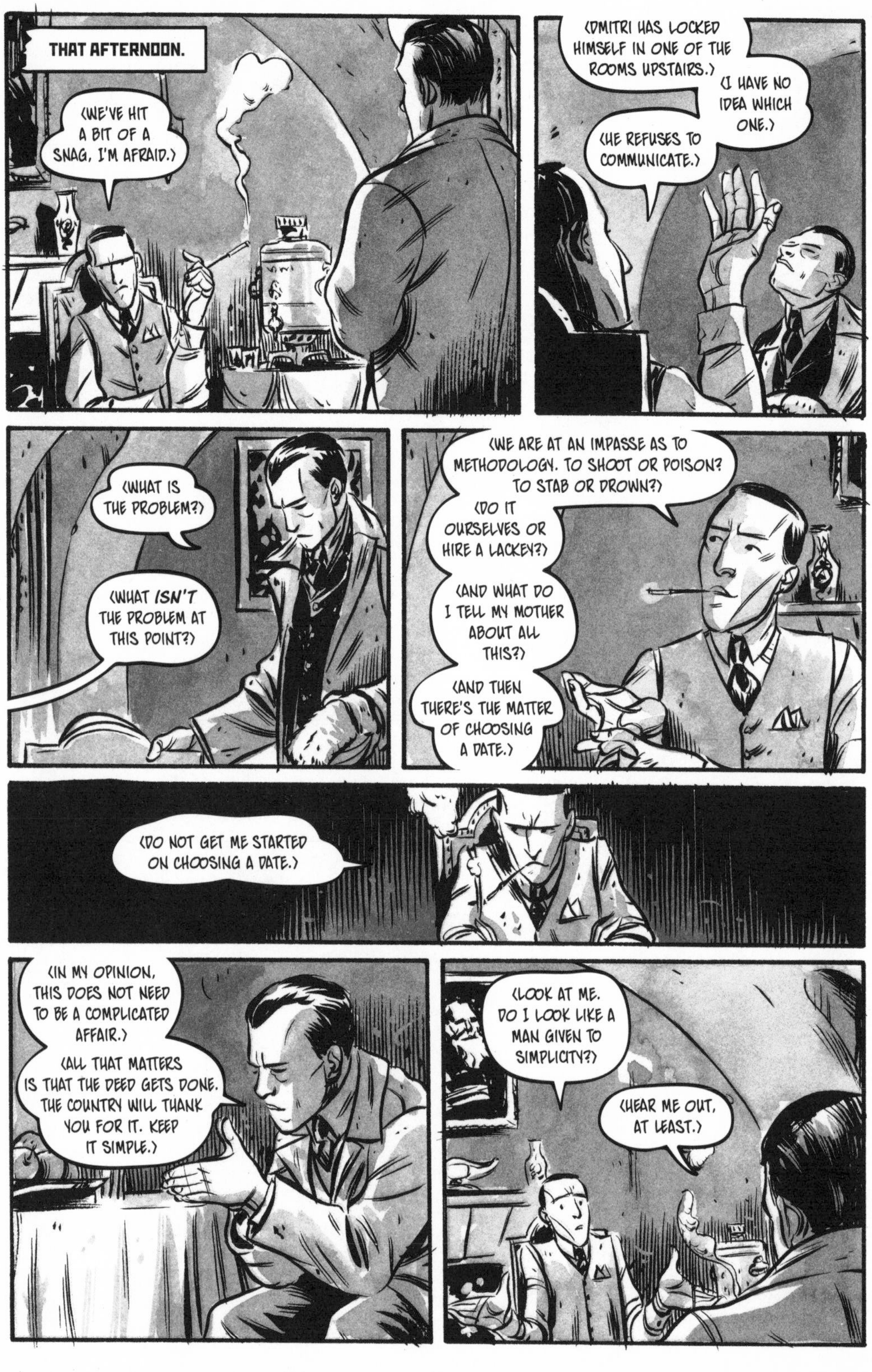
THAT AFTERNOON.
⟨WE'VE HIT A BIT OF A SNAG, I'M AFRAID.⟩
⟨DMITRI HAS LOCKED HIMSELF IN ONE OF THE ROOMS UPSTAIRS.⟩
⟨I HAVE NO IDEA WHICH ONE.⟩
⟨HE REFUSES TO COMMUNICATE.⟩
⟨WHAT IS THE PROBLEM?⟩
⟨WHAT ISN'T THE PROBLEM AT THIS POINT?⟩
⟨WE ARE AT AN IMPASSE AS TO METHODOLOGY. TO SHOOT OR POISON? TO STAB OR DROWN?⟩
⟨DO IT OURSELVES OR HIRE A LACKEY?⟩
⟨AND WHAT DO I TELL MY MOTHER ABOUT ALL THIS?⟩
⟨AND THEN THERE'S THE MATTER OF CHOOSING A DATE.⟩
⟨DO NOT GET ME STARTED ON CHOOSING A DATE.⟩
⟨IN MY OPINION, THIS DOES NOT NEED TO BE A COMPLICATED AFFAIR.⟩
⟨ALL THAT MATTERS IS THAT THE DEED GETS DONE. THE COUNTRY WILL THANK YOU FOR IT. KEEP IT SIMPLE.⟩
⟨LOOK AT ME. DO I LOOK LIKE A MAN GIVEN TO SIMPLICITY?⟩
⟨HEAR ME OUT, AT LEAST.⟩

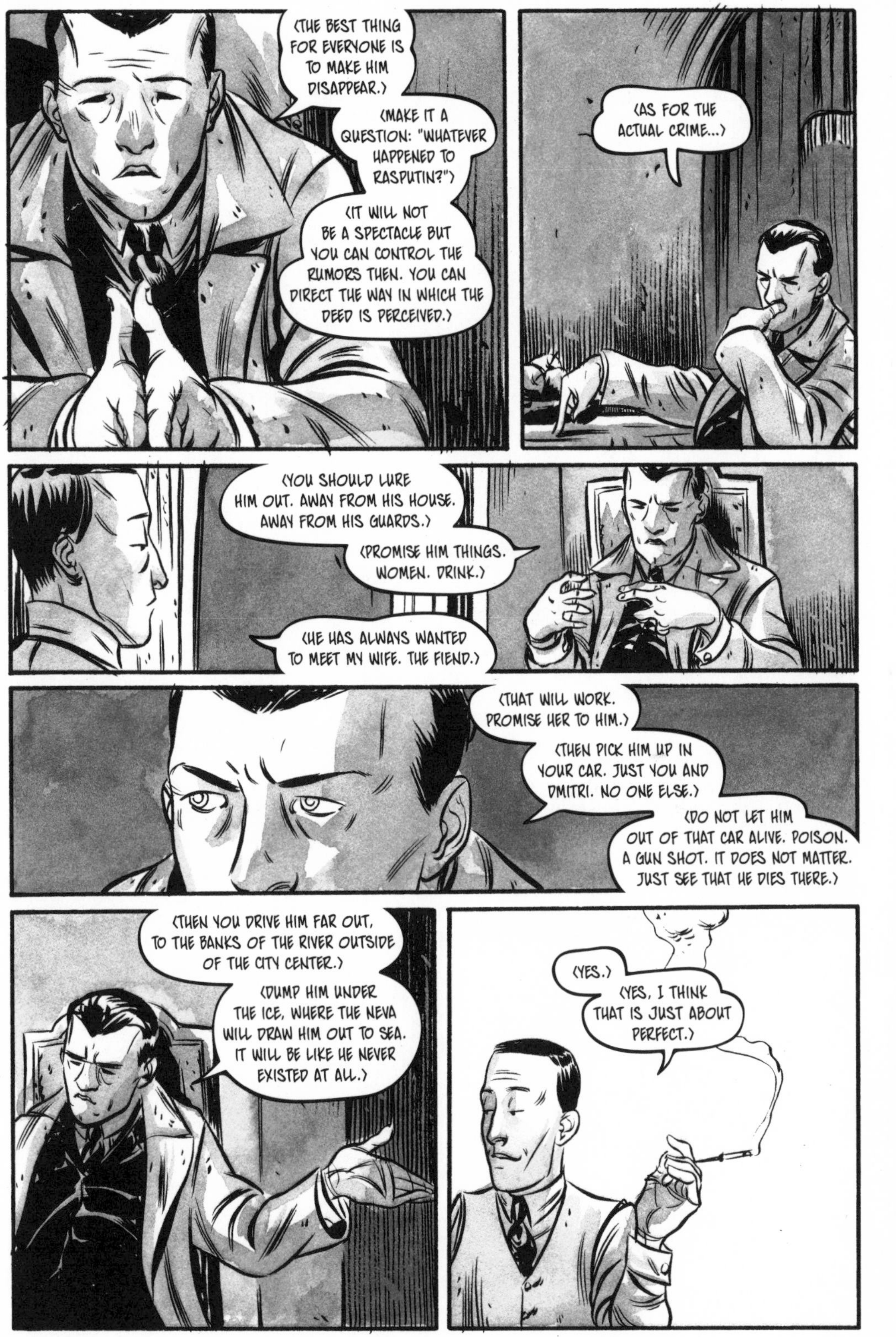
(THE BEST THING FOR EVERYONE IS TO MAKE HIM DISAPPEAR.)
(MAKE IT A QUESTION: "WHATEVER HAPPENED TO RASPUTIN?")
(IT WILL NOT BE A SPECTACLE BUT YOU CAN CONTROL THE RUMORS THEN. YOU CAN DIRECT THE WAY IN WHICH THE DEED IS PERCEIVED.)
(AS FOR THE ACTUAL CRIME...)
(YOU SHOULD LURE HIM OUT. AWAY FROM HIS HOUSE. AWAY FROM HIS GUARDS.)
(PROMISE HIM THINGS. WOMEN. DRINK.)
(HE HAS ALWAYS WANTED TO MEET MY WIFE. THE FIEND.)
(THAT WILL WORK. PROMISE HER TO HIM.)
(THEN PICK HIM UP IN YOUR CAR. JUST YOU AND DMITRI. NO ONE ELSE.)
(DO NOT LET HIM OUT OF THAT CAR ALIVE. POISON. A GUN SHOT. IT DOES NOT MATTER. JUST SEE THAT HE DIES THERE.)
(THEN YOU DRIVE HIM FAR OUT, TO THE BANKS OF THE RIVER OUTSIDE OF THE CITY CENTER.)
(DUMP HIM UNDER THE ICE, WHERE THE NEVA WILL DRAW HIM OUT TO SEA. IT WILL BE LIKE HE NEVER EXISTED AT ALL.)
(YES.)
(YES, I THINK THAT IS JUST ABOUT PERFECT.)

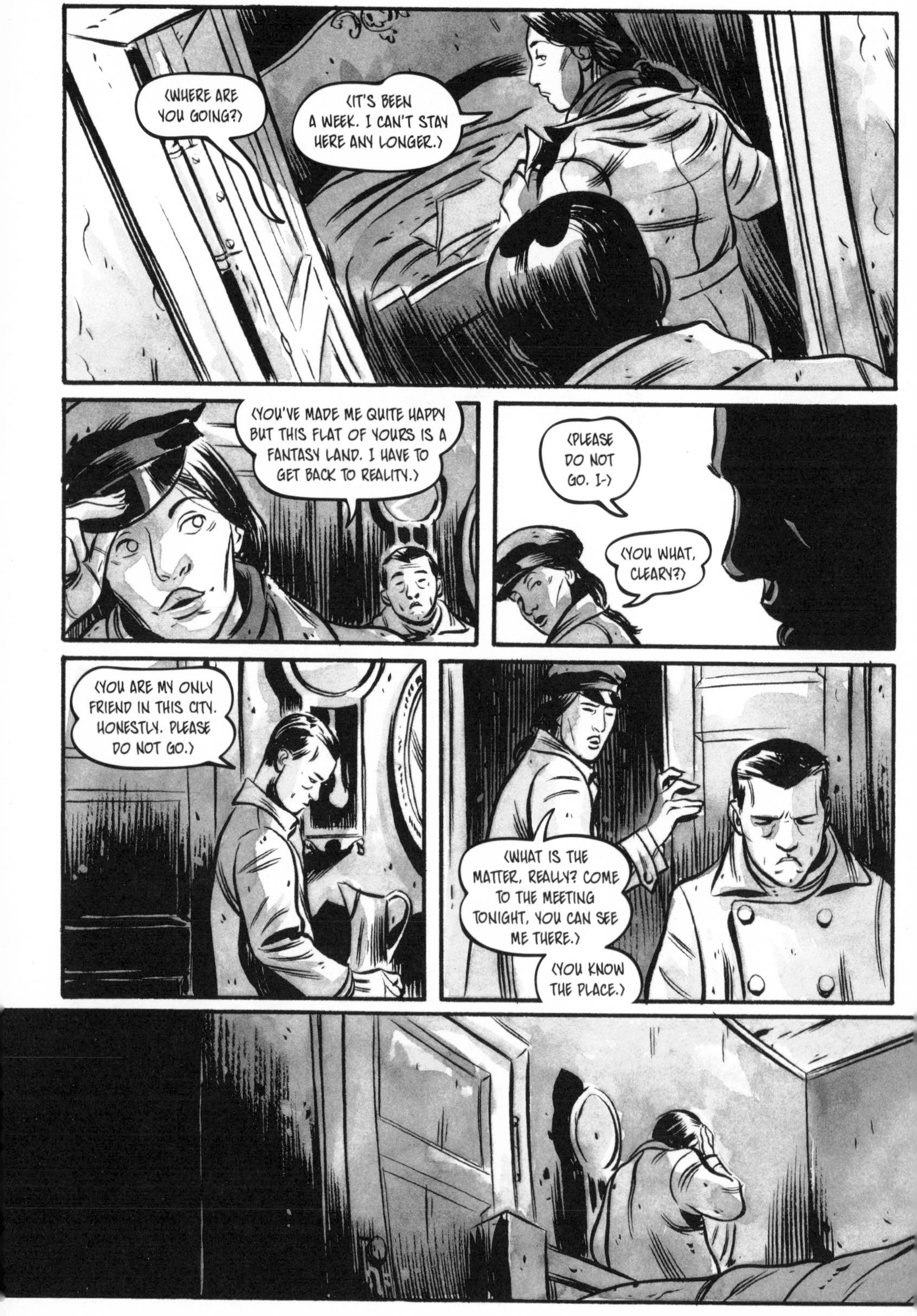

‹WHERE ARE YOU GOING?›
‹IT'S BEEN A WEEK. I CAN'T STAY HERE ANY LONGER.›
‹YOU'VE MADE ME QUITE HAPPY BUT THIS FLAT OF YOURS IS A FANTASY LAND. I HAVE TO GET BACK TO REALITY.›
‹PLEASE DO NOT GO. I-›
‹YOU WHAT, CLEARY?›
‹YOU ARE MY ONLY FRIEND IN THIS CITY. HONESTLY. PLEASE DO NOT GO.›
‹WHAT IS THE MATTER, REALLY? COME TO THE MEETING TONIGHT, YOU CAN SEE ME THERE.›
‹YOU KNOW THE PLACE.›

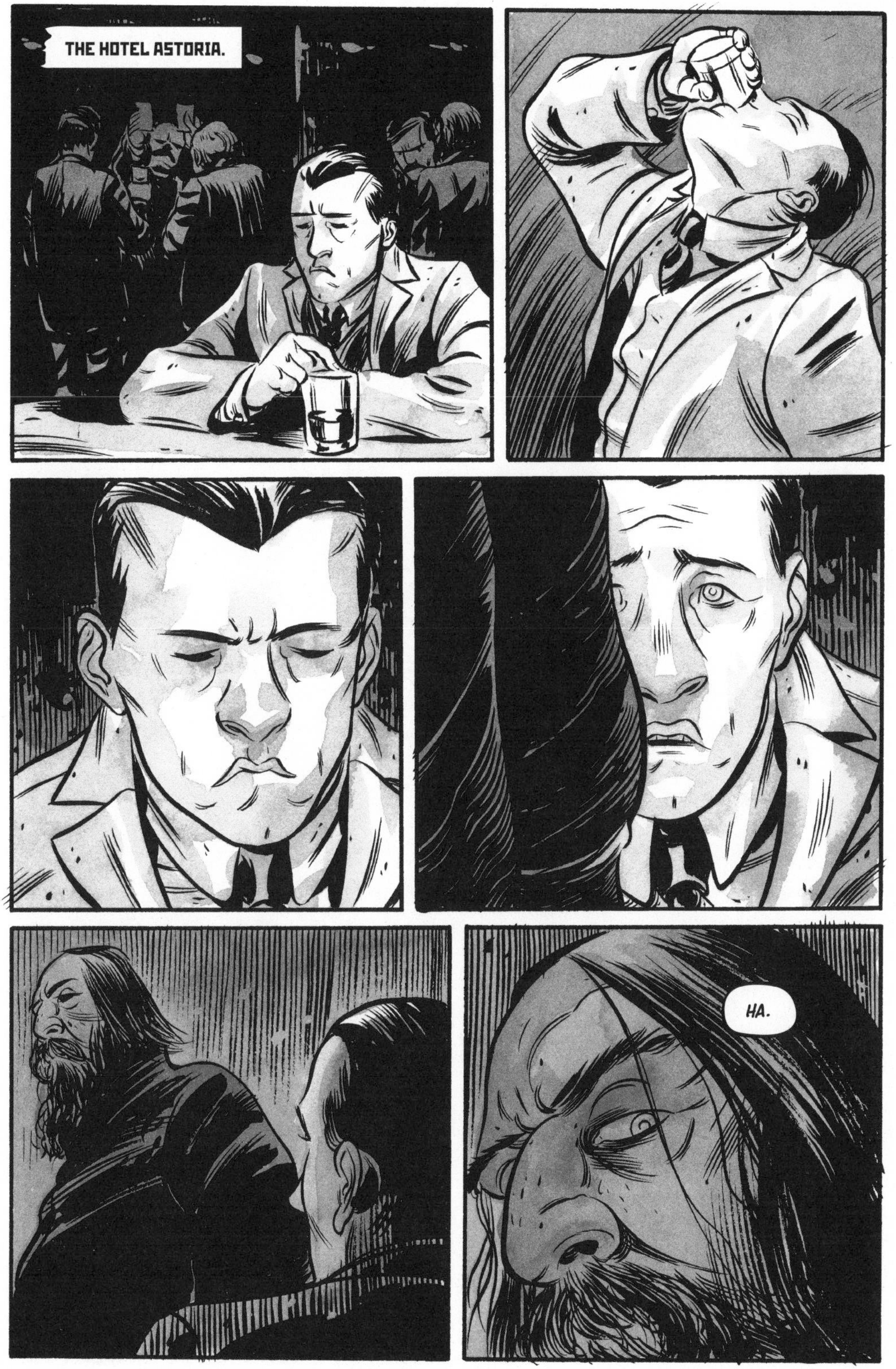
THE HOTEL ASTORIA.
HA.

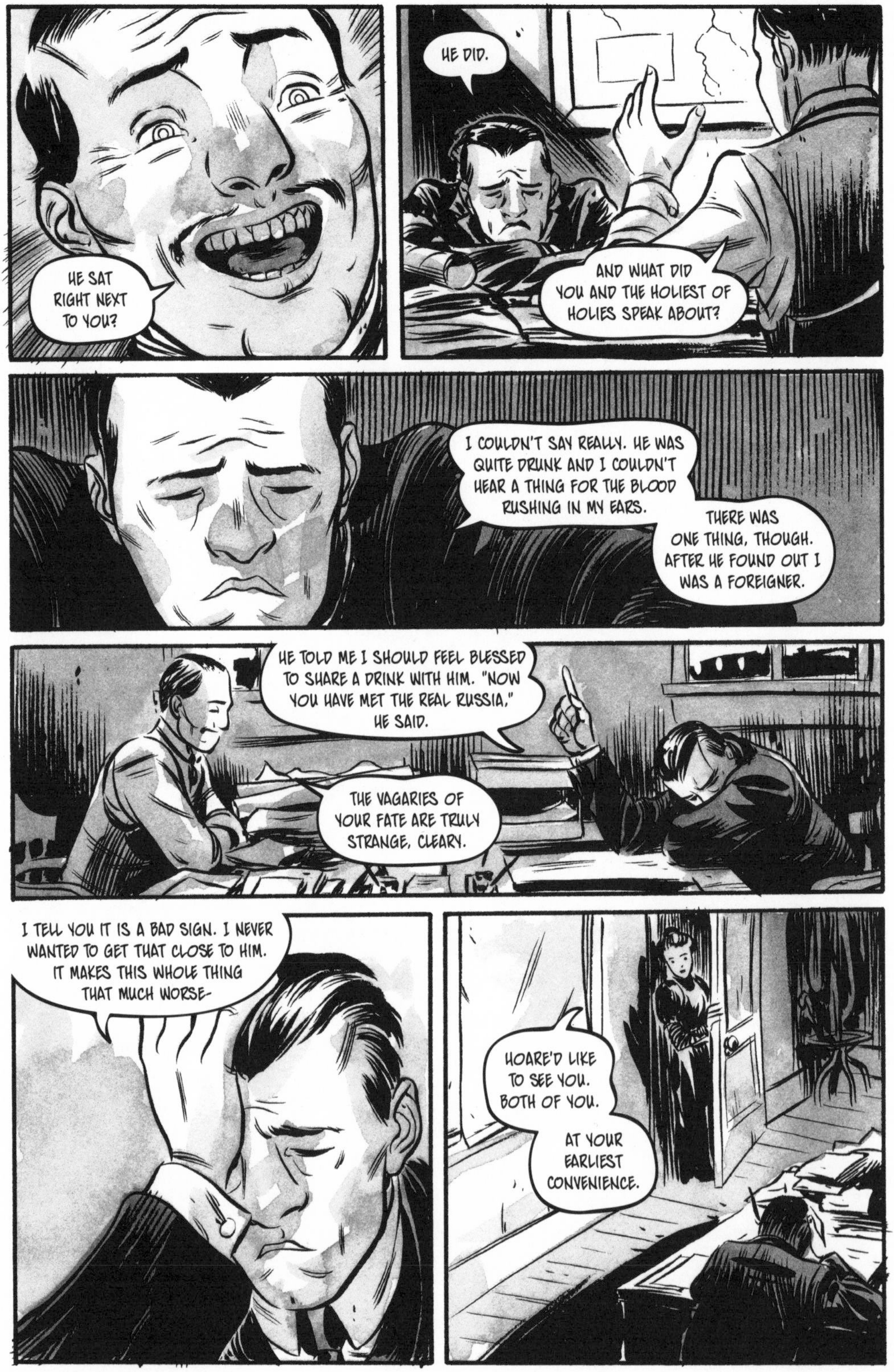
HE SAT RIGHT NEXT TO YOU?
HE DID.
AND WHAT DID YOU AND THE HOLIEST OF HOLIES SPEAK ABOUT?
I COULDN'T SAY REALLY. HE WAS QUITE DRUNK AND I COULDN'T HEAR A THING FOR THE BLOOD RUSHING IN MY EARS.
THERE WAS ONE THING, THOUGH. AFTER HE FOUND OUT I WAS A FOREIGNER.
HE TOLD ME I SHOULD FEEL BLESSED TO SHARE A DRINK WITH HIM. "NOW YOU HAVE MET THE REAL RUSSIA," HE SAID.
THE VAGARIES OF YOUR FATE ARE TRULY STRANGE, CLEARY.
I TELL YOU IT IS A BAD SIGN. I NEVER WANTED TO GET THAT CLOSE TO HIM. IT MAKES THIS WHOLE THING THAT MUCH WORSE-
HOARE'D LIKE TO SEE YOU. BOTH OF YOU.
AT YOUR EARLIEST CONVENIENCE.

YOU TWO ARE *THE* INTELLIGENCE MISSION IN PETROGRAD, YES?

WHILE MY EARS DO NOT EXTEND BEYOND THIS OFFICE, YOURS ARE EVERYWHERE, CORRECT?

YOU FLATTER US, SIR.

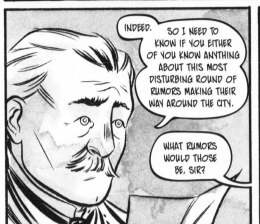

INDEED. SO I NEED TO KNOW IF YOU EITHER OF YOU KNOW ANYTHING ABOUT THIS MOST DISTURBING ROUND OF RUMORS MAKING THEIR WAY AROUND THE CITY.

WHAT RUMORS WOULD THOSE BE, SIR?

CONSPIRACY, ALLEY.

PARDON ME, BUT CONSPIRACY IS THE TURBINE THAT MAKES THIS CITY RUN. COULD YOU BE MORE SPECIFIC?

CERTAINLY, ALLEY. THESE RUMORS CONCERN A CONSPIRACY TO MURDER THIS RASPUTIN FELLOW...

...A CONSPIRACY INVOLVING NOBLES, DUMA MEMBERS...

AND MEMBERS OF THE BRITISH MISSION IN PETROGRAD. *THIS* OFFICE.

I THINK, SIR...

WE DON'T KNOW ANYTHING ABOUT IT.

ANY PLOT THAT GOES THROUGH THIS OFFICE GOES THROUGH YOU.

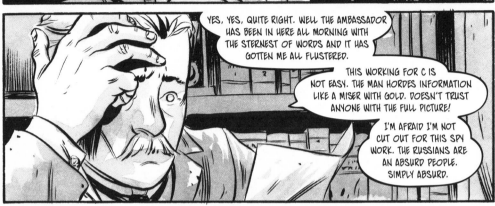

YES, YES, QUITE RIGHT. WELL THE AMBASSADOR HAS BEEN IN HERE ALL MORNING WITH THE STERNEST OF WORDS AND IT HAS GOTTEN ME ALL FLUSTERED.

THIS WORKING FOR C IS NOT EASY. THE MAN HORDES INFORMATION LIKE A MISER WITH GOLD. DOESN'T TRUST ANYONE WITH THE FULL PICTURE!

I'M AFRAID I'M NOT CUT OUT FOR THIS SPY WORK. THE RUSSIANS ARE AN ABSURD PEOPLE. SIMPLY ABSURD.

DAMNED UNGENTLEMANLY BUSINESS. ALL OF THIS.

I CURSE THE DAY I WAS HANDED THIS POST.

PERHAPS YOU WOULD LIKE US TO LOOK INTO THIS RUMOR, SIR?

RASPUTIN HAS ENEMIES EVERYWHERE I DON'T DOUBT THAT THERE IS AT LEAST ONE PLOT TO KILL HIM CURRENTLY GOING.

YES... YES... THAT MIGHT BE WORTHWHILE.

PERHAPS IF YOU FOUND ANYTHING OUT, WE COULD USE IT TO GET SOMETHING FROM THE RUSSIANS.

THE PLOT STEMS FROM A FRIEND OF YOURS, CLEARY. THIS FELIX YUSSUPOV FELLOW.

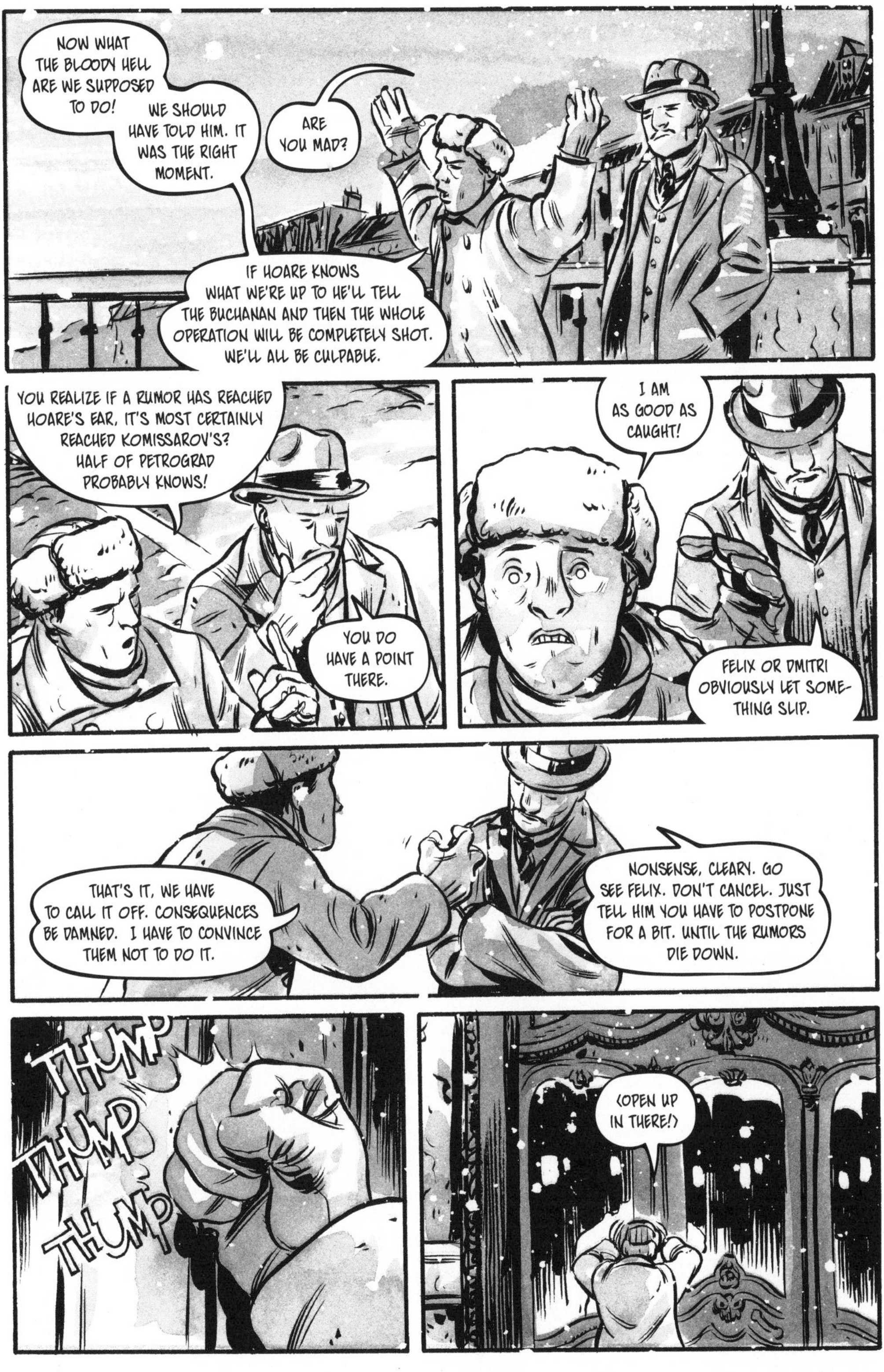

NOW WHAT THE BLOODY HELL ARE WE SUPPOSED TO DO!
WE SHOULD HAVE TOLD HIM. IT WAS THE RIGHT MOMENT.
ARE YOU MAD?
IF HOARE KNOWS WHAT WE'RE UP TO HE'LL TELL THE BUCHANAN AND THEN THE WHOLE OPERATION WILL BE COMPLETELY SHOT. WE'LL ALL BE CULPABLE.
YOU REALIZE IF A RUMOR HAS REACHED HOARE'S EAR, IT'S MOST CERTAINLY REACHED KOMISSAROV'S? HALF OF PETROGRAD PROBABLY KNOWS!
YOU DO HAVE A POINT THERE.
I AM AS GOOD AS CAUGHT!
FELIX OR DMITRI OBVIOUSLY LET SOME-THING SLIP.
THAT'S IT, WE HAVE TO CALL IT OFF. CONSEQUENCES BE DAMNED. I HAVE TO CONVINCE THEM NOT TO DO IT.
NONSENSE, CLEARY. GO SEE FELIX. DON'T CANCEL. JUST TELL HIM YOU HAVE TO POSTPONE FOR A BIT. UNTIL THE RUMORS DIE DOWN.
THUMP
THUMP
THUMP
<OPEN UP IN THERE!>

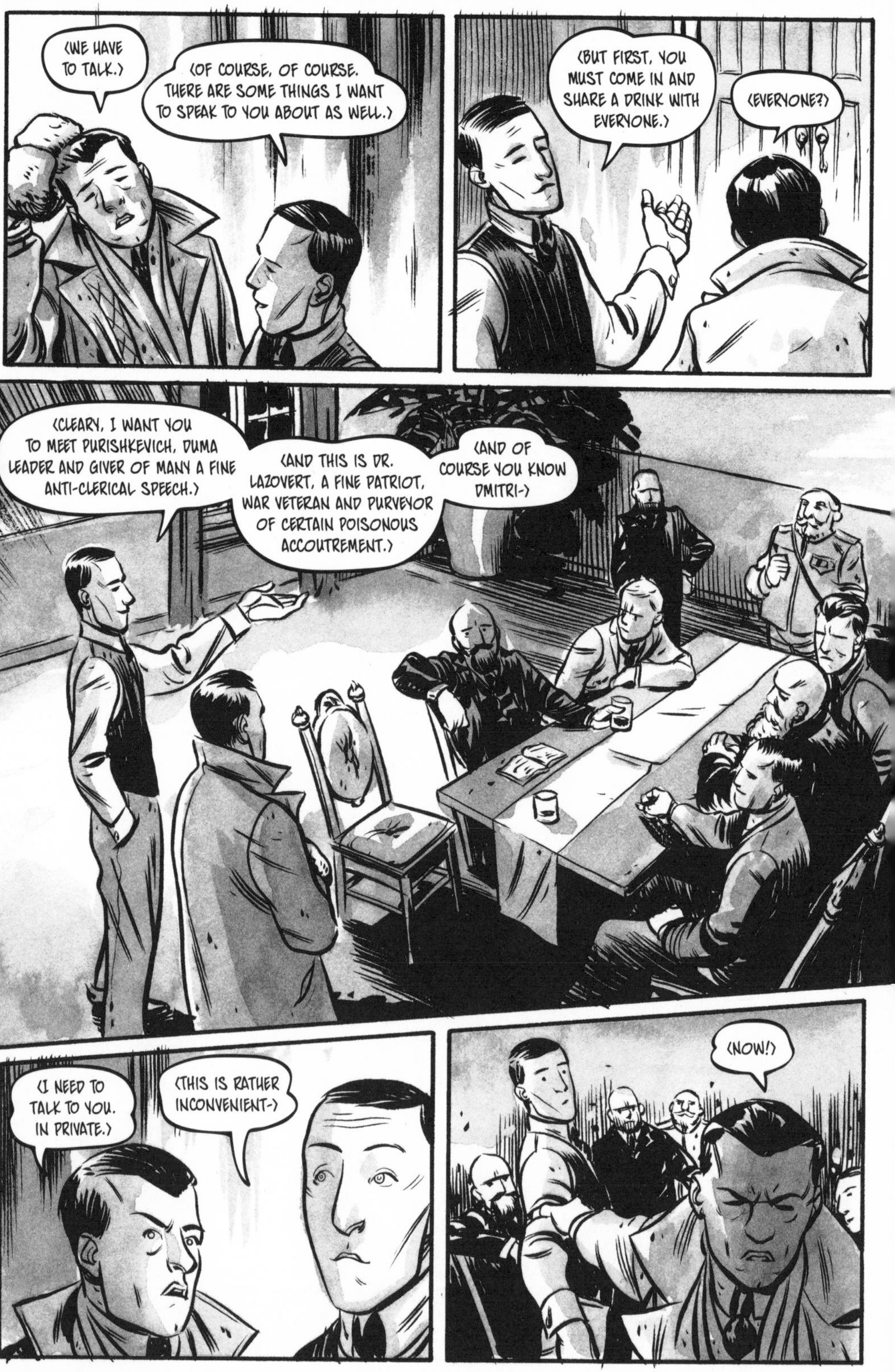
‹WE HAVE TO TALK.›
‹OF COURSE, OF COURSE. THERE ARE SOME THINGS I WANT TO SPEAK TO YOU ABOUT AS WELL.›
‹BUT FIRST, YOU MUST COME IN AND SHARE A DRINK WITH EVERYONE.›
‹EVERYONE?›
‹CLEARY, I WANT YOU TO MEET PURISHKEVICH, DUMA LEADER AND GIVER OF MANY A FINE ANTI-CLERICAL SPEECH.›
‹AND THIS IS DR. LAZOVERT, A FINE PATRIOT, WAR VETERAN AND PURVEYOR OF CERTAIN POISONOUS ACCOUTREMENT.›
‹AND OF COURSE YOU KNOW DMITRI-›
‹I NEED TO TALK TO YOU. IN PRIVATE.›
‹THIS IS RATHER INCONVENIENT-›
‹NOW!›

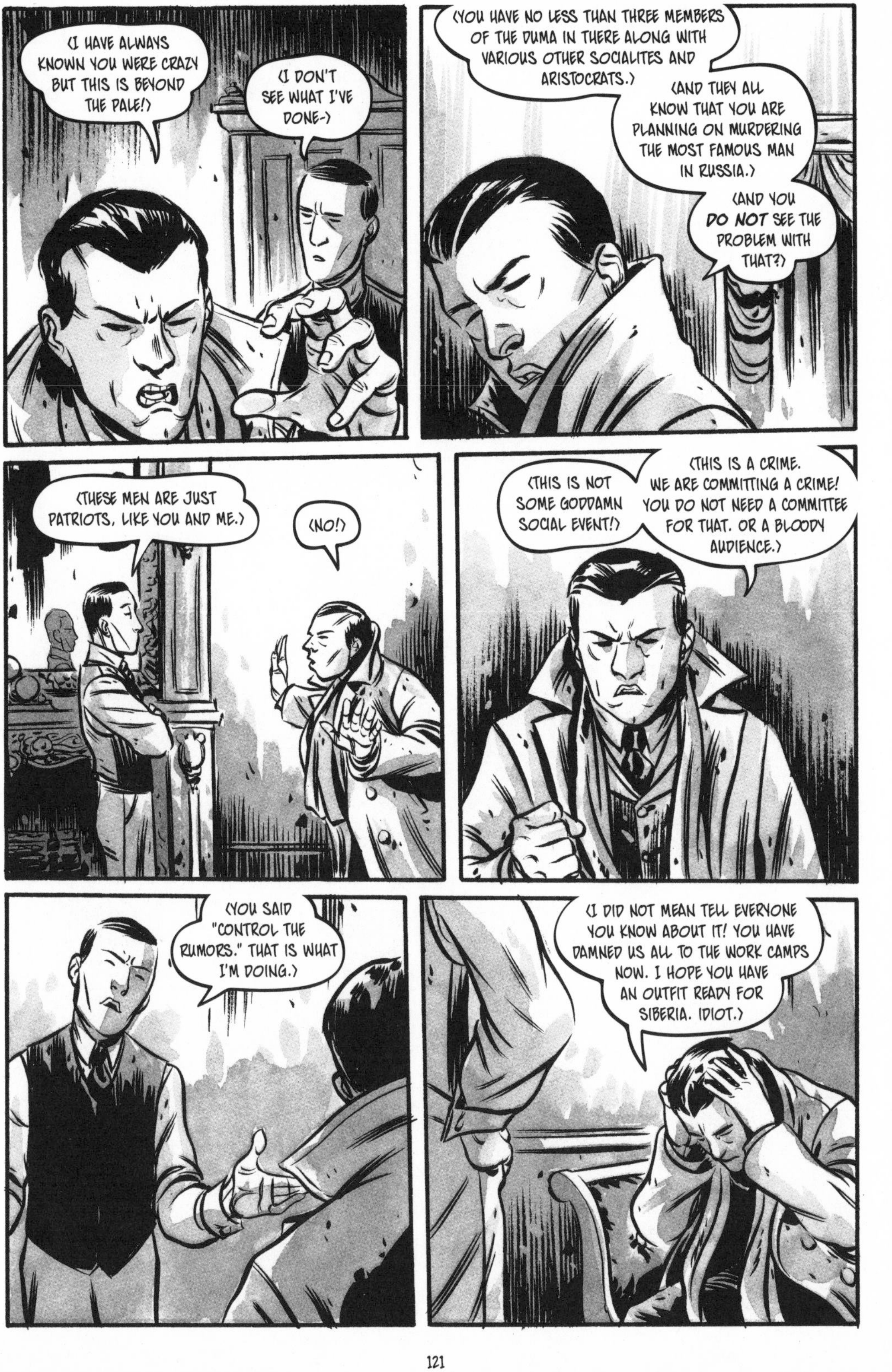

(I HAVE ALWAYS KNOWN YOU WERE CRAZY BUT THIS IS BEYOND THE PALE!)
(I DON'T SEE WHAT I'VE DONE-)
(YOU HAVE NO LESS THAN THREE MEMBERS OF THE DUMA IN THERE ALONG WITH VARIOUS OTHER SOCIALITES AND ARISTOCRATS.)
(AND THEY ALL KNOW THAT YOU ARE PLANNING ON MURDERING THE MOST FAMOUS MAN IN RUSSIA.)
(AND YOU **DO NOT** SEE THE PROBLEM WITH THAT?)
(THESE MEN ARE JUST PATRIOTS, LIKE YOU AND ME.)
(NO!)
(THIS IS NOT SOME GODDAMN SOCIAL EVENT!)
(THIS IS A CRIME. WE ARE COMMITTING A CRIME! YOU DO NOT NEED A COMMITTEE FOR THAT. OR A BLOODY AUDIENCE.)
(YOU SAID "CONTROL THE RUMORS." THAT IS WHAT I'M DOING.)
(I DID NOT MEAN TELL EVERYONE YOU KNOW ABOUT IT! YOU HAVE DAMNED US ALL TO THE WORK CAMPS NOW. I HOPE YOU HAVE AN OUTFIT READY FOR SIBERIA. IDIOT.)

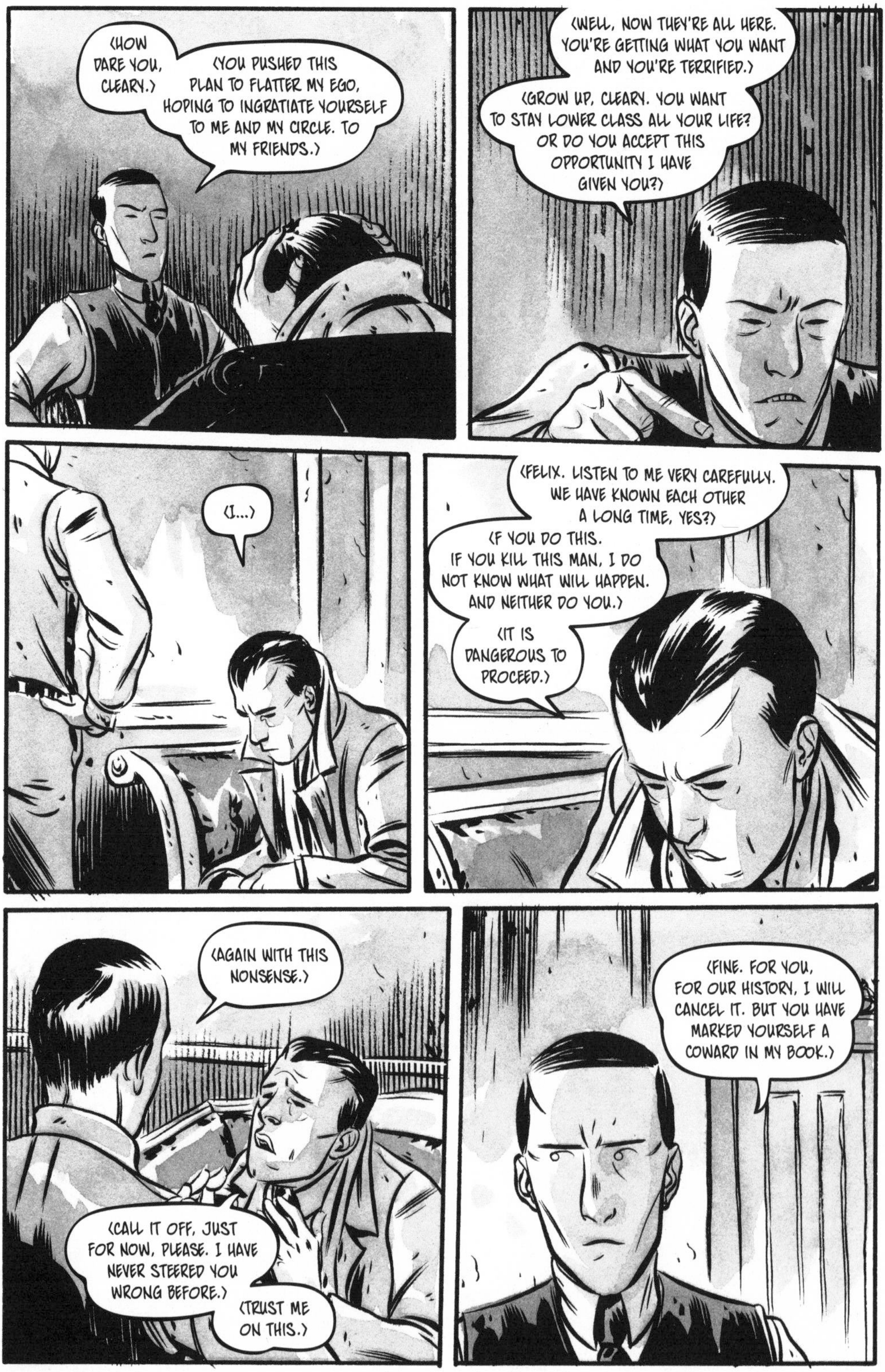
‹HOW DARE YOU, CLEARY.›
‹YOU PUSHED THIS PLAN TO FLATTER MY EGO, HOPING TO INGRATIATE YOURSELF TO ME AND MY CIRCLE. TO MY FRIENDS.›
‹WELL, NOW THEY'RE ALL HERE. YOU'RE GETTING WHAT YOU WANT AND YOU'RE TERRIFIED.›
‹GROW UP, CLEARY. YOU WANT TO STAY LOWER CLASS ALL YOUR LIFE? OR DO YOU ACCEPT THIS OPPORTUNITY I HAVE GIVEN YOU?›
‹I...›
‹FELIX. LISTEN TO ME VERY CAREFULLY. WE HAVE KNOWN EACH OTHER A LONG TIME, YES?›
‹IF YOU DO THIS. IF YOU KILL THIS MAN, I DO NOT KNOW WHAT WILL HAPPEN. AND NEITHER DO YOU.›
‹IT IS DANGEROUS TO PROCEED.›
‹AGAIN WITH THIS NONSENSE.›
‹CALL IT OFF, JUST FOR NOW, PLEASE. I HAVE NEVER STEERED YOU WRONG BEFORE.›
‹TRUST ME ON THIS.›
‹FINE. FOR YOU, FOR OUR HISTORY, I WILL CANCEL IT. BUT YOU HAVE MARKED YOURSELF A COWARD IN MY BOOK.›

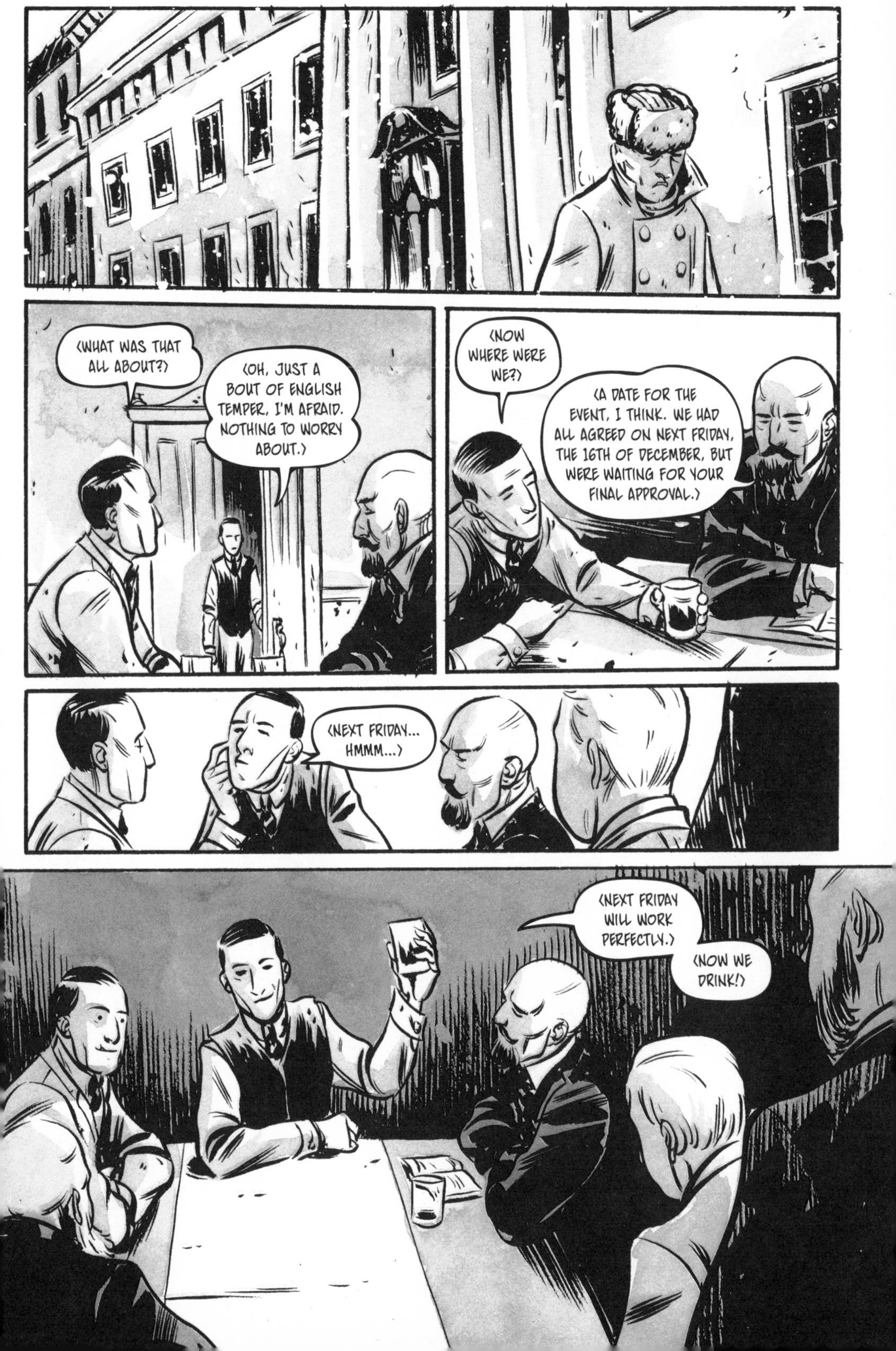

‹WHAT WAS THAT ALL ABOUT?›
‹OH, JUST A BOUT OF ENGLISH TEMPER, I'M AFRAID. NOTHING TO WORRY ABOUT.›
‹NOW WHERE WERE WE?›
‹A DATE FOR THE EVENT, I THINK. WE HAD ALL AGREED ON NEXT FRIDAY, THE 16TH OF DECEMBER, BUT WERE WAITING FOR YOUR FINAL APPROVAL.›
‹NEXT FRIDAY... HMMM...›
‹NEXT FRIDAY WILL WORK PERFECTLY.›
‹NOW WE DRINK!›

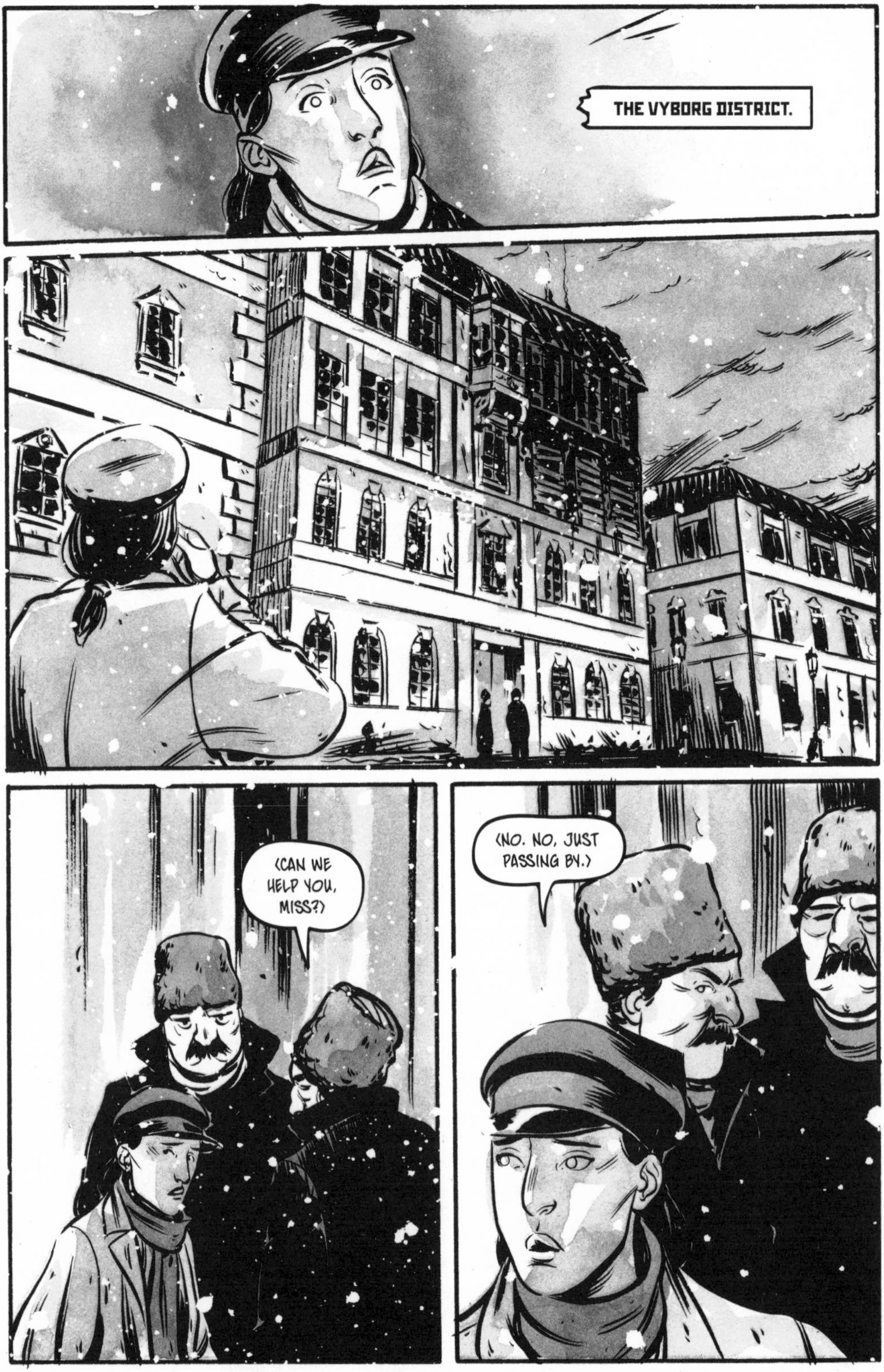
THE VYBORG DISTRICT.
‹CAN WE HELP YOU, MISS?›
‹NO. NO, JUST PASSING BY.›

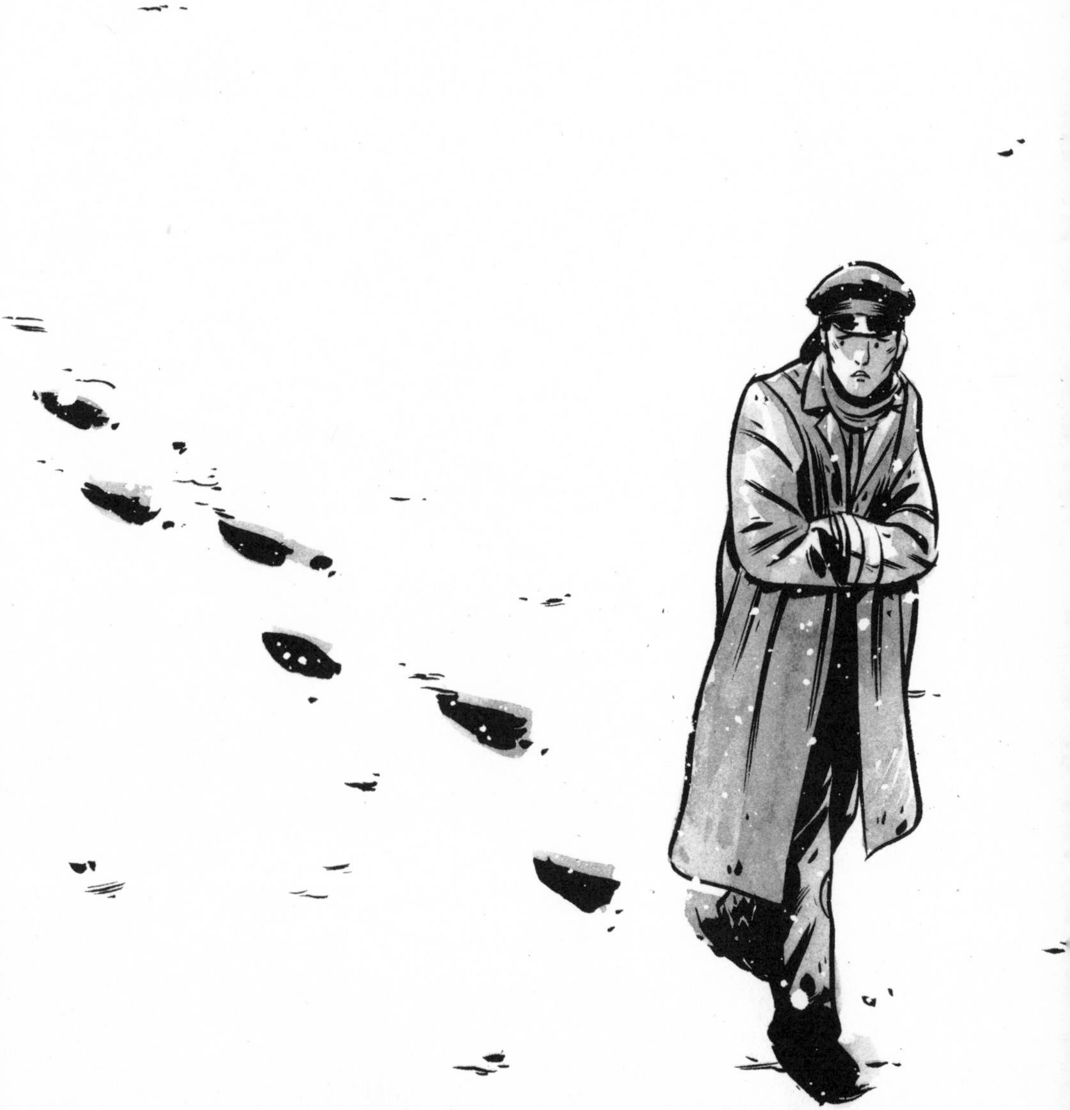

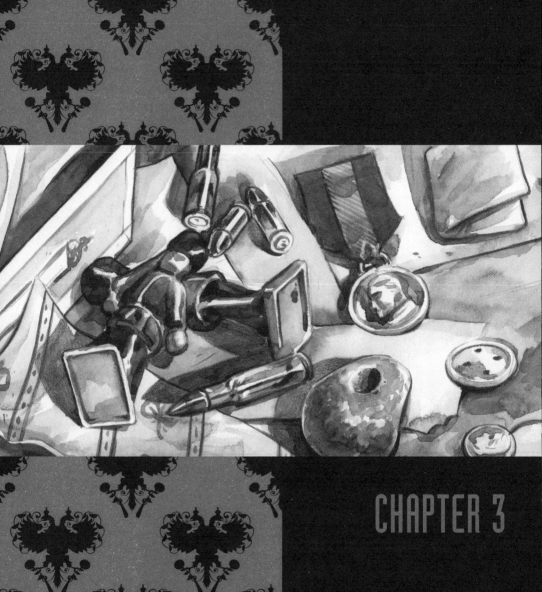

CHAPTER 3

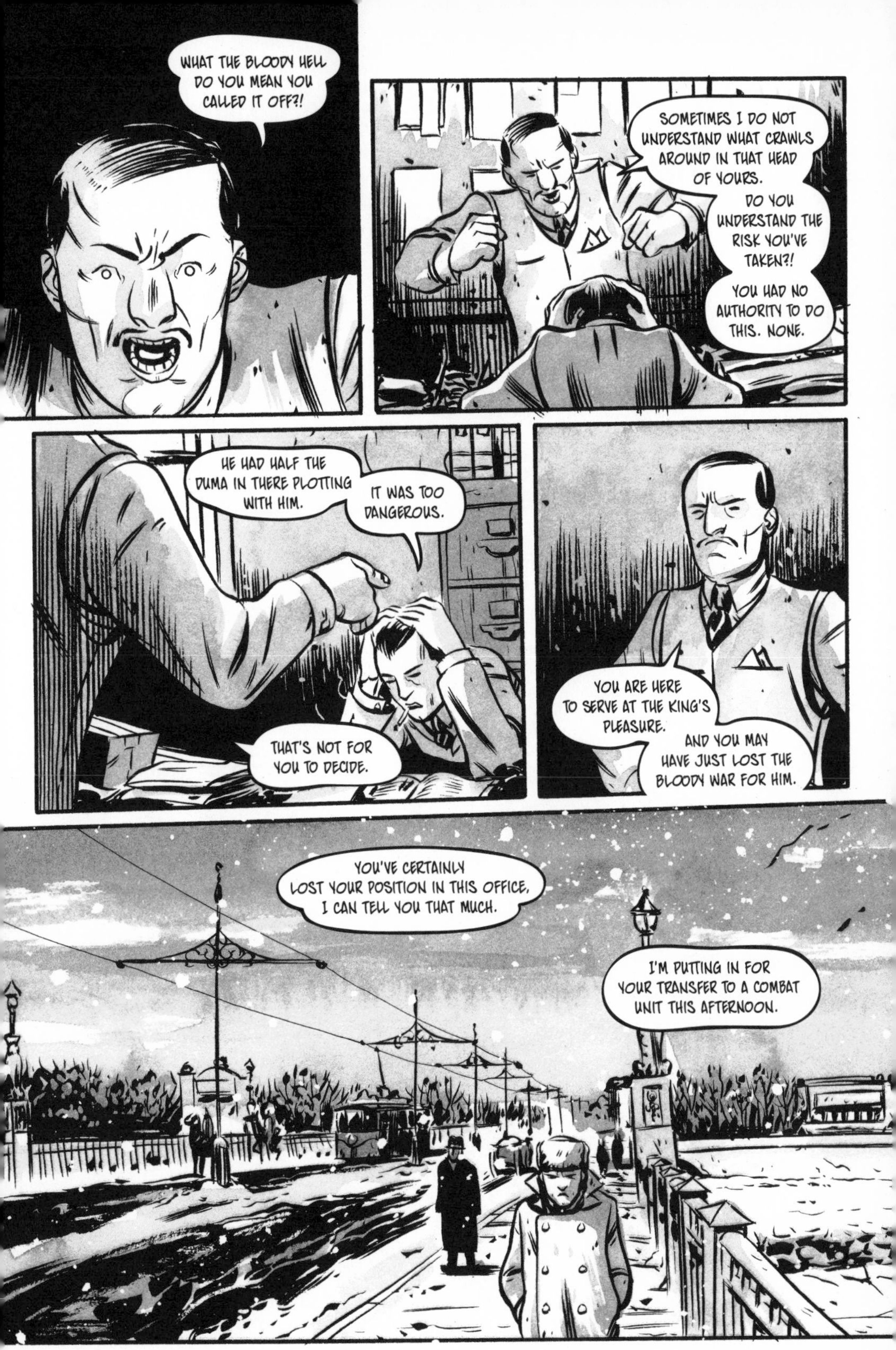
WHAT THE BLOODY HELL DO YOU MEAN YOU CALLED IT OFF?!
SOMETIMES I DO NOT UNDERSTAND WHAT CRAWLS AROUND IN THAT HEAD OF YOURS.
DO YOU UNDERSTAND THE RISK YOU'VE TAKEN?!
YOU HAD NO AUTHORITY TO DO THIS. NONE.
HE HAD HALF THE DUMA IN THERE PLOTTING WITH HIM.
IT WAS TOO DANGEROUS.
THAT'S NOT FOR YOU TO DECIDE.
YOU ARE HERE TO SERVE AT THE KING'S PLEASURE.
AND YOU MAY HAVE JUST LOST THE BLOODY WAR FOR HIM.
YOU'VE CERTAINLY LOST YOUR POSITION IN THIS OFFICE, I CAN TELL YOU THAT MUCH.
I'M PUTTING IN FOR YOUR TRANSFER TO A COMBAT UNIT THIS AFTERNOON.

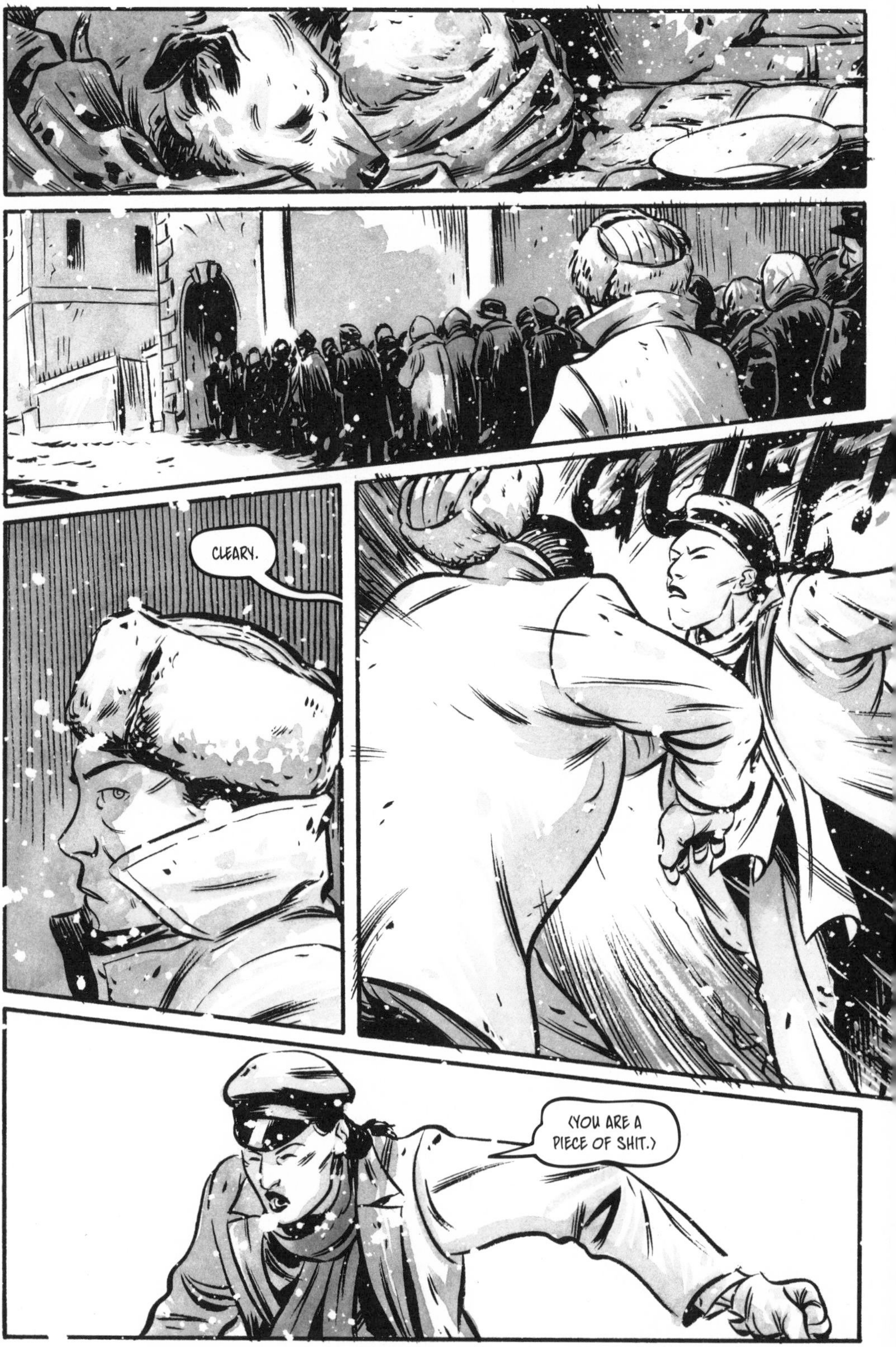
CLEARY.
(YOU ARE A PIECE OF SHIT.)

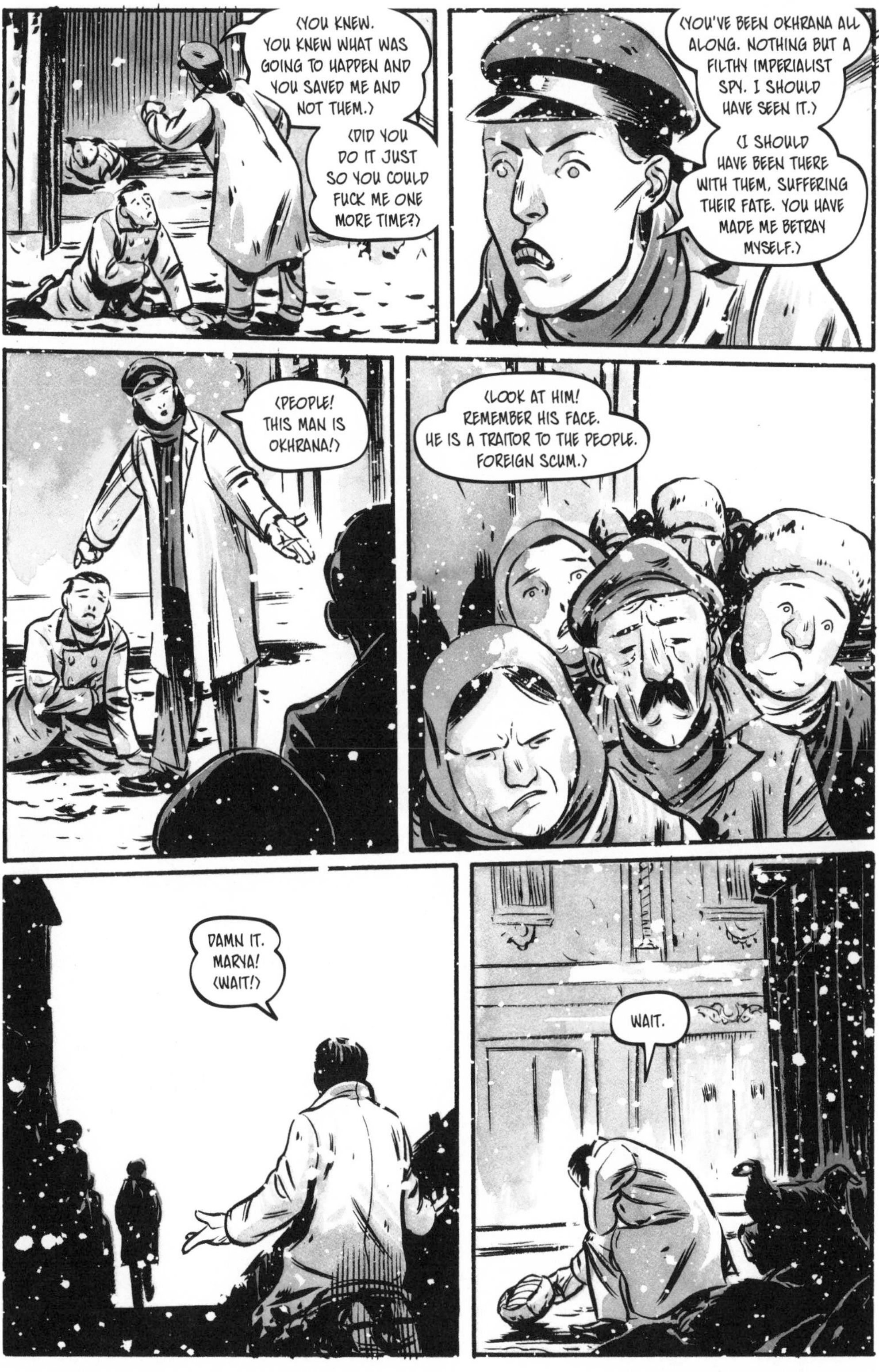

‹YOU KNEW. YOU KNEW WHAT WAS GOING TO HAPPEN AND YOU SAVED ME AND NOT THEM.›
‹DID YOU DO IT JUST SO YOU COULD FUCK ME ONE MORE TIME?›
‹YOU'VE BEEN OKHRANA ALL ALONG. NOTHING BUT A FILTHY IMPERIALIST SPY. I SHOULD HAVE SEEN IT.›
‹I SHOULD HAVE BEEN THERE WITH THEM, SUFFERING THEIR FATE. YOU HAVE MADE ME BETRAY MYSELF.›
‹PEOPLE! THIS MAN IS OKHRANA!›
‹LOOK AT HIM! REMEMBER HIS FACE. HE IS A TRAITOR TO THE PEOPLE. FOREIGN SCUM.›
DAMN IT. MARYA! ‹WAIT!›
WAIT.

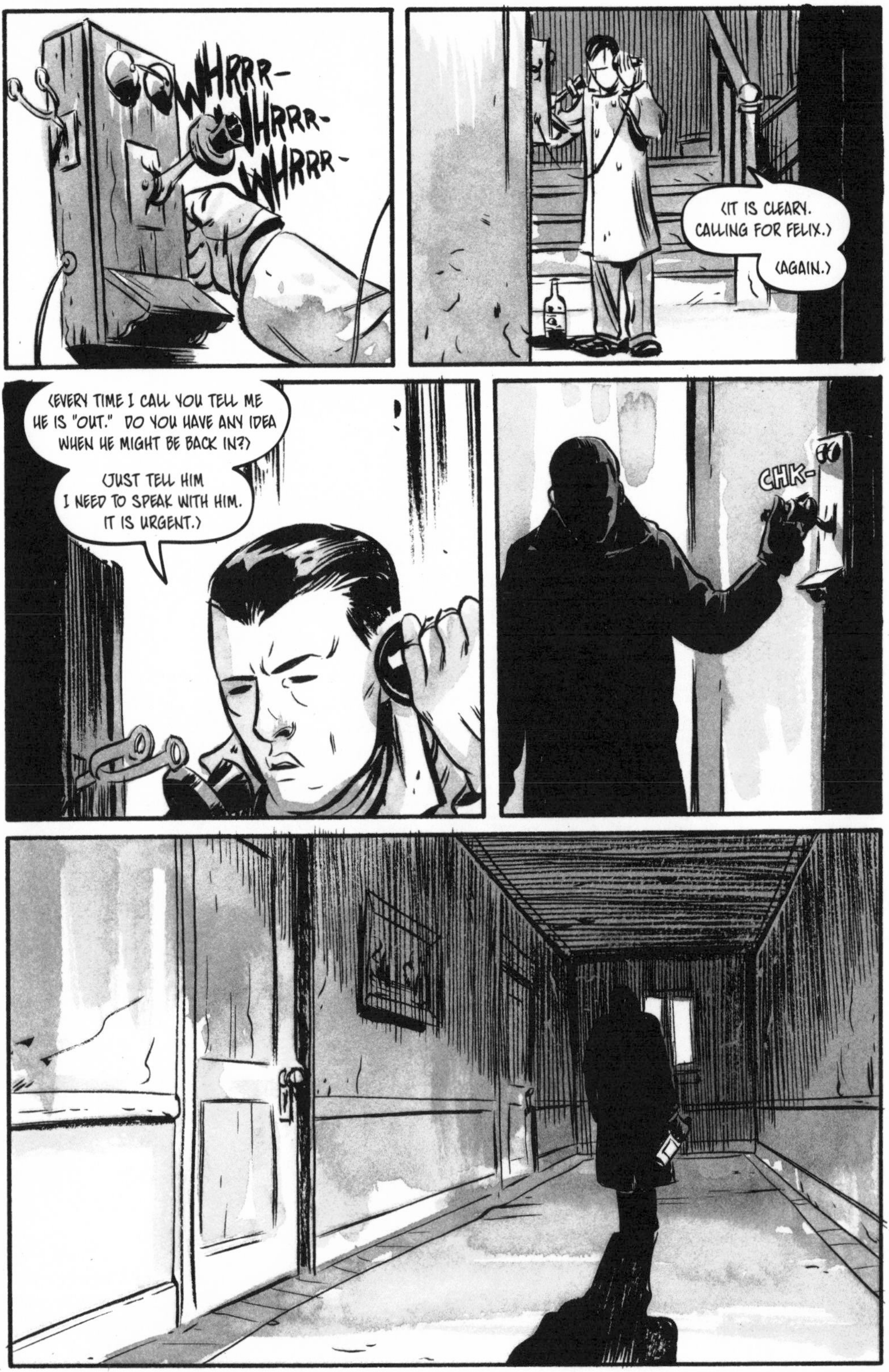
WHRRR-
WHRRR-
WHRRR-
‹IT IS CLEARY. CALLING FOR FELIX.›
‹AGAIN.›
‹EVERY TIME I CALL YOU TELL ME HE IS "OUT." DO YOU HAVE ANY IDEA WHEN HE MIGHT BE BACK IN?›
‹JUST TELL HIM I NEED TO SPEAK WITH HIM. IT IS URGENT.›
CHK-

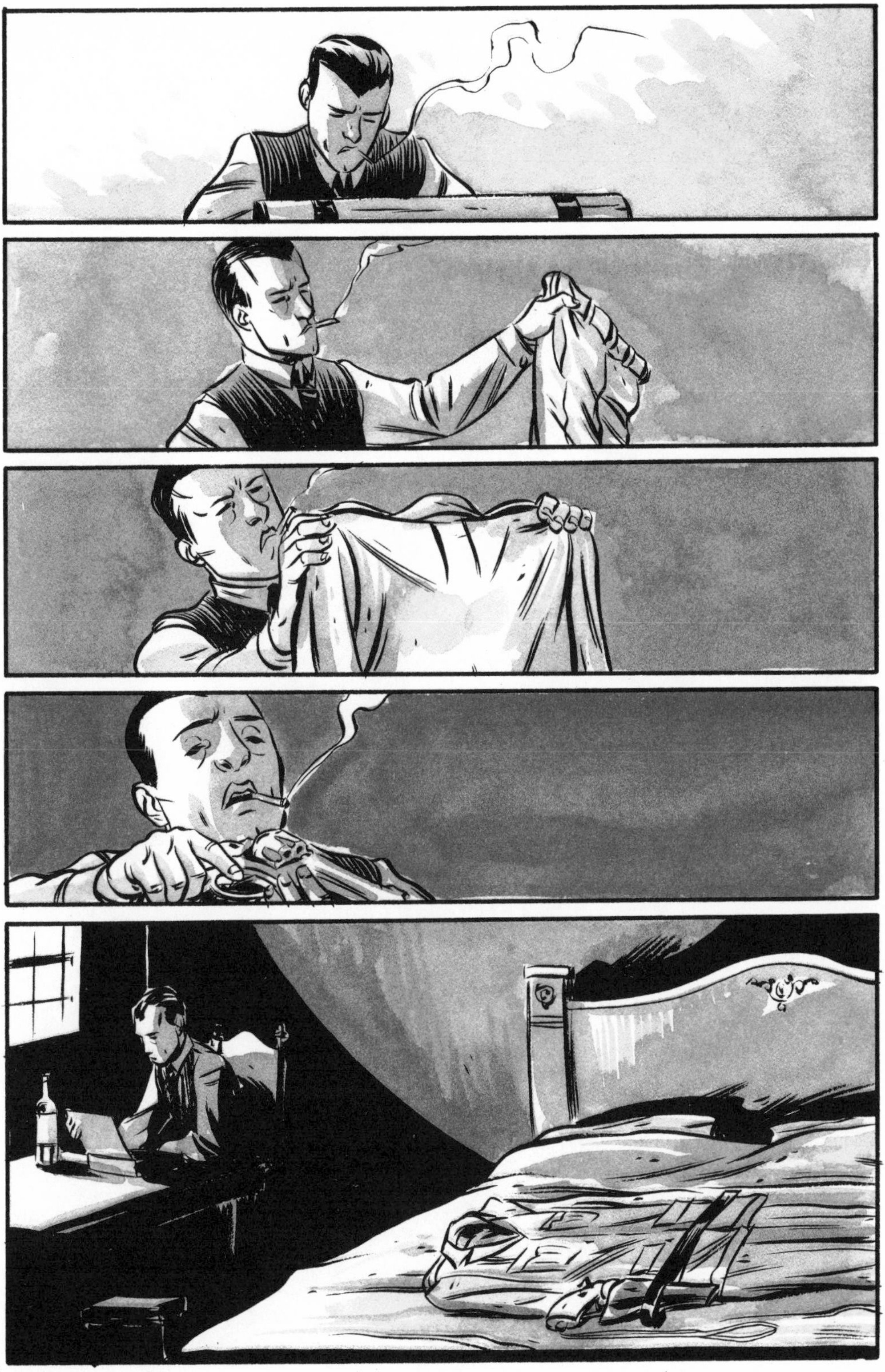

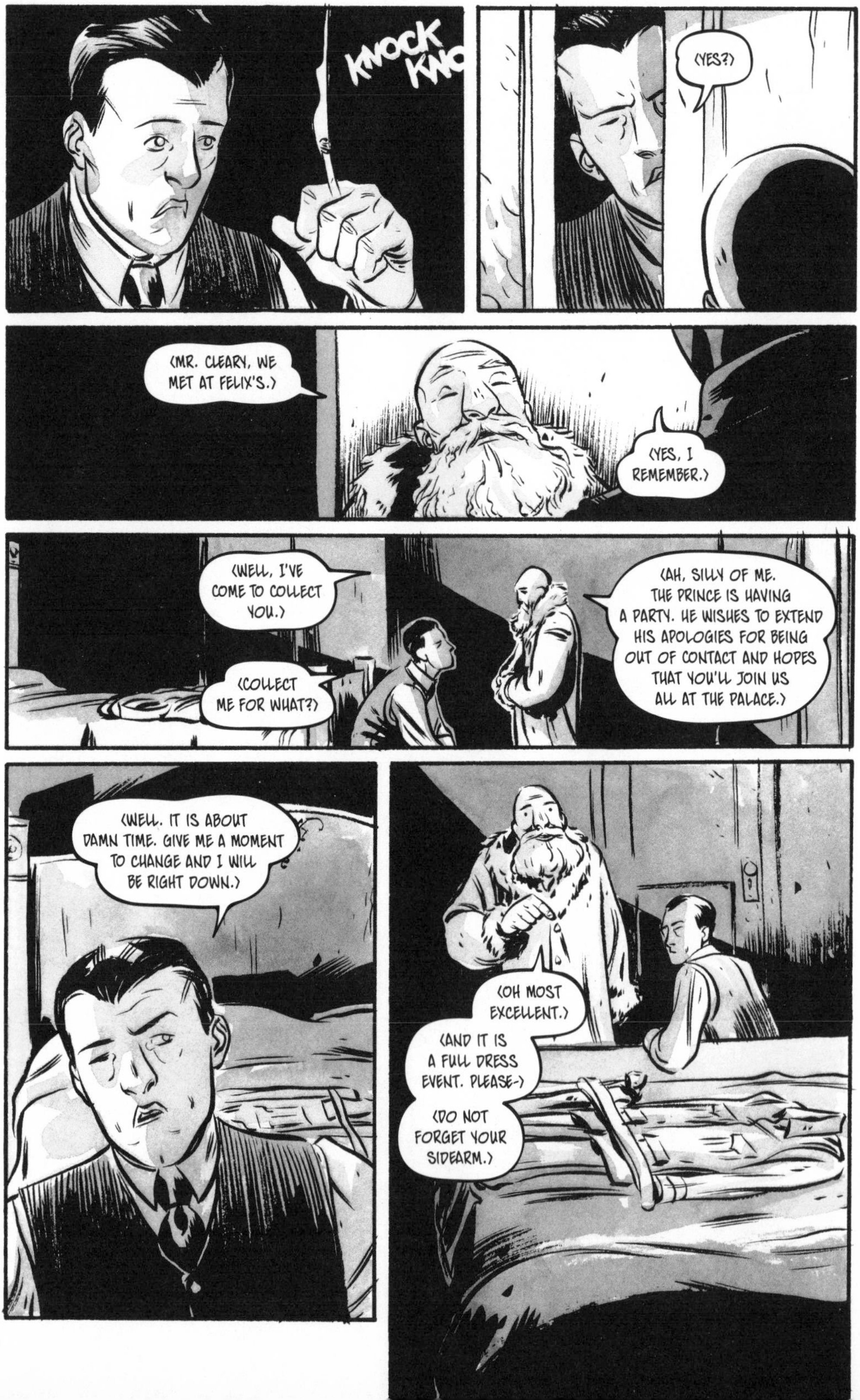
KNOCK KNO
⟨YES?⟩
⟨MR. CLEARY, WE MET AT FELIX'S.⟩
⟨YES, I REMEMBER.⟩
⟨WELL, I'VE COME TO COLLECT YOU.⟩
⟨COLLECT ME FOR WHAT?⟩
⟨AH, SILLY OF ME. THE PRINCE IS HAVING A PARTY. HE WISHES TO EXTEND HIS APOLOGIES FOR BEING OUT OF CONTACT AND HOPES THAT YOU'LL JOIN US ALL AT THE PALACE.⟩
⟨WELL. IT IS ABOUT DAMN TIME. GIVE ME A MOMENT TO CHANGE AND I WILL BE RIGHT DOWN.⟩
⟨OH MOST EXCELLENT.⟩
⟨AND IT IS A FULL DRESS EVENT. PLEASE-⟩
⟨DO NOT FORGET YOUR SIDEARM.⟩

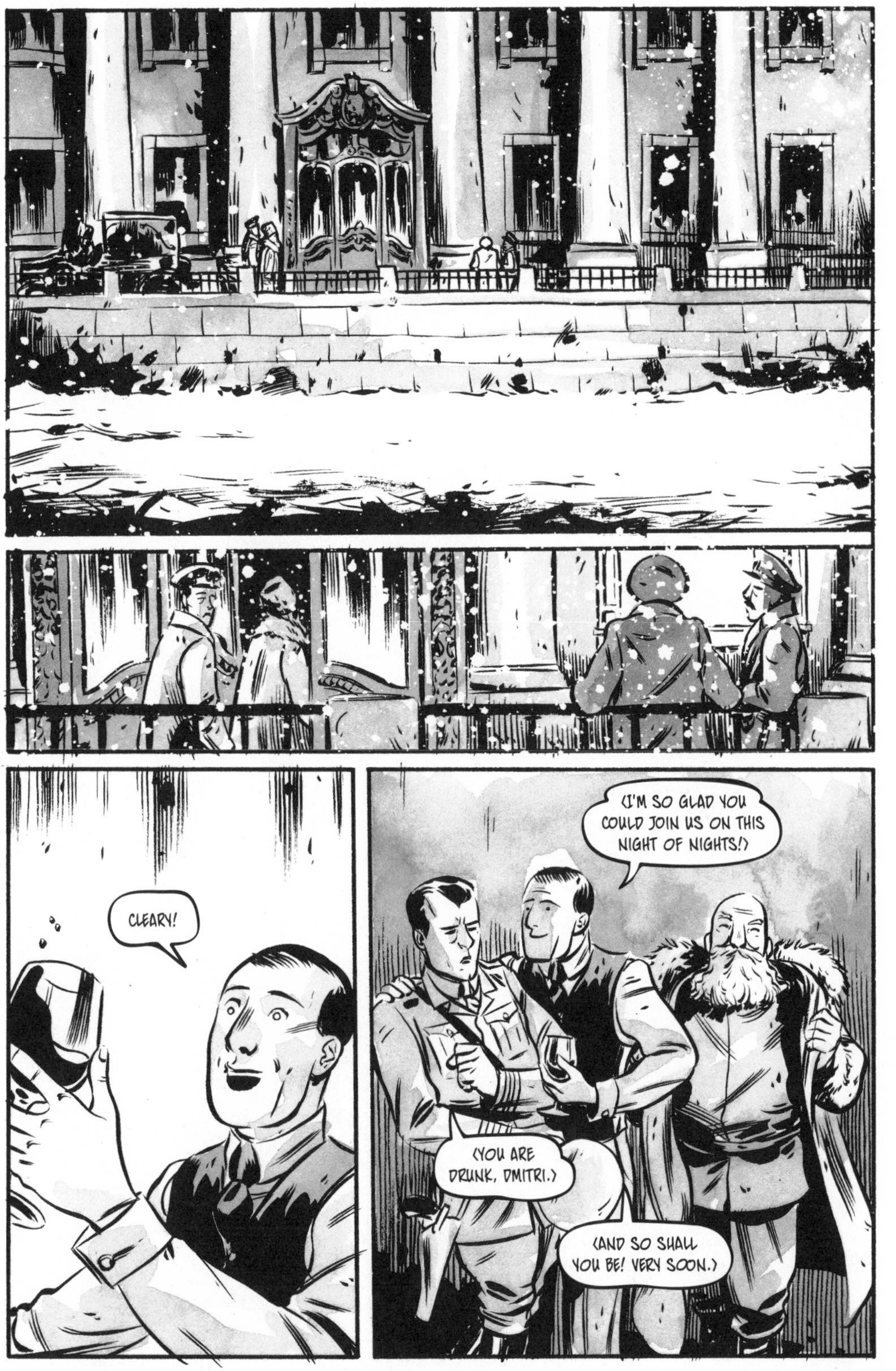
CLEARY!
‹I'M SO GLAD YOU COULD JOIN US ON THIS NIGHT OF NIGHTS!›
‹YOU ARE DRUNK, DMITRI.›
‹AND SO SHALL YOU BE! VERY SOON.›

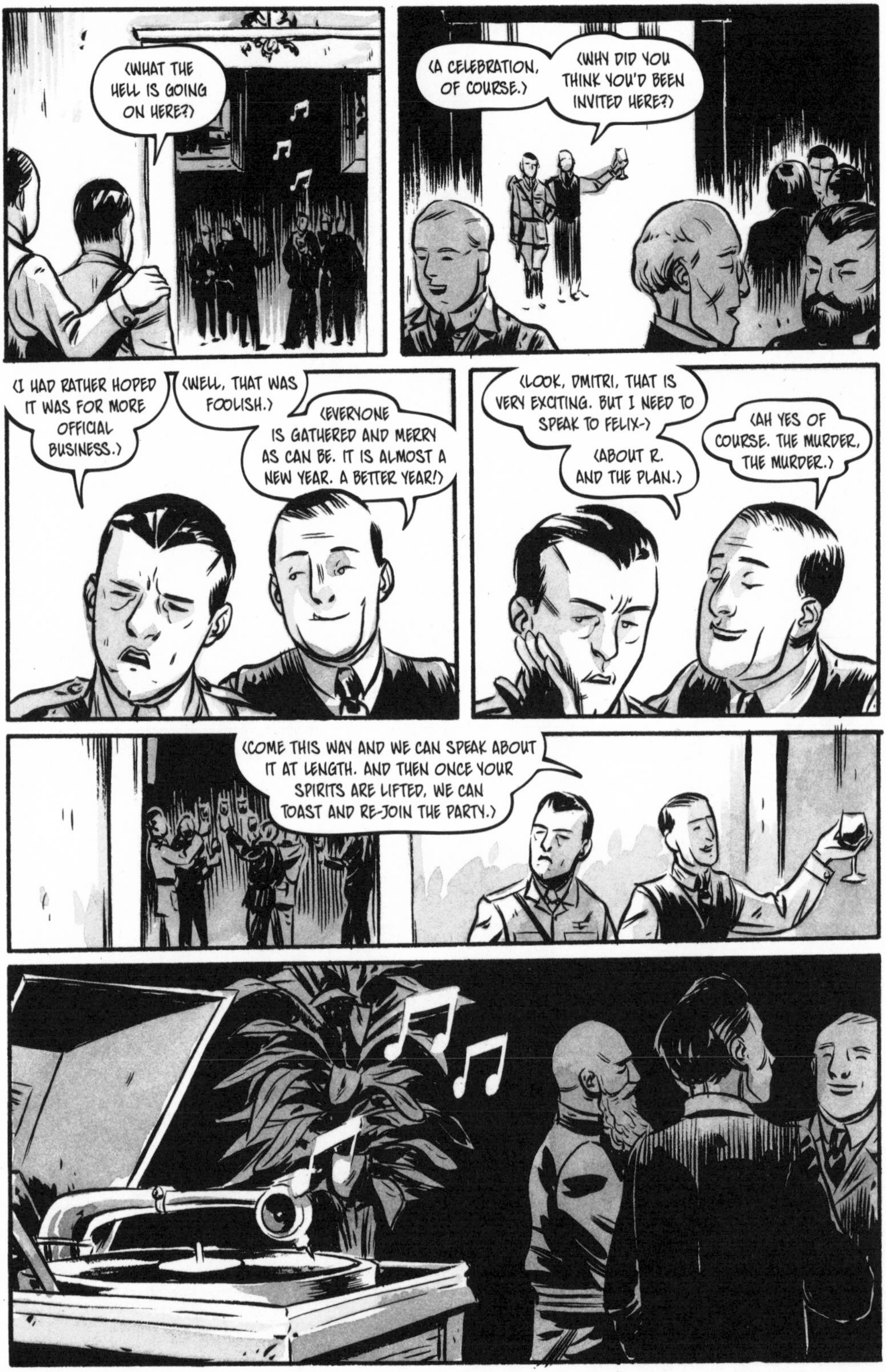

‹WHAT THE HELL IS GOING ON HERE?›
‹A CELEBRATION, OF COURSE.›
‹WHY DID YOU THINK YOU'D BEEN INVITED HERE?›
‹I HAD RATHER HOPED IT WAS FOR MORE OFFICIAL BUSINESS.›
‹WELL, THAT WAS FOOLISH.›
‹EVERYONE IS GATHERED AND MERRY AS CAN BE. IT IS ALMOST A NEW YEAR. A BETTER YEAR!›
‹LOOK, DMITRI, THAT IS VERY EXCITING. BUT I NEED TO SPEAK TO FELIX-›
‹ABOUT R. AND THE PLAN.›
‹AH YES OF COURSE. THE MURDER, THE MURDER.›
‹COME THIS WAY AND WE CAN SPEAK ABOUT IT AT LENGTH. AND THEN ONCE YOUR SPIRITS ARE LIFTED, WE CAN TOAST AND RE-JOIN THE PARTY.›

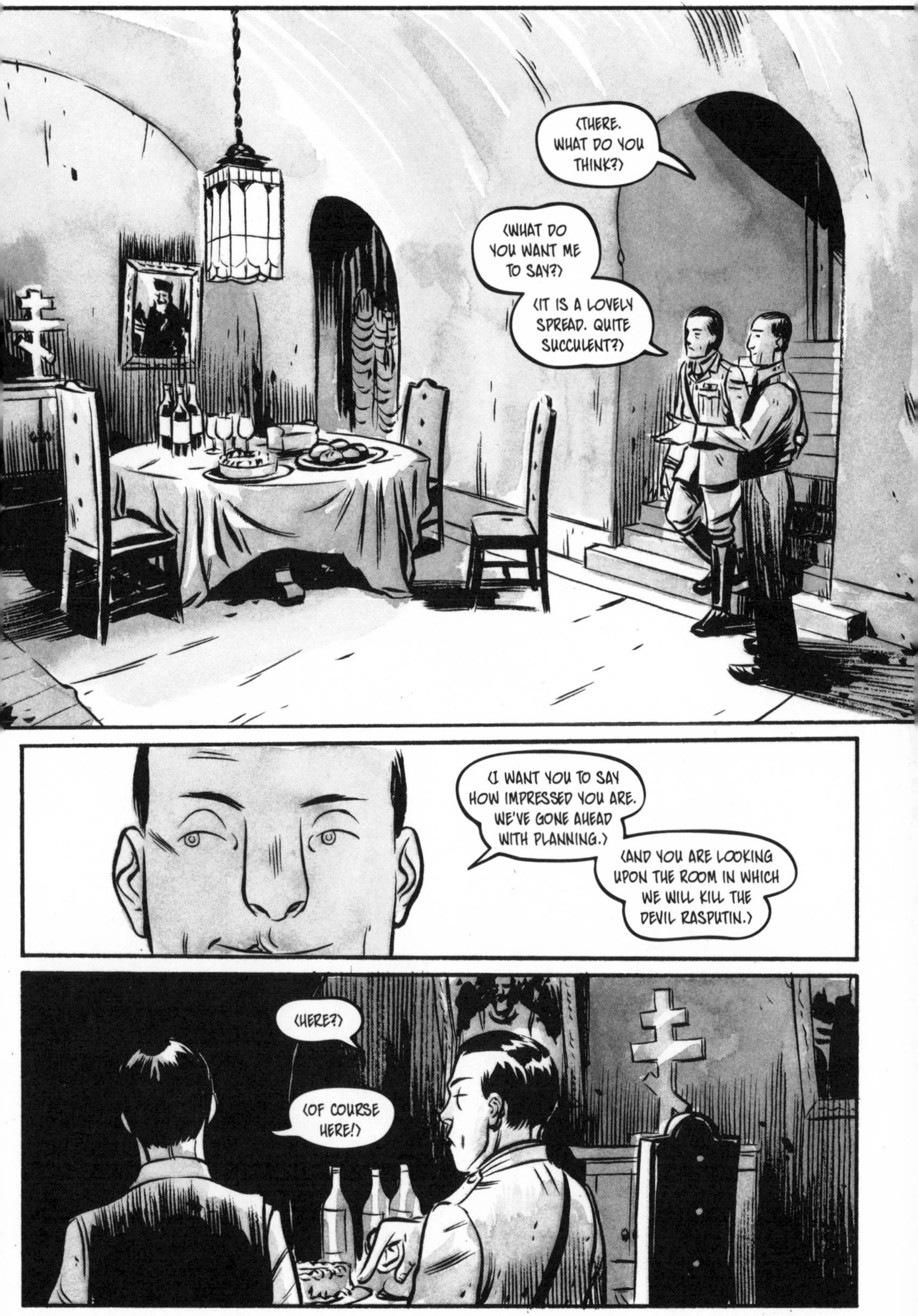

‹THERE. WHAT DO YOU THINK?›
‹WHAT DO YOU WANT ME TO SAY?›
‹IT IS A LOVELY SPREAD. QUITE SUCCULENT?›
‹I WANT YOU TO SAY HOW IMPRESSED YOU ARE. WE'VE GONE AHEAD WITH PLANNING.›
‹AND YOU ARE LOOKING UPON THE ROOM IN WHICH WE WILL KILL THE DEVIL RASPUTIN.›
‹HERE?›
‹OF COURSE HERE!›

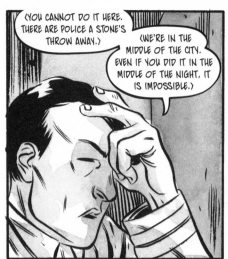

〈YOU CANNOT DO IT HERE. THERE ARE POLICE A STONE'S THROW AWAY.〉

〈WE'RE IN THE MIDDLE OF THE CITY. EVEN IF YOU DID IT IN THE MIDDLE OF THE NIGHT, IT IS IMPOSSIBLE.〉

〈POISON, CLEARY. POTASSIUM CYANIDE, OR SOME SUCH, IN HIS WINE AS WELL AS LACED INTO SWEET CAKES. HE'LL BE DEAD AFTER A SINGLE TASTE.〉

〈THEN WE'LL MAKE IT LOOK AS THOUGH HE'S GONE TO SEE THE GYPSIES AND WE'LL DUMP HIM IN THE RIVER.〉

〈IT IS YOUR PLAN, YES? BUT MADE JUST A TOUCH MORE BRILLIANT.〉

〈NO. NO. WHEN FELIX GETS BACK WE CAN ALL SIT DOWN TOGETHER, GET THESE GUESTS OUT OF HERE AND WE WILL MAKE A *REAL* PLAN. SOMETHING SENSIBLE-〉

〈WHAT?〉

〈YOU DON'T UNDERSTAND, DO YOU?〉

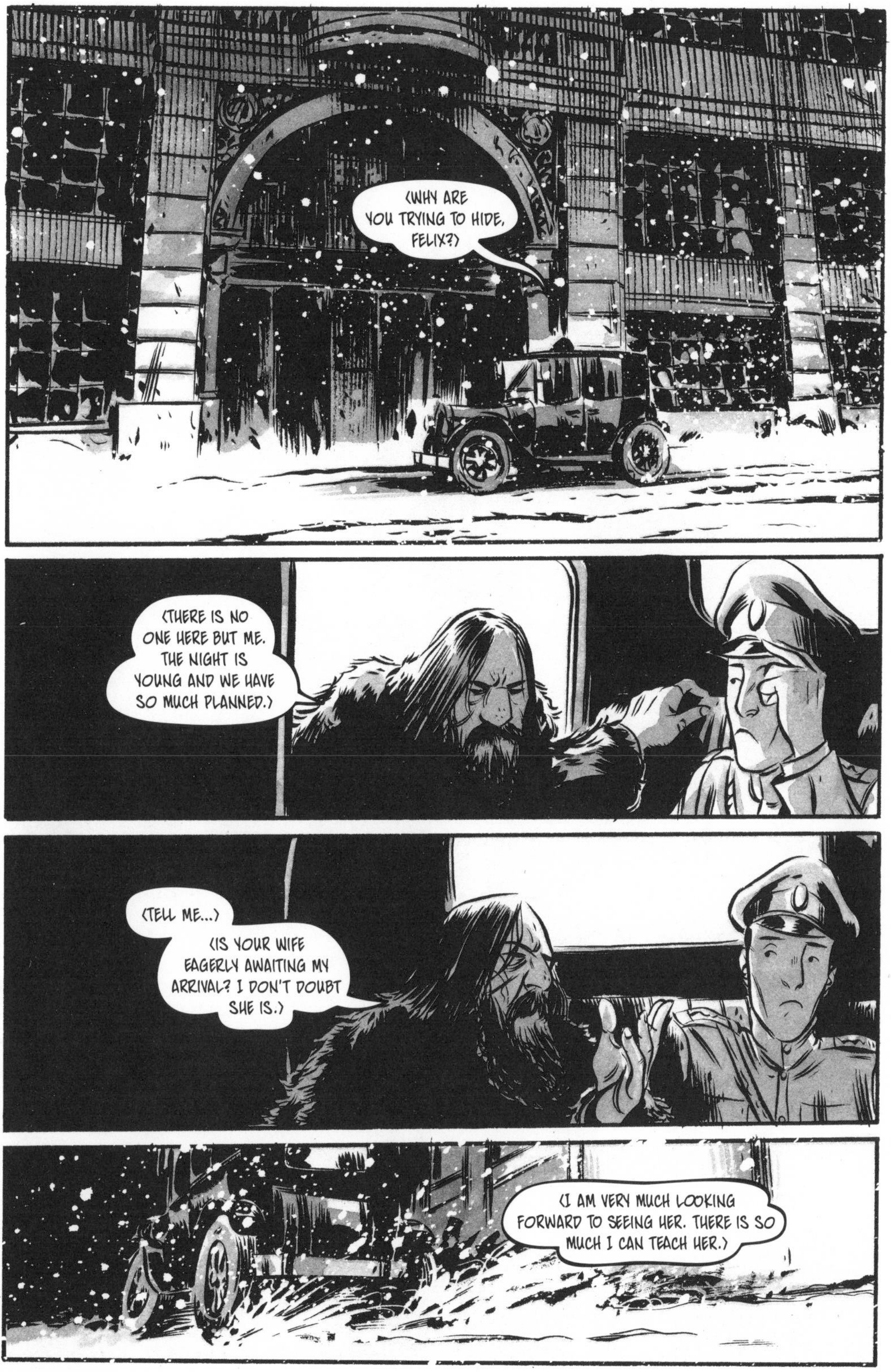
<WHY ARE YOU TRYING TO HIDE, FELIX?>
<THERE IS NO ONE HERE BUT ME. THE NIGHT IS YOUNG AND WE HAVE SO MUCH PLANNED.>
<TELL ME...>
<IS YOUR WIFE EAGERLY AWAITING MY ARRIVAL? I DON'T DOUBT SHE IS.>
<I AM VERY MUCH LOOKING FORWARD TO SEEING HER. THERE IS SO MUCH I CAN TEACH HER.>

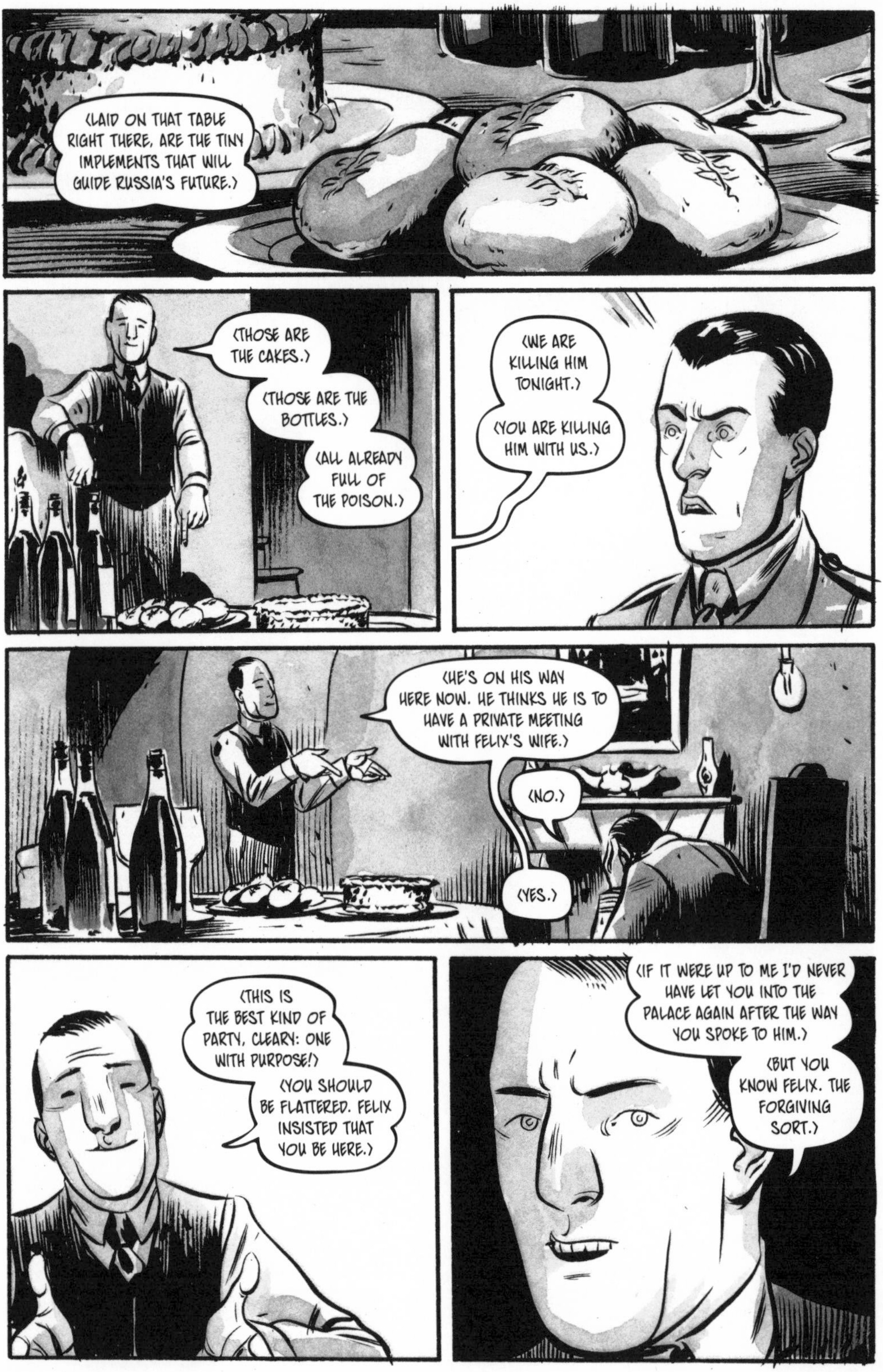

<LAID ON THAT TABLE RIGHT THERE, ARE THE TINY IMPLEMENTS THAT WILL GUIDE RUSSIA'S FUTURE.>
<THOSE ARE THE CAKES.>
<THOSE ARE THE BOTTLES.>
<ALL ALREADY FULL OF THE POISON.>
<WE ARE KILLING HIM TONIGHT.>
<YOU ARE KILLING HIM WITH US.>
<HE'S ON HIS WAY HERE NOW. HE THINKS HE IS TO HAVE A PRIVATE MEETING WITH FELIX'S WIFE.>
<NO.>
<YES.>
<THIS IS THE BEST KIND OF PARTY, CLEARY: ONE WITH PURPOSE!>
<YOU SHOULD BE FLATTERED. FELIX INSISTED THAT YOU BE HERE.>
<IF IT WERE UP TO ME I'D NEVER HAVE LET YOU INTO THE PALACE AGAIN AFTER THE WAY YOU SPOKE TO HIM.>
<BUT YOU KNOW FELIX. THE FORGIVING SORT.>

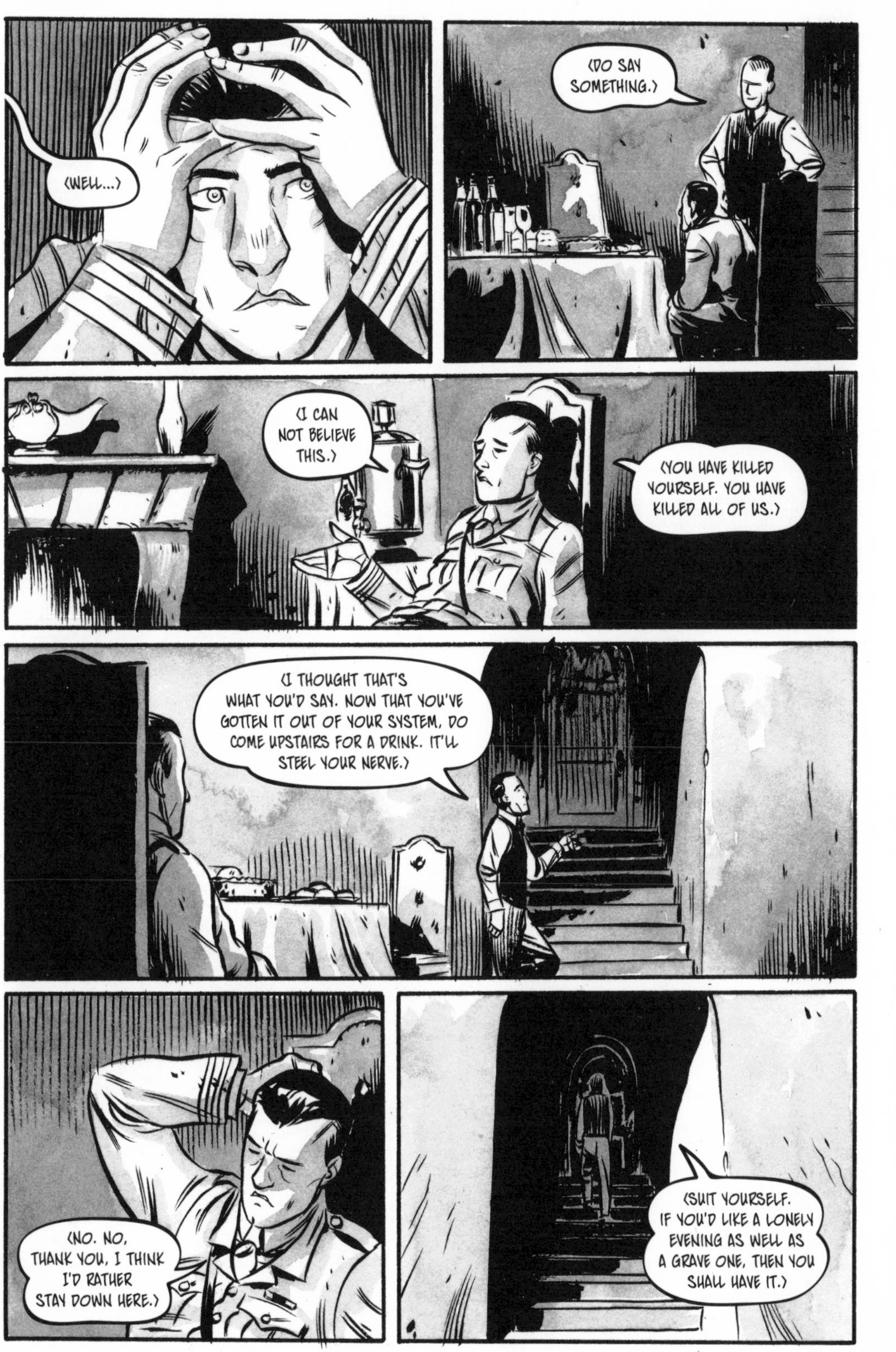

〈WELL...〉
〈DO SAY SOMETHING.〉
〈I CAN NOT BELIEVE THIS.〉
〈YOU HAVE KILLED YOURSELF. YOU HAVE KILLED ALL OF US.〉
〈I THOUGHT THAT'S WHAT YOU'D SAY. NOW THAT YOU'VE GOTTEN IT OUT OF YOUR SYSTEM, DO COME UPSTAIRS FOR A DRINK. IT'LL STEEL YOUR NERVE.〉
〈NO. NO, THANK YOU, I THINK I'D RATHER STAY DOWN HERE.〉
〈SUIT YOURSELF. IF YOU'D LIKE A LONELY EVENING AS WELL AS A GRAVE ONE, THEN YOU SHALL HAVE IT.〉

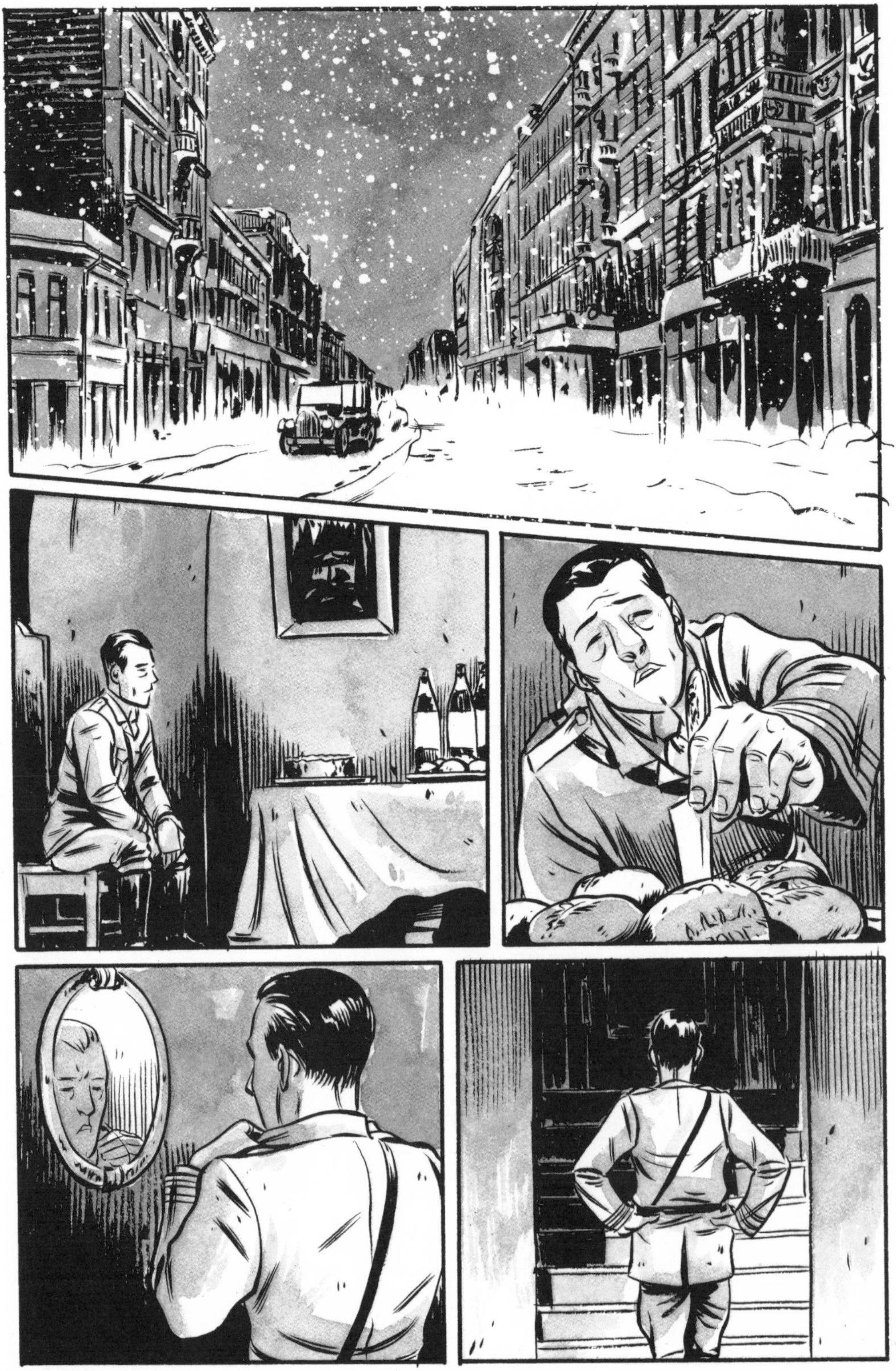

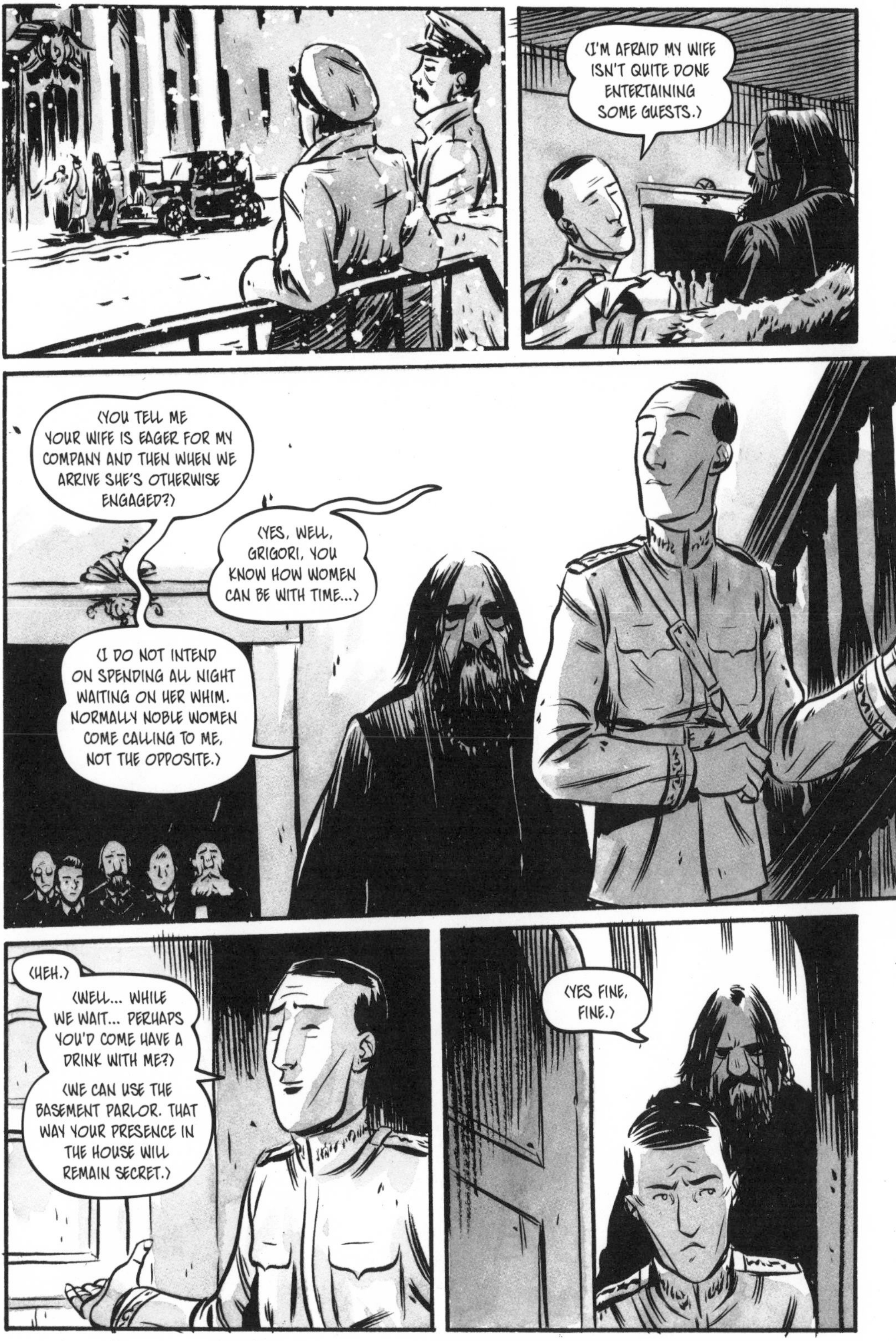

<I'M AFRAID MY WIFE ISN'T QUITE DONE ENTERTAINING SOME GUESTS.>
<YOU TELL ME YOUR WIFE IS EAGER FOR MY COMPANY AND THEN WHEN WE ARRIVE SHE'S OTHERWISE ENGAGED?>
<YES, WELL, GRIGORI, YOU KNOW HOW WOMEN CAN BE WITH TIME...>
<I DO NOT INTEND ON SPENDING ALL NIGHT WAITING ON HER WHIM. NORMALLY NOBLE WOMEN COME CALLING TO ME, NOT THE OPPOSITE.>
<HEH.>
<WELL... WHILE WE WAIT... PERHAPS YOU'D COME HAVE A DRINK WITH ME?>
<WE CAN USE THE BASEMENT PARLOR. THAT WAY YOUR PRESENCE IN THE HOUSE WILL REMAIN SECRET.>
<YES FINE, FINE.>

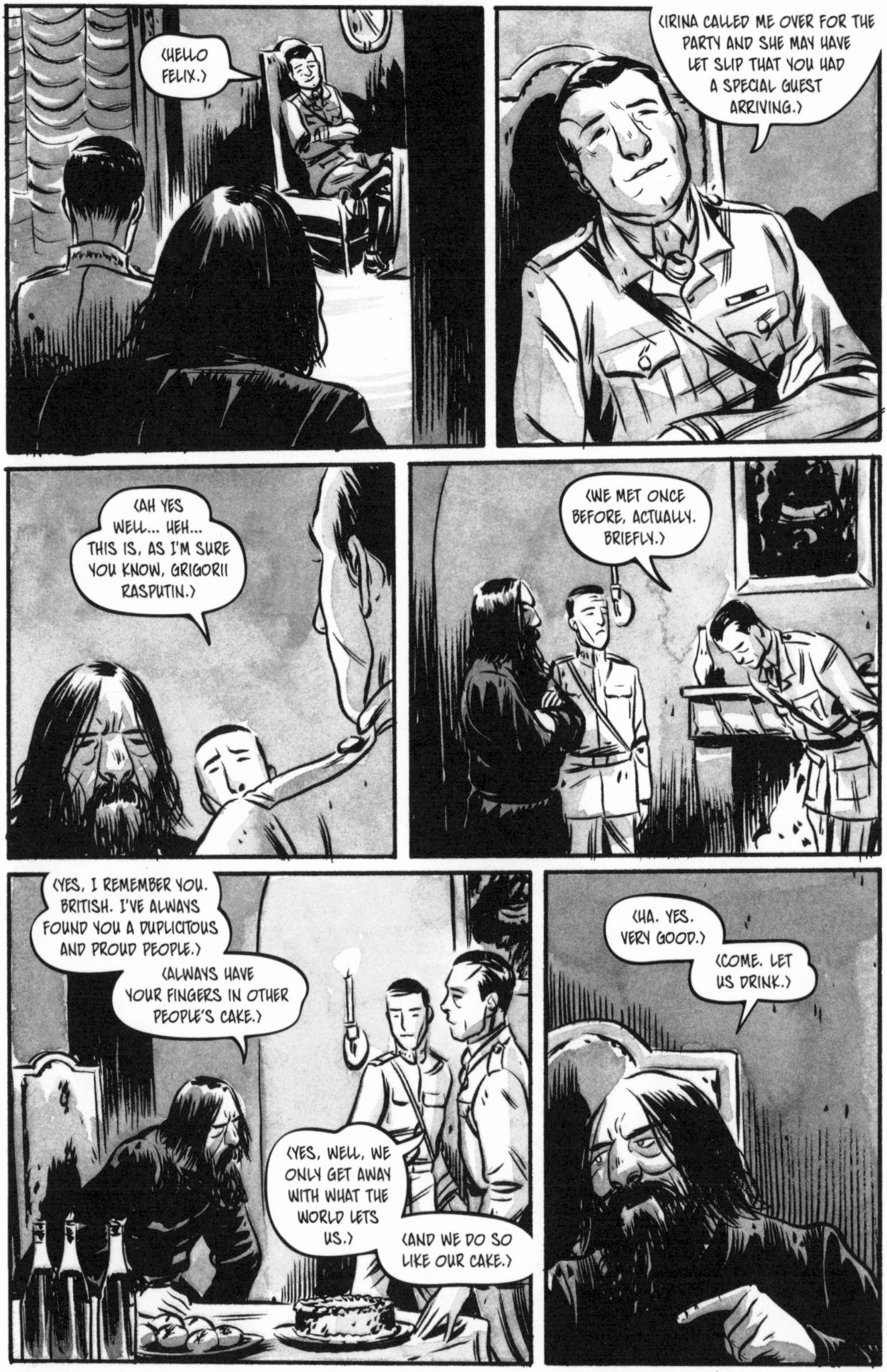
‹HELLO FELIX.›
‹IRINA CALLED ME OVER FOR THE PARTY AND SHE MAY HAVE LET SLIP THAT YOU HAD A SPECIAL GUEST ARRIVING.›
‹AH YES WELL... HEH... THIS IS, AS I'M SURE YOU KNOW, GRIGORII RASPUTIN.›
‹WE MET ONCE BEFORE, ACTUALLY. BRIEFLY.›
‹YES, I REMEMBER YOU. BRITISH. I'VE ALWAYS FOUND YOU A DUPLICITOUS AND PROUD PEOPLE.›
‹ALWAYS HAVE YOUR FINGERS IN OTHER PEOPLE'S CAKE.›
‹YES, WELL, WE ONLY GET AWAY WITH WHAT THE WORLD LETS US.›
‹AND WE DO SO LIKE OUR CAKE.›
‹HA. YES. VERY GOOD.›
‹COME. LET US DRINK.›

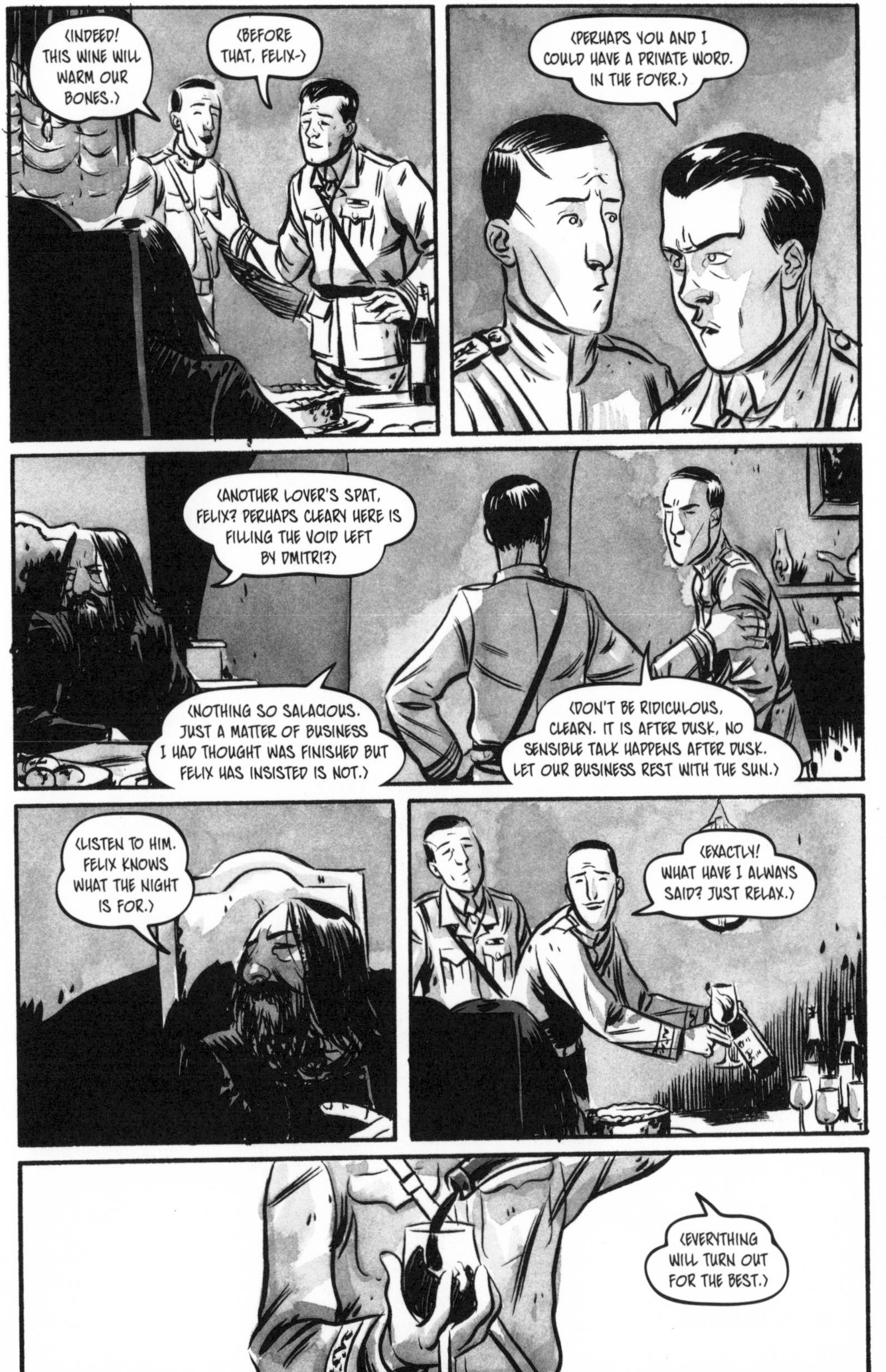

<INDEED! THIS WINE WILL WARM OUR BONES.>
<BEFORE THAT, FELIX->
<PERHAPS YOU AND I COULD HAVE A PRIVATE WORD. IN THE FOYER.>
<ANOTHER LOVER'S SPAT, FELIX? PERHAPS CLEARY HERE IS FILLING THE VOID LEFT BY DMITRI?>
<NOTHING SO SALACIOUS. JUST A MATTER OF BUSINESS I HAD THOUGHT WAS FINISHED BUT FELIX HAS INSISTED IS NOT.>
<DON'T BE RIDICULOUS, CLEARY. IT IS AFTER DUSK, NO SENSIBLE TALK HAPPENS AFTER DUSK. LET OUR BUSINESS REST WITH THE SUN.>
<LISTEN TO HIM. FELIX KNOWS WHAT THE NIGHT IS FOR.>
<EXACTLY! WHAT HAVE I ALWAYS SAID? JUST RELAX.>
<EVERYTHING WILL TURN OUT FOR THE BEST.>

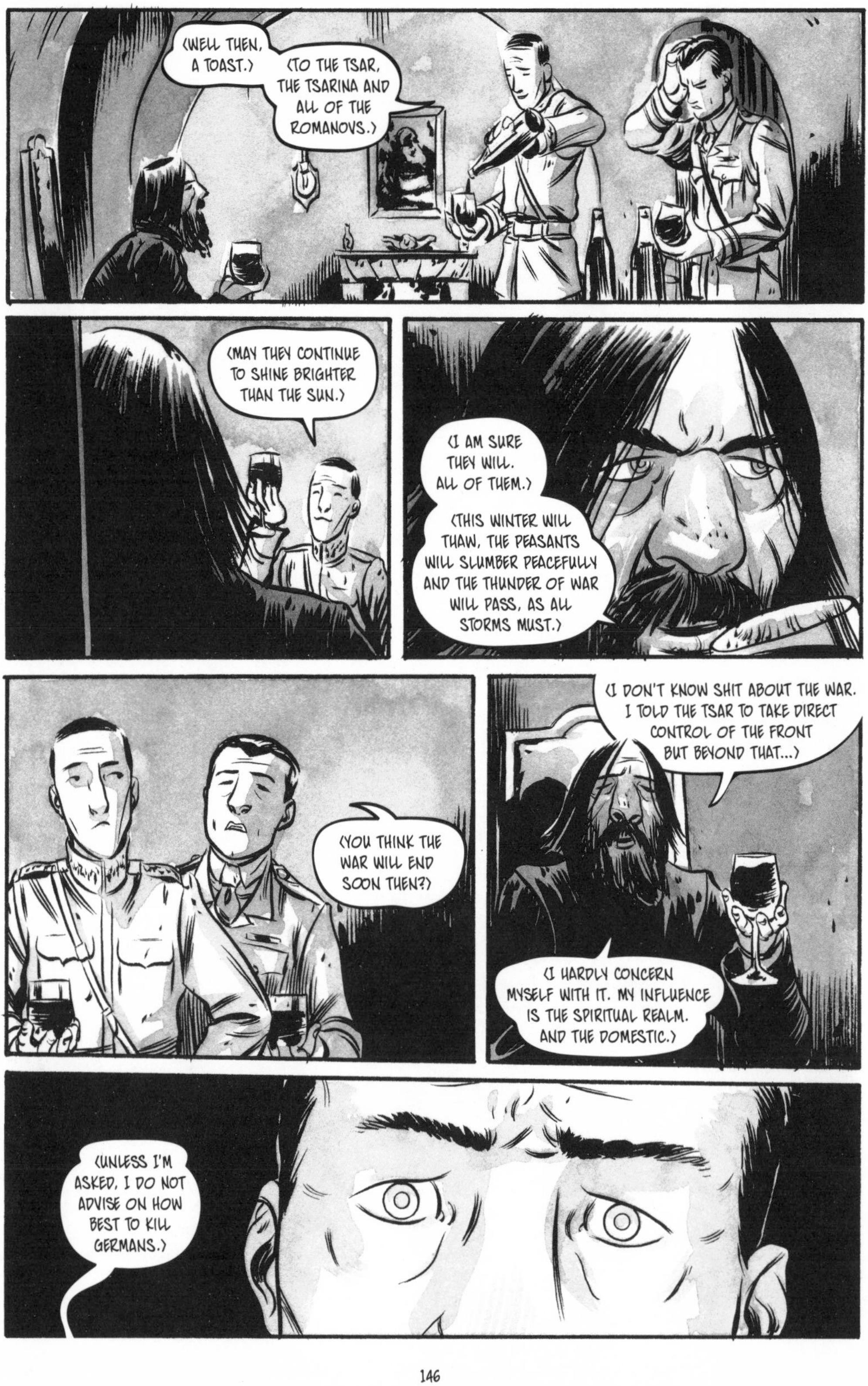
‹WELL THEN, A TOAST.›
‹TO THE TSAR, THE TSARINA AND ALL OF THE ROMANOVS.›
‹MAY THEY CONTINUE TO SHINE BRIGHTER THAN THE SUN.›
‹I AM SURE THEY WILL. ALL OF THEM.›
‹THIS WINTER WILL THAW, THE PEASANTS WILL SLUMBER PEACEFULLY AND THE THUNDER OF WAR WILL PASS, AS ALL STORMS MUST.›
‹YOU THINK THE WAR WILL END SOON THEN?›
‹I DON'T KNOW SHIT ABOUT THE WAR. I TOLD THE TSAR TO TAKE DIRECT CONTROL OF THE FRONT BUT BEYOND THAT...›
‹I HARDLY CONCERN MYSELF WITH IT. MY INFLUENCE IS THE SPIRITUAL REALM. AND THE DOMESTIC.›
‹UNLESS I'M ASKED, I DO NOT ADVISE ON HOW BEST TO KILL GERMANS.›

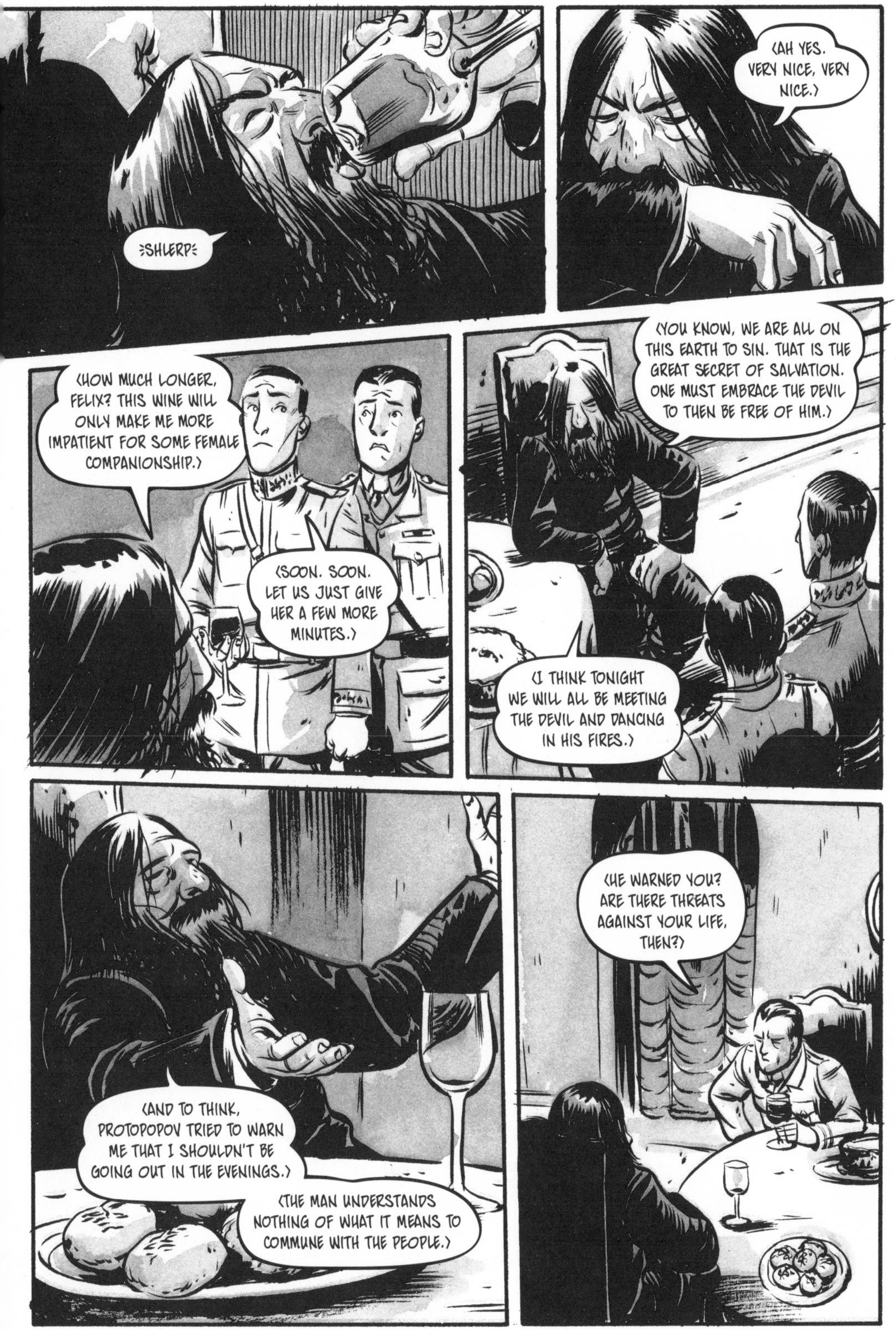
SHLERP
‹AH YES. VERY NICE, VERY NICE.›
‹HOW MUCH LONGER, FELIX? THIS WINE WILL ONLY MAKE ME MORE IMPATIENT FOR SOME FEMALE COMPANIONSHIP.›
‹SOON. SOON. LET US JUST GIVE HER A FEW MORE MINUTES.›
‹YOU KNOW, WE ARE ALL ON THIS EARTH TO SIN. THAT IS THE GREAT SECRET OF SALVATION. ONE MUST EMBRACE THE DEVIL TO THEN BE FREE OF HIM.›
‹I THINK TONIGHT WE WILL ALL BE MEETING THE DEVIL AND DANCING IN HIS FIRES.›
‹AND TO THINK, PROTOPOPOV TRIED TO WARN ME THAT I SHOULDN'T BE GOING OUT IN THE EVENINGS.›
‹THE MAN UNDERSTANDS NOTHING OF WHAT IT MEANS TO COMMUNE WITH THE PEOPLE.›
‹HE WARNED YOU? ARE THERE THREATS AGAINST YOUR LIFE, THEN?›

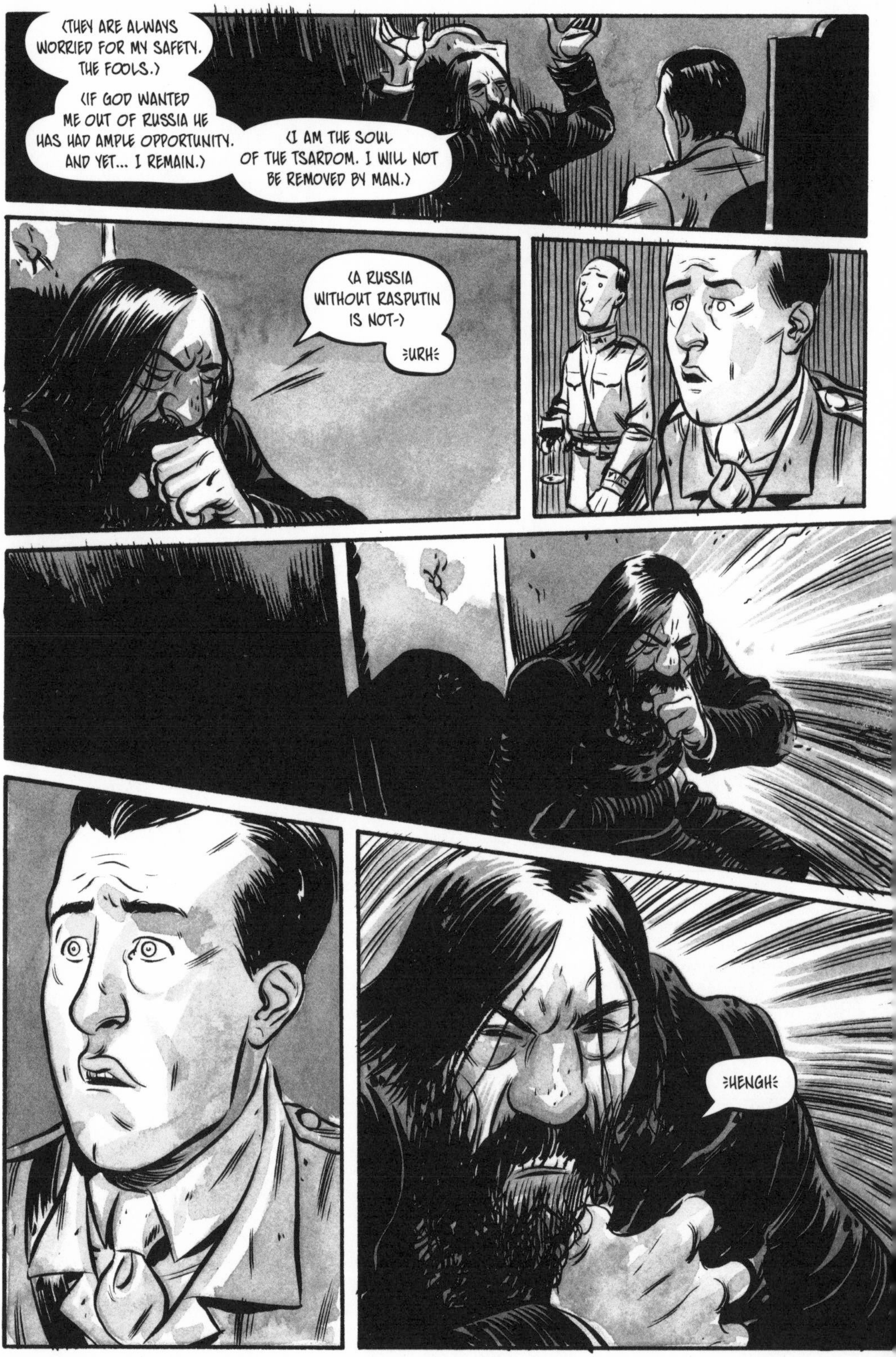
‹THEY ARE ALWAYS WORRIED FOR MY SAFETY. THE FOOLS.›
‹IF GOD WANTED ME OUT OF RUSSIA HE HAS HAD AMPLE OPPORTUNITY. AND YET... I REMAIN.›
‹I AM THE SOUL OF THE TSARDOM. I WILL NOT BE REMOVED BY MAN.›
‹A RUSSIA WITHOUT RASPUTIN IS NOT-›
URH
HENGH

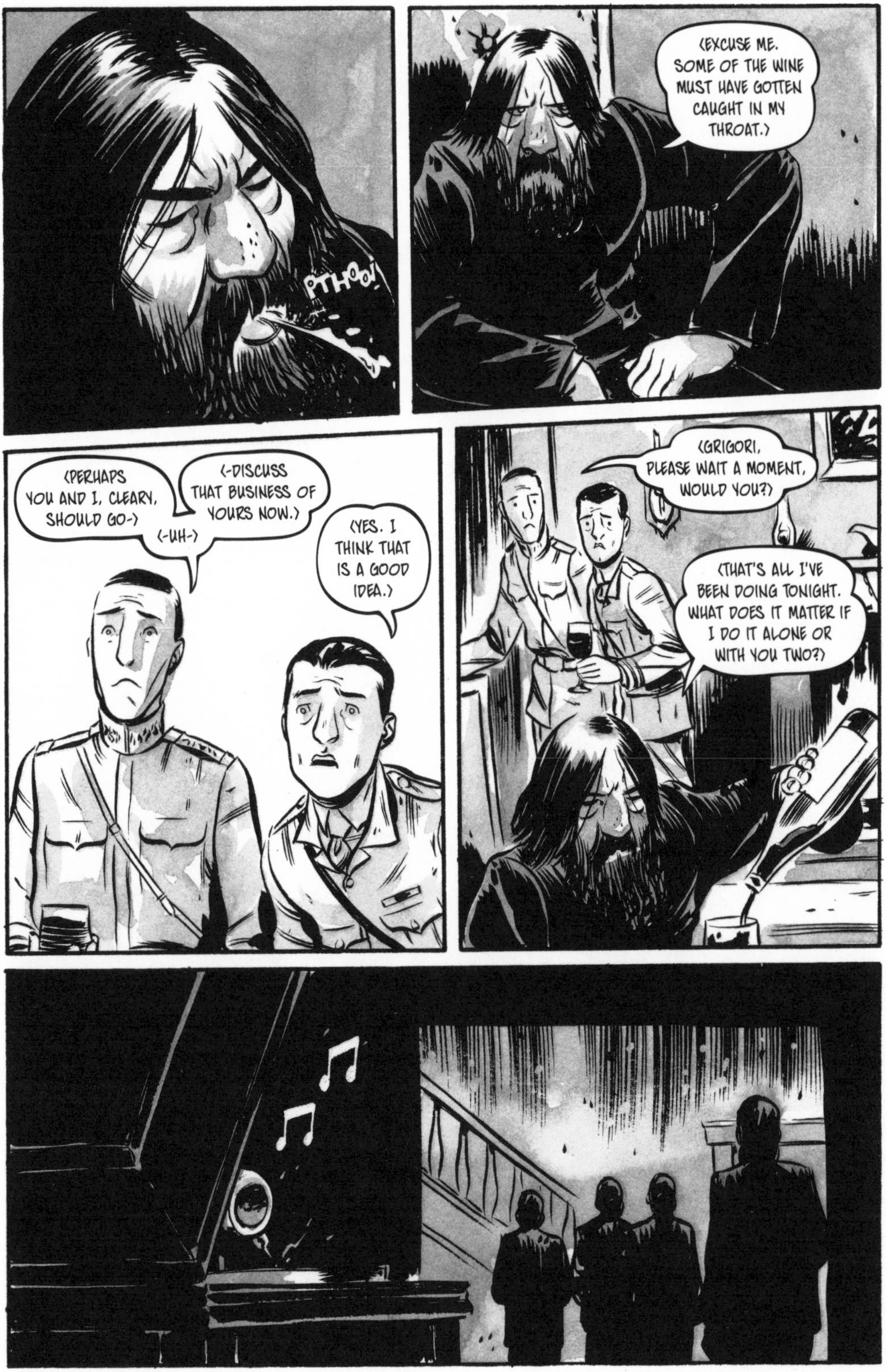
PTHOO!
(EXCUSE ME. SOME OF THE WINE MUST HAVE GOTTEN CAUGHT IN MY THROAT.)
(PERHAPS YOU AND I, CLEARY, SHOULD GO-)
(-UH-)
(-DISCUSS THAT BUSINESS OF YOURS NOW.)
(YES. I THINK THAT IS A GOOD IDEA.)
(GRIGORI, PLEASE WAIT A MOMENT, WOULD YOU?)
(THAT'S ALL I'VE BEEN DOING TONIGHT. WHAT DOES IT MATTER IF I DO IT ALONE OR WITH YOU TWO?)

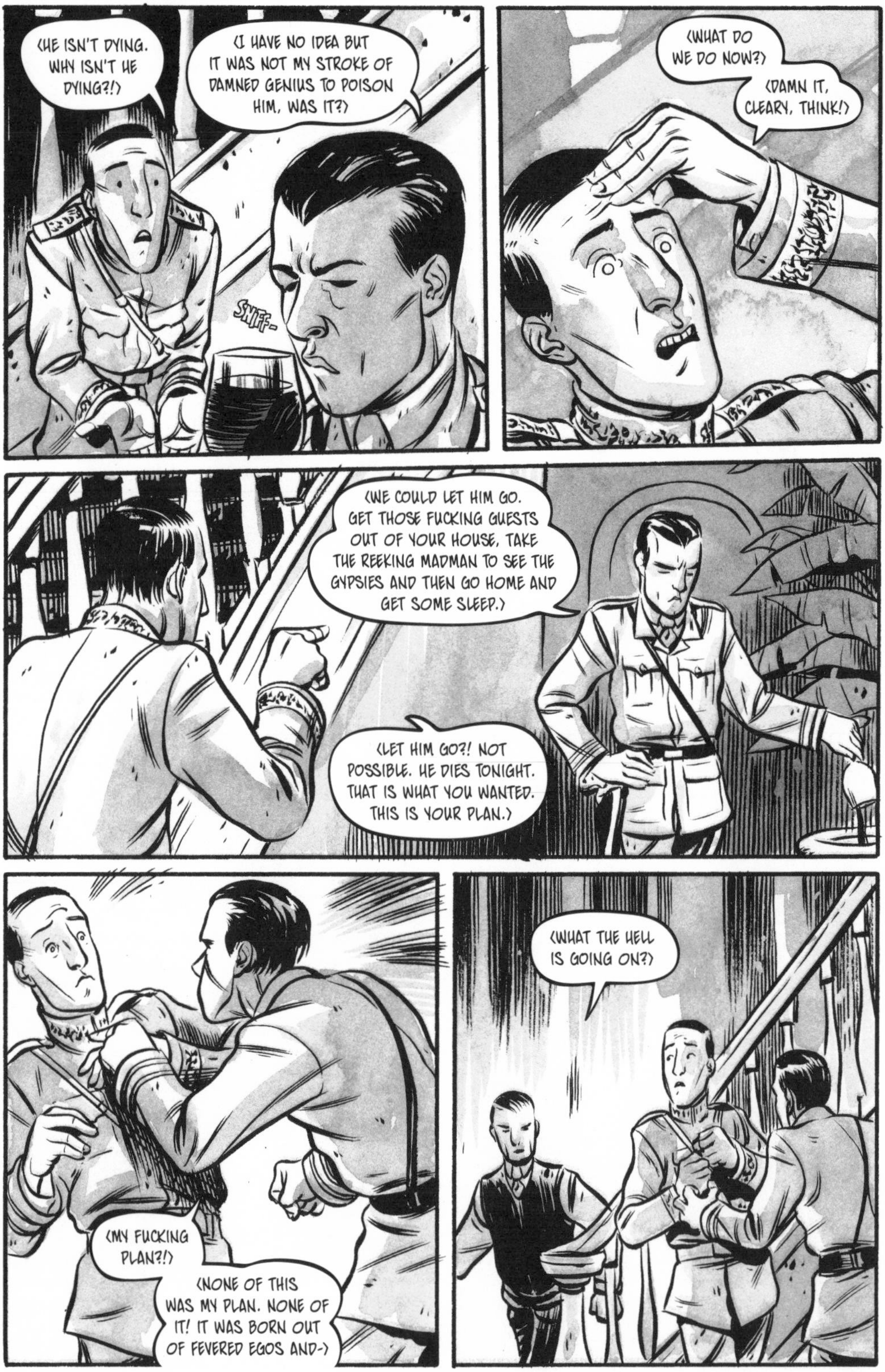
⟨HE ISN'T DYING. WHY ISN'T HE DYING?!⟩
⟨I HAVE NO IDEA BUT IT WAS NOT MY STROKE OF DAMNED GENIUS TO POISON HIM, WAS IT?⟩
SNIFF-
⟨WHAT DO WE DO NOW?⟩
⟨DAMN IT, CLEARY, THINK!⟩
⟨WE COULD LET HIM GO. GET THOSE FUCKING GUESTS OUT OF YOUR HOUSE, TAKE THE REEKING MADMAN TO SEE THE GYPSIES AND THEN GO HOME AND GET SOME SLEEP.⟩
⟨LET HIM GO?! NOT POSSIBLE. HE DIES TONIGHT. THAT IS WHAT YOU WANTED. THIS IS YOUR PLAN.⟩
⟨MY FUCKING PLAN?!⟩
⟨NONE OF THIS WAS MY PLAN. NONE OF IT! IT WAS BORN OUT OF FEVERED EGOS AND-⟩
⟨WHAT THE HELL IS GOING ON?⟩

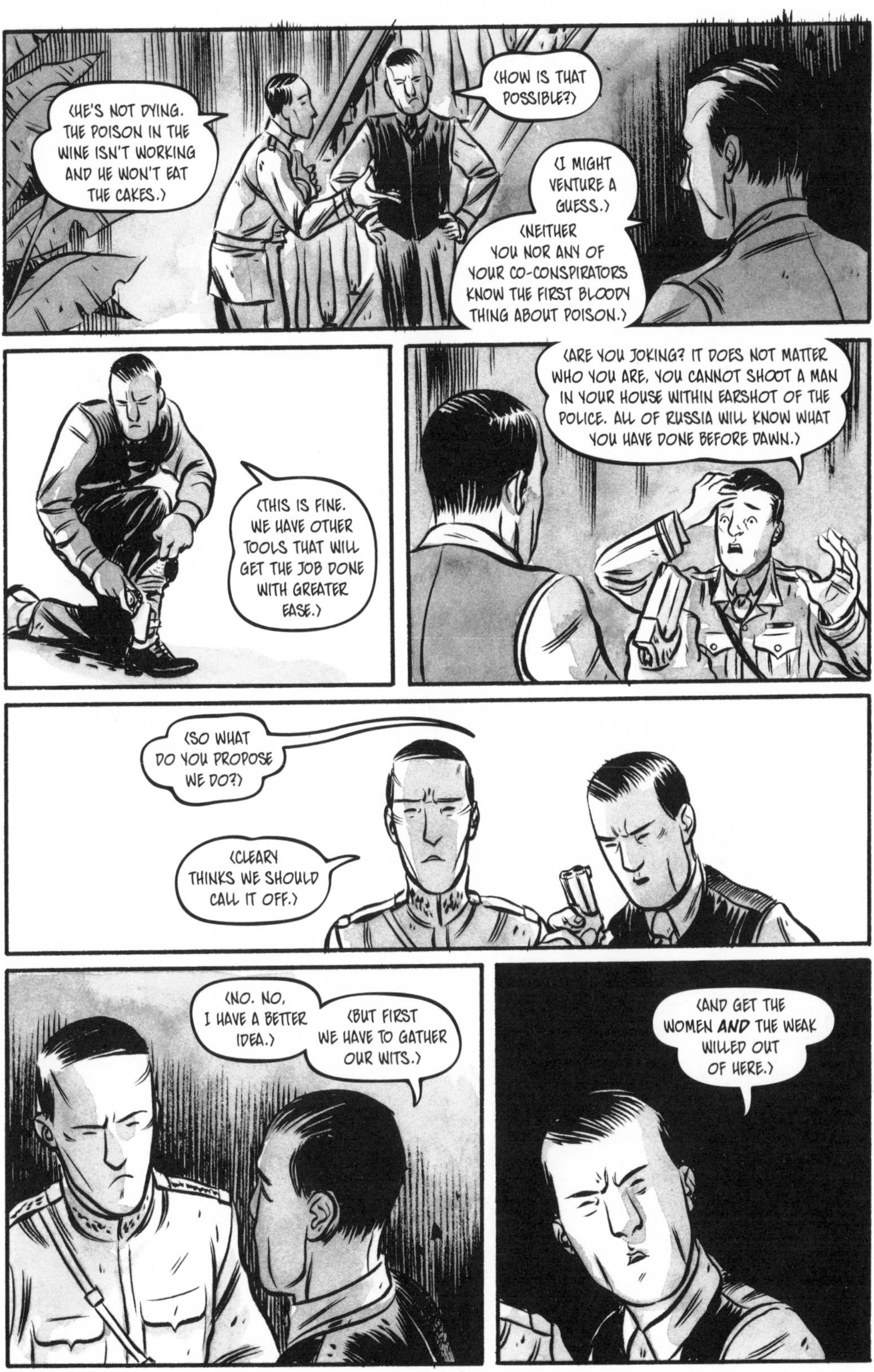
‹HE'S NOT DYING. THE POISON IN THE WINE ISN'T WORKING AND HE WON'T EAT THE CAKES.›
‹HOW IS THAT POSSIBLE?›
‹I MIGHT VENTURE A GUESS.›
‹NEITHER YOU NOR ANY OF YOUR CO-CONSPIRATORS KNOW THE FIRST BLOODY THING ABOUT POISON.›
‹THIS IS FINE. WE HAVE OTHER TOOLS THAT WILL GET THE JOB DONE WITH GREATER EASE.›
‹ARE YOU JOKING? IT DOES NOT MATTER WHO YOU ARE, YOU CANNOT SHOOT A MAN IN YOUR HOUSE WITHIN EARSHOT OF THE POLICE. ALL OF RUSSIA WILL KNOW WHAT YOU HAVE DONE BEFORE DAWN.›
‹SO WHAT DO YOU PROPOSE WE DO?›
‹CLEARY THINKS WE SHOULD CALL IT OFF.›
‹NO. NO, I HAVE A BETTER IDEA.›
‹BUT FIRST WE HAVE TO GATHER OUR WITS.›
‹AND GET THE WOMEN **AND** THE WEAK WILLED OUT OF HERE.›

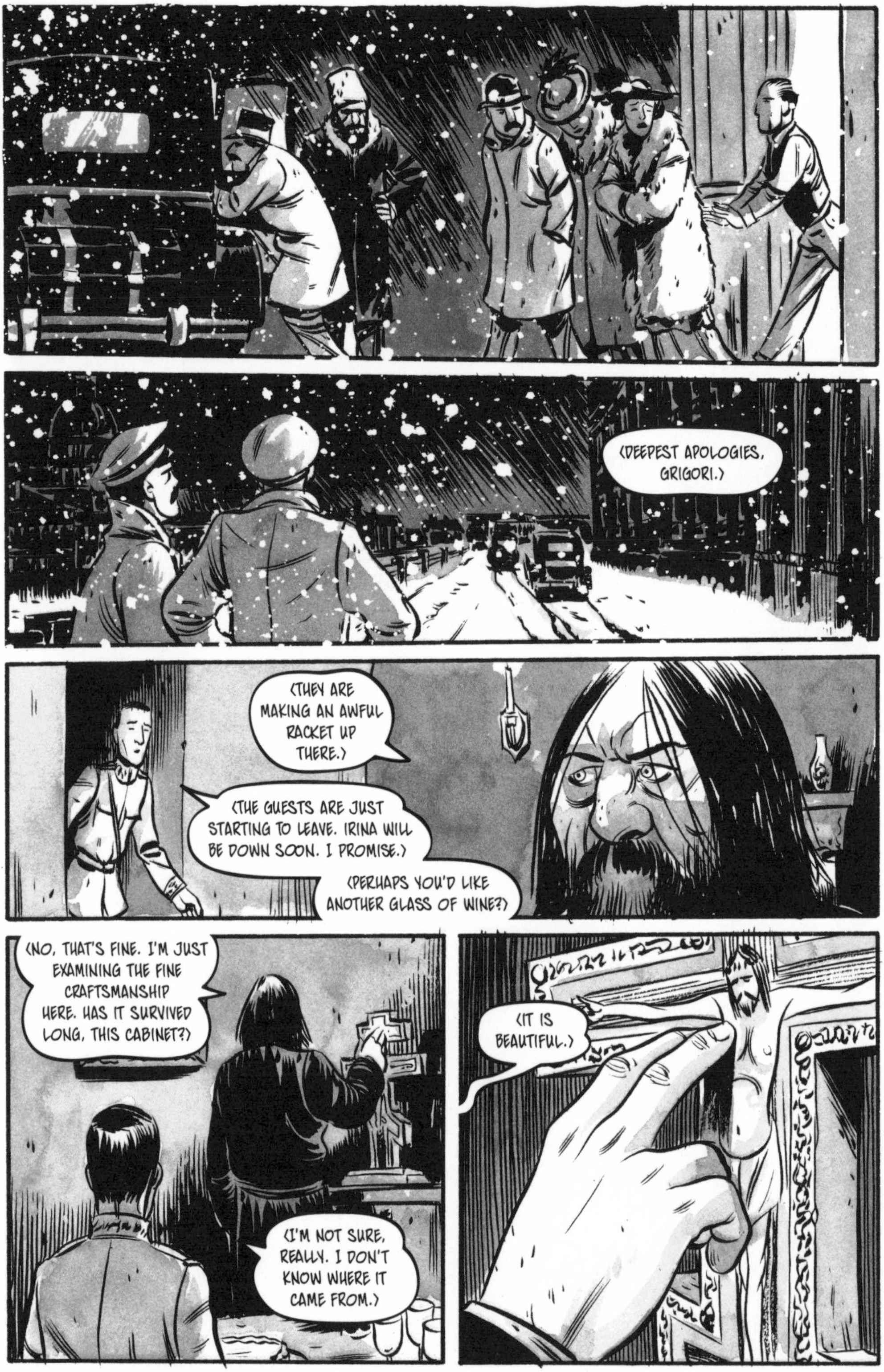
<DEEPEST APOLOGIES, GRIGORI.>
<THEY ARE MAKING AN AWFUL RACKET UP THERE.>
<THE GUESTS ARE JUST STARTING TO LEAVE. IRINA WILL BE DOWN SOON. I PROMISE.>
<PERHAPS YOU'D LIKE ANOTHER GLASS OF WINE?>
<NO, THAT'S FINE. I'M JUST EXAMINING THE FINE CRAFTSMANSHIP HERE. HAS IT SURVIVED LONG, THIS CABINET?>
<I'M NOT SURE, REALLY. I DON'T KNOW WHERE IT CAME FROM.>
<IT IS BEAUTIFUL.>

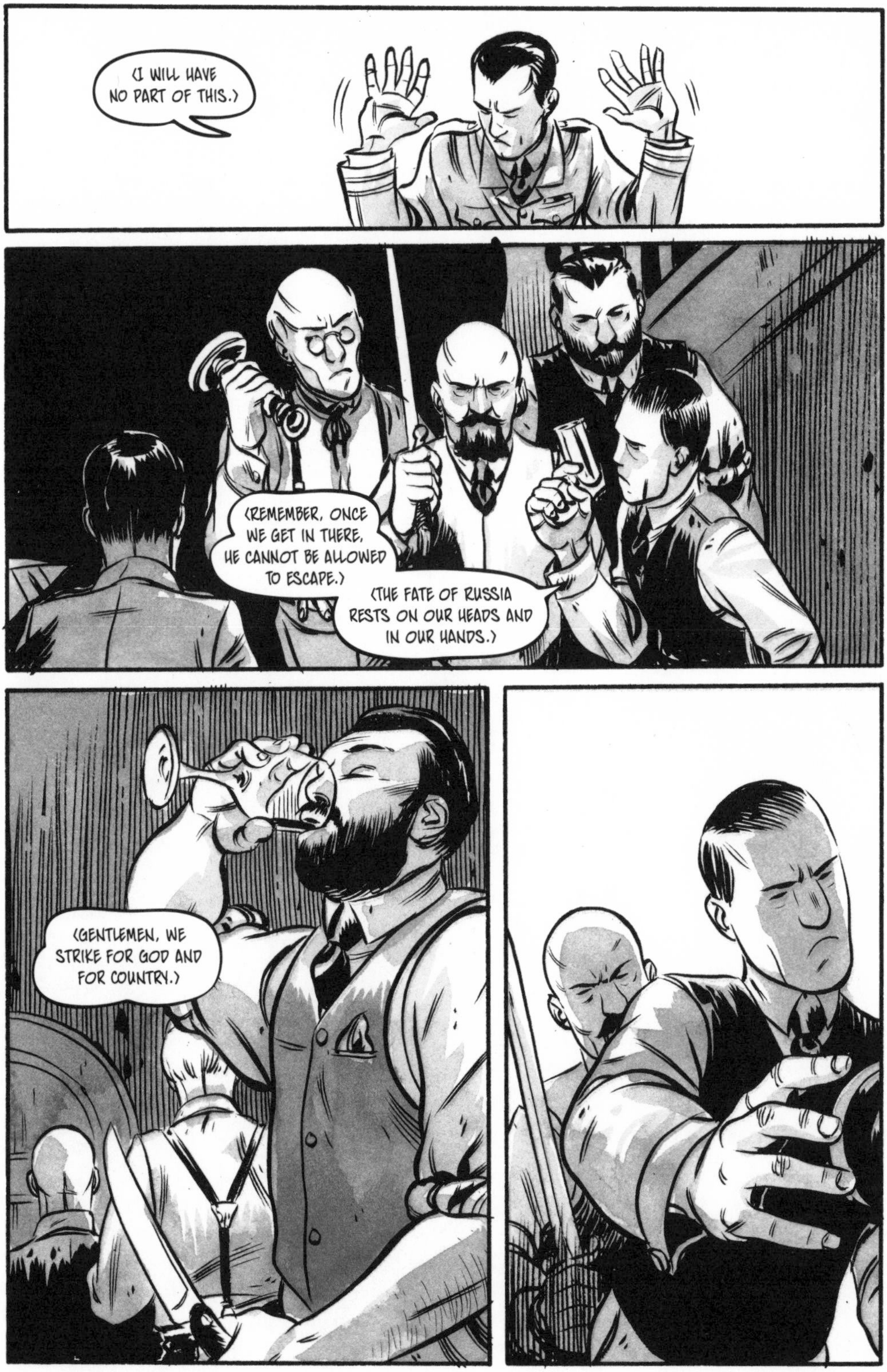
‹I WILL HAVE NO PART OF THIS.›
‹REMEMBER, ONCE WE GET IN THERE, HE CANNOT BE ALLOWED TO ESCAPE.›
‹THE FATE OF RUSSIA RESTS ON OUR HEADS AND IN OUR HANDS.›
‹GENTLEMEN, WE STRIKE FOR GOD AND FOR COUNTRY.›

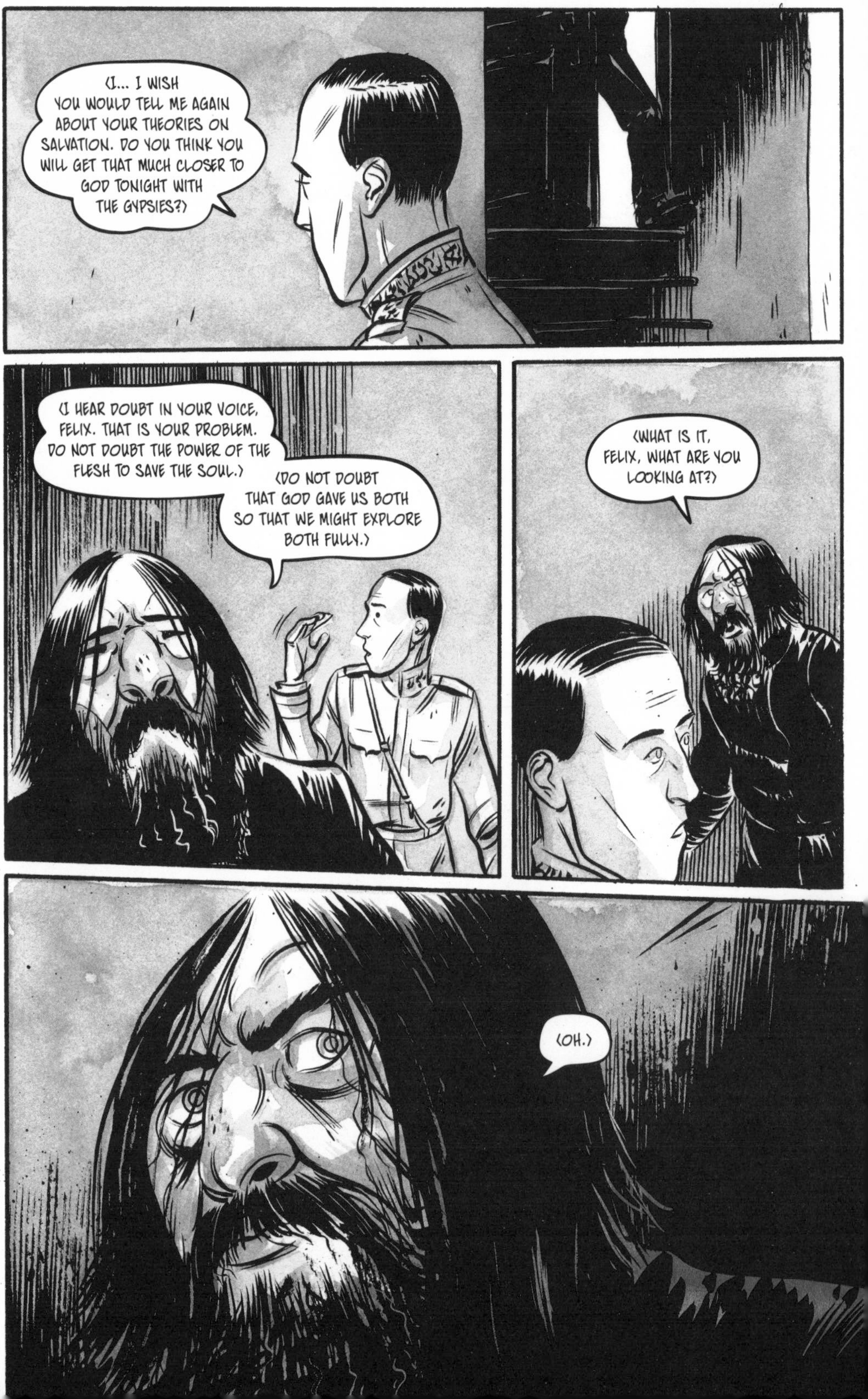
(I... I WISH YOU WOULD TELL ME AGAIN ABOUT YOUR THEORIES ON SALVATION. DO YOU THINK YOU WILL GET THAT MUCH CLOSER TO GOD TONIGHT WITH THE GYPSIES?)
(I HEAR DOUBT IN YOUR VOICE, FELIX. THAT IS YOUR PROBLEM. DO NOT DOUBT THE POWER OF THE FLESH TO SAVE THE SOUL.)
(DO NOT DOUBT THAT GOD GAVE US BOTH SO THAT WE MIGHT EXPLORE BOTH FULLY.)
(WHAT IS IT, FELIX, WHAT ARE YOU LOOKING AT?)
(OH.)

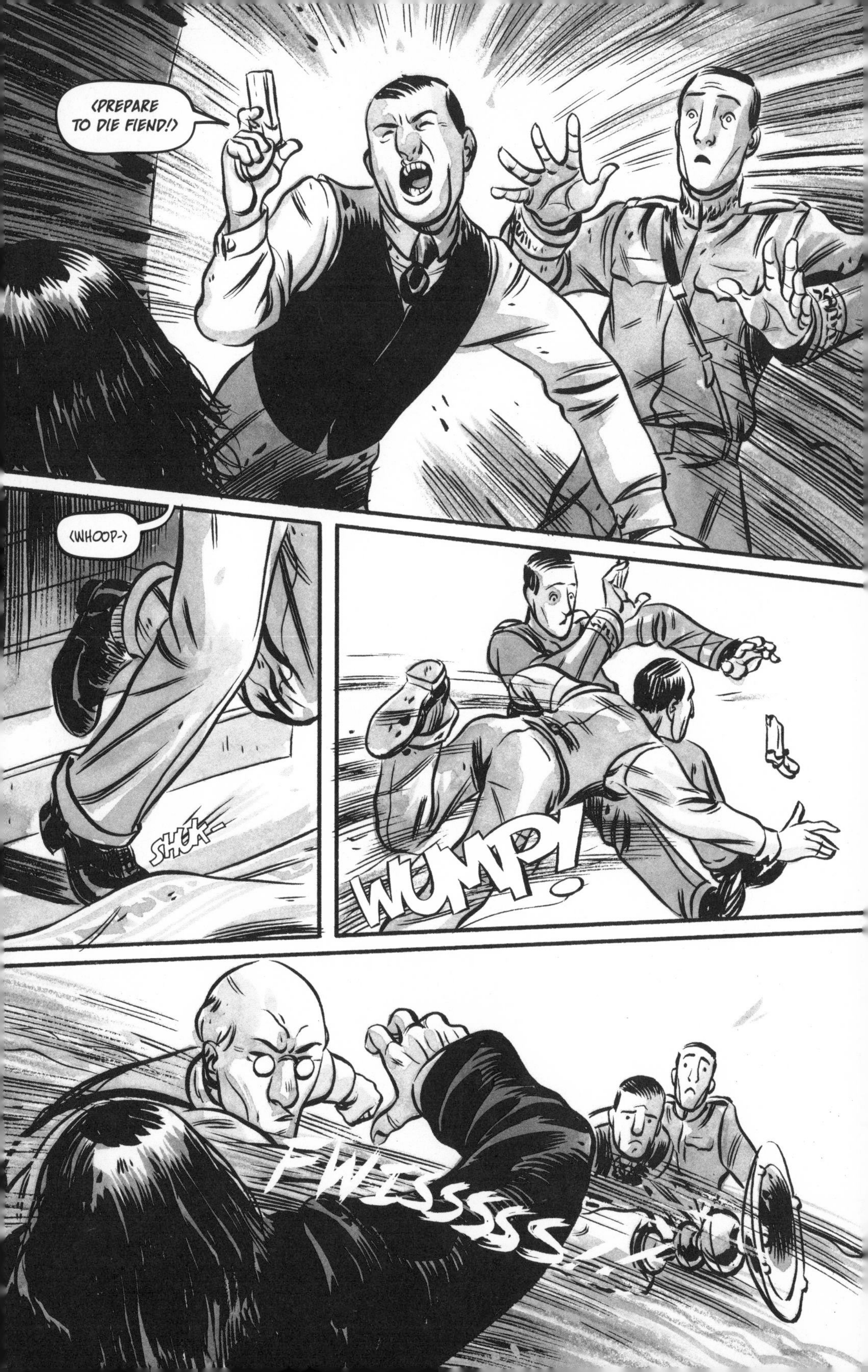

<PREPARE TO DIE FIEND!>
<WHOOP->
SHUK-
WUMP!
FWISSSS!!

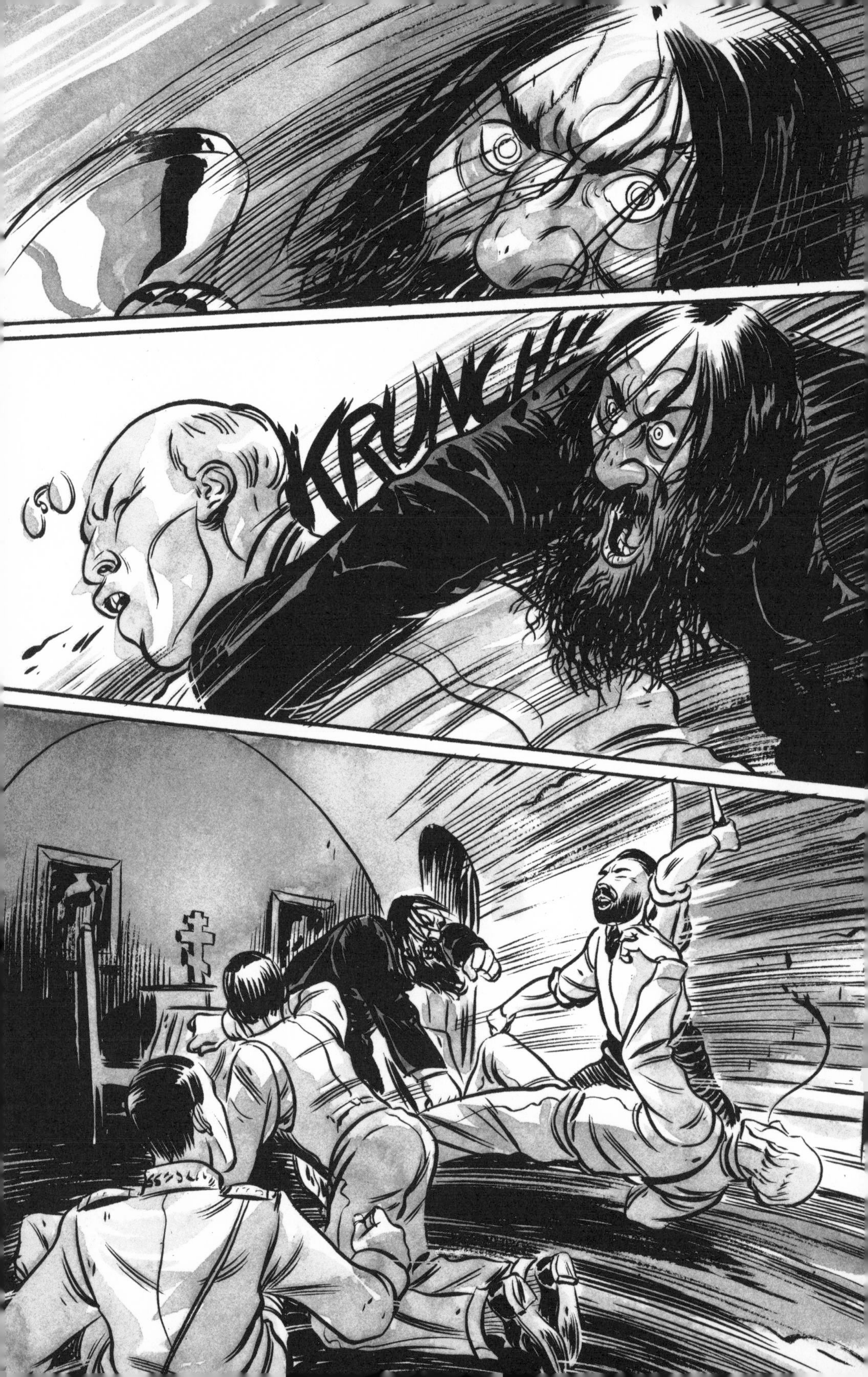
KRUNCH!!

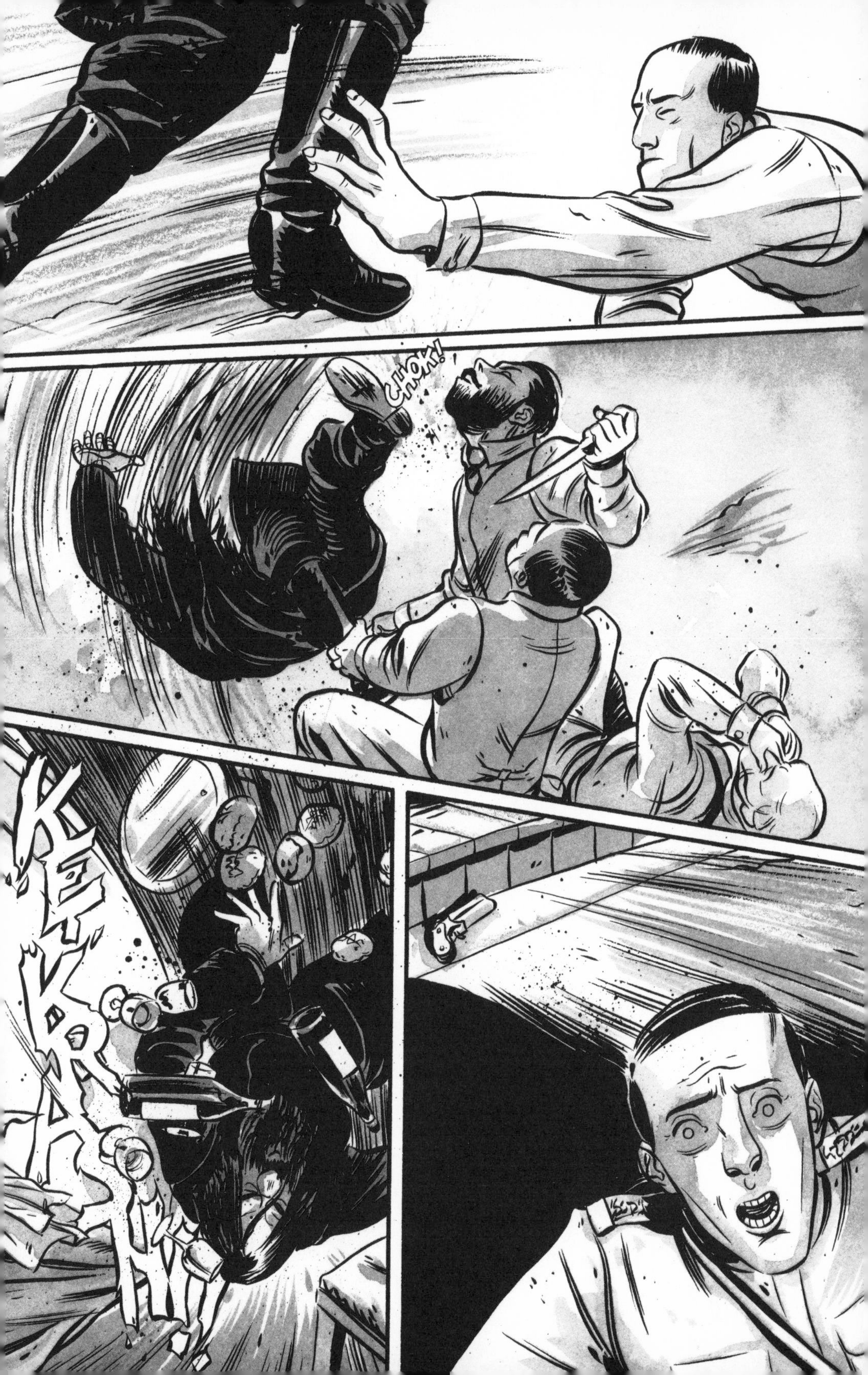
CHOK!

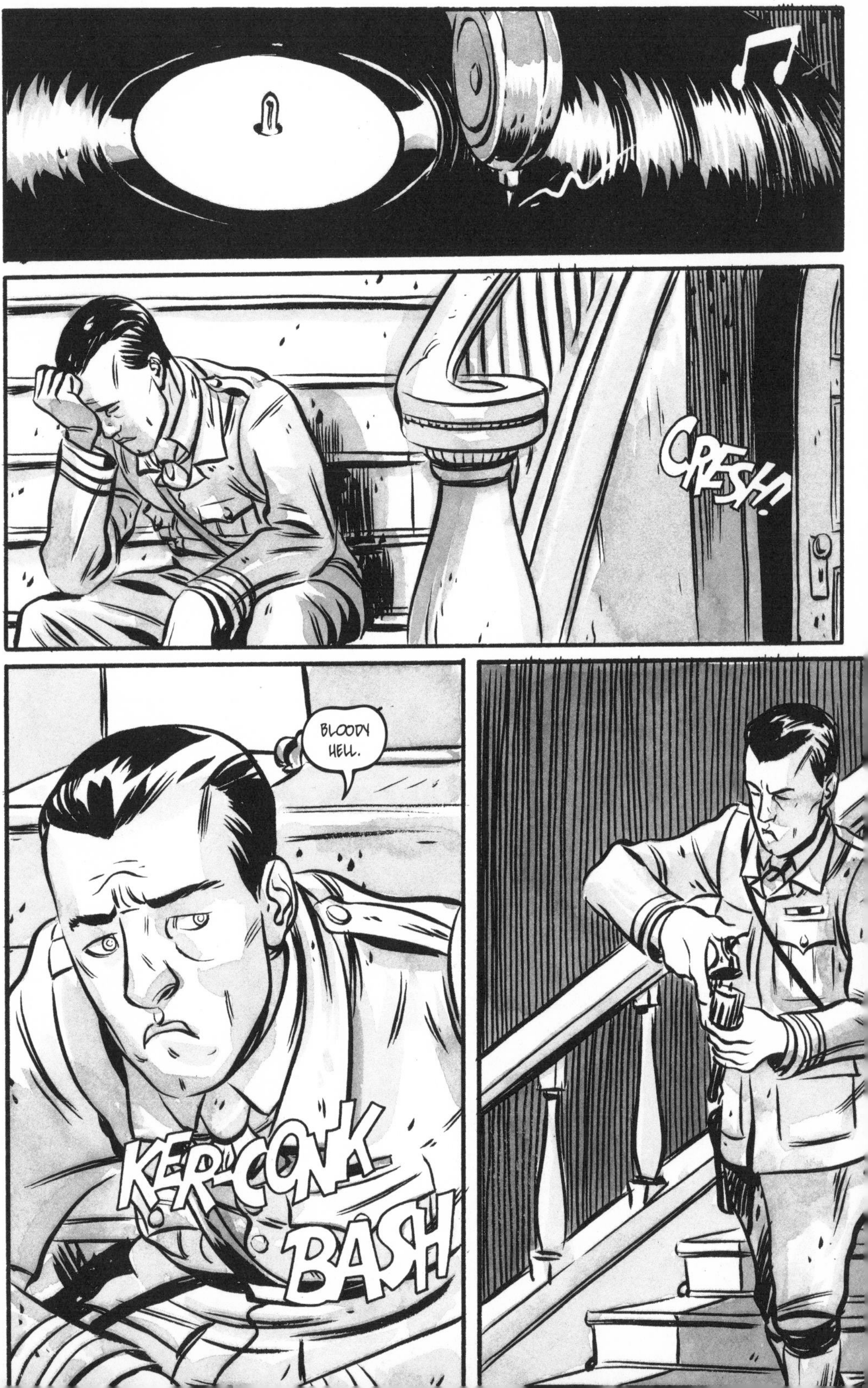
CRESH!
BLOODY HELL.
KER-CONK
BASH

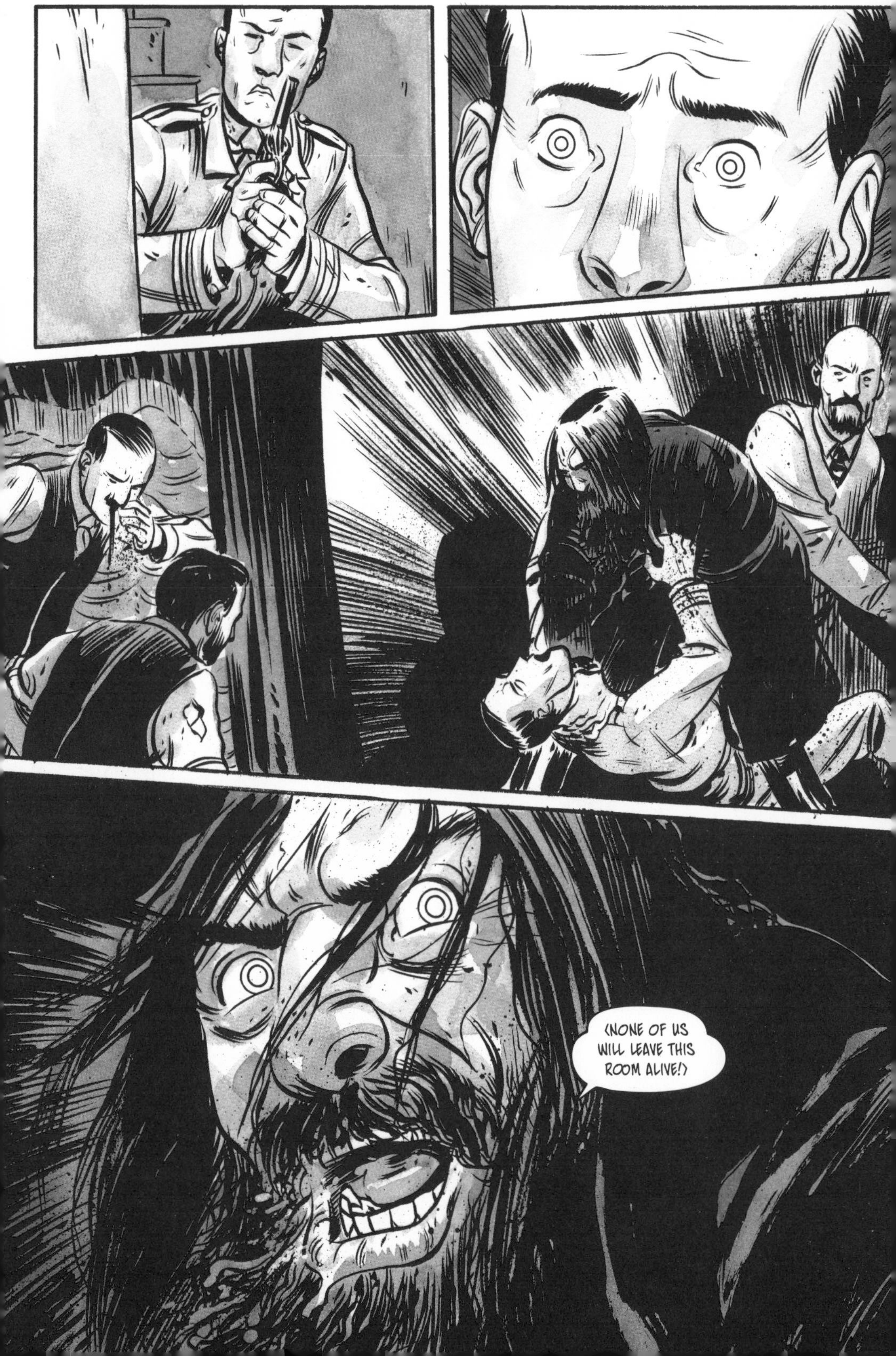
(NONE OF US WILL LEAVE THIS ROOM ALIVE!)

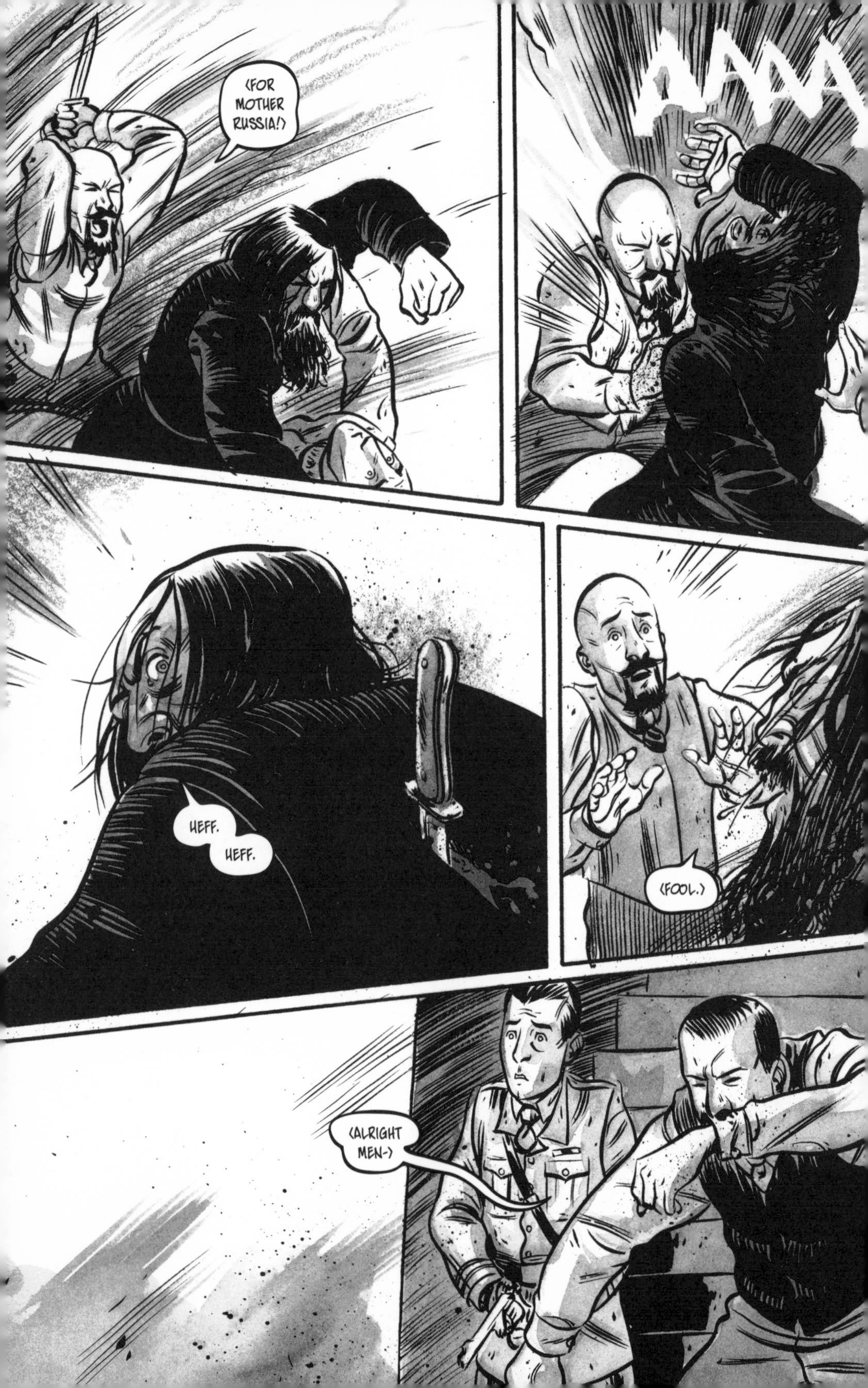
‹FOR MOTHER RUSSIA!›
HEFF. HEFF.
‹FOOL.›
‹ALRIGHT MEN-›

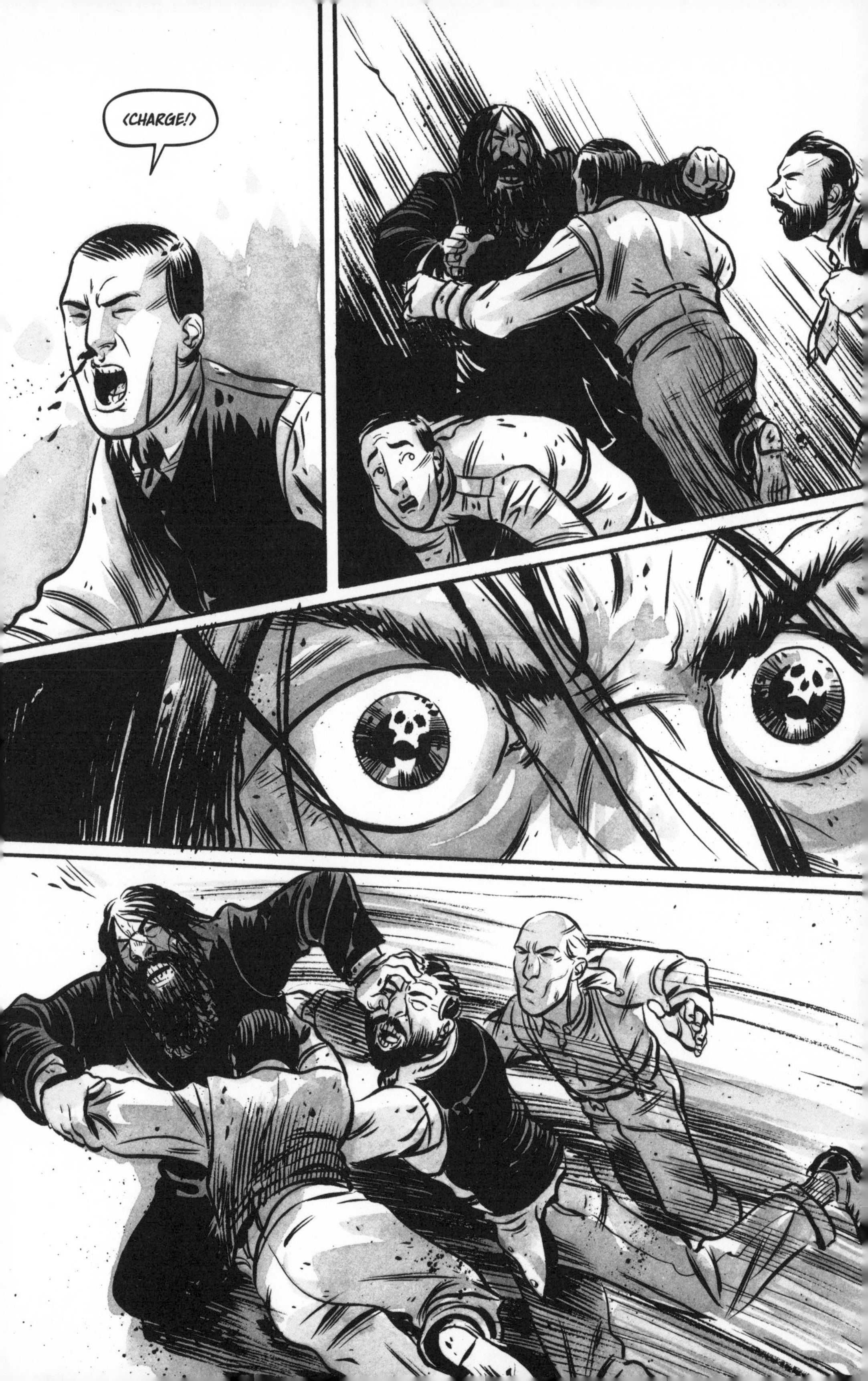
‹CHARGE!›

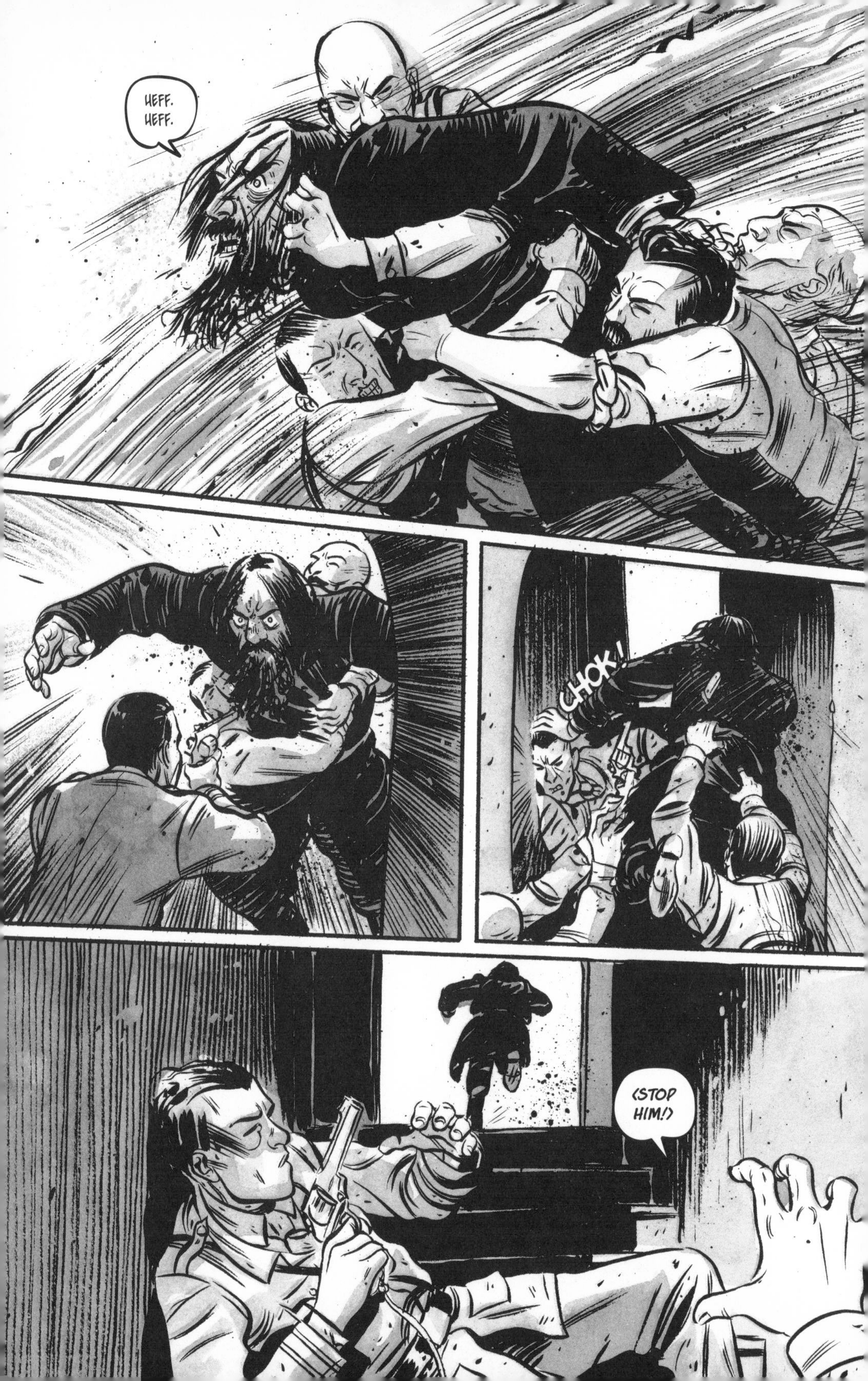
HEFF.
HEFF.
CHOK!
<STOP
HIM!>

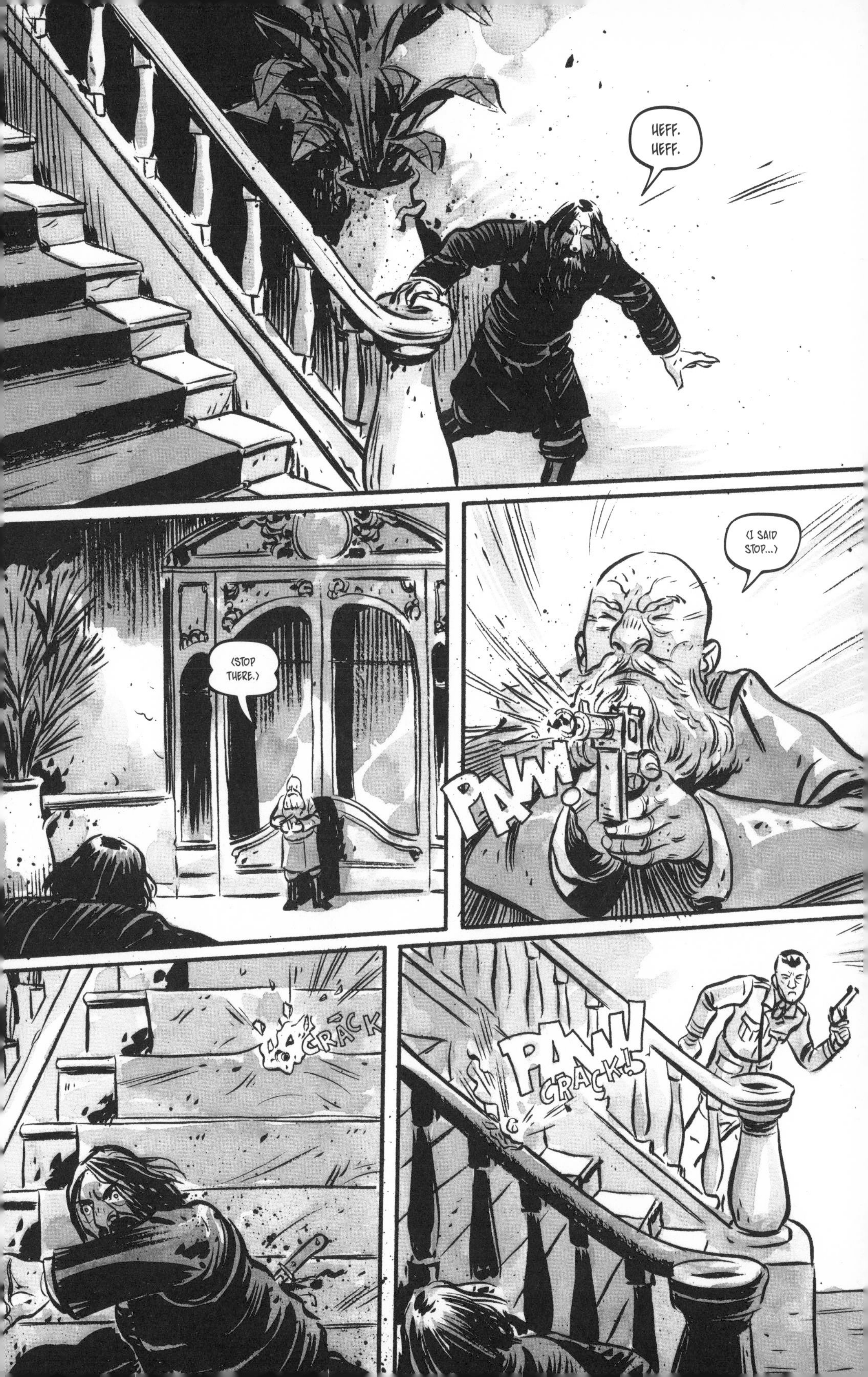
HEFF.
HEFF.
‹STOP THERE.›
‹I SAID STOP...›
PAW!
CRACK
PAW!
CRACK!

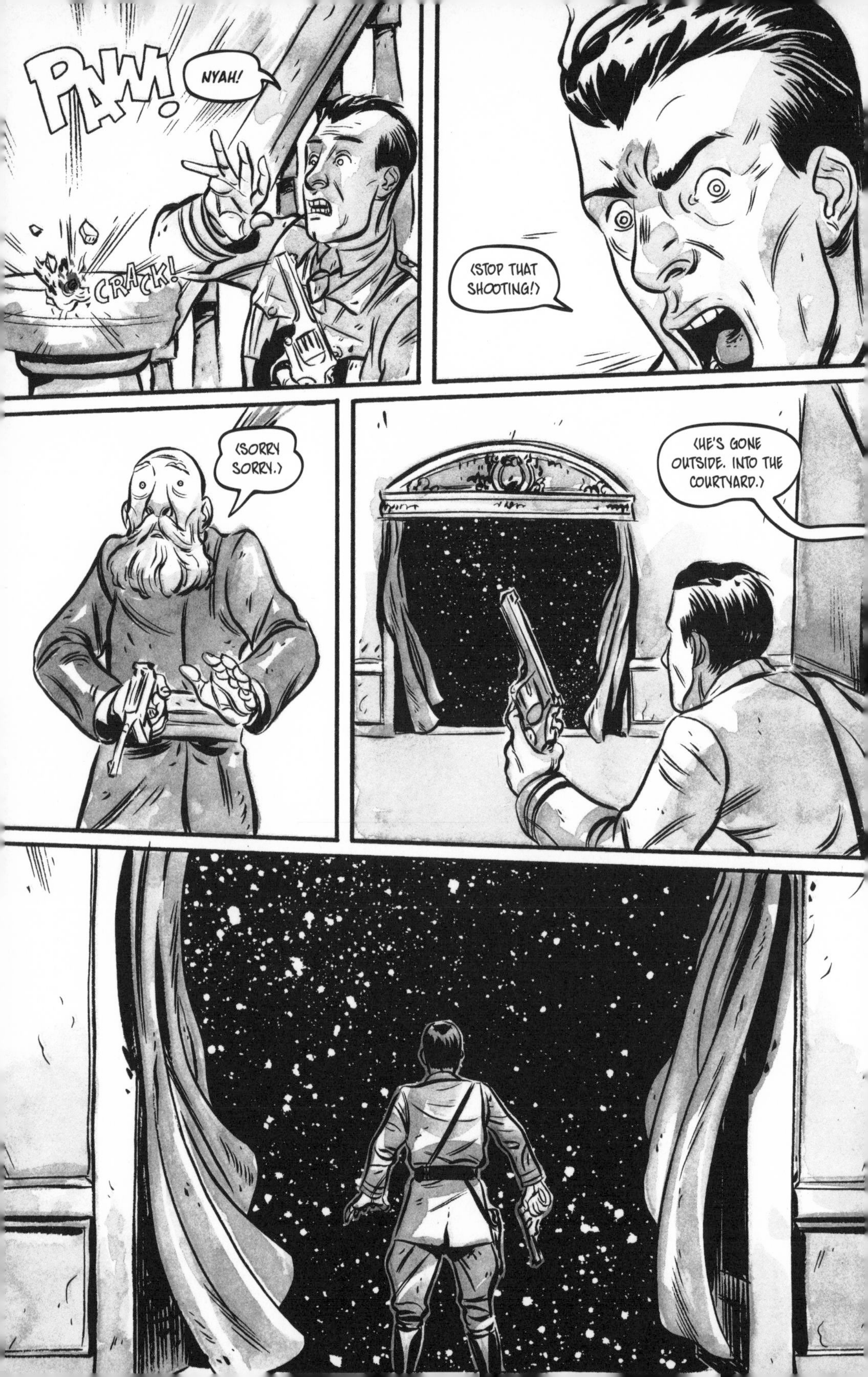
PAW!
NYAH!
CRACK!
‹STOP THAT SHOOTING!›
‹SORRY SORRY.›
‹HE'S GONE OUTSIDE. INTO THE COURTYARD.›

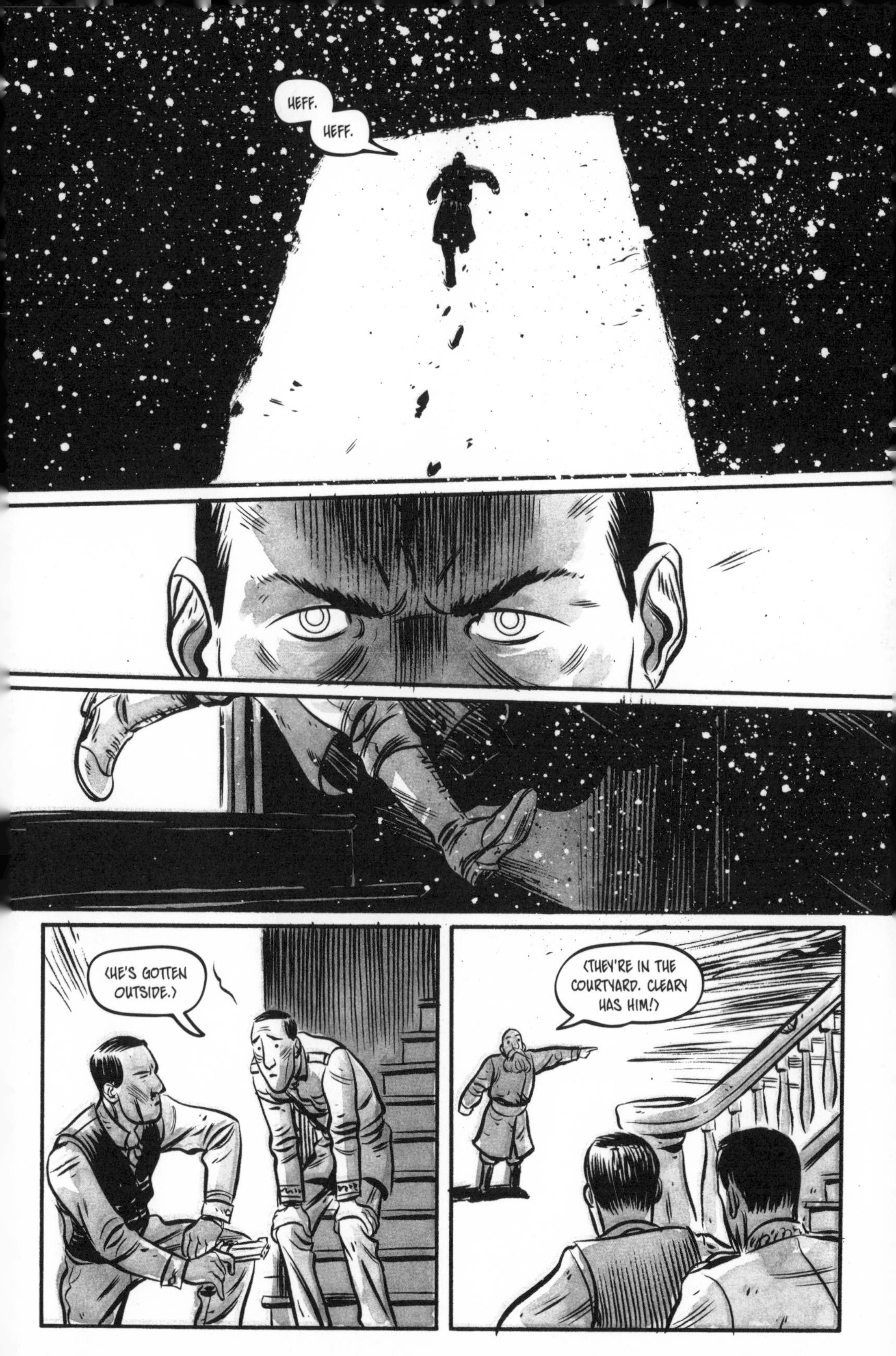
HEFF.
HEFF.
‹HE'S GOTTEN OUTSIDE.›
‹THEY'RE IN THE COURTYARD. CLEARY HAS HIM!›

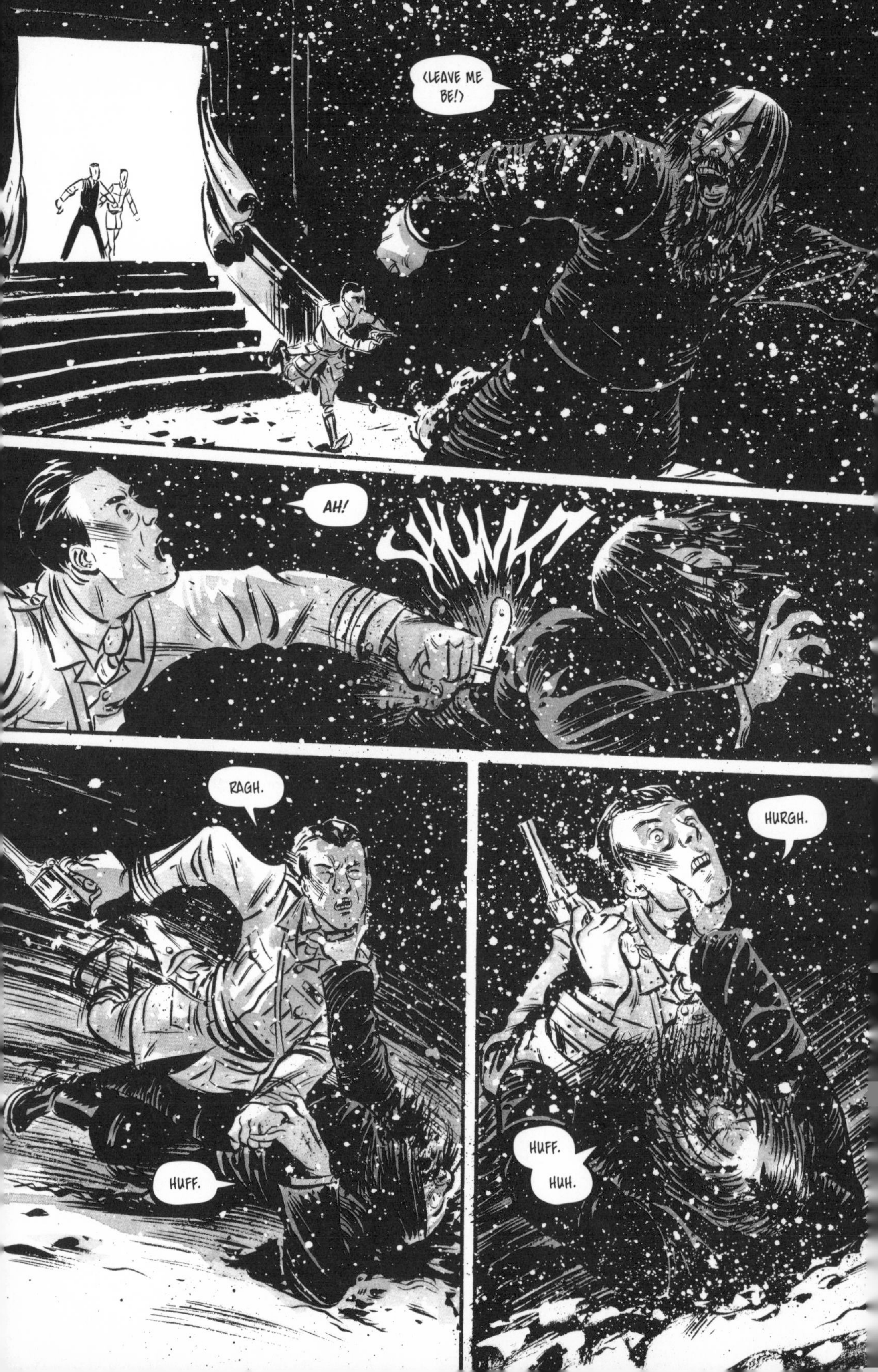
<LEAVE ME BE!>
AH!
SHUNK!
RAGH.
HUFF.
HURGH.
HUFF.
HUH.

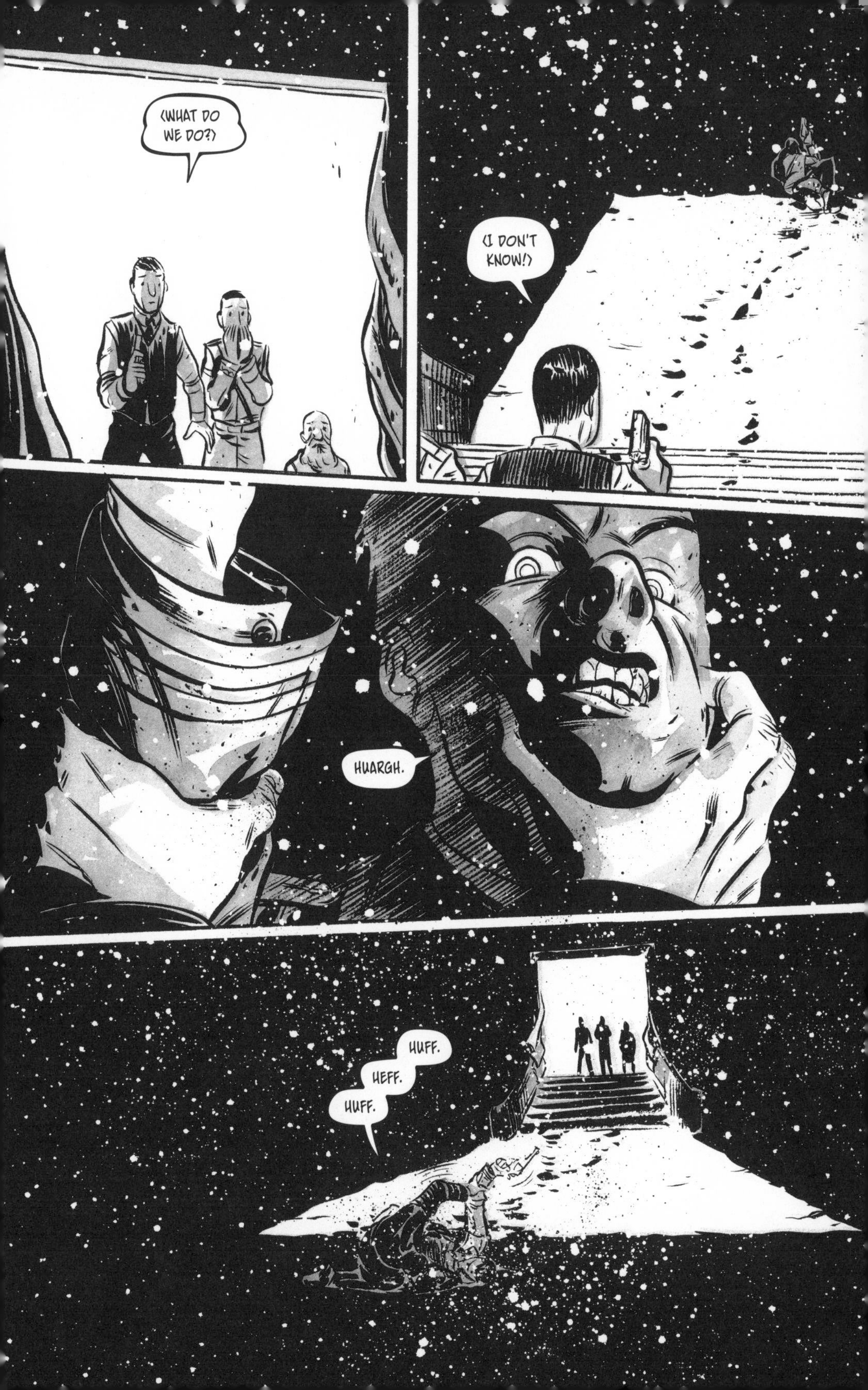

<WHAT DO WE DO?>
<I DON'T KNOW!>
HUARGH.
HUFF.
HEFF.
HUFF.

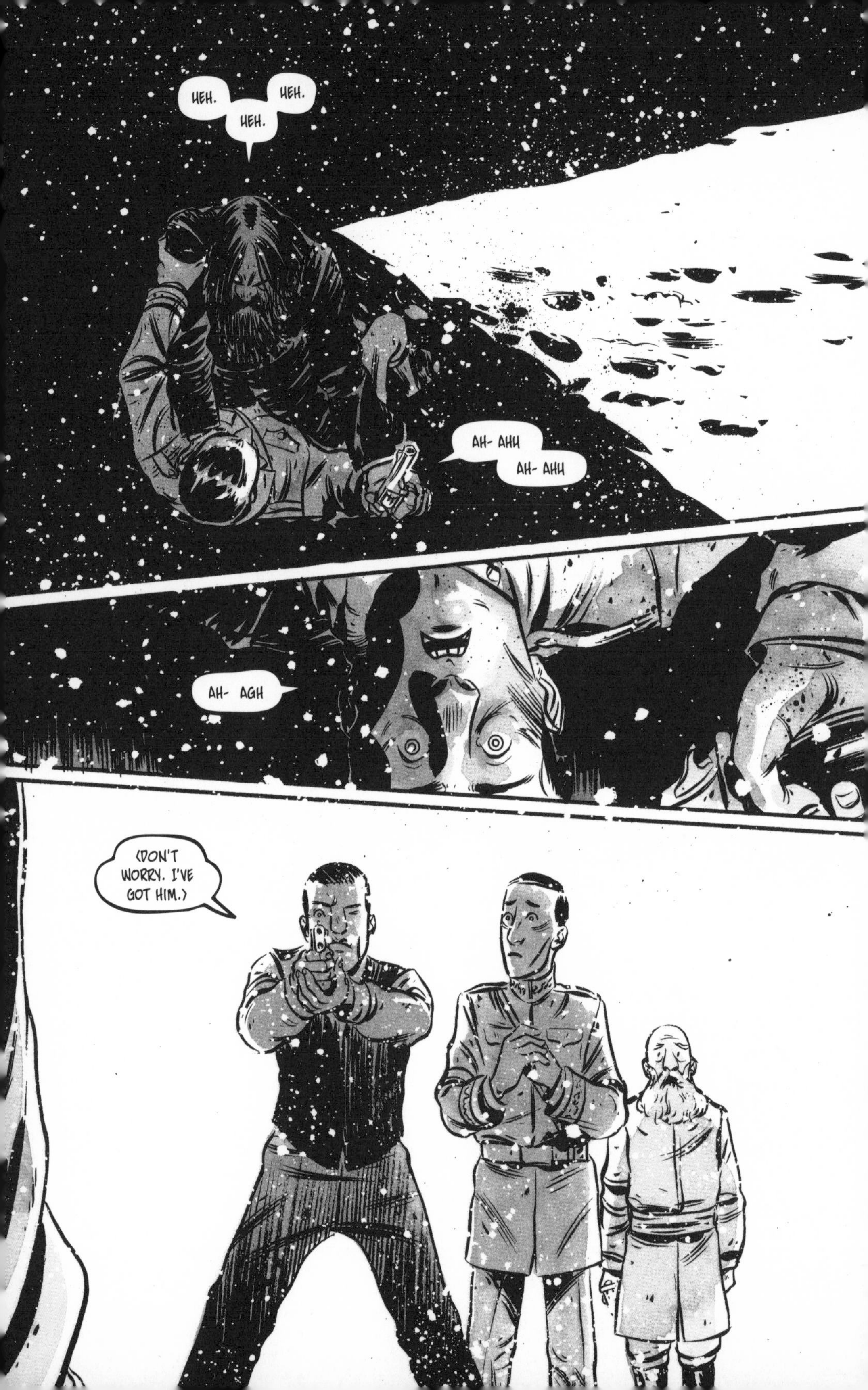
HEH.
HEH.
HEH.
AH- AHH
AH- AHH
AH- AGH
<DON'T WORRY. I'VE GOT HIM.>

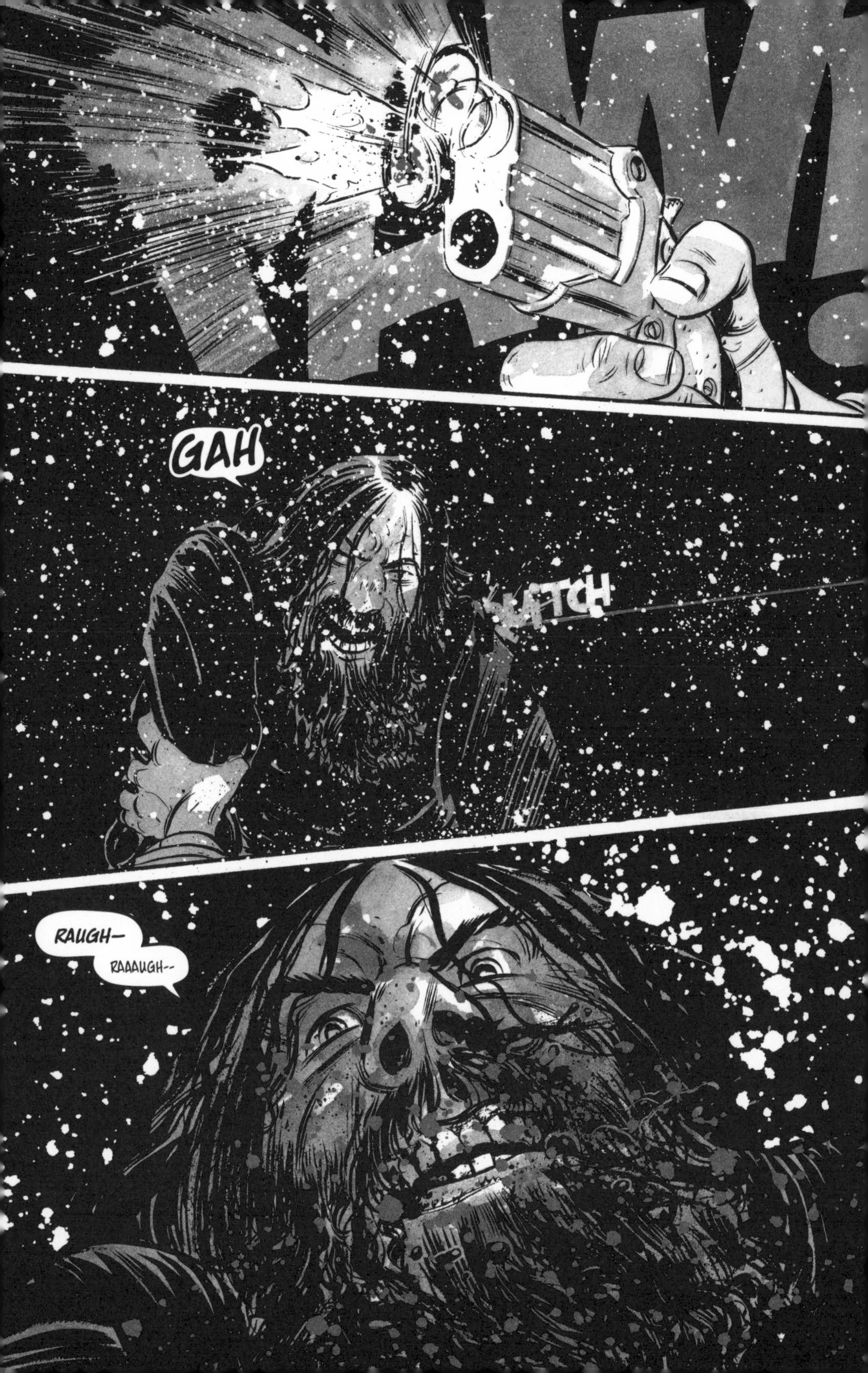
GAH
RAUGH—
RAAAUGH--

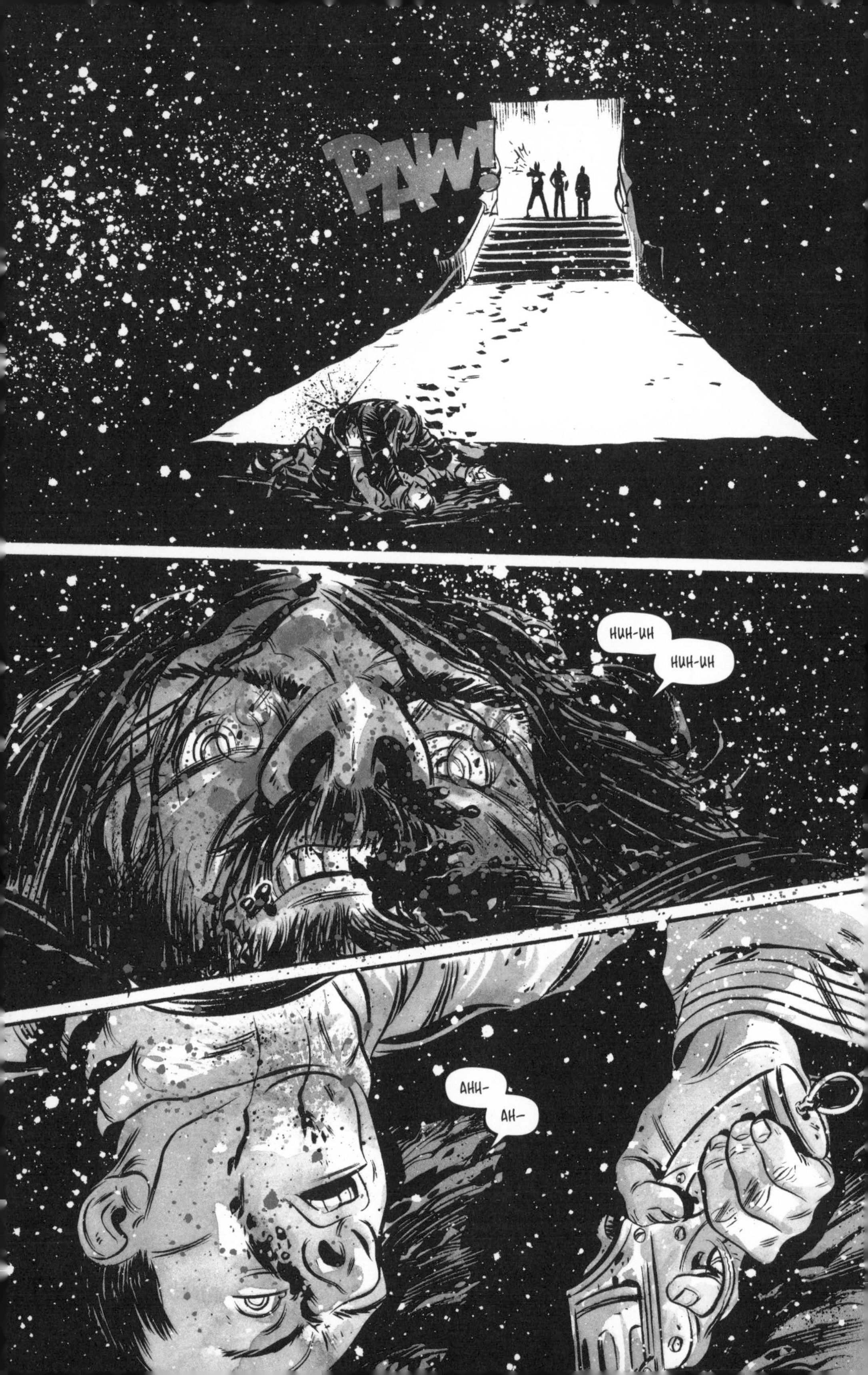
PAW!
HUH-UH
HUH-UH
AHH-
AH-

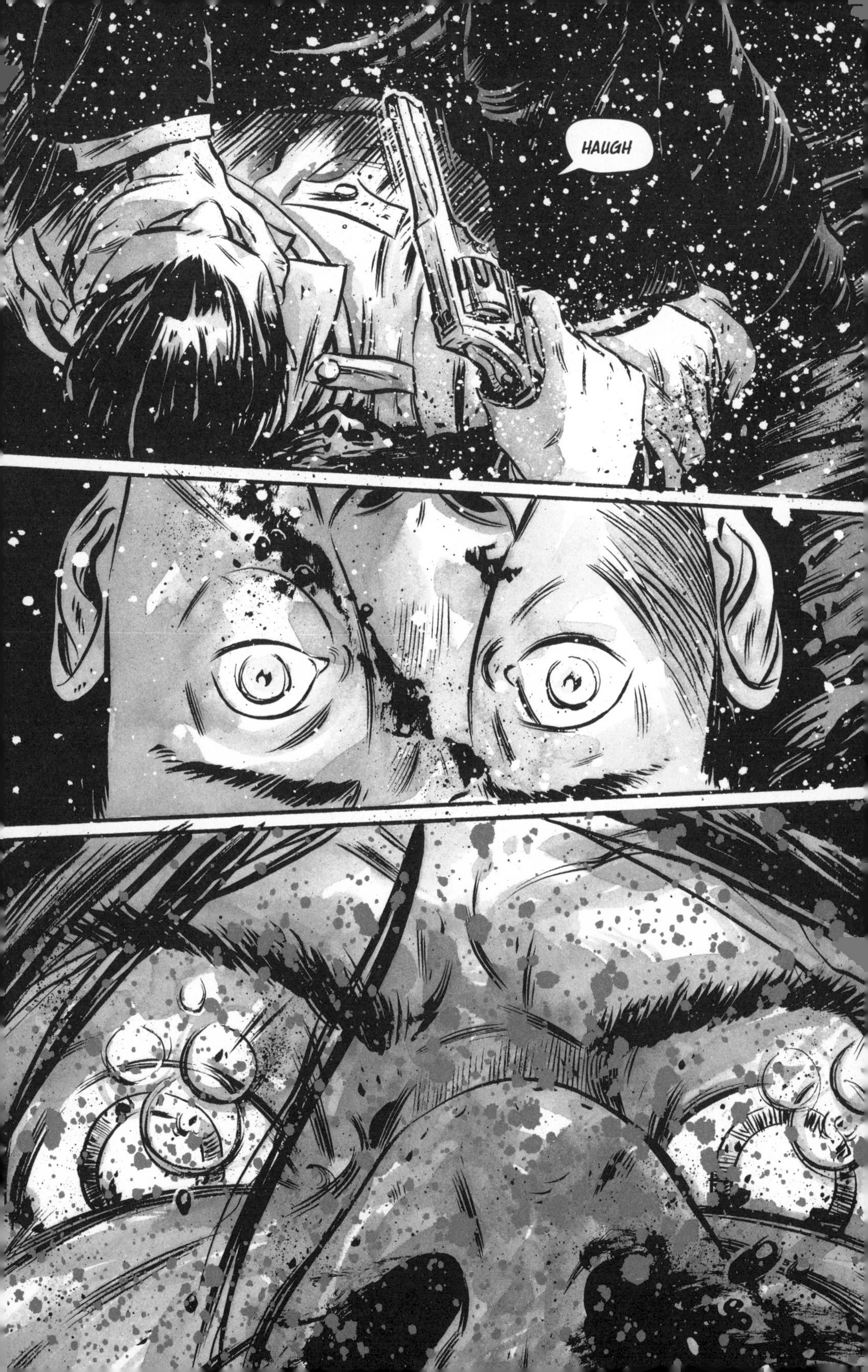
HAUGH

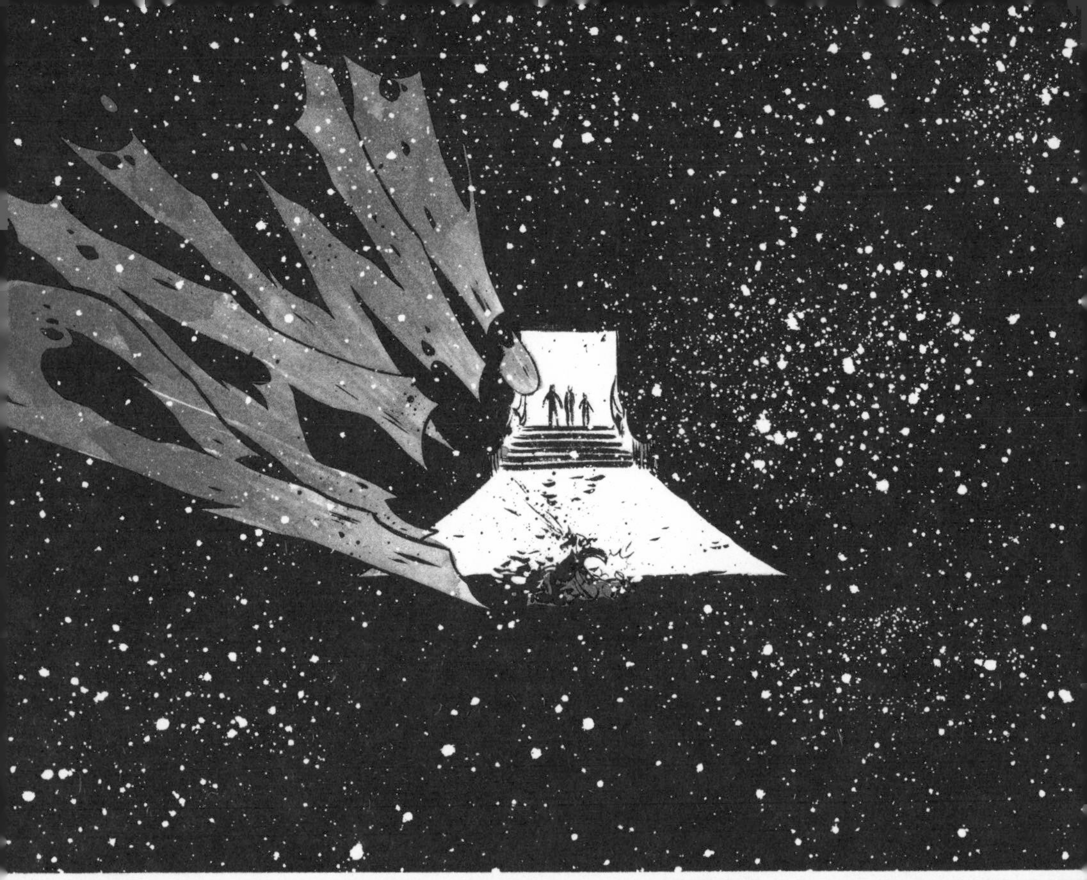
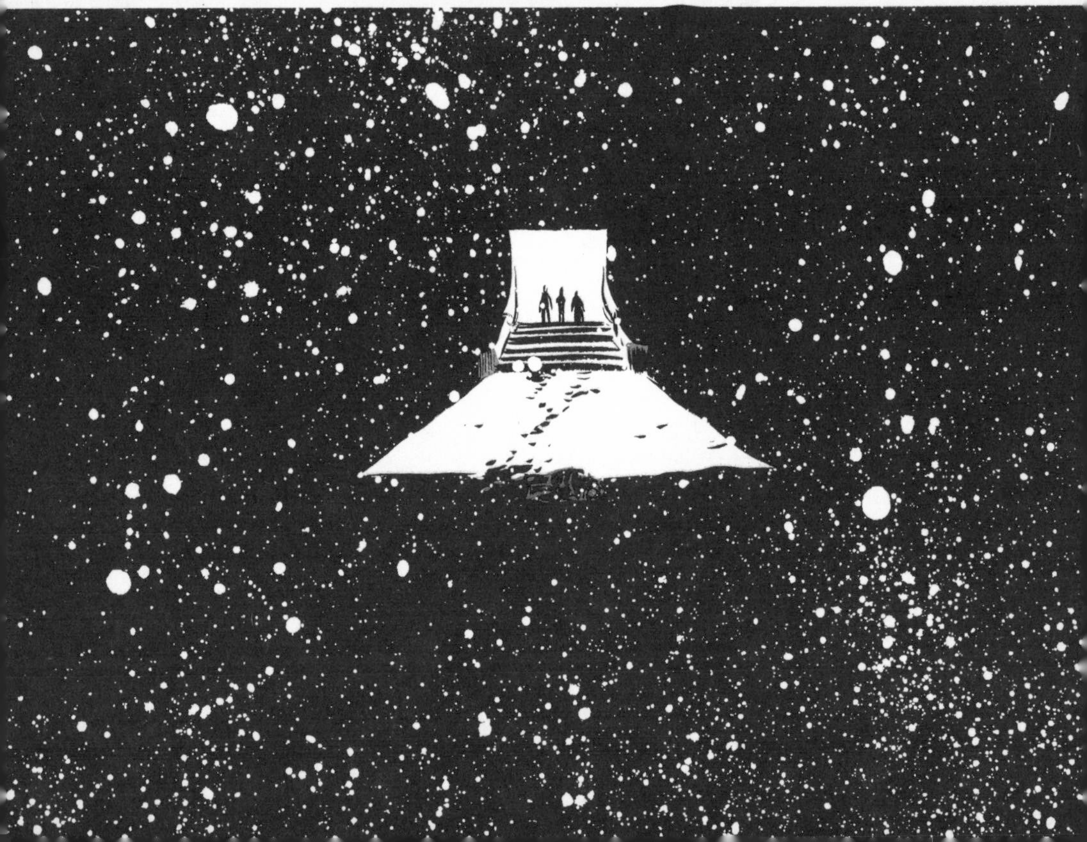

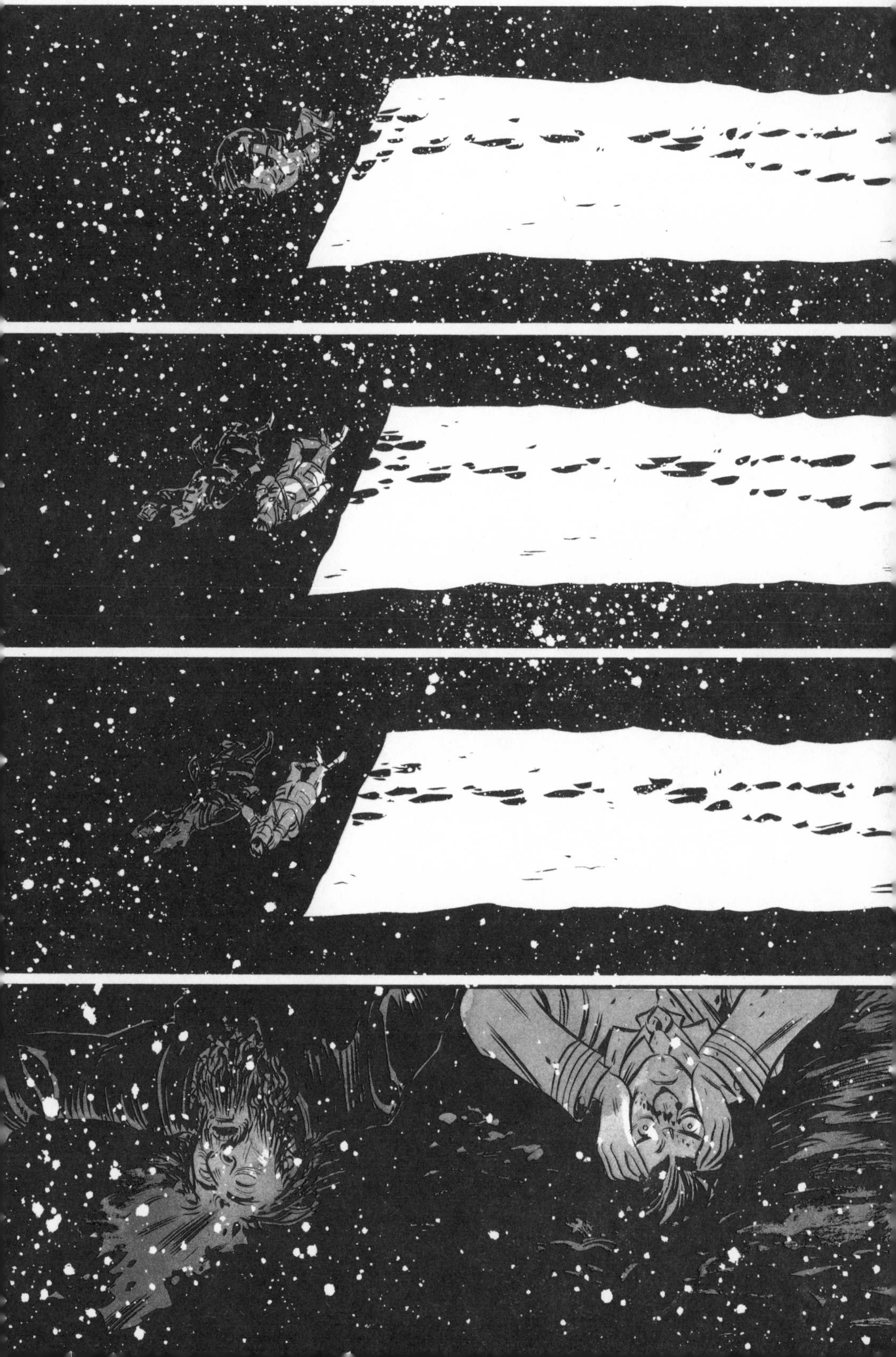

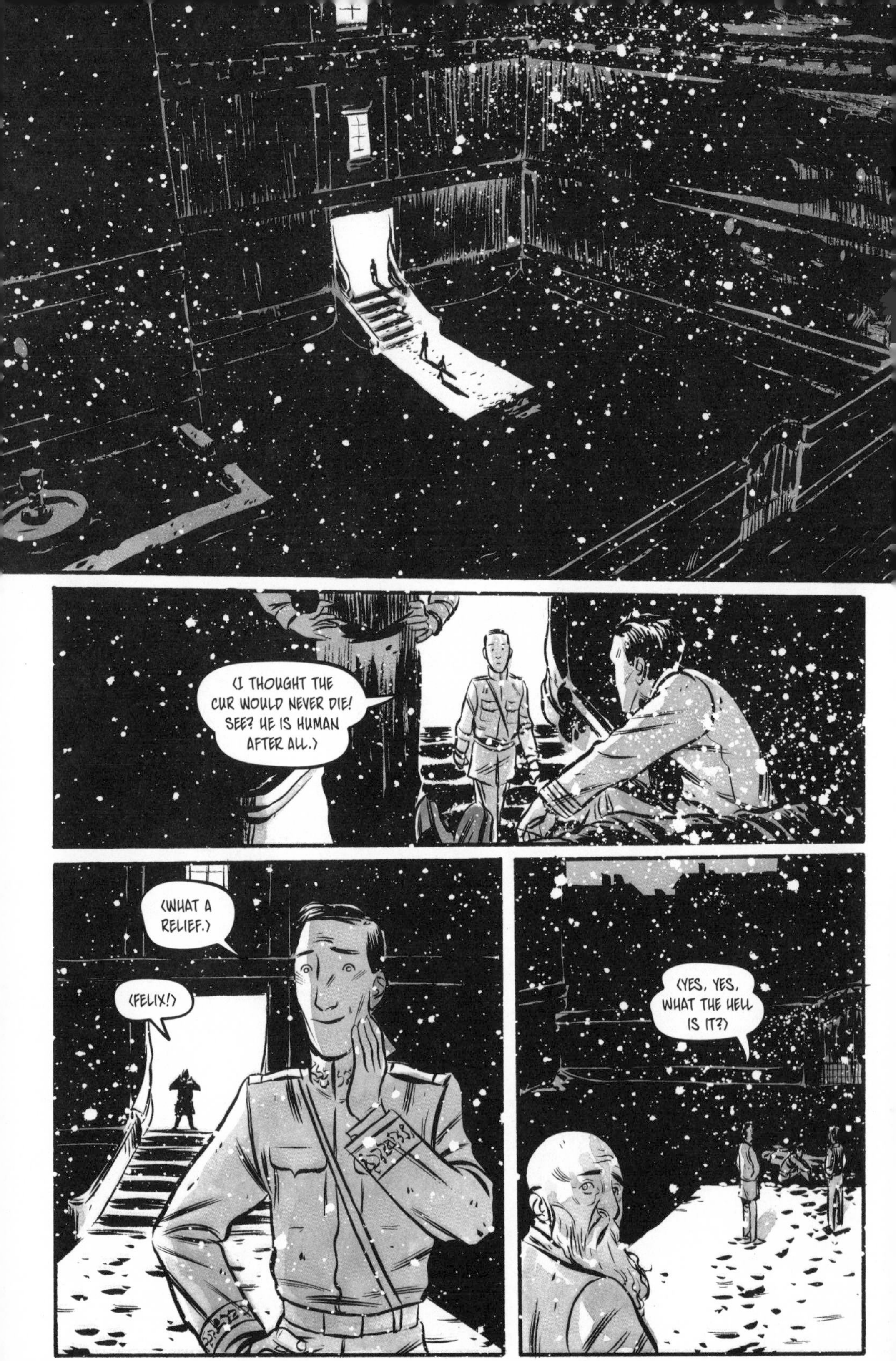

<I THOUGHT THE CUR WOULD NEVER DIE! SEE? HE IS HUMAN AFTER ALL.>
<WHAT A RELIEF.>
<FELIX!>
<YES, YES, WHAT THE HELL IS IT?>

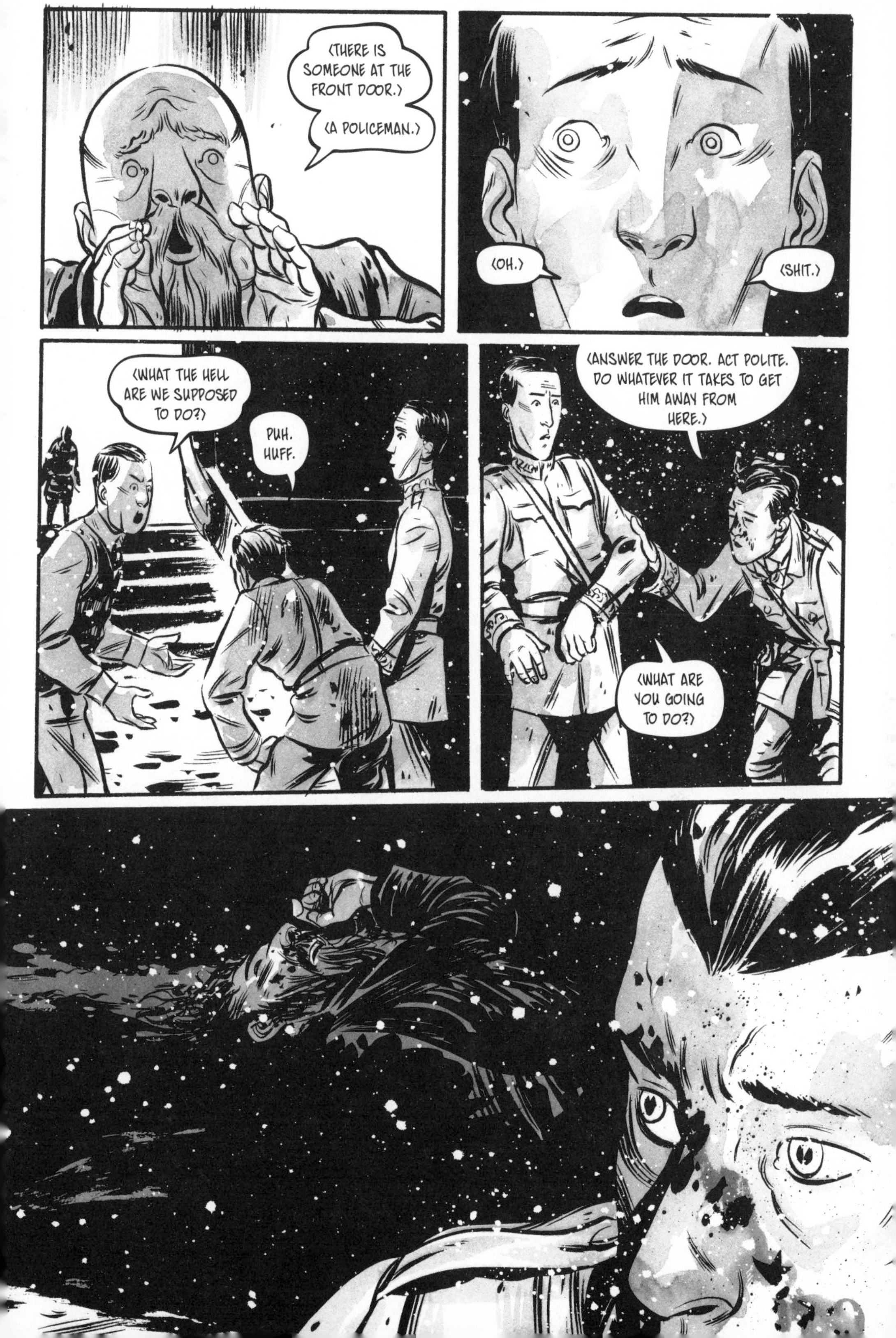

‹THERE IS SOMEONE AT THE FRONT DOOR.›
‹A POLICEMAN.›
‹OH.›
‹SHIT.›
‹WHAT THE HELL ARE WE SUPPOSED TO DO?›
PUH. HUFF.
‹ANSWER THE DOOR. ACT POLITE. DO WHATEVER IT TAKES TO GET HIM AWAY FROM HERE.›
‹WHAT ARE YOU GOING TO DO?›

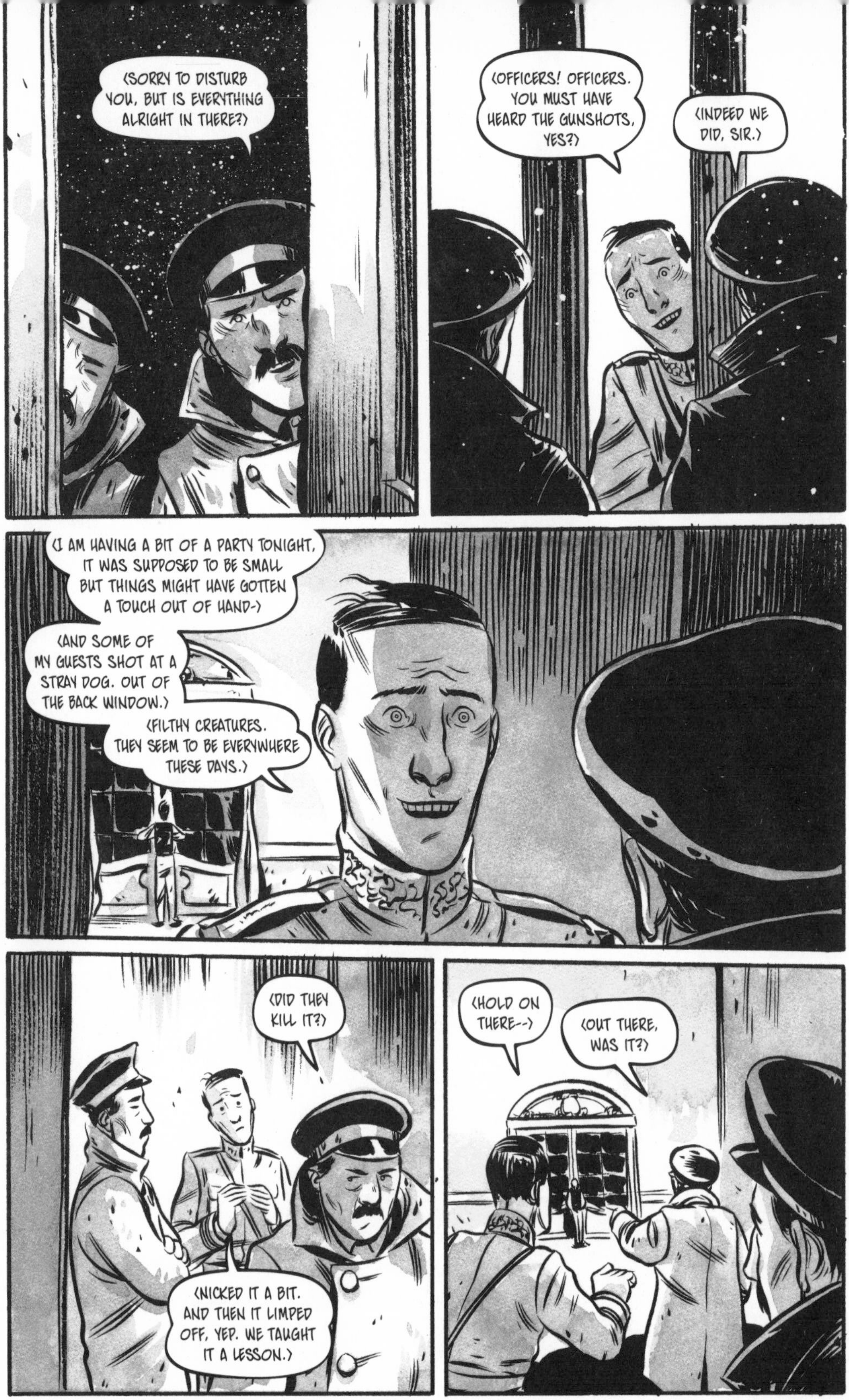
(SORRY TO DISTURB YOU, BUT IS EVERYTHING ALRIGHT IN THERE?)
(OFFICERS! OFFICERS. YOU MUST HAVE HEARD THE GUNSHOTS, YES?)
(INDEED WE DID, SIR.)
(I AM HAVING A BIT OF A PARTY TONIGHT, IT WAS SUPPOSED TO BE SMALL BUT THINGS MIGHT HAVE GOTTEN A TOUCH OUT OF HAND-)
(AND SOME OF MY GUESTS SHOT AT A STRAY DOG. OUT OF THE BACK WINDOW.)
(FILTHY CREATURES. THEY SEEM TO BE EVERYWHERE THESE DAYS.)
(DID THEY KILL IT?)
(NICKED IT A BIT. AND THEN IT LIMPED OFF, YEP. WE TAUGHT IT A LESSON.)
(HOLD ON THERE--)
(OUT THERE, WAS IT?)

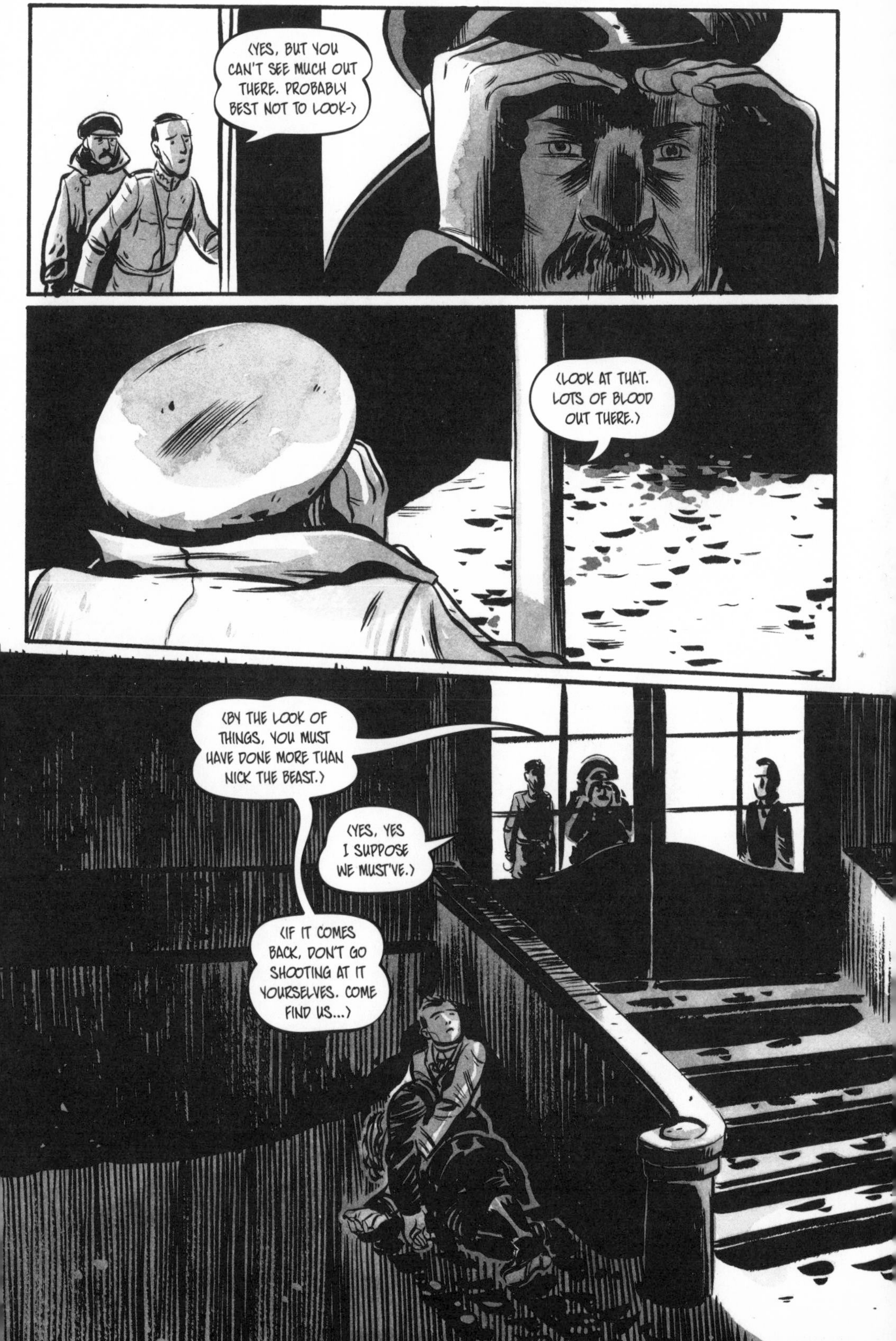
‹YES, BUT YOU CAN'T SEE MUCH OUT THERE. PROBABLY BEST NOT TO LOOK-›
‹LOOK AT THAT. LOTS OF BLOOD OUT THERE.›
‹BY THE LOOK OF THINGS, YOU MUST HAVE DONE MORE THAN NICK THE BEAST.›
‹YES, YES I SUPPOSE WE MUST'VE.›
‹IF IT COMES BACK, DON'T GO SHOOTING AT IT YOURSELVES. COME FIND US...›

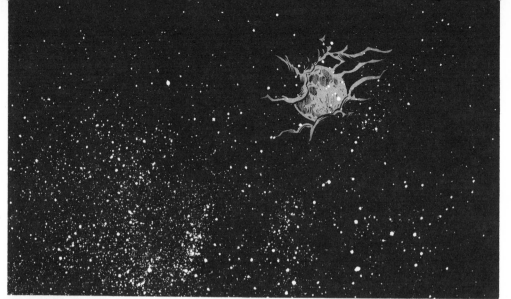

(WELL THAT WAS DAMNED CLOSE WASN'T.)

(I THOUGH WE WER CAUGHT F SURE.)

(NICE ORK CLEARY. DIDN'T THINK OU HAD IT IN YOU.)

(DMITRI ALMOST RUINED THE WHOL THING. I DIDN'T KN YOU COULD BE SO CLUMSY!)

(HOW THE HELL DID YOU TRIP, DMITR WHAT WERE YOU THINKING?)

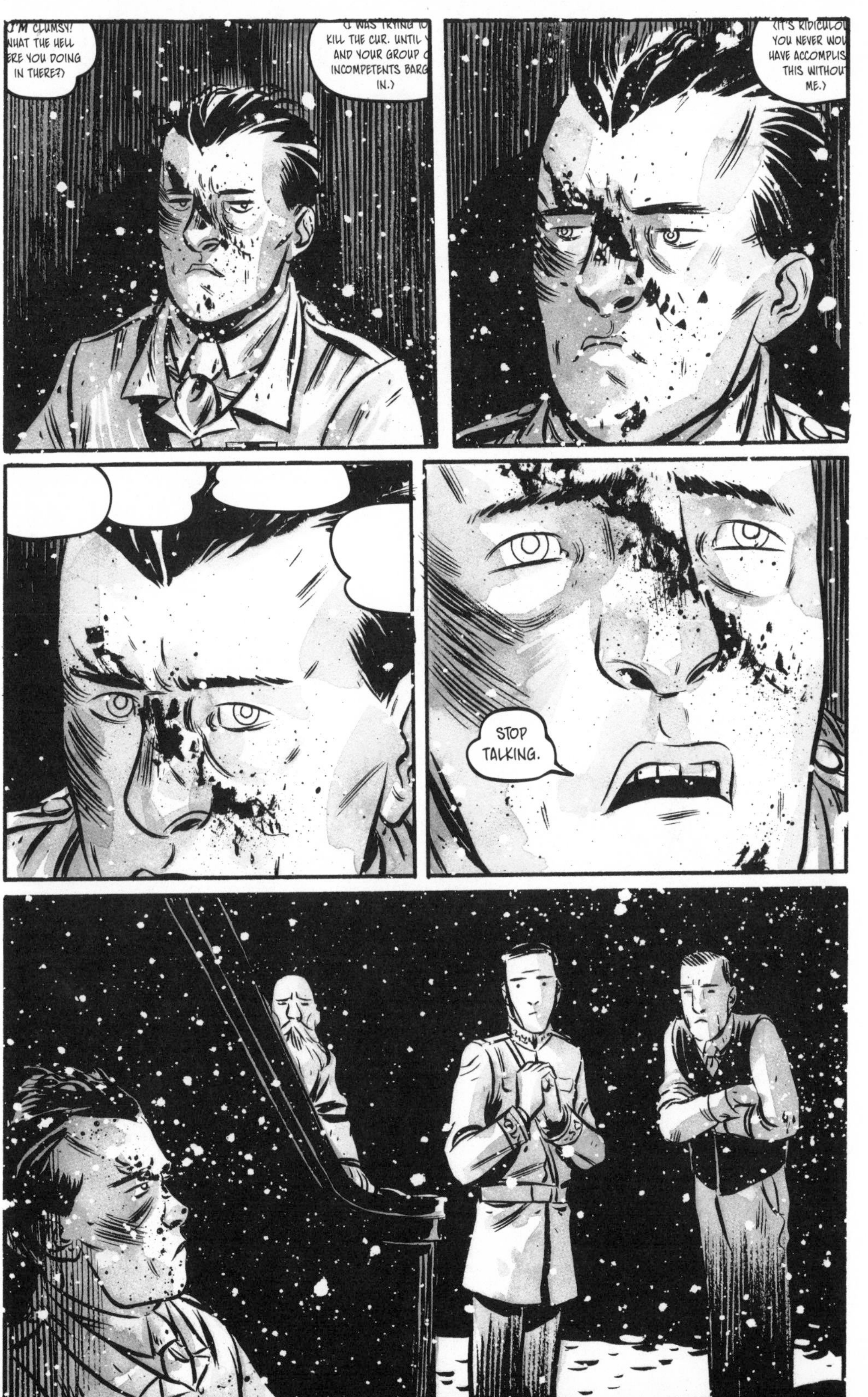
I'M CLUMSY! WHAT THE HELL ERE YOU DOING IN THERE?>
<I WAS TRYING TO KILL THE CUR. UNTIL Y AND YOUR GROUP O INCOMPETENTS BARG IN.>
<IT'S RIDICULOU YOU NEVER WOU HAVE ACCOMPLIS THIS WITHOUT ME.>
STOP TALKING.

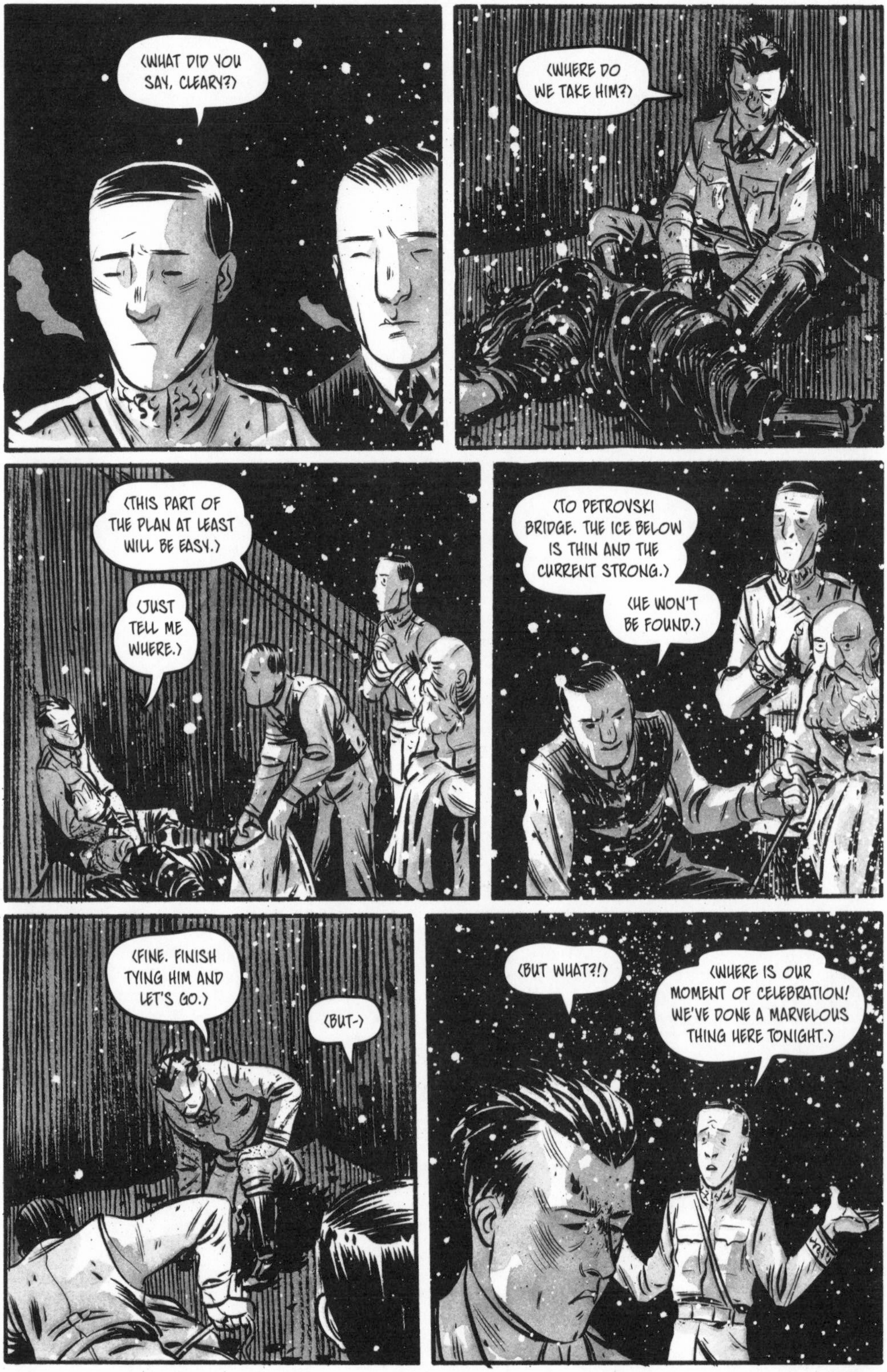
‹WHAT DID YOU SAY, CLEARY?›
‹WHERE DO WE TAKE HIM?›
‹THIS PART OF THE PLAN AT LEAST WILL BE EASY.›
‹JUST TELL ME WHERE.›
‹TO PETROVSKI BRIDGE. THE ICE BELOW IS THIN AND THE CURRENT STRONG.›
‹HE WON'T BE FOUND.›
‹FINE. FINISH TYING HIM AND LET'S GO.›
‹BUT-›
‹BUT WHAT?!›
‹WHERE IS OUR MOMENT OF CELEBRATION! WE'VE DONE A MARVELOUS THING HERE TONIGHT.›

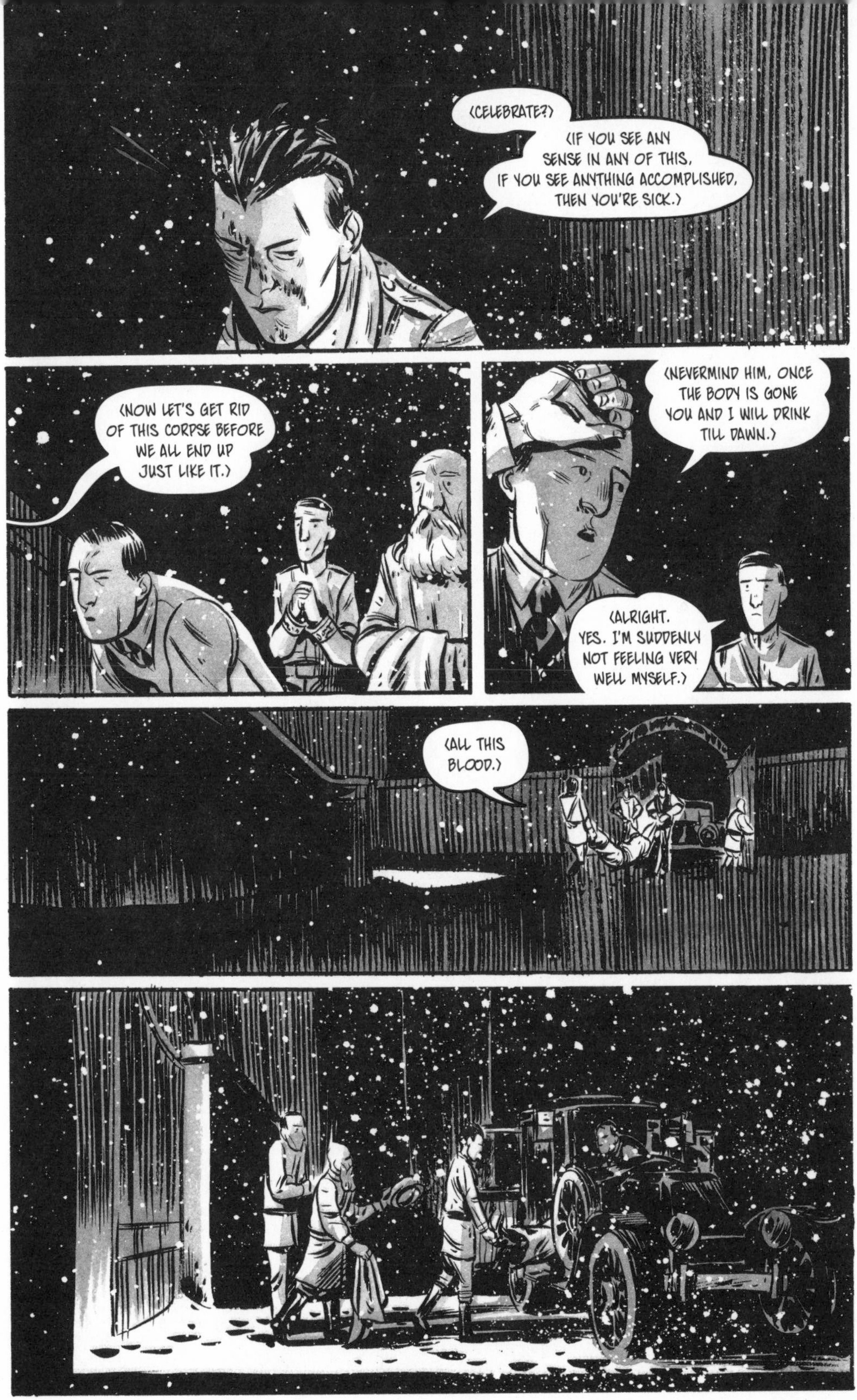
‹CELEBRATE?›
‹IF YOU SEE ANY SENSE IN ANY OF THIS, IF YOU SEE ANYTHING ACCOMPLISHED, THEN YOU'RE SICK.›
‹NOW LET'S GET RID OF THIS CORPSE BEFORE WE ALL END UP JUST LIKE IT.›
‹NEVERMIND HIM, ONCE THE BODY IS GONE YOU AND I WILL DRINK TILL DAWN.›
‹ALRIGHT. YES. I'M SUDDENLY NOT FEELING VERY WELL MYSELF.›
‹ALL THIS BLOOD.›

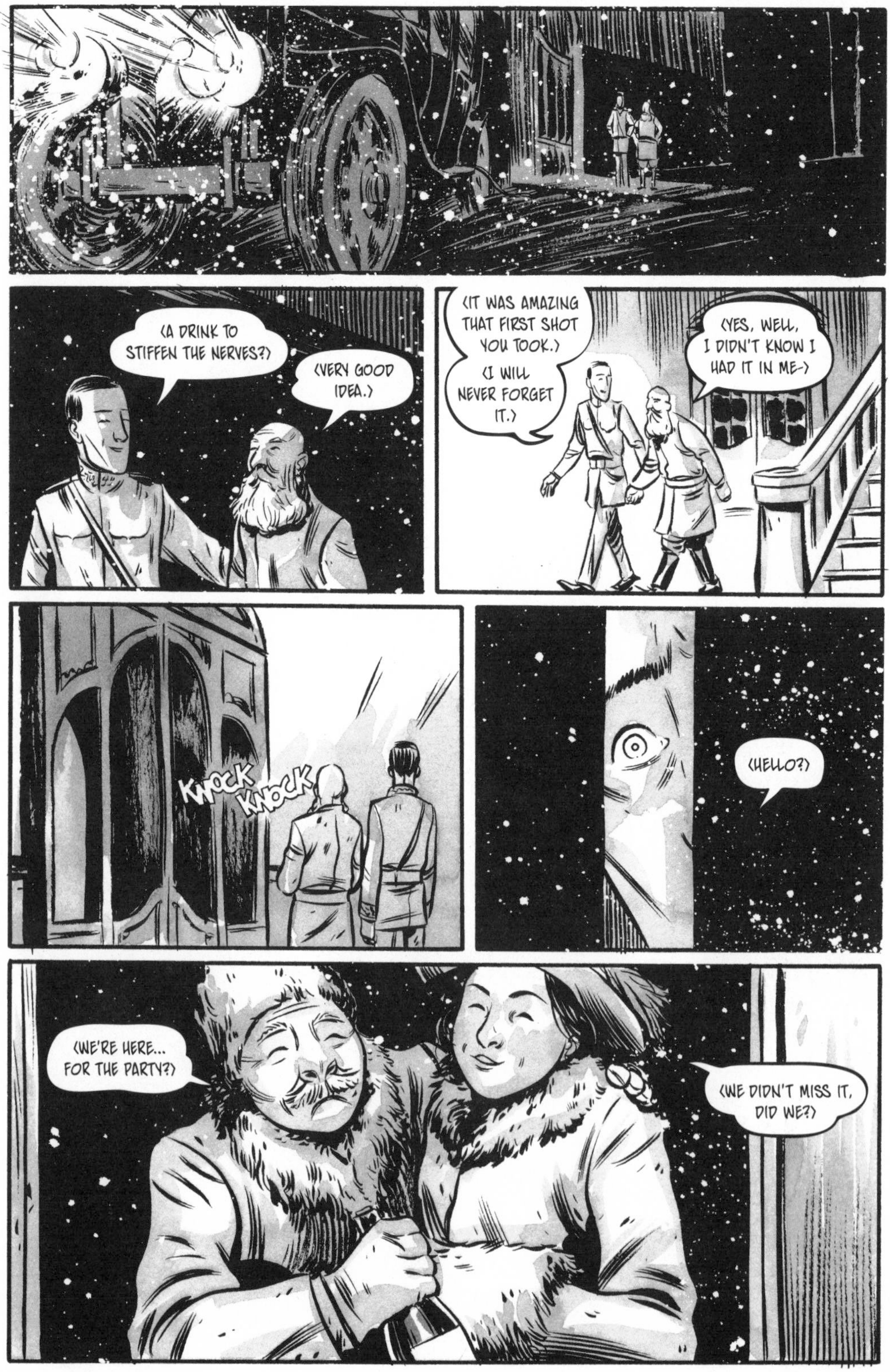

<A DRINK TO STIFFEN THE NERVES?>
<VERY GOOD IDEA.>
<IT WAS AMAZING THAT FIRST SHOT YOU TOOK.>
<I WILL NEVER FORGET IT.>
<YES, WELL, I DIDN'T KNOW I HAD IT IN ME->
KNOCK KNOCK
<HELLO?>
<WE'RE HERE... FOR THE PARTY?>
<WE DIDN'T MISS IT, DID WE?>

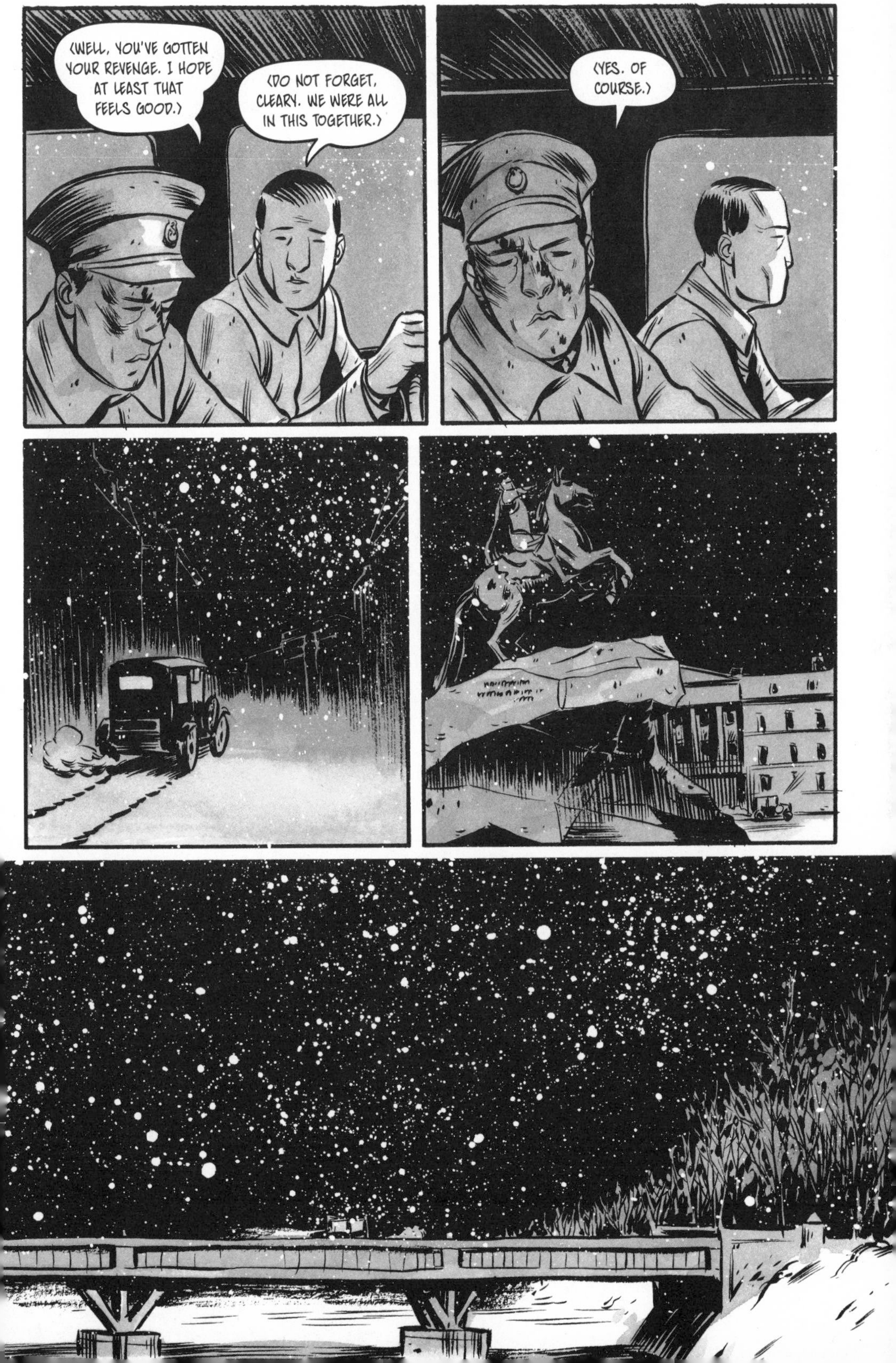

‹WELL, YOU'VE GOTTEN YOUR REVENGE. I HOPE AT LEAST THAT FEELS GOOD.›
‹DO NOT FORGET, CLEARY. WE WERE ALL IN THIS TOGETHER.›
‹YES. OF COURSE.›

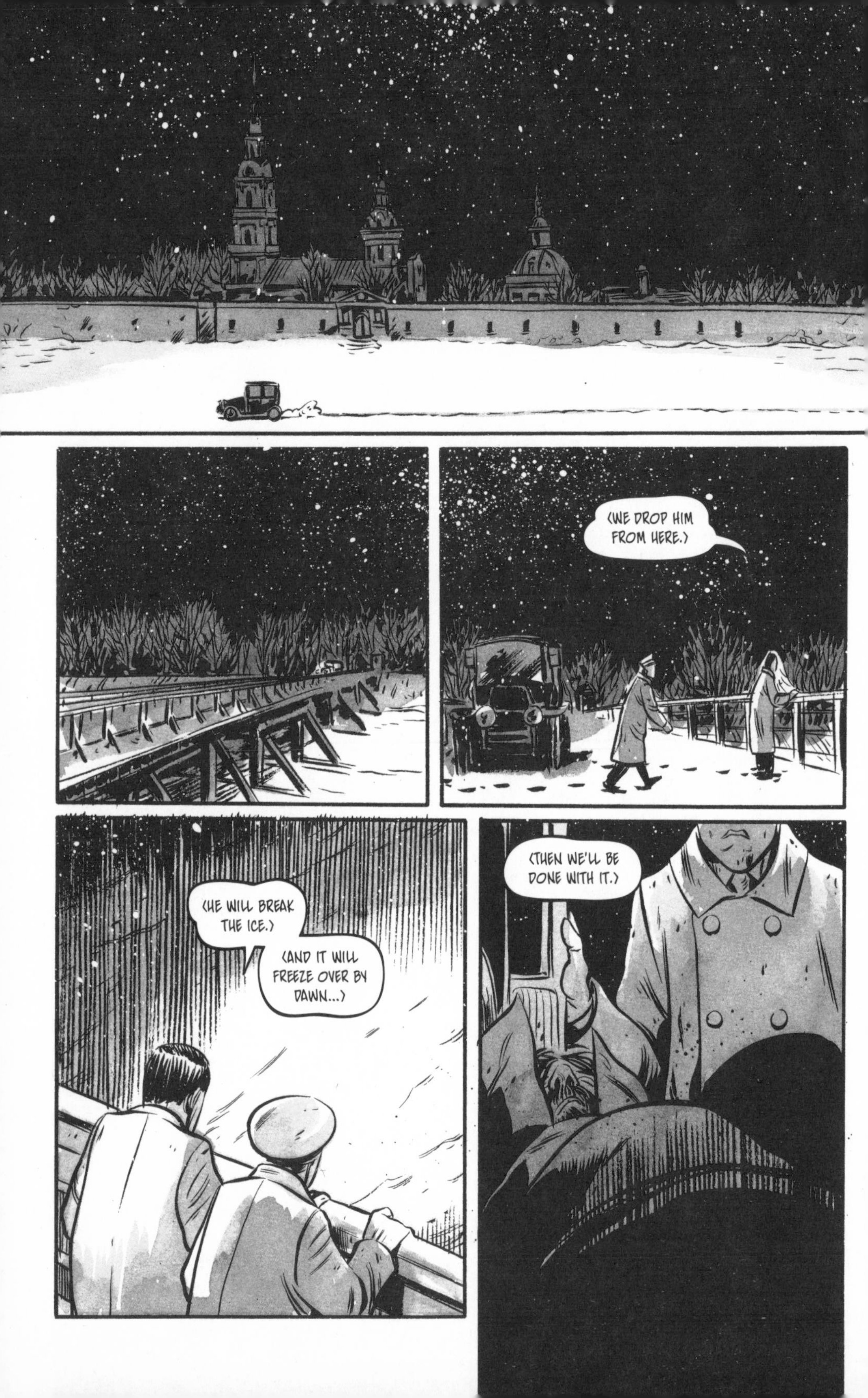
‹WE DROP HIM FROM HERE.›
‹HE WILL BREAK THE ICE.›
‹AND IT WILL FREEZE OVER BY DAWN...›
‹THEN WE'LL BE DONE WITH IT.›

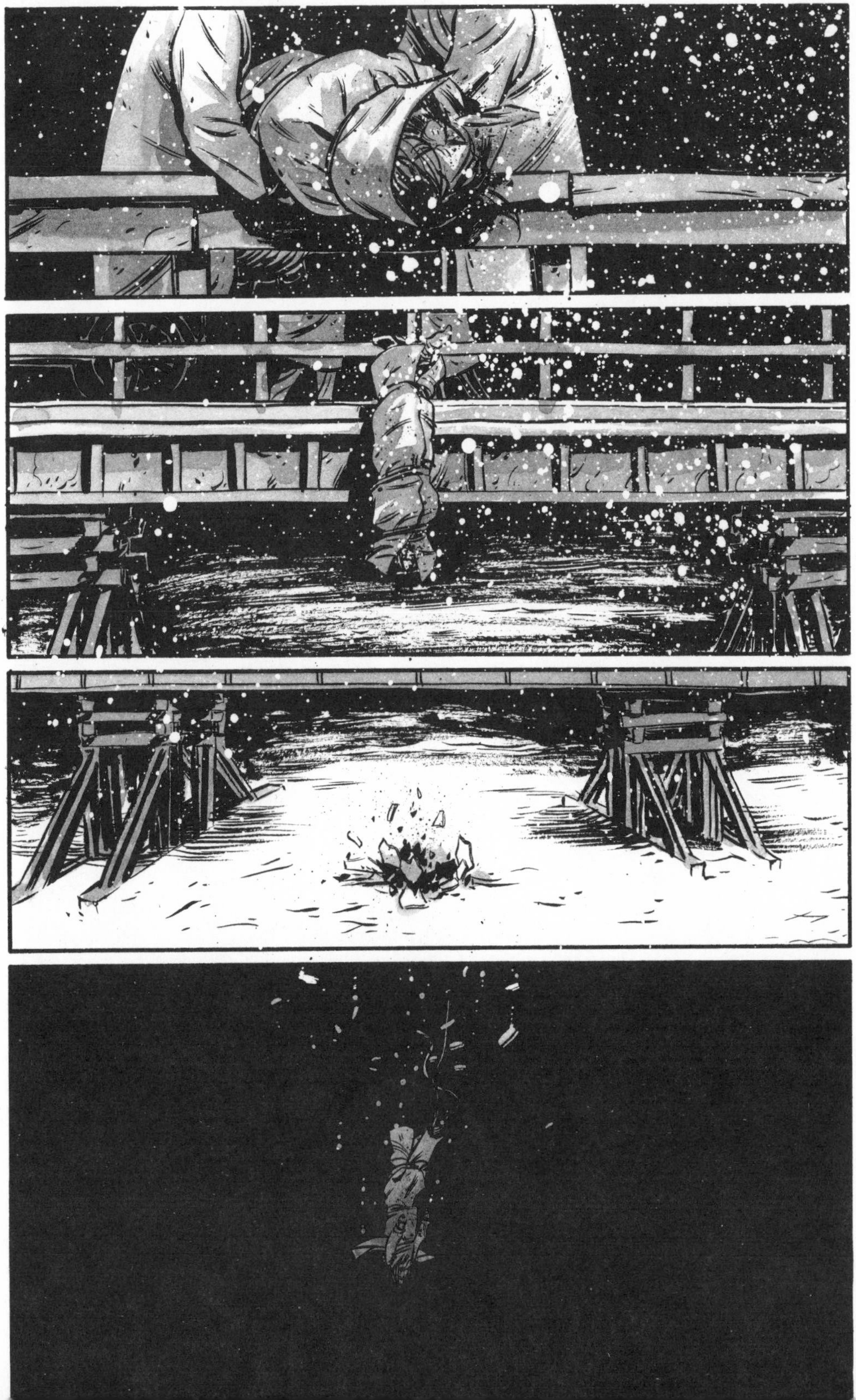

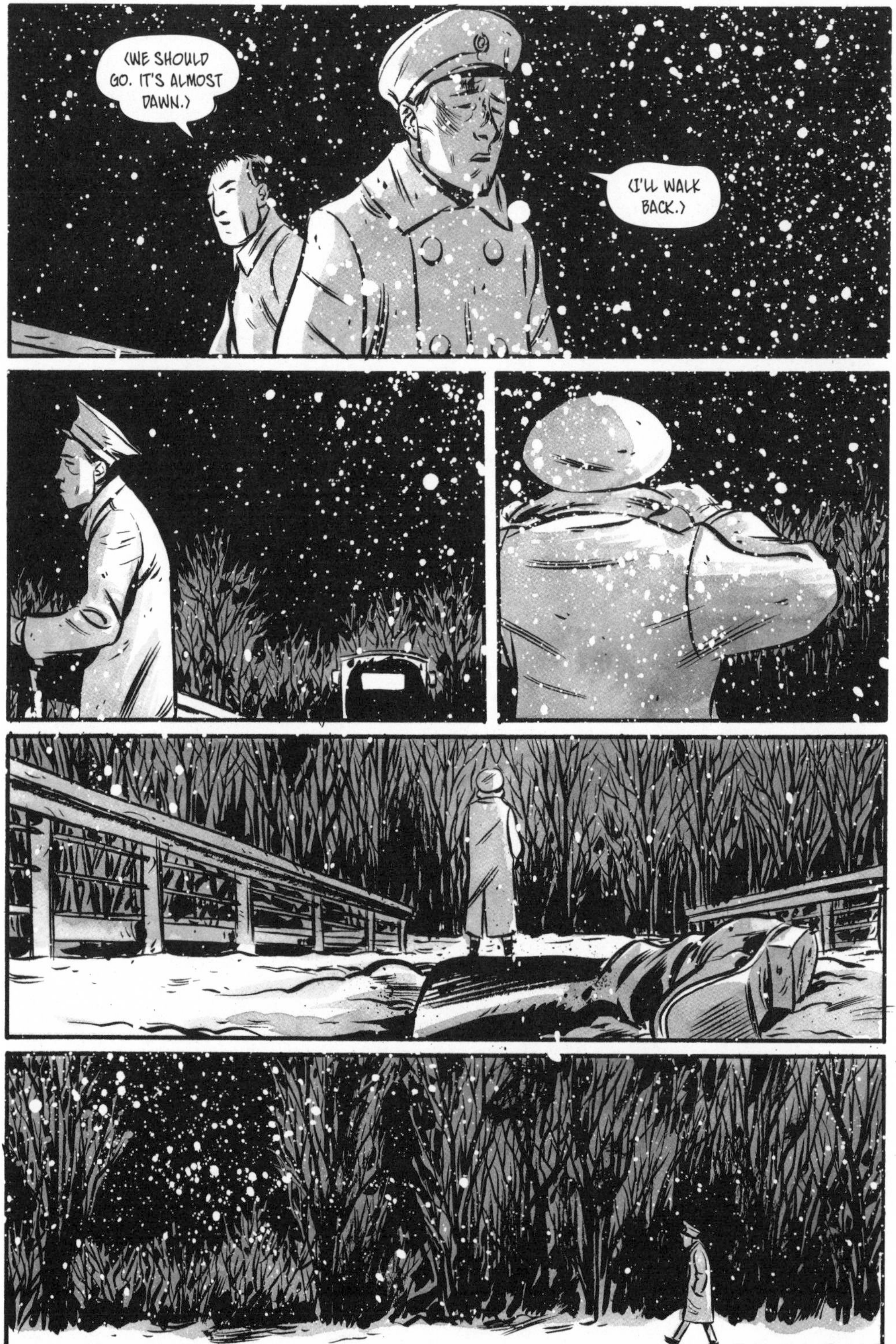
<WE SHOULD GO. IT'S ALMOST DAWN.>
<I'LL WALK BACK.>

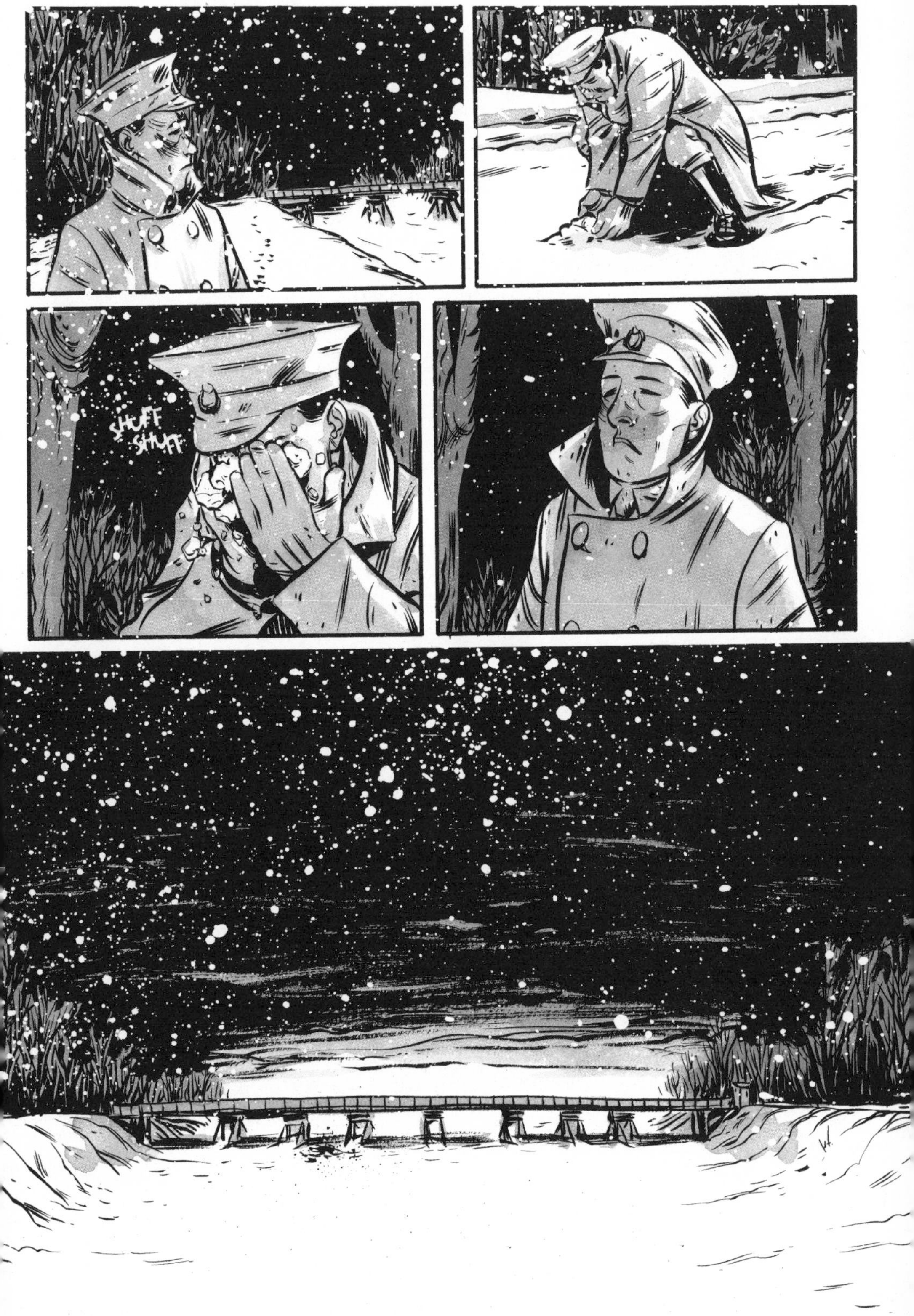
SHUFF
SHUFF

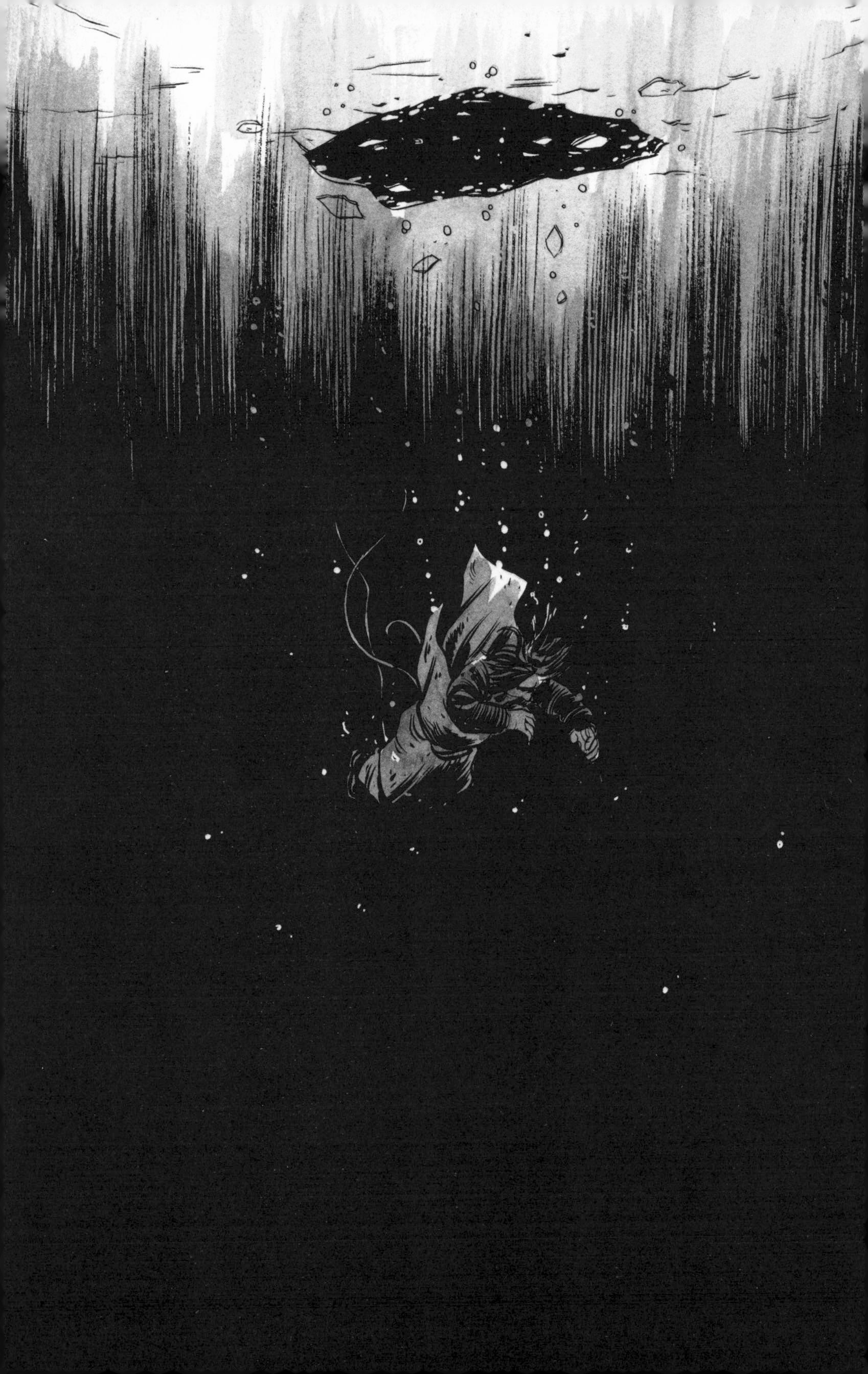

CHAPTER 4

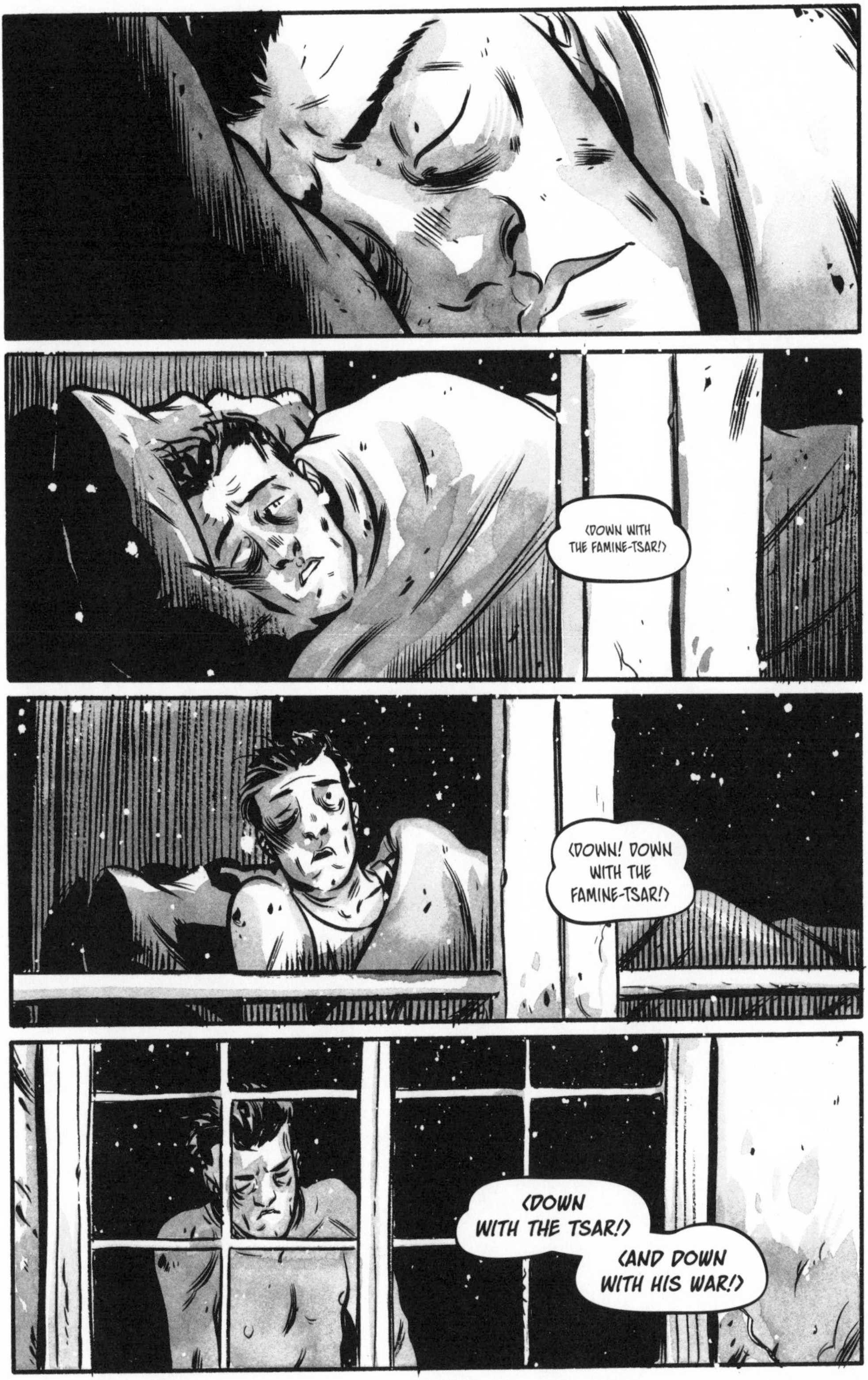
‹DOWN WITH THE FAMINE-TSAR!›
‹DOWN! DOWN WITH THE FAMINE-TSAR!›
‹DOWN WITH THE TSAR!›
‹AND DOWN WITH HIS WAR!›

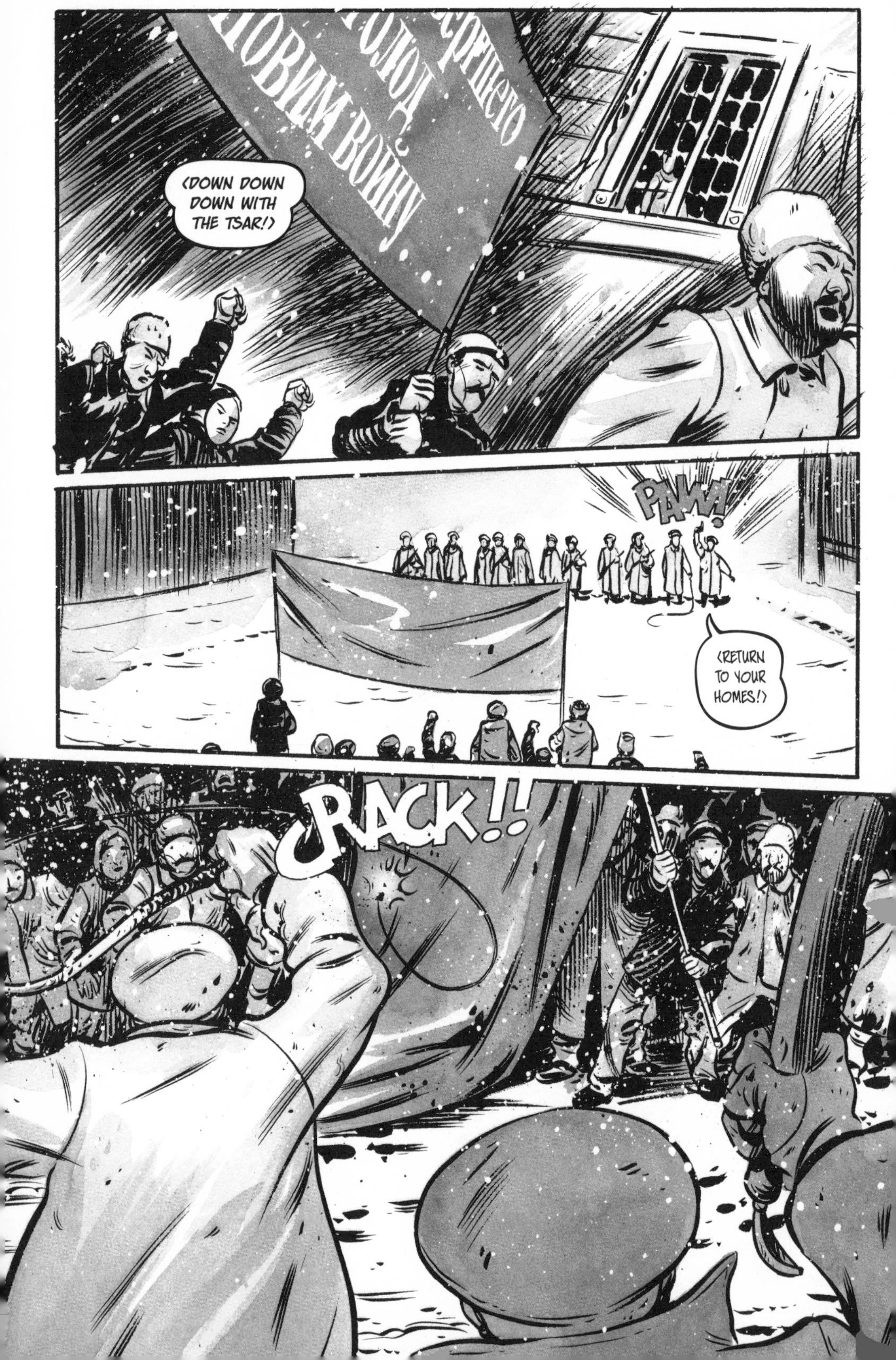
‹DOWN DOWN DOWN WITH THE TSAR!›
PAW!
‹RETURN TO YOUR HOMES!›
CRACK!!

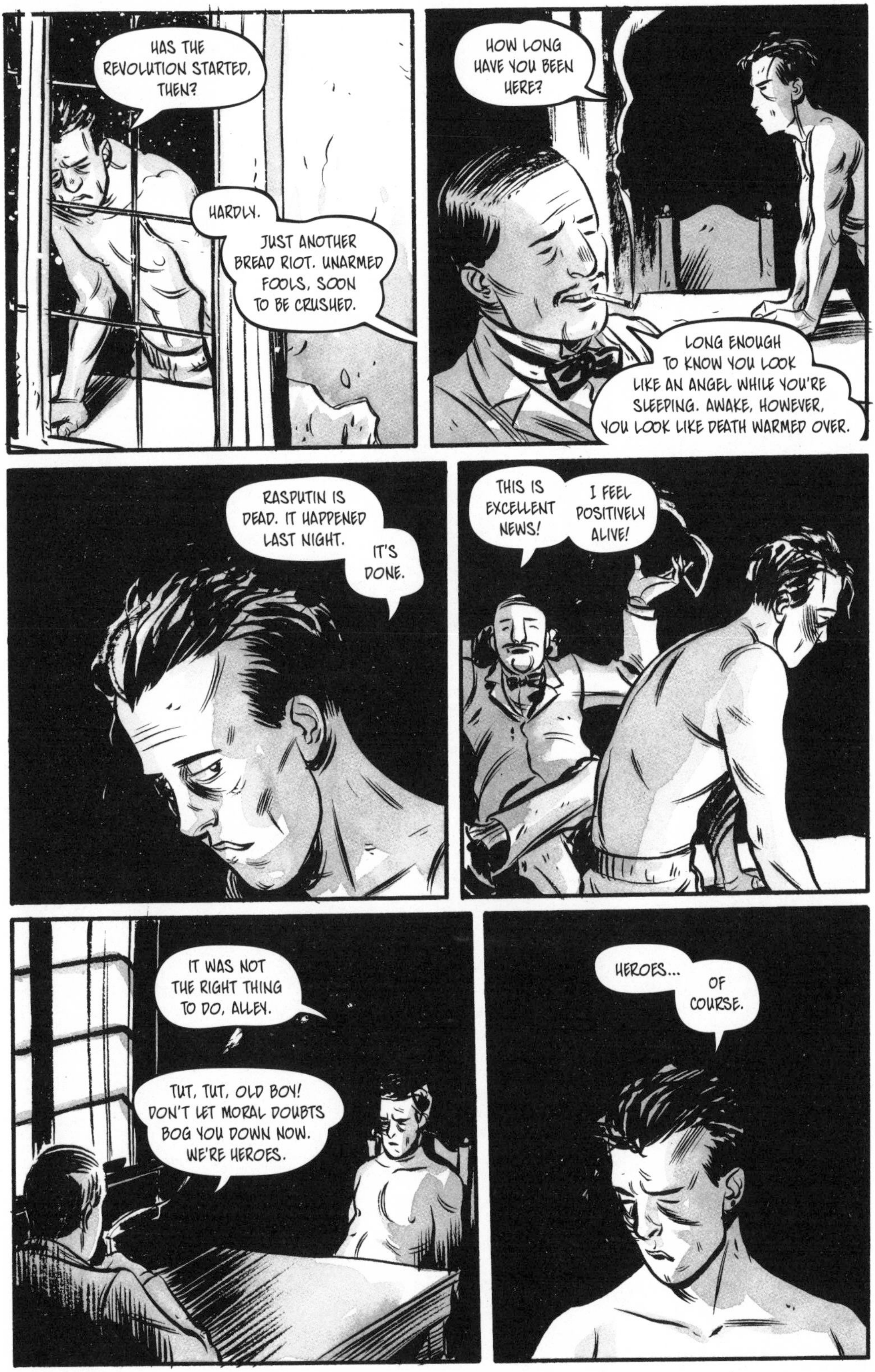
HAS THE REVOLUTION STARTED, THEN?
HARDLY.
JUST ANOTHER BREAD RIOT. UNARMED FOOLS, SOON TO BE CRUSHED.
HOW LONG HAVE YOU BEEN HERE?
LONG ENOUGH TO KNOW YOU LOOK LIKE AN ANGEL WHILE YOU'RE SLEEPING. AWAKE, HOWEVER, YOU LOOK LIKE DEATH WARMED OVER.
RASPUTIN IS DEAD. IT HAPPENED LAST NIGHT.
IT'S DONE.
THIS IS EXCELLENT NEWS!
I FEEL POSITIVELY ALIVE!
IT WAS NOT THE RIGHT THING TO DO, ALLEY.
TUT, TUT, OLD BOY! DON'T LET MORAL DOUBTS BOG YOU DOWN NOW. WE'RE HEROES.
HEROES...
OF COURSE.

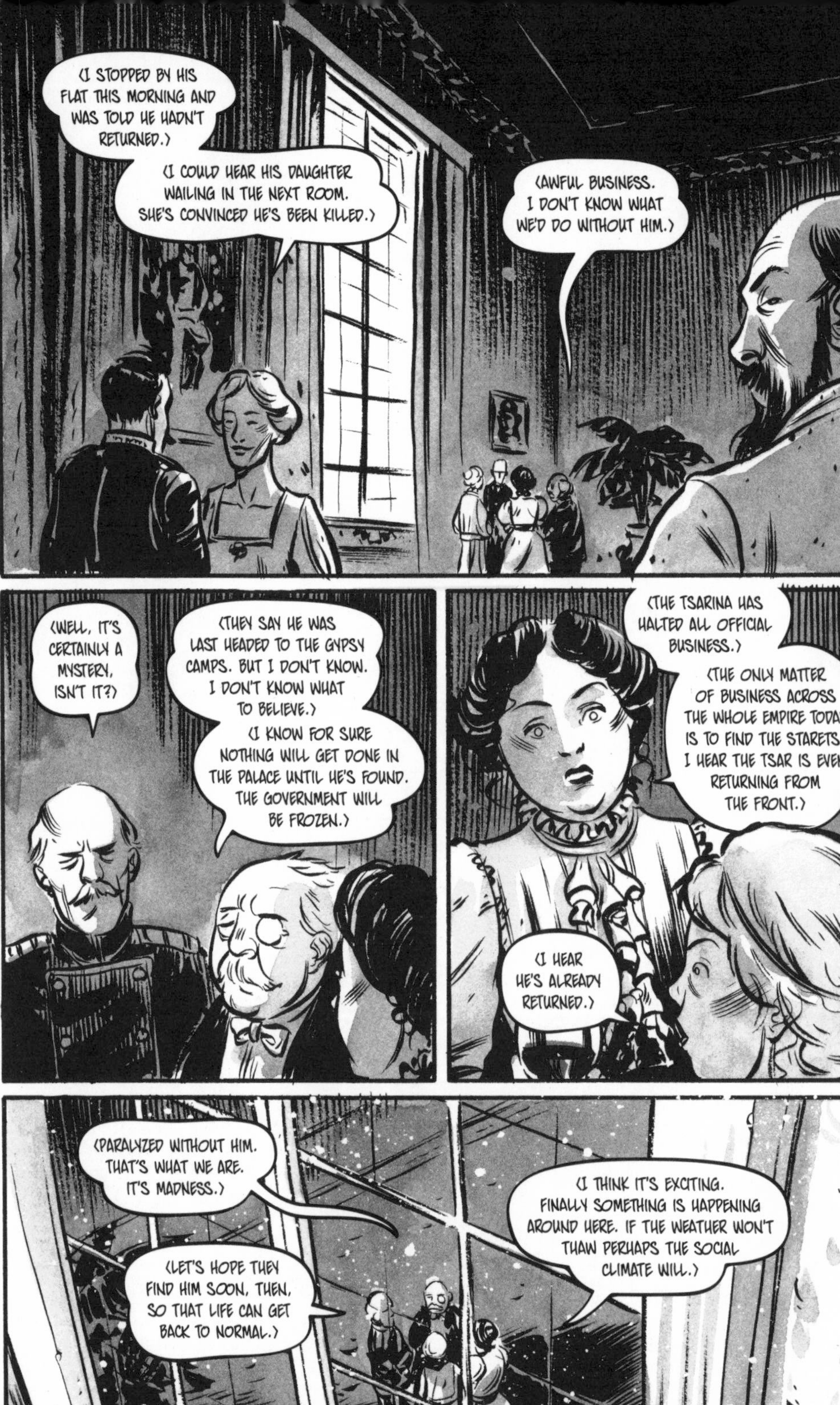

<I STOPPED BY HIS FLAT THIS MORNING AND WAS TOLD HE HADN'T RETURNED.>
<I COULD HEAR HIS DAUGHTER WAILING IN THE NEXT ROOM. SHE'S CONVINCED HE'S BEEN KILLED.>
<AWFUL BUSINESS. I DON'T KNOW WHAT WE'D DO WITHOUT HIM.>
<WELL, IT'S CERTAINLY A MYSTERY, ISN'T IT?>
<THEY SAY HE WAS LAST HEADED TO THE GYPSY CAMPS. BUT I DON'T KNOW. I DON'T KNOW WHAT TO BELIEVE.>
<I KNOW FOR SURE NOTHING WILL GET DONE IN THE PALACE UNTIL HE'S FOUND. THE GOVERNMENT WILL BE FROZEN.>
<THE TSARINA HAS HALTED ALL OFFICIAL BUSINESS.>
<THE ONLY MATTER OF BUSINESS ACROSS THE WHOLE EMPIRE TODAY IS TO FIND THE STARETS. I HEAR THE TSAR IS EVEN RETURNING FROM THE FRONT.>
<I HEAR HE'S ALREADY RETURNED.>
<PARALYZED WITHOUT HIM. THAT'S WHAT WE ARE. IT'S MADNESS.>
<LET'S HOPE THEY FIND HIM SOON, THEN, SO THAT LIFE CAN GET BACK TO NORMAL.>
<I THINK IT'S EXCITING. FINALLY SOMETHING IS HAPPENING AROUND HERE. IF THE WEATHER WON'T THAW PERHAPS THE SOCIAL CLIMATE WILL.>

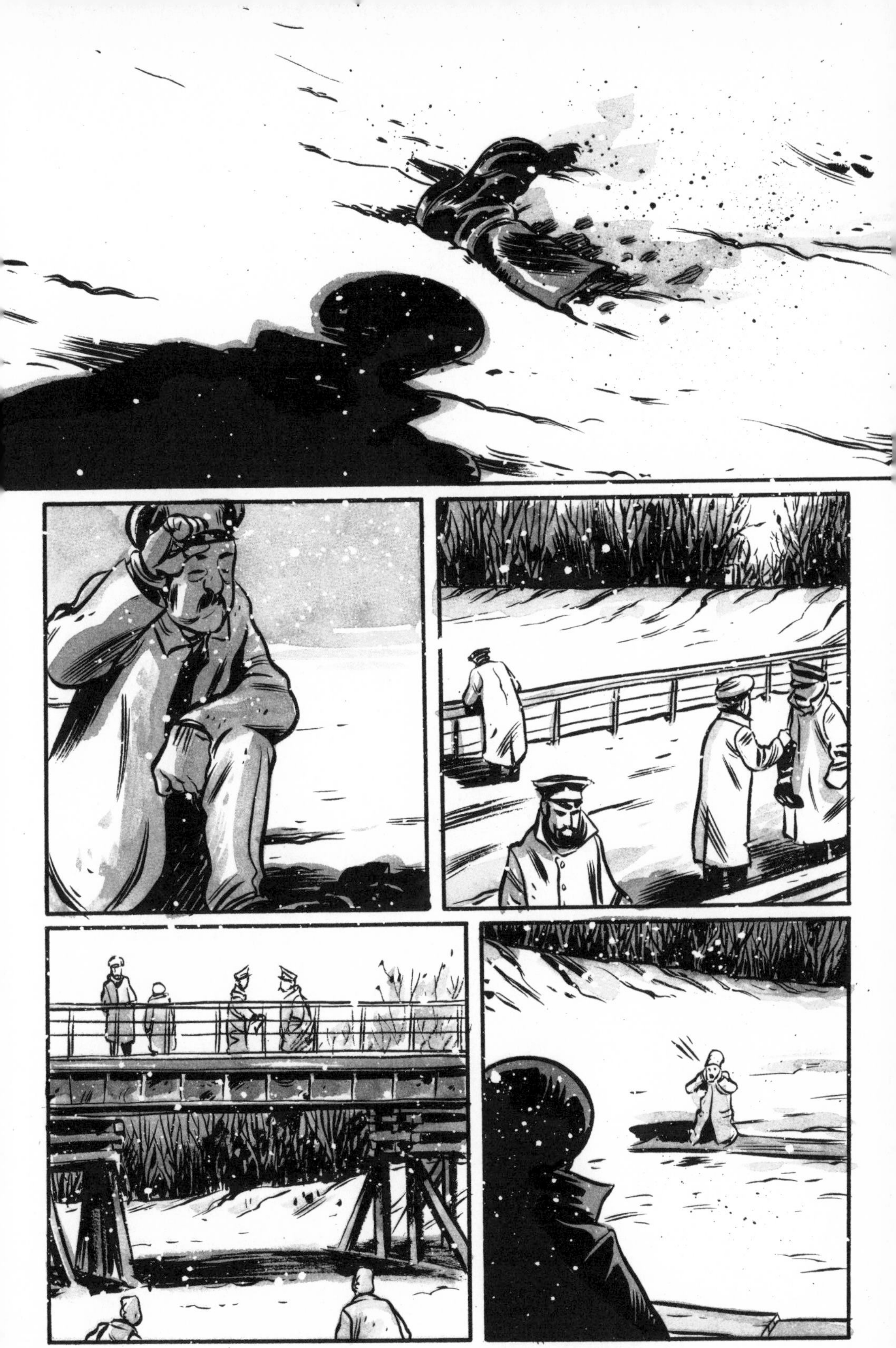

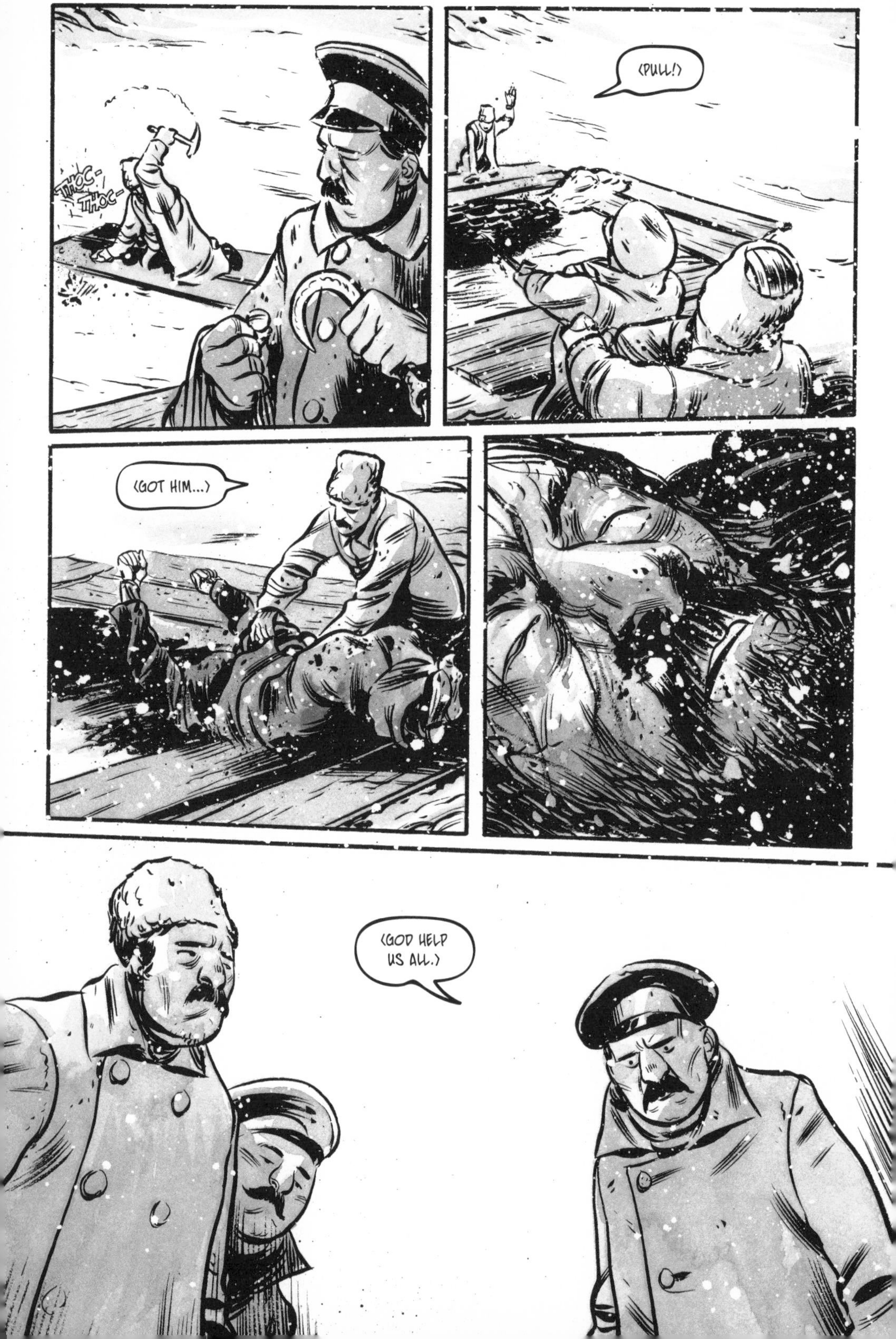
THOC-
THOC-
‹PULL!›
‹GOT HIM...›
‹GOD HELP US ALL.›

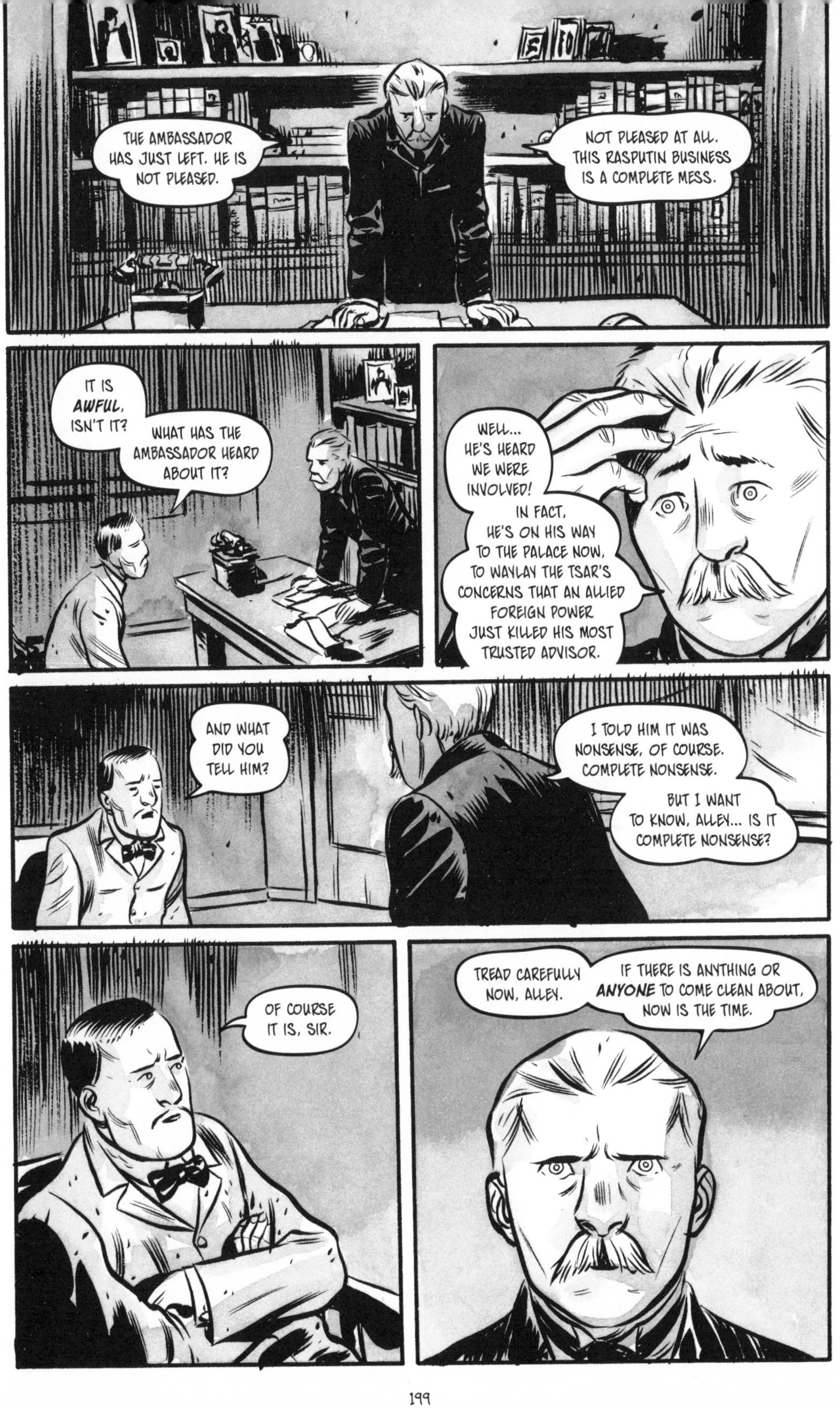
THE AMBASSADOR HAS JUST LEFT. HE IS NOT PLEASED.
NOT PLEASED AT ALL. THIS RASPUTIN BUSINESS IS A COMPLETE MESS.
IT IS **AWFUL**, ISN'T IT?
WHAT HAS THE AMBASSADOR HEARD ABOUT IT?
WELL... HE'S HEARD WE WERE INVOLVED!
IN FACT, HE'S ON HIS WAY TO THE PALACE NOW, TO WAYLAY THE TSAR'S CONCERNS THAT AN ALLIED FOREIGN POWER JUST KILLED HIS MOST TRUSTED ADVISOR.
AND WHAT DID YOU TELL HIM?
I TOLD HIM IT WAS NONSENSE, OF COURSE. COMPLETE NONSENSE.
BUT I WANT TO KNOW, ALLEY... IS IT COMPLETE NONSENSE?
OF COURSE IT IS, SIR.
TREAD CAREFULLY NOW, ALLEY.
IF THERE IS ANYTHING OR **ANYONE** TO COME CLEAN ABOUT, NOW IS THE TIME.

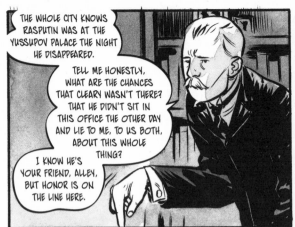

THE WHOLE CITY KNOWS RASPUTIN WAS AT THE YUSSUPOV PALACE THE NIGHT HE DISAPPEARED.

TELL ME HONESTLY, WHAT ARE THE CHANCES THAT CLEARY WASN'T THERE? THAT HE DIDN'T SIT IN THIS OFFICE THE OTHER DAY AND LIE TO ME, TO US BOTH, ABOUT THIS WHOLE THING?

I KNOW HE'S YOUR FRIEND, ALLEY, BUT HONOR IS ON THE LINE HERE.

CLEARY HAS ALWAYS BEEN AN EFFECTIVE AGENT BECAUSE HE KNOWS HOW TO GO A BIT NATIVE. BUT YOU'RE RIGHT, SIR.

I FEAR IN THIS CASE HE HAS FORGOTTEN HIS ROOTS.

SO WHAT DO WE DO ABOUT HIM!

WELL, WE CAN'T GIVE HIM TO THE RUSSIANS.

LORD NO!

BUT WE CAN'T HAVE HIM IN THIS OFFICE ANY LONGER.

THE TSARINA WILL MOVE MOUNTAINS TO HAVE THIS CRIME AVENGED AND KEEPING HIM HERE WILL ENDANGER OUR WHOLE OPERATION.

IF HE IS CAUGHT, IT WILL HAVE TO SEEM AS IF HE IS NO LONGER A SERVANT OF THE BRITISH CROWN.

I AGREE COMPLETELY.

WE CAN'T HAVE ANY ROGUE AGENTS AROUND THIS OFFICE. HE'LL SIMPLY HAVE TO FEND FOR HIMSELF FROM HERE ON OUT.

AGREED. AND, IF YOU DON'T MIND, SIR, I THINK I'D BETTER TELL HIM MYSELF.

BEST TO KEEP YOUR HANDS AS FAR AWAY FROM THIS MESS AS POSSIBLE.

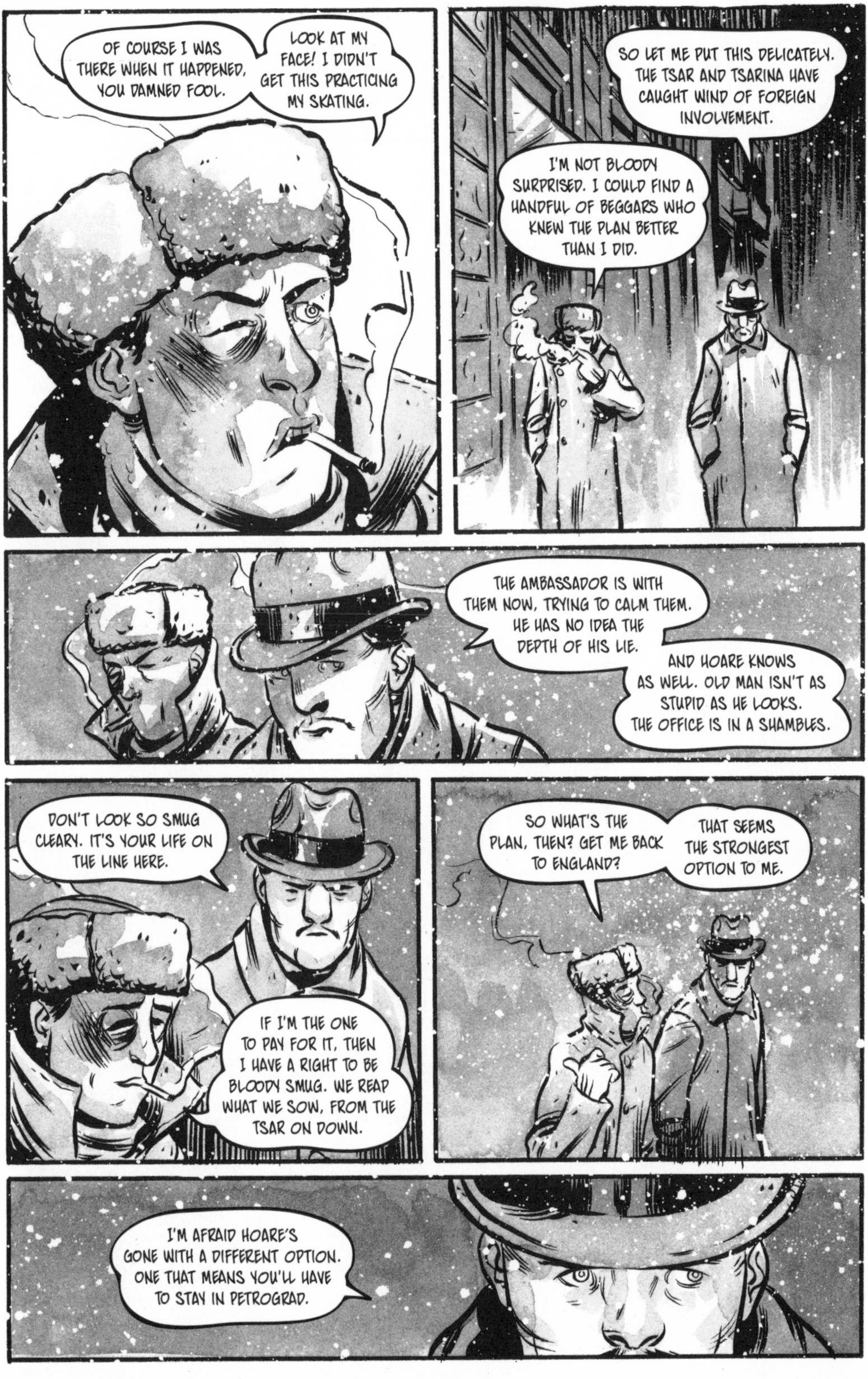
OF COURSE I WAS THERE WHEN IT HAPPENED, YOU DAMNED FOOL.
LOOK AT MY FACE! I DIDN'T GET THIS PRACTICING MY SKATING.
SO LET ME PUT THIS DELICATELY. THE TSAR AND TSARINA HAVE CAUGHT WIND OF FOREIGN INVOLVEMENT.
I'M NOT BLOODY SURPRISED. I COULD FIND A HANDFUL OF BEGGARS WHO KNEW THE PLAN BETTER THAN I DID.
THE AMBASSADOR IS WITH THEM NOW, TRYING TO CALM THEM. HE HAS NO IDEA THE DEPTH OF HIS LIE.
AND HOARE KNOWS AS WELL. OLD MAN ISN'T AS STUPID AS HE LOOKS. THE OFFICE IS IN A SHAMBLES.
DON'T LOOK SO SMUG CLEARY. IT'S YOUR LIFE ON THE LINE HERE.
IF I'M THE ONE TO PAY FOR IT, THEN I HAVE A RIGHT TO BE BLOODY SMUG. WE REAP WHAT WE SOW, FROM THE TSAR ON DOWN.
SO WHAT'S THE PLAN, THEN? GET ME BACK TO ENGLAND?
THAT SEEMS THE STRONGEST OPTION TO ME.
I'M AFRAID HOARE'S GONE WITH A DIFFERENT OPTION. ONE THAT MEANS YOU'LL HAVE TO STAY IN PETROGRAD.

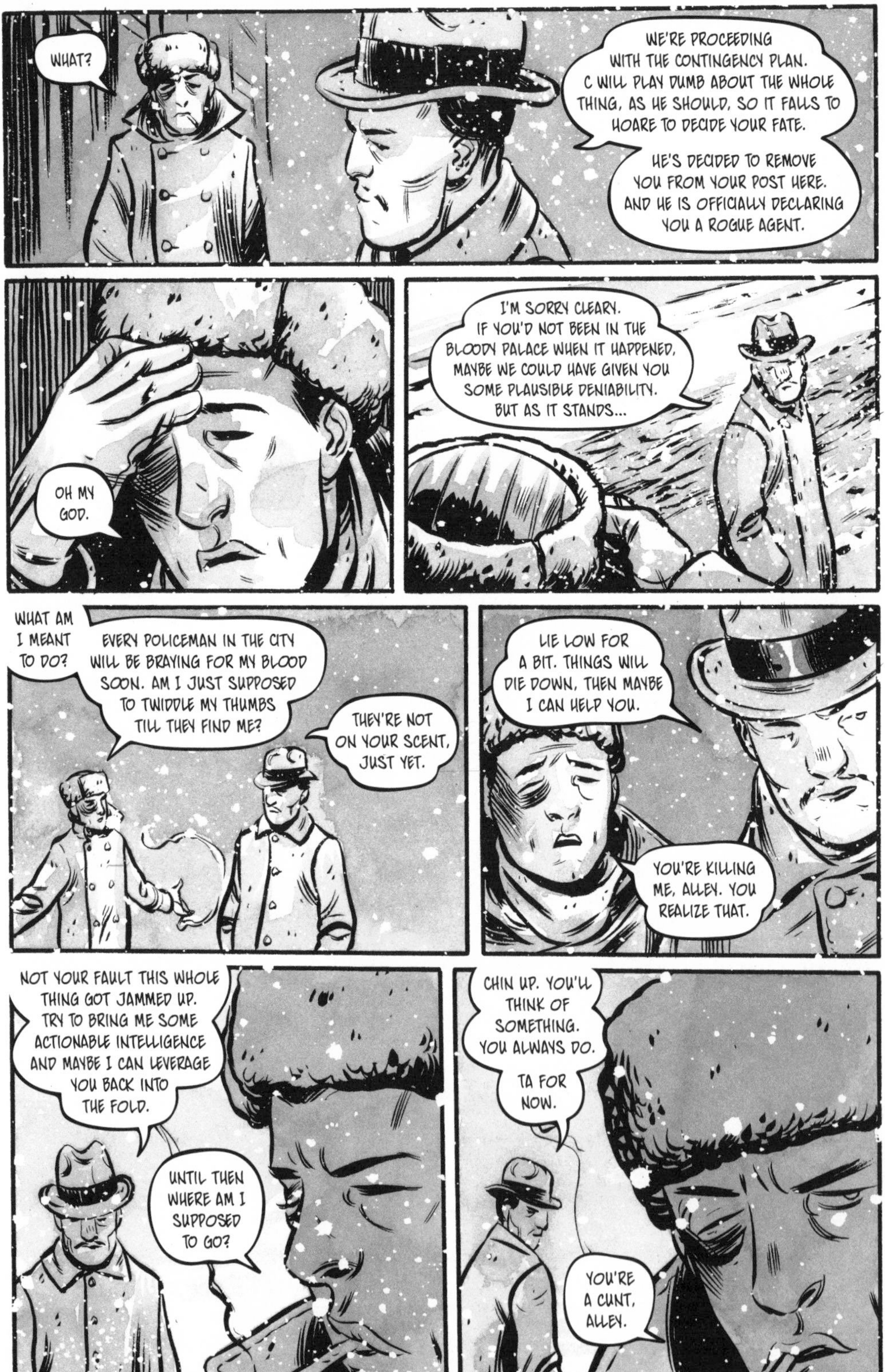
WHAT?
WE'RE PROCEEDING WITH THE CONTINGENCY PLAN. C WILL PLAY DUMB ABOUT THE WHOLE THING, AS HE SHOULD, SO IT FALLS TO HOARE TO DECIDE YOUR FATE.
HE'S DECIDED TO REMOVE YOU FROM YOUR POST HERE. AND HE IS OFFICIALLY DECLARING YOU A ROGUE AGENT.
OH MY GOD.
I'M SORRY CLEARY. IF YOU'D NOT BEEN IN THE BLOODY PALACE WHEN IT HAPPENED, MAYBE WE COULD HAVE GIVEN YOU SOME PLAUSIBLE DENIABILITY. BUT AS IT STANDS...
WHAT AM I MEANT TO DO?
EVERY POLICEMAN IN THE CITY WILL BE BRAYING FOR MY BLOOD SOON. AM I JUST SUPPOSED TO TWIDDLE MY THUMBS TILL THEY FIND ME?
THEY'RE NOT ON YOUR SCENT, JUST YET.
LIE LOW FOR A BIT. THINGS WILL DIE DOWN, THEN MAYBE I CAN HELP YOU.
YOU'RE KILLING ME, ALLEY. YOU REALIZE THAT.
NOT YOUR FAULT THIS WHOLE THING GOT JAMMED UP. TRY TO BRING ME SOME ACTIONABLE INTELLIGENCE AND MAYBE I CAN LEVERAGE YOU BACK INTO THE FOLD.
UNTIL THEN WHERE AM I SUPPOSED TO GO?
CHIN UP. YOU'LL THINK OF SOMETHING. YOU ALWAYS DO.
TA FOR NOW.
YOU'RE A CUNT, ALLEY.

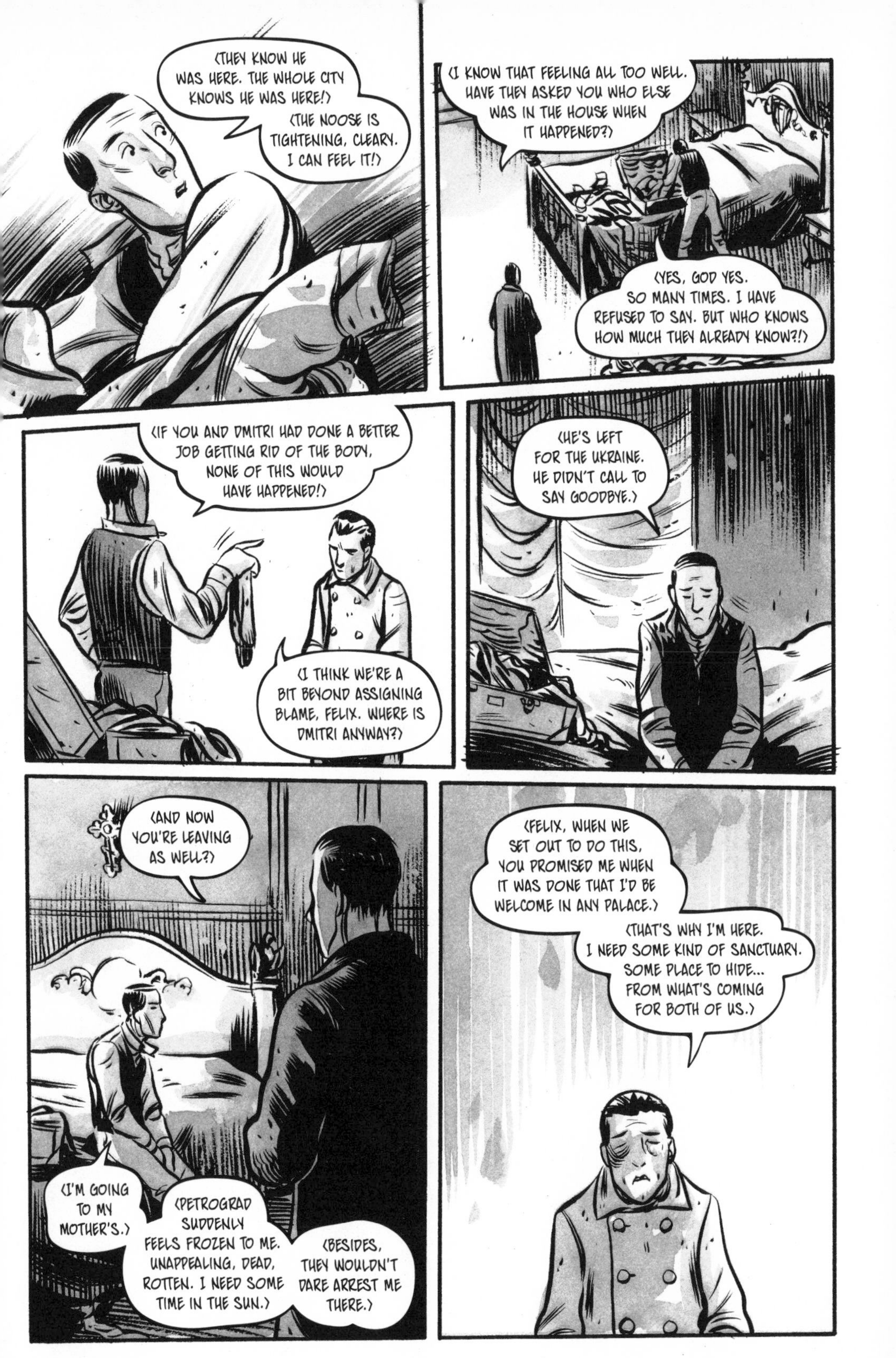

⟨THEY KNOW HE WAS HERE. THE WHOLE CITY KNOWS HE WAS HERE!⟩
⟨THE NOOSE IS TIGHTENING, CLEARY. I CAN FEEL IT!⟩
⟨I KNOW THAT FEELING ALL TOO WELL. HAVE THEY ASKED YOU WHO ELSE WAS IN THE HOUSE WHEN IT HAPPENED?⟩
⟨YES, GOD YES. SO MANY TIMES. I HAVE REFUSED TO SAY. BUT WHO KNOWS HOW MUCH THEY ALREADY KNOW?!⟩
⟨IF YOU AND DMITRI HAD DONE A BETTER JOB GETTING RID OF THE BODY, NONE OF THIS WOULD HAVE HAPPENED!⟩
⟨I THINK WE'RE A BIT BEYOND ASSIGNING BLAME, FELIX. WHERE IS DMITRI ANYWAY?⟩
⟨HE'S LEFT FOR THE UKRAINE. HE DIDN'T CALL TO SAY GOODBYE.⟩
⟨AND NOW YOU'RE LEAVING AS WELL?⟩
⟨I'M GOING TO MY MOTHER'S.⟩
⟨PETROGRAD SUDDENLY FEELS FROZEN TO ME. UNAPPEALING, DEAD, ROTTEN. I NEED SOME TIME IN THE SUN.⟩
⟨BESIDES, THEY WOULDN'T DARE ARREST ME THERE.⟩
⟨FELIX, WHEN WE SET OUT TO DO THIS, YOU PROMISED ME WHEN IT WAS DONE THAT I'D BE WELCOME IN ANY PALACE.⟩
⟨THAT'S WHY I'M HERE. I NEED SOME KIND OF SANCTUARY. SOME PLACE TO HIDE... FROM WHAT'S COMING FOR BOTH OF US.⟩

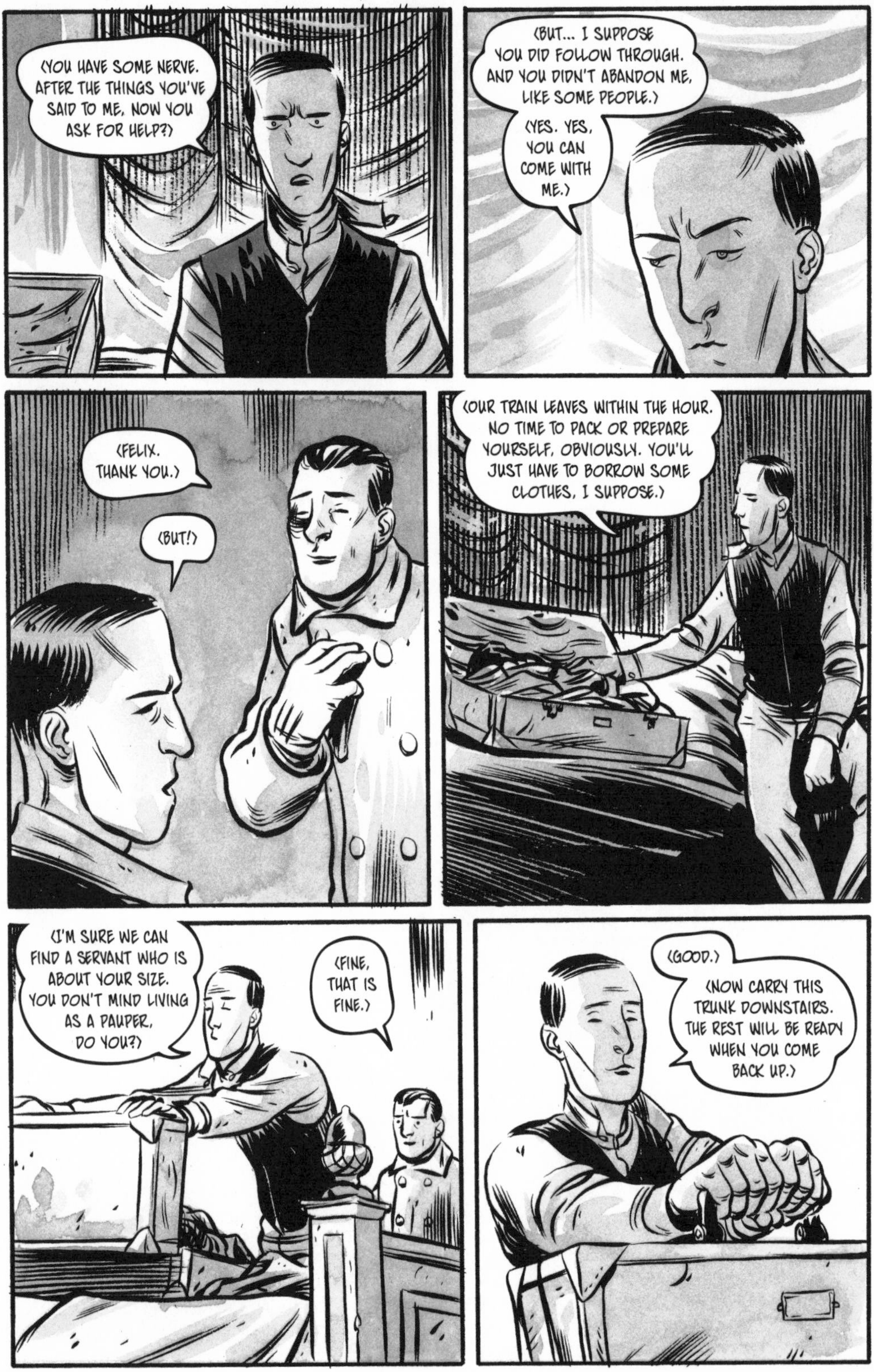
(YOU HAVE SOME NERVE. AFTER THE THINGS YOU'VE SAID TO ME, NOW YOU ASK FOR HELP?)
(BUT... I SUPPOSE YOU DID FOLLOW THROUGH. AND YOU DIDN'T ABANDON ME, LIKE SOME PEOPLE.)
(YES. YES, YOU CAN COME WITH ME.)
(FELIX. THANK YOU.)
(BUT!)
(OUR TRAIN LEAVES WITHIN THE HOUR. NO TIME TO PACK OR PREPARE YOURSELF, OBVIOUSLY. YOU'LL JUST HAVE TO BORROW SOME CLOTHES, I SUPPOSE.)
(I'M SURE WE CAN FIND A SERVANT WHO IS ABOUT YOUR SIZE. YOU DON'T MIND LIVING AS A PAUPER, DO YOU?)
(FINE, THAT IS FINE.)
(GOOD.)
(NOW CARRY THIS TRUNK DOWNSTAIRS. THE REST WILL BE READY WHEN YOU COME BACK UP.)

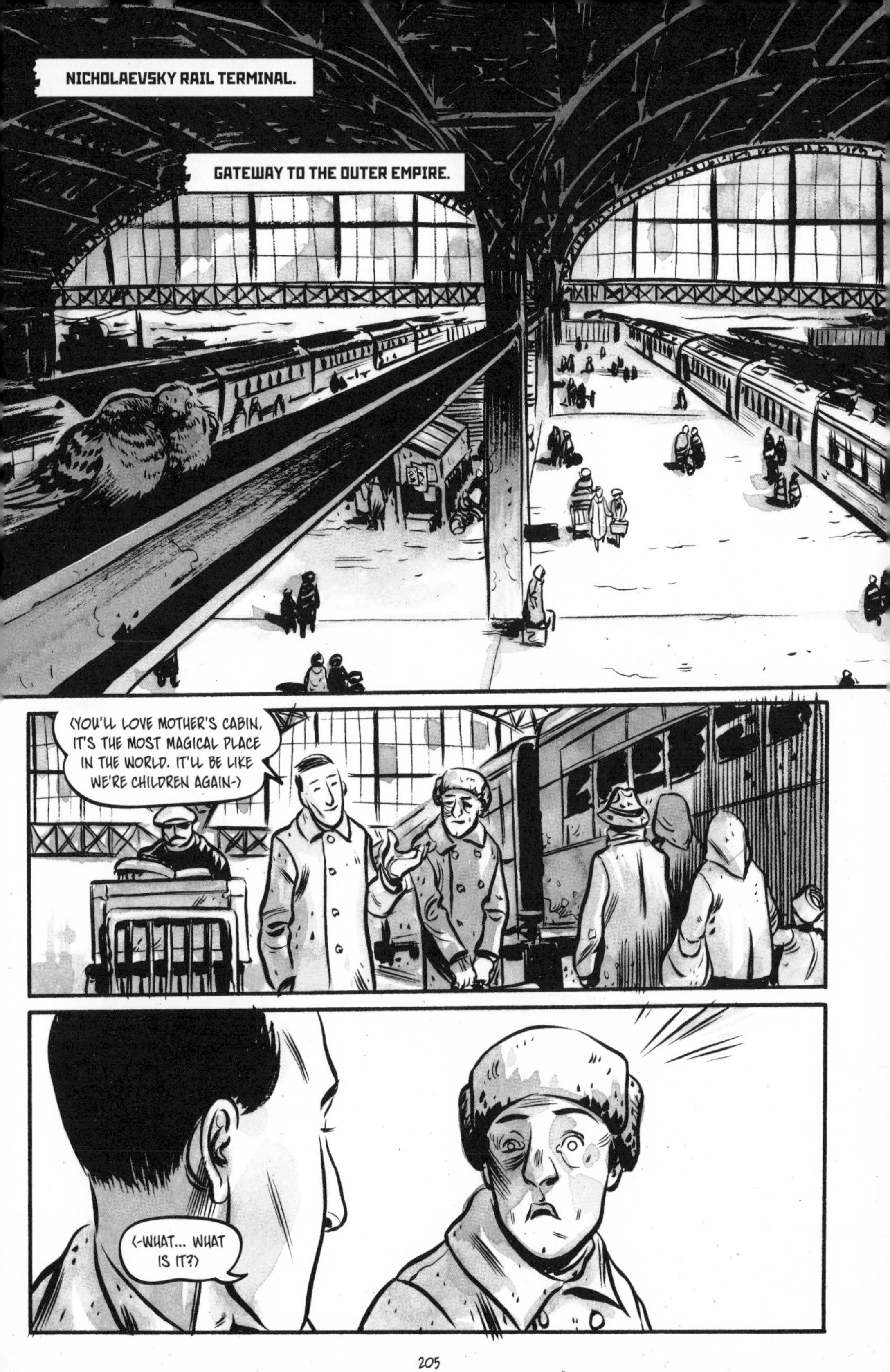
NICHOLAEVSKY RAIL TERMINAL.
GATEWAY TO THE OUTER EMPIRE.
‹YOU'LL LOVE MOTHER'S CABIN, IT'S THE MOST MAGICAL PLACE IN THE WORLD. IT'LL BE LIKE WE'RE CHILDREN AGAIN-›
‹-WHAT... WHAT IS IT?›

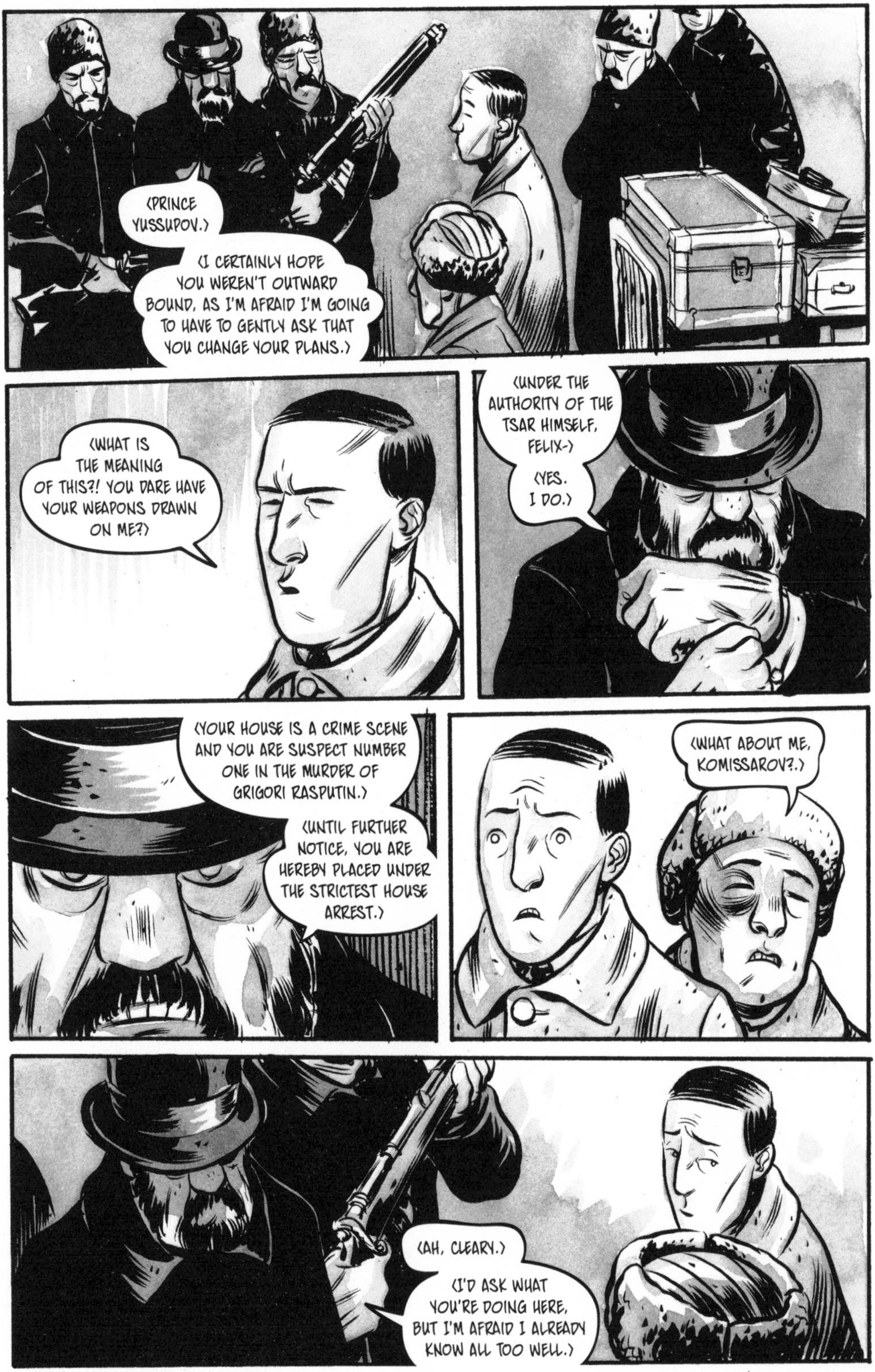

<PRINCE YUSSUPOV.>
<I CERTAINLY HOPE YOU WEREN'T OUTWARD BOUND, AS I'M AFRAID I'M GOING TO HAVE TO GENTLY ASK THAT YOU CHANGE YOUR PLANS.>
<WHAT IS THE MEANING OF THIS?! YOU DARE HAVE YOUR WEAPONS DRAWN ON ME?>
<UNDER THE AUTHORITY OF THE TSAR HIMSELF, FELIX->
<YES. I DO.>
<YOUR HOUSE IS A CRIME SCENE AND YOU ARE SUSPECT NUMBER ONE IN THE MURDER OF GRIGORI RASPUTIN.>
<UNTIL FURTHER NOTICE, YOU ARE HEREBY PLACED UNDER THE STRICTEST HOUSE ARREST.>
<WHAT ABOUT ME, KOMISSAROV?.>
<AH, CLEARY.>
<I'D ASK WHAT YOU'RE DOING HERE, BUT I'M AFRAID I ALREADY KNOW ALL TOO WELL.>

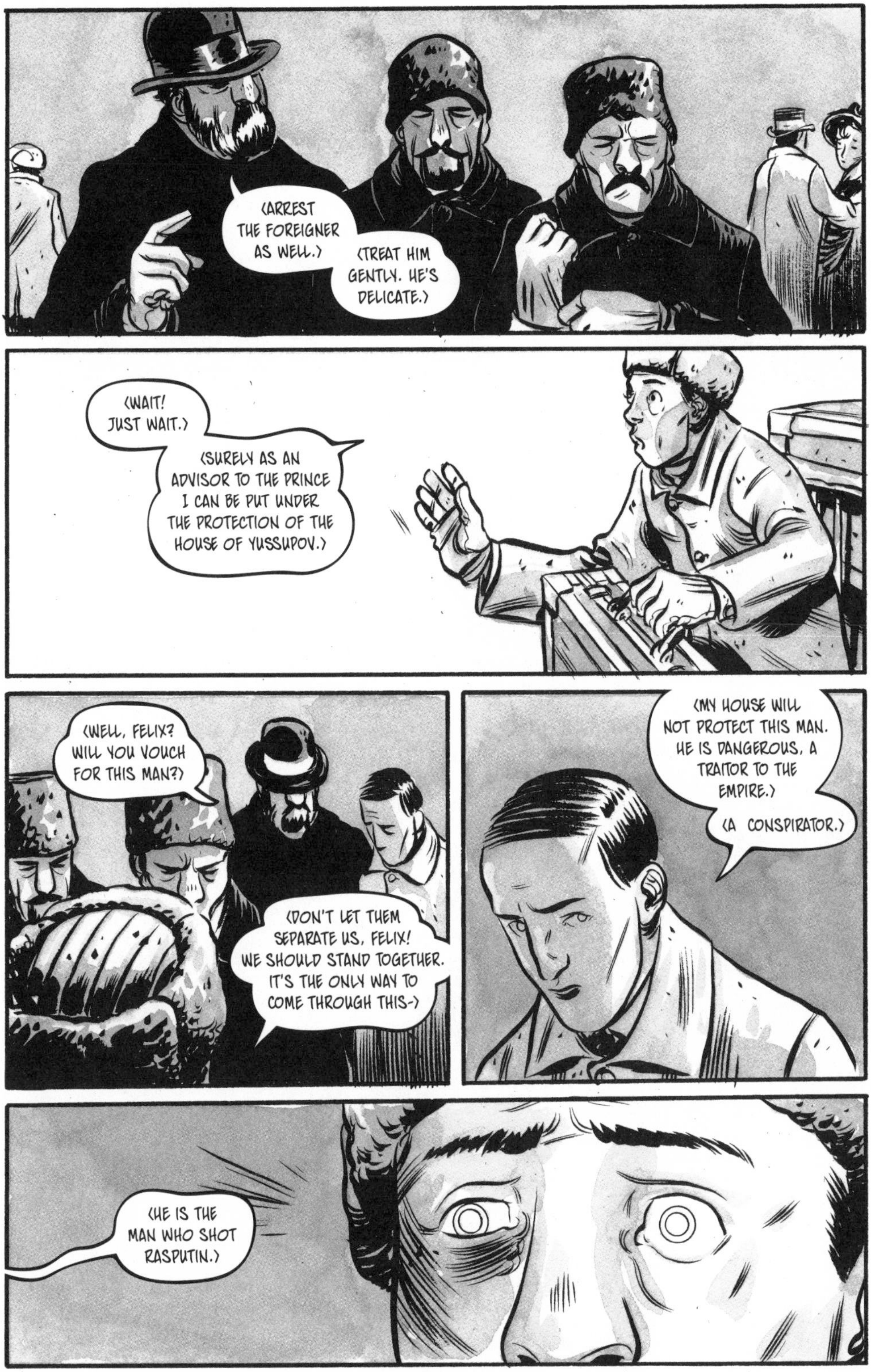

‹ARREST THE FOREIGNER AS WELL.›
‹TREAT HIM GENTLY. HE'S DELICATE.›
‹WAIT! JUST WAIT.›
‹SURELY AS AN ADVISOR TO THE PRINCE I CAN BE PUT UNDER THE PROTECTION OF THE HOUSE OF YUSSUPOV.›
‹WELL, FELIX? WILL YOU VOUCH FOR THIS MAN?›
‹DON'T LET THEM SEPARATE US, FELIX! WE SHOULD STAND TOGETHER. IT'S THE ONLY WAY TO COME THROUGH THIS-›
‹MY HOUSE WILL NOT PROTECT THIS MAN. HE IS DANGEROUS, A TRAITOR TO THE EMPIRE.›
‹A CONSPIRATOR.›
‹HE IS THE MAN WHO SHOT RASPUTIN.›

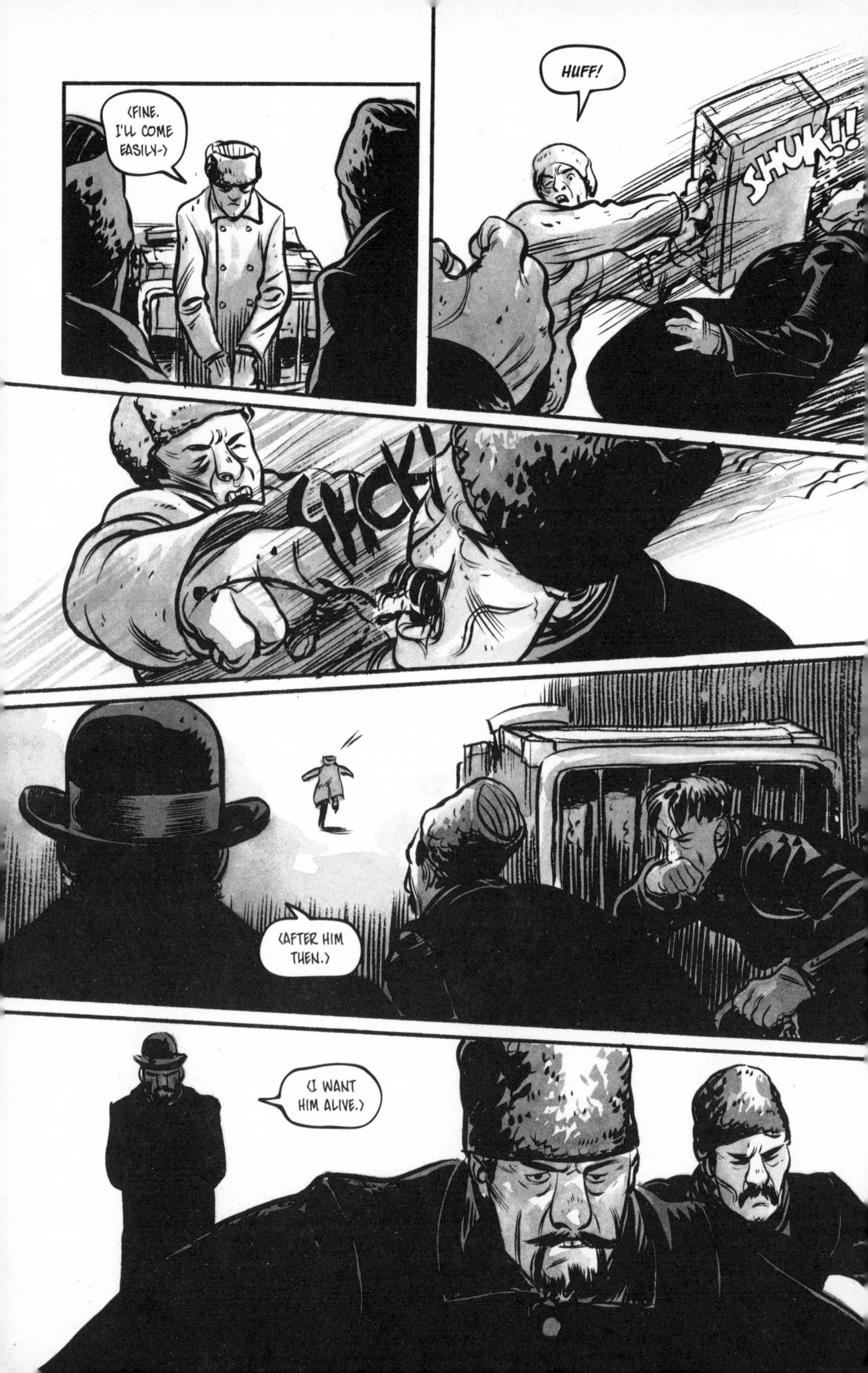
<FINE. I'LL COME EASILY->
HUFF!
SHUK!!
SHCK!
<AFTER HIM THEN.>
<I WANT HIM ALIVE.>

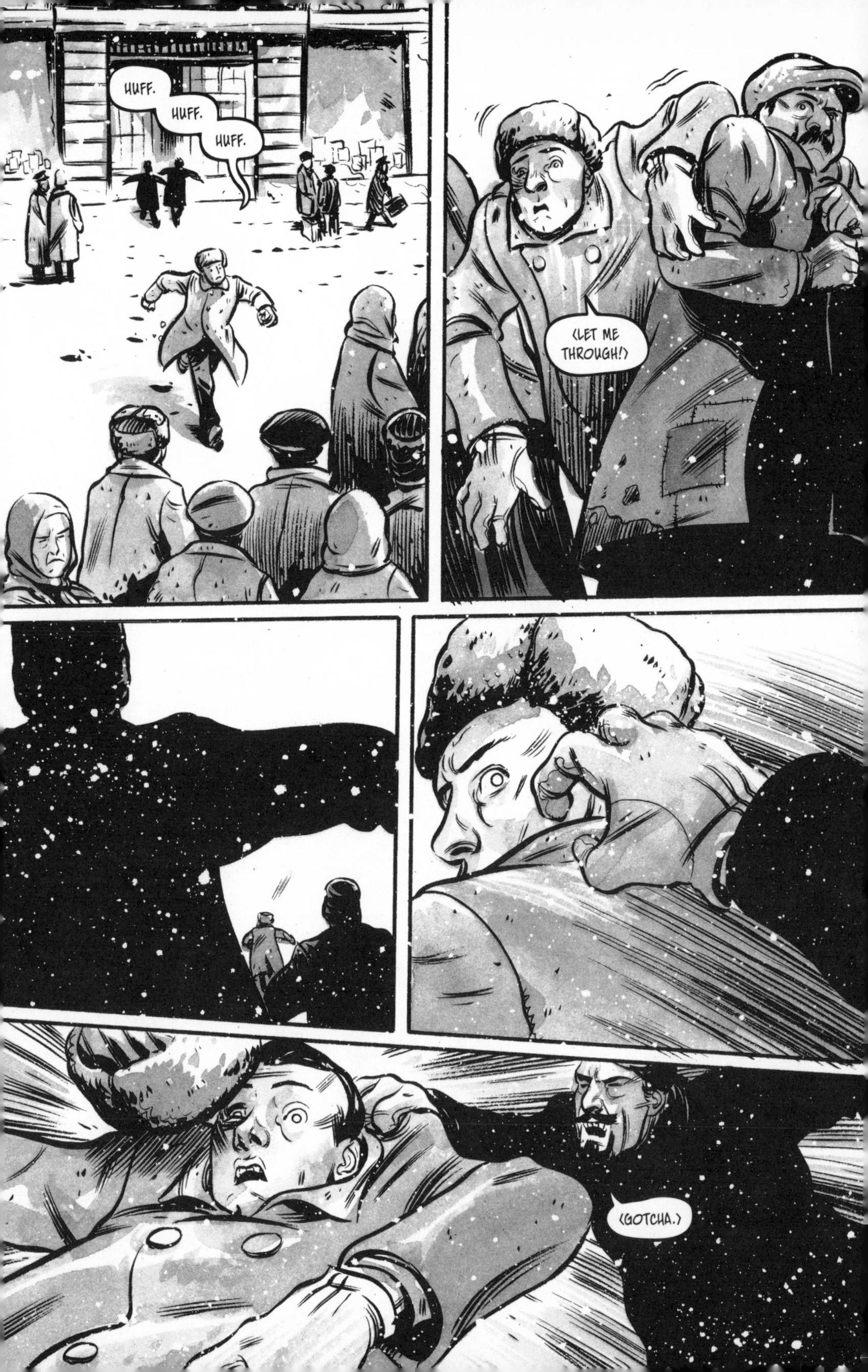
HUFF.
HUFF.
HUFF.
‹LET ME THROUGH!›
‹GOTCHA.›

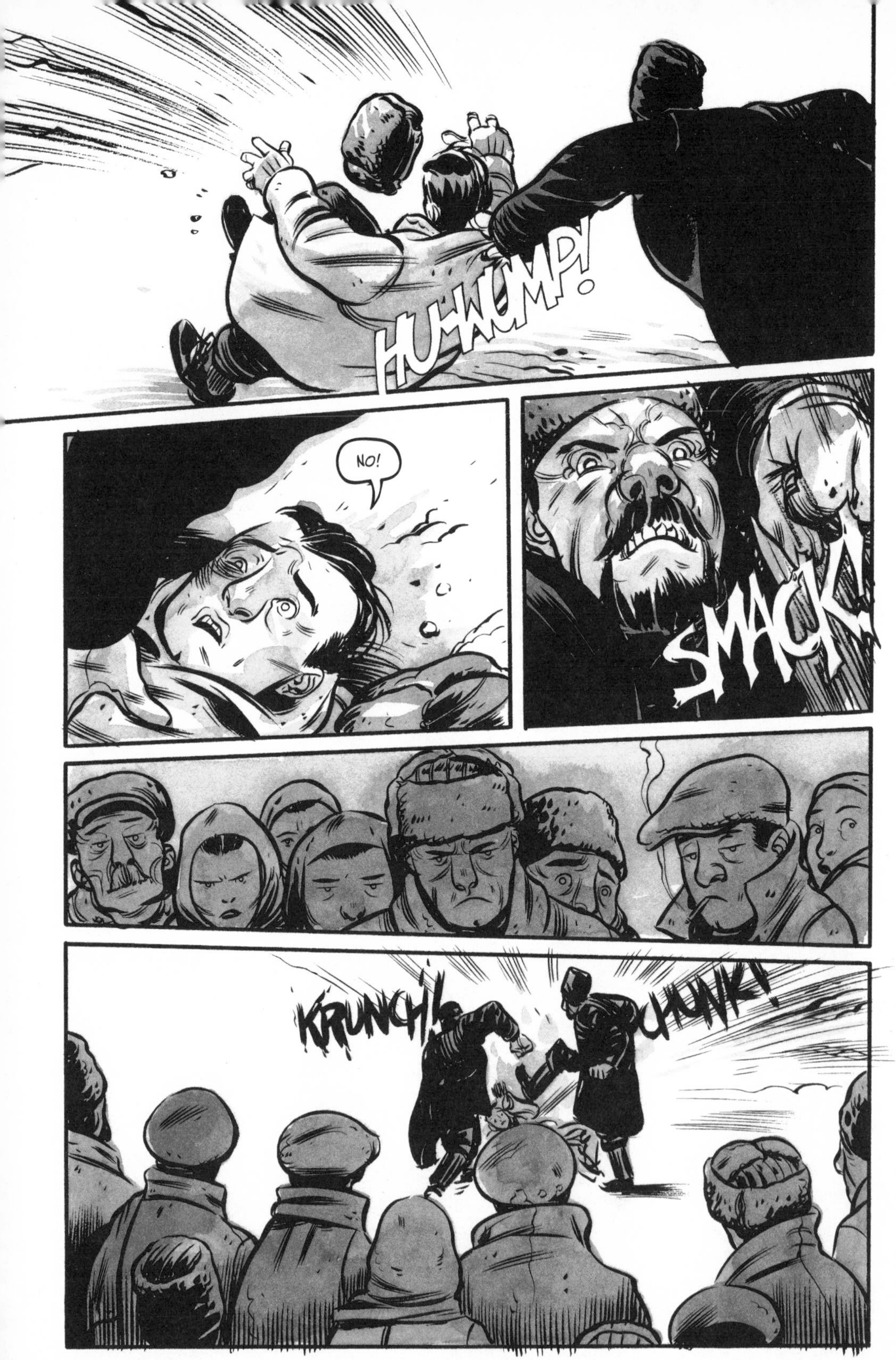
HU-WUMP!
NO!
SMACK!
KRUNCH!
CHUNK!

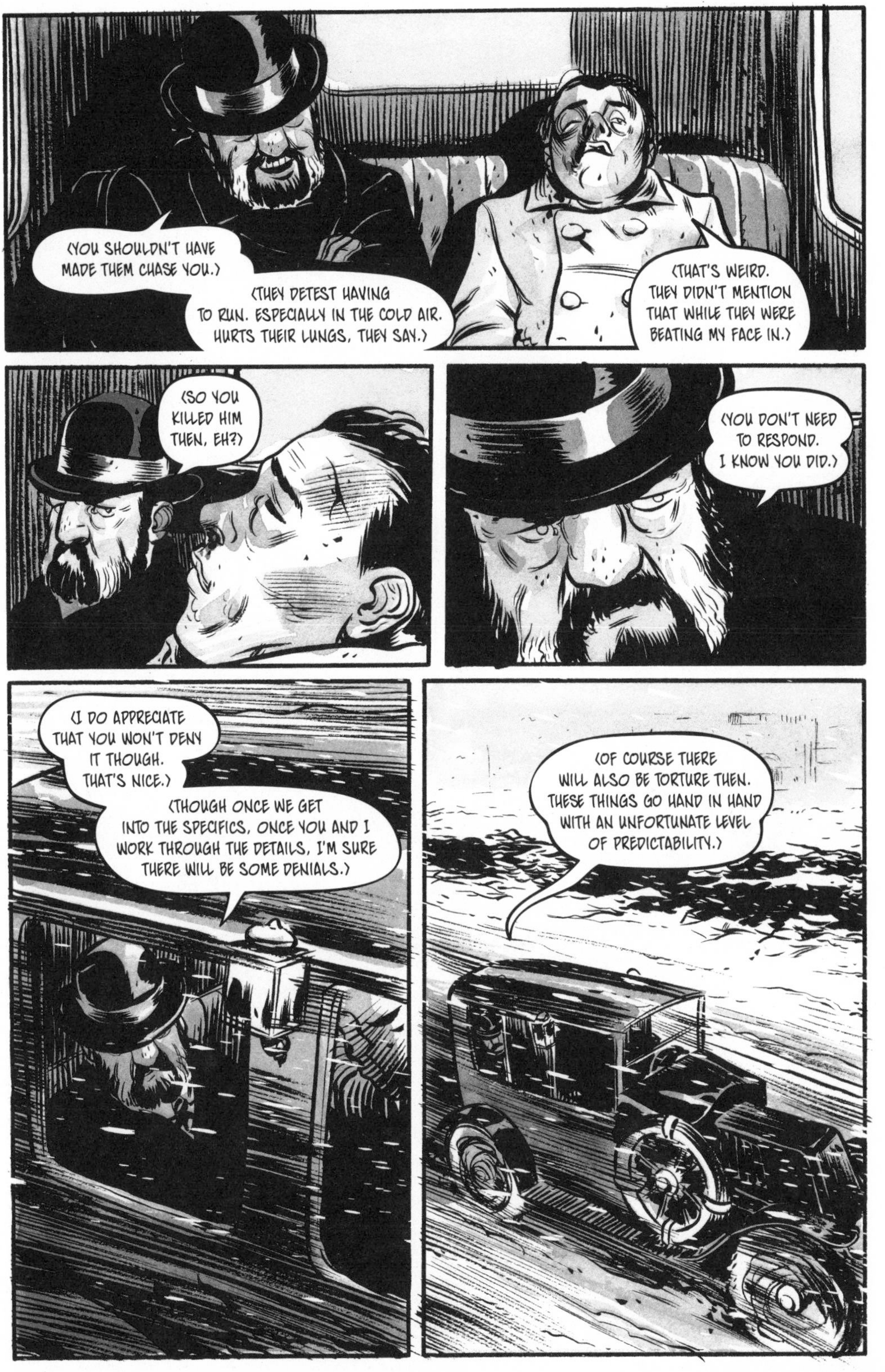

‹YOU SHOULDN'T HAVE MADE THEM CHASE YOU.›
‹THEY DETEST HAVING TO RUN. ESPECIALLY IN THE COLD AIR. HURTS THEIR LUNGS, THEY SAY.›
‹THAT'S WEIRD. THEY DIDN'T MENTION THAT WHILE THEY WERE BEATING MY FACE IN.›
‹SO YOU KILLED HIM THEN, EH?›
‹YOU DON'T NEED TO RESPOND. I KNOW YOU DID.›
‹I DO APPRECIATE THAT YOU WON'T DENY IT THOUGH. THAT'S NICE.›
‹THOUGH ONCE WE GET INTO THE SPECIFICS, ONCE YOU AND I WORK THROUGH THE DETAILS, I'M SURE THERE WILL BE SOME DENIALS.›
‹OF COURSE THERE WILL ALSO BE TORTURE THEN. THESE THINGS GO HAND IN HAND WITH AN UNFORTUNATE LEVEL OF PREDICTABILITY.›

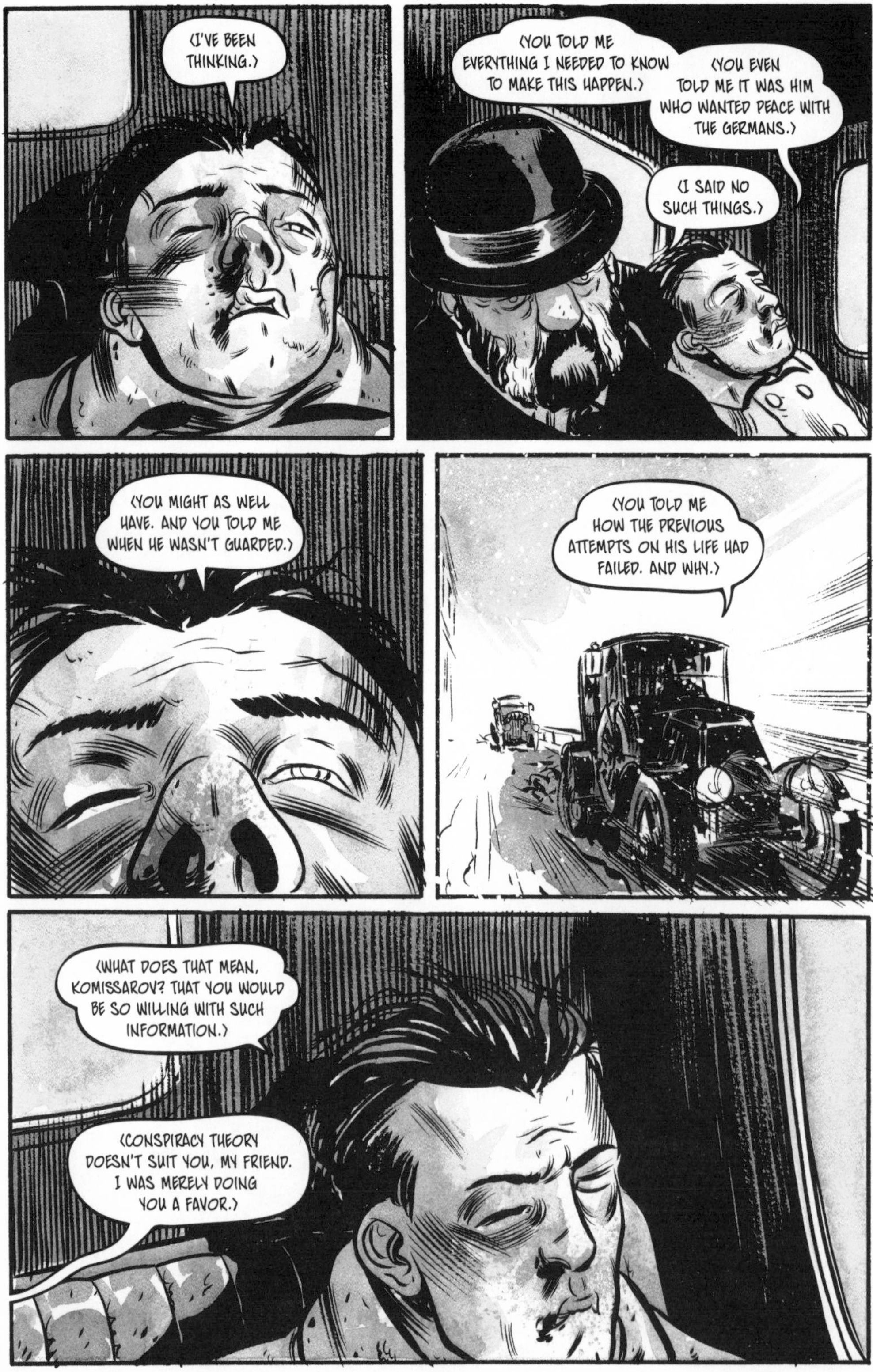
⟨I'VE BEEN THINKING.⟩
⟨YOU TOLD ME EVERYTHING I NEEDED TO KNOW TO MAKE THIS HAPPEN.⟩
⟨YOU EVEN TOLD ME IT WAS HIM WHO WANTED PEACE WITH THE GERMANS.⟩
⟨I SAID NO SUCH THINGS.⟩
⟨YOU MIGHT AS WELL HAVE. AND YOU TOLD ME WHEN HE WASN'T GUARDED.⟩
⟨YOU TOLD ME HOW THE PREVIOUS ATTEMPTS ON HIS LIFE HAD FAILED. AND WHY.⟩
⟨WHAT DOES THAT MEAN, KOMISSAROV? THAT YOU WOULD BE SO WILLING WITH SUCH INFORMATION.⟩
⟨CONSPIRACY THEORY DOESN'T SUIT YOU, MY FRIEND. I WAS MERELY DOING YOU A FAVOR.⟩

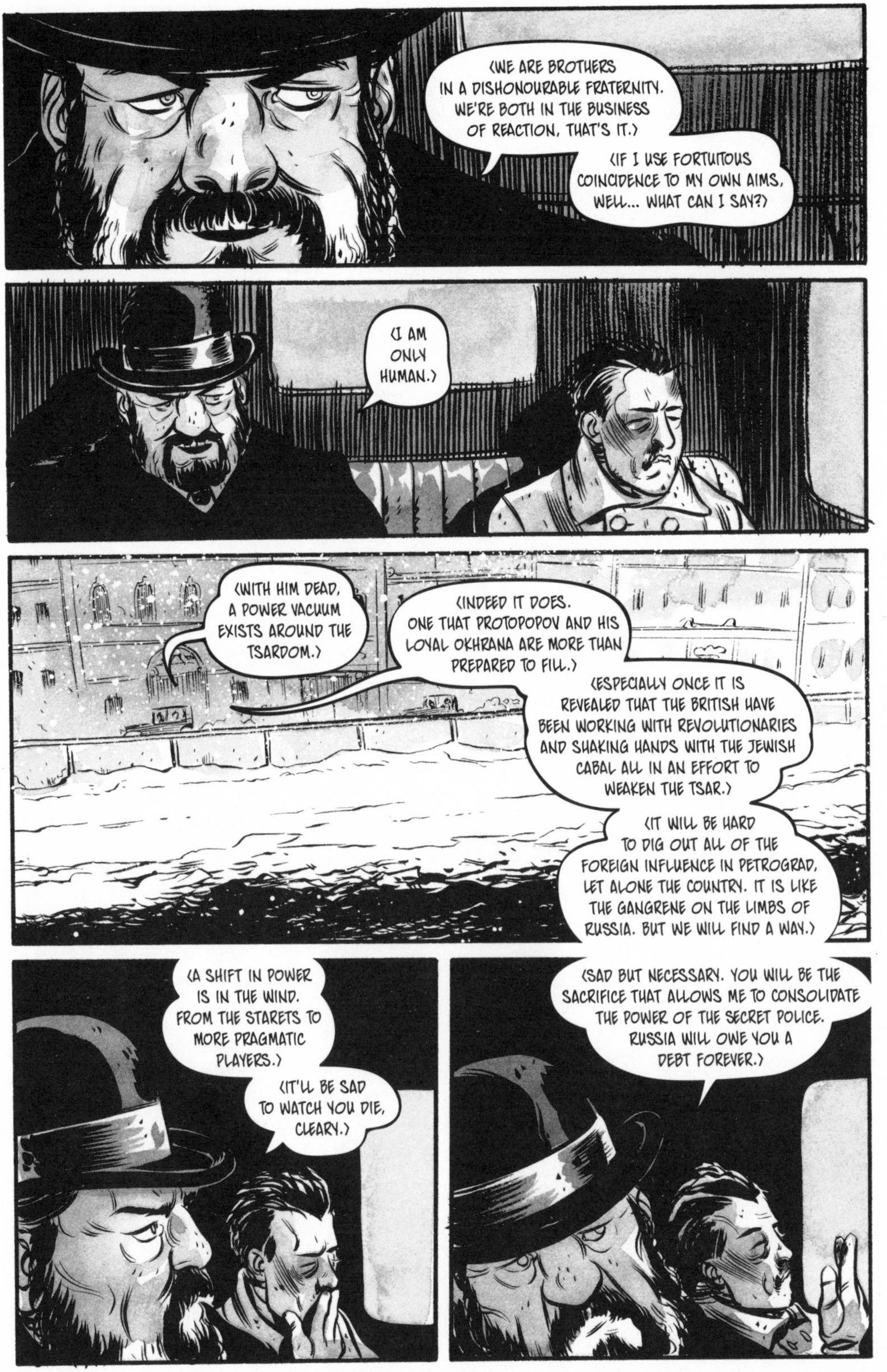

‹WE ARE BROTHERS IN A DISHONOURABLE FRATERNITY. WE'RE BOTH IN THE BUSINESS OF REACTION, THAT'S IT.›
‹IF I USE FORTUITOUS COINCIDENCE TO MY OWN AIMS, WELL... WHAT CAN I SAY?›
‹I AM ONLY HUMAN.›
‹WITH HIM DEAD, A POWER VACUUM EXISTS AROUND THE TSARDOM.›
‹INDEED IT DOES. ONE THAT PROTOPOPOV AND HIS LOYAL OKHRANA ARE MORE THAN PREPARED TO FILL.›
‹ESPECIALLY ONCE IT IS REVEALED THAT THE BRITISH HAVE BEEN WORKING WITH REVOLUTIONARIES AND SHAKING HANDS WITH THE JEWISH CABAL ALL IN AN EFFORT TO WEAKEN THE TSAR.›
‹IT WILL BE HARD TO DIG OUT ALL OF THE FOREIGN INFLUENCE IN PETROGRAD, LET ALONE THE COUNTRY. IT IS LIKE THE GANGRENE ON THE LIMBS OF RUSSIA. BUT WE WILL FIND A WAY.›
‹A SHIFT IN POWER IS IN THE WIND. FROM THE STARETS TO MORE PRAGMATIC PLAYERS.›
‹IT'LL BE SAD TO WATCH YOU DIE, CLEARY.›
‹SAD BUT NECESSARY. YOU WILL BE THE SACRIFICE THAT ALLOWS ME TO CONSOLIDATE THE POWER OF THE SECRET POLICE. RUSSIA WILL OWE YOU A DEBT FOREVER.›

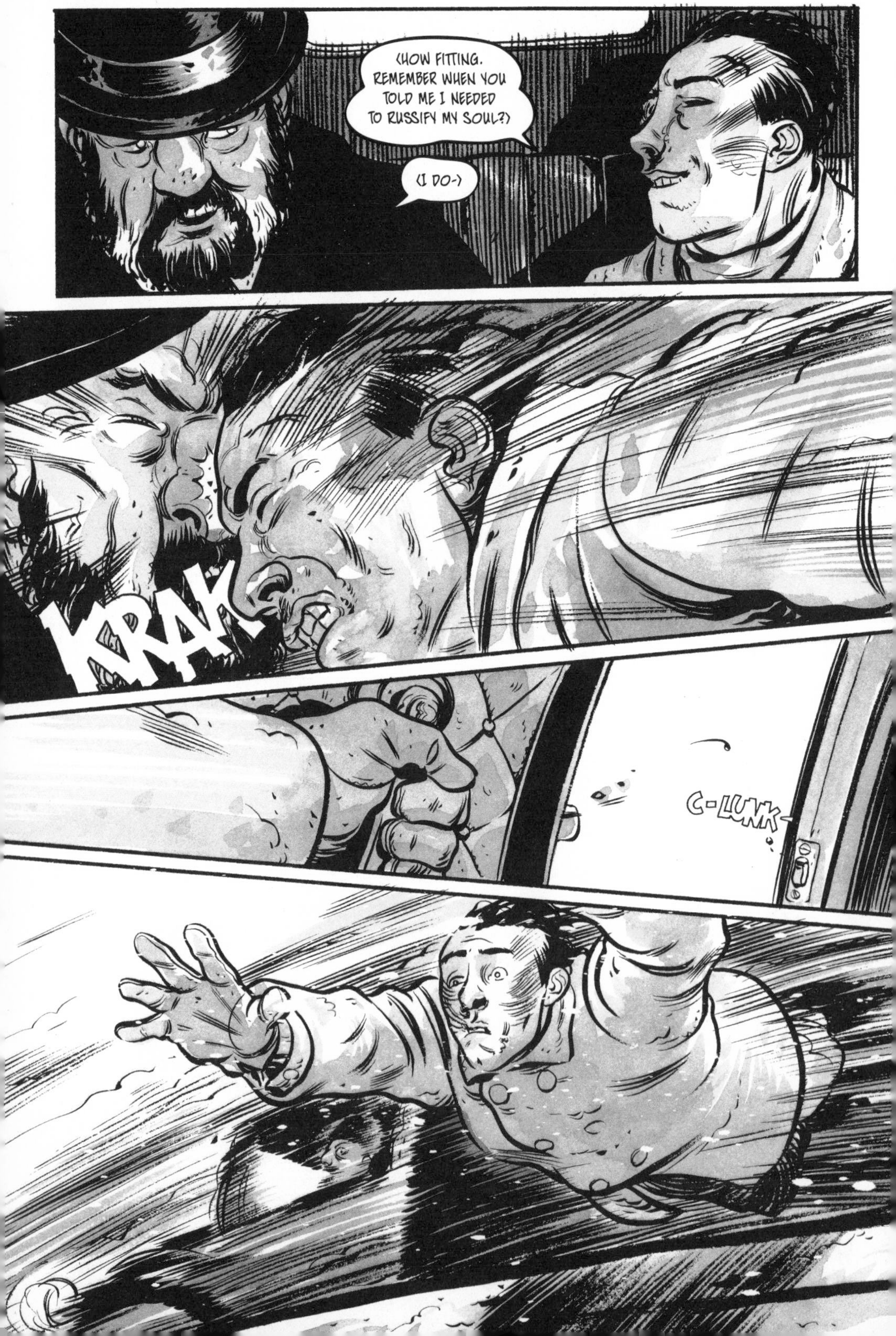

‹HOW FITTING. REMEMBER WHEN YOU TOLD ME I NEEDED TO RUSSIFY MY SOUL?›
‹I DO-›
KRAK
C-LUNK

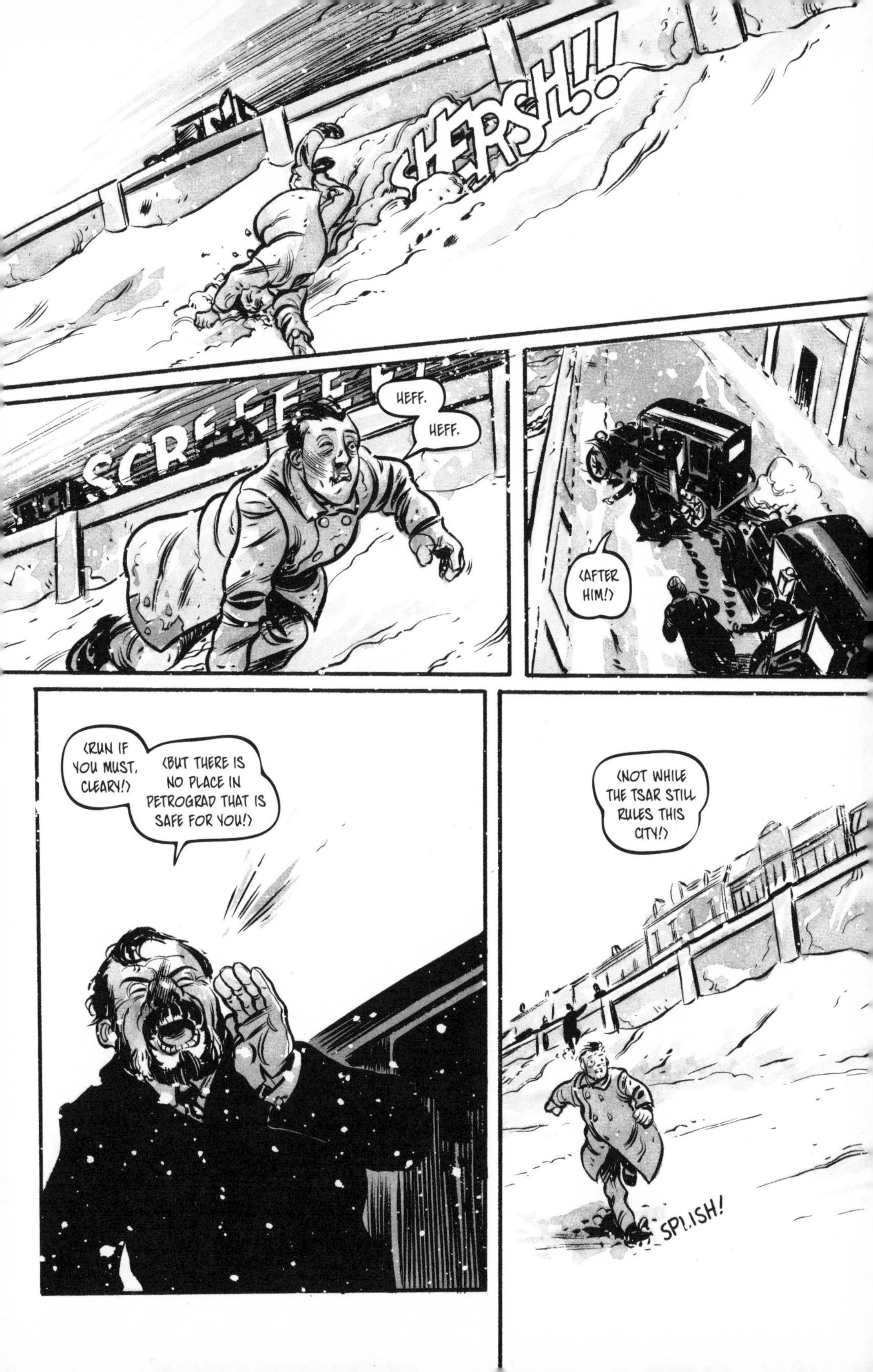
SHERSH!!
SCREEEEE
HEFF.
HEFF.
‹AFTER HIM!›
‹RUN IF YOU MUST, CLEARY!›
‹BUT THERE IS NO PLACE IN PETROGRAD THAT IS SAFE FOR YOU!›
‹NOT WHILE THE TSAR STILL RULES THIS CITY!›
SPLISH!

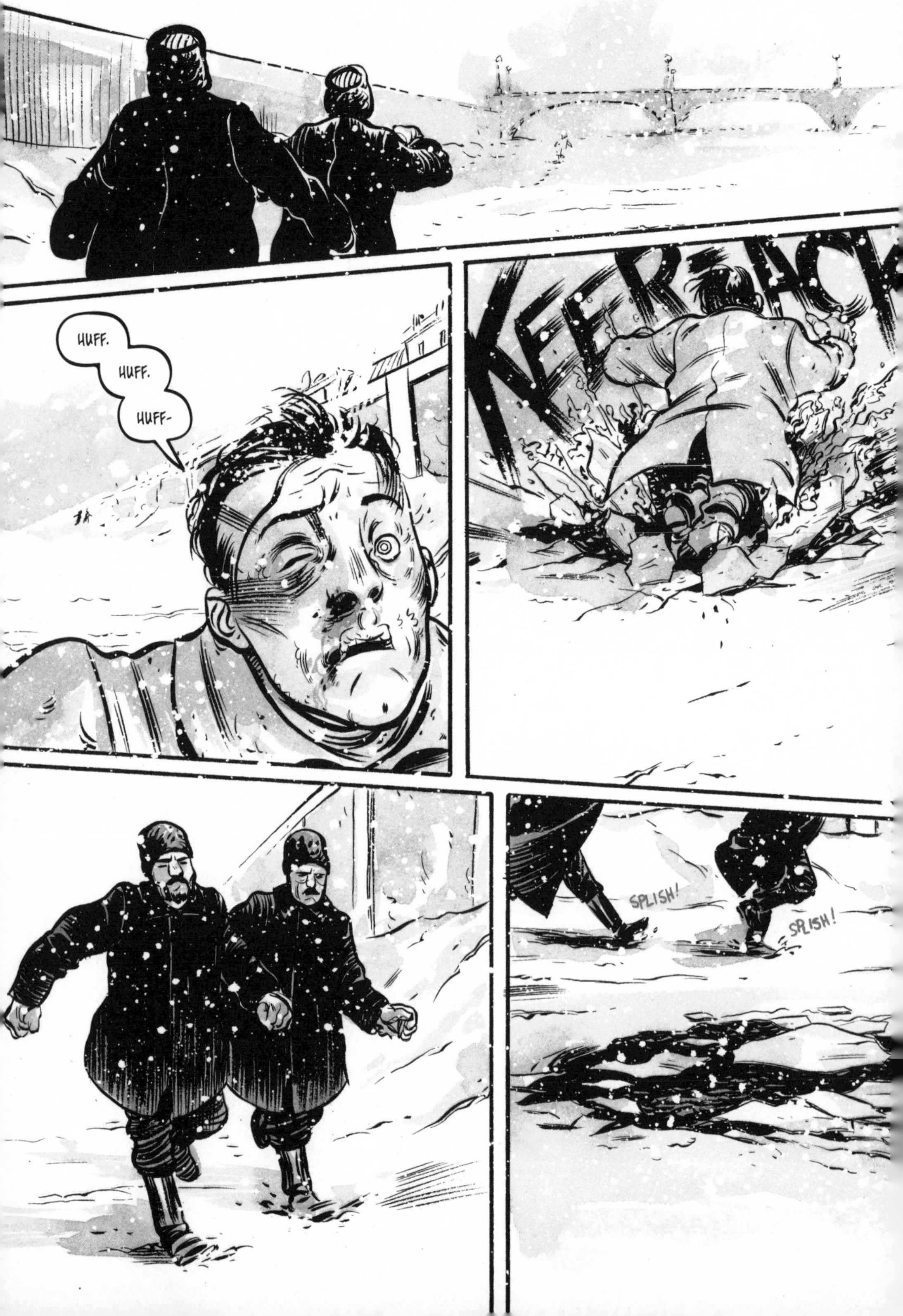
HUFF.
HUFF.
HUFF-
KEER-ACK
SPLISH!
SPLISH!

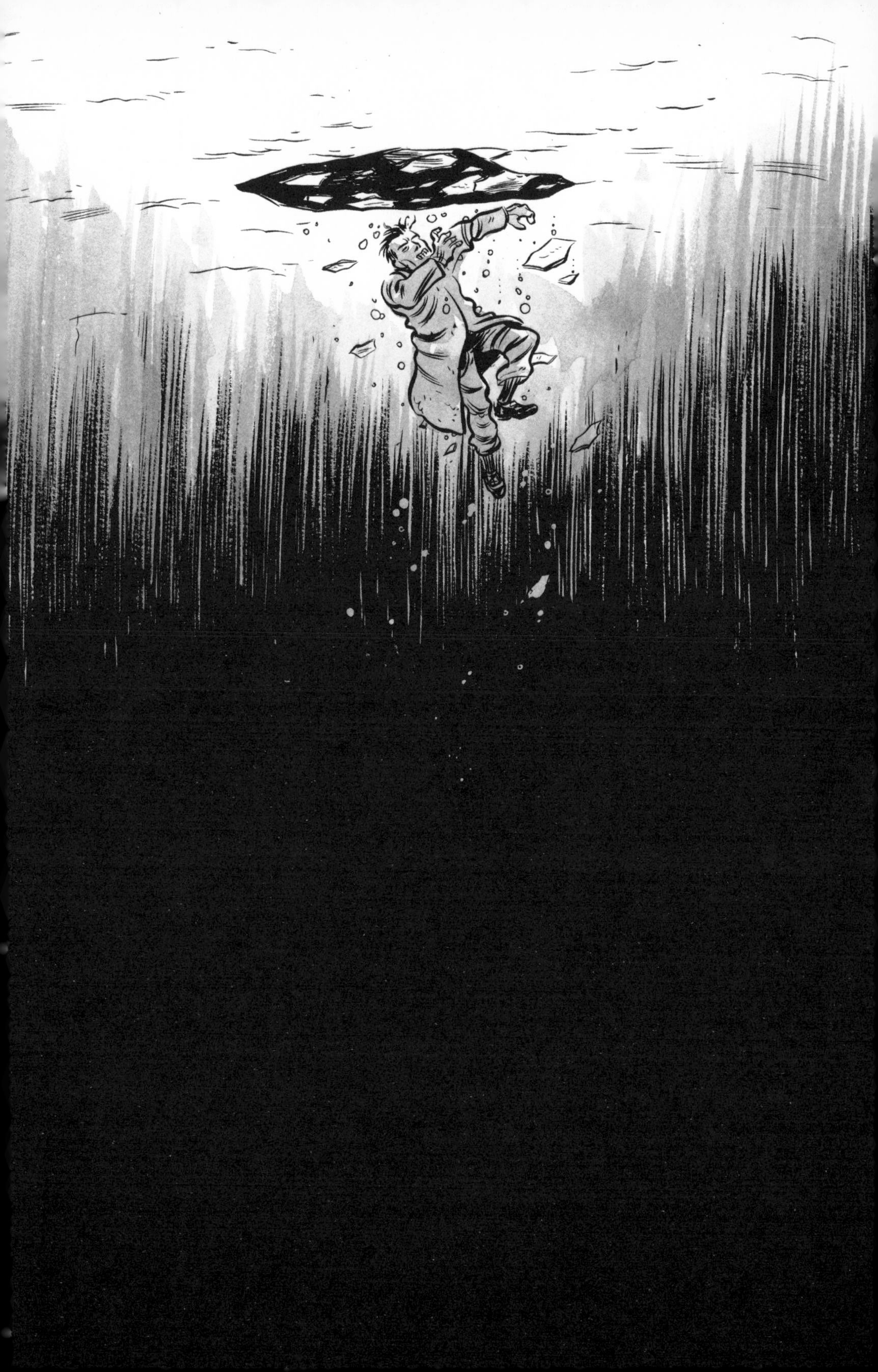

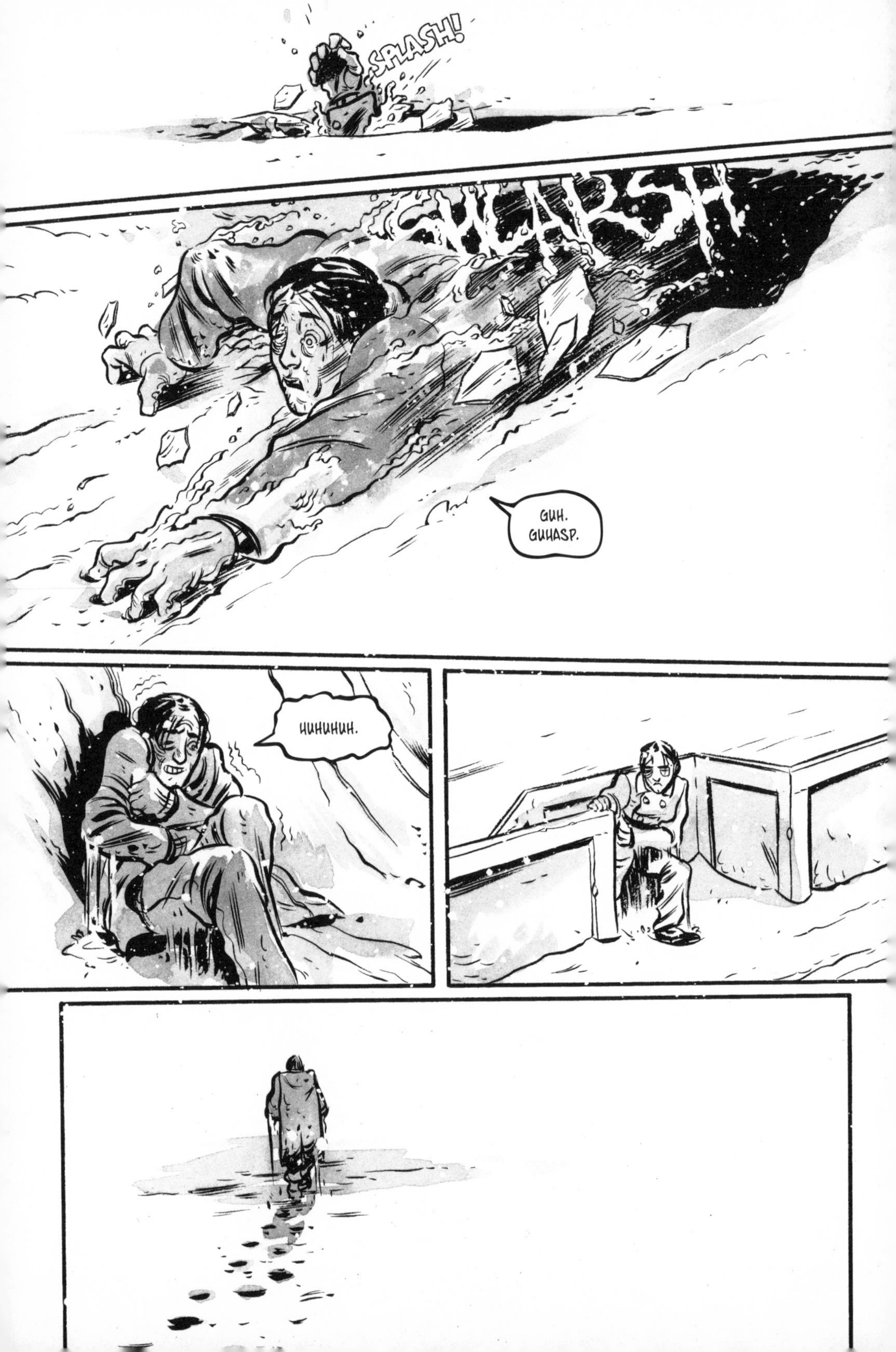
SPLASH!
SHARSH
GUH.
GUHASP.
HUHUHUH.

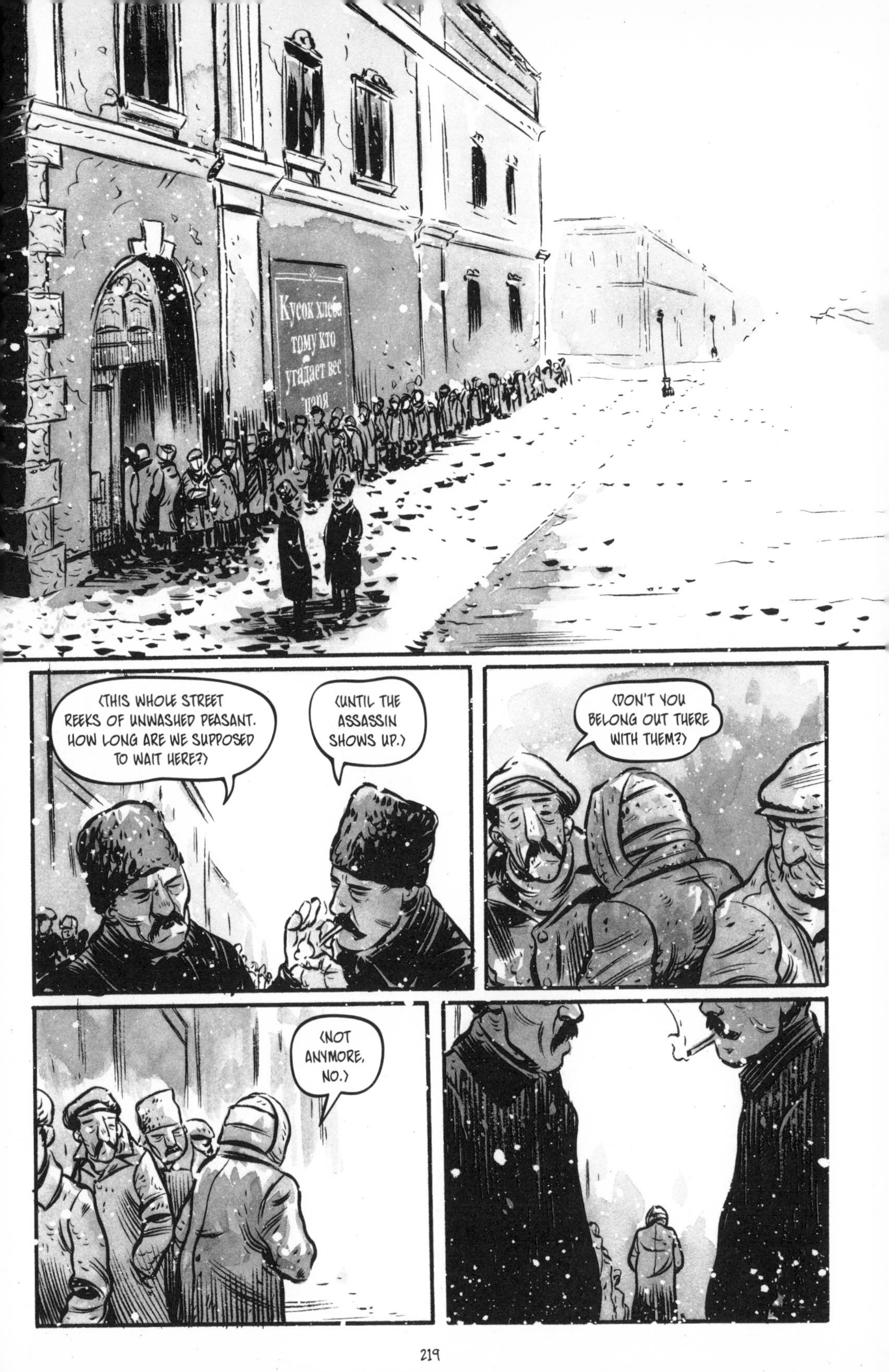
Кусок хлеба
тому кто
угадает вес
‹THIS WHOLE STREET REEKS OF UNWASHED PEASANT. HOW LONG ARE WE SUPPOSED TO WAIT HERE?›
‹UNTIL THE ASSASSIN SHOWS UP.›
‹DON'T YOU BELONG OUT THERE WITH THEM?›
‹NOT ANYMORE, NO.›

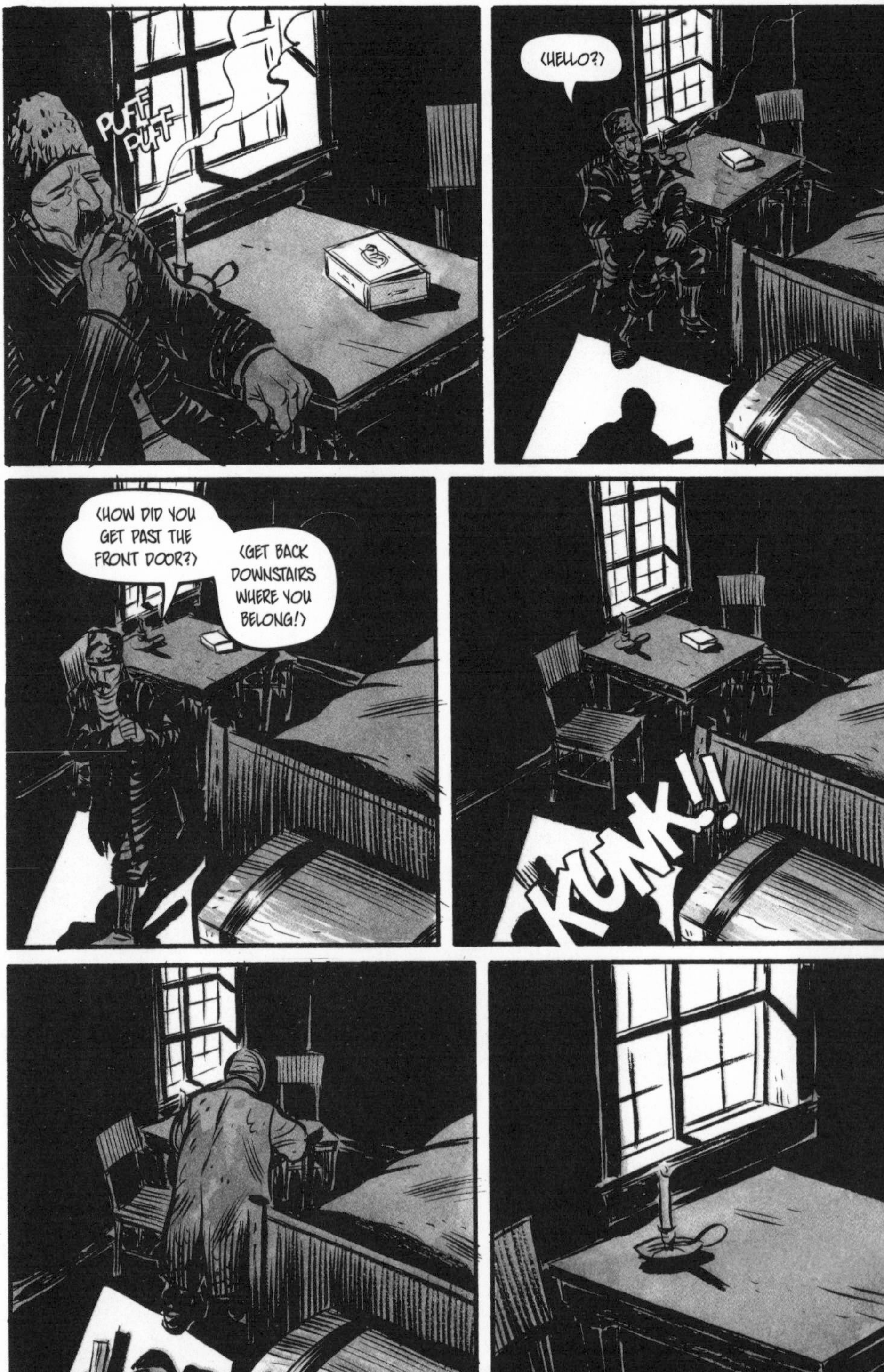
PUFF PUFF
(HELLO?)
(HOW DID YOU GET PAST THE FRONT DOOR?)
(GET BACK DOWNSTAIRS WHERE YOU BELONG!)
KUNK!!

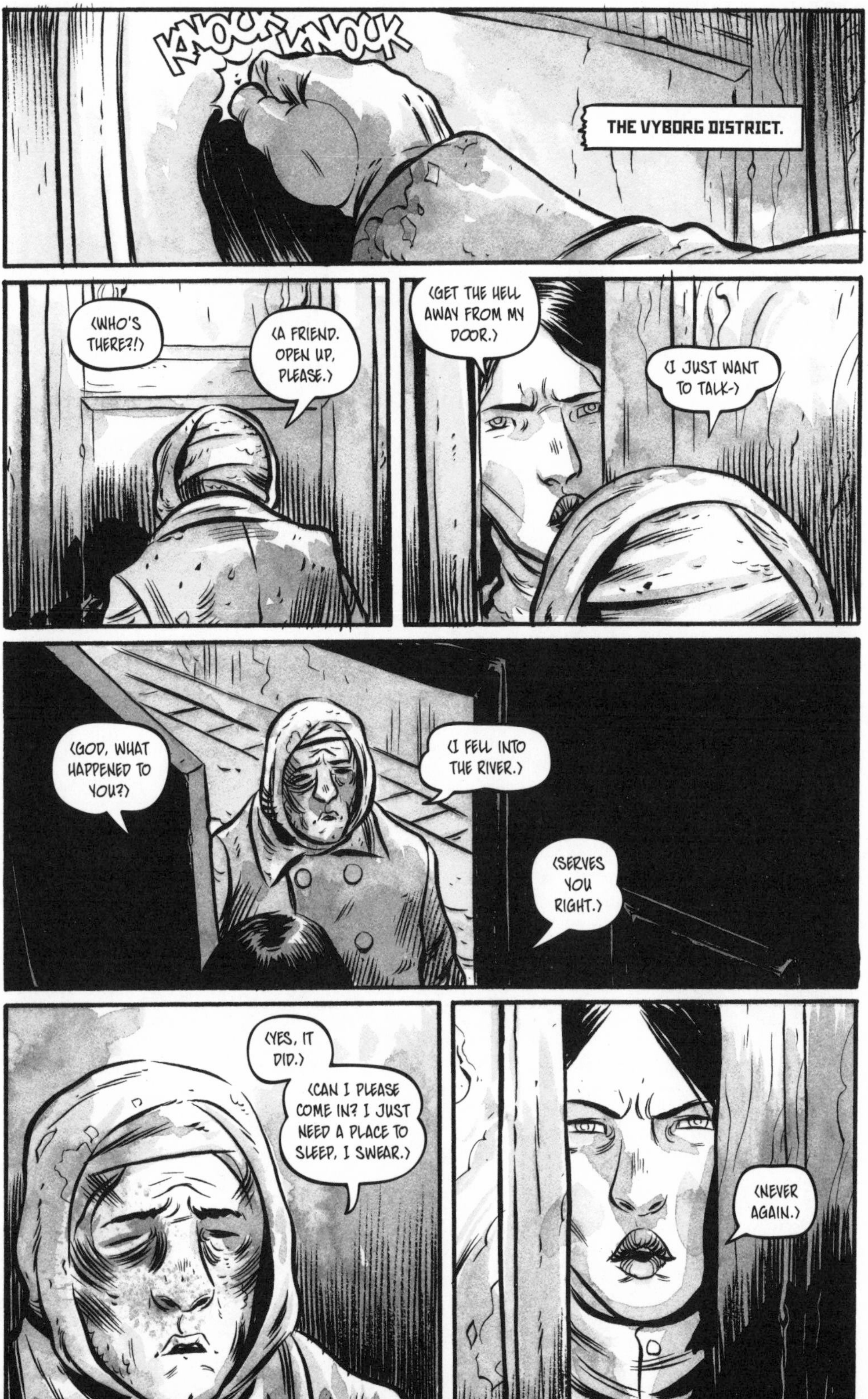
KNOCK KNOCK
THE VYBORG DISTRICT.
<WHO'S THERE?!>
<A FRIEND. OPEN UP, PLEASE.>
<GET THE HELL AWAY FROM MY DOOR.>
<I JUST WANT TO TALK->
<GOD, WHAT HAPPENED TO YOU?>
<I FELL INTO THE RIVER.>
<SERVES YOU RIGHT.>
<YES, IT DID.>
<CAN I PLEASE COME IN? I JUST NEED A PLACE TO SLEEP, I SWEAR.>
<NEVER AGAIN.>

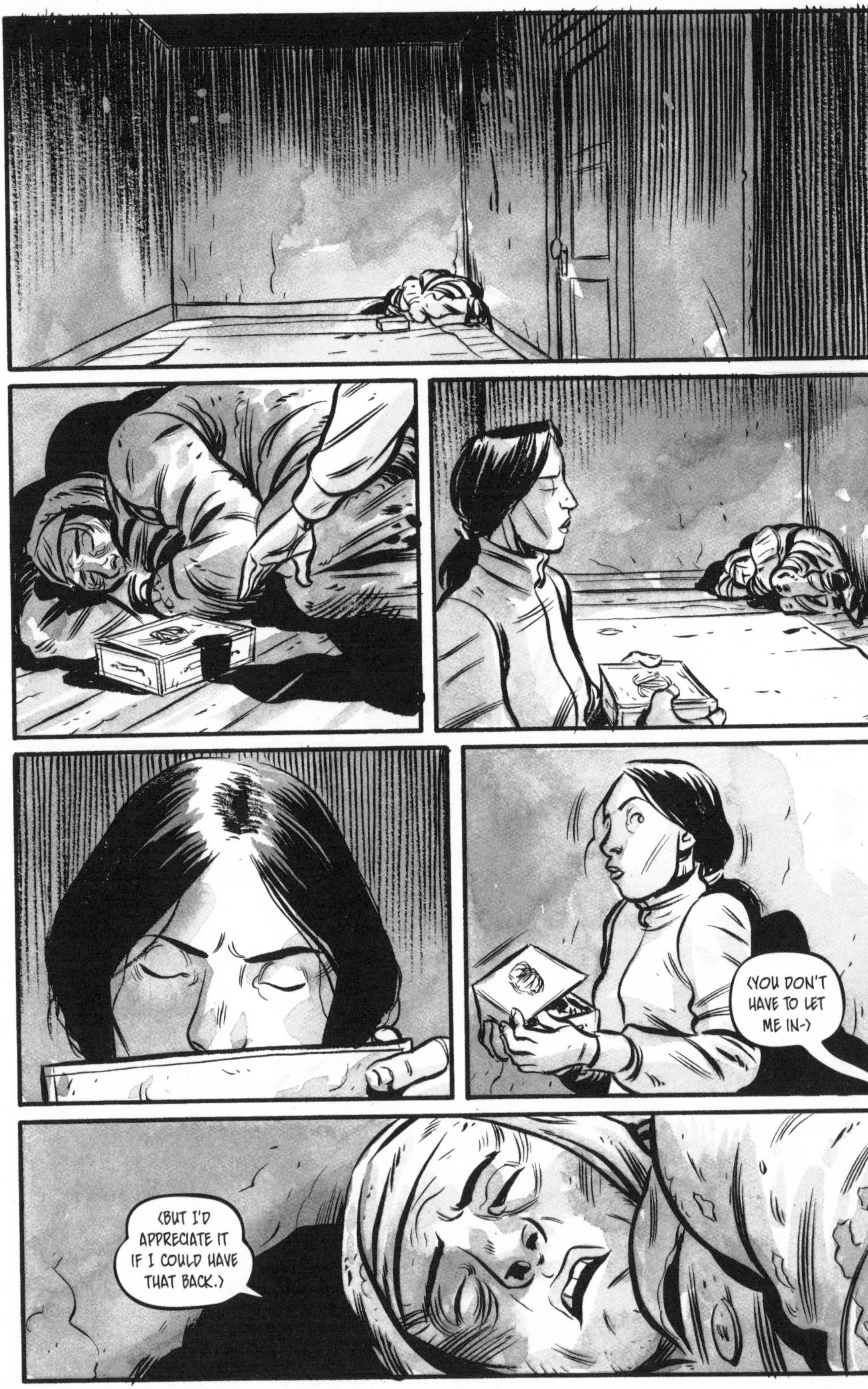
‹YOU DON'T HAVE TO LET ME IN-›
‹BUT I'D APPRECIATE IT IF I COULD HAVE THAT BACK.›

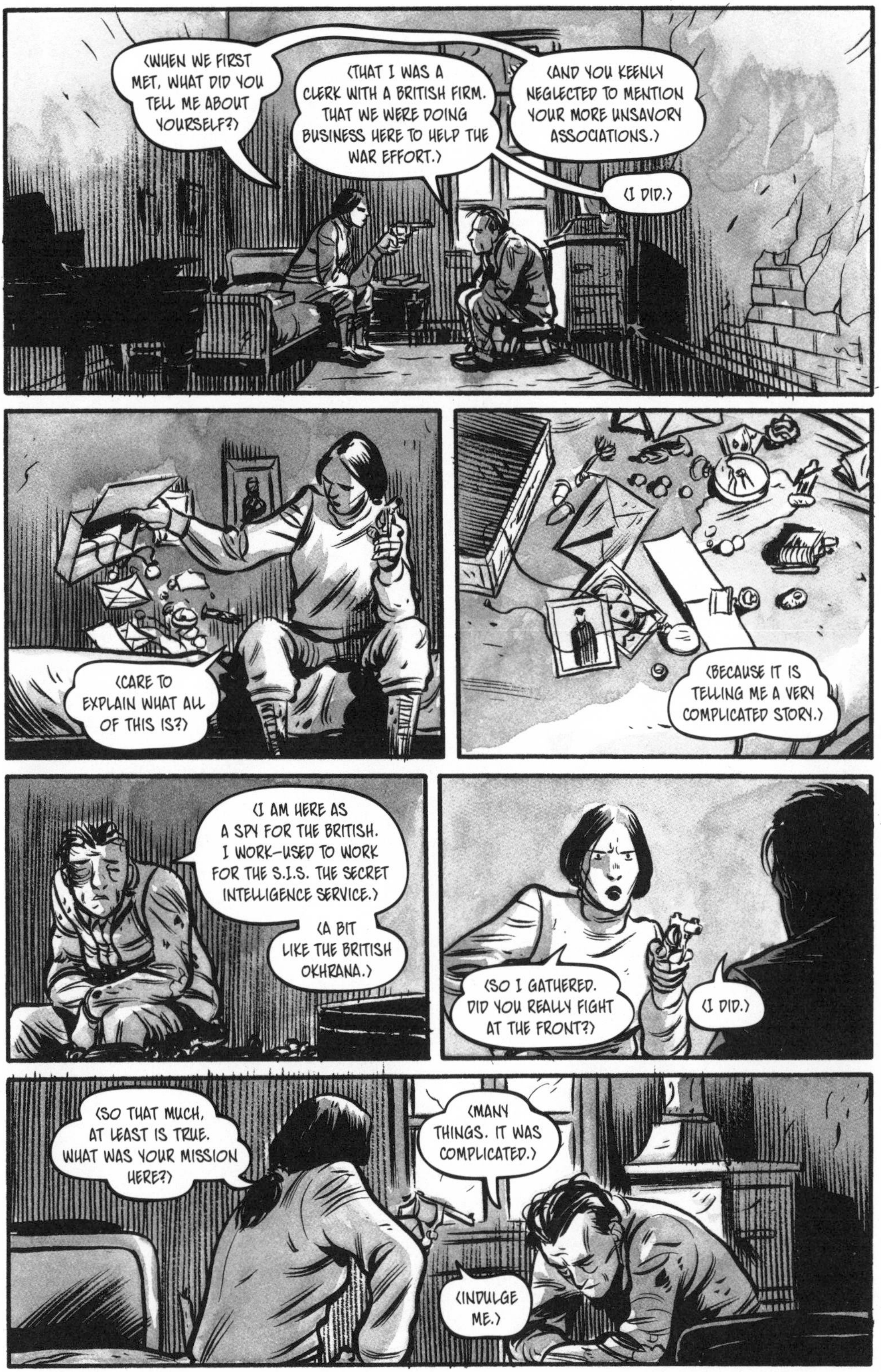

‹WHEN WE FIRST MET, WHAT DID YOU TELL ME ABOUT YOURSELF?›
‹THAT I WAS A CLERK WITH A BRITISH FIRM. THAT WE WERE DOING BUSINESS HERE TO HELP THE WAR EFFORT.›
‹AND YOU KEENLY NEGLECTED TO MENTION YOUR MORE UNSAVORY ASSOCIATIONS.›
‹I DID.›
‹CARE TO EXPLAIN WHAT ALL OF THIS IS?›
‹BECAUSE IT IS TELLING ME A VERY COMPLICATED STORY.›
‹I AM HERE AS A SPY FOR THE BRITISH. I WORK–USED TO WORK FOR THE S.I.S. THE SECRET INTELLIGENCE SERVICE.›
‹A BIT LIKE THE BRITISH OKHRANA.›
‹SO I GATHERED. DID YOU REALLY FIGHT AT THE FRONT?›
‹I DID.›
‹SO THAT MUCH, AT LEAST IS TRUE. WHAT WAS YOUR MISSION HERE?›
‹MANY THINGS. IT WAS COMPLICATED.›
‹INDULGE ME.›

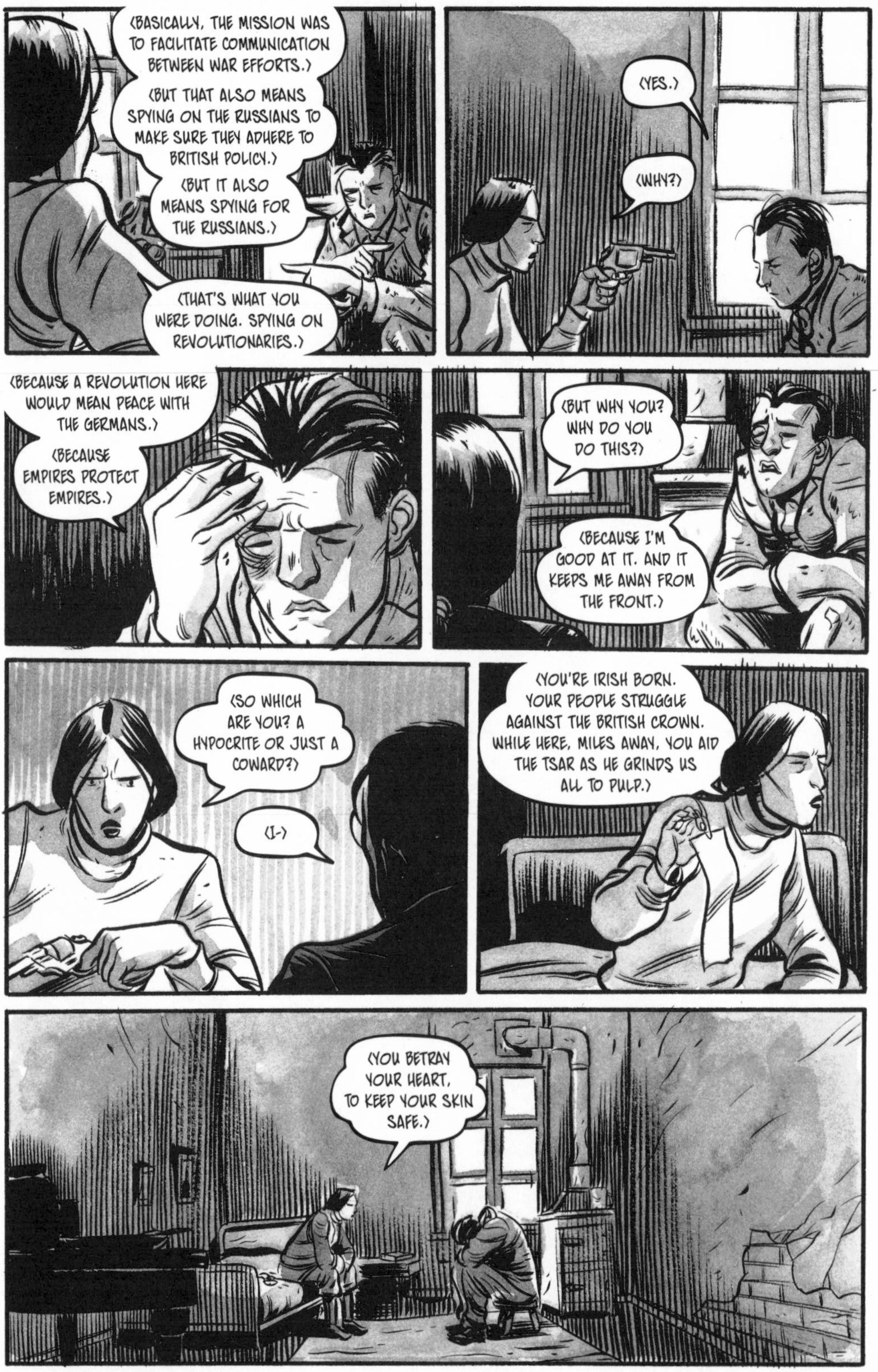
(BASICALLY, THE MISSION WAS TO FACILITATE COMMUNICATION BETWEEN WAR EFFORTS.)
(BUT THAT ALSO MEANS SPYING ON THE RUSSIANS TO MAKE SURE THEY ADHERE TO BRITISH POLICY.)
(BUT IT ALSO MEANS SPYING FOR THE RUSSIANS.)
(THAT'S WHAT YOU WERE DOING. SPYING ON REVOLUTIONARIES.)
(YES.)
(WHY?)
(BECAUSE A REVOLUTION HERE WOULD MEAN PEACE WITH THE GERMANS.)
(BECAUSE EMPIRES PROTECT EMPIRES.)
(BUT WHY YOU? WHY DO YOU DO THIS?)
(BECAUSE I'M GOOD AT IT. AND IT KEEPS ME AWAY FROM THE FRONT.)
(SO WHICH ARE YOU? A HYPOCRITE OR JUST A COWARD?)
(I-)
(YOU'RE IRISH BORN. YOUR PEOPLE STRUGGLE AGAINST THE BRITISH CROWN. WHILE HERE, MILES AWAY, YOU AID THE TSAR AS HE GRINDS US ALL TO PULP.)
(YOU BETRAY YOUR HEART, TO KEEP YOUR SKIN SAFE.)

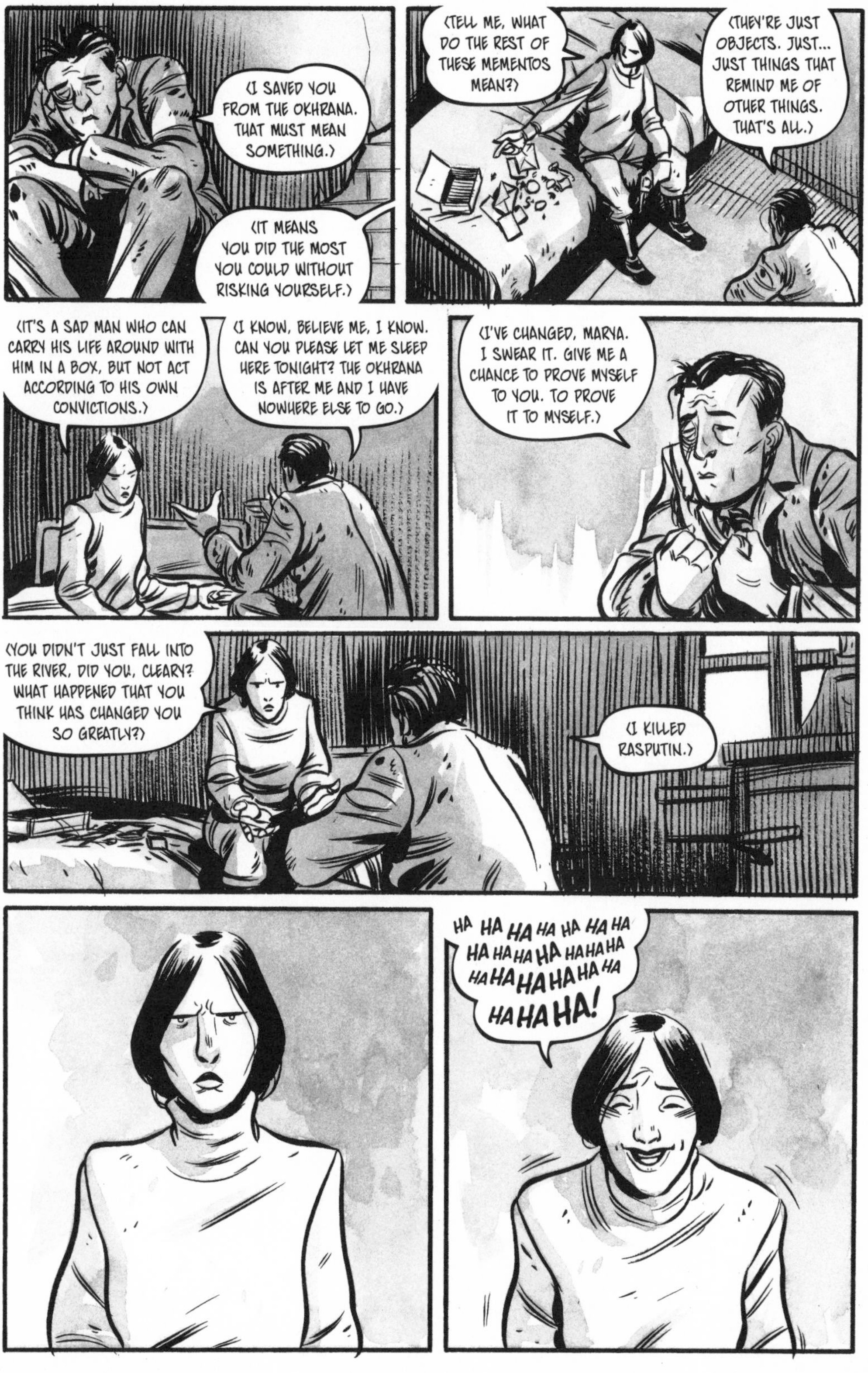
‹I SAVED YOU FROM THE OKHRANA. THAT MUST MEAN SOMETHING.›
‹IT MEANS YOU DID THE MOST YOU COULD WITHOUT RISKING YOURSELF.›
‹TELL ME, WHAT DO THE REST OF THESE MEMENTOS MEAN?›
‹THEY'RE JUST OBJECTS. JUST... JUST THINGS THAT REMIND ME OF OTHER THINGS. THAT'S ALL.›
‹IT'S A SAD MAN WHO CAN CARRY HIS LIFE AROUND WITH HIM IN A BOX, BUT NOT ACT ACCORDING TO HIS OWN CONVICTIONS.›
‹I KNOW, BELIEVE ME, I KNOW. CAN YOU PLEASE LET ME SLEEP HERE TONIGHT? THE OKHRANA IS AFTER ME AND I HAVE NOWHERE ELSE TO GO.›
‹I'VE CHANGED, MARYA. I SWEAR IT. GIVE ME A CHANCE TO PROVE MYSELF TO YOU. TO PROVE IT TO MYSELF.›
‹YOU DIDN'T JUST FALL INTO THE RIVER, DID YOU, CLEARY? WHAT HAPPENED THAT YOU THINK HAS CHANGED YOU SO GREATLY?›
‹I KILLED RASPUTIN.›
HA HA HA HA HA HA HA HA HA HA HA HA HAHAHA HA HA HA HA HA HA HA HA HA HA!

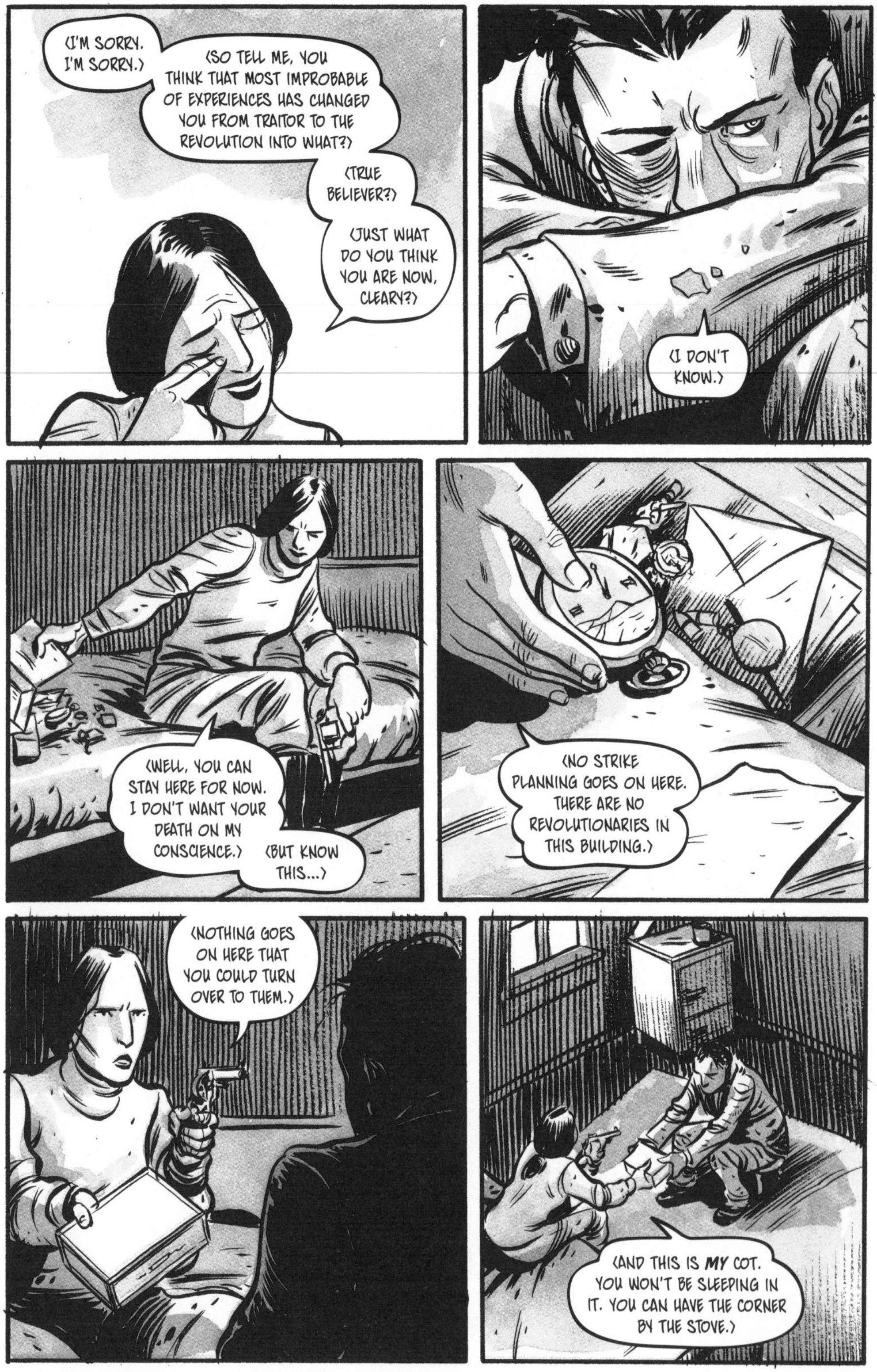
‹I'M SORRY. I'M SORRY.›
‹SO TELL ME, YOU THINK THAT MOST IMPROBABLE OF EXPERIENCES HAS CHANGED YOU FROM TRAITOR TO THE REVOLUTION INTO WHAT?›
‹TRUE BELIEVER?›
‹JUST WHAT DO YOU THINK YOU ARE NOW, CLEARY?›
‹I DON'T KNOW.›
‹WELL, YOU CAN STAY HERE FOR NOW. I DON'T WANT YOUR DEATH ON MY CONSCIENCE.›
‹BUT KNOW THIS...›
‹NO STRIKE PLANNING GOES ON HERE. THERE ARE NO REVOLUTIONARIES IN THIS BUILDING.›
‹NOTHING GOES ON HERE THAT YOU COULD TURN OVER TO THEM.›
‹AND THIS IS MY COT. YOU WON'T BE SLEEPING IN IT. YOU CAN HAVE THE CORNER BY THE STOVE.›

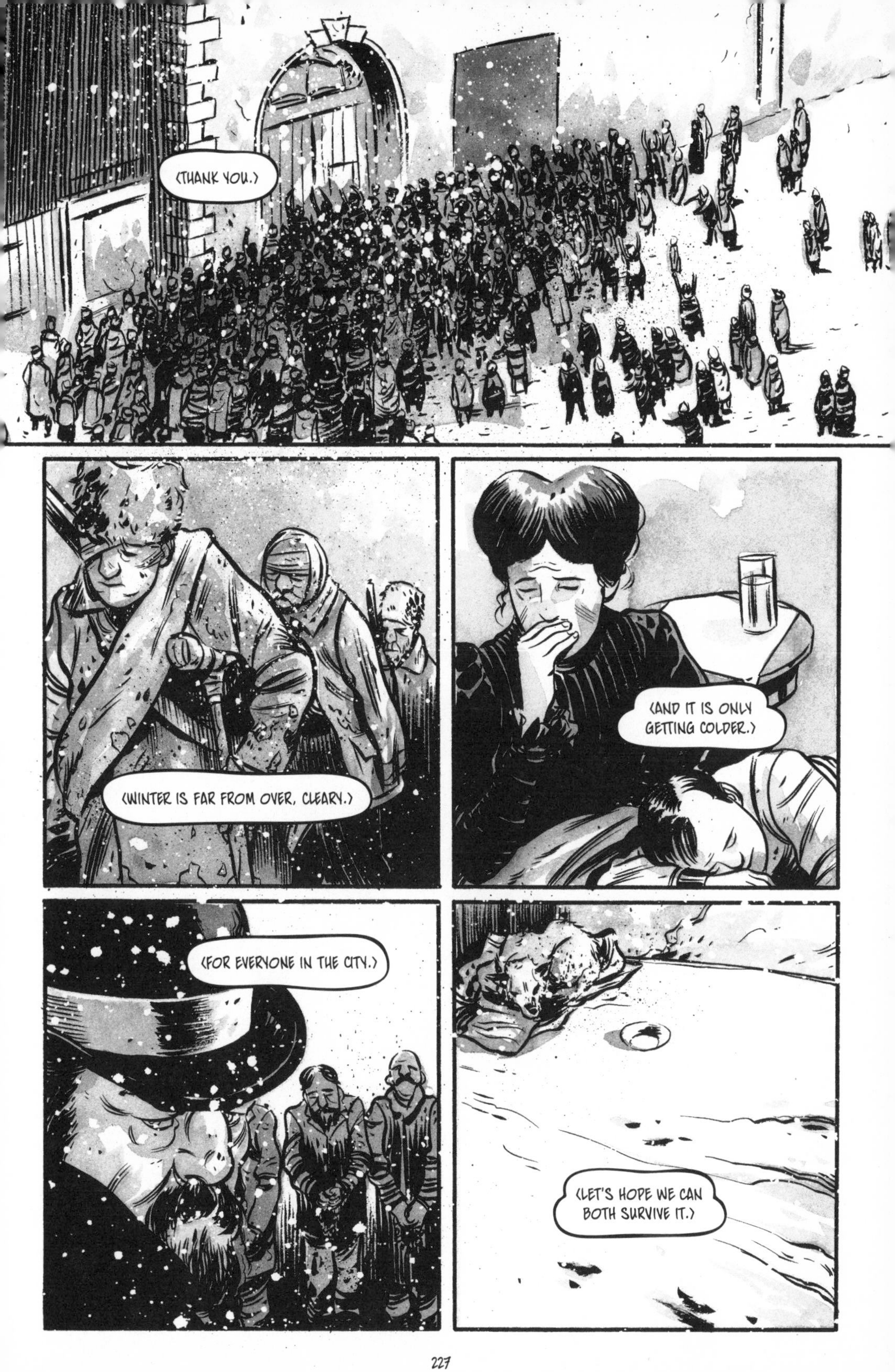
(THANK YOU.)
(WINTER IS FAR FROM OVER, CLEARY.)
(AND IT IS ONLY GETTING COLDER.)
(FOR EVERYONE IN THE CITY.)
(LET'S HOPE WE CAN BOTH SURVIVE IT.)

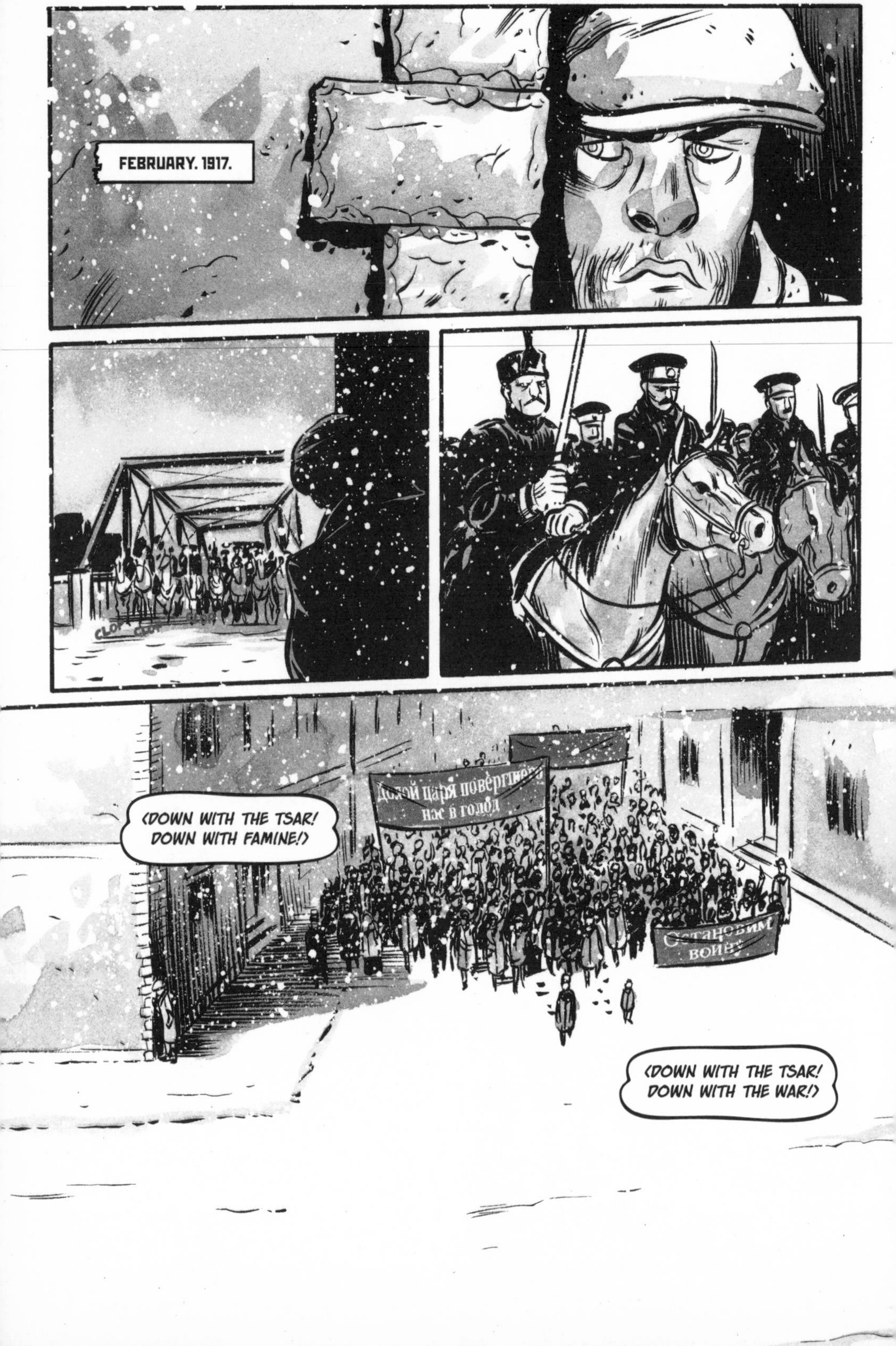
FEBRUARY. 1917.
CLOP CLOP
‹DOWN WITH THE TSAR! DOWN WITH FAMINE!›
‹DOWN WITH THE TSAR! DOWN WITH THE WAR!›

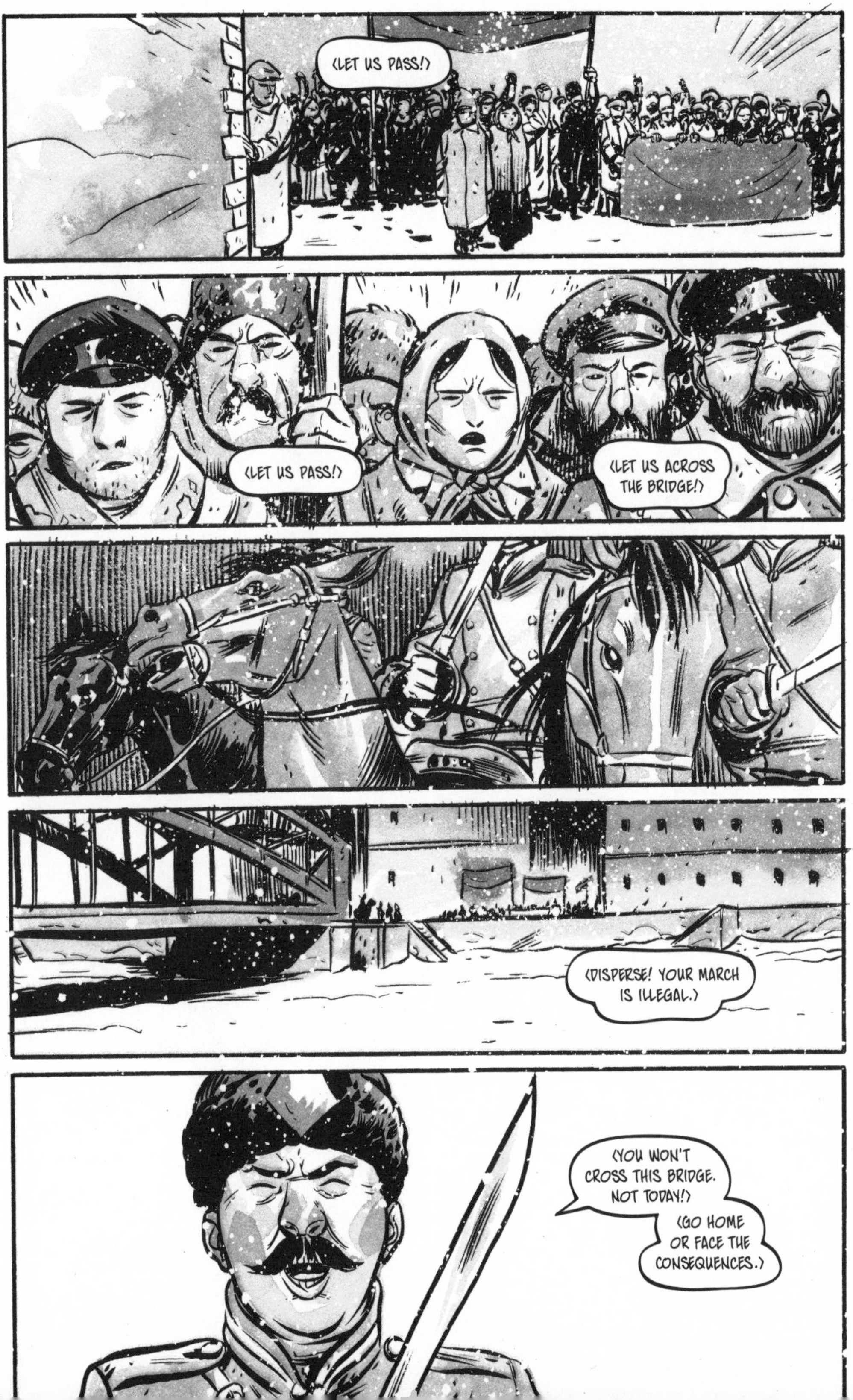
‹LET US PASS!›
‹LET US PASS!›
‹LET US ACROSS THE BRIDGE!›
‹DISPERSE! YOUR MARCH IS ILLEGAL.›
‹YOU WON'T CROSS THIS BRIDGE. NOT TODAY!›
‹GO HOME OR FACE THE CONSEQUENCES.›

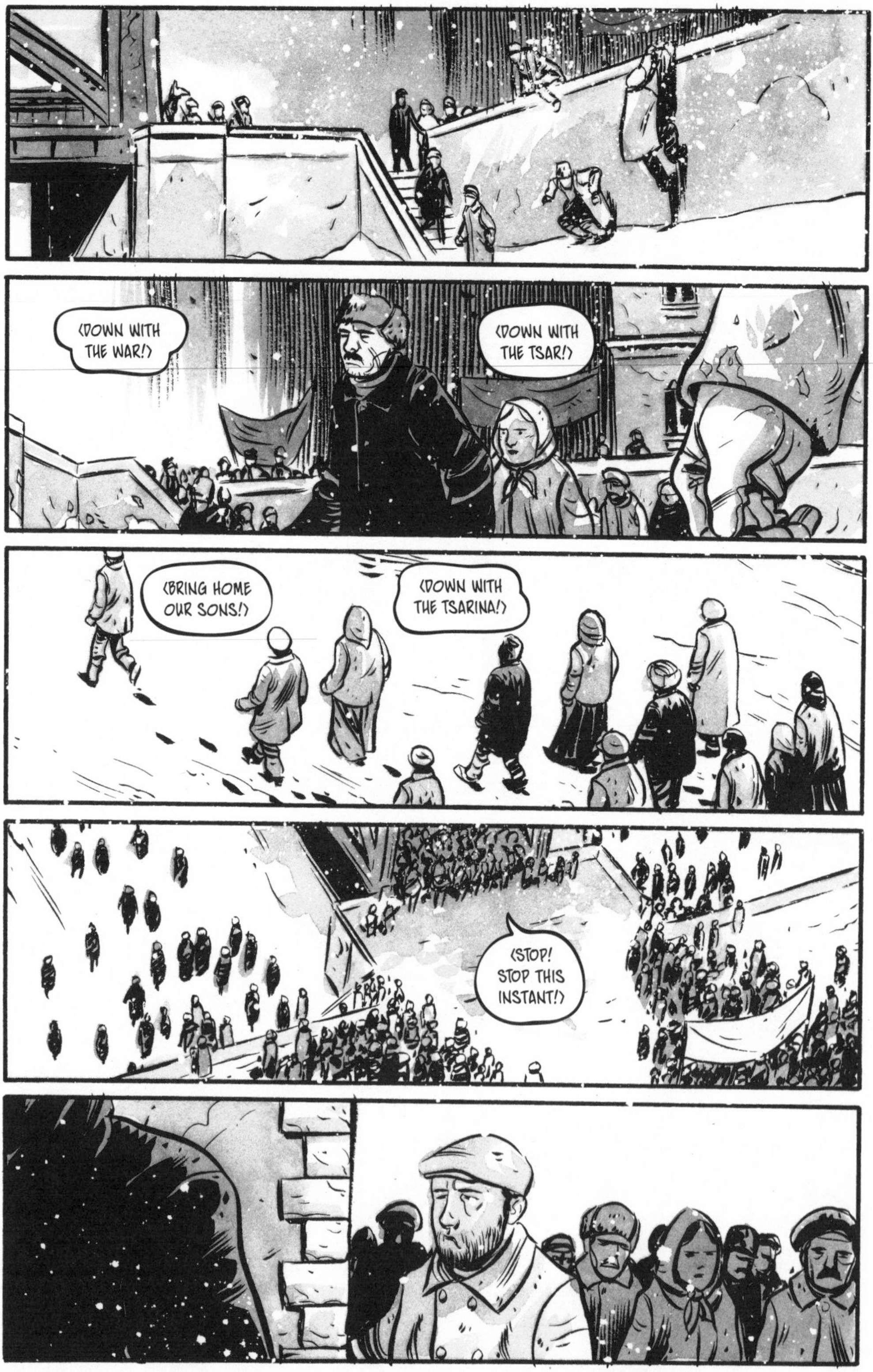
‹DOWN WITH THE WAR!›
‹DOWN WITH THE TSAR!›
‹BRING HOME OUR SONS!›
‹DOWN WITH THE TSARINA!›
‹STOP! STOP THIS INSTANT!›

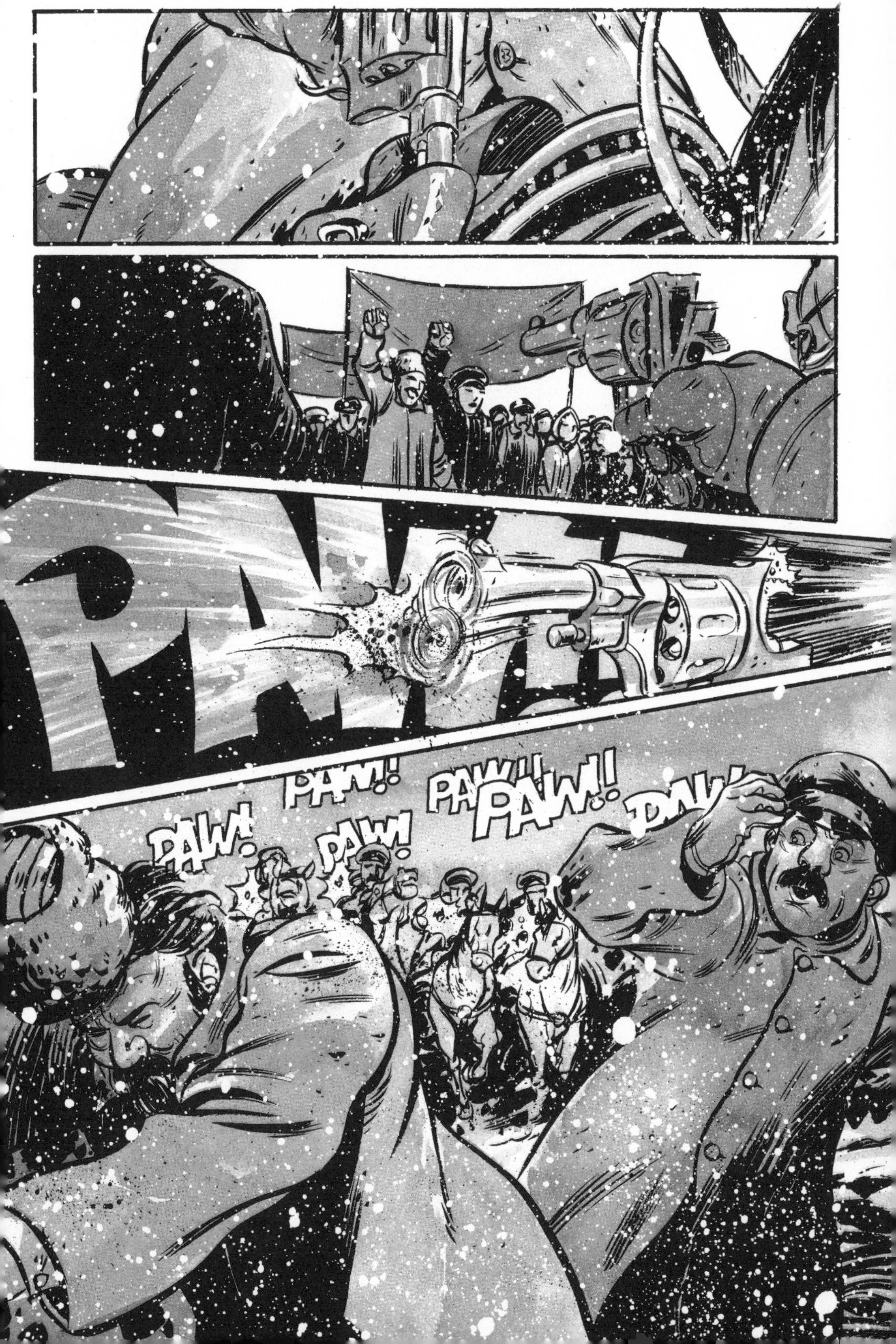
PAW!
PAW!
PAW!
PAW!
PAW!
PAW!

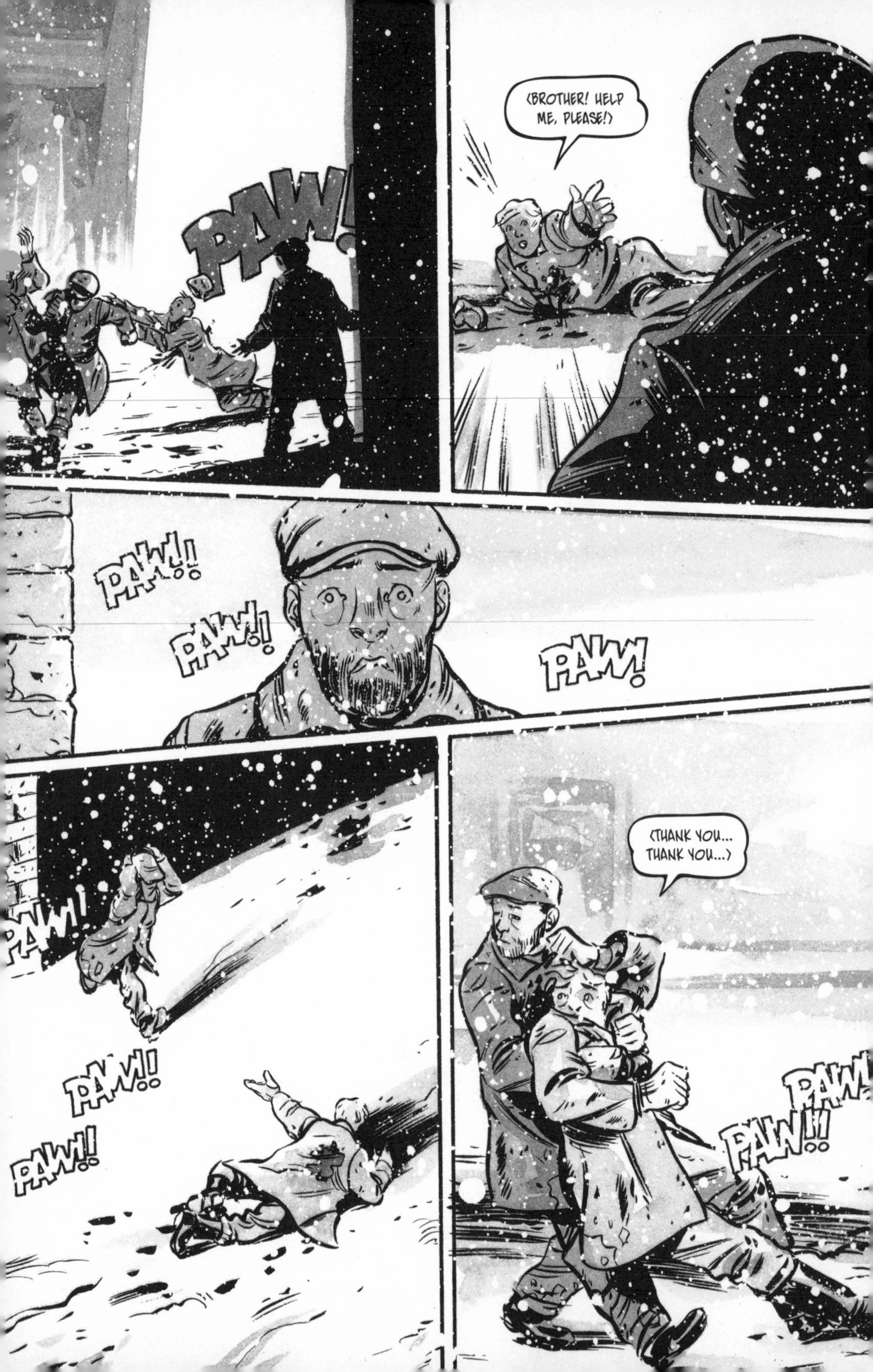
PAW!
‹BROTHER! HELP ME, PLEASE!›
PAW!!
PAW!!
PAW!
PAW!
PAW!!
PAW!!
‹THANK YOU... THANK YOU...›
PAW
PAW!!

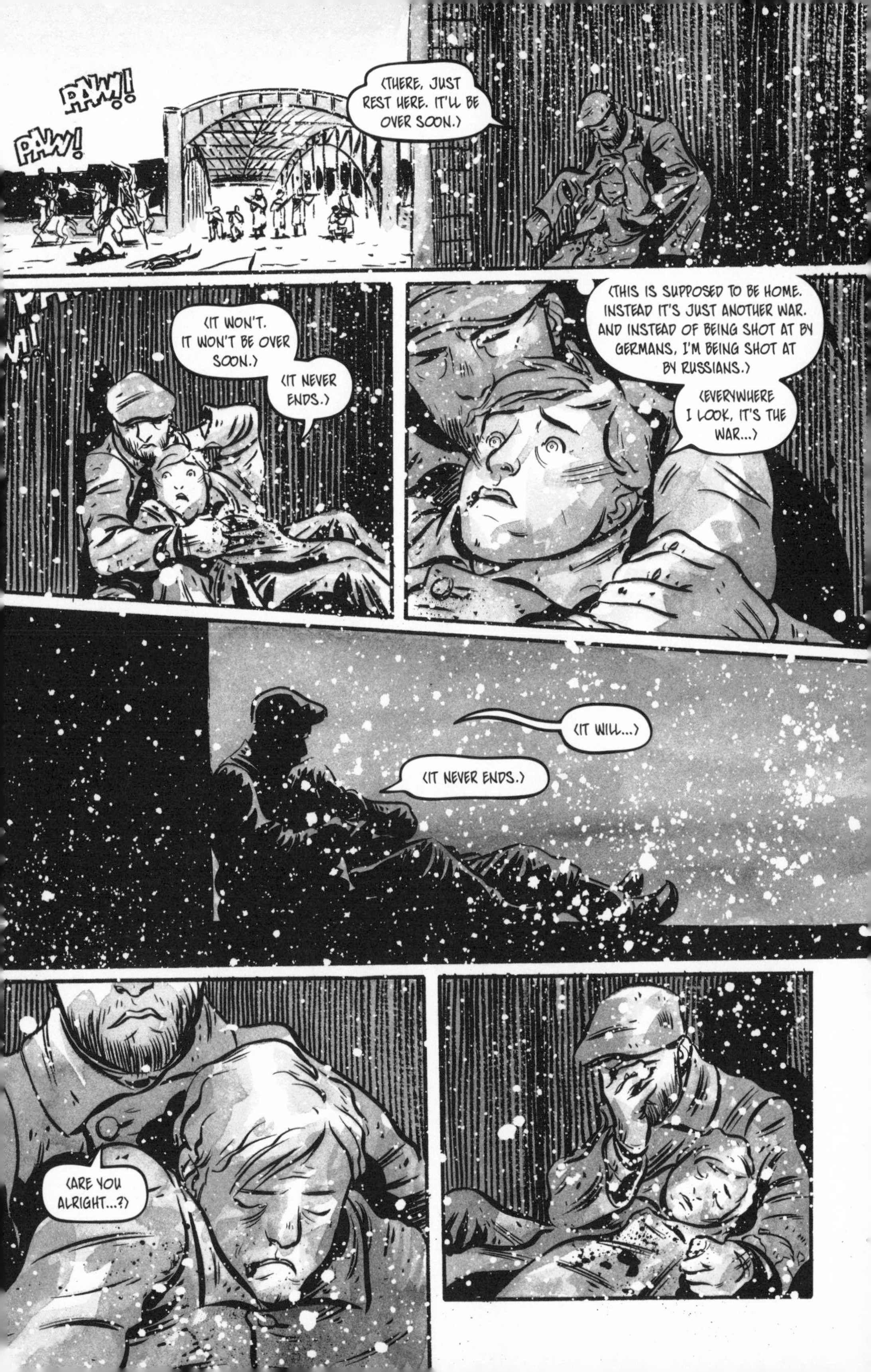
PAW!
PAW!
‹THERE, JUST REST HERE. IT'LL BE OVER SOON.›
‹IT WON'T. IT WON'T BE OVER SOON.›
‹IT NEVER ENDS.›
‹THIS IS SUPPOSED TO BE HOME. INSTEAD IT'S JUST ANOTHER WAR. AND INSTEAD OF BEING SHOT AT BY GERMANS, I'M BEING SHOT AT BY RUSSIANS.›
‹EVERYWHERE I LOOK, IT'S THE WAR...›
‹IT WILL...›
‹IT NEVER ENDS.›
‹ARE YOU ALRIGHT...?›

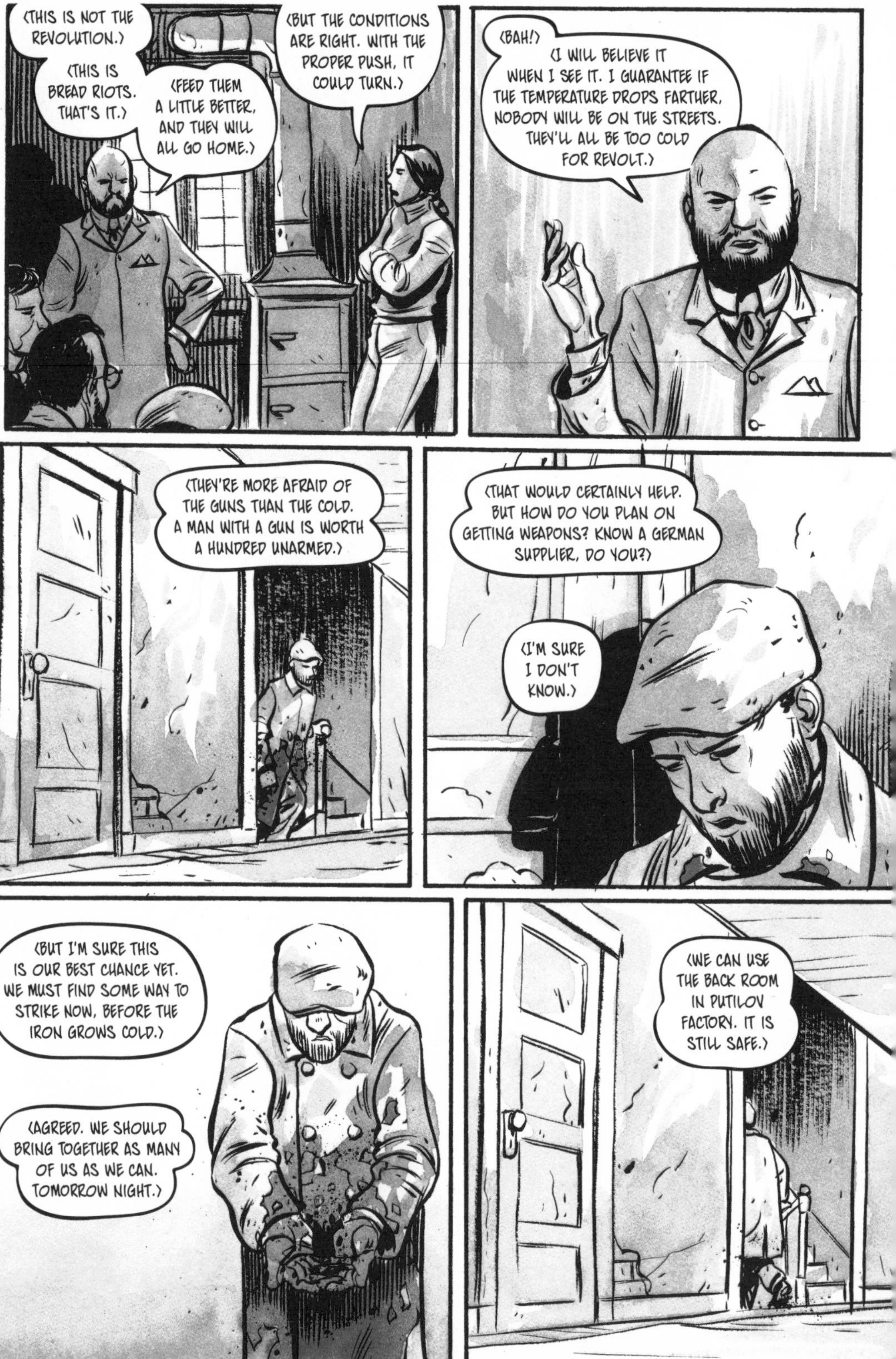
‹THIS IS NOT THE REVOLUTION.›
‹THIS IS BREAD RIOTS. THAT'S IT.›
‹FEED THEM A LITTLE BETTER, AND THEY WILL ALL GO HOME.›
‹BUT THE CONDITIONS ARE RIGHT. WITH THE PROPER PUSH, IT COULD TURN.›
‹BAH!›
‹I WILL BELIEVE IT WHEN I SEE IT. I GUARANTEE IF THE TEMPERATURE DROPS FARTHER, NOBODY WILL BE ON THE STREETS. THEY'LL ALL BE TOO COLD FOR REVOLT.›
‹THEY'RE MORE AFRAID OF THE GUNS THAN THE COLD. A MAN WITH A GUN IS WORTH A HUNDRED UNARMED.›
‹THAT WOULD CERTAINLY HELP. BUT HOW DO YOU PLAN ON GETTING WEAPONS? KNOW A GERMAN SUPPLIER, DO YOU?›
‹I'M SURE I DON'T KNOW.›
‹BUT I'M SURE THIS IS OUR BEST CHANCE YET. WE MUST FIND SOME WAY TO STRIKE NOW, BEFORE THE IRON GROWS COLD.›
‹AGREED. WE SHOULD BRING TOGETHER AS MANY OF US AS WE CAN. TOMORROW NIGHT.›
‹WE CAN USE THE BACK ROOM IN PUTILOV FACTORY. IT IS STILL SAFE.›

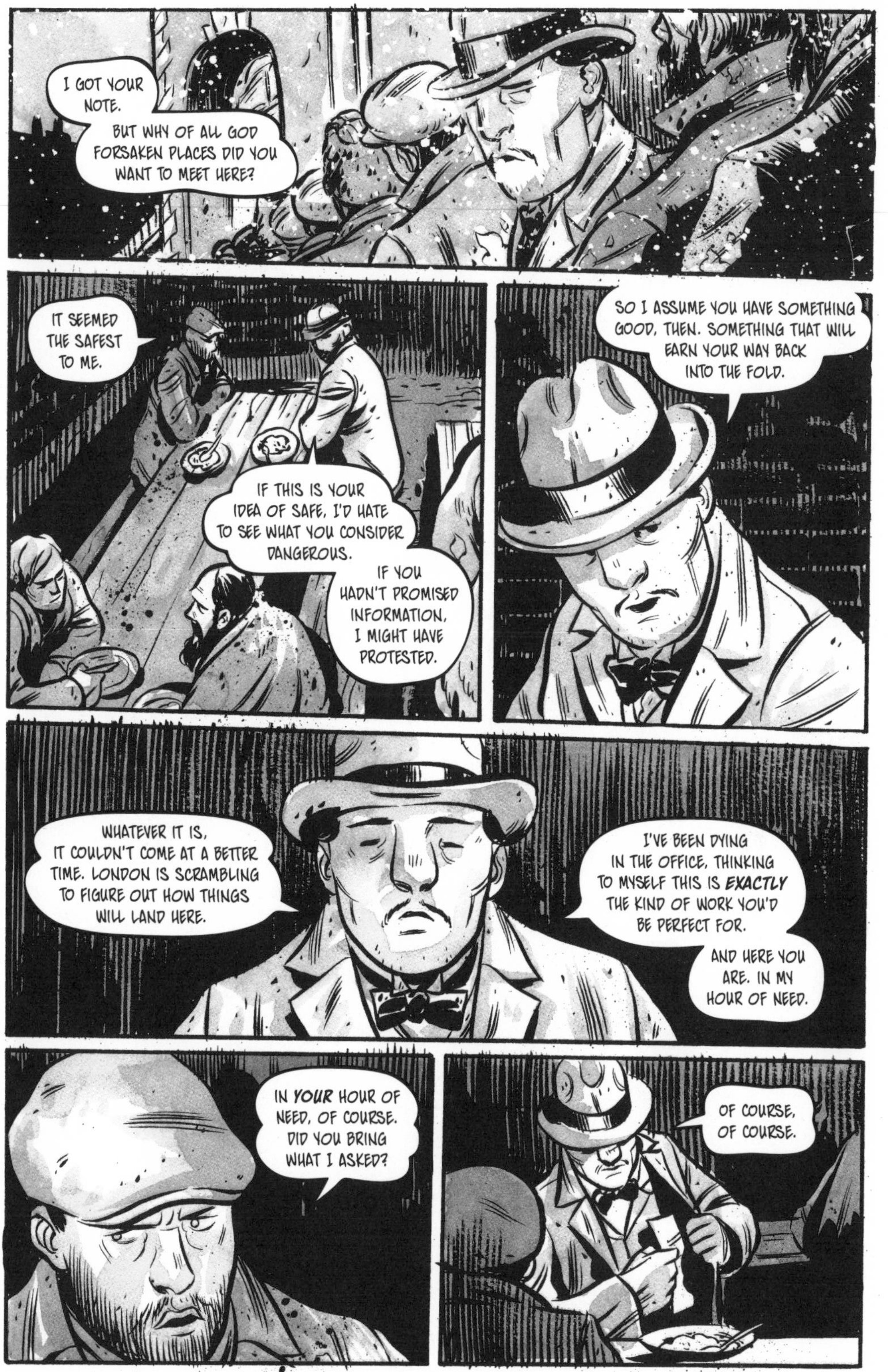
I GOT YOUR NOTE.
BUT WHY OF ALL GOD FORSAKEN PLACES DID YOU WANT TO MEET HERE?
IT SEEMED THE SAFEST TO ME.
IF THIS IS YOUR IDEA OF SAFE, I'D HATE TO SEE WHAT YOU CONSIDER DANGEROUS.
IF YOU HADN'T PROMISED INFORMATION, I MIGHT HAVE PROTESTED.
SO I ASSUME YOU HAVE SOMETHING GOOD, THEN. SOMETHING THAT WILL EARN YOUR WAY BACK INTO THE FOLD.
WHATEVER IT IS, IT COULDN'T COME AT A BETTER TIME. LONDON IS SCRAMBLING TO FIGURE OUT HOW THINGS WILL LAND HERE.
I'VE BEEN DYING IN THE OFFICE, THINKING TO MYSELF THIS IS EXACTLY THE KIND OF WORK YOU'D BE PERFECT FOR.
AND HERE YOU ARE. IN MY HOUR OF NEED.
IN YOUR HOUR OF NEED, OF COURSE. DID YOU BRING WHAT I ASKED?
OF COURSE, OF COURSE.

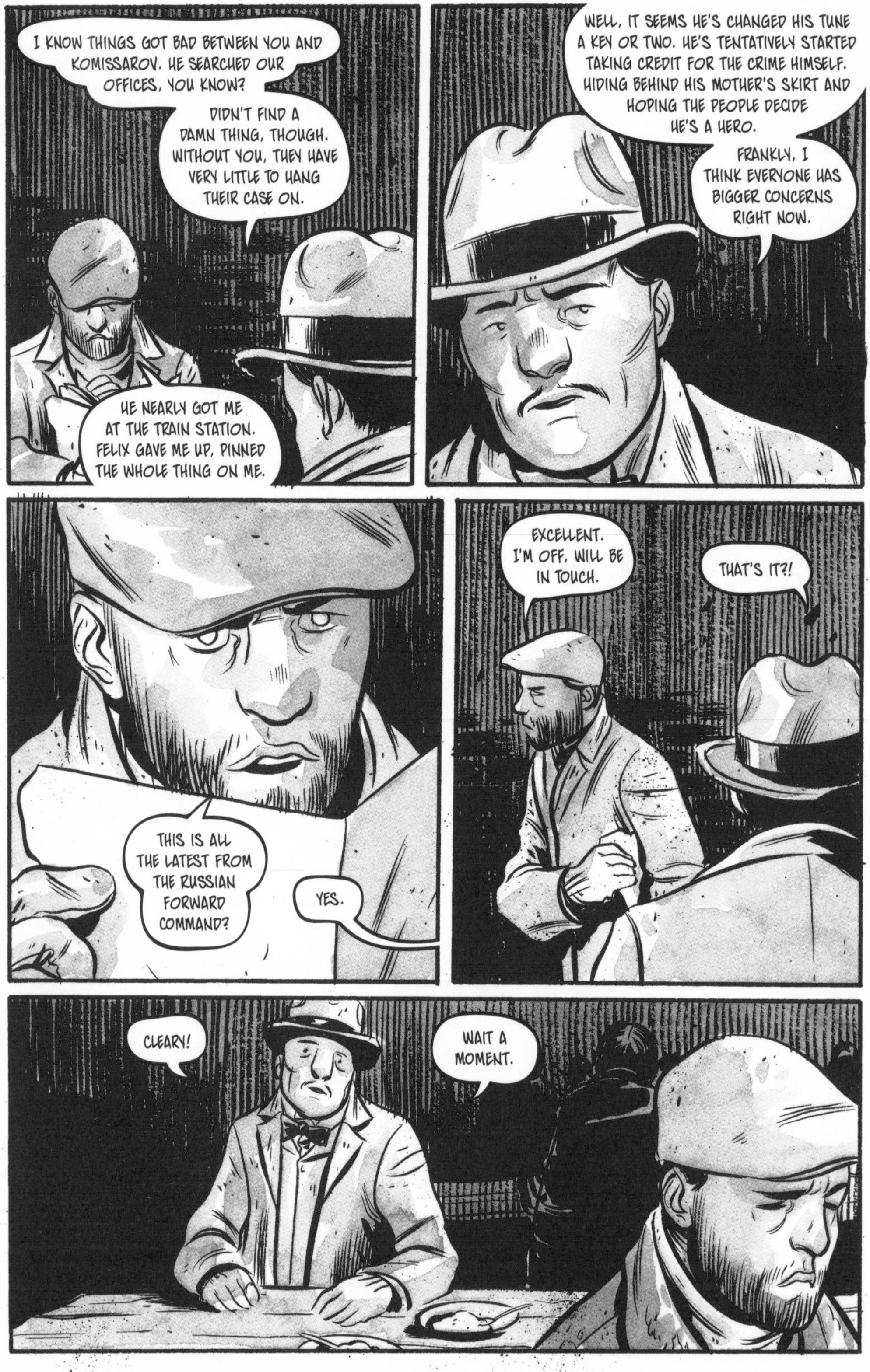
I KNOW THINGS GOT BAD BETWEEN YOU AND KOMISSAROV. HE SEARCHED OUR OFFICES, YOU KNOW?
DIDN'T FIND A DAMN THING, THOUGH. WITHOUT YOU, THEY HAVE VERY LITTLE TO HANG THEIR CASE ON.
HE NEARLY GOT ME AT THE TRAIN STATION. FELIX GAVE ME UP, PINNED THE WHOLE THING ON ME.
WELL, IT SEEMS HE'S CHANGED HIS TUNE A KEY OR TWO. HE'S TENTATIVELY STARTED TAKING CREDIT FOR THE CRIME HIMSELF. HIDING BEHIND HIS MOTHER'S SKIRT AND HOPING THE PEOPLE DECIDE HE'S A HERO.
FRANKLY, I THINK EVERYONE HAS BIGGER CONCERNS RIGHT NOW.
THIS IS ALL THE LATEST FROM THE RUSSIAN FORWARD COMMAND?
YES.
EXCELLENT. I'M OFF, WILL BE IN TOUCH.
THAT'S IT?!
CLEARY!
WAIT A MOMENT.

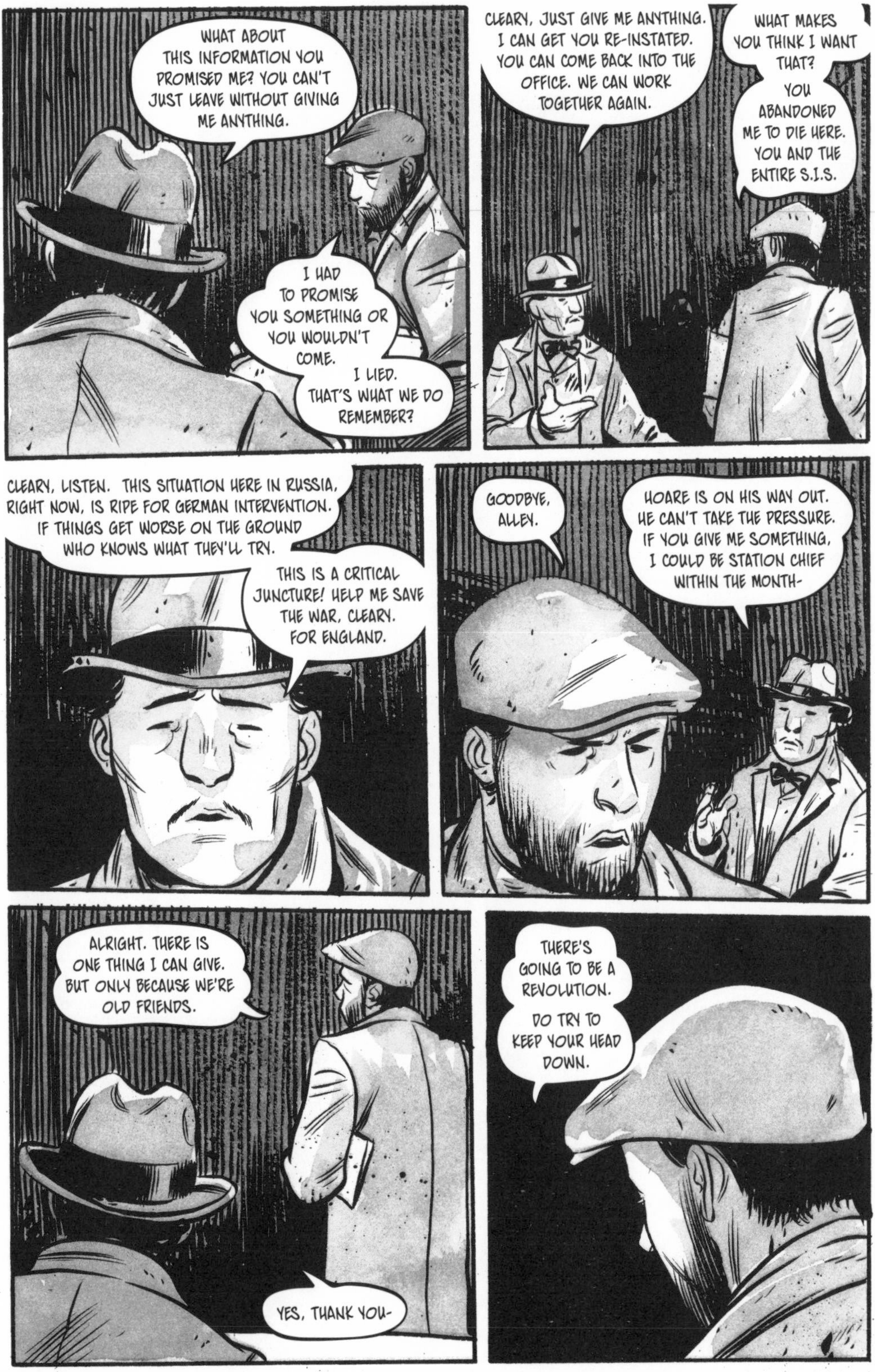
WHAT ABOUT THIS INFORMATION YOU PROMISED ME? YOU CAN'T JUST LEAVE WITHOUT GIVING ME ANYTHING.
I HAD TO PROMISE YOU SOMETHING OR YOU WOULDN'T COME.
I LIED. THAT'S WHAT WE DO REMEMBER?
CLEARY, JUST GIVE ME ANYTHING. I CAN GET YOU RE-INSTATED. YOU CAN COME BACK INTO THE OFFICE. WE CAN WORK TOGETHER AGAIN.
WHAT MAKES YOU THINK I WANT THAT?
YOU ABANDONED ME TO DIE HERE. YOU AND THE ENTIRE S.I.S.
CLEARY, LISTEN. THIS SITUATION HERE IN RUSSIA, RIGHT NOW, IS RIPE FOR GERMAN INTERVENTION. IF THINGS GET WORSE ON THE GROUND WHO KNOWS WHAT THEY'LL TRY.
THIS IS A CRITICAL JUNCTURE! HELP ME SAVE THE WAR, CLEARY. FOR ENGLAND.
GOODBYE, ALLEY.
HOARE IS ON HIS WAY OUT. HE CAN'T TAKE THE PRESSURE. IF YOU GIVE ME SOMETHING, I COULD BE STATION CHIEF WITHIN THE MONTH-
ALRIGHT. THERE IS ONE THING I CAN GIVE. BUT ONLY BECAUSE WE'RE OLD FRIENDS.
YES, THANK YOU-
THERE'S GOING TO BE A REVOLUTION.
DO TRY TO KEEP YOUR HEAD DOWN.

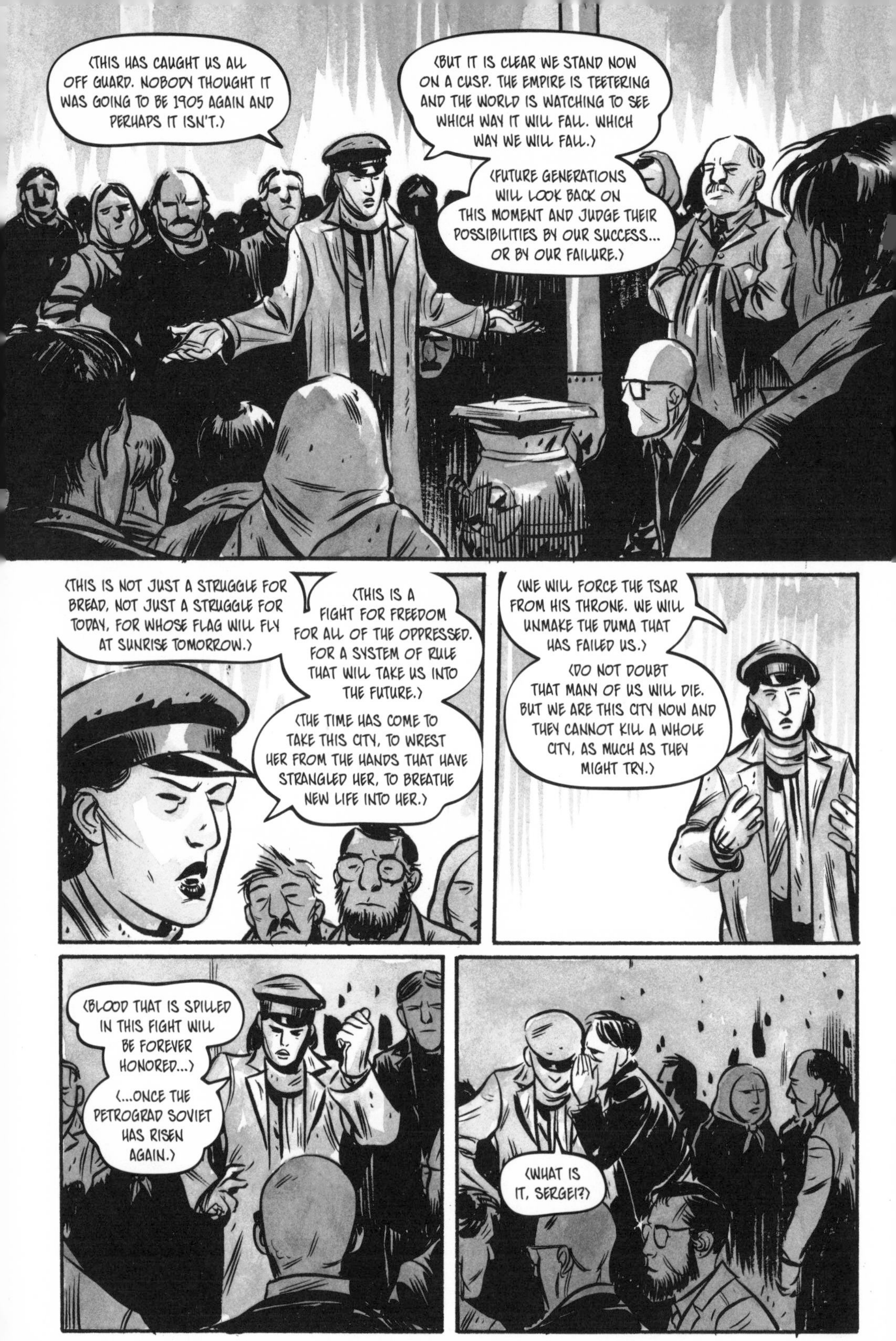
‹THIS HAS CAUGHT US ALL OFF GUARD. NOBODY THOUGHT IT WAS GOING TO BE 1905 AGAIN AND PERHAPS IT ISN'T.›
‹BUT IT IS CLEAR WE STAND NOW ON A CUSP. THE EMPIRE IS TEETERING AND THE WORLD IS WATCHING TO SEE WHICH WAY IT WILL FALL. WHICH WAY WE WILL FALL.›
‹FUTURE GENERATIONS WILL LOOK BACK ON THIS MOMENT AND JUDGE THEIR POSSIBILITIES BY OUR SUCCESS... OR BY OUR FAILURE.›
‹THIS IS NOT JUST A STRUGGLE FOR BREAD, NOT JUST A STRUGGLE FOR TODAY, FOR WHOSE FLAG WILL FLY AT SUNRISE TOMORROW.›
‹THIS IS A FIGHT FOR FREEDOM FOR ALL OF THE OPPRESSED. FOR A SYSTEM OF RULE THAT WILL TAKE US INTO THE FUTURE.›
‹THE TIME HAS COME TO TAKE THIS CITY, TO WREST HER FROM THE HANDS THAT HAVE STRANGLED HER, TO BREATHE NEW LIFE INTO HER.›
‹WE WILL FORCE THE TSAR FROM HIS THRONE. WE WILL UNMAKE THE DUMA THAT HAS FAILED US.›
‹DO NOT DOUBT THAT MANY OF US WILL DIE. BUT WE ARE THIS CITY NOW AND THEY CANNOT KILL A WHOLE CITY, AS MUCH AS THEY MIGHT TRY.›
‹BLOOD THAT IS SPILLED IN THIS FIGHT WILL BE FOREVER HONORED...›
‹...ONCE THE PETROGRAD SOVIET HAS RISEN AGAIN.›
‹WHAT IS IT, SERGEI?›

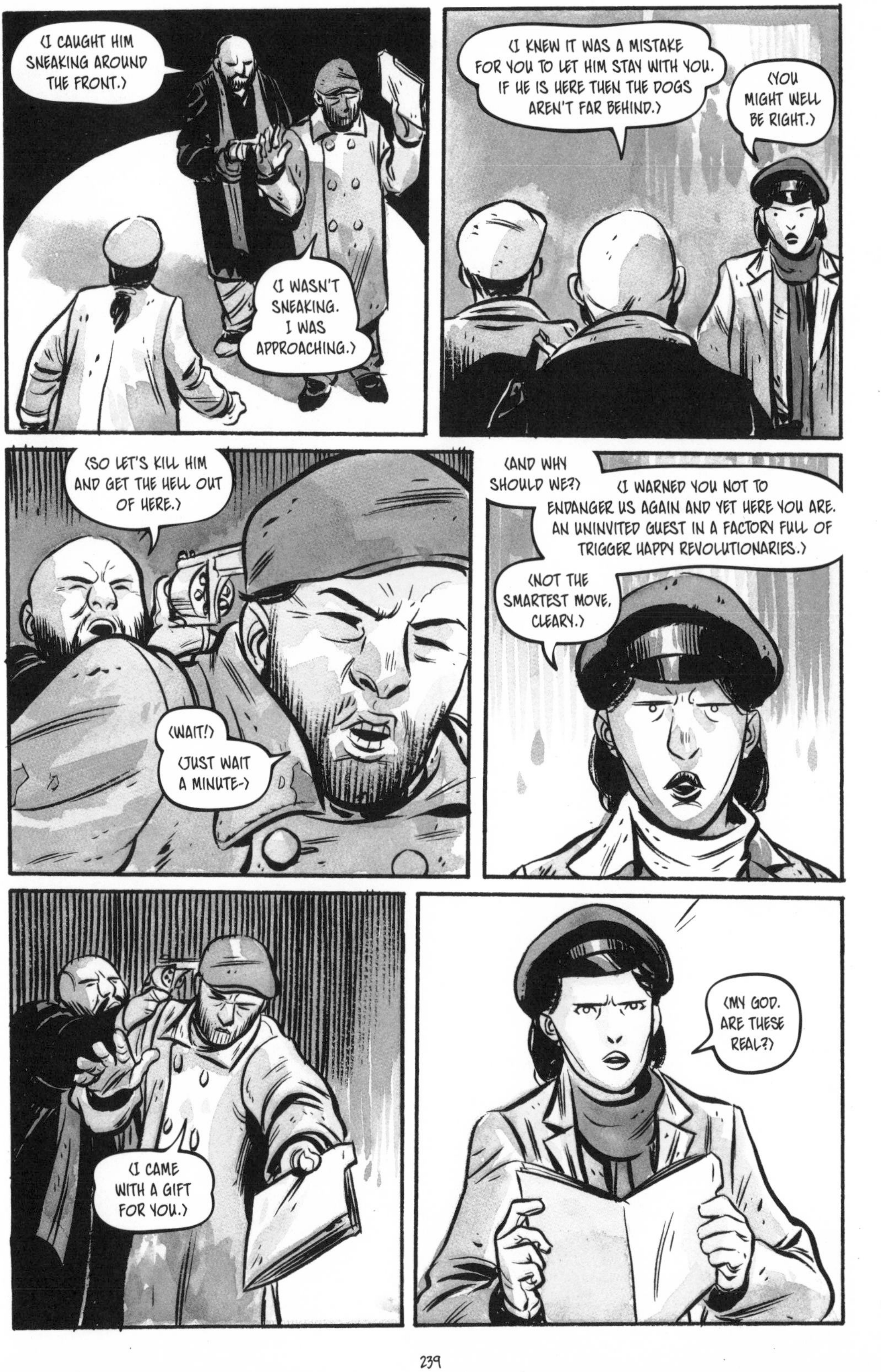
‹I CAUGHT HIM SNEAKING AROUND THE FRONT.›
‹I WASN'T SNEAKING. I WAS APPROACHING.›
‹I KNEW IT WAS A MISTAKE FOR YOU TO LET HIM STAY WITH YOU. IF HE IS HERE THEN THE DOGS AREN'T FAR BEHIND.›
‹YOU MIGHT WELL BE RIGHT.›
‹SO LET'S KILL HIM AND GET THE HELL OUT OF HERE.›
‹WAIT!›
‹JUST WAIT A MINUTE-›
‹AND WHY SHOULD WE?›
‹I WARNED YOU NOT TO ENDANGER US AGAIN AND YET HERE YOU ARE. AN UNINVITED GUEST IN A FACTORY FULL OF TRIGGER HAPPY REVOLUTIONARIES.›
‹NOT THE SMARTEST MOVE, CLEARY.›
‹I CAME WITH A GIFT FOR YOU.›
‹MY GOD. ARE THESE REAL?›

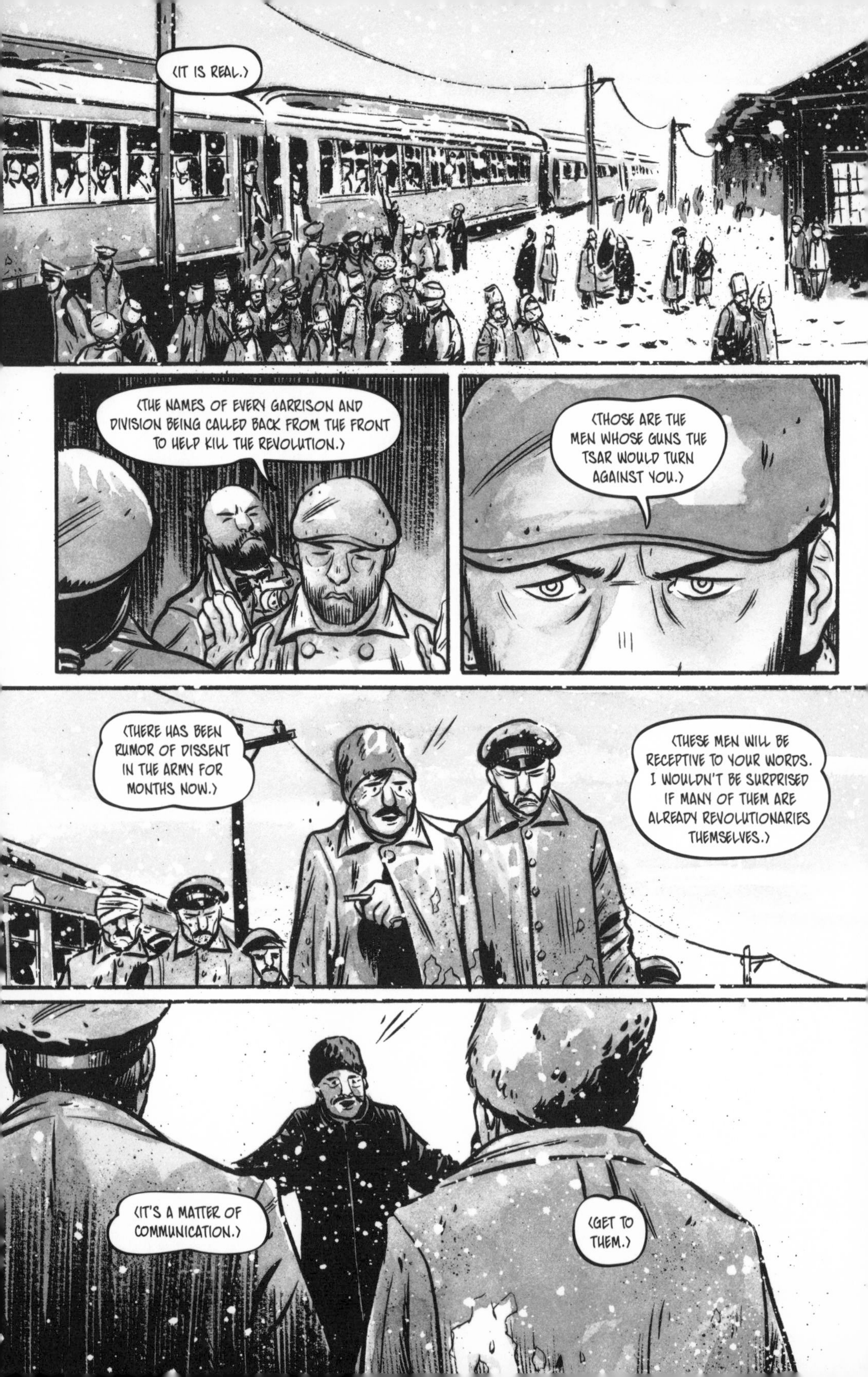

(IT IS REAL.)
(THE NAMES OF EVERY GARRISON AND DIVISION BEING CALLED BACK FROM THE FRONT TO HELP KILL THE REVOLUTION.)
(THOSE ARE THE MEN WHOSE GUNS THE TSAR WOULD TURN AGAINST YOU.)
(THERE HAS BEEN RUMOR OF DISSENT IN THE ARMY FOR MONTHS NOW.)
(THESE MEN WILL BE RECEPTIVE TO YOUR WORDS. I WOULDN'T BE SURPRISED IF MANY OF THEM ARE ALREADY REVOLUTIONARIES THEMSELVES.)
(IT'S A MATTER OF COMMUNICATION.)
(GET TO THEM.)

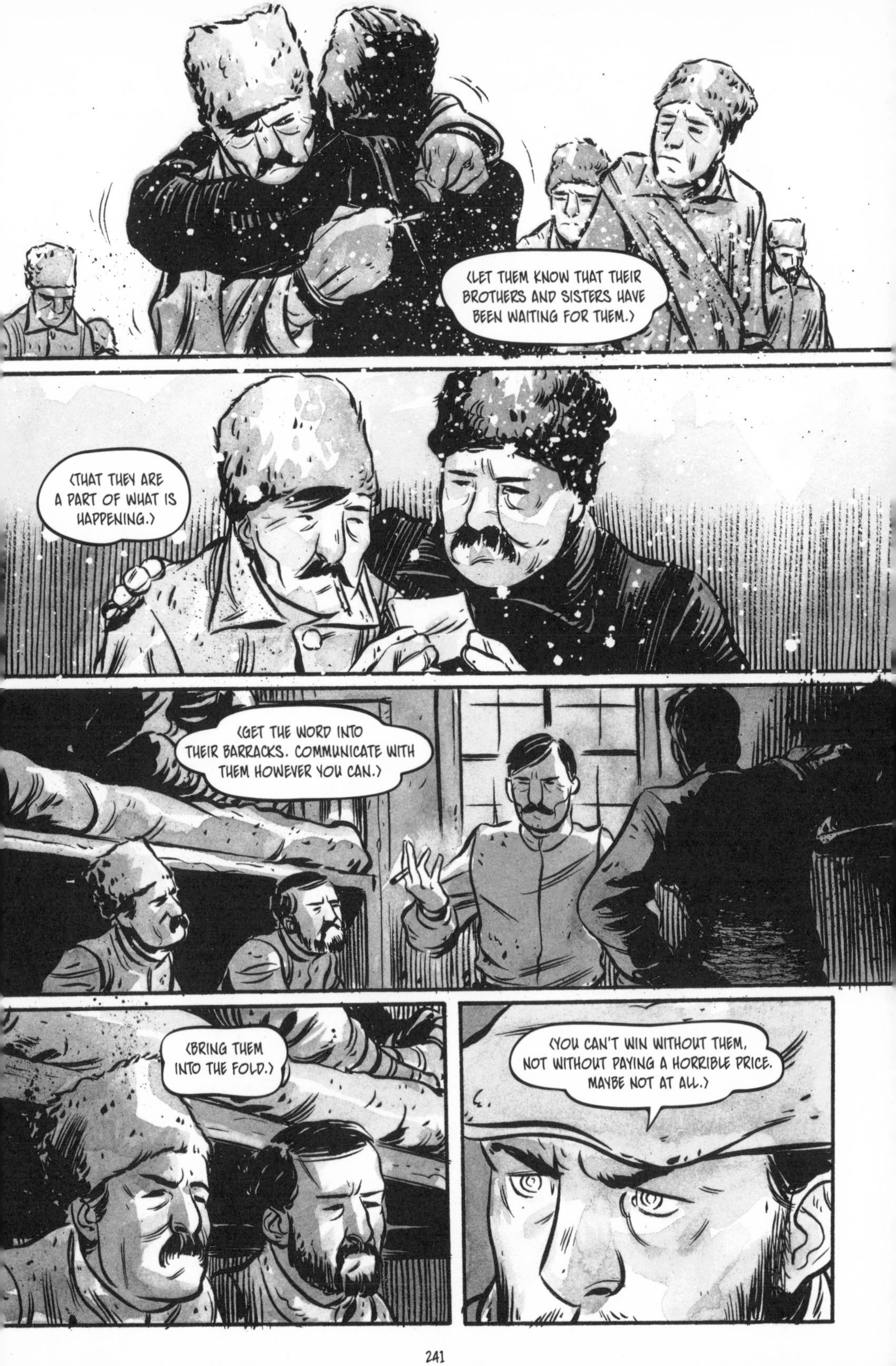

⟨LET THEM KNOW THAT THEIR BROTHERS AND SISTERS HAVE BEEN WAITING FOR THEM.⟩
⟨THAT THEY ARE A PART OF WHAT IS HAPPENING.⟩
⟨GET THE WORD INTO THEIR BARRACKS. COMMUNICATE WITH THEM HOWEVER YOU CAN.⟩
⟨BRING THEM INTO THE FOLD.⟩
⟨YOU CAN'T WIN WITHOUT THEM, NOT WITHOUT PAYING A HORRIBLE PRICE. MAYBE NOT AT ALL.⟩

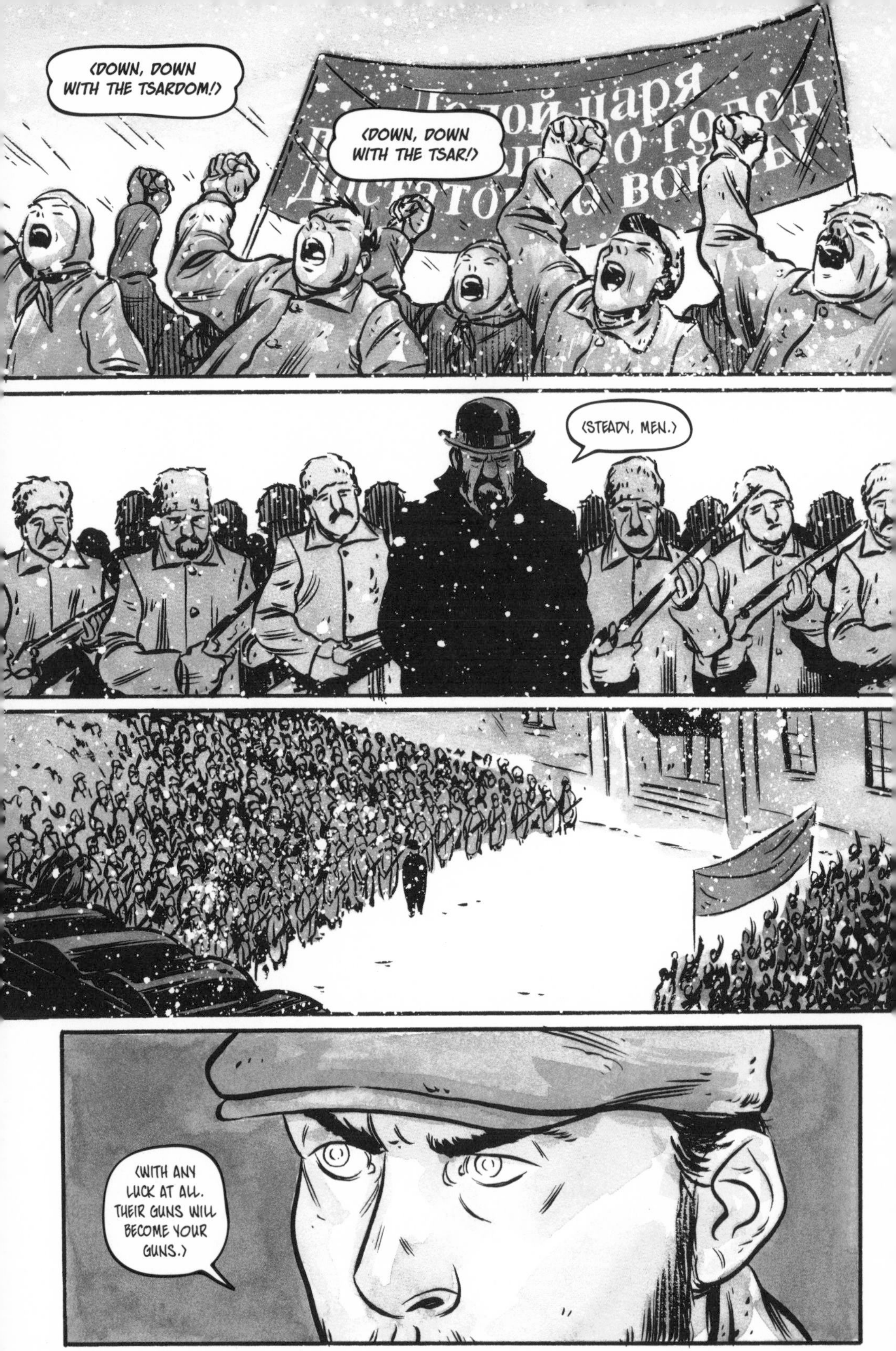
‹DOWN, DOWN WITH THE TSARDOM!›
‹DOWN, DOWN WITH THE TSAR!›
‹STEADY, MEN.›
‹WITH ANY LUCK AT ALL. THEIR GUNS WILL BECOME YOUR GUNS.›

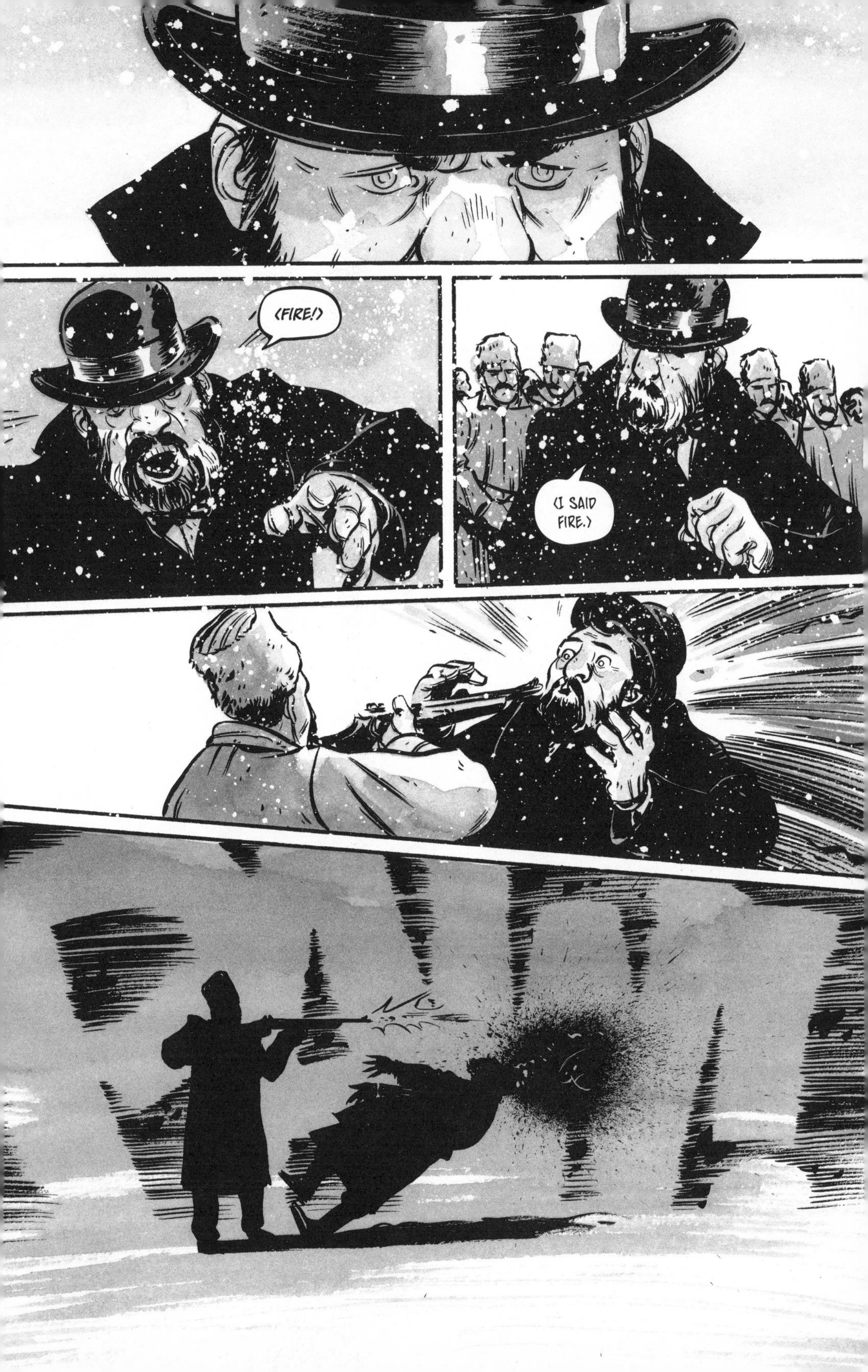
‹FIRE!›
‹I SAID FIRE.›

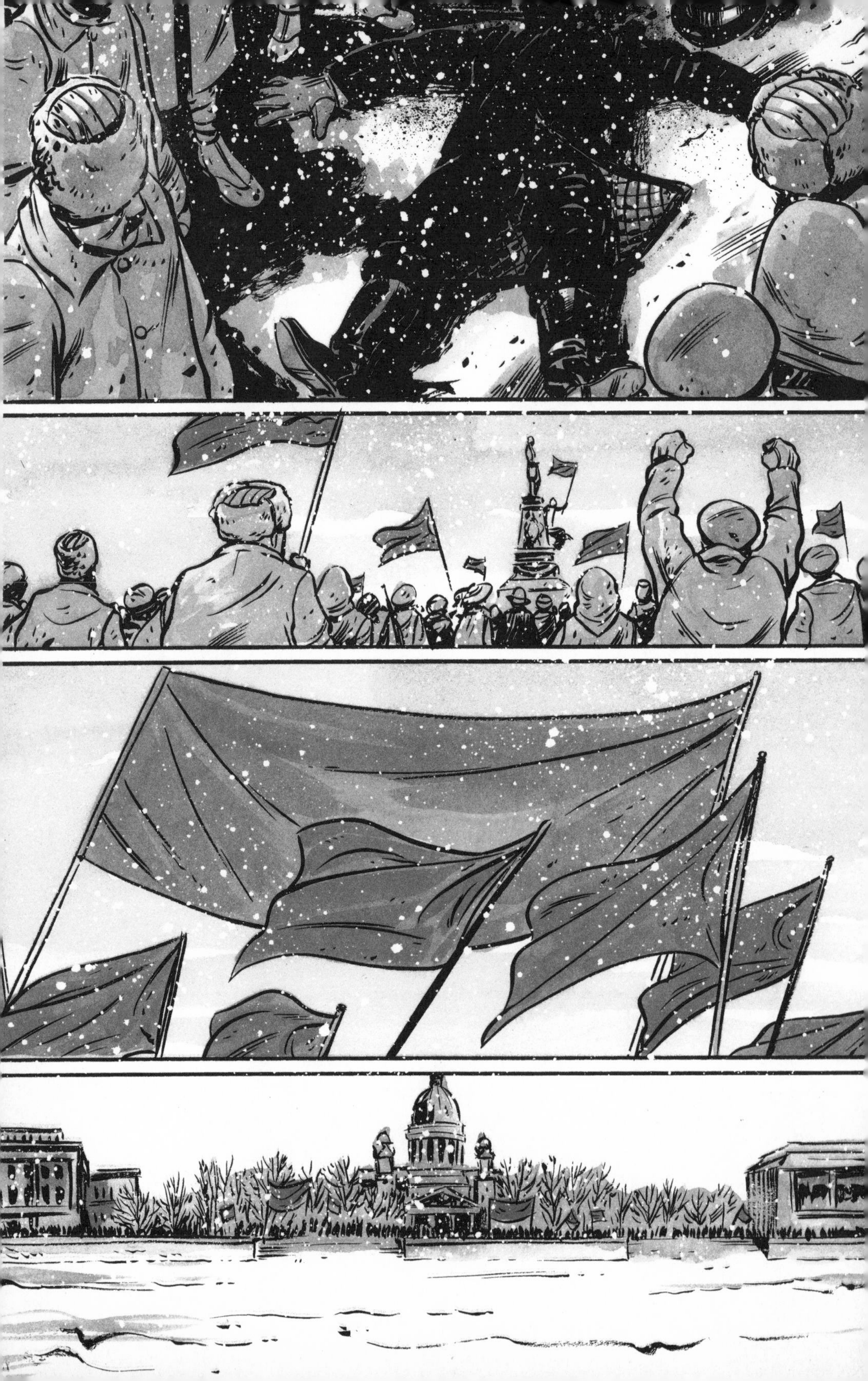

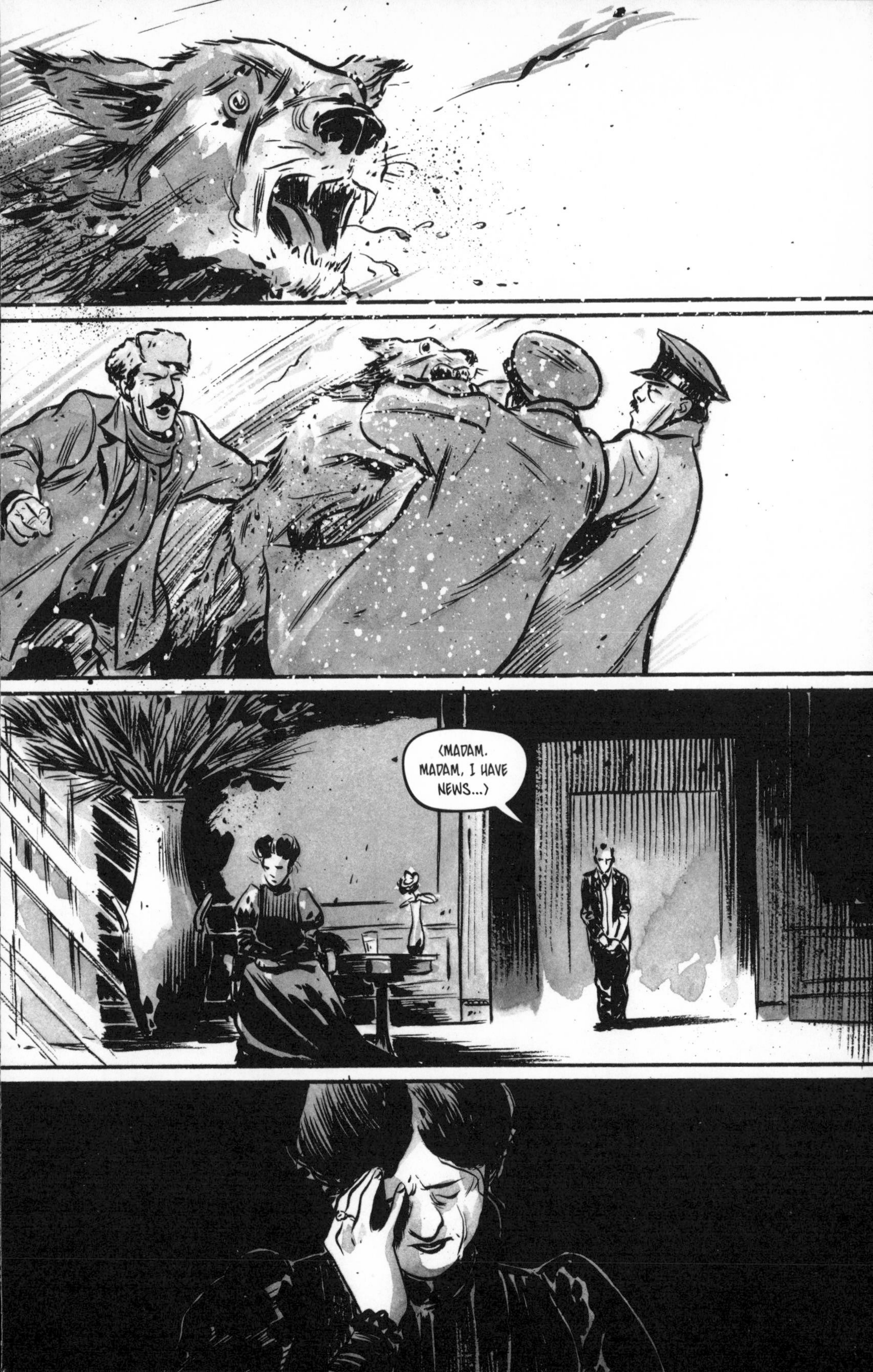
<MADAM. MADAM, I HAVE NEWS...>

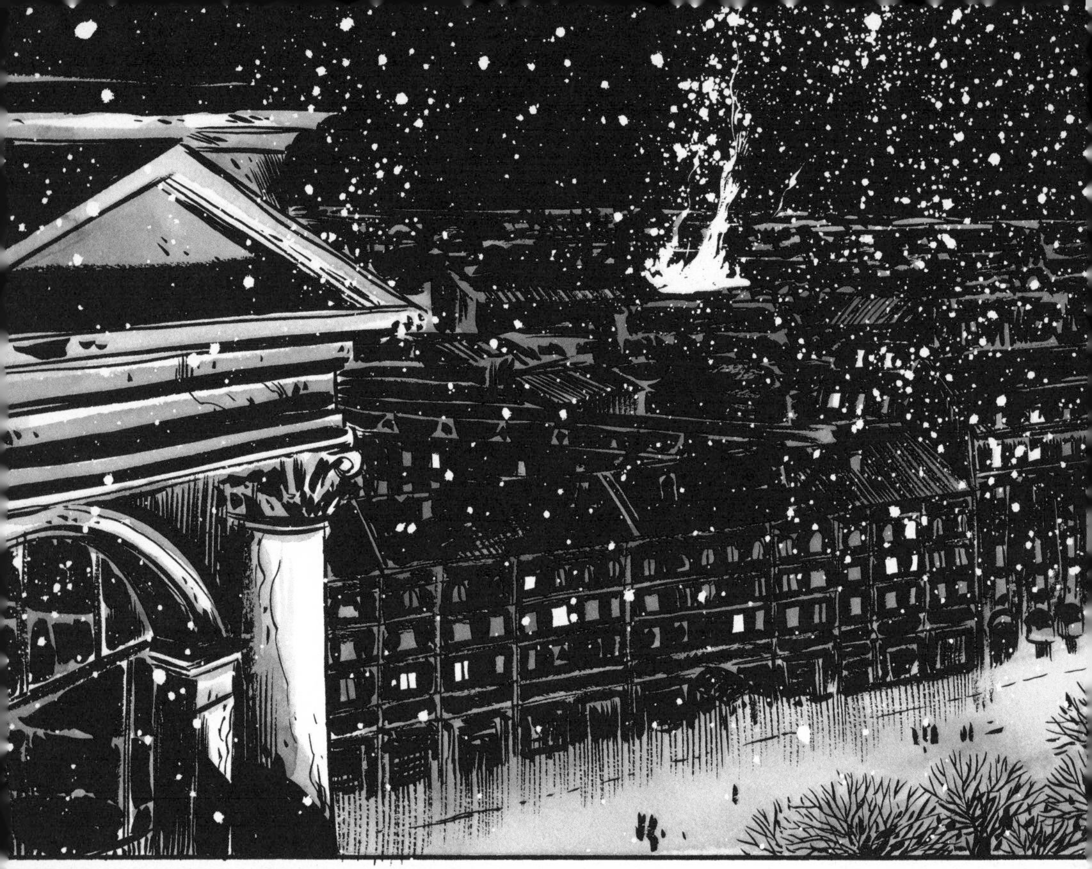

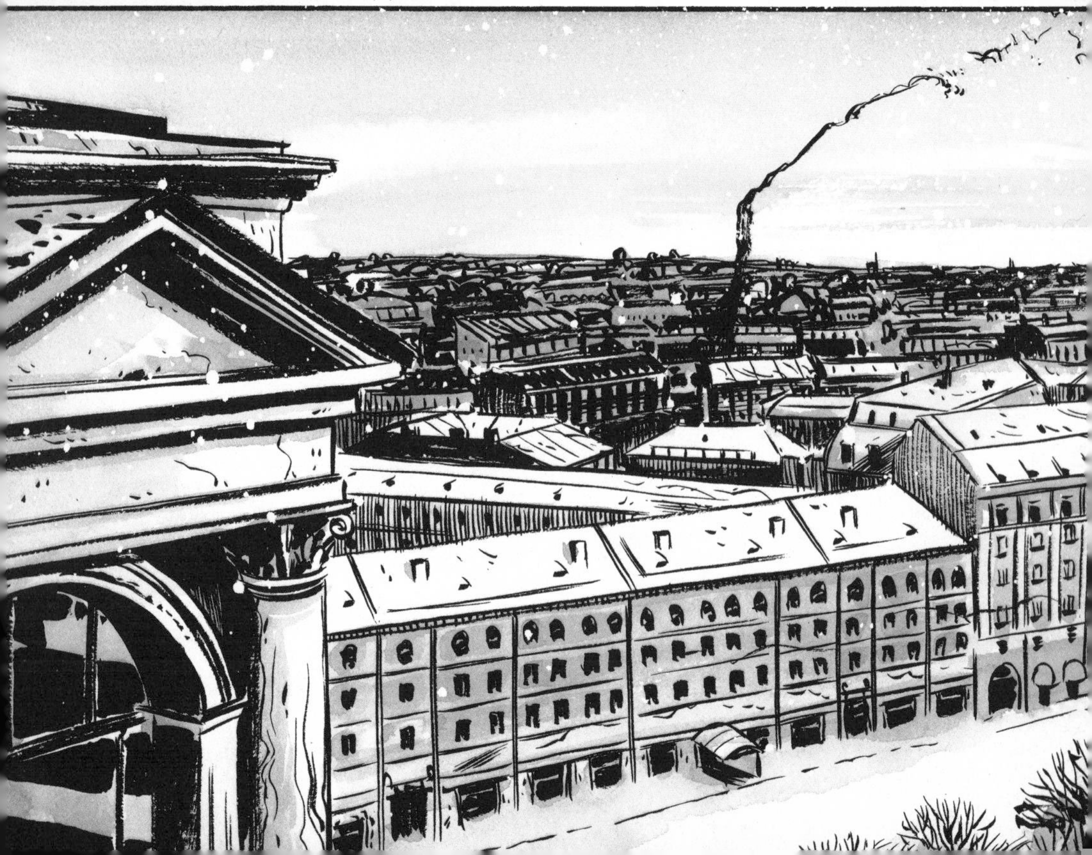

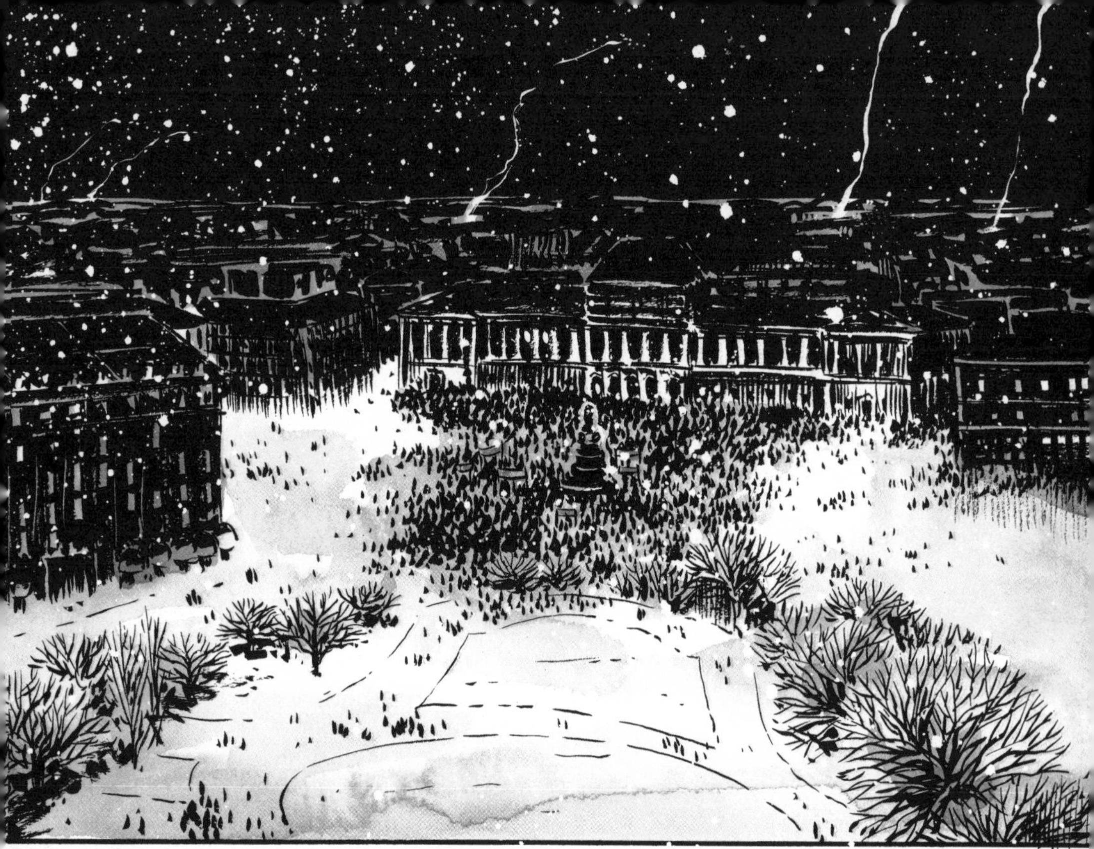
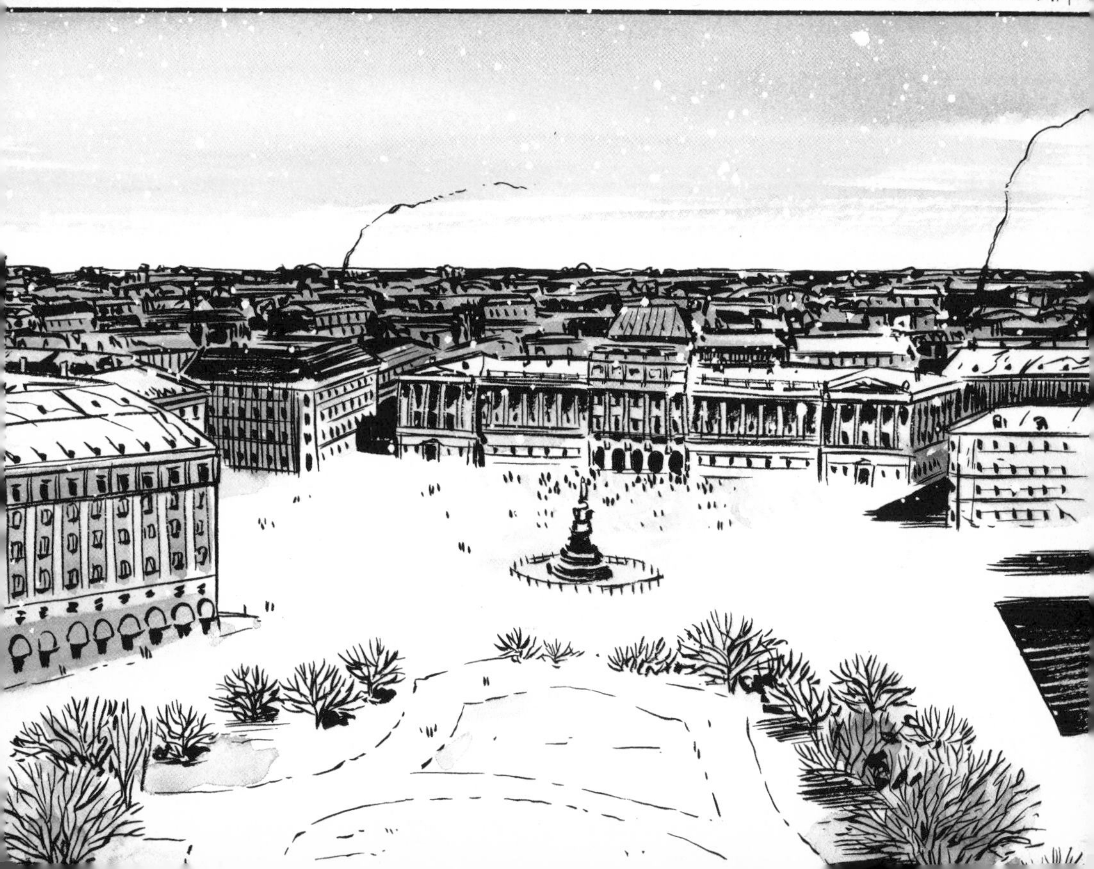

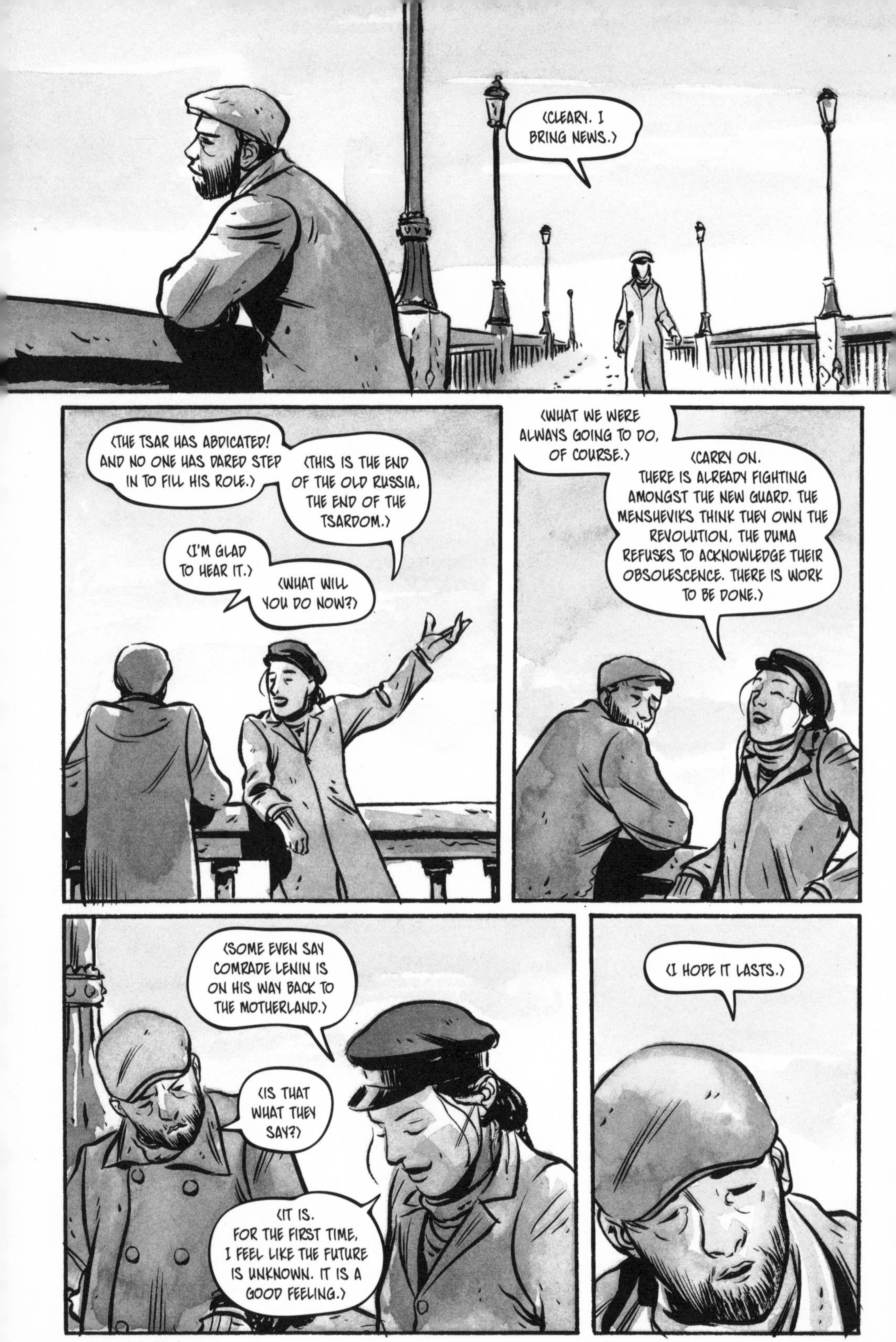

<CLEARY. I BRING NEWS.>
<THE TSAR HAS ABDICATED! AND NO ONE HAS DARED STEP IN TO FILL HIS ROLE.>
<THIS IS THE END OF THE OLD RUSSIA, THE END OF THE TSARDOM.>
<I'M GLAD TO HEAR IT.>
<WHAT WILL YOU DO NOW?>
<WHAT WE WERE ALWAYS GOING TO DO, OF COURSE.>
<CARRY ON. THERE IS ALREADY FIGHTING AMONGST THE NEW GUARD. THE MENSHEVIKS THINK THEY OWN THE REVOLUTION, THE DUMA REFUSES TO ACKNOWLEDGE THEIR OBSOLESCENCE. THERE IS WORK TO BE DONE.>
<SOME EVEN SAY COMRADE LENIN IS ON HIS WAY BACK TO THE MOTHERLAND.>
<IS THAT WHAT THEY SAY?>
<IT IS. FOR THE FIRST TIME, I FEEL LIKE THE FUTURE IS UNKNOWN. IT IS A GOOD FEELING.>
<I HOPE IT LASTS.>

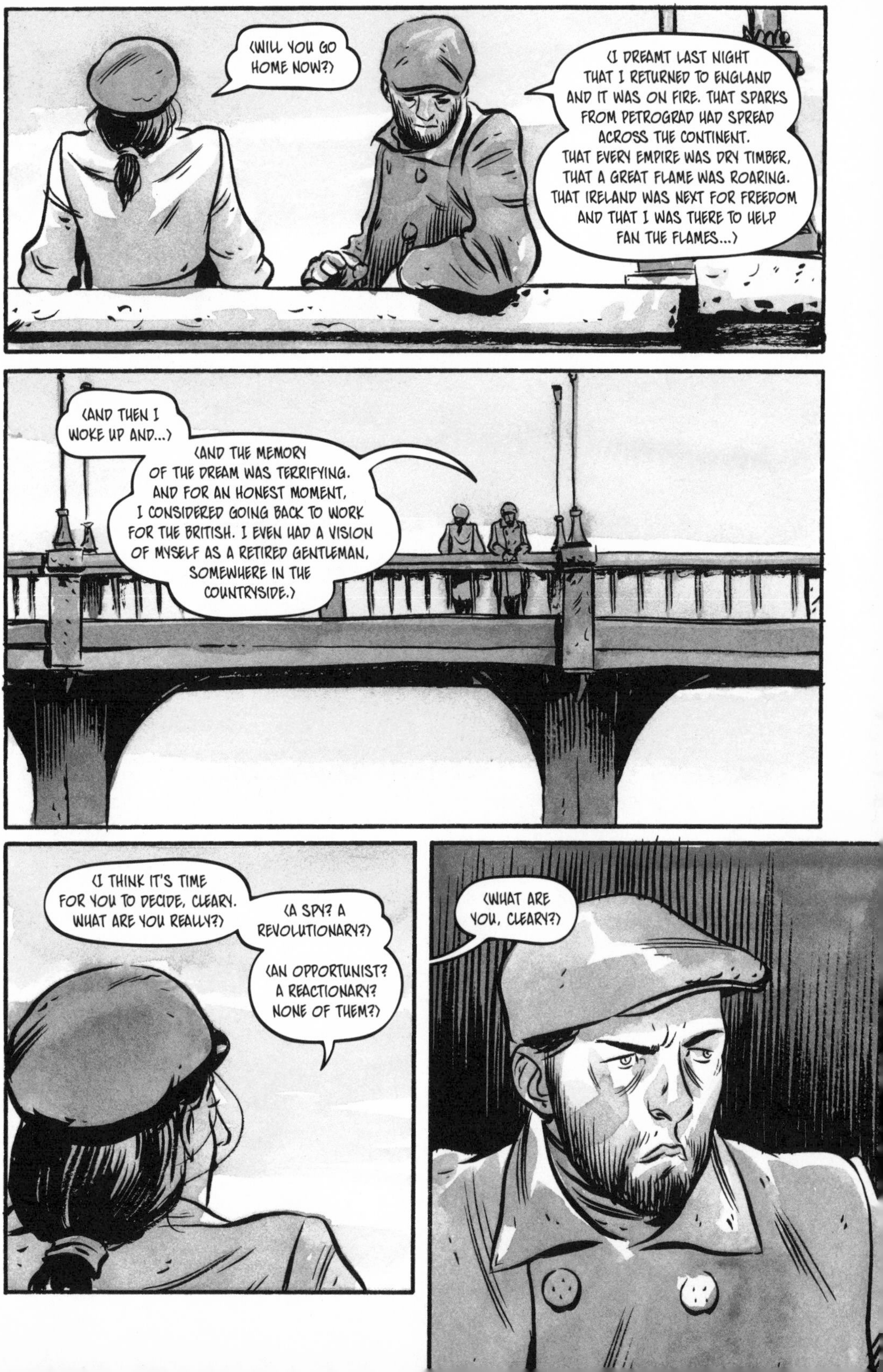

‹WILL YOU GO HOME NOW?›
‹I DREAMT LAST NIGHT THAT I RETURNED TO ENGLAND AND IT WAS ON FIRE. THAT SPARKS FROM PETROGRAD HAD SPREAD ACROSS THE CONTINENT. THAT EVERY EMPIRE WAS DRY TIMBER, THAT A GREAT FLAME WAS ROARING. THAT IRELAND WAS NEXT FOR FREEDOM AND THAT I WAS THERE TO HELP FAN THE FLAMES...›
‹AND THEN I WOKE UP AND...›
‹AND THE MEMORY OF THE DREAM WAS TERRIFYING. AND FOR AN HONEST MOMENT, I CONSIDERED GOING BACK TO WORK FOR THE BRITISH. I EVEN HAD A VISION OF MYSELF AS A RETIRED GENTLEMAN, SOMEWHERE IN THE COUNTRYSIDE.›
‹I THINK IT'S TIME FOR YOU TO DECIDE, CLEARY. WHAT ARE YOU REALLY?›
‹A SPY? A REVOLUTIONARY?›
‹AN OPPORTUNIST? A REACTIONARY? NONE OF THEM?›
‹WHAT ARE YOU, CLEARY?›

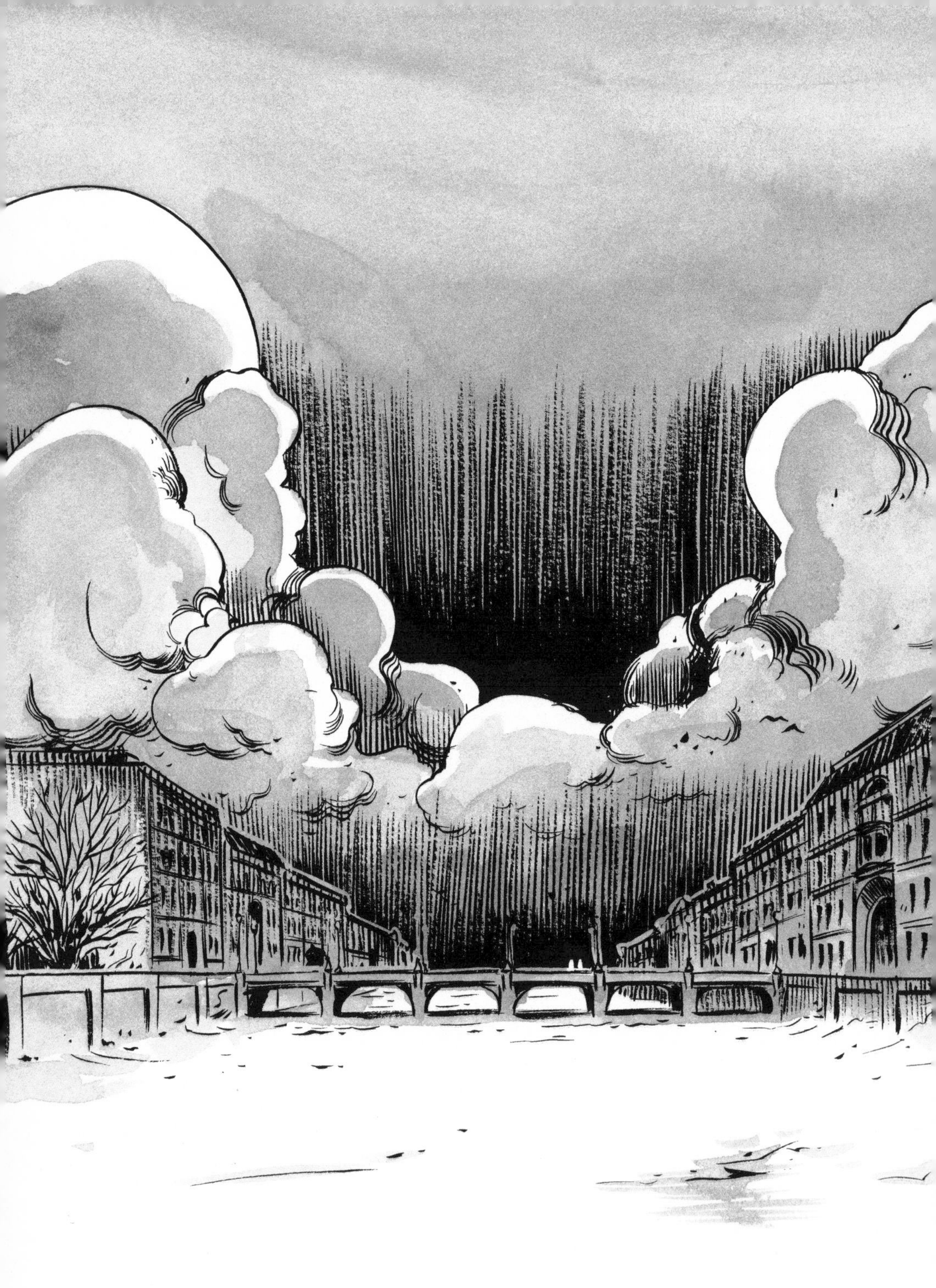

PHOTO BY CHARLIE CH

PHILIP GELATT

Philip Gelatt was born in Wisconsin and lives in Brooklyn His apartment is small and his book collection is large. He has been intrigued by Rasputin and spies for as long as he can remember. His secret dream is to begin a collection of assassination memorabilia which would include both the bullet that killed Rasputin and the ice axe that killed Trotsky He has no Russian blood. He once claimed that his favorite James Bond was George Lazenby. He writes graphic novels and screenplays for a living.

Philip would like to thank Avery G. and Lee E. for early and informative Rasputin discussions; everyone at Oni for being top notch; and his wife Victoria D. for constant encouragement.

PHOTO BY CHARLIE CHU.

TYLER CROOK

Mr. Tyler Crook is an artist. He lives on the Oregon coast with his one wife, two cats, three legged dog, four legged dog and the many smells they provide. He has a deep appreciation for all Russian literature but prefers the comic stylings of Dostoevsky. He hopes to someday work on a book that is so powerful and moving that schools will force children to read and hate it.

Tyler has contributed many wonderfully intriguing and technically proficient pages of art to his regular gig, *B.P.R.D.*, for Dark Horse Comics, as well as to his occasional gig, doing one-shot stories of *The Sixth Gun*, for Oni Press.

mrcrook.com

Tyler would like to thank his wife, Ma'at for being the best wife in the world and helping with scanning and setting up the digital files, Ryan Benjamin for hooking him up with a big ole scanner, Max Horbul for his Russian translations, Robbi Rodriguez for his advice and encouragement, Rhode Montijo for his awesome critiques, Randy Jarrell for starting us off on the right foot and Jill for stopping us on the other right foot.

BIBLIOGRAPHY

Books

Andrew, Christopher. Her Majesty's Secret Service: The Making of the British Intelligence Community. New York, NY: Viking Penguin Books, 1987.

Cook, Andrew. To Kill Rasputin. Gloucestershire, England: Tempus Books, 2006.

Figes, Orlando. A People's Tragedy: The Russian Revolution 1891-1924. New York, NY: Penguin Books, 1996.

Judd, Alan. The Quest for C: Mansfield Cumming and the Founding of the Secret Service. London, England: Harper-Collins Publishers, 1999.

Radzinksy, Eduard. The Rasputin File. New York, NY: Anchor Books, 2000.

Ruud, Charles and Sergei Stepanov. Fontanka 16: The Tsars' Secret Police. Montreal, Quebec, McGill-Queen's University Press, 1999.

Spence, Richard. Trust No One: The Secret World of Sydney Reilly. Los Angeles, CA: Feral House Publishing, 2002.

Strachan, Hew. The First World War. New York, NY: Penguin Books, 2003.

Bolt, John E. Moscow & St. Petersburg: 1900 – 1920 Art Life & Culture of the Russian Silver Age. New York, NY: The Vendome Press, 2008.

Rossif, Frederic and Chapsal, Madeleine. Portrait of a Revolution: Russia 1896 – 1924. Boston, MA: Little, Brown and Company, 1969.

Kurth, Peter. The Lost World of Nicholas and Alexandra: Tsar. Boston, MA: Little, Brown and Company, 1995.

Gosling, Nigel. Leningrad. Studio Vista, 1965.

DVDs

Russia: Land of the Tsars. Prod. Campbell, Don. DVD. History Channel, 2003.

Reilly: Ace of Spies. Dir. Goddard, Jim & Campbell, Martin. DVD. A&E, 2005.

Internet

www.nevsky-prospekt.com
(Vintage Nevsky Postcard Collection)

images.google.com

www.alexanderpalace.org

Felix's own account of the crime is called "Lost Splendor" and can be found here: http://www.alexanderpalace.org/lostsplendor/intro.html

OTHER BOOKS BY PHIL GELATT

ABOR DAYS, VOLUME 1
y Philip Gelatt & Rick Lacy
44 pages, 6"x9" trade paperback, black and white
SBN 978-1-932664-92-8

ABOR DAYS, VOLUME 2: JUST ANOTHER DAMN DAY
y Philip Gelatt & Rick Lacy
52 pages, 6"x9" trade paperback, black and white
SBN 978-1-934964-22-4

MORE BOOKS FROM ONI PRESS

OCAL - DELUXE HARDCOVER
y Brian Wood & Ryan Kelly
84 pages, hardcover, black and white
SBN 978-1-934964-00-2

NORTHWEST PASSAGE - SOFTCOVER
y Scott Chantler
272 pages, 6"x9" trade paperback, black and white
SBN 978-1-932664-35-4

QUEEN & COUNTRY, VOLUME 1: DEFINITIVE EDITION
y Greg Rucka, Steve Rolston, Brian Hurtt & Leandro Fernandez
76 pages, 6"x9" trade paperback, black and white
SBN 978-1-932664-87-4

UNION STATION
y Ande Parks & Eduardo Barreto
28 pages, 6"x9" trade paperback, black and white
SBN 978-1-934964-27-9

ONE SOUL
y Ray Fawkes
76 pages, hardcover, black and white
SBN 978-1-932664-70-6

AVAILABLE AT FINER COMIC BOOK SHOPS AND BOOK-SELLERS EVERYWHERE!

LABOR DAYS
Philip Gelatt | Rick Lacy

LABOR DAYS
Philip Gelatt | Rick Lacy

BRIAN WOOD ★ RYAN KELLY
LOCAL

NORTHWEST PASSAGE
by Scott Chantler

GREG RUCKA
QUEEN & COUNTRY
DEFINITIVE EDITION
VOLUME 01

UNION STATION
Ande Parks
Eduardo Barreto

Ray Fawkes
ONE SOUL

For additional information on these and other fine Oni Press comic books and graphic novels visit www.onipress.com. To find a comic specialty store in your area visit www.comicshops.us.

ONI PRESS
REVOLUTIONIZE COMICS
www.onipress.com

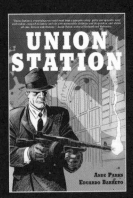